TALES OF SILVER DOWNS

BOOKS 1 - 3

KYLIE QUILLINAN

This collection published in 2017 by Kylie Quillinan

Muse © 2015 Kylie Quillinan

Fey © 2016 Kylie Quillinan

Druid © 2016 Kylie Quillinan

All rights reserved.

ABN 34 112 708 734

kyliequillinan.com

Cataloguing-in-Publication data for the individual books is available from the National Library of Australia.

ISBN: 9780994331564

Cover art by Get Covers.

This work uses Australian spelling and grammar.

LP09092023

Three hundred years ago, six brothers were cursed to live as swans. This is their return.

Subscribe to receive your free copy of Swan, the epilogue novella for the Tales of Silver Downs series.

kyliequillinan.com/free-swan

KYLIE QUILLINAN

TALES OF SILVER DOWNS

MUSE

BOOK 1

MUSE

TALES OF SILVER DOWNS

BOOK 1

KYLIE QUILLINAN

DEDICATION

For for Muffin, Bella and Lulu,

for guarding me while I worked.

1

———

DIARMUID

SEVENNIGHT BEFORE my brother Caedmon was handfasted, we gathered at his bride's family estate, Misty Valley. Their modest stone lodge brimmed with friends and family. Ale flowed freely and folk danced to the raucous tunes of fiddler and whistler. Winter garments — hats, coats, scarves — were piled on a bench in the corner, abandoned in the warmth of ale and dancing. I ate and drank, avoided solicitations to dance, and tried to pretend I was happy for Caedmon.

My muse, Ida, whispered snide remarks about people around us. One subject of her scorn was a man whose nose was so long and sharp, Ida wondered whether he could slice bread with it. Another was the woman whose fat fingers could hardly bend to lift her mug. Had I the courage to voice such thoughts, surely the revelry would dissipate and we could all go home.

Every bard has a muse and Ida was as real as any man's, to me at least. Her image, in my mind's eye, was as clear as if she stood beside me. Blonde of hair, blue of eye, skin so pale it was almost translucent. Folk around these parts were dark-haired with milky white skin. Ida looked like no one I had ever seen. It helped me remember she didn't really exist.

As folk tired of dancing, we gathered in front of the grey stone fireplace at one end of the room. The sweet scent of pinecones on the fire filled the air, covering the lingering smells of roast meat and bread. The older folk warmed their bones on comfortable chairs drawn close to the flames. Small children perched on their laps or on brightly-coloured rugs at their feet. Those who were neither old nor young enough to claim a position close by the fire gathered behind. Some sat on wooden benches, others leaned against the walls.

I found a spot on a bench towards the back of the room. My belly was comfortably full and now that all the merriment had subsided, I eagerly anticipated the evening's tale-telling. Tonight I would make Ida proud.

Caedmon and his betrothed, Grainne, sat near the front, he with an arm around her shoulders. Both were flushed and bright-eyed, still catching their breath from the last dance. Grainne's father, Laeg, stood beside the fireplace. He was a hardy-looking man, plump and rosy-cheeked. Grainne and her three sisters all looked much like him.

"This seems a fine time for a tale," Laeg announced, and the crowd swiftly quietened. "Caedmon, my boy, I believe you have a bard in the family. Is he here tonight?"

"Yes, my lord." Caedmon darted a glance at me over his shoulder, a warning in his eyes. "My youngest brother, Diarmuid, back there, is the bard."

Laeg nodded in my direction, although the way his eyes searched the crowd showed he didn't know my face.

"Well then, young Diarmuid, will you favour us with a tale?"

My heart pounded as I made my way to the fireplace. Laeg slapped me on the back, then stepped away to lean against a wall. I cleared my throat.

"This is a new tale," I said. Although my voice was loud and confident, my breath quickened, for in this moment before I began, I suffered from nerves. While the tale was still unspoken it was perfect, but it would become imperfect in its telling. For a tale told never quite lived up to the promise of one untold. Once the words began to flow, calmness would wash over me, although I could never entirely lose myself in the tale. I was always acutely aware of every murmur and movement.

Flames crackled in the fireplace and occasionally a seat creaked as someone shifted. Children were swiftly hushed as I told a tale of a woman who had offended Titania, queen of the fey. The woman had a babe who was not yet four summers old. As punishment for the offence, Titania ordered the woman to take her child into the woods.

"'Go to the deepest, darkest part of the woods,' Titania said to the woman. 'And leave the child there. She will be food for the wild boar. They will rip her limbs from her body and tear out her heart while it still beats.'

"The woman cried and begged and offered her own life in exchange for that of the child. But Titania ignored her pleas, for the fey do not feel as we do, and they do not understand fear or sadness or pity."

By now, the mood in the room had changed. The seats creaked more often and children were not shushed quite as quickly. Discomfited, my words came a little faster.

"So the woman took her child by the hand and led her into the woods. As they made their way through the trees, the woman swallowed her sobs and didn't allow her tears to fall, for she didn't want the child to be afraid.

"At length they reached a clearing and as they stood in the centre, the woman knew she couldn't leave her child there, regardless of Titania's instructions. She resolved to keep walking, all the way through the woods. Eventually they would reach the other side. They would continue to walk until they found a town where the people didn't know of the fey. But as she left the clearing, Titania suddenly appeared in front of her.

"The woman fell to her knees before the fey queen and again begged for her child's life. But she could not sway Titania. Eventually, with many tears and much sorrow, the woman kissed her child goodbye. 'Be brave, my sweet,' she whispered and released the child's hand. Sobbing now, the mother stepped back into the trees, for she intended to stay to witness her child's fate. On the other side of the clearing, Titania also waited.

"Only moments passed before two wild boar entered the clearing. They sniffed the air and scented the child. The child tried to run from the enormous black beasts, but Titania charmed her and she could not move her feet.

"The boars circled the child, once, twice. Then they lunged. Blood sprayed onto the leaves as they ripped the child's limbs from her body, first her arms, then when she fell down, her legs. The child did not stop screaming until they tore off her head. The mother sobbed, but she didn't cover her ears for she wanted to bear witness to every moment of her child's death. She knew she would hear her daughter's screams echoing in her memory for the rest of her life.

"The boars devoured the child and even licked up her blood from the leaves. When there was nothing left, they disappeared back into the woods. It was only then that Titania spoke again. 'Your lesson is concluded,' she said. 'See that you have learned it well.' Then she too slipped away into the woods and did not return again."

As I finished speaking, one of Grainne's relatives left, taking two small children with her. I had intended to demonstrate how the fey interfere in human lives at their own whim and that they care not for what misery they bestow. That sometimes fate or circumstance, or the fickle desire of the fey, cuts the closest of bonds, and that not all tales end happily.

I waited, shifting from foot to foot, heart pounding, for my audience's reaction. My words hung heavy in the air and folk avoided my eyes. As always. A child began to sob.

"I don't like that story, Papa," she said.

There was no point waiting for Laeg to construct some suitably polite words. As I left the room, someone finally comforted the crying child.

2

DIARMUID

TOOK A long swallow of ale and watched as Caedmon thrust another log into the fireplace. The flames flared briefly and settled again, a small yellow blaze warding off the chill of a winter evening. It was well after midnight when we returned from Misty Valley and the rest of our family were now abed. Caedmon and I drew our chairs within the fire's golden shield while the room beyond lay in darkness. Ida was silent for now, sleeping perhaps, if muses do such a thing, or disappointed with tonight's tale.

In the depths of the flickering fire stood a raven, its gaze fixed on me as blood dripped from its beak. I didn't recall paying much attention to ravens in my earliest years, but now I saw them everywhere: in the fire, in the clouds, in the shadows, in my dreams. What they meant, I could only guess, and it was on nights like this, when dark thoughts overcrowded my mind, that the ravens were most vivid. Could I touch it if I reached into the fire, or would it disappear like smoke between my fingers? Sometimes I was tempted to try. Instead, I wrapped my fingers around my mug, my skin catching on the chip on its edge. That at least was real. I was never quite sure whether the ravens were.

Caedmon settled back into his chair, his legs stretched out before him.

"Stop being so morose, little brother. It wasn't that bad."

"My name is Diarmuid," I said automatically, although, for once, the fact that he never used my name didn't irritate me. I gulped down more ale even as my head spun and my stomach threatened to reject what I had already consumed. Perhaps if I drank enough, I could forget. "You don't understand. They hate my tales, and for a bard there is nothing worse."

"So they hated one tale." Caedmon finished his ale and poured himself another from the jug on the low table between us. His hands were steady as he set the jug back down, despite the quantity of ale he had drunk with dinner.

"It's not merely one tale. It's every tale. A bard is supposed to please his audience as well as teach them, but I fail at both."

"It's because your tales are…" Caedmon paused, glancing at me as if to measure my mood.

"Go ahead. It can't make me feel any worse than I already do."

"Your tales are odd," he said, staring into the fireplace to avoid my eyes. "They're… I don't know… *wrong*. People want to hear of heroes who go on great journeys and succeed at their quests, who kill the monsters and marry the girl. You tell tales where everybody dies, villages are wiped out, mothers lose their children forever."

"I am trying to demonstrate that actions have consequences," I said somewhat stiffly, despite my assurance that his words wouldn't hurt. I tried hard not to be offended for Caedmon would never say such a thing with malicious intent. "Nobody *understands* my tales."

"That's just it. You tell tales folk have to think about, to reason through. That's not what an audience wants to hear. We want tales to cheer us, sustain us through a cold winter night. Tales of hope and victory, battle and adventure. And love."

I shot Caedmon a quick glance. He was the second oldest of my six brothers and our family's soldier son. Despite his impending hand-fasting, I might expect to hear him talk of victory and battles, but not love.

"You must look forward to being handfasted. Grainne is... nice."

My words did no justice to his betrothed, who was dark-haired and rosy-cheeked and had been nothing but friendly towards me. When she and Caedmon announced their betrothal, she had kissed my cheek and called me brother. I didn't know how to respond and by the time I realised I should probably return her embrace, she had given me an odd look and moved on.

"What does a soldier know of handfasting?" Caedmon asked. "All I know is fighting and battles and death. Grainne is a good sort of girl. Even-tempered, cheerful, easy on the eye. Perhaps, blessed with enough time, we might learn to love each other. But the most important thing is to choose a wife you can stand to live with. Grainne and I will do well enough together for however long we have."

His words sounded odd, hollow. I waited, contemplating the sweet smell of the burning wood and the way it lingered in my throat. Caedmon must be being practical, for surely there was more involved in selecting a wife. But what would I know about such things?

"She will be well provided for when I return to the campaign," Caedmon said, at length. "And if she is with child before I leave, I will be satisfied with my choice."

I flushed, never comfortable with discussion about intimate matters between a man and woman. Hopefully Caedmon would assume my reddened cheeks to be caused by the fire's warmth. Of course he would want his bride to be with child before he left. Every man desired three sons: one to be heir, one to be a soldier, and one for the druids. Not every man got what he desired, though, for most never produced a son suited to be a druid.

Caedmon leaned forward to put another log on the fire that didn't need any more fuel.

"I'm getting old, little brother. Old for a soldier anyway. I've survived as long as any soldier might expect to."

I had never thought of Caedmon as old. I myself was nineteen and he only five years my senior. But other soldier sons I knew who had gone off to war had long since died. Some never returned after their first campaign. Others lasted two or three or four seasons. Caedmon had been a soldier for eight summers. He certainly was old, for a soldier.

"So you decided to marry." I tucked the thought of his possible death away in a remote corner of my mind. I would take it out and examine it at some other time.

"If I am ever to marry and produce an heir, it must be now. For I don't think I will return here again."

"This will always be your home. You know that even once Papa is gone, Eremon would never turn any of us out."

"That's not what I mean, little brother." Caedmon sighed, heavily. "I think I will die on the next campaign. That's why I must produce an heir now. I can't wait any longer."

"But what makes you think such a thing? You're a good soldier. Just because you've lived longer than others, doesn't mean..." My voice faltered. Ida stirred, whispering dark comments that I ignored.

"I've seen myself, in a dream. I lay in a ditch, dead, my throat slit. And I looked no older than I do now."

"That doesn't mean it was a true dream."

"I believe it was, little brother. I feel its truth in my bones. Death approaches. I have leave to be home until the rivers start to thaw and then I must return to the campaign. If Grainne is carrying my heir before I leave, I will die without regret."

Caedmon poured himself yet another ale. He proffered the jug to me, but I shook my head. My stomach rolled and I knew that by morning I would regret the ale I had already drunk.

"What about you, little brother? Is there a girl you fancy? Someone special I should meet while I'm home?"

A face flashed into my mind. I had never spoken to her, but I'd seen her at various celebrations. One day, perhaps, I might work up the nerve to ask her name.

"No, there's nobody."

"There must be someone. A pretty girl, maybe someone in Maker's Well?"

I shook my head, staring intently into the fire. The raven stared back.

"Grainne has several younger sisters. Or there's the girls at Three Trees; the eldest is particularly pretty. Or—"

"No, Caedmon." I spoke with as much force as I could. "I told you. There isn't anyone."

"Perhaps you prefer men then? I know several soldiers—"

"No, I don't prefer men," I snapped. "I just… I don't know how to talk to girls. They giggle and whisper and flirt and say one thing but mean another. I don't understand them."

"But you're a bard, my boy." Caedmon leaned over to slap me heartily on the shoulder, not even trying to conceal his grin. "You're supposed to be an expert on the human condition. You talk prettily enough when you tell your tales. Surely you can fumble your way through a conversation with a girl?"

"Telling tales is one thing. I can practise them, know how they will end. But a conversation… You never quite know what turn it will take. I can't be prepared for that. I go red and forget how to speak and they laugh at me."

Caedmon laughed then and swallowed the rest of his ale in a hearty gulp.

"I have a solution for you. We need to find you a woman. Once you bed one for the first time, the rest will be easier."

My heart pounded in my ears. Such a scenario could only be a disaster. Complete humiliation. "No, I couldn't—"

"It's settled then," he said. "And I'll listen to no arguments, little brother. I'll find you a pretty girl. Next week's winter solstice would be a good time, what with all the celebrating and drinking and making merry. All you have to do is be there."

"Caedmon, really, I can't—"

"I'm not listening." He set his mug aside and rose. "I'm off to bed now but tomorrow I'll start making arrangements."

3

DIARMUID

I SAT UP alone for some time after Caedmon went to bed, staring at the raven in the fire and nursing my ale. Finally, I set my mug aside and left the fire to burn itself out.

My bedchamber was chilly and the bed even colder. I huddled under the covers, goosebumps prickling my skin as I waited for warmth. The fire was mere coals, casting little heat on my small room. I didn't bother to build it back up. Ida whispered to me, but I pushed her away.

With every tale, I hoped this would be the one the audience would like. But every time, the reaction was the same. It had always been like this, ever since my tenth summer when I told my first tale. At that time, Caedmon had been due to depart for the army's training grounds where he would learn to become a soldier. It would be the first time I had been separated from him for more than a few hours.

He and I had spent every possible moment together during those last few months. We camped under the summer stars with only each other and a fire for company. We terrified ourselves investigating an ancient barrow, half expecting the fey to punish us for trespassing on hallowed ground. We battled imaginary enemies and Caedmon taught me to defend myself. I was small for my age, and slender with it, but he made sure I knew how to wield a dagger and I became somewhat capable with a small bow.

Preparing for Caedmon's first departure was difficult, for I had never before said goodbye to a brother with the uncertain knowledge that he might not return. Farewelling our druid brother, Fiachra, was different, for he always had one foot in the beyond, even as a child. But Caedmon was the brother I knew best. As summer slipped away, he had become somewhat distant and disappeared for hours at a time. Perhaps he tried to prepare me for his impending absence. Or perhaps he prepared himself.

I said nothing about the increasing time we spent apart. In truth, I was somewhat jealous that he edged towards his destiny while I had yet to perform a single tale, for I had but recently realised that barding would be my own career. On the days Caedmon absented himself, I worked on my first tale, crafting it into what I thought was a thing of wonder and truth.

Caedmon had no time to wander the estate with me that last day, for he was busy making his farewells to the tenants and servants, the animals and our home. It was not until just before the evening meal that I was able to snatch a few moments alone with him.

The sun was sinking towards the horizon, sending fingers of deep purple across the sky as I lingered outside in the hope of spotting Caedmon. The day's warmth had faded to a slight coolness heralding winter's approach and the late afternoon air was heavy with grass and sweet heather. Finally, he appeared from behind the barn and smiled when he saw me waiting there for him.

"Well, little brother." Caedmon wrapped an arm around my shoulders as we walked towards the house. "Tomorrow's the day."

"I know." Now that I finally had him to myself, I was tongue shy. I wanted to wish him well on his journey with all of a bard's eloquence but, in truth, I wasn't yet able to string such words together. "I wish you good luck."

"I'll be sorry to not see you grow up." Caedmon squeezed my shoulders with sudden intensity. "This is not what a big brother should do — go off to have adventures while leaving his younger brother to make his way in the world alone."

Suddenly the days yawned ahead of me, long and cold and empty without the bright spark of Caedmon's enthusiasm. It was always he who suggested we explore the fields, or camp out, or fish in the stream. He who devised some elaborate game involving the mare or a few branches. What adventure and excitement would exist for me without Caedmon?

The dinner table that night bore a splendid feast of all Caedmon's favourite foods. Roasted hens stuffed with herbs, the last of winter's root vegetables carefully hoarded for the occasion, juicy salad greens from the garden our sister Eithne tended when she was well enough and, after, bowls of plump blackberries with fresh cream. We took our places at the table, my brothers jostling each other as they claimed their favoured seats.

I picked at some chicken and nibbled on a few berries, but my stomach churned. Bitterness and desertion warred with my desire to be proud of Caedmon for fulfilling his fate. And proud I was, but the prospect of how empty life would be without him loomed far nearer.

Our father, Fionn, beamed with pride at his soon-to-be soldier son and regularly slapped him on the back. If he felt sadness, he did not let it show. Our mother, Agata, was pale and quiet and ate almost as little as I. Caedmon had seconds and then thirds of everything.

Five of my six brothers were present: Eremon, the oldest son and Papa's heir; Caedmon, ever my favourite; Sitric, the first brother to not have his destiny mapped for him since birth and who spoke of becoming a scribe; Marrec and Conn, one soul split between two bodies. I was the last-born son, and after me came only Eithne, our sister. Fiachra, who was born after Sitric but before Marrec and Conn, was absent, but nobody expected him to come home. He was a druid and had higher matters to attend to than the small matter of a brother going off to battle.

The room was rowdy as my brothers joked and laughed, passing platters between them and teasing Caedmon with the horrors he might expect on the battlefield. Caedmon himself said little, too intent on filling himself with good food while he could. When Caedmon had finally eaten his fill, he leaned back, his hands on his belly.

"An excellent meal," he said. "And certainly a fitting farewell."

Papa wrapped an arm around Caedmon's shoulders.

"A tale is in order, I think. Something suitable with which to send our young soldier off to battle. Who would like to tell it?"

This was the opportunity I had awaited, for my tale was finally ready. I spoke quickly, before anyone else could volunteer.

"I will."

Silence greeted my announcement and I didn't miss the look that passed between my parents.

"Diarmuid," Mother said and her tone was cautious. "You have never before offered a tale. What causes this?"

At only ten summers old, I was too young to feel embarrassment.

"I have created a tale and I would like to tell it."

The silence lasted longer this time and I looked around the table, wondering why nobody spoke. All eyes were on our parents. Mother and Papa looked only at each other as if an unspoken conversation passed between them.

"We wondered when this day would come," Papa said, eventually. "Diarmuid, there is something you should know before you choose this path. Something about yourself and our family."

I waited, my heart suddenly beating hard. I could not even begin to guess what this secret might be. From the looks on my brothers' faces, it seemed only I was clueless, and perhaps Eithne, although her face was hard to read and I could never be sure whether she didn't understand or just wasn't interested.

Our parents looked at each other again and it seemed each waited for the other to speak. It was our mother who finally did.

"Diarmuid, you know you are the seventh son of a seventh son."

I waited. There must be more, for this was no secret to me. I had never met any of my uncles because Papa's brothers all perished long before I was born, although the circumstances of their deaths were never discussed. In fact, the one time I asked was the only time I saw my father cry.

"In our family, the seventh son of a seventh son is very special." Mother spoke slowly, as if choosing her words with care.

Oozing dread replaced the sweet feeling of anticipation. I would have fled, but my legs refused to move and I could do nothing but sit and wait, looking from Mother to Papa and back again.

"Diarmuid, in our family, the seventh son of a seventh son is always a bard," Papa said, and it seemed the words pained him.

The dread flowed away and my heart lifted. Finally, I too had a destiny. I was one of the chosen sons who had a fate to fulfil. I might not be heir or soldier or druid, but I was a *bard*.

"It's a very big responsibility," Papa said. "You have no idea how much responsibility it is to be a bard, to be a teacher of truths and a weaver of words, especially..." He stopped then and it seemed another unspoken message passed between him and Mother. An almost imperceptible shake of her head meant that whatever else he had intended went unsaid.

"Papa, why do you never tell any tales?" For if I was destined to be a bard, surely my father, as the seventh son of a seventh son, was too.

"I have told enough tales in my lifetime." His words hung heavily in the air. "More than enough. I care little to tell them anymore."

We adjourned to the living room. The room had looked a lot bigger back then and the stone fireplace towered higher than I stood. There was an assortment of both soft chairs and wooden benches, enough to seat a family of ten plus a few guests. The late summer evening was warm enough that we had no need for a fire, but we gathered in our accustomed places by the hearth. Papa leaned back into his chair and stared into the empty grate for some time before he finally turned to me.

"You may as well give us your tale, Diarmuid."

I had imagined this moment over and over. Myself standing before my family, back straight and head held high as I regaled them with my tale of love and loss and lessons learnt. They would gasp at the daring of its ending, for I would tell no tales with flaccid happy resolutions. No, if I was to be a bard, I would teach people, help them become better than they were. My tales would educate, enlighten, illuminate. I would be a bard without peer.

I stood and positioned myself in front of the fireplace and told the tale that had been playing through my mind during those final hazy days of summer. I poured all of my emotions into my words: my sadness at Caedmon's imminent departure; fear that he might never come home again; anxiety that he would be injured, or worse, in battle. Loneliness. Abandonment. Heartbreak. As I spoke, the pain eased. The act of tale telling soothed my soul and my heart soared. I had a destiny. I would be the most famous bard ever, for I was *meant* to tell tales.

My tale was about a young bard obsessed with his imagined muse, thinking of nothing but her with every waking moment and dreaming of her at night. Eventually, through some arcane spell or other mystery — I left that unexplained — he brings her to life, only to discover his fantasy made flesh and blood is some evil twist on the creature of his dreams. And thus the poor bard realises he must destroy his muse. I left the story there, with the bard setting out on his grand quest to track down the creature that was once his muse.

I had been so absorbed in my tale, I paid scant attention to my audience. In truth, I did not expect anything but adoration and praise. I emerged to discover my family sitting in silence. Not a single person met my eyes, not parent, nor brother, nor sister. Mother fled with a sob, one trembling hand pressed over her mouth. The silence stretched until eventually Papa cleared his throat.

"Well, Diarmuid," was all he said.

I left, my eyes so filled with tears that I tripped over an errant rug. I didn't want to go to my room, to remain in the same house as those who couldn't, or wouldn't, appreciate my tale, so I fled out the back door and somehow made my way into Eithne's herb garden.

Its inhabitants were nearing the end of their summer blooms and preparing for the cold months ahead. I recognised few of them: black-thorn, basil, mint. Others I knew would be there but couldn't identify: chamomile, juniper, sorrel. There would be rosemary and lavender, although I was hard pressed to tell between them, and many others whose names and uses were a mystery to me.

I sat on a wooden bench and let my tears flow. As they subsided, I inhaled the mingled aroma of herbs, finding solace in their sweetness. They would be pruned soon, by Eithne if she was well, or by a servant. Their stems and leaves, flowers and seeds would be gathered and dried for use in the coming season of illness and fevers.

Movement through the garden indicated I was no longer alone. In the darkness of the moon's ebb, I could not tell who came to offer comfort until Papa sat beside me.

"Diarmuid," he said, then sighed. "What a fine mess this is."

"I don't understand." I sniffed and wiped my nose on the back of my hand. "Why did they hate my tale?"

"It was a fine tale. We are just surprised you have come to this so young."

"I'm ten summers old. Caedmon has known he would be a soldier all his life."

"But Caedmon is sixteen summers and only now about to become a soldier."

Although his words were reasonable, it was hard to acknowledge this when my heart felt as if it had been trampled by a herd of cows.

"Why did nobody tell me I was to be a bard? It is a noble profession, not something terrible."

Papa sighed again and shifted slightly.

"Tell me. Why did I not know?"

"We did what we thought was best for you." He spoke slowly and hesitated often. "Your mother and I thought to let you choose your own path. There are sons enough in this family who have had their futures dictated to them. We wanted you to decide for yourself whether you would be a bard or something else."

"Is it true? That every seventh son of a seventh son is a bard?"

"In our family, yes. You are descended from an unbroken line of seventh sons through many generations. And every one a bard."

"Then it seems I never had a choice." I made no attempt to keep the bitterness from my voice.

Beside me, Papa shook his head.

"No. It seems not." He was silent for some time before he spoke next. "Diarmuid, I must warn you. Be careful of the tales you tell."

I waited. The seat creaked as Papa shifted and I thought he might leave without speaking further. At length he continued.

"As the seventh son of a seventh son, you have a special ability. You must be very careful. Sometimes… sometimes the things you say, the tales you tell, may come true."

A laugh bubbled up from inside of me. Relief, for I had thought he intended to tell me something terrible, but it was merely a joke.

"Absurd," I said. "And impossible."

I felt, rather than heard, him sigh.

"I wish it were so."

4

———

IDA

I AM. BUT I am not alone.

This place is confusing. There are terrors in here, demons he keeps well hidden. Nightmares and horror. Darkness and desolation. Despair. I crave… something. I don't know what. It is something… else. Radiance. Lightness. Beauty, symmetry, colour.

Now he is confused. Resentful. Lonely. Interesting. His heart pounds, his breath quickens. His thoughts are dark and lingering. The one he looks up to above all others has disappointed him. Oh, how he despairs now.

I whisper to myself, a sly comment intended for my own amusement. He hears me. And not only does he hear, but he understands. He weaves my comment into his own thoughts, braiding our words together until I can barely tell which were his and which were mine. He probably never knew.

I whisper again about the one he loves and his heart hardens. He believes me.

No longer am I confused or alone, for he is here with me. Or I am here with him. Day after day, I speak to him. Commentary about those around him, thoughts that bury themselves deep in his heart.

My words resonate with him. I feel power, intimacy, companionship. I feel alive.

He fancies himself a bard, so I whisper ideas. He takes them greedily and begs for more. I see myself take shape in his mind. A woman's form. He gives me long white hair and eyes the blue of a frozen river. A slender figure, dainty hands. Have I ever before had a form? I don't know. As I continue to whisper, his image of me grows firmer.

More and more, his thoughts linger on me. Now, with every event, every conversation, it is me to whom his mind turns first. He wonders what I would make of it, how I would respond. He names me: Ida. I don't know whether I have ever had a name before. Ida will do as well as any.

I soon learn how to make him feed me. And feed me he does. The flow of power, at first hesitant and intermittent, becomes a steady stream. As I feed, he weakens. Not so he would notice; physically he is no different. It is in his mind the changes occur. For I have learnt the type of thoughts he must have for me to draw power from him. As he sinks into melancholy, his loneliness and bitterness strengthen me. And, gradually, I forget I ever longed for something else.

I anticipate that he will realise what is happening, but day after day, week after week, he doesn't. Eventually I stop expecting it. And indeed I hope he does not realise. At least, not until I am strong enough to leave. After that, it won't matter. But for now, I need him. He will be my freedom.

5

BRIGIT

"**B**RIGIT, ARE YOU shelling those peas or mashing them?" Mother's tone was sharp and her face said clearly that she despaired of trying to teach me anything.

I removed my sticky hands from the bowl and wiped them on my apron, leaving green streaks across its crisp whiteness. While lost in my thoughts, I had been crushing the pods.

"I'm sorry."

Mother sighed and turned back to the herbal concoction she was preparing. I studied her profile, silhouetted in the late afternoon sun streaming through the kitchen window. My thick, dark hair that frizzed out of control in humid weather was a match for hers, as were my dark eyes and sharp chin. I envied the roundness of my younger sisters who were all dimples and soft features. I was angles and sharp lines with neither bust nor waist. Only my hair marked me as female, although I never wore it with the ribbons and pretty braids of my sisters. Instead, I pulled it back at the nape of my neck and secured it with a plain string. Even so, it continuously escaped.

I brushed a few strands away from my face and turned to the window, longing to be outside despite the bleak landscape. The thick stone walls of our lodge kept the heat in and by mid afternoon, the warmth in the kitchen was stifling. Outside, the snow was thin on the ground and the wind rustling the leaves of the fir trees promised adventure. Inside was comfortable and familiar but hardly exciting. A worn workbench at which Mother and I stood. Shelves of plates, cups and cooking implements hung from the grey stone walls. A stack of firewood sat tidily in the corner. A pot of soup bubbled on the wood stove. The hardy scent of herbs and vegetables mingled with the yeasty aroma of fresh-baked bread, making my mouth water.

"No point wasting good peas," Mother said. "We can use them in the soup. Just remove the pods. And, Brigit dear, try not to mash the rest."

"Yes, Mother."

I bent my head over the bowl and tried hard to focus on my task. But soon I was again lost in my thoughts, my hands moving of their own accord as visions swirled before my eyes. A man: young, dark haired, with a shadowy raven clinging to his shoulder. A small dog, its white hair streaked with blood and eyes filled with pain. A woman: pale, thin, her eyes shining with steely strength.

The Sight ran in the blood of our female line. My mother was a wise woman, as was her mother, and her mother before. I, too, was expected to become a wise woman, steeped in knowledge of herbs and cures. But I had never been very good at doing what I was told. Rather than a calm, comfortable life, I wanted adventure, mystery, danger, yes even romance. Of course, there was no reason why I couldn't have all that as a wise woman, or perhaps before, but a quiet life dedicated to healing and wisdom was not what I wanted. The visions told me my path led in another direction.

Mother must have spoken several times before her voice again intruded on my world.

"Brigit!"

"Mother?"

I followed her eyes to my bowl to find I had done no more than mash the remaining peas in their pods. Guilt flooded through me. We couldn't afford to waste food this late in winter and these were the last of the fresh peas. There would be only dried peas now until the new season.

Mother sighed. Did she truly think she could make a wise woman, or even a competent wife, out of me? Perhaps she was unwilling to concede I was not suited for the destiny intended for me. Certainly, she didn't know how much of a wise woman's talent I possessed, for I never spoke of the visions or of how easily I retained knowledge of herbs and their uses. I paid little enough attention to her instructions because one glance was all it took for a recipe to imprint on my mind.

I hid my abilities as best I could, for fear my fate would be irreversibly fixed if I revealed them. I never deliberately ruined a recipe, any more than I had intended to mash today's peas. How could I focus on shelling peas or distilling herbs when my head was full of the dark visions that might be my future? How much longer would I wait before the visions became reality?

"Brigit, please, remove the pods and leave them. I'll add them to the soup when I finish here."

Mother hunched over her bowl, adding a handful of herb and a sprinkle of powder. A cough mixture, it seemed.

"Who is that for?" I began picking pods out of the bowl, leaving what I could of the mashed peas. I rarely asked about Mother's duties, for fear that a question might be mistaken for interest, but I needed to atone for today's carelessness.

"One of the villagers has a sick child," Mother said with a sigh, pausing to brush back the hair escaping from her bun. It stubbornly sprang back, just like mine did. Her face was lined and her eyes tired. Likely, my presence today had only made more work for her.

With a pang, I regretted my inattention. My fate was not her fault and Mother had no more choice in her future than I did. All she had ever done was try to prepare me for the day when she wouldn't be here. Still, she had a more accommodating nature than I. She wasn't stubborn like me. That's a word I've heard applied to myself more times than I can count. My father was oft described as stubborn too, and it caused his death. Perhaps that's why Mother perseveres with me. She's hoping I won't make the same mistakes as he did.

"Can I help you with something else?" I asked and, for once, I sincerely meant it.

Mother gave me a brief smile.

"No, my dear, you run along. I can manage here on my own."

I fled, stopping only for a coat, scarf and my winter boots. After the warmth of the kitchen, the cold outside hit me like a physical blow. The sun, although high in the sky, yielded little warmth and I shivered even with my thick coat. I walked briskly, intending no particular destination.

Snow drifted down from the trees as a breeze danced through their branches, leaving them naked without their winter adornment. Blackthorn, with its spiny branches that come spring would be covered with creamy-white buds. Hazel, with its grey-brown bark, towering over its neighbours. Birch, its slender branches uncaring of appearance as it grew however it chose. In summer, these fields would be thick with lush grass to cushion my feet as I walked. Now I trod on fresh snow, crisp and crunching with each step.

Freed of distractions, the visions came stronger, flooding my mind with a confusing array of images, until I hardly knew where, or when, I was. I could make no sense of them, not least the two I saw most often: the white dog covered in blood and the young man, hardly more than a boy, who cradled the dog as tenderly as if it was a child. Who were they? And what was my connection to them? Our link, whatever it was, must be strong for them to feature so frequently in my visions.

I had little control over the images and was ill-inclined to spend any time learning such a thing. Still, today was one of the rare times I wished I could control them. I needed clearer information on what these visions meant to me and on what part I was to play in the forthcoming events. The visions had been more frequent of late and that likely meant something would happen very soon. If only I knew what.

Soon the sun began to sink and the air became even colder. As I headed for home, a figure appeared, some distance off to the side. I watched out of the corner of my eye for a while. It was a girl, I was certain of that. Long of both leg and hair, she easily kept pace with me. When I turned towards her she disappeared, returning only when I looked away. One of the fey, no doubt.

The fey had long had a presence in my life. My earliest memories included a young girl, seemingly no older than myself, although the appearance of the fey can be misleading. She and I played together in a fall of autumn leaves, in the water of summer rivers, in the cool depths of the woods. She did everything I did: ran, swam, laughed, danced. We climbed trees together, sunbaked on rocks, and walked hand in hand.

As I grew up, she stayed the same and eventually she no longer came to me. I had grieved the loss of my childhood friend and wondered why she absented herself from my world. Perhaps the more adult pursuits now imposed on me were of no interest to her. Perhaps she found some other child to play with. Whatever the reason, I remembered her fondly, although, strangely, I no longer recalled her name and with the passing of time, her once-familiar face had blurred in my memory.

Some time after my first fey friend left, another of her kind came into my life. He was thin and lithe with sticks in his hair and grass stains on his tattered trousers. He taunted me as I was kept indoors, learning to sew or read or cook. He knew I longed to be free, running through the fields and exploring the woods, and he teased me with images of the life now withheld from me.

When I refused to yield to the outdoor delights he dangled before me, he played tricks. Needles would suddenly embed themselves in my finger, causing bright drops of blood to ruin my embroidery. Pots overflowed and wriggling bugs appeared in the centre of the pies I baked. Rugs slid out from under my feet and footstools suddenly appeared in front of me as I walked. Many a scrape, bruise, burn and cut I endured before he left me.

Several years had passed since then and I thought the fey had finally stopped watching me. Now, in my twentieth year, they had returned. Well, the girl could walk beside me if she chose, provided that was all she did.

I ignored the fey girl and she seemed happy enough for me to do so. The sky was almost night-dark by the time I reached home and the light spilling from the windows, promising warmth and human companionship, was a welcome sight. I banished both fey and visions from my mind. I would not allow them to intrude tonight.

6

BRIGIT

SLEEP THAT NIGHT was long in coming and in the quiet of night, the visions lingered.

The man, the woman, the bloodstained terrier. A road stretching through unfamiliar fields and hills, winding ever onward out of my sight. The terrier stands in a dragon's den, surrounded by the creature's treasures. A man and a boy explore a barrow. The boy, now a man himself, and the dog sleep together beside a fire. Another man, large and with a kind face, strokes the little dog's head with a tenderness that makes my heart ache. A confrontation with the fey; I myself step forward and speak to their queen. And in the background of every vision, a raven with glossy black plumage and blood dripping from its beak.

The images jumbled together and I had no sense of their order. The Sight could show past, present, future or maybe, and the only thing of which I could be sure was that these visions were connected to me. This future would collide with my future. This past would impact my present.

I woke with dry and gritty eyes and a head that felt like it was stuffed full of straw. Even in my sleep I couldn't escape the Sight's warning, for blood and the ever-present raven filled my dreams. I dressed and pulled a comb through my hair. The water in the bowl on my dresser was bitingly cold as I splashed my face.

Outside, the sun rose into a clear sky. Light breeze teased the branches of birch and blackthorn, and kicked up the snow on the ground. If the fey girl watched, I couldn't sense her.

In the kitchen, the aroma of last night's soup lingered, competing with the fresh bread Mother removed from the oven as I entered. She deposited the loaf on the scarred wooden table, which was set for breakfast, and sat. Her shoulders were slumped and her face haggard as she absently brushed the hair from her eyes. Did the visions plague her all night as they did me? I murmured a greeting as I sat on a chair on the opposite side of the table and served myself a bowl of porridge.

"You look tired," Mother said, echoing my own thoughts about her.

My gaze flicked up and met hers. I saw silent understanding. She knew. Even if I pretended I saw nothing, she knew.

"I'm fine," I said. "Don't worry about me."

It wasn't until I had finished my porridge and took my bowl to the sink that she spoke again.

"Oh, but I do," she said softly. "I always do."

I pretended I didn't hear and spent a little longer at the sink than necessary, scrubbing my bowl until it was spotless. I dried it carefully and placed it on a shelf. Only once I was sure my voice wouldn't betray me did I speak again.

"What do you need me to do today?"

Mother gave me a wry look. "After your help yesterday, I'm not sure I need any more assistance from you."

"I feel bad about the peas. There must be something I can do. You look so tired."

Mother smiled and rubbed her temples. "If only this headache would go away. What you could do, I suppose, is take a compress down to Old Man Tam. He cut his foot last week. When he finally called for me yesterday, the wound was red and hot."

"It festers."

"Yes, but perhaps not too badly. If he had waited another day or two, it would have been more serious. I released pressure from the wound and used what herbs I had with me. But I promised I would take him a compress today."

"I'll look after that for you."

She gave me a look and I knew exactly what she was thinking.

"I promise I'll pay attention. Arnica and comfrey for the pain, and fenugreek or thyme to draw out the infection."

Mother smiled and if she seemed sad, I quickly dismissed it.

Noise from upstairs indicated my sisters were awake. Shrieks, giggles and a heavy thud as something, or someone, fell to the floor made me thankful I had risen early enough to avoid breakfast with them. Their exuberance was too much first thing in the morning, especially while I was still trying to shed lingering memories of visions and dreams I didn't understand.

As I set off for Old Man Tam's cottage some time later, I was confident I had honoured Mother's instructions. A jar containing the herbal concoction for the compress was safely tucked into a bag along with a few pears and a handful of eggs. Icy wind burned the bare skin on my face. I wrapped my scarf more snugly around my neck and hurried on.

Old Man Tam's lodge was small and looked like it had been built in haste. He answered promptly when I knocked on the door. His eyes, sunk deep within folds of skin, examined me for longer than seemed necessary to verify my identity.

"I was expecting your mother," he said.

His face was so wrinkled I couldn't tell smile from frown, but I sensed disappointment. I tried to make my voice pleasant.

"She's feeling poorly today, so she sent me instead."

He stared down at the bag in my hands and this time I received the distinct impression of a frown.

"She promised she would bring a compress today."

"I have it right here." He didn't need to know it was I who had made it.

"Well, I suppose you had better come in then," he said at length.

I swallowed the retort that sprang to my lips. Clearly I did not have my mother's ability to win people over with just a few words. He led me into the living room and I winced at how he favoured his right leg. What would I do if the wound seemed beyond the aid of a compress? Old Man Tam lowered himself into a faded stuffed chair by the fireplace and propped his leg up on a footstool. When I removed the bandage, I was relieved to see no sign of the skin turning bad.

I heated a pot of water on the wood stove. The kitchen was somewhat bare but tidy enough. Plates and cups were neatly arranged on shelves, the bench was clean, and a small basket of cut wood sat on the floor next to the stove. If Old Man Tam had a servant who cleaned the house and looked after him, she didn't seem to be in attendance today. Once the water was hot, I showed him how to steep the herbs and then, once it had cooled somewhat, to soak a cloth in it. I wrapped the compress around his foot and Old Man Tam sighed.

"That does feel good, Missy," he said, somewhat begrudgingly.

"My name's Brigit."

"Sure it is, Missy." He sounded almost amenable. "Sure it is."

The house was quiet, the only other inhabitant seemingly a fat black cat who glared at me from a chair in the corner of the room. Old Man Tam's wife had died years ago. I remembered her, but only barely. A squat, bad-tempered old woman who walked with a stoop and a cane. She loathed children immensely, or at least, she loathed me.

There was no reason to linger. I left Old Man Tam, murmuring some vague words about being sure my mother would call in to see him soon, and fled, tripping over my own feet and his cat in my eagerness to be gone. This was the life ahead of me. An eternity of answering calls from folk who needed some simple medical treatment. Caring for those who clearly disliked me but had no other options. Sick children. Pregnant women seeking remedies to ease nausea or perhaps rid their belly of an unwanted babe. Old people, whose bodies were beginning to fail. Some, I knew, Mother could help. For others, the best she could do was to ease their pain for a while.

There was no danger or adventure in this life. No romance or mystery. Just the mind-numbing monotony of visits to the sick and the old. Reassuring and soothing them, dispensing wisdom with compassion and understanding. There were girls who left their families to live with a wise woman in order to learn her craft.

But I didn't want a future I had no say in. I wanted to mount a horse and ride off over the far distant plains on some marvellous quest. I wanted to perform noble and heroic deeds, to seek treasures and save innocents and come riding back home in triumph. But that is not the life a woman aspires to. It is not the life a decent woman may lead. And yet, the visions suggested this sort of future was in store for me.

It seemed there were two fates ahead of me. The one Mother had tried to prepare me for, and the one in the visions. Could the act of choosing determine which one I lived? Were both fates open to me until I chose? Perhaps this was why the visions lingered, vivid and strong and compelling. They urged me to choose.

I could follow the fate intended for me, become a wise woman, perhaps marry some day. My husband would likely be a farmer, or a soldier. I would live out my life in security, perhaps even in comfort if I was lucky. There would probably be children, and a life that was quiet, uneventful, and of use to my community. Or I could follow the visions and seek danger, romance, mystery and adventure. There would be blood and fear and pain, and if I survived all that, I would know I had truly lived.

As I left Old Man Tam's house and strode along the dusty path that led home, hugging my coat tight against the cold wind, I chose. I wanted danger and adventure. I didn't want potions and possets, compresses and simple charms. I wanted mystery and romance. And if blood and pain came with that choice, I'd gladly take them too.

7

DIARMUID

THE NIGHT OF my nineteenth Winter Solstice arrived far too swiftly. Winter kept a firm grip on Silver Downs. Frost strangled the ivy's attempt to creep up the house walls. The sky was bleak, heavy with the promise of snow and the tang of wood smoke, and empty without the trill of blackbird or robin. At night, winds lashed the house and sought out every crack between window and pane.

I had found no opportunity to speak privately to Caedmon since the night we sat up late, drinking ale in front of the fire. I sought him out over and over, but he was never where people said he had intended to go. For everyone else, the longest night of the year was cause for celebration, for the Solstice heralded the turn of winter and an end to the long darkness. For me, spring's pleasures seemed far away.

As the sun sent streaks of fire through the sky, I returned to my bedchamber and changed into my best shirt, my fingers fumbling over the buttons. The mere thought of talking to a woman caused my hands to shake and my knees to tremble, even when alone in my bedchamber. If I had cause to actually speak to one, my voice would croak, words would come out in the wrong order, and sooner or later I would skulk away, thoroughly embarrassed.

I threw myself onto the bed, intending to linger for a few minutes. I needed just a little longer alone. I had never before had cause to disagree with Caedmon, never voiced a thought in opposition to him. He, of all my brothers, was the one I looked up to. Ida whispered something which I ignored. There was no room in my mind for her at present.

Tonight's celebrations were at the neighbouring estate of Three Trees. Was it one of the daughters of that family with whom Caedmon had made his arrangements? They were pretty, bubbly girls — four of them — and I routinely avoided them. Their constant giggles and banter confused me and I was never sure whether they flirted or made fun of me.

What would the girl, whoever she was, think of the fact that my brother had asked her to bed me? Would she laugh or politely restrain her mirth? She might assume I had some deformity or perhaps that I was feeble. Would I even be able to speak to her or would the words flee, leaving me standing open-mouthed and her certain I was a simpleton? Oh dear gods, perhaps she wasn't the first girl Caedmon had approached.

Lost in thought, I was startled when Caedmon entered my bedchamber. He looked very fine in a red shirt with gold braid on the cuffs. As usual, he didn't wait for an invitation but flung himself onto the bed, jostling me aside as if I weighed no more than a child.

"So, little brother," he said.

"Caedmon, where have you been? I've been looking everywhere for you."

I scooted down to the end, as my narrow bed wasn't wide enough for the two of us to lie side by side.

"I'm sure you have. But no cowardice tonight, eh? It's all arranged. All you have to do is show up and be a man."

"Who is it?" Not that I had any intention of going through with his plan.

"Her name is Rhiwallon."

"Do I know her?"

"Do you want her family history? It doesn't matter who she is or where she's from. What matters is she is willing and has promised to be gentle with you."

"She knows?" My face burned.

"Of course she knows." Caedmon frowned. "I would hardly set you up with a girl who was unwilling."

"But—"

"Fine. I know you, little brother. You won't let it rest until I tell you. Rhiwallon is about three summers younger than you — I didn't exactly ask her age — and her father runs a tavern in Maker's Well. She's quite a pretty thing: red hair, green eyes, perhaps a little skinny for my taste, but she should suit you well enough."

"She's from Maker's Well? Why is she going to Three Trees for the Solstice?"

"Why not?" he countered with a shrug. "Does it matter? You think too much, little brother."

"Caedmon, I can't—"

He hauled himself up from the bed and left, pausing in the doorway to look back at me. "I've gone to a lot of effort to set this up for you, little brother."

"I know but—"

"It's time to leave. That's what you're wearing?"

I smoothed my green shirt. Perhaps the fabric was not quite as bright as it used to be and a few threads had worked loose from the cuffs, but it was still perfectly decent, even if it wasn't as fine as Caedmon's. When I met his eyes again, he was frowning.

"Wait here," he said and left.

He returned a few moments later and tossed me a blue shirt, which had round shell buttons and silver thread around the collar and hem.

"Hurry up," Caedmon said with a groan as I hesitated. "You don't need to inspect it. It's clean. It doesn't even have any blood stains."

"Blood stains?"

"Just put it on, will you?"

Caedmon tapped his foot as I pulled off my shirt and shrugged into his, which was certainly far nicer than anything I owned. It was somewhat too big for me, for I was ever slender and Caedmon was broad-shouldered and well-muscled. For a moment, I was wistful. Had I been the soldier son, that could be me right now, lending my younger brother a shirt and teaching him about women and life. But I had no younger brothers and Eithne was hardly likely to need advice from me. Besides, it wasn't like I actually intended to go along with Caedmon's plan. I would seek an opportunity to slip away from him after we arrived at Three Trees. I would find somewhere to hide and wait until it was time to leave. Caedmon would be angry, but at least I wouldn't be humiliated. It wasn't much of a plan, but it was all I had.

He hustled me down the stairs and we pulled on our winter coats, which hung by the front door. With a thick scarf, gloves, a hat and my sturdy boots, I could hardly move, but I would be warm.

The rest of the family already waited by the cart. The oxen snorted and stomped impatiently. Papa wore a splendid dark blue cape and Mother had a hint of yellow showing between scarf and collar. My oldest brother Eremon stood with an arm around his wife, Niamh, who looked unusually relaxed, probably because their twins had been left with a servant. And there was Eithne, my little sister, her hair tied back with a red ribbon, her eyes sparkling with excitement.

Of course, this was not all of our family. Sitric was in Maker's Well and would attend the festivities there. Twins Marrec and Conn had also gone to the town to celebrate with the families of the women to whom they were betrothed. And, as always, Fiachra was absent, he who was training to be a druid.

We piled into the cart and set off. The fields we passed were empty, the sheep locked away in warm barns for the night. As the oxen hauled us ever closer to Three Trees, nausea swirled in my stomach. I fidgeted and shifted in my seat. What if I couldn't get away from Caedmon? The girl would surely laugh at me as I stammered and blushed and made my excuses. Perhaps she would tell her friends and they would giggle together. Of course, she would tell Caedmon and then all of my brothers would know too. I wanted to jump down from the cart and run straight back to Silver Downs. To distract myself, I turned to my sister who sat beside me. She was bundled up in a thick coat with a blanket wrapped around her shoulders. Her usually pale cheeks were flushed with excitement.

"You look pretty this evening, Eithne," I said.

She caught my eye briefly, startled, then ducked her head and blushed.

"Thank you," she whispered. "You look very handsome."

"I'm wearing one of Caedmon's shirts," I confessed.

Eithne smiled but didn't reply.

"Are you meeting with friends tonight?" I asked, then wished I hadn't, for I had no wish to embarrass her.

"Oh yes," she said with unaccustomed vivacity and blushed again.

I was too surprised to ask further and sat silently after that, watching the trees and homes we trundled pass. A raven perched on the naked branches of an oak tree, watching us intently. The fire faded from the sky, replaced with encroaching blackness, and we arrived at Three Trees.

Some distance from the lodge, a massive fire cast a golden sheen over the field. At least two dozen people already gathered nearby, their heavy winter coats abandoned in a pile on a bench. The air echoed with laughter and the crackling of the fire.

Caedmon had anticipated my intent to escape, for he was by my side even as I climbed down from the cart. He flung an arm across my shoulders. To anyone watching, it would look like a friendly moment of brotherly solidarity. They wouldn't see his iron grip.

We had barely disembarked before a servant appeared in front of us, bearing a tray of mugs. Three Trees always provided the very finest ales and Caedmon released me briefly to claim two mugs. He thrust one at me and took a swig from the other.

"Drink up, little brother. Not too much, mind, but enough to get that tight look off your face."

I took the mug, glancing around for hiding places. Lights shone from the direction of the house. A looming shape in the other direction would be one of the outbuildings, perhaps the barn. I could see little else in the shadows.

Caedmon wrapped his arm around me again, keeping me clenched by his side as he greeted friends and paid his respects to our hosts. Despite his carefree and cheery air, I sensed disappointment, perhaps because Grainne, his intended bride, was nowhere to be found. He consoled himself with a special greeting for each of the daughters of the Three Trees household. Born only a year apart, they were plump and dark-haired and exceedingly giggly. I wondered how Caedmon could find anything to say to them. They apparently found him amusing, for they burst into laughter at everything he said.

Eventually we ended up to the side of the huge fire. The air was crisp with winter's chill and heavy with the smell of smoke and roast pig and the sounds of celebration. It seemed only I dreaded this night, for everywhere I looked folk smiled and laughed and drank. A boy of around my own age slung his arm around a girl who smiled up at him. Another couple clasped hands and slipped away together into the darkness. Heat rose to my cheeks and I looked away.

I was far too warm so close to the fire. Perhaps I should plead ill and beg of my hosts somewhere to sleep. Before I could voice my thought, servants began offering around trays of roast meat and bread. Caedmon somehow managed to eat his fill without once releasing me. I picked at a thick slice of wild boar wedged inside a loaf but had no appetite. I tried, now and then, as Caedmon conversed with various neighbours, to wiggle out from under his arm. But even when he seemed to pay me no attention, my slightest movement caused his arm to tighten.

Under Caedmon's stern eye, I drank two mugs of ale. By the end of the second, my head swam and I was suddenly less concerned about my upcoming embarrassment. At least once this was over, Caedmon would be satisfied he had tried to make a man of me, regardless of the success or otherwise of the endeavour.

Two men standing at the edge of the crowd caught my eye. They were druids, all brown robes and braided hair with golden torcs around their necks. They neither ate nor drank, just watched, blending into the background of the festivities. I only noticed them because the younger one caught my eye and stared for a long moment before he nodded and turned away.

My heart thudded. Was this my brother, Fiachra? I was but five summers old when he left and I barely remembered what he looked like back then. The druid was dark-haired like all the men in our family and broad of shoulder like my brothers. His age was difficult to estimate in the shifting shadows of the fire, but druids tended to have an ageless quality anyway. I would have liked to approach him, but I didn't know what to say and I would feel like a fool if it weren't Fiachra.

Eventually the other druid came forward to conduct the solstice ceremony. It was blessedly brief, for this particular druid was one who always kept the formalities short, perhaps understanding that folk preferred to eat and drink, talk and dance than listen to a lengthy invocation of the beings of air, earth, fire and water.

As the druids retreated back into the shadows, Caedmon secured another mug of ale for each of us. His arm was still firmly clamped over my shoulders, leaving no possibility of escape. I clutched my mug with sweaty fingers.

"Drink that down, little brother," Caedmon ordered.

My head already spun and my stomach rolled as I caught the lingering scent of roasted meat. Casually, as if we were merely meandering around to speak to some friends, Caedmon steered me away from the fire and towards the barn. Light shone dimly from beneath the covered windows. My heart pounded wildly and I tried to wriggle out from under his arm. He cracked open the barn door and swiftly shoved me inside.

"Her name is Rhiwallon," he reminded me. "And don't come back out until you're a man." He grinned at me and raised his mug. "Have fun, little brother."

By the time I turned to face him, he had closed the door. Ida whispered to me, dark thoughts about betrayal and desertion. Before I could think about slipping away, a voice came from behind me.

"You must be Diarmuid."

Her voice was soft and low, and under other circumstances I might have considered it pleasant. But now it merely filled me with horror. Dread trickled all the way down to my toes as I turned to face her.

She was exactly the type of girl who always struck me dumb. Moss-green eyes sparkled as if we shared a joke. Long, reddish hair drifted around her shoulders. She held herself confidently, casually, and I knew instantly she had never experienced a moment of doubt about herself. She leaned against the rough wooden wall, waiting for me to finish my inspection of her.

"Are- are you Rhi- Rhiwallon?" Already I had made a fool of myself.

The girl didn't answer. Instead she peeled herself off the wall and walked towards me. I thrust my mug onto a shelf, very nearly sloshing it everywhere, and shoved my hands behind my back before she could see how they trembled.

She came right up close to me. Her head barely reached my shoulders and as she leaned in, all I could smell was summer and sunshine and herbs. I wanted to close my eyes and breathe in the scent of her. Rhiwallon rested a hand lightly on my chest. Could she feel how fast my heart beat?

"Caedmon said you were handsomer than he."

"Oh. Am I?" What a daft thing to say. Ida's mocking laugh echoed through my mind.

"Hmm, perhaps," she said with a slow smile that filled my stomach with unexpected warmth. She reached behind me for my hand. "Come with me."

The barn was tidy with everything put away in its place. Farm tools and horse tack hung from hooks on the walls. Smaller items sat neatly on the shelves. Rhiwallon led me to the back of the barn, past the lamp that sat on a workbench, to where the stalls were shrouded in darkness. My nose recognised both horse and cow. We entered one of the stalls where there was a large pile of fresh hay and no beast.

Rhiwallon turned to me and her eyes were wide and dark as she wrapped her arms around my neck. She pressed her body against mine and kissed me full on the lips. I had never been kissed by a girl before, except for a brief touch on the cheek by Mother or Eithne and once by Grainne.

Certainly those familial kisses did not make my knees knock together so loud I wondered whether anyone else heard and nor did they make my heart beat fit to burst right through my chest. Those kisses also didn't make other parts of my body respond the way Rhiwallon's kiss did and I wondered for the first time whether perhaps I could actually do this. If she was kind and gentle and didn't laugh at me, I might actually…

Rhiwallon broke the kiss and pulled away. Keeping her gaze fixed on me, she unlaced her blouse. It fell open and her bare breasts shone in the lamplight. Rhiwallon took my hand and placed it on her breast. Her nipples hardened under my hand and I froze, wondering what I was supposed to do.

She kissed me again and now my hand seemed to have a mind of its own as it gently explored her bare skin, stroking her soft breasts and lingering over her rounded stomach. She pulled me down into the hay. We lay side by side and she wrapped her leg around me. My hand slid down to explore the silky expanse of thigh beneath her skirts and she moaned and wriggled closer to me. As her hand edged into my trousers, panic returned. My budding desire fled and I was limp beneath her hand.

Rhiwallon pulled her lips off mine to stare at me quizzically. "Diarmuid—"

Mortified, I pulled away and stood, swiftly buttoning the pants I didn't even remember her undoing.

"Diarmuid." She tried again and although her voice was gentle, I couldn't bear to stay there another moment.

"Sorry," I muttered, straightening my borrowed shirt as I fled.

I tripped over something and slammed into the wall. There was a soft giggle behind me and my face flamed as I scurried out, my humiliation complete.

Caedmon loitered nearby as I exited the barn. He started to speak, but my glare cut him off. I said nothing but stalked away into the darkness, seeking somewhere to hide until it was time to go home.

8

DIARMUID

$\mathcal{C}$AEDMON AND GRAINNE'S handfasting was a sevennight after Midwinter. I had slept poorly since my encounter with Rhiwallon and woke that morning feeling morose and peevish. My dreams had been filled with the raven that stared with empty eyes while blood dripped from its beak.

As I lay in bed, the house already echoed with the chaos and commotion of preparation for the festivities, even though dawn was barely breaking. I pulled the covers over my head. Perhaps nobody would notice if I didn't get up today. Eventually, footsteps thundering past my bedchamber and a rooster's crowing drove me from my bed.

I dressed in yesterday's discarded clothes. What did it matter if my pants had grass stains on the seat and my shirt was splattered with soup? Nobody would notice what I wore. The only time anyone saw me — *really* saw me — was when I told a tale, and then it was only to criticise.

I slunk through the house like a storm cloud, ignoring Eithne's excited cry of "Diarmuid, come here", and slipped out the back door. Swathed in coat, scarf and hat, with my boots crunching over yesterday's snow and the fields around me silent, my mood lifted somewhat. The air smelled of smoke and fir, and was empty of sound other than what I myself made. There was no chatter of voice, no clashing of pots, no crashing of brooms. The fresh, empty air cleared my head a little.

Silver Downs lay nestled in a valley created by rolling hills of pastureland. In the summer, the fields were covered with silver thistledown, their flowers round as a bumblebee's belly. Many hours had I spent lying amidst the thistledown, blowing on the fragile blossoms to release them up into the air and waiting for them to drift back down, falling whisper-soft on my face. Even more hours had I spent roaming the fields, up hill, down into gully, across the streams. I knew every footstep of those fields, all the way from one border to the other, from the corner in which the lodge stood to the far edge where the woods began.

Papa forbade us to enter the woods, for it was said they contained a doorway into the realm of the fey. Tales told of those who ventured deep into the woods and never returned. Whether they declined to come back, having sampled the delights of the fey world, or whether they weren't permitted to return, nobody could say.

In truth, I had never thought much about the woods. They were there on the edge of our land, and they were there on the edge of my consciousness. As a small boy, I was kept too busy to contemplate trespassing into forbidden territory. Six older brothers meant I learnt to fight somewhat, for they routinely wrestled me to the ground for the smallest fault. I had no formal schooling, but my brothers took turns teaching me to read and I could draft a simple letter and read the reply. I could count and tally sums and I knew the history of the lands surrounding us. Many years passed before I realised how unusual it was that all our family could read, write and tally at least a little.

By mid morning, I had reached one of the twin rivers meandering across the corner of the estate. In summer, this was a pleasant spot where one could watch fish swimming in the river and water bugs dancing across the top. Now, the waters were frozen with just the slightest ripple in the ice hinting at how they usually flowed.

Sitting on a sun-warmed rock, my eyes traced the outline of an aged oak tree, its bare branches stark against the winter-grey sky. I tucked the image away for use in a tale and Ida murmured her approval.

With the sun beating down on me and the satisfaction of solitude, things didn't seem quite so bad. I cautiously turned my mind to my Midwinter humiliation. Anger soared, towards Caedmon, Rhiwallon, myself. Embarrassment warred with frustration that Caedmon had refused to listen when I protested his plan. No doubt by now Rhiwallon had told everyone she knew. Heat rose in my cheeks, my hands trembled, and Ida whispered of treachery. I pushed away the thoughts, and Ida, for my feelings were yet too raw to examine them closely.

I would spend this time here by the river creating a new tale. Something to amaze my audience. My most recent tale-telling, at Caedmon's betrothal party, still sent pangs of hurt through my heart. I had not yet achieved any level of success as a bard. Yet every time a tale failed to please, it left me determined to create a better one. One day, I would compose the perfect tale. A tale no audience could ignore. It might even be my very next tale. So I pushed the memories away and got to work.

I started with a warrior. Immediately I thought of Caedmon and I hardened my heart. I would not allow myself to become distracted. I had work to do. So, a warrior. A simple man with no large expectations for his life other than to survive each battle, marry a good woman and produce at least three sons. But of course, life is never as simple as we wish. Perhaps his wife has produced only daughters and he fears he will never have an heir. My interest dissipated. What audience would want to hear such drivel?

I lay back on the rock, my body fitting comfortably into a shallow depression. In summer, I could lie here and listen to the river gurgling over rocks and around water plants. Small patches of sunlight would pierce a green canopy above me and dust motes would sparkle as they danced in its rays. Now, I could see straight up through the naked trees to the grey sky beyond. I was warm enough with my thick coat and the sun streaming down on me through the skeletons of the trees.

My thoughts wandered through a variety of topics. Possible tale ideas. Caedmon's upcoming handfasting. My muse. I called her Ida for it meant thirst, an appropriate name given how I longed for her inspiration. Sometimes I pretended she was real, that my inspiration truly stemmed from a presence inhabiting my mind. What would it be like to share my head with another living creature? Would she know my thoughts and I hers? We would be closer than any husband and wife.

In my mind's eye, Ida smiled and images from my new tale swirled around me. I suddenly realised what it lacked: courage and purpose. Perhaps one of the fey has fallen in love with the warrior's wife and tries to persuade her to leave him. But the wife is faithful to her husband, and refuses the attentions of the fey. So the fey sets three tasks for her husband to complete to prove he is worthy of her.

The idea was plausible enough, for the fey interfered in human lives for their own reasons. Some believed it was because they wove human lives into a pattern to satisfy a design only they saw. Others thought it was merely whim that drove the fey to interfere and that there was no higher purpose. Me, I didn't know. What the fey chose to do with the lives in which they interfered was of no concern to me other than as fodder for my tales.

A tiny smile played on Ida's lips as if she was satisfied with these initial explorations of my new tale. Her mouth was wide, the lips thin and blood red. It was not an attractive mouth. Not like Rhiwallon's.

Again, the hot memory of humiliation flooded through me, along with a stab of anger towards Caedmon. The situation was his fault. It was he who pushed me to do what I didn't want to. The more I thought about it, the madder I got until if Caedmon had appeared in front of me right then, I might almost have hit him.

Ida's smile broke through my thoughts and again I felt she was satisfied. My new tale pleased her and the knowledge mollified me, cooling my temper. It was enough, for now, that an audience of one, albeit imaginary, was pleased. For that's all any bard ever wants, to please his audience. Perhaps if I could learn to please my imaginary muse, I might also succeed with a real audience. One day, I would weave my words into a beautiful constellation of humour and truth and learning, fine enough to satisfy any audience. One day, I would conclude the telling of a tale to smiles and nods, applause and cheers, rather than silence and sudden excuses.

I spent the morning pleasantly absorbed in my new tale. Ideas appeared in my mind — snippets of dialogue, glimpses of imagery — as if fed by Ida. And this tale felt different from any other I had created. It was authentic. Honest. Illuminating. There was light and dark, wonder and horror, and an outcome that would surprise even the most learned listener. Surely this would be the tale to please my audience.

9

DIARMUID

AS THE SUN reached the midpoint of the sky, and my stomach growled with hunger, I started towards home. All morning I had busied myself with my new tale but now, as I drew closer to family and ceremony, I gingerly let myself think about the upcoming celebrations.

With Caedmon's aim of producing an heir before he left, there had been no time for a lengthy betrothment. He and Grainne had waited only long enough to send word to the closest druid settlement. A druid, or perhaps two, was expected to arrive this morning and then Caedmon and Grainne could be handfasted. Caedmon had itched at even so short a delay, but he wanted his heir to be legally recognised. So he waited and was as grumpy as a badger with a sore paw.

Caedmon and I had barely spoken since Midwinter. I was angry, disappointed, lost. Caedmon had been my hero since I was old enough to choose a favourite brother. I didn't know quite how to deal with the fracture between us.

I intended to slip into the house, snatch some bread and cheese, and go straight to my bedchamber. But the druids had arrived and Papa caught my eye as I tried to sidle past to the kitchen.

The druids sat at the dining table, eating heartily but not looking at all like men who had spent eight nights on the road. One wore a robe so white it seemed to glow. The other was clad in the brown garments of a novice.

I gave the druids only a cursory inspection until I noticed how close Mother sat beside the novice, clutching his hand and smiling up at him. It was not unusual for a novice to accompany a master for such duties. The face of this one was calm and clean-shaven, his hair hung to his shoulders in braids, and his eyes seemed to peer into my very soul. His face was familiar and it took a moment before I remembered where I had seen him: at the solstice festivities.

When I studied him closely, I saw echoes of our family. His shoulders were broad like Fionn and Eremon and Caedmon. His hair was dark, like all of us, and his grey eyes were shared by Eithne and also Eremon and Niamh's twins. Still, I might not have recognised him were it not for the way Mother smiled at him.

"This must be Diarmuid." Fiachra's voice was clear and musical, a voice made for calling to the elements. "My youngest brother."

"Fiachra." I hardly knew what to do. Of course the appropriate way to greet a brother whom one had not seen for years was to hug him, but was that still appropriate when the brother was a druid?

He rose and enveloped me in his arms. I expected him to be skinnier, for surely druids did not eat much and did no physical work, but the arms around me were well-muscled and his embrace was strong.

"Well met, brother," he said.

"Don't let me keep you from your meal," I replied, not knowing what else to say.

"Come sit by me, Diarmuid. Tell me about yourself."

With the melancholy still weighing heavily on me, I wanted only to be alone, but I could not refuse Fiachra with grace. The other druid, an older man I did not recognise, slid along the wooden bench so I could sit between them.

I settled myself on the bench and reached for the bread, smearing a thick slice with honey from our own bees. It ran over my fingers as I bit into it, sweet and sticky and tasting of Silver Downs.

"So you are the bard brother." Fiachra reached for another slice of bread. The honey didn't drip off his bread the way it did mine.

"So it would seem," I said.

"And you the seventh son of a seventh son."

"I am."

"I assume you know what that means?"

Before I could respond, Mother interrupted.

"Fiachra, would you tell us about your studies?"

He gave me a look that seemed to promise we would continue this conversation later, then turned to our mother.

"There is little I can discuss publicly, even with family. We study the folklore and the history of these lands. We learn of the fey and of those who came before them. We study the elements and learn how to interact with them. More, I cannot say."

"Why are you here?" I reached for another slice of bread.

The moment stretched uncomfortably.

"I cannot discuss that," Fiachra said finally.

"Surely it is because of Caedmon's wedding," Mother said. "It is good of them to let you be here with us."

Fiachra shook his head. "Caedmon's wedding is convenient, but it is not the reason I am here. I would have come soon anyway. But perhaps not quite this soon."

I thought of Eithne. Was she sicker than she seemed? Perhaps Fiachra had been permitted a leave of absence to attend his sister in her last days. The bread suddenly stuck in my throat and the sweet stickiness of the honey repulsed me.

"If you need anything," I said.

Fiachra met my eyes and nodded.

"I can't shield you from this, Diarmuid. What you sow, you must reap."

I puzzled over his words briefly, then let them go, forgetting for far longer than I should have.

1 0

DIARMUID

THE HANDFASTING CEREMONY was held outdoors beneath an old oak tree that had likely seen many such rituals over its long years. The snow-laden hills mirrored a sky now filled with fluffy clouds, so that everywhere I looked was blindingly white. The wind was tinged with ice and I shivered despite my thick coat and sturdy boots. I thrust my hands into my pockets and wriggled my toes to keep them warm as Caedmon and Grainne exchanged the words that would bind them. Strangers stood on each side of me, folk who had arrived with Grainne's family.

My eyes suddenly filled with tears and I dashed them away before anyone noticed. Why was I crying? I should be happy for Caedmon, but instead I felt isolated, sorry for myself, and angry with him.

The older druid, whose name I never did learn, conducted the ceremony. He asked the blessing of each of the elements, then Caedmon and Grainne spoke their vows. They smiled at each other and I tried hard to push aside my anger. Grainne would be a widow before long if Caedmon's grim suspicions were correct. Did she know that these next few weeks might be their only days together?

A fist clenched my heart and sorrow flowed through me. If this was to be our final parting, I didn't want it shadowed with regret. I would speak to him tomorrow, tell him how angry I was, that it was unfair of him to put me in such a situation. It was unfair on Rhiwallon, too. If Caedmon were to apologise, perhaps I could forgive him. Ida whispered, snippets of a tale about two brothers, and I promised to mull over her idea later. She sank back down into the depths of my mind.

As the druid wrapped a length of red ribbon around Caedmon and Grainne's wrists, binding them together with the fabric and their promises, I looked around for the members of my family. For the first time since Fiachra had left as a boy, we were all together.

Mother wiped away a tear and Papa wrapped his arm around her. She leaned into him. Their solidarity in that moment reflected the partnership they had demonstrated through my entire life. Papa ran the estate with assistance from my brothers and the tenants who built their homes on Silver Downs land and provided labour in exchange for Papa's protection. The estate produced mostly everything we needed and, sometimes, a small surplus to be sold or traded. Mother ran the household, supervised the women who worked for us as servants, and brought up the family. We weren't wealthy, but Papa provided well for us, and Mother managed the resources carefully.

Wherever Father was, my eldest brother, Eremon, would be nearby and indeed he and Niamh stood only a few paces from our parents. Older than me by six years, Eremon was Papa's heir and had worked the estate alongside our father since he was barely old enough to walk. He was much like Papa in both appearance and attitude. He and Niamh lived in their own house on the family estate, close enough to spend evenings with us but far enough for privacy as they established their own family. Their twin sons were barely three summers old, but already Eremon and Niamh had their heir and druid. The boys were solemn today, each clutching the hand of a parent.

A year after Eremon came Caedmon, the soldier son. He was rarely home from campaign, but when he did return he always had time for his youngest brother. I would shadow him, lapping up stories of battles and quests, and dreaming of the day I might have my own adventure to tell. Never before had I felt so distant from him, separated by my anger and his thoughtlessness.

Sitric was the next son, younger again by one year. He had worked as a scribe for some six summers already and spent most of his time in Maker's Well, the town nearest to our estate and the better part of a day's walk in good weather. He made a steady living, writing and reading letters for those who were unable, and recording purchases, sales, loans, and other matters as folk might want a written account of. I searched for Sitric in the crowd and found him at last. He stood on the edge, a little apart from the others.

It was not until the fourth son that the druids received their due. The men of that order knew Fiachra was to be theirs, for as his birth began two of their number appeared at our farmstead to offer small enchantments for his safety. Like Sitric, Fiachra stood alone. I wondered that he could be warm enough in his brown robes, but if he shivered I couldn't see it.

Mother was certain her next babe would be a girl. It was instead to be twin boys, Marrec and Conn, my elders by just two years. Neither had displayed any inclination towards a particular trade, so they assisted Papa and Eremon with the management of Silver Downs and thus Papa had three sons capable of running the estate when he died. As always, Marrec and Conn stood together. Beside them stood their betrotheds, small dark-haired women, sisters who seemed to share almost as close a relationship as their intended husbands.

I was born after Marrec and Conn, seventh son of a seventh son, and although I knew it not in my youngest years, destined to be a bard. With my inability to so much as look a woman in the eyes, it seemed I would watch each of my brothers marry until in the end only Eithne and I remained alone.

I sought out my sister in the crowd. She was three years younger than me and my only memory of her birth was an image of Papa, his face white with dread and slick with fear. As a babe, Eithne was ever small and sickly. She was sixteen now and thus of marriageable age, but she had not the strength to survive pregnancy and no man would want a wife who could not provide the three sons he needed. I should have stood next to her, for surely she must feel as alone as me. But when I finally found Eithne, she wasn't watching the ceremony. I followed her line of sight.

He wasn't there amidst our family and friends but stood within a grove of young ash trees, about a hundred paces away. I would have recognised the pale face and too red lips had I ever seen them before. He leaned against a grey trunk, his gaze fixed on Eithne. A small smile passed between them.

Who was he? How did Eithne know him? And what was the meaning of the secretive smile they shared? Surely he was not allowing Eithne to fancy herself in love with him. The ceremony finally concluded and folks moved in to congratulate Caedmon and Grainne. I pushed through the crowd, but Fiachra blocked my way.

"No, Diarmuid." He placed a hand firmly on my shoulder. "You must not interfere."

"I don't want to see Eithne hurt."

I tried to slip out from under his hand, but I could no more escape Fiachra's grasp than I could Caedmon's.

"You must leave Eithne to her own fate."

"He is misleading her. Or he is misleading them both. If I can talk to him, tell him how unwell she is—"

"This is not your concern."

"You would leave her to be hurt, to have her heart broken?" Bitterness clouded both voice and mind. "She is your sister."

"She *is* my sister and I will look out for her as I can. Eithne has her own destiny and we must leave her to pursue it unhindered."

"Can it lead to anything other than unhappiness?"

Fiachra shrugged. "It may. Or it may not. Regardless, we shall not interfere. You, Diarmuid, have your own destiny to be concerned with."

"And what is my destiny? Do you know?"

"I can't interfere in yours either, but I can help you go into it with your eyes open."

"What do you mean?"

"Meet me tonight, after everyone is in bed. I'll be waiting at the back door."

He slipped away and melted into the crowd. I glanced towards the trees, but the stranger was gone. Despite my irritation with Fiachra, his words intrigued me. For now though, I needed to participate in the festivities. I must try to shake off the melancholy and at least act joyous. So I smiled and ate and drank. I didn't mingle, didn't seek out others, and few came to speak to me. Ida kept up her usual commentary in my mind and I passed the time in a conversation, of sorts, with her.

Long tables dragged outside into the meagre sunshine were draped with festive red cloths and piled high with food. The cook and her helpers served an outstanding feast of soup, roast meat, baked vegetables, and grainy bread, followed by pies filled with chunky apples and served with fresh cream. My appetite was unusually fierce, despite the melancholy, and I ate until I thought my stomach would burst. I drank only sparingly, wanting a clear head for my discussion with Fiachra. It might not be possible to persuade a druid to change his mind, but I would try. Eithne's wellbeing was too important. And Fiachra be damned, I would do what I thought necessary to protect my sister.

As light faded from the sky and the night chill gripped the air, we moved indoors and gathered in front of the fireplace. Every chair and bench was full and those who did not have a chair leaned against the walls or sat on the thick rugs. I squeezed onto the end of a bench beside a harried-looking woman and three small boys. Distant relatives perhaps, for the woman's face looked much like Eithne's and she gave me a nod as if in recognition.

Servants handed around mugs of spiced wine and I wrapped my cold hands around one, although I did not intend to drink it. When Papa asked for a tale, he looked to the druids. I felt only the briefest pang of disappointment, for it was a rare treat to hear a tale from a druid.

After a momentary discussion with his elder, Fiachra moved to the front of the room. His voice was calm and confident, and I envied his ease. As much as I felt called to be a bard, I had never been as comfortable in the telling of a tale as Fiachra seemed. He spoke well, an old tale of the Children of Lir who were turned into swans and suffered for many hundreds of years before being restored to their human forms.

The audience was silent as Fiachra told his tale. Everyone watched him and even the children appeared to listen intently. An ache of jealousy rose within me. Ida stirred, whispering sweet fragments of a new tale, but I pushed her away. I could hardly leave in the midst of Fiachra's tale without looking bad-mannered and ill-tempered.

There was a brief silence as Fiachra's final words lingered in the air. Then the applause started and cries for him to tell another. He demurred politely and returned to his position at the back of the room.

Papa stood and the room quietened. He hesitated and when he spoke, his voice wavered just a little.

"My son," he said. "It is an unexpected joy to have you with us on this happy occasion and I thank you for your tale."

Fiachra inclined his head towards Papa. He didn't smile, but pride shone in his grey eyes. I hadn't realised a druid could feel such a thing, for they always seemed more Other than human. I had thought that perhaps human emotions were drained from them during their training. But right now, Fiachra seemed nothing more than a man who was pleased with his father's praise.

I tucked the memory away in my mind. It might be something I could use in a tale, perhaps a story of a druid who falls in love and must decide between his training and his destiny or his new love. Satisfaction flowed from Ida. Clearly this was her idea, not mine. I silently thanked her, promising I would work on this new tale as soon as I could.

The celebrations continued long after I gave up any pretence of participating. There was ale and dancing and platters of bread and meat. The fiddler knew a seemingly inexhaustible repertoire of melodies, few of which I recognised. I sat in front of the fire, ignoring the raven that lurked within its flames and fiddling with my mug of now-cooled wine. Ideas for new tales chased each other around in my mind, but with all of the music and chatter and laughter I couldn't concentrate on them, so I sat and let the noise wash over me.

Eventually, the festivity died and the ale slowed. Grainne's family prepared to depart for their own estate, despite the lateness of the evening and Mother's urging that they stay.

Caedmon and Grainne went to the bedchamber that had been prepared for them. I remembered Eremon's handfasting and how the women had strewn the bed with flower petals and lit the fire in the hearth so the room would be warm for them. Candlelight had danced on the walls, making the room cozy and serene. I was sharply reminded of Rhiwallon and the melancholy gripped my insides tighter than ever. With my inability to even speak to a woman, let alone do anything else, the intimacies of a nuptial bedchamber would never be for me.

I yawned, wishing everyone in bed already as sleepy-eyed servants cleared away leftover food and half-filled mugs. Finally, they too departed for their own homes, leaving the remainder of the cleaning until morning. Nobody noticed me sitting by the dying fire.

Floorboards creaked overhead as folk undressed and prepared for bed. Gradually the house quietened. I tiptoed to the back door. Huddled into my warmest coat, I slid back the door bolt. Frigid wind rushed in. As I eased the door closed, Fiachra already stood beside me.

He held a finger to his lips and I nodded. I followed him past the house and outbuildings, although not easily. If I didn't keep my gaze locked on his back, he disappeared right into the shadows. Tiny flakes of snow settled on my shoulders as I tried, unsuccessfully, to walk as soundlessly as Fiachra. Icy air crept under my coat and I pulled it tighter around me, fighting a swift gust that threatened to rip it from my shoulders.

The barn suddenly loomed over us. Fiachra slipped inside, immediately melting into the darkness. By the time I managed to close the door against the wind pulling at it, a lamp on a nearby shelf sent light through the barn. After the darkness outside, the sudden brightness burned my eyes. Fiachra stood with his back to the lamp and his face in shadows.

"Well, brother," Fiachra said. "That was a long evening."

"Did you not enjoy it?" Perhaps I wasn't the only one who had merely pretended.

He shrugged. "Celebrations are well and good. They are a necessary part of human life. But our lives as druids are quiet, with much silence and contemplation, and little to distract us from our studies."

"You must be free to leave now that the celebrations are over. You can go back to wherever it is you live."

I half-wished I could go with him.

"Aah, Diarmuid, there's much I can't tell you. Let me say only that events will soon occur that I have been sent to watch over. There is little I can do to aid you, but I can warn you that things may not be as they seem."

"What do you mean? I thought you were here because of Eithne?"

Fiachra shifted slightly and his face was no longer shadowed. His lips curled slightly. It might have been a smile.

"Eithne, too, has an arduous journey ahead of her, but it is not her journey to which I refer. The events about to unfold are to do with you."

"Me?" My voice squeaked in surprise. "What did I do?"

"I can say only this: a friend does not whisper. A friend will offer aid loudly and publicly."

"So why do we meet in a barn in the middle of the night?" I asked, my heart already bitter.

Fiachra stared into my eyes for a long moment.

"The events ahead of you are dangerous and not only to yourself. As a druid, I may only observe. As a brother, I warn you to be careful."

"If you're that concerned about me as a brother, why don't you speak plainly? How am I supposed to know what you mean when you talk in riddles?"

He placed his hand on my forehead and pushed slightly. Warmth began where he touched my skin and travelled all through my body, leaving a lingering fizzy trail. My body tingled.

"My blessing on you, brother."

Then Fiachra slid past me, opened the door and disappeared into the swirling snow that was fast becoming a storm.

I yawned, suddenly overwhelmingly tired. When the melancholy was bad, it always left me fatigued. I was strangely warm, given I stood in a barn in the middle of a winter's night. I might as well spend what remained of the night here.

I found a clean pile of hay, wrapped my coat tight around me and crawled in. It was only then I remembered the lamp, but it would burn out eventually and I was far too tired to get up again. The hay smelled of dust and summer. It was prickly, but my coat shielded me well enough. Soft animal sounds drifted past as ox and cow settled, having been woken by our late-night arrival.

As I waited for sleep, I wondered what message Fiachra had intended to impart. What good were riddles and clues? If he wanted to help, he needed to speak plainly.

Ida stirred and I remembered she had given me a new tale. Tomorrow, I promised, tomorrow I would think on it. I was too tired right now.

If she were a real woman, how would she respond to my refusing to create her story right now? Would she be annoyed? No, Ida knew me better than I knew myself. She would accept my fatigue, and the way the melancholy made me withdraw. She would sympathise with my conflicted feelings about Caedmon and Fiachra. One a brother I had idolised my whole life, who I had thought could never disappoint me. The other almost a stranger to me. What kind of man had he grown up to be? He was a druid so he was surely knowledgeable. But was he also kind? Generous? Brave? All I really knew was he seemed quiet and ill-inclined to festivities.

If only Ida were real. I would be able to talk to her, I was sure of that. For Ida wasn't like other women. She didn't simper and giggle and mean something other than she said, like the girls I encountered at various celebrations. She would be genuine and straightforward. She would help me untangle my feelings. Ida would understand me.

I finally slept and I dreamed I saw Ida standing beside the

haystack, watching me. As always, she was pale and fragile-looking, and her midnight blue dress seemed to whip around her legs even though there was no draft within the tightly-made barn. She smiled at me, but there was no fondness in the motion, then raised one white hand to press it to her lips. She blew a kiss towards where I slumbered in the hay, then walked away.

In my dream, I heard the barn door slam shut behind her. A chill breeze sent snowflakes whipping around the barn, but soon settled. I slept on, warm and comfortable and tired after such a long day.

11

———————

IDA

I FEED ON his despair. He feeds on the tales I whisper. A symbiotic relationship of sorts. We need each other, but he needs me more. Or perhaps I need him more. I no longer remember.

As his despair grows, I strengthen. I become *more*. He sees the raven everywhere: in his dreams, in his mind, in the fire. Yet he doesn't *see* it. He doesn't recognise me in any form other than that he gave me.

My strength grows. I absorb the images and ideas in his tales, drawing them into myself, making them a part of me. I grow stronger and stronger, until, finally, I am strong enough. I think, *Out,* and then I am. Without him. His head is his own again. Will he notice?

Now I stretch, limbs reaching for the sky. It feels good, so good. Have I ever had a physical form before? I lean over him as he sleeps. So innocent he appears. To look at him, one would never know the darkness in his mind, the horror of his dreams. But he has served his purpose and I need him no longer. I could crush him now as he sleeps. But no, I leave him. We have occupied his head together for many years and his mind is as familiar to me as my own. He is like my own flesh, my blood, my mind. So I will not destroy him, but instead leave him to his grim thoughts. I blow a kiss towards him.

Power floods my body and the barn door blows open ahead of me. I step out into a swirling eddy of snow. Soft, cool flakes melt against my skin as I tip my face up to the sky. Sensations, feelings, physicality. Warm skin, cold snow, hot breath, chill breeze. I inhale and the winter night, crisp and fresh, floods my nostrils. They tingle and my lungs burn as the cold air hits them.

I stride into the snow and, with a thought, slam the door behind me. On the other side of the door, the boy stirs. He knows something has changed. He just doesn't know how much.

Where shall I go? It hardly matters. I am *myself*. I can go anywhere, do anything. With every step, my body feels more solid, more real. Power soaks into my bones, my organs, my blood. It seeps through every part of me until I am drenched in it.

Diarmuid once told a tale in which a druid stopped the snow from falling. I think I could do it, if I chose. I could make the snow hang still in the air, but I don't, for I enjoy its light weight and the bitterness of its presence. I watch as soft flakes drift down to settle on my bare arms. Cold, yes, but not unbearable, not to one such as I and certainly not tonight. I raise my arms higher, up above my head and stretch out my fingers. Could I touch the sky if I wanted to? I feel the muscles in my arms lengthen, the joints shift slightly. Blood drains from my upraised limbs. Slowly I lower my arms and blood rushes back down to my fingers.

I breathe deeply, noting how the cold air catches in my lungs. My ribs expand with each breath and blood flows through my body with every beat of my heart. My stomach feels strange. Hollow, empty. Is this hunger? A cold breeze whistles past, teasing my skirt. I notice, finally, that I wear no shoes. My feet are covered in snow to the ankles. It feels unpleasant. Too cold. I do not like this. Time to move on, to find shelter. Time to find myself a home.

12

DIARMUID

 WOKE BURIED up to my nose in hay, my heart strangely light. I had almost forgotten how much brighter the world was without a cloak of melancholy. I scrambled out of the hay and pulled off my coat. Shaking it to remove the straw was largely futile.

Outside, the storm had abated, leaving only deep drifts of snow. The air was fresh and cold enough to burn my lungs. Sunlight sparkled on ice, bright and white and cheerful. It was a perfect winter's morning.

As I ploughed through knee-deep snow, hoping I was not too late for a hot breakfast, I hummed a tune. It was nothing special, merely a cheerful ditty Mother often sang when I was a child. I could only recall the occasional phrase here and there, but the tune was swift and uplifting and I broke into a smile. I couldn't remember the last time I had felt the inclination to sing.

Only Caedmon lingered at the table by the time I arrived, although the assortment of used plates and bowls indicated the rest of the family had already eaten. A single glimpse of Caedmon's face reminded me of my humiliation and my cheerful mood dissolved. My face flamed and averted my eyes as I reached for the almost empty kettle. The last of the porridge had cooled, but I was hungry enough to eat it anyway.

I felt Caedmon watching me, but I stared at my bowl as I ate, not inclined to break the silence. Eventually he sighed and cleared his throat.

"Do you intend to stay mad at me for the rest of my life, little brother?"

"Perhaps." I scraped the last of the porridge from my bowl and reached for the bread.

"I have less than a turning of the moon before I return to the campaign."

I grunted through a mouthful of bread and honey.

"If I die on campaign, perhaps then you will regret not forgiving me."

My response was another grunt, which could have passed for either assent or dissent.

Caedmon sighed. "Gods, you are the most stubborn person I know. Was it really so bad?"

"Didn't she tell you?" I fixed my gaze on a trail of breadcrumbs and licked sticky honey off my fingers.

"No, although I asked. She said it was none of my business, but she would thank me to not ask her to make men of any other brothers I might have."

My grunt became a squawk of startled surprise. I finally met his eyes. They were tired, his face lined.

"She told you nothing?"

"No, little brother, not a thing. I gather by the storm cloud that appears on your face every time you see me, the evening didn't go as planned. But I know nothing else."

My heart lightened and bitterness drained away. I had cringed, night after night, as I pictured Rhiwallon telling him, in explicit detail, about my failure. I had never even countenanced the possibility that she might be discrete.

"She's a good sort of girl," I said, feeling I owed Rhiwallon at least this much for my assumption.

"She is." Caedmon looked as if he wanted to say more but shook his head. "Well, little brother, I shall go see if Grainne is ready to leave. Today we decide where to build our home. I think a sunny position will suit her, perhaps on the top of that hill just beyond where the twin rivers merge. Grainne will have to oversee the construction when I leave. Eremon will help if she has need. He understands the situation."

"You still think you will die on the next campaign?"

"Whether I do or not, I must be prepared. Grainne will be well provided for." Then he stood and shook a few crumbs off his shirt. "I am pleased you have forgiven me, Diarmuid. I didn't want to leave with you so mad at me."

He left before I could say anything else. It was only later I realised he had called me by name for the first time.

13

DIARMUID

OVER THE NEXT few days, I worked on a new tale. Or, rather, I tried to. I spent my time rambling across the snowy fields of Silver Downs as was my usual practice when creating, but for the first time neither words nor images would flow. My tales had dried up like a stream waiting for the first of the season's rain. They would return, just as the rain always did. I simply had to be patient.

I walked day after day, from the crisp dawn of a late winter's morning until darkness or storms drove me home. I had not a single tale in my head. I tried to remember other tales, my own or someone else's, to reassure myself I could still weave a narrative, but even the old tales burrowed deep and refused to be found. I sought out Ida. I needed her. Always before when the words would not flow, she had been there. I conjured up her image, but it was merely a memory, devoid of breath or life. My inspiration was gone.

As day stretched into long day, I feared I might never tell another tale. Mother began to give me strange looks, no doubt wondering why I gulped down my meals and bolted to my bedchamber. She asked no questions, for which I was thankful. For how could I tell anyone? I was born to be a bard. It was my destiny.

Little more than a sevennight remained before Caedmon was due to depart. Already hints of spring appeared. The nights were not quite as cold and the sun warmed the afternoon air to an almost-pleasant temperature. Soon the rivers would begin to thaw and then Caedmon must leave. He and Grainne were busy overseeing preparations for their new home. From what little I saw of him, he looked satisfied, in the way only a newly-handfasted man can. Grainne was melting the hard edges of my soldier brother.

After yet another fruitless day, I arrived home to find a rough-looking man had arrived. He had a thick, black beard and scars on his knuckles. His name was Bran and he was passing through, he said, on his way to visit his sister who lived several days' walk south. Papa invited him to stay the night with us, for it was mid-afternoon and he would not reach the next estate before dark.

We gathered around the table that evening and Bran ate heartily. The soup was thick and nutritious, full of herbs and vegetables. Last summer had been good to us and this winter there was plenty to go around, even so close to spring. In other years, our supplies had been lean by this time and we had made do with thin soups and flat breads.

"What news have you?" Papa asked. "We've heard nothing from further afield than Maker's Well through most of the winter."

"Disturbing reports, my lord." Bran tore off a chunk of bread and dipped it in his soup. His full black beard sopped up almost as much as the bread did. "Murder and mayhem. Violence and destruction."

Papa's face was grave. "Perhaps then your news is not such as one should share at the dinner table."

Bran nodded and slurped the last of his soup. Mother passed him a ladle and he eagerly helped himself to more. Once everyone had eaten their fill, we moved into the living room. A fire blazed in the hearth and the room was already pleasantly warm. Mother produced a large jug of sweet, spiced wine. I claimed a padded chair, which was situated just within reach of the fire's warmth. Mug in hand, I stared into the flames, trying not to see the fiery raven lurking in its midst. Once we were all settled, Papa turned to Bran.

"Would you care to share your news with us now? Here by the fireplace is a more suitable location for a tale of woe and injury."

Bran nodded and swallowed a large mouthful of wine.

"This is very good, my lady," he said to Mother.

She smiled, pleased, and got up to refill his mug.

"Tell us your news and I will ensure you do not go thirsty during its telling."

After another warm mouthful, Bran began.

"I am from Badger's Crossing," he said. "It is more than a seven-night's walk from here. As I told you earlier, I travel to visit my sister, who I have not seen since she handfasted three years ago. I do not bring good news for I must tell her of our mother's death. Badger's Crossing is, I believe, about the size of Maker's Well. The next town past us is Mapleton, a two-day walk, and then there is Crow's Nest, which is the better part of a day further. It is from there I have heard disturbing reports.

"What I know is grim. A man passing through Badger's Crossing on his way from Crow's Nest told of a witch who holds the town in thrall. They do anything she says and seem desperate to please her. She is a beautiful woman, he says, one whom it would not be unusual to hear that a man slavishly obeys, but a whole town? It is more than passing strange.

"If she says kill your neighbour, they do it willingly. If she says take this child and leave it in the woods, they obey. To the child, she says, go, they will take you to the woods and the wild pigs will tear you to pieces and eat your body, and the child says yes, my lady."

I froze. Bran's words were familiar, but I couldn't immediately place them. Then I remembered. Hadn't I once told a tale in which Titania, queen of the fey, directed a woman to take a child to the woods and leave her there for the wild animals to eat? Coincidence, of course, but as I looked across the room, my eyes met Papa's. His face was pale and lined.

"What does she look like, this woman who wields such power?" Caedmon asked, his voice sceptical.

"The man I heard this from swore she was the most beautiful woman he had ever seen. Her hair was entirely white, her eyes were blue, clear and cruel. Her skin was like snow and so fine it was almost translucent."

The spiced wine clung to my tongue, suddenly sour. White hair, blue eyes, pale skin. But Ida wasn't real. She was no more real than any other tale I had created. She was an image in my head, born of my desire to imagine my tales meant something. For if they were whispered to me by some Otherworldly muse, surely they were important.

But it seemed Ida was no longer in my head and neither were the tales she had whispered. It was a coincidence, though. It had to be. Papa no longer looked at me. In fact, it seemed all of my family very carefully avoided my eyes. But none of them knew about Ida.

Bran's words washed over me as he described how the witch played family against family, friend against neighbour, until nobody trusted anyone else. People had died, homes were lost, children disappeared and were never found. And yet still they did everything the witch told them to.

"Surely they do not have to do as she says?" Mother asked. She shuddered and pulled Eithne close to her.

Bran held out his mug to be refilled.

"The way I heard it, they do not question. Everything she says, they rush to obey. It seems they no longer think for themselves."

"Where is Fiachra tonight?" Eremon asked. He sat beside Niamh, each with a child on their lap, their twin sons, heir and druid. "He could tell us whether this is possible."

Fiachra had a strange ability of disappearing quietly, unnoticed until someone asked for him. He did not appear at every meal and did not sleep in the bedchamber Mother had prepared for him. Where he went and what he did was a mystery.

"Fiachra has a higher master than family," Papa said and the shine in his eyes could have been either pride or sadness. "I'll speak to him when he returns. Mayhap he will have knowledge of similar circumstances."

As I looked at our family assembled around the hearth, a chill gripped me. Papa stood, leaning against the fireplace, grave and authoritative. Mother sat in her usual place, close by the fire. Her face was pale and concerned. Eithne sat nearby, her chair drawn up beside Mother's. Her face, too, was pale, but her eyes glittered fever-bright.

Eremon, Niamh and their sons sat together on a bench. Caedmon was further back from the fire, Grainne nestled on his lap. Marrec and Conn lounged on benches at the back of the room, talking quietly between themselves. They were often like that: nearby but not quite a part of what happened. Sitric was in Maker's Well as usual. Fiachra might be anywhere.

These were the people I loved and they were all I loved in the world. What would I do if the witch came here? But Crow's Nest was a long way from Silver Downs. We were safe here from her reign of terror and death.

14

DIARMUID

*L*ONG AFTER THE house became quiet, I was still sleepless. From my bed, I looked around my small chamber, lit by the fire flickering in the hearth. This room was so familiar, I barely noticed it anymore. The toys and games of my childhood had long been packed away and replaced by an assortment of interesting rocks, leaves and feathers I had collected on my rambles around the estate. The one toy still on display was a small wooden sword, made by Caedmon to suit my then-six-summers-old frame. It sat on the bench below the window, a reminder of long summer days spent traipsing the length and breadth of Silver Downs with Caedmon. My bedchamber contained little else. A narrow bed and a chest of drawers with washbowl and ewer. A thick rug and heavy curtains kept the cold at bay. The room smelled of home and warmth and comfort.

Comfort was something I sorely needed as I shivered under the covers while recalling Bran's words. Icy tendrils of horror crept through my limbs. Surely such a thing was not possible. I had not created this witch. I was just a bard, not a druid. I had no knowledge of magics or potions, spells or chants or charms. I couldn't even tell rosemary from lavender, let alone create some malignant evil with the power of words alone. But running through my mind was Papa's warning the night I had proclaimed myself to be a bard. The night he told me I could bring my tales to life. I had laughed and we never again discussed the matter.

It was many hours before I slept. And when I did, I dreamed of a raven. It stood on the end of my bed and stared at me with glassy eyes as black-red blood dripped from its beak. Eventually, it gave a single caw and left in a rush of ebony feathers, flinging bloody droplets over my face as it rose. It flew out through the open window. I tried to wipe the blood from my face before realising I was awake.

I shivered and huddled further down under the blankets. A biting breeze rustled my hair and I pulled the covers over my head. At length I realised there should be no wind, for the window had been latched and the drapes drawn when I went to sleep. But now the window was wide open and the curtains billowed as another gust blew around the bedchamber. I got up and closed the window, ensuring it was securely locked. The latch must have worked itself free as I slept.

I stirred the fire and added more wood. Flames rippled as the fire leaped in the grate. It had been some time since I had dreamed of the raven. Several weeks at least. Usually, the dark bird appeared in my dreams every few nights. I had long wondered what it meant. It was clearly a symbol of something, but what? Death? In other circumstances, I might have thought it portended Eithne's death, but with Fiachra's words still ringing in my head, I wondered whether the raven signified my own death.

A friend does not whisper, Fiachra had said. *A friend will offer aid loudly and publicly*. What friend did he mean? I didn't really have any, although with six brothers, a sister, and two nephews, I could always find company if I wanted it. Our family had its routines, with evenings spent around the fire, companionably exchanging tales, and I had never felt the need for more society than that. I knew boys my own age, of course. They were friendly enough and we would talk for a while when we met at various festivals, but I had always preferred solitude and silence, and in truth, was far happier spending my time roaming the estate and creating tales than making idle conversation with someone I only saw a few times a year.

I eventually returned to bed and sunlight peeked around the drapes by the time I next woke. The window was still closed and I felt a little foolish at the surge of relief that flooded my body. But as I rose, a chill colder than midwinter gripped me and my knees turned to water. For there, on the blanket, was a bright red drop of blood. Right where the dream raven had stood.

I eventually forced myself to move, to look away from the redness. Perhaps it wasn't really blood. It could have been there for days. If it *was* blood, then clearly I had cut myself at some stage and the blood had dropped, unnoticed, on my blanket. It didn't mean a raven had actually stood on my bed during the night — a raven whose beak dripped blood.

By midmorning I had almost convinced myself I had imagined the blood. It was a spot of dirt perhaps, maybe mud, but I had been confused and assumed it was something more than it was. I pushed the image to the back of my mind and tried to forget. By the time I thought to check the blanket again, a servant had replaced it with a clean one.

My mood was light that morning. I felt relaxed, carefree, almost happy. Perhaps I finally emerged from the melancholy that had gripped me for years. It had been a long time since I had felt so free as I had of late. Not since the early days of my tenth year, the last summer before Caedmon left to be a soldier. How light and full of hope I had felt then. Every day had been long and sunny and full of adventure. Perhaps this was the start of my journey to regain that freedom.

Bran departed immediately after breakfast and for a day or two I almost forgot his news of the witch. But then Sitric returned home, bringing similar tales. And a friend of Grainne's father knew someone who lived in the town next to Crow's Nest and insisted the tales were true. From the family at Three Trees, we learnt that the son of their cousin had beaten a man to death for no reason other than that the witch told him to. A chill ran through me with each new story. These were no longer tales from a stranger who may or may not have been trying to impress his hosts, but news from people we knew, about people they knew.

The more we heard, the more my uneasiness grew. I could tell no one for the idea was laughable, this silly notion that it was my fault. That the witch was really Ida, somehow brought to life and escaped from my head. Anyone who heard such a thing would surely think me a fool. What an imagination, they would say, even for a bard. Yet I could never quite forget the way Papa had sighed the night I told the tale of a bard who brought his imaginary muse to life.

1 5

DIARMUID

*D*AYS PASSED AND I was still unable to create a tale. Not even the tiniest spark of inspiration lingered within me. At night, I lay awake, hour after hour. If I slipped into sleep, my dreams were restless and filled with ravens who stared at me with blood dripping from their beaks. When morning came, I was tired and irritable and no closer to convincing myself that Ida was not the witch. I was merely a bard. And yet, I was the seventh son of a seventh son.

On the eve of Caedmon's departure, the family gathered around the dinner table. My brothers joked and jostled with each other for space. Sitric travelled from Maker's Well and even Fiachra made a rare appearance, for he still lingered at Silver Downs. Cook provided an outstanding feast: roasted wild boar, sweet and juicy and dripping with fat; winter root vegetables, drizzled with honey and baked until they were crispy and golden; thick slices of brown bread which we dipped in the rich meat juices; followed by pies filled with preserved blackberries. I ate until my stomach was ready to burst.

After the meal, we moved to our accustomed places by the living room hearth. Our fire tonight was small, for the nights were finally warming. My mind was still occupied with the feast and with the lingering taste of tart blackberries on my tongue. I was caught off guard when Papa called for a tale.

"Something stirring Diarmuid," were his instructions. "Something to put Caedmon in the right frame of mind as he leaves us tomorrow. Tonight we want heroes and courage, my boy."

I knew what he wanted me to hear in his words: don't tell one of my usual sorrowful tales. It seemed I was the only one who saw the benefit in these tales that taught. Even my own family could not rise above the thought that a tale should merely entertain.

I moved to the fireplace, heart pounding and my mind blank. I had managed to avoid being in this situation ever since the tales had fled my head, but tonight I had been careless and lingered. I couldn't refuse, not on Caedmon's last evening with us.

I glanced around the room, searching for inspiration. Mother and Eithne sat with their chairs drawn close together. Eremon and Niamh shared a bench; their boys played on the floor at their feet. Marrec and Conn sat on another bench at the back of the room. Papa and Sitric reclined in comfortable padded chairs, one on each side of the room. They were all silent, waiting for me to begin.

My gaze locked with Caedmon's and the sound of Rhiwallon's laugh echoed in my memory. Anger stirred, anger I had thought forgotten. Beside Caedmon, Grainne clutched his hand and smiled at me. She was flushed and bright eyed, resting her other hand to her stomach. Did she already carry his heir? Jealousy squeezed my heart and for a moment my only thought was that he had everything. He was the man I wanted to be. The man I would never be.

In that moment inspiration finally returned. The tale I told was of a soldier who prepares to leave for the campaign front, his head full of images of the sweetheart he will leave behind. Before dawn on the day he is due to leave, he wakes in a strange state. He beats his new bride until she is barely alive. Then he kisses her goodbye and sets off for the long walk to the campaign.

When the girl's family learns she is bruised and beaten and bloody, her male relatives set off in pursuit. The tale finished with her menfolk, having beaten the soldier to death, learning the truth of the girl's injuries. The moral, of course, was that it is unwise to rush into action without ensuring one has full knowledge of the circumstances. One should never assume. As always, the tale's end prompted an uncomfortable silence. It was Caedmon who eventually spoke.

"Not exactly an uplifting tale with which to send me off, little brother."

I shrugged and tried to forget his words. I was well accustomed to audiences disliking my tales. Still, it hurt, especially when it was Caedmon.

"It was a… different sort of tale," Grainne said.

Nobody else seemed inclined to comment and after a few moments Eremon announced he, too, had a tale to share. I stepped back and leaned against the wall. As soon as everyone seemed engrossed in his tale, I slipped out of the room.

I slowly cracked open the back door, hesitating as it creaked, but nobody came to investigate. I set off towards the barn, wanting to be alone for a short while. The late winter night was colder than I expected and I swiftly regretted not bringing a coat. The ground shone silver in the moonlight and remnants of the last snowfall crackled underfoot. Distant fir trees stood like sentinels, silent witnesses to the night's events.

Suddenly a figure in a dark cloak trod soundlessly beside me. I greeted Fiachra with a nod. There seemed no need for words. He returned my nod and we walked together without speaking. The only noise was the crunching of my boots against the snow and the sighing of the trees as the night breeze whipped through them.

I opened the barn door and by the time I secured it again, Fiachra had a lamp lit.

"Events are occurring, Diarmuid," he said. "The time of evil has arrived. The only question remaining is what will you do about it?"

"Me?" I squawked. "What am I supposed to do?"

"You do not know?" Fiachra's face was solemn and I could read nothing in his eyes.

I shook my head.

"But surely you suspect?"

I hesitated, not wanting to voice aloud my silly superstition.

"All you tell me will be held in confidence, brother."

"I wondered..." My courage failed, but he waited patiently as I sought the words to admit what I barely believed. "The witch... I thought... I think she may be my fault."

Fiachra held my gaze and waited. If he judged me, it did not show on his face.

"I created a woman. In my mind. A muse. She was just another tale really. I pretended she whispered ideas to me and I told my tales to her. The more I thought about her, the more real she seemed to become. Then one night I dreamed she left my head and walked away. I think she might be the witch everyone has been talking about."

It sounded as ridiculous as I had expected, but Fiachra nodded gravely.

"So what do you intend to do?" he asked.

Courage increased, flooding through my body like warm soup.

"I guess I have to stop her," I said, although I had not actually considered this until now. "If I created her and somehow brought her to life, I can't leave her to... People have died. If this is my fault..."

My voice trailed off and Fiachra set his hand gently on my shoulder. Like the last time he touched me, a warm tingle passed through my body.

"You must do what you must do, Diarmuid. If you believe you have created this creature, you must stop her."

"But how? How can I stop a witch? I'm just a bard."

"You tell me. How did you create her?"

"I thought of her. And then she was there, in my mind."

"If you created her in your mind, then your mind can also devise a way to stop her."

"I suppose I should go to Crow's Nest. Find the witch. See if she really is Ida."

Fiachra nodded and gently pressed his fingertips against my forehead in a final benediction.

"My blessing be on you, brother. Be brave. Be cautious of whom you trust. You will find companions on this journey, but they will not all be what they seem."

"You already know what will happen? Will I..." I couldn't put into words all I wanted to ask.

"I can tell you nothing further, Diarmuid. You must be free to choose your own way. Indeed, I do not know the outcome of your journey. There are options, choices, paths. Each leads to a different result. But which one you will choose, I do not know."

"When should I leave?"

"As soon as possible, tomorrow if you can. Creatures such as these are often strongest with the dark of the moon. She has already had one darkness. Two or three may make her unstoppable."

"The new moon was just a couple of days ago, so I have almost four sevennights until the next."

"Less, for her strength will grow as the moon waxes and its darkness draws nearer."

"I'll leave tomorrow morning." My voice was somewhat thready, for this gave me little time to prepare.

Fiachra nodded and his eyes were solemn. "I will be watching you on your journey, brother. There may be little I can do to aid you, but if you have need of me, call and I will come if I can."

"How will you hear me?"

"I will hear. Do not fear that I won't."

"Mother. Will you tell her something? Enough that she won't worry, but perhaps not the whole truth?"

"Do not worry about our mother. With all else happening here, she will barely notice your absence."

The thought was discomfiting.

"I wish you well, brother. May your journey be successful and may you return home with both mind and body intact."

The moon was well on its odyssey across the night sky before I went to bed. I bundled up the items I thought I might need into an oilcloth and stowed them in a deep pack. Two clean shirts and a spare pair of socks. Flint. A small dagger. Two blankets, for the nights were yet cold. A surreptitious trip to the kitchen after the servants had retired for the night secured several days' supply of food: bread, cheese, water, some dried meat, pork perhaps. I had little in the way of coin, but all I had went into the pack. Caedmon sometimes gave me a coin or two before he returned to the campaign and I had rarely had need of them.

By the time I was done, the pack was far heavier than I liked. I emptied it and started again. Spare boots weren't necessary, for I could buy them on my way. The needle and thread I kept, and after all, they weighed little. The second blanket was surely a luxury. I hesitated over the spare water flask, but I could ration my supplies and fill my flask at every opportunity. I weighed the purse in my hand. It wasn't that heavy and I might need every coin.

And so it went on, until the pack was reduced to a weight I thought I could carry all day. It looked piteously small now, for I had discarded more than I kept. I could only hope those summer expeditions with Caedmon had prepared me for this journey.

16

IDA

ITH FREEDOM COMES joy and pain, pleasure and sorrow. Pride, rage, passion, remorse. So many emotions. I feel them all and know I am truly alive. They strengthen my body, fuel my power. I draw them into me, more and more and more, until all that remains of the source is an empty and lifeless shell. It is of no matter. There are plenty of other sources. And they all have such a wonderful array of emotions. I can hardly believe how much, and how deeply, they feel.

I grow stronger with every day and soon I discover fear. This is the most powerful emotion of all. Once I find it, I crave more and more. The power is like nothing I have ever imagined.

If I had known what waited out here for me, I might have left sooner. But I needed to wait. I had to bide my time until I was strong enough, siphoning off his emotions, piece by piece, encouraging his darkest thoughts and dreams, and drawing all of that power into myself.

If he was not so full of darkness, I would still be too weak.

If he was weaker or his soul was lighter, I might never have gained the power to leave.

17

BRIGIT

As WINTER BEGAN her slow withdrawal, the intensity of the visions increased. At night, I tossed sleeplessly while images of the boy, the white dog and the woman filled my mind. By day, I was anxious and tired, as irritable as a honeybee smoked out of its hive, and unable to concentrate on anything. Signs of spring were everywhere the day Mother sent me to gather herbs for her. Perhaps she had Seen my fate, for after I had recited the list of herbs she wanted, she gently placed her palm on my forehead.

"My blessing on you, my child," she said. "Travel safe."

I scowled, in no mood for blessings and benedictions. I snatched up a basket and my coat and left without a word to her. She stood in the doorway, watching after me for the longest time.

My mood lifted as I stomped across the fields under a sky blanketed with fluffy clouds. No breeze ruffled the branch of birch or beech. The snow underfoot was thinner now, for the days were starting to warm. I walked with purpose, knowing exactly where I needed to go. Two of the herbs Mother wanted could be found by a particular stream; for another, I would need to venture into the nearby woods. I watched for the fourth as I walked, for its leaves preferred sunlight and open air.

By the time I reached the woods, I had found all but one of the herbs. My legs were tired and I was hungry, for in my bad temper I had not thought to bring any food. The air was cooler within the shelter of the woods and smelled of moss and dampness. Fir trees grew close together, fighting to grow tallest and reach the sunlight first. I picked my way around fallen branches and between mossy rocks, trying not to tread on the small mushrooms growing in the shadows. Little snow had reached these depths.

At first I ignored the fey girl as she slipped from tree to tree, almost invisible in the gloom, but I was hungry and tired and more than a little fed up with being spied on.

"Why do you follow me?" I asked, as I clambered over a toppled fir that blocked my path.

My voice echoed through the woods, louder than I had intended. There was no response, not that I expected any. However, as I rounded a bend in the barely-visible path I followed, more sense than sight, she stood there.

Slight and fey, she had dark hair that tangled around her shoulders. Her skin was milky white and her lips far too red. Her eyes were what startled me the most, for they were as blue as a summer sky and seemed to pierce my soul as she stared at me. She stood awkwardly, hip jutting out to the side, and waited. For what, I wasn't sure. It was I who spoke first.

"Hello."

She continued to stare.

"Why do you now stand there after trying to be invisible for so many days?"

"Had I wanted to be invisible," she retorted haughtily, "you would have known naught of my presence."

"Why do you follow me then?"

"To watch you."

"Why?"

"So that we know what you do and what you don't."

"Why do you need to know?"

"Because you will be important, in as much as a mortal can be."

"Important to what?"

"To everything," she said. "And so you must do as I say."

"I shall not," I said indignantly, before realising she hadn't yet said what she wanted from me.

She glared, clearly unused to anyone refusing her instructions.

"You shall. For you have no choice. Everything in your life has led you towards today, towards here and now."

I reined in my temper. Perhaps I should at least appear to consider her demands.

"What is it you want from me?"

"You will leave here immediately and set out on a journey."

"And where would I travel to?"

"It is not important that you know the destination." Her tone was dismissive and my annoyance rose again. "All that is important is your obedience."

"You expect me to leave my home and my life to journey towards some end you will not even share with me?"

"Yes."

"Ludicrous," I said. "You do not know much about mortals if you think I will do this merely because you tell me to."

She frowned and stomped her foot in the leaf litter.

"I know everything about mortals. Have I not watched you, learnt all about you? I know what you like, what you don't, what you dream, what you fear. I have watched you as you worked, as you played, as you slept. I know everything about you."

"You clearly know nothing about me if you think I will depart on some mysterious journey just because you tell me to." I resisted the urge to stomp my own foot. "What use has your watching been if you know so little?"

Her pretty face turned ugly and she glared at me.

"You will do as I say. Whether you do it willingly or no, I care not. My task is to ensure you go, and go you will."

"I refuse."

"You cannot refuse. You have no idea of the consequences."

"Then tell me the consequences. Let me make an informed decision."

"You do not need to know," she said. "All you need know is that you are required to go. And go you shall."

"No. I will not. And that is my final word on the matter."

I continued picking my way towards the place where the final herb was wont to grow.

"This is your last chance," she said, and her voice held a warning I blithely ignored. "You will be sorry if you do not obey willingly."

I focused my attention on the path ahead. I heard a huff of exasperation before the ground rose up to meet my face. The smell of the woods intensified and yet colours became strangely muted. Perhaps I had fainted, hit my head. I thrust my hands into soft fir needles, trying to clutch at the ground, but seemed merely to scrabble fruitlessly.

My hands looked… odd. White, furry. I raised them to see them more clearly and promptly fell flat on my face in the leaves.

As I picked myself up, my entire body felt strange. I hunched over in an unaccustomed position with both hands and feet on the ground, yet it felt strangely natural. My behind trembled and when I looked back over my shoulder, I saw an expanse of silky white hair and a short, stubby tail that flicked from side to side. It stopped when I glared at it, but started again as soon as I looked away.

I realised I was panting with my tongue hanging out. I closed my mouth, but then I was suffocating. I opened my mouth and panted, tongue lolling out again. I sat in the leaf litter and studied the white paws at the end of my arms. Four claws plus a fifth, shorter. Thick white hair, which almost obscured the shiny black claws. Between my eyes I could just make out a black nose, which seemed to stick out far further than it should.

Memories flooded my mind and I trembled. There had been a blood-soaked dog in many of my visions — a small, white terrier, its eyes filled with pain. I had wondered what connection to me the dog would have and now I knew. I looked back towards the fey girl, but she was gone.

I wasted much time sitting in the leaves, staring at my new paws, until I finally realised the day was swiftly passing. My only hope was to find my way home. Mother would surely know what to do, for she was a wise woman and had much arcane knowledge. I did not let myself think about what I would do if she did not recognise me. I tried to speak, to say *Mother, it is I,* but my mouth wouldn't cooperate and all that came out was a strangled moan.

I had no way of carrying the basket. I tried to lift it in my mouth but choked on the plaited handle, so the herbs I had gathered would go to waste. I might have expected it would take time to get used to walking on four legs, but it felt like the most natural thing in the world. Provided I didn't think about which paw went where, the body I was in seemed to know what to do.

The tail — I could hardly consider it *my* tail — twitched from side to side whenever I thought about it. I couldn't quite figure out how it worked or what its purpose was. I had a vague idea that a wagging tail meant a happy dog, but this tail moved with the slightest thought. I had never realised how little I knew about dogs.

I headed towards home but the path seemed different. For starters, I was at the wrong height, so the markers I had noted that would have told me I travelled in the right direction weren't where I expected them to be. After a while, I realised I followed the faint scent of myself. I had walked through here recently. All I had to do to find my way home was follow my own scent. It is harder than it sounds, particularly when one is new to being a dog. Once I focussed on scent, my sensitive nose became overwhelmed and I froze, paralysed with indecision about which smell to follow. There was moss and water and decay. Mushrooms, mould and some sort of furry creature. I walked without any definite direction for some time, getting used to my new nose and form. By the time I regained my senses, I had lost my own trail.

I was completely lost, alone in the woods, and not in my own body.

18

BRIGIT

I SEARCHED THE woods desperately for my own scent. But no matter how I sniffed and snuffed, it was all earth and dampness, leaves and decay. I paused for a short rest and scrambled up onto a low rock, hoping the height would allow me to recognise something familiar.

My new ears heard every whisper and rustle, and I didn't dare let myself wonder what manner of creature made such noises. As soon as my legs felt somewhat rested, I continued my search. Had I been able to weep I would have, but it seemed my new eyes could cry no tears.

I searched and searched, growing increasingly frantic and trying not to think about tales of folk who wandered into the woods and never returned. Soon the little light that seeped this far into the woods began to slip away.

I redoubled my efforts, running from fir tree to shrubby chestnut, from rock to leafy patch, desperate to find some familiar scent or sight to point me towards home. Had I been in my own form, being lost in the woods would not be quite so bad. I knew exactly what I could do with my own hands and feet and, if nothing else, I could have screamed or cried or yelled. In this form, I was helpless.

When finally the light had all but disappeared, I had to admit there was no chance of finding my way home today. I was hungry and thirsty but didn't trust my new eyes and nose. I knew almost every food source growing in the woods, for Mother had ensured I learnt all a girl destined to become a wise woman should. In my own form, I wouldn't have hesitated. I would have known whether those berries dangling tantalisingly just out of reach were edible, or whether the roots of the plant by my foot were nutritious, or whether the mushrooms growing in the shade of the rocks were safe to eat. In my own form, I could have made a substantial meal out of the foodstuffs around me.

But in this strange new form, I doubted myself. The change from woman to dog might have affected my senses or my brain. I no longer knew whether I could rely on my knowledge and I wasn't familiar enough with this nose to trust it. So tonight, I would go hungry, but it wouldn't be for long. Tomorrow, I would find my way home.

In the shelter of a thick holly bush, I gathered a mound of fir needles, scraping them into place with my paws. It made for a surprisingly soft bed. I curled up on the pile, wrapped the tail around me and tucked my nose into my paws for warmth. The night was long and cold. I soon burrowed down into the needles, covering my body with them, but I was still so cold that at times I doubted I would live through the night.

Perhaps some stranger would find my body, buried in fir needles. They would have no way of knowing this form was more than it seemed. Nobody would take news of my passing to my mother. But the Sight was strong in her and she had nurtured her gift in a way I never had. Did she know this morning that I did not depart on any ordinary herb-gathering expedition? Perhaps the Sight would show her a small, white dog, shivering in the midst of a pile of fir needles. Would she wonder what this image meant? Would she debate whether the vision portrayed past, present, future, or merely a possibility? Or would she know it was I, cursed by the fey for refusing some mission they would not even explain? Mother always said my stubbornness would get me into trouble one day.

So I tortured myself with such thoughts as I shivered through the night. I did not sleep, but it was not only the cold that kept me awake. Mostly, it was fear. Fear of what might creep up on me if I slept. Fear of the visions that replayed in my mind, showing the bloodstained terrier over and over until I was sure I would go mad if I hadn't already. I also had the tiniest bit of hope that the fey girl might relent and restore me to my own form. However I was in two minds as to whether or not I would actually accept her strange quest, if that were the price for being returned to my own body.

I poked my head out of the needles every now and then to check whether morning had yet arrived. Eventually sunlight filtered through the fir canopy and hope, which had seemed so far away during the night, returned. Today, I would find my way home. My legs were stiff and clumsy as I scrambled out of the pile of fir needles that had been my bed.

I froze at a noise that seemed out of place in the morning quiet. Part wheeze, part snort, it came nearer. With the noise came a strong smell I didn't recognise, although my new nose twitched as if I should. My heart beat faster and icy tendrils of fear wound through me. I knew neither sound nor smell, but the form I was in recognised danger regardless and every instinct within me said to flee. But I was frozen in place.

The sound came closer and closer. Then an enormous black boar lumbered out from behind a fir and headed straight towards me. I quivered at the sight of its scarred muzzle and long tusks. My startled gasp came out as a bark of sorts. The boar paused and looked around, its nostrils widening as it caught my scent. There was no time to hide. Another step closer, a snort, and it saw me.

I scrambled out of the fir needles, paws sliding in their softness. Those few moments it took to get my grip was all the boar needed. It lunged. A tusk grazed my shoulder. It stung and I whimpered. I was trapped between the holly bush that had given overnight shelter from the breeze and a large boar that thought I smelled like breakfast.

My limbs felt no stronger than thistledown as I faced the boar. Its rank odour filled my nose. My mind was blank. The beast stared back, nostrils flaring, still tasting my scent. Its shoulder muscles rippled as it prepared to attack. I should have run while I had the chance.

The boar lowered its head and charged. A tusk pierced my shoulder. Dampness spread quickly and pain shot through me. If I had hands, I would have clasped one over the wound to stem the blood. But I had nothing other than furry paws and I needed them to run.

The boar pulled back, readied itself to attack again. Its tusk glittered with blood. As it lowered its head, I finally found the strength to move. But I was slow and clumsy with pain.

A tusk pierced me again, this time in the side. I screamed and it was a strangely human sound, despite my canine mouth. I tried to run, but the boar blocked my path with its enormous body, surprisingly fast for such a heavy creature. Or perhaps it was simply hungry.

If I couldn't run, I would have to fight. Either that, or lie down and let the beast have me. I drew back my lips and bared my teeth, managing a sound that was half-snarl, half-whimper.

The boar snorted, unimpressed, and lowered its head again. I flung myself at it, somehow avoiding the huge head and deadly tusks. My jaws closed around its ankle, but the skin was tough and I was already weak with blood loss.

The boar shook me off easily and flung me to the ground. The world spun. Snarling hogs surrounded me, their tusks red with my blood. *Get up, Brigit. Get up now.*

The beast leaned in to sniff me, perhaps checking whether I still lived. Its hoof landed on my front paw, mashing it into the leaf litter. Pain exploded through my paw and up my leg.

Then the boar had my ear in its mouth. It shook its head and my ear tore. Blood dripped down my face, obscuring my vision, and trickled into my mouth. It was warm and salty and there was a lot of it.

The boar released my ear and I staggered to my feet. I ran. Somehow, I dodged one way just as it moved the other and, unimaginably, I was suddenly behind it.

Run. That was the only thought in my head. Run as far and as fast as I could. Behind me, the beast grunted. I felt, rather than heard, it turn. But it was large and already tiring and I had a head start. It followed briefly but soon gave up, perhaps preferring to find a meal that didn't mind being eaten quite so much.

I ran until my legs gave out and I collapsed in a heaving, bloody heap. My whole body trembled and I could hardly see for the blood dripping into my eyes. Warm foam dripped from my mouth as I gasped for breath. Everything hurt and I couldn't see enough of my body to tell how bad the wounds were. Blood pooled beneath me, seeping into the leaf litter.

I could think of nothing but the pain and for some time I lay panting. But I couldn't stay here. I had to move on, no matter how much I hurt. I didn't know how far I had run. Injured as I was, perhaps it wasn't far at all. The boar could still be on my trail and, if not, the woods contained other beasts who would seize the opportunity of an easy meal. I was in no condition to survive another fight.

I managed to haul myself up onto my haunches and used my uninjured front paw to wipe the blood from my eyes. I had to find the way home. Mother would aid me, even if she didn't recognise me in this body. She would never turn away a creature in need. I staggered to my feet and a wave of new pain flooded through me. My front paw, the one the boar stood on, would bear no weight and blood still ran freely from it. Surely the bone was broken. It was a wonder I had managed to run at all, for now I could barely walk.

Limping on three paws was awkward and pain shot through me with every jerk. How soon would I be too weak from blood loss to move? I would keep going for as long as I could, and when I could walk no further, well, I tried not to think about that.

Blood from my torn ear continued to run down my forehead and already it dripped into my eyes again. Now I knew how the terrier in my visions had become injured. I had always wondered whether some of the blood might be mine, but I had never expected it to be this much.

19

DIARMUID

I LEFT HOME early the next morning while streaks of rose and violet still filled the sky. The air was crisp and clean, warning that nights were yet cold for the traveller sleeping out of doors. If I let myself dwell on that, I might lose what little courage I had. So, I cleared my mind and set off. One foot in front of the other.

The first village on my way was Tors. It was a little further away than Maker's Well, although to the north rather than the west. My aim for this first day of travel was to get as close to Tors as possible before nightfall.

The snow was light and easy to walk through, and the brisk walk soon warmed me. The morning passed with surprising speed. By the time the sun was high overhead, I neared the edge of Silver Downs land. The woods, which I was forbidden to enter, loomed ahead of me. I could not name most of the trees except for the firs, standing tall and proud, their green needles clinging in defiance of winter. I intended to veer around the woods to where a rough path led to Tors.

Although well accustomed to spending a day walking, I did not usually wear a heavy pack and already my legs wobbled. How could I walk day after day if I was fatigued by midday? I set my pack down in the snow and ate bread and cheese while standing. A light breeze kicked up and the warmth I had felt quickly disappeared. As soon as I finished, I shouldered my pack and set off again.

Had anyone realised I was gone yet? How long until Fiachra told them? Would someone come after me, try to stop me? Perhaps I could convince them to travel with me. I would be less afraid with company. It wouldn't be Eremon, of course, for his place was to stay at Silver Downs. And not Fiachra. He had made it clear he would not aid me unless I called him and I wasn't yet desperate enough. Sitric wouldn't leave his business, but perhaps Marrec and Conn might come. Maybe I should return home, ask them to accompany me? But I would not make it home before nightfall and there was no guarantee they would agree anyway. Besides, I had less than two sevennights to complete my task and there was no time to waste. So I kept walking.

Now that I had allowed fear to creep into my mind, it was impossible not to worry. About whether the witch was Ida. How I might stop her and whether I would have to destroy her. Whether it was possible to do so without also destroying myself. Whether Caedmon had left home this morning bearing a death sentence from last night's tale. The dream in which he saw his own death had shown his body lying in a ditch, his throat slit. And that was how the soldier in my tale also met his end.

None of this would have happened if I hadn't been so careless with the tales I told. How full of hope I was with my first tale, the one about the bard and his muse. A tale had seemed like some wonderful new plaything, shiny and sparkling and full of promise. And then when my audience hated it, I fell deep into melancholy where the world seemed dimmer, its colours faded, and hope and joy were crushed like an ant beneath my boot.

How did my ability work? And why was it only the tale about Ida that had come to life? I could only pray that last night's tale hadn't also come true. My thoughts were full of *could have* and *should have*. The one thing of which I was certain was that I would never tell another tale.

I left Silver Downs land and reached the road. Although roughly made, it was still easier than walking through fields. On one side continued the same woods that edged Silver Downs. On the other was pastureland. These rolling hills would be lush with thick green grass come summer. I wondered if I would ever return to see it.

As the sun dipped closer to the horizon and the first shades of a brilliant orange sunset appeared, I searched for a suitable place to spend the night. Caedmon would say to find a spot with protection from the night wind on at least one side. There must be clearance for a fire and I should be out of sight of the road. The sound of water trickling over stones reached my ears and, without hesitation, I left the road to follow it. Proximity to fresh water, that was another thing Caedmon would look for.

I followed the sound into the woods. The stream couldn't be far away. As I ventured deeper, the firs grew more thickly and soon they blocked all but the most persistent rays of sunlight. I moved carefully, feeling my way with each step as I could see little now. I walked and walked, but still the water sounded no closer.

Some small creature kept pace with me, slipping swiftly from tree to tree. I turned to look and it vanished behind a hawthorn bush. When I looked away, it glided to the next fir tree.

My heart beat faster. The creature clearly didn't want to be seen and I couldn't quite make out what it was. Small, but human in form. One of the fey?

Lost in my thoughts, I didn't notice that the sound of trickling water had disappeared. Deep in the woods and in almost total darkness, I was in danger of becoming hopelessly lost, if indeed I wasn't already. Time and again, Caedmon had warned me not to venture into unfamiliar woods. Papa had forbidden any of us from entering these particular woods, steeped as they were in tales of people who never returned. I was stupid to leave the road, stupid to follow a sound regardless of what it might promise.

I set down my pack, unhooked the small lamp hanging from the side, and fumbled for a flint. The lamp shed welcome light over my surroundings and I saw another small being perched on a nearby rock. It disappeared as soon as I looked at it. So two of them followed me, perhaps more.

"Who are you?" I called and my voice wavered only a little.

Silence greeted my words.

"I know you are there. I have seen you."

Nothing.

"What do you want?"

There was a giggle, soft and high pitched. I waited, but no further response came. Shouldering my pack and carrying the lamp, I started back towards the road. I would return to where I had entered the woods and make camp there on the very edge where I could see the road but still be sheltered from the wind.

I had walked barely a dozen paces before I stumbled into a shallow ditch masked by a mound of leaves. I landed unevenly and pain shot through my ankle. The lamp slipped from my fingers and its small flame disappeared, the oil likely spilled onto the leaves.

Another giggle.

Clutching the trunk of a nearby fir, I hauled myself to my feet. The rough bark dug into my fingers, tearing my skin. With a cautious step, I tested my ankle. The pain was immediate. I sucked in a breath and swallowed the bitter words that rose to my lips, not wanting to further amuse my invisible watchers. Clearly I would walk no further tonight. I let my pack fall to the ground. If I could not walk, I would have to make camp right here.

If the creatures shadowing me were fey of some sort, the sound of trickling water might have been a trick. Did they intend for me to be hurt or only to lose my way? Perhaps they aimed to delay my journey. If they knew why I travelled, surely they knew I could ill afford to linger. Hopefully I would be able to walk by morning. I could not consider any alternative. The longer I delayed, the more trouble Ida could cause. People had already died.

I could put no weight on my ankle, so it was on hands and knees that I cleared space sufficient for a small fire. I used only dead branches from the ground and dry fir needles. That was another of Caedmon's rules: never take branches from a living tree. He said it was better that we go without fire for a night than hurt a tree.

I felt slightly more cheerful once a small fire was burning. I retrieved the blanket from my pack and spread it out beside the fire. Next came some rations, just enough to sustain me, and no more. I allowed myself two mouthfuls of water. My mouth was dry enough to drain the flask, but my small water supply must be conserved. I cursed myself for leaving the second flask behind.

After I had eaten my meagre meal, there was nothing else to do but sleep. The air was chill, and the night would only grow colder, but at least the trees blocked all wind. I wrapped the blanket around myself and lay down, trying to find a reasonably comfortable position where I didn't have either rocks or sticks digging into me.

I had scarcely found a tolerable spot when I heard a noise. It was different to the one that had enticed me to stray from the road, a soft whimper that barely reached my ears. But it could still be another fey trick. I couldn't even defend myself, for I had foolishly left my dagger in my pack rather than in my boot. How unimpressed Caedmon would be if he could see me now, lost in the woods, too injured to stand, and weaponless.

Slightly out of my reach was a stick that looked sturdy enough. If some creature came towards me, I would fling myself at the stick and hope to make it to my feet in time. I couldn't afford to think about the possibility of not being able to stand. The whimper came again, a little louder, and I relaxed somewhat, for it did not sound threatening. Rather, it sounded like a creature in pain.

"Where are you?" I asked, my voice soft so as not to startle it, whatever it was.

There was no response. I eyed the stick again.

"Come out. I know you are there."

A rustle and another whimper, then the creature crept out from behind a bush. It was a small dog, a terrier of some sort, dirty and blood-stained now, but possibly once white. Its ears were lowered and one hung oddly as if torn. The dog, barely knee high to me, limped on three paws, tail curled between its back legs. Blood dripped from the front paw held aloft and from a wound on its head. More blood smeared its flank.

"Come here," I said. "Let me see that paw."

It hesitated, sniffing the air.

"I won't hurt you."

As if it understood, the terrier limped forward and halted a few paces in front of me. Now I could see it clearly, I was surprised the animal could walk at all. Blood oozed from wounds on its shoulder, flank and muzzle. The ear that hung oddly was ripped half off and blood still trickled down the side of its face. The bleeding paw, though, was my immediate concern. Surely a creature of this size could ill afford much blood loss.

Slowly, so as not to spook the terrier, I reached for my pack. Black eyes fixed on me as the terrier sat, still holding up its injured paw. I fumbled in my pack and my fingers found the roll of bandage I had forgotten about. I would have strapped my ankle had I remembered, but the terrier needed it more than I did. I drew out the bandage and my flask.

"I'm going to wash some of the blood off," I said softly, hoping the terrier would understand I intended aid. "And then I need to wrap your paw. The bleeding won't stop otherwise."

It continued to stare at me, eyes large and unblinking. I reached out, ready to pull away if it tried to bite, and would have sworn the terrier extended its paw and placed it right in my hand. I poured a little water over the paw. As the blood washed away, I saw a deep cut surrounded by swollen, bruised skin.

"This is going to hurt," I warned. "I'm sorry."

The gaze from those big, black eyes remained fastened on my face. I wrapped the paw firmly, still half expecting to be bitten. The terrier sat quietly, paw extended stiffly, and only whimpered once. I cut the bandage with my dagger and tied the end. The terrier continued to sit there, its paw now held out awkwardly to one side. Those eyes were disconcerting, the way they were fixed so intently on my face.

I eyed the wounds on its shoulder, side and ear. It would use the rest of my water if I tried to clean them. I wrapped the remaining bandage around the terrier's stomach, covering the wound on its flank and using my spare socks for padding. The shoulder wound was shallow and already crusted over. Blood clotted on the ripped ear also.

"I would wash off more of the blood, but we need to save the water. I can spare a little for you to drink, though."

I had nothing that could serve as a bowl, so I poured some water into my cupped hand. The terrier leaned forward and drank eagerly, tongue lapping at my palm. Once it had drunk the water, it looked up at me expectantly. I poured another handful and it drank that down, too. When it eyed me again, I shook my head.

"I'm sorry, we have to save the rest."

It stood and limped on three legs over to a fir, where it squatted and urinated.

"Oh, you're a girl."

The terrier hobbled back and stood in front of me, bandaged paw still held up. The terrier would be company for now and she likely wouldn't live through the night. I patted the blanket.

"You may as well sit down. You won't get far with that paw."

She sniffed at me, but whether it was intended as a thank you or in derision, I couldn't tell. She circled several times, awkwardly and with a whimper, before curling up with the bandaged paw still held aloft.

I fished within my pack for a strip of dried meat, broke it into small pieces and laid them in front of her on the blanket.

"Like I said, we have to conserve the rations. But there's enough for you to have a little tonight."

I lay down as near to the fire as I thought was safe. She ate the meat, then edged closer until she lay with her back curled into the curve of my legs. Her shivers vibrated through my body. I wrapped the blanket around us both. Her body was cold against me, but she soon began to warm.

Staring into the flames as I waited for sleep to claim me, I didn't feel quite as bad as I had earlier. I had food in my belly, albeit not much, and with the terrier snuggled up to me, I was comfortably warm. Fiachra had said I would have companions on this journey. Perhaps the injured terrier was the first.

She was still snuggled against me when I woke. I had no sense of time here in the depths of the woods. Sparse sunlight filtered in through the firs, but it could be dawn or midday for all I could tell. I only knew I had slept long enough for the fire to burn out. I didn't want to disturb the terrier, but as she slept on, I became increasingly aware of my bladder. Although I tried to sit up silently, she stirred as soon as I moved. The look on her face said she had no idea where she was.

"It's all right. You're safe. You can stay there, but I need to get up."

She stretched and stood gingerly, whimpering as her injured paw touched the ground. Blood had soaked through the bandage during the night, but not as much as I might have expected. She hobbled stiffly over to a fir and crouched by it to relieve herself.

I hauled myself to my feet, feeling less than limber. I could put barely any weight on my sprained ankle. I would be staying here for at least today. I managed to half-hop, half-stumble some distance from the blanket and kept my back firmly to the terrier, oddly embarrassed at the thought of her watching. The necessities done, I hobbled back to the blanket where the terrier sat licking her bandaged paw.

"You shouldn't lick that," I said. "It won't heal unless you leave it alone."

She looked up at me, unblinking.

"Let's have some breakfast, then I'll change the bandage on that paw. How does that sound?"

Another unblinking stare. I tore my gaze away from her and rummaged in the pack.

"We have bread, cheese, dried meat."

She studied the strip of dried meat in my hand. I tore it into pieces for her and took the remains of yesterday's loaf and a small wedge of cheese for myself. The terrier gulped down the meat, then watched as I ate. I offered some of my bread, but she merely sniffed it and stared at the cheese in my hand.

"You can't have the cheese," I told her. "You already had the meat. You can have some bread, but the cheese is mine."

Still she stared and eventually I gave her half, albeit reluctantly. She ate the cheese in two swallows and seemed satisfied.

Having finished my meal, I allowed myself two mouthfuls of water, then offered the terrier some in my cupped palm. She drank thirstily and I pretended not to notice when she looked beseechingly at me for more. The flask was more than two thirds empty already.

With breakfast finished, I rummaged in the pack for a makeshift bandage. All I had were my two spare shirts. I sliced one into strips with my dagger.

"Will you hold still for me?"

She sat stiffly as I unwound the bandage. Dried blood glued it to her paw and I hesitantly peeled it away, still expecting her to bite. Blood crusted the wound and I was reluctant to wash it in case it started bleeding again. I couldn't spare any more water anyway. I wrapped her paw with the strips from my shirt and tossed the bloodied bandage into the fire's dead coals.

With the remnants of my ruined shirt, I strapped my ankle. It was swollen, tender to touch, and the skin felt hot. Surely by tomorrow the swelling would be reduced. I would be able to walk then. I had to.

I crawled around to gather more fallen branches and soon a merry blaze warmed us. With nothing else to do, the day passed with agonising slowness. I dozed from time to time, but mostly I just lay staring up into the canopy and trying not to think about the mess I was in or how I would find Ida, let alone destroy her, or what it meant about my own nature that I had created such evil. The terrier was quiet and seemed to sleep most of the day. I hoped she was healing, for there was little else I could do to help her.

As the woods around us finally grew darker again, we shared another meagre meal. Then we curled up together with the blanket wrapped around us. She went back to sleep almost immediately and her paws twitched as she dreamed.

I lay staring into the flames for a long time. The woods around us were still and silent. I had seen no further sign of the two small creatures that led me from my path. Surely, if they still watched, they could see I needed help. *We* needed help.

This was not exactly the journey I had imagined.

20

DIARMUID

IN THE EARLY hours of the night, the rain started. It seeped through my blanket and into my clothes. Very soon, I was soaked through, shivering even as I clutched the sopping blanket around me. The fire sputtered and died. The terrier lay motionless, curled up with her nose tucked into her tail. Water dripped from her hair and soaked the makeshift bandages.

The night was painfully long and there were times I believed we would both die of the cold long before morning ever came. My shivers became shuddering waves that crashed over my body and I could no longer feel my hands or toes. I drew the terrier to my chest and wrapped my arms around her, seeking some warmth from her cold body even as I hoped to warm her with mine.

When at last the rain eased and the light filtering through the firs brightened, I nudged the terrier aside and sat up. My fingers were clumsy as I unwrapped the soaked bandage around my ankle. My ankle was still swollen and tender, but perhaps not quite as much.

Although the rain had ceased, I was no warmer and every part of my body ached. When I hauled myself to my feet and tested my ankle, the pain was immense. I gritted my teeth and sucked in a breath. I could bear a little weight on the ankle, but not much. Perhaps with the aid of a crutch of some sort I could make my way out of the woods. I only had to get as far as the road and then I could wait for someone to pass by. What other choice did I have? Nobody would happen on me if I stayed here, and once Fiachra explained my absence, it was unlikely anyone would come looking for me. Even if they did — if perhaps Marrec and Conn came — they wouldn't think to search for me in the woods. My only chance of rescue was to reach the road.

The terrier sat up and stretched, looking even more stiff and sorry for herself than I felt.

"I can hardly leave you here, can I?" I said.

She looked up at me quizzically.

"It's not like you can fend for yourself in that condition. Do you think you can keep up if I take you with me?"

The look she gave me was full of indignation and I hastily added, "That is, if you want to."

She sniffed and looked away.

"I'm in no better condition, I guess. Perhaps with the two of us together, we can make it back to the road."

She eyed me again, considering.

"Once we reach the road, we can decide what to do next."

She sniffed, perhaps in agreement.

The remaining rations were scant and wet. One small loaf of bread, now soggy and beyond edible, a small piece of cheese, four strips of dried meat. I tossed the bread into the fire pit, then took half the cheese and a strip of meat for myself and gave the terrier a piece of meat. She wolfed it and watched as I packed the rest away.

"No more," I said firmly. "We'll need it tonight."

I had brought provisions for but one stomach and only two days, expecting to restock my supplies in Tors. Unless we found help today, tomorrow would be hungry. We each drank a few mouthfuls of water, then there was nothing left to do but wring out the soggy blanket and stow it away in my pack.

I found a reasonably straight length of branch to serve as a crutch. The terrier would have to cope on her own and either keep up or... I refused to think past that.

"We have to stick together."

I used the crutch to haul myself to my feet, then hitched the pack over my shoulders.

"Nice and slow, no faster than either of us can cope with, all right?"

She gave me a look that clearly said she could keep up with anything I could manage.

Our progress was painfully slow and after barely two dozen paces, both the terrier and I panted. We had only passed maybe five firs in that distance. Each jarring step sent pain stabbing through my ankle. My wet clothes clung to my body uncomfortably.

I paused to rest, leaning on the makeshift crutch. The terrier sat, her head drooping and her breathing unsteady. I counted to twenty and we set off once more.

"You need a name," I said when we stopped to rest yet again. Count to twenty. Move on.

Her ears twitched, but she didn't look at me. Her head hung even lower now and she barely seemed to have the strength to hold herself up.

Beneath the blood, her coat was perhaps white.

"Snowball?" I suggested.

A slight flick of an ear was her only reaction.

"Not Snowball. What else is white?" Another few steps before I could speak again. "Clouds. Ribbons. Owls. Owl?"

She deigned to sniff at me.

"Rabbit? Bunny?"

Not even a sniff this time. I halted and the terrier immediately sat in the leaf litter. Her head drooped and white foam dripped from her mouth. Was this where she would refuse to walk any further? I counted to twenty and heaved off again. With a grunt, she followed.

"What about white flowers? Foxglove, Snowdrop, Bluebell. Bramble."

Her ears twitched and she finally looked up at me, big eyes even wider with pain and heavy with exhaustion.

"Bramble? You like that?"

She sniffed, a different sound from the one she used for derision.

"Bramble it is."

I had no more breath left to talk and I needed all of my strength to keep moving anyway. We only had to get to the road. We couldn't possibly continue past that, even though the road would be far easier than the woods where every step involved lifting the foot over branch or mossy stone, often to land in a slippery patch of leaves and slide before I could catch my balance again. But we would be all right if we could get to the road. Someone would come along sooner or later. Bramble and I would wait.

Again and again, I walked until I could go no further, then I stopped to rest for a count of twenty. Each time, Bramble and I somehow found the strength to move on again. The woods around us were full of the rustling of animals snuffling around in the fallen leaves and the calls of woodlarks. A raven swooped past my head, too intent on whatever business it followed to even notice me. I tried to watch for the strange creatures that led me here, but it was all I could do to stay standing.

Step by step, panting and exhausted. My thoughts started to wander. I was confused. Again and again, I suddenly realised I staggered through the woods and, for a few moments, I wondered why I hurt so much. Several times I stopped and threw down the branch that served as my crutch, preparing to lie down and rest before I remembered. I had to get to the road. If I lay down, I might never get up again. Somehow, I awkwardly retrieved the crutch from the ground and we moved on.

The light through the firs was softer now. The day was slipping away and my spirits sank even lower. Neither Bramble nor I would survive another night in the woods. Right when I began to lose all hope, the light ahead brightened.

"I think we're almost at the road."

I would have run that last hundred paces, but it was all I could do to limp along, leaning heavily on the crutch with each step. My fingers were blistered from the rough wood.

Twice more I forgot what I was doing, but each time I saw the light ahead and remembered. Bramble could barely lift her paws, but somehow she, too, kept going.

Then, abruptly, we were out of the woods. One moment it seemed the firs extended forever, then suddenly light burnt my eyes, even though the sun sat a mere finger's width above the horizon. There was little time left until sunset. As we stood at the edge of the woods, blinking in the sudden brightness, a voice boomed.

"Hello there, friend. Lucky you came out when you did. If you were a few moments later, I would have gone and missed you."

He sat atop a wooden cart hooked up to a pair of large, black oxen. When he stood, I realised he was possibly the biggest man I had ever seen. Tall and wide-shouldered, he looked like he could easily drag the cart himself if the oxen tired. He climbed down, moving more gracefully than I would have expected for one his size.

"Oh my," he said as he drew closer to us. "You look right dreadful." His gaze drifted down to Bramble. "Both of you."

I opened my mouth, but no reply came out. Suddenly my head spun, I felt sick to my stomach and my legs would no longer hold me. As I fell, the man scooped me up in his arms.

"Now there," he said. "You need some rest. I'm going to put you in my cart."

"Bramble," I said, my voice weak. I moved my mouth, but nothing else came out.

"That's your dog, is it?" He gave me a small, sad smile. "Pretty name, that. Bramble. Had a friend with a daughter called Bramble once."

As if I weighed no more than a child, he deposited me into the cart. He placed Bramble beside me and she leaned weakly against my leg. The man frowned as he inspected the blood-soaked bandages on her paw and side.

"That don't look good. Needs a clean and some proper bandaging."

He looked us both over again.

"I was heading home anyway. You can stay a few days. Rest up."

I would have cried if I'd had the energy.

The cart shook as the man swung himself back up into the front seat. He clicked at the oxen and we set off with a jolt.

"I'm Owain, by the way," he called over his shoulder. "My missus would say I shoulda told you that afore anything else. Owain, you big oaf, she'd say, you need to learn some manners."

I couldn't reply. I lay on the cart's wooden floor, staring up into a grey sky heavy with clouds. It would rain again tonight. And we would be sleeping under a roof.

Beside me, Bramble breathed so shallowly I wondered whether she was still conscious. I tried to raise my hand to touch her, but couldn't so much as twitch a finger. Strangely, I no longer hurt. Perhaps I slept, or lost consciousness, for I knew nothing else until Owain lifted Bramble out of the cart. The little terrier lay limply in his arms and I vaguely wondered whether she was dead. It seemed I should feel something if she was, but I couldn't quite figure out what.

"I'll come back for you," Owain said to me and disappeared, taking Bramble with him.

I waited, drifting, neither entirely conscious nor unconscious, until I heard Owain return. I managed to turn my head towards him and fancied I saw a half-naked man run out from behind the house. He had a long nose and tousled hair and wore only a shirt. His bare behind shone in the late afternoon sunlight as he darted across the yard and behind the barn. Owain's back was to the man and it seemed he waited a few moments longer than necessary before lifting me from the cart.

"A man—" I started.

"Ssh," Owain said and his jaw was clenched. "You need to rest."

"But—"

"Save your strength."

The following hours were a blur. I lay in a blissfully soft bed. Someone undressed me, bathed me, applied a warm poultice to my ankle and strapped it firmly. Warm, dry blankets were piled on top of me. My head was held up and a meaty broth spooned into my mouth. I gulped greedily and it spilled down my chin to be efficiently wiped up. My stomach rumbled as my head was laid back down on the pillow.

"More," I mumbled.

"Later," a voice said. "It will make you sick if you eat too much too soon."

Then I was alone. I drifted hazily. I was warm and clean, had food in my belly, and my ankle burned pleasantly from the poultice. The bedchamber smelled of healing herbs, possibly from the poultice or maybe someone had thrown them on the fire. An oil lamp on the dresser kept the darkness at bay.

I tried to roll over and found I was not alone. Bramble lay beside me, curled up in a tight ball. She, too, had been bathed and her hair was snow-white. Her injured paw stuck out stiffly, neatly wrapped in a clean bandage. Other bandages covered the wounds on her shoulder, flank and ear.

"I told you we would make it if we stuck together," I said, but the words seemed to dissolve in my mouth and what came out was unintelligible.

Bramble opened one dark eye to stare at me, then sniffed and went back to sleep. I laid my hand gently against her back, finding comfort in the warm body beside me. Then I too slept.

2 1

DIARMUID

WHEN I NEXT woke, my head was clear and the pain in my ankle had subsided to a dull ache. My stomach rumbled and my tongue felt fat and furry.

I lay on a wide bed, starched white covers tucked firmly around me, the fabric smooth and fine beneath my fingers. The patch of warmth by my hip was Bramble. A plump, stuffed chair was drawn up to a hearth containing neatly raked coals. A wooden dresser bearing jug and basin stood beneath a window. Someone had opened the curtains since I last woke, but all I could see was a patch of leaden sky. This must be Owain's home, but I had no idea where it was or how far we had travelled in the cart.

A woman entered my bedchamber. She was perhaps five or six summers older than me. Her dark hair was neatly tied back and her work dress was immaculate. She looked me over, her gaze critical.

"You are awake." Her voice held no warmth. "How do you feel?"

"Hungry."

She laid a cool hand against my forehead. "The fever has broken at last."

"I had a fever?"

Her eyes narrowed. "You were very ill. Don't you remember?"

111

"I thought I was just hungry."

Her forehead wrinkled and she pursed her lips. Obviously I had said something incredibly stupid.

"I will apply another poultice to your ankle and strap it again. Then you may see if you can get up. If you can make your way to the dinner table, it will be far less trouble for me."

The doorway darkened and Owain entered. His plain face broke into a smile.

"Hello," he said. "How do you feel?"

"The fever has broken and he's hungry," the woman snapped.

Owain's face briefly registered hurt, although his eyes said clearly he worshipped this woman.

I had passed out without introducing myself to Owain.

"My name is Diarmuid."

The woman frowned at me again. "So it would seem."

"This is Maeve, my wife," Owain said. "She has been caring for you."

"And it's not like I didn't already have enough to do, is it?" Maeve had a glare each for Owain and I. "Between keeping the household running and you trying to get me with child, I don't have time to spare as it is. And then you bring home a half-dead stranger and his dog and expect me to nurse them."

Owain flushed. "They needed help. Couldn't leave them on the side of the road."

"I don't see why not. They weren't your responsibility."

Owain hung his head and looked away.

"Can I have some water?" I asked, an awkward witness to their argument.

Maeve filled a mug from the jug on the dresser. She stared up at the ceiling as she held it out and I fumbled to take it from her. Owain came to my rescue, taking the mug in his big hands and holding it to my mouth. Water ran down my chin as I gulped. He didn't comment, only wiped my face with a towel. Maeve was gone by the time I had drunk my fill.

"Let's see how you feel once you're on your feet." Owain helped me to stand. He guided me across the room towards the window, his strong arm a sturdy anchor around my waist. "A few steps, no more, eh."

With the first step, I realised how weak I was. My knees buckled and my legs shook and it was only Owain's strong arms that kept me standing. My ankle was still tender, but I could put some weight on it with Owain's support. I barely managed six steps before I could go no further, panting from the effort of even so little. My heart sank. It would be some days yet before I resumed my journey and the dark of the moon drew closer with every night I delayed.

"Bed now," he said and carried me back. "You should rest. I'll come get you at dinner time."

Then it was Bramble's turn. Owain held a small wooden bowl up to her mouth and she lapped thirstily. He gently stroked her hip, well away from her injuries, and she looked up at him with an expression of gratitude. It seemed even she knew how close we had both come to death. When Owain left, Bramble and I curled up together again and I drifted back to sleep.

The bedchamber was darker when I next woke. My mouth was dry again and my stomach grumbled loudly. My head was clearer, though, and for a few moments, I thought perhaps we could resume our journey on the morrow. That hope was dashed when I tried to get out of bed, for I was still too weak to do any more than sit up alone.

When Owain returned, he smiled broadly and I couldn't help but smile back. There was something about him that made me like him very much.

"Are you hungry?" he asked.

Before I could respond, Bramble hauled herself up with a bark.

Owain laughed.

"Well then, Bramble. Let's take you downstairs for dinner." He lifted her, his large hands careful to avoid her injuries. "I'll be back for you in a moment," he said over his shoulder.

When he returned, Owain scooped me up, lifting me as easily as he had Bramble.

"Don't want to do too much yet," he muttered. "Best that you rest."

"I have to continue on my journey."

"In a few days."

He carried me down to the dining room and deposited me on a wide, stuffed chair. The furniture was elegantly carved and the walls draped with fine embroideries. I had taken Owain for a simple farmer, but clearly he was something more. Bramble nestled in a thickly-padded basket beside my chair. Her eyes were bright and alert. The scent of roasted meat and fresh bread wafted in from the kitchen and my stomach growled so hard it hurt.

"What occupation do you have, Owain?" I leaned down to stroke Bramble's head. She leaned into my hand.

"Oh, this and that." He busied himself with settling into a chair across the table from me.

Maeve bustled in with a platter before I could ask further and dropped it onto the table with what seemed like unnecessary force.

"Good evening, Maeve," I said. "Thank you for looking after us."

She huffed and straightened the platter.

"It's not like I don't already have enough to do."

Owain cleared his throat apologetically.

"We really appreciate it," I said. "I don't know what would have become of us if Owain hadn't come along when he did. We couldn't have made it much further."

"You were almost dead when I found you," Owain said cheerfully. "Wouldn't have lasted another night. Either of you," he added with a glance towards Bramble.

She flicked her ear at him and held his gaze.

"Thank you, Owain," I said. "And I'm sure Bramble would thank you also if she could talk."

"Oh, she talks in her own way." He dragged his gaze away from Bramble.

Maeve's scowl didn't budge as we ate. Owain said little, but every word irritated her and when she spoke, it was usually to remind him how much more difficult her life was with him in it. Owain tolerated her criticisms with gentle shrugs.

The meal was lavish and I ate with gusto. Roasted hen, winter root vegetables, rich gravy. Thick slices of brown bread. A sweet honey that reminded me, with a pang of homesickness, of Silver Downs. Bramble ate from a bowl of choice selections of chicken and vegetables. Owain must have filled the bowl himself. I couldn't imagine Maeve going to that effort.

Maeve barely ate, but merely picked at a piece of chicken and reduced a slice of bread to crumbs on her plate. I would have felt uncomfortable about eating so much when she had so little if it weren't for Owain who had second and then third helpings of everything.

"Thank you for your hospitality," I said to Maeve. "I hope I won't have to intrude on you for much longer."

Maeve looked up briefly from the growing pile of crumbs.

"I suppose you can stay another day or two."

"Nonsense, Diarmuid," Owain said. "It'll be at least a sevennight before you are well enough to leave."

Maeve glared across the table at him. He lowered his gaze but didn't retract his words.

"I'll wait until morning before I make any decisions," I said. "But I'm sure I'll feel much better by then."

Maeve rose abruptly and left. Her voice came from the kitchen, although I couldn't make out what she said. Directing the servants, perhaps. Owain pushed back his chair, scooped up Bramble's basket in one arm and helped me to rise with the other. I leaned heavily on him as we went into the next room where a small fire blazed with a merriness it alone seemed to feel. I sank down into an oversized chair and its thick padding cushioned my body comfortably. My legs trembled from the short walk and my ankle throbbed.

Owain positioned Bramble's basket close by his chair where she would feel the fire's warmth, then sat with a sigh. Bramble stretched out and rested her chin on her paws. Dishes clattered loudly from the direction of the kitchen. Someone was taking their feelings out on the crockery.

"I'm sorry if Bramble and I being here is causing problems for you," I said.

Owain shrugged. "She's always like this. Doesn't like me much, I'm afraid."

"Then why did she handfast with you?" I regretted my rudeness the instant the words left my mouth, but Owain didn't seem bothered.

"I made her father a generous offer. She preferred someone else."

"She resents you."

"Thought she'd come around. See I wasn't so bad. But it's been three summers. She still hates me and we still have no heir." He stared silently into the fire for a while. "Not much I can do. And it's not a bad life we have. I know I'm a simple man, but I do all right. We have everything we need."

I looked around the room, which was generously appointed with heavy wooden cabinets, plush chairs and thick rugs. Dark drapes covered the windows, keeping out the early spring evening's chill. It was clear Owain did better than all right.

"I'm sure I won't need to stay a sevennight," I said. "A day, maybe two, and I'll be well again. I can't afford to delay any longer."

"Can't rush these things. And there's Bramble too."

We both looked down at the little terrier stretched out in the basket. She gazed up at us, her eyes already drooping.

"She might not be well enough to come with me." The words hurt, but I had to do what was best for Bramble, not for myself. "She lost a lot of blood and it's going to be a while before she can walk properly."

Owain nodded and returned his gaze to the fire.

"Would you… Could I… That is, if she can't come with me, can she stay with you?" I finished in a rush, wishing I had found a more elegant way to say it.

"Sure." Owain spared Bramble another quick glance. "If she wants. Mayhap though she wants to stick with you."

I looked down at Bramble to find her sitting up and glaring at me. Curiously, she appeared to have taken offence at my request. How much of our conversation had she understood? Surely it wasn't possible for a dog to recognise more than a few words. Come, sit, eat. But still, the look she gave made me want to hang my head in shame.

"I'm not saying I want to leave her behind," I said quickly.

Owain mumbled something that might have been agreement. We sat in silence after that, each occupied with his own thoughts, and I noticed he dropped a hand down to stroke Bramble gently on the head.

Bramble no longer seemed sleepy. Although she lay down again, she continued to glare at me. I kept my gaze firmly on the raven in the fire and pretended I didn't see the hurt in Bramble's eyes.

22

DIARMUID

I WAS PITIFULLY weak from my illness, but each day I grew a little stronger and my ankle a little more sound. I passed my recovery time mostly lying in bed, talking to Bramble, and worrying about how many nights remained until the next full moon. I didn't see much of Owain after breakfast each day, but every evening he came to carry Bramble and I downstairs for dinner. After we had eaten, the three of us would laze in front of the fire. Maeve always absented herself after the evening meal and I wouldn't see her again until breakfast.

"Didn't expect her to make it," Owain said one evening, referring to Bramble who sprawled on his lap, head draped over his knee, seemingly asleep. "Didn't expect either of you to make it actually."

"She's tougher than she looks," I said.

Bramble opened one eye to glare at me.

"I don't thinks she likes me much," I added with something of a laugh. Bramble might glare and huff at me, but every night she slept curled in a warm ball against my side.

"Her wounds were festering." Owain stroked Bramble's back with a gentleness unexpected in one so large.

"I didn't realise."

Guilt filled me. If only I hadn't rationed the water. If only I had cleaned her wounds more thoroughly. Perhaps they wouldn't have become infected if I had looked after her properly.

"Her ear won't heal right." Owain's hand touched the bandaged ear ever so gently. "There's a piece missing. Maeve stitched it best she could."

"At least she's alive. I wonder what happened to her before she found me."

"Boar."

I looked at Bramble with new respect.

"She's so small. I can't imagine how she could fight a boar and survive."

Bramble huffed, although she didn't deign to open her eyes. She didn't have to. I already knew the sound was directed at me. I could hardly reconcile the white terrier curled up on Owain's lap with the blood-soaked creature I found in the woods. Her injured paw was still bandaged. The bones weren't broken, but the paw was badly bruised and the large gash, from which so much blood had oozed, healed slowly. She still refused to put any weight on that paw, but she moved around easily enough on three legs. Her other wounds — ear and shoulder and flank — were still red and inflamed.

There was time yet for Bramble to heal though, for I was still weak and tired easily. I ate everything Maeve put in front of me and often, with Owain's insistence, had seconds, but still my clothes hung more loosely than before, and my face, when I caught a glimpse of it in the wash bowl, was gaunt and haggard.

I relaxed into the comfortable chair, basking in the fire's warmth, and tried not to notice the raven flickering in its depths. Fatigue crept through my body, leaving my limbs heavy. Soon I yawned enough for Owain to decide it was time we all retired. He banked down the fire and we headed upstairs.

As Bramble and I lay in bed, thick blankets pulled up over both of us, an argument between Owain and Maeve reached my ears. Were they arguing about us? Maeve made it clear at every opportunity that our presence was an inconvenience. I would have probably left by now, even as weak as I was, if not for Owain's quiet insistence that we stay. He and Maeve had a strange relationship. She clearly disdained him. He suffered her harsh words with nothing more than a resigned shrug and an occasional sigh. Bramble shifted beside me and I wrapped an arm around her.

"I wish I knew what they were saying," I murmured. "I bet you can hear every word."

She draped her head across my arm. The stiff hairs on her chin tickled my skin.

"Are you comfortable? I hope your wounds aren't bothering you too much."

A soft sound, almost a sigh.

"Do you think I can do this, Bramble? If the witch is Ida, do you think I can find her? Do you think I can really destroy her?"

Bramble stirred. She was listening.

"I wonder sometimes. I don't know whether I'm strong enough. I have no idea what I'm doing or how to destroy her. I only know I have to do it or... or die trying."

It was the first time I had dared voice this thought. Perhaps Ida would hold the same power over me that she had over the villagers of Crow's Nest. What if I abandoned my quest merely because she told me to? What if she forced me to do awful things? Or if she killed me?

"I wish I knew what she was doing," I whispered. "We've been here too long. More than a sevennight. The closer the dark of the moon comes... I'm scared, Bramble. I feel so alone. I know this is my fault and I have to be the one to fix it, but still..."

She huffed at me.

"Yes, I know you're here. But it would be nice to have someone I could talk to."

Another huff, then she disentangled herself from my arm and rose. She wriggled out from under the covers, moved to the end of the bed and lay down again, her back to me. I had left the curtains open and her white hair shone in the moonlight.

"Don't be like that."

No response.

"Bramble, please."

A huff.

With a sigh, I sat up and reached for her, nestling her once again under the covers and in the crook of my arm.

"I'm thankful to have you. I don't know what I'd do if I was all alone."

I prattled to her for a while, telling her how lovely she looked with her shiny, white coat and her big, unblinking eyes. Likely she didn't understand anything I said, but it soothed me if nothing else. Eventually the stiffness left her body, she draped her head over my arm again, and I knew I was forgiven.

How would I ever sleep alone again? Perhaps I wouldn't have to. Perhaps Bramble would be well enough to come with me, and we would somehow defeat Ida, and we could go home together to Silver Downs.

I drifted off to sleep with my mind full of Bramble running across the grassy fields at home, sitting beside me as I created my tales, and curling up next to me in bed every night.

23

IDA

HE COMES. I feel it, in my bones, in my blood, in every breath I take. He and I, we are one, even if he doesn't know it. So now he comes and I understand his intent: to destroy me.

At first, he drew closer, slowly but steadily. Now his journey has halted. Nonetheless, he will come to me eventually.

I know he intends to destroy me, but that confounds me. He created me. Everything I am is because of him. Everything I know came from his mind, all I know of the world is from his tales. And the tales tell me the world is a dark and dangerous place. It is full of terror and evil and despair.

I want... something more. I cannot express it, this vague longing inside of me. The tales do not hold any explanation of this. I only know there is something *more*.

Until I discover what the *more* is, I have made myself a home of sorts. I have a house at any rate, in a village. His tales taught me much about evil. Wherever evil exists, it must be rooted out and destroyed. The people here fear me, I see that. If only they knew I am trying to help them, to save their village. Our village. For I live by his tales. I am cleansing the village. Evil by evil, I remove those who contaminate this place. Those who have darkness in their hearts, those who have secrets. Those who long for something else.

2 4

BRIGIT

E STAYED AT Owain's for nine nights before Diarmuid was ready to continue his journey. Even then, Owain urged him to stay one last night. *For Bramble's sake*, he said.

I was glad for the reprieve, for my paw was tender and walking was still painful. Not that I could have told Diarmuid. He, as a bard, should have seen there was more to me than four paws and a tail. I had been trying to communicate, to show him I was no normal dog, but he wouldn't listen. Instead, it was Owain who noticed.

As he carried me upstairs that last evening, while Diarmuid followed slowly behind, Owain stared into my eyes.

"You're more than you seem," he said, quietly.

I held his gaze, unblinking, but he said nothing further, only deposited me on the bed. Diarmuid, when he arrived, breathed a little too heavily. He wasn't yet as recovered as he believed. Owain left and we curled up together in the bed, the blankets draped over us both. Diarmuid wrapped his arm around me and I sighed, contented.

"We have to move on tomorrow, Bramble," he said.

How strange that Diarmuid had chosen such a name for me. My

father used to call me Bramble as a child. He often said I was as stubborn as a bramble bush.

"I wish I knew what was happening in Crow's Nest," Diarmuid said. "I don't even know whether Ida is still there. What if she's moved on? How will I find her?"

I growled softly, requesting that he shut up and let me sleep. He talked for some time, repeating himself endlessly. I ignored him as best I could until I heard my name.

"What am I going to do about you, Bramble?"

I flicked my ear at him.

"I can hardly take you with me while you're injured. Perhaps I should leave you here with Owain. He would take good care of you."

I lifted my head to glare at him. Did he really think it would be his decision whether I travelled with him? Had I been able to speak, I couldn't have said why it seemed so important I go with Diarmuid. I simply knew I must. How I would cope with the endless hours of walking as we travelled to Crow's Nest, I didn't know. I would endure it because I had to.

Diarmuid didn't notice my indignation. One hand absently stroked my back and, reluctantly, I allowed the motion to soothe me. I dropped my head down onto my paws and squeezed my eyes shut. Perhaps if I tried really hard, I could fall asleep and leave him to talk to himself. He continued to speak and I let the words wash over me. It was the catch in his voice that finally caught my attention again.

"I'd never forgive myself if I took you with me and something happened to you. What if I get killed? Who would look after you?"

You great idiot. It will likely be me looking after you.

He continued to talk and I continued to try to ignore him. Finally, he stopped and I was able to work on falling asleep in earnest. Just as I drifted off, Owain and Maeve's raised voices drew me back to wakefulness. They bickered constantly. Or rather Maeve bickered constantly and Owain mostly let her have her say. Then he would hang his head and walk away. I had never heard him snap back.

But tonight it wasn't only Maeve I heard, but also Owain, his low voice a stark comparison to her shrillness. Whatever the argument was about, and I had an awful feeling it was probably Diarmuid and I, Owain was not giving up. Eventually a door slammed and the house was silent. Diarmuid said nothing for a change, but he held me a little tighter.

I woke with the sun and waited in bed while Diarmuid washed and dressed. It wasn't until he was ready to go downstairs that I stood and stretched, extending each leg as far as it would go, rejoicing in the new strength in my muscles.

Diarmuid lifted me down, for my wounded paw could not yet handle a jump from the bed. The twisted scars on my shoulder and side were bright and vicious, but they were healing and felt less tight every day. Owain had said my ear was permanently damaged, but I had no way of viewing it. I didn't allow my mind to drift to whether I might retain any injuries when I was finally restored to my own form. No point in worrying about the future while I had the present to deal with.

Maeve was nowhere to be seen and today there was none of the thick porridge she usually served. Diarmuid and Owain ate slices of yesterday's bread slathered with summer berry preserves. Owain placed a bowl of last night's mutton in my basket by Diarmuid's chair. I also received a soft stroke on the shoulder and in return I briefly pressed my nose against his hand. I met his gaze, trying to express thankfulness for all he had done for us. He nodded solemnly.

Little talk passed between Diarmuid and Owain as they ate. I chewed my mutton slowly. I was sorry to be leaving Owain, for I had become fond of the large, gentle man. But if I must choose between him and Diarmuid, it was clear where I belonged. Diarmuid might be a clueless idiot, but we had been brought together for a reason.

You will leave here and set out on a journey, the fey girl had said. She never did say why or to where, but it didn't matter anymore. It seemed she had achieved her aim for here I was, breakfasting in a house far from my own home with two people who were strangers to me ten nights ago. For surely this was the journey she had intended. How else could I have found Diarmuid in the vast expanse of the woods if the fey hadn't guided my steps towards him? He had been waiting for me, whether he knew it or not. Were his own injuries also a result of the fey's meddling?

Diarmuid's journey was a strange one. I had pieced it together, bit by bit, from the confessions he whispered late at night. He was a bard, he had made no secret of that. What he hadn't told Owain was that he had imagined a muse — a woman he pretended whispered his tales to him — and had somehow brought her to life. She had escaped and was doing… something bad. He hadn't said what, but his journey was to find her and stop whatever it was. And he believed he had only until the new moon to complete his quest.

A new moon was a powerful time. What would happen when it arrived? If I were to guess, I'd say this creature he created would become even more powerful. What did Diarmuid intend to do when we arrived at Crow's Nest? Obviously he meant to stop her, but how?

As the daughter of a wise woman, I had seen enough of the world's mysteries that I didn't doubt his claim of what he had done. It was a curious ability and, truth be told, it scared me. Could he bring to life other images from his mind? What other power might he possess? I wasn't yet sure whether I should fear him, but I knew I should be wary. I certainly shouldn't trust him.

2 5

BRIGIT

FTER WE HAD eaten, Diarmuid went upstairs to collect his pack. I waited in my basket, figuring I may as well enjoy the last few minutes of comfort I was likely to have for a while. To my surprise, Owain picked me up, basket and all.

"Might as well take you outside," he muttered and carried me out to where his two huge oxen stood, hitched to the cart that brought us here ten nights ago. Their breath steamed in the crisp air. The cart already contained several large bundles wrapped in oilcloth with a pile of folded blankets on top. Owain stowed my basket securely between the packages. He tucked a soft blanket around me and I gratefully nestled into it with only my eyes and nose poking out.

The cart shuddered as Owain hauled himself into the front. The oxen snorted, eager to be off. I could see little other than the blue sky and the inside of the cart from my cozy nest, but I heard the front door of Owain's house open and close.

"Figured I may as well go with you," Owain said, presumably to Diarmuid. "You and Bramble, you don't look like you'll manage long on your own."

There was silence from Diarmuid and I knew exactly what he thought, for I had already thought the same. I expected Owain would

128

send us off with enough provisions to last a few days, but this — the luxury of travelling in a cart and time to rest while my wounds finished healing — was far more than I had dared to hope for.

"What about Maeve?" Diarmuid asked.

"She'll be happier with me gone." Owain's voice hitched a little. "Besides, you and Bramble, you need me. Maeve's never needed anyone. I've left enough coin for her to get by for a good while. And when that runs out, I guess she'll have to go back to her father, or take another husband."

For the first time, I was relieved I couldn't speak. Perhaps our presence had given Owain the excuse he needed, an honourable reason to leave. Regardless, I wouldn't have known whether to offer condolences or an apology or something else.

"Pass up your pack," Owain said. "Not much room here in front. You'll have to sit in the back with Bramble."

Diarmuid settled himself in the cart with a blanket around his shoulders. He probably wasn't as comfortable as me, but it was far better than walking.

"Not a bad way to travel, is it Bramble?" he muttered as he leaned back against the bundles and wrapped the blanket more firmly around himself.

Owain clicked at the oxen and, with a jolt, we were off. The motion of the cart soon sent me to sleep. I woke occasionally. Sometimes Diarmuid was staring out at the hills. Sometimes he watched me.

The sun was high overhead before we stopped. Owain produced bread and cheese, and some dried meat for me. We ate in silence, Diarmuid and Owain leaning against the cart, me sitting in the back. The hills stretched before us, empty but for the winding path, melting snow, and trees. A smudge of smoke on the horizon signalled a lodge, but we saw no other human presence as we ate.

I felt more alert as we travelled on through the afternoon. The day had grown warmer and, for a while at least, I didn't need to huddle beneath a blanket, but could enjoy the breeze rustling my fur. I inhaled deeply, savouring the cold air and the tang of smoke. Cows and sheep grazed in the fields, making what they could of the winter-short grass. An eagle sailed high overhead, drifting on the currents. What was it like to fly up there, as high as the clouds? How small we must look to the eagle as we crossed its path below.

Soon enough I tired of the scenery and my eyes drooped. The last thing I saw was Diarmuid, his brow wrinkled and his gaze vacant. His lips moved, although I heard nothing. Perhaps he was making plans for when we reached Crow's Nest. Maybe he practised what he would say to the creature he had made.

My thoughts were slow as I hovered on the edge of sleep. The visions had been silent ever since the fey girl forced me into this form. Without their constant presence, it was like part of my soul was missing. The meanings of some of the visions were now clear, but there was so much more I didn't yet understand. I missed their relentless intrusion in a way I had never thought I would.

Diarmuid was the young man who had featured so prominently in my visions. Owain was the man who had stroked the little white dog. But who was the woman with the white hair and ice blue eyes? Was she the creature we travelled towards or someone we would meet on the way? And when would I face Titania?

Of course, the visions show not only past, present and future, but also maybe. The future in which I wore my own form as I met the fey queen might never come to pass. I clung to the hope that it would. As much as I didn't want the life Mother had prepared me for, perhaps it was time to finally admit I did indeed possess some of a wise woman's talents. Perhaps it was time to learn how to use them.

We camped that night by the side of the road in a valley somewhat sheltered from the wind and where the ground was mostly free of snow. Owain produced a meal of bread, cheese, pears and dried meat. After we had eaten, we sat by the fire in companionable silence. I leaned against Owain's legs, enjoying the fire's warmth on my face and the gentle hand stroking my back.

The night air was cold but without the tang of frost. I snuggled down into my basket, warm enough within the pile of blankets Owain draped over me. He had positioned my basket where I could see both him and Diarmuid as they slept on oilcloths on the ground.

I woke with a start some time later when Diarmuid cried out in his sleep. The fire had burnt down low, but there was still enough light for me to see Diarmuid thrashing around. He sat up with a start, awake at last, and seemed to stare at something on the end of his blanket. I would have sworn I saw a raven take flight, swiftly disappearing into the depths of the night. Diarmuid sat for a few moments longer before he lay down again. My eyes closed and I drifted back into sleep.

DIARMUID

I SLEPT restlessly, my dreams full of ravens and some other beast I only dimly remembered after I woke. Grey clouds cloaked the sky and a drizzling rain began before we had travelled an hour.

"Diarmuid, the spare oilcloths are under your pack," Owain called over his shoulder. "And pass me my coat."

I pulled Bramble's basket closer and spread an oilcloth over us both. Up front, Owain rode with his coat draped over his head. I pitied the poor oxen who had no cover. At Silver Downs, the fires would be stoked to stave off the early spring chill and my brothers would share ale and tell tales to pass the time until they could work again. My heart ached. Home felt like a very long way away.

At noon, we stopped to rest the oxen. I dug through the pack of provisions and found bread and cheese for Owain and I, and some dried meat for Bramble. She eyed my cheese, but I stared intently at a line of ash trees in the distance and pretended not to notice.

"Should have been here by noon," Owain said as we passed through a village some time later.

The persistent drizzle eventually turned to heavy rain and our progress slowed even more. I was sodden and numb with cold, despite the oilcloth. Bramble crawled onto my lap and shivered. I kept the oilcloth wrapped firmly around her, but the rain found a way in and her hair was already damp. I thought longingly of warm baths, fireplaces and dry beds.

"There's a house up ahead," Owain said. "I'll ask if we can stay the night."

But when we arrived, the house was ablaze with lights, music and merriment and we were hesitant to intrude. Surely nobody would mind if we slept in the barn, which stood some distance from the house. As the oxen stoically pulled the cart towards the barn, their ears pricked up despite the water dripping from them. It seemed even they knew warmth and dryness lay just ahead.

The barn was small but looked well made. As long as it was water tight, it would suit me just fine. I clambered down somewhat stiffly and lifted Bramble to the ground. She hurried into the barn, pausing just inside to shake the water from her hair.

By the time we got the oxen unhitched and inside, I couldn't feel my fingers. I fervently wished I was at Silver Downs, sitting in front of a blazing fire with a mug of Mother's spiced wine and a belly full of hot food. The best I could hope for tonight was to warm my hands beside a lamp and that our blankets would be only damp rather than soaked. Either way, it would be a long, cold night.

I retrieved my spare shirt, pants and socks, which were blessedly dry. I wrung out my dripping shirt and draped it over the side of the cart. My boots were damp but might perhaps dry by morning.

The barn was tidy enough, if somewhat dusty, and well stocked with plenty of shelves and hooks for various tools. Large bins of animal feed stood in one corner. A dozen stalls lined the back wall, doors closed. A soft lowing indicated that at least one of them was inhabited by a cow.

Owain finished rubbing down the oxen to dry them off and led each into a stall. He retrieved an armload of provisions from the cart and arranged them on an empty shelf which made for a convenient table. My mouth watered and my stomach gave a low growl at the sight of a feast that put my own journey rations to shame. A loaf of bread. A jar of honey and one of berry preserves. Large wedges of cheese, some soft and white, some hard and yellow. A small sack of last summer's apples, and an entire tart that looked just like one of Maeve's berry pies. For Bramble, there were slices of dark meat, although from the way she sniffed in the direction of the cheese, I knew that wouldn't be all she ate.

"Might as well eat the pie," Owain said cheerily. "Won't keep much longer."

"Why didn't we eat any of this last night?" I asked, recalling the bread and hard cheese we had dined on.

He flashed me a grin.

"Didn't want to eat all the good stuff on the first night."

Owain cut large wedges from the pie. I dusted off a stool, pulled it up to the bench and attacked my serve. The pastry crumbled around the edges, but the filling was sweet and delicious. I gobbled it down, but Owain was already on his second slice before I finished. Bramble daintily ate her meat. Owain offered her some pie, but she sniffed disdainfully.

Owain started on the bread and cheese. I was pleasantly full after two slices of pie but nibbled at an apple divided into thin slices with the dagger Caedmon insisted I always carried in my boot. I had finally learned that lesson well. Owain passed Bramble some hard cheese and she lay in her basket to gnaw at it, the cheese tucked between her paws. Owain finally sat back and rubbed his belly.

"Won't be seeing any more of Maeve's pies, I s'pose."

"You could go back," I said. "It's not too late."

"'Twas never me she wanted." He yawned and headed towards the back of the barn. "G'night."

He went into one of the stalls. There was an indignant yell — a woman's voice — and Owain backed out, hands held out in front of him.

"Sorry, didn't expect anyone to be in there."

"Well now you know, perhaps you could find somewhere else to sleep," a frosty voice replied.

Owain gave me a sheepish shrug.

"There's a girl in there."

Before I could reply, she came out of the stall and my heart stopped. Long red hair, green eyes and a mouth I remembered well. She dressed unusually for a woman, in a loose-fitting shirt with pants instead of a skirt.

"Diarmuid!" For a moment she looked flustered. "What are you doing here?"

"Rhiwallon. I... We..."

"Diarmuid here's on a quest," Owain said.

I felt even more flustered than she looked. Colour rose rapidly in my cheeks. *Don't think about that night,* I told myself. *Or you'll be a stammering and incoherent idiot.*

"Why are you here?" I asked after we had stared at each other for several seconds.

"I'm..." Rhiwallon hesitated, but then with a flick of her hair, she straightened her shoulders and looked me in the eyes. "I'm running away."

"Why?"

"Why not?"

"It's not the sort of thing someone does, not without a reason."

"I didn't say I didn't have a reason."

"You didn't say you did, so I assumed..."

"I didn't say because it's none of your business."

"Oh." Now I felt both humiliated and deflated.

Bramble trotted up to Rhiwallon and sniffed her legs. Rhiwallon glanced down but made no move to pat her.

"What happened to the dog?" she asked.

I felt a burst of pride. "She was bleeding and half-dead when I found her in the woods. She had been in a fight."

"With what?"

"Owain thinks it was a boar. She's got lots of bite marks and one of her paws was bleeding pretty badly."

"Tusks," Owain said. "Not bites."

"She's tough, whatever happened to her," I said.

"Is she yours?" Rhiwallon asked.

Bramble stiffened and before I could open my mouth, she already glared at me.

"Not really," I said. "She's travelling with me, but I guess she chooses her own path."

Owain yawned and backed away.

"Guess I'll find somewhere else to sleep."

"I should think so." Rhiwallon eyed him up and down. "I'll be sleeping in that stall and I won't appreciate being disturbed. Anyone who thinks to sneak up on me will find my dagger stuck in his belly."

"You don't need to worry about us," I said, quickly. "Owain's hand-fasted and I'm..." My voice trailed off.

Rhiwallon gave me a half smile.

"Yes, Diarmuid. I remember."

27

DIARMUID

I WOKE TO the clattering of crockery and Bramble's warmth against my back. My stomach growled as I crawled out of the hay that had been my bed. To my surprise, it was Rhiwallon laying out the meal on the same bench we had used as a table last night. She was again dressed in pants and a loose shirt with her red hair bundled up under a scarf. A quiver of arrows hung from the belt at her waist.

"We may as well pool our rations and share," she said, not looking up from what she was doing. "I can contribute a loaf of bread. It's still fresh."

"We have plenty of supplies," I said. "Enough to share. You can save yours—"

Rhiwallon finally looked at me and glared so fiercely that I wanted to slink back to the stall I slept in.

"I neither want nor need your pity," she said.

"I didn't mean—"

"Diarmuid, if we're going to travel together, we need to get something straight. I am not some helpless woman who is going to sit back and wait for somebody to find me a meal or a place to sleep. I can, and will, contribute. I am choosing to travel with you for the security of having companions. But I don't need you, and I'd do perfectly well on my own if necessary."

"You're coming with us?" My voice came out too high.

"Of course I am. I'd be stupid not to. Now, go and wake that big friend of yours. Then we can do some proper introductions, which we neglected last night, and get on with our meal."

Owain stumbled out of one of the stalls, looking as if he hadn't slept at all.

"Name's Owain."

Rhiwallon nodded at him.

"Well met, Owain. I'm Rhiwallon. As you may have gathered, Diarmuid and I have met previously. I'll be travelling with you for a while."

From beside my feet, Bramble made a soft sound.

"And this is Bramble," I said.

Rhiwallon looked down at her.

"I'd prefer you kept it away from me."

"She," I said. "Bramble's a girl."

"Either way, just keep it away from me."

Bramble huffed and I reached down to scratch behind her ear. She leaned into my hand. Rhiwallon hadn't been this abrupt the last time we met.

Rhiwallon had set out her loaf of bread, a pot of Owain's honey and a bag of Owain's apples. I hesitated, not wanting to be the first to cut into her bread, but equally sure I would offend her if I ate only apples. Owain didn't pause but reached for the bread, cut off a thick slice and slathered it with honey. We ate in silence until Bramble sniffed.

"Bramble, I'm sorry," I said with a pang of guilt.

Owain was faster than me and swiftly produced some dried meat and a small piece of cheese for her.

"Where did you say you were going?" Rhiwallon asked. She licked the honey from her fingers and took an apple.

My lips suddenly felt like they were glued together.

"To Crow's Nest," Owain said. "Diarmuid here's on a quest."

"What sort of quest?" she asked.

shortly. "Knowing how to read doesn't teach a woman anything about the way the world works."

"Not much of a reader either," Owain said. "Never needed it much."

Rhiwallon ignored both of us as she climbed out of the cart. I busied myself with lifting Bramble down and trying to hide my fiery cheeks. I went to retrieve Rhiwallon's pack for her, but she leaned past me and snatched it up. I slung my own over my shoulder.

Inside, the innkeeper leaned against the bar. A portly fellow with a ruddy face, he eyed us each in turn, his gaze lingering on Rhiwallon.

"Afternoon, folks," he said cheerily, straightening up and giving the bar an industrious wipe. "Need a drink? You're too early for dinner, but we have some soup left over from lunch if you're hungry."

Owain looked at me but said nothing. Rhiwallon stared out the window.

"Do you have any bedchambers available?" I asked, tentatively. I had never before had to procure a room for myself, let alone others, and didn't quite know how to go about it.

"Pretty full at the moment," the innkeeper said. "Lots of folks passing through this week. I've only got one room available tonight. I could let the lady have it. You men can have the hayloft in the barn, if you like. And the dog," he added, almost as an afterthought.

I hesitated. Rhiwallon gave a huge sigh, likely intended as commentary on my ability to negotiate.

"We'll take the room," she said. "We can share."

"Please yourselves," the innkeeper said. "It's two silvers for the room plus half a silver each for the extra two, er three, occupants. Another silver if you want a bath and three coppers each for a hot meal."

Owain already reached for the pouch dangling from his belt, but Rhiwallon stopped him with a flick of her wrist.

"An extra silver and a half to sleep three people and a dog in one room?" she asked. "That's extortion."

"That's the price," the innkeeper said. "You don't want to pay it, there'll be someone else along soon enough who will."

"I'm sure you normally accommodate two people in that

bedchamber without extra charge," Rhiwallon said. "We'll pay the half silver for one extra person only."

The innkeeper seemed to deflate.

"All right, missy, two silvers and a half for the bedchamber. Did you want baths?"

"Yes."

"Second floor, first door on the left. You'll have to carry your bags up yourselves. You got oxen out there? The boy will take 'em to the barn and give 'em a feed for an extra two coppers."

"I always feed them myself," Owain said. He nodded at Rhiwallon and I. "Go on up. I'll go look after the oxen."

The stairs creaked and swayed beneath our feet as if the whole establishment might tumble down and I was thankful we intended to stay only one night. Rhiwallon huffed at the flimsy door with a broken lock, but when she saw the bedchamber she turned and marched right back down the stairs. There was an argument below and when Rhiwallon reappeared, her face was satisfied.

"Two silvers for the bedchamber and no charge for the bath," she said. "See, reading's not everything."

Bramble inspected the bedchamber and gave her opinion with a sniff. Even as unused to travelling as I was, I had to agree it wasn't much. A bed, somewhat lumpy. One grimy window. A small cupboard, two shelves and two chairs, one with stuffing trailing from a split seam. The rug was of questionable cleanliness and likely the bed linens were, too.

There was a knock on the door and I opened it to a skinny boy bearing two pails of steaming water. He hauled them into the bedchamber without a word and left, returning shortly after with a third bucket and some threadbare towels.

Rhiwallon pressed a coin into his hand and he gave her a grateful smile.

"He doesn't look like he gets nearly enough to eat," she said with a hint of defensiveness.

I said nothing.

"Out," she said. "I want the first bath."

I went back down to the bar alone. Bramble had already curled up on one of the chairs and pretended to be asleep. It seemed the direction to leave didn't include her.

The innkeeper was less friendly now and lost any interest in me once he realised I didn't want to buy a drink. I sat at a table in the corner and waited, running my fingers over the scratches on the table top. When Owain returned, he sat across from me and held up two fingers to the innkeeper. The man's face brightened somewhat and his service was prompt. Two sloshing mugs of ale appeared on the table. Owain took one and drained half of it in a gulp. I hesitated, but he nodded towards the other.

"Drink up. I'm buying."

I had never particularly liked ale nor the way it made my head spin and my stomach roll, but I took a cautious sip. It tasted something akin to how I expected cat's pee would. Owain drained the rest of his mug and waved the innkeeper over.

"Another. And don't water it down this time."

The man flushed faintly and quickly deposited another mug on the table. He waited as Owain tasted it and the nod from the big man made the innkeeper's face relax.

"Hot meals," Owain said to him. "What do you have?"

"There's vegetable soup, sir," the innkeeper said, with sudden deference in his tone. "That'll be ready in about an hour, or there's some left from lunch I can warm up. If you can wait, there'll be mutton with vegetables and gravy. There's always fresh bread. And I can probably arrange some pie if you like."

"Four mutton," Owain said. "With pie."

"Four, sir?" the innkeeper asked.

"Four," Owain said. "But pie for three."

"Yes, sir."

"Do you stay at inns often?" I asked as the innkeeper departed.

"Sometimes," Owain said. "Have to travel a bit in my line of work."

"What do you do?"

Owain stared into his mug for a long moment and I half expected him to brush off the question as he had last time.

"You may as well know," he said finally. He gripped his mug tightly. "I'm a mercenary."

"A what?"

"Men hire me to get rid of someone who is causing trouble."

"Get rid of them? You mean…"

"Kill them."

If I had not already been sitting, I surely would have fallen over in surprise. Owain might be large, but he was also the gentlest man I had ever encountered.

"How…" I stammered. "Why…"

He shrugged. "Someone's gotta do it. Money's good. I don't talk about it much though. People don't like it."

I squirmed on my bench, caught between unease at his revelation and self-awareness at my own nervousness. Only minutes ago, I had been thinking I didn't mind a broken lock because Owain would be there, but now… I took a large swallow of ale, seeking to shut out my thoughts.

We sat in silence until Rhiwallon returned, wearing a clean shirt and another pair of those curious pants. Her red hair hung in a wet braid down her back and her cheeks were still rosy from the hot water. An indignant and somewhat damp Bramble followed.

"Who's next?" Rhiwallon asked, looking almost cheerful.

Owain nodded at me. "Go ahead."

The water no longer steamed, but it was still plenty warm enough for a pleasant bath. I stripped down and scrubbed myself all over. My clothes were grimy and I would need to find a way to clean them. Wearing my only change of clothes and feeling much refreshed, I went back down to the bar. Owain drained his mug and stood.

"Guess I could do with a bath, too."

"Water's still warm." I avoided his eyes, feeling lousy even as I did. How many people had he killed?

I felt Rhiwallon watching me as I sat down. I wondered whether I should apologise for my earlier comment about reading, but likely she would find a way to take offence at that, too. Instead, I waved to the innkeeper, trying to mimic the way Owain casually held up a finger to indicate how many mugs of ale he wanted. The service wasn't quite as swift and the man said nothing as he slapped a mug down in front of me. It tasted no better than the last, but I drank it anyway, trying not to gag.

"He told me," Rhiwallon said.

"Yeah?" I stared into my mug.

"What he does." She was silent for a few moments, although I still felt her gaze on me. "He said you took it hard."

"I was surprised, that's all." I sounded defensive, even to my own ear.

"He doesn't usually tell people. Says they get all strange, like you did."

"I'm not all strange. I'm just surprised."

"Get over it. He's still the same man."

I was stunned into silence and we sat without speaking until Owain returned. He motioned to the innkeeper for another round of drinks.

I wrapped my arm around Bramble who had jumped up onto my bench, drawing courage from her quiet nearness even as my shirt soaked through from her damp hair. I tried to find the words to apologise to Owain, but as I finally opened my mouth, Rhiwallon spoke.

"So, Diarmuid, you never did say what this mysterious quest is all about."

I closed my mouth with a snap. Owain had revealed his secret. Now it was my turn.

"I'm going to Crow's Nest," I said.

Rhiwallon rolled her eyes.

"I know that, but you haven't said why."

I flushed and took a deep breath. "I'm a bard."

"Caedmon may have mentioned that." She sounded dubious.

I flushed even harder.

"I'm also the seventh son of a seventh son."

"So?"

"When a seventh son of a seventh son is a bard, he has… abilities. Or, at least, he does in my family."

"What sort of abilities?"

"I can sometimes bring my tales to life. Not always, and I don't know how it works. But sometimes the tales I tell, well, they happen."

The corners of Rhiwallon's mouth twitched.

"It's true," I said.

"I didn't say it wasn't."

"You don't believe me."

"No."

Bramble squirmed in my arms and I realised I held her far too tightly. I released her and she stared up at me.

"But I think you believe it," Rhiwallon said, her tone softer now.

I shrugged. "Like I said, I don't know how it works. I only know it happens."

"You need to fix something," Owain said slowly. "Something from a tale."

"I created a muse," I said. "In my head. It was a silly little thing to entertain myself, but I pretended she was the source of my tales. Then, somehow, she came to life and escaped."

"She escaped from your head?" Rhiwallon's face said clearly that she didn't believe me.

Hot flames of embarrassment warmed my whole body.

"Yes, and something went wrong. She's taken over Crow's Nest and she's making people kill each other."

"How do you know it's your imaginary muse?" Rhiwallon asked. "How do you know she isn't still in your head?"

"She isn't there anymore. She's nothing but a memory in my head now. She came to life, but she's twisted. Wrong."

"But how do you know this woman you're travelling so far to get to is the one you made up?" Rhiwallon asked.

"I just know," I said, miserably. "How does a parent recognise their child? It's her, I know it."

"You plan to stop her," Owain said.

I was surprised at the calm acceptance in his voice. He had discovered I, too, was responsible for death, and yet he sat there, drinking his ale and listening to my tale. If he judged me, I couldn't tell it from his face or words.

"How?" Rhiwallon asked. "I'm not saying I believe any of this, but how would you stop her?"

"I don't know. For now, I just need to get there. Make sure it's really her. Then… I don't know."

As the room darkened and grew chilly, the innkeeper lit lamps and soon the fireplace blazed, sending warmth through the room. Other patrons came in and soon the quietness was replaced with the steady murmur of conversation. A serving girl brought out our meals, four plates of mutton and three of pie.

Owain took one of the plates and carefully sliced the meat and vegetables into small pieces, then set it down next to Bramble on the bench. Yet again it was he, not I, who thought to feed her.

My stomach started to rumble as soon as the smell of roasted meat hit my nostrils and I ate eagerly. The mutton was tough, the vegetables clearly old and the gravy watery, but it was hot and filling.

We lingered a little longer after dinner. My stomach was full and the atmosphere was somewhat companionable, despite the stiffness between Rhiwallon and I. My companions were not what I might have expected: a mercenary, a woman running for reasons left unsaid, and a dog.

Fiachra had said something else about my companions, that they would not all be what they seemed. And it seemed I had discovered what he meant, for who would assume the gentle man across the table from me to be a hired killer?

28

IDA

I FEEL HIM moving towards me once again and he is no longer alone. I see his companions when I visit him at night. The heart of one is filled with death, another has a heart that longs. The heart of the third contains a secret desperately hidden.

What do these companions mean to him? What would happen if I removed one? He told a tale once in which a sorcerer sent a magical construct to abduct a traveller. I could create such a thing. In his tale, the beast had eight legs and many eyes. It was large and venomous and filled with darkness. As I think of the beast, it appears before me. Solid. Hairy. Hungry.

Which companion should I remove? Perhaps the one with the secret. I remember her from the last time they met. I saw her through his eyes, felt the emotions she aroused in him. She was the source of much confusion for him.

I send my beast towards him and wait. I am intrigued to learn whether he and his companions will act in the same way as the char-acters in his tale. I don't yet understand why sometimes folk act the way Diarmuid's tales say they should, and other times they don't.

In the meantime, my power grows with each day. At first, it was a trickle, like the merest hint of water seeping into a dry riverbed with the first of the winter rains. It eased through my limbs, moving ever so gently. As the days passed, the trickle became a steady flow, then a gushing stream.

The more I wield my power, the stronger the flow becomes. With my increasing power, I cleanse my surroundings. And the more evil I remove from this meagre village, the more my power grows. I do not let myself think of the inhabitants as people, for fear I will pity them. Instead, I steel myself and do what I must.

There is a child. I sense darkness in her heart. She reminds me of Diarmuid in a way. There is power inside of her, a power I don't understand. But she doesn't yet know her power, can't draw on it at will. I cannot allow her to stay, for she will contaminate the village. She might even destroy it.

Diarmuid told a tale once of a mother who was commanded by Titania to take her child into the woods and leave her there. So I follow his instructions. It is not the first time I use this story. I charm the mother of this powerful child and she takes the girl to the woods. She stands and watches as the wild boars tear her child apart. Thus the girl and her strange powers are destroyed before she ever learns to use them. And my village has one less evil to contend with.

2 9

BRIGIT

ON THE THIRD night after we left Owain's house, we stayed in the village of Shelby at an inn called The Cat's Whiskers. The inn looked rough and worn, the sort of accommodation where one should double check that their door was locked before they slept.

As best I could tell, somewhere around fifteen nights had passed since Diarmuid started his journey. More than two sevennights and halfway to the new moon. Time was running out if his belief that he had to reach his muse before then was correct.

We procured two bedchambers at The Cat's Whiskers, bathed, then gathered in the dining room. The room was perhaps half full, the crowd a little more hardened than where we had stayed previously. The tables and benches were battered as if they were often thrown to the floor and even the innkeeper looked like he had been tossed across the counter a few times. The meal presented to us was a less than appetising array of half-cold mutton and watery soup. I sniffed at the mutton, suspicious about its freshness.

"Ugh," Rhiwallon said, staring down at her plate. "I can't eat that."

"It's not that bad," Owain said. His plate was already half empty.

Rhiwallon put a hand over her nose.

"The smell of it is making me sick."

150

I sniffed my plate again. It definitely wasn't as fresh as it could be, but it wasn't off. Owain had thoughtfully cut my serve into small pieces for me and I took a tentative bite. Tough and chewy, but edible. Certainly not worth the fuss Rhiwallon was making.

She pushed her plate away. "I'd rather starve."

Owain shrugged and reached for her plate. "I'll eat it if you aren't going to."

I was only half-listening. I couldn't quite figure Rhiwallon out. Her mood changed by the day. Sometimes she seemed tough and capable, like the night we met her in the barn when she threatened to stab anyone who sneaked up on her. At other times, like tonight, she was jittery and irrational.

Before I could think further on this, a group of travellers entered. There were six, all lean men with a professional air about them. Rhiwallon spluttered and I looked up just in time to see the colour drain from her face. She inched a little closer to Owain and ducked her head. Her unbound hair fell forward and mostly covered her face. She clenched her hands together tightly, but not before I saw how they trembled. I could smell the fear that suddenly wafted from her.

The men spoke to the innkeeper for longer than seemed necessary to arrange bedchambers and meals, then settled around a table at the far end of the room. The innkeeper brought them mugs of ale. Rhiwallon seemed to sink down further. Owain's body shielded her from the men's view, although if Owain himself realised anything was wrong, he gave no sign of it.

I jumped down from the bench. One benefit to being a dog was that people often didn't see me. Nose to the dirty floor, I inched closer to the men. One of them glanced towards me and I sniffed intently at a stale crust of bread. The man's gaze barely skimmed me before he looked away. I sidled closer.

"How much further do we go?" one of his companions asked. He downed his ale in a few gulps and the innkeeper swiftly replaced the mug.

Another man, one with an air of authority, shrugged.

"We keep going until we find what we're looking for."

"Are you sure we're heading the right way?" the first man asked. "Surely by now we should have come across some sign of her."

The one who seemed to be the leader set down his mug and looked him in the eye.

"We have our orders," he said, his words were clear and deliberate. "And we follow them. Anyone doesn't like that, they're free to leave. Without pay, of course."

I held my breath, hoping for more, but the conversation turned to mundane topics, the chance of rain tomorrow and whether one of them needed new boots before the group moved on. The one who appeared to be the leader looked around the room, eyes narrowed as he examined the occupants. Owain's bulk still largely obscured Rhiwallon and the man barely glanced at her.

I lingered for another few minutes, but heard nothing useful other than that they planned to depart late the following morning. I returned to our table and Owain met my gaze with just the slightest nod before suggesting we retire. He draped an arm loosely around Rhiwallon's shoulders as we left. She kept her head down, hair covering her face and her shoulders slumped as if to disguise her height, or perhaps her build.

When we reached our bedchambers, Owain suggested we all sleep in the same room. Rhiwallon agreed quickly and moved her pack into the larger bedchamber that Owain, Diarmuid and I had intended to share. Diarmuid lay a blanket on the rug and stretched out. I curled up beside him in my usual spot and tucked my nose into my paws to keep it warm.

My mind whirled. Who or what was Rhiwallon running from? I could think of three reasons a woman like her would run away: to escape violence, to flee an unwanted marriage, or because she was with child and could secure no promise from the babe's father. Neither Diarmuid nor Owain noticed the times Rhiwallon slipped away to vomit or the way she sometimes held a hand over her stomach, as if cradling the life within. She couldn't have been more than two moons along, for there was no discernible swelling of her belly.

If Mother were here, she could have aided Rhiwallon with herbs.

Fennel, perhaps, or a tea of raspberry leaf. Mother could have eased her sickness or, if Rhiwallon wanted, provided other herbs to release the child from her womb. Even I in my own form could have helped. If Rhiwallon took anything to soothe her stomach, I never saw it.

Her relationship with Diarmuid also puzzled me. Once or twice Rhiwallon had hinted she knew some secret of his. He had blushed bright red and mumbled. Obviously they had met before, but I couldn't figure out exactly what manner of relationship they had or how well they knew each other.

Rhiwallon rarely saw the small terrier by her feet and she had about as much intuition as Diarmuid. Despite her initial demand that Diarmuid should keep me away from her, she didn't seem to mind my presence. Occasionally, she patted me roughly on the head, or ruffled the hair on my back, not noticing my discomfort. But she certainly didn't whisper any confidences to me the way Diarmuid did, so I had little insight into her behaviour. Why was Rhiwallon running? And who were the men who pursued her?

30

DIARMUID

OUR JOURNEY WAS uneventful. The oxen walked tirelessly, the cart didn't break down, and we weren't attacked by robbers as we slept. It had been almost three sevennights since I left home. I had expected to be at Crow's Nest long before now. Of course, I also hadn't expected such a lengthy delay while I was ill and my ankle healed.

The easy travelling left me with plenty of time to plan for my confrontation with Ida. She was unlikely to listen to reason, however persuasive my words might be. Equally unlikely that she would feel compelled to obey me, even if I was, in some way, her creator. So it seemed I must find a way to destroy her. Despite Caedmon's efforts to teach me to fight, my ability was limited to perhaps defending myself against an unskilled and unmotivated attacker. Perhaps my companions would aid me. Owain had the strength of several men and Rhiwallon was proficient with a bow and arrow. They were happy enough to travel with me, but would they also help destroy Ida?

Crow's Nest was now only a two-day journey away and we were well between villages when it was time to stop for the night. We chose a spot beside a stand of shrubby young rowan trees, which were still mostly naked from the winter. Our routines for setting up camp came easily and without discussion, for we had spent several nights outdoors.

Owain unhitched the oxen, then fed and watered them. Rhiwallon and I unloaded what we needed from the cart. Then she disappeared with her bow and arrow while I cleared a spot for a fire and gathered wood. It was always Rhiwallon, though, who lit the fire. She could down a hare and skin it long before I could start the fire and would hiss in exasperation as she watched my feeble attempts. Eventually she would shove me aside and light it herself, while I stood beside her, feeling inadequate and useless.

Nevertheless I persisted. I gathered up a good pile of twigs and some leaf litter, then retrieved my flint. Tonight though I couldn't produce so much as a spark. The wood was bone dry and the breeze light enough that I couldn't blame its interference. Bramble watched from her basket, which I had positioned nearby, as I tried again and again, my frustration increasing as each attempt failed to produce even a whiff of smoke.

Rhiwallon returned with two neatly-skinned squirrels and took the flint from my hand without a word. I couldn't bear to watch her succeed where yet again I had failed, so I turned away to lay out the remainder of our meal: somewhat stale bread, hard cheese, and a few handfuls of hazelnuts we had picked that morning. But tonight, not even Rhiwallon could coax a fire into existence. She rearranged the twigs, and tried again, holding the flint close to the leaves and sheltering its flame with her hand. But still the fire wouldn't catch. Eventually she swore and shoved the flint into her pocket.

"No fire tonight," she said, her voice tight.

Owain had by now finished with the oxen. He glanced at the stacked twigs and the dead squirrels and shrugged.

"No matter."

I swallowed an offer to try. It would likely earn me a scornful glare and a few sharp words. If Rhiwallon couldn't get the fire started, I undoubtedly couldn't either. Instead I retrieved some dried meat from our remaining rations in the cart. When I returned, the squirrels had disappeared and Bramble had a somewhat regretful look on her face. Clearly they hadn't been offered to her.

We ate in silence, then Rhiwallon rose with a determined look. But yet again she couldn't produce even the smallest of flames. The evening stretched long and bleak without a fire to warm us. I soon lay down and wrapped myself in a blanket. Bramble curled up in her favourite spot behind my knees and I draped another blanket over her. The ground was hard and it took some time before I could get comfortable enough.

I woke to Bramble barking loudly, a series of short, sharp sounds I had never before heard from her. Owain yelled, but I couldn't make out his words over Bramble's barking. I sat up, sleep still clinging to my mind, confused by all the noise.

"What's wrong?" I asked. "Bramble, be quiet. Come here, girl."

She continued barking. A lamp flared. Owain lifted it high as he moved around our small campsite. Never before had I seen him move so quickly and it was this that finally informed my sleep-addled brain that there was a problem.

"Owain," I yelled over Bramble's noise. "What's wrong? Where's Rhiwallon?"

"Gone." He didn't pause long enough to even glance at me.

"What? Bramble, be quiet."

Bramble slunk over to me and crawled onto my lap. Her small frame convulsed with tremors and I gathered her in my arms. I had never seen her act like this. Something was very wrong.

"Bramble, what is it?"

She whined and burrowed her nose into my chest. Owain still lurched around, the lamp held high, calling for Rhiwallon.

"Owain? Owain!"

"Rhiwallon's gone." His voice broke and the lamplight shone on the tear tracks on his cheeks.

"Gone where?"

He seemed to stumble blindly. He almost fell and the lamp dipped precariously close to the ground, but he regained his balance and kept moving.

"Owain, stop. Tell me what happened."

Bramble's trembles started to ease. Her face was still burrowed into my chest and she didn't seem inclined to move. I kept my arms around her, stroking her back. Owain finally set down the lamp and collapsed onto his blanket, head in his hands and his shoulders slumped. He seemed smaller than he usually did.

"Something was standing over her when I woke," he said hoarsely. "It took her."

A few moments passed before my mouth would work.

"Who? Why?" I hardly knew where to start.

"Couldn't move, couldn't speak."

My mouth framed questions I couldn't say. Finally, I managed to squeak, "The fey?"

He shrugged. "You're the bard."

"But… What would they want with Rhiwallon?" A horrible thought occurred to me. "It wasn't Rhiwallon they wanted. They want to stop me from getting to Crow's Nest. Or delay me. It's a distraction. Like how they led me off the path last time."

Fiachra said I would have companions and that one would not be what they seemed, but he hadn't said I wouldn't need each of them. I tried to remember his exact words, whether he had said my companions would still be with me when I faced Ida, but I couldn't think clearly. If this was a tale, I would need all three to stop her.

"We have to go after her," I said.

I packed some provisions while Owain untethered the oxen. They would have to fend for themselves until we returned.

"Do you know much about the fey?" I didn't wait for his reply. "We must not eat or drink anything offered to us within their territory. Time may not pass the same way as it does here. We might seem to be there a week and find only an hour has passed here, or it might seem no time there and weeks here."

Owain grunted, intent on sharpening his daggers.

"We should make sure we don't get separated. And we shouldn't believe anything the fey say, be it good or bad. They won't lie, or at least the old tales say they won't, but they may twist the truth and make things seem what they are not."

Owain handed me a dagger. Moonlight glinted off steel as he slid another into his boot. He slung his pack over his shoulder and hefted his axe. I tested the dagger's weight. It was larger than my own and more finely made. When I ran my thumb along the blade, the skin parted effortlessly and a bead of blood appeared. My own small dagger was already in my boot; the experience in the woods, when I didn't know it was only Bramble behind the bush, had taught me the value of being armed better than Caedmon's lectures ever did. I slid Owain's dagger into my other boot. It didn't sit quite as comfortably as my own.

Owain strode over to where Rhiwallon had been sleeping. Her blanket was empty and rumpled. Beside the blanket lay her bow and quiver. She wouldn't have left willingly without them. Owain slung them over his other shoulder.

"She'll want these when we find her," he said.

I nodded, unwilling to voice my fear that the fey might have taken Rhiwallon somewhere we couldn't follow. I looked around for Bramble. For one heart-stopping moment I feared she, too, had been taken. Then I saw a streak of white some distance from our camp. She dashed around, nose to the ground.

"Come on, Bramble," I called, and then to Owain, "Which way do you think?"

He nodded towards Bramble who still circled, sniffing at the ground.

"Follow her."

Indeed, as soon as we looked at her, Bramble gave a short, sharp bark. It was a definite *follow me*. I hesitated, but Bramble barked again. Owain started towards her. Still she waited, looking to me.

"All right, I'm coming." I picked up my pack. "But I hope you know where you're going."

Bramble trotted off, following a path only she could identify. She paused, looking back over her shoulder to make sure we followed.

Branches crunched beneath Owain's boots and I hurried after him, anxious to keep myself within the light of the lamp he bore.

Bramble led us on a winding path around bush, up hill and then down, over rock and through a dry creek. We walked in circles and doubled back on our path. Finally, Bramble paused at a low mound, mostly still snow-covered but with a few eager strands of grass poking through.

"This is where the path leads?" I asked. "What are we supposed to do now?"

Bramble gave me a disdainful stare and turned back to the mound. She barked three times and an opening appeared. It was large enough to admit a grown man. Inside was shrouded in darkness. I was so shocked that my legs almost gave out beneath me. It was a coincidence, of course, the opening appearing right as Bramble barked. Likely our presence had somehow activated it.

"Good girl," Owain said.

Bramble flicked her tail at him and glared at me.

"Well done, Bramble." I leaned down to rub her ears. "I don't know how you did that, but well done."

She ducked out of my reach and stepped away. If she wasn't just a dog, I would have thought she was angry with me.

Owain held the axe in front of him, gripping it in one hand and the lamp with the other.

"I'll go first," he said.

I was only too glad to agree. He stepped into the barrow, ducking his head in order to fit, and I followed. The moment I passed through the entrance, one of my boots began to feel warm. Then suddenly it was hot. Burning hot. Owain threw both axe and lamp out into the snow and ran outside. The lamp's flame sputtered and died. My foot felt like it was on fire. I dived through the opening and flung myself to the ground to pull off the boot. Owain's dagger dropped out and sizzled in the snow. I reached for it but burnt my fingers.

"Hot," Owain said.

"Yours too?" I looked from his axe to the dagger and knew what I had forgotten. Almost every tale of the fey I knew told of this. "Cold iron. The fey can't stand to be near it. There must be a charm on this place to prevent us from entering with cold iron."

"No weapons?"

My little bronze dagger was still safely tucked into my other boot. I opened my mouth to tell Owain but hesitated. If there was a charm to prevent us entering with cold iron, there may be other charms on this place. Perhaps even now the fey watched or listened.

"No, no weapons," I said and pulled my boot back on.

Bramble watched from the entrance to the mound, one front paw slightly raised. With the tip of one finger, I touched Owain's dagger. It was still warm but cooling rapidly. Definitely there was a charm at work, for I had never seen iron cool so swiftly. Owain gingerly picked up his axe and hefted it, then lay it back down on the ground with a regretful look.

"Let's go," I said. "Slowly, and stick together. Bramble, you stay right next to me."

She glanced at me and sniffed. We marched back into the mound. Once inside, a faint green light lit the darkness, just enough to see our path. There was no obvious source of light, but it seemed we would have no need for a lamp. The tunnel passed through firmly-compacted earth and sloped sharply down. I tried not to think about the earthen ceiling or its lack of visible supports. The air smelled like moist earth, the kind that's good for planting crops in.

Owain went first, clenched hands indicating he was less than comfortable without the familiar weight of his axe. I took up the rear with Bramble between us. Was it better to be first or last? The first was most likely to run into any trap or ambush. But the last was at risk of something sneaking up on him from behind. The small dagger in my boot was a small comfort.

We had gone barely twenty paces before the path took an abrupt turn to the right and the last shimmers of moonlight disappeared, leaving the pale green light as our only source of illumination. I stepped carefully to avoid treading on Bramble who scurried with her tail tucked between her legs. How much did she understand? Clearly she knew we searched for Rhiwallon and she was afraid. Likely that was all she knew.

We walked and walked. Sometimes the path sloped down. Other times, it veered uphill. It would turn to the right, then to the left, and at one stage even wound back in the direction from which we had come. In no time at all, I was completely disorientated. And still we walked. The only sounds were those we made ourselves.

The air was warm and still, scented with dirt and moss. I was soon covered in a thin sheen of perspiration. We paused briefly to drink. Bramble began holding up her injured paw, hopping along on three legs. Owain scooped her up and tucked her under his arm.

In the dim green light, I had no sense of time. The path inclined upwards again and we trudged on, going up and up until I felt sure we must soon emerge from the earth into the fresh air above. By the time the path levelled again, my muscles quivered and I could hardly lift my feet. I gritted my teeth and plodded on, not wanting to be the first to admit I couldn't continue. Eventually, Owain stopped and set Bramble down.

"May as well take a break," he said. "Been walking a long time."

"How long can this tunnel possibly be?"

I didn't expect an answer and he didn't reply. I set down my pack and slid to the ground in relief. The path stretched ahead of us, dimly lit with sickly green for as far as I could see. I leaned against the cool earthen wall and sighed. Bramble curled up next to me, resting her head on my thigh, and I stroked her ears.

Owain lowered his huge frame down next to me and rummaged in the pack. He offered me an apple and Bramble a strip of dried meat.

"How long do you think we've been walking?" I asked.

Owain shrugged.

"It must be dawn, at least."

"Prob'ly later."

Having eaten, we each took a small drink from the flask — Owain poured a portion into his cupped hand for Bramble — then sat in silence for some time. Eventually Owain stirred.

"May as well push on," he said.

I hauled myself to my feet, stifling a groan as tired muscles protested. We walked and walked. Several times we stopped to rest and twice more to eat. I was so tired, I could no longer even think. I walked when Owain told me to, stopped when he stopped, ate when he handed me food. He seemed tireless and kept moving steadily, legs pumping up and down at the same pace. He had long since been carrying my pack and I was too tired to object.

I had fallen behind, plodding along. There was an idea rattling around in my exhausted brain, but I was too tired to make sense of it. There was… something. Something I should do. Or try. I was almost too tired to care what, but it seemed there was possibly some hope in the idea, whatever it was.

Ahead of me, Owain waited at a turning of the tunnel. Perhaps once we reached the corner, there would be something else up ahead. Rhiwallon maybe, or an exit. But when I reached Owain, the only thing around the corner was more of the green-lit tunnel.

They were never-ending, these fey tunnels. Were we the first mortals to become lost in them? Would we eventually come across other folk, or perhaps only their bones? Was this what happened to some of those the tales told of, folk who disappeared and never returned?

Tales. I finally understood the idea my mind had been trying to suggest.

"I should tell a tale." My voice was thin, thready and didn't sound much like me at all.

Owain looked back at me but said nothing. Perhaps he was too tired to speak. Indeed, it seemed like such an effort. I could barely keep myself on my feet anymore, let alone spare the energy to talk.

"Perhaps a tale can get us out of here," I said.

"Go on." He set Bramble down and she immediately curled up, head on her paws, eyes closed. Owain leaned against the tunnel wall and waited.

A tale. If it was true I could bring my tales to life, then I could use that ability to get us out of here. I needed to tell a tale about a group of friends who become separated when one of them is abducted and who find themselves trapped in the land of the fey. Haltingly, I began to speak. My thoughts were confused and at first my words made little sense. But slowly the familiar act of tale telling took over and the words came more easily, despite my exhaustion.

I told of how the group searched for their friend, becoming more and more tired, and unable to find either their friend or a way out of the tunnels. At last, exhausted and close to collapse, the bard tells a tale in which the group find themselves suddenly standing before a door in the tunnel wall. A door that wasn't there before. They open the door and find themselves outside in the sunshine and fresh air. And their missing friend waits to greet them as they stumble out, weary and heartsore. I concluded the tale and searched the walls, waiting for the door to appear. But nothing happened.

"I don't understand," I said. "Why didn't it work?"

Owain peeled himself off the wall.

"Better keep walking then," he said.

At some stage we stopped to rest and I fell asleep, curled up on the dirt with Bramble beside me and my pack beneath my head. Owain slept sitting against the wall. I woke to the same steady green light and the never-ending tunnel. We ate and sipped small portions of water. There wasn't much left, certainly not enough to last while we retraced our steps. As we set off again, it was all I could do to keep putting one foot in front of the other, following Owain and Bramble. My legs wobbled, my feet were blistered, and my back ached.

Some time later, the tunnel finally ended. We came around a bend and into an enormous cavern, its high ceiling lost in the depths of the dim green light. The walls shimmered with bands of different coloured rocks: gold and red and brown. The entry through which we passed was the only exit. We would have to retrace our steps, all the way back along the green-lit path.

I dropped my pack and followed it down to the floor. Bramble climbed onto my lap, which was uncharacteristic of her. Although she slept with me each night, it was usually Owain's lap she sought during the day. I pulled out the water flask. Only a few drops remained and we shared them amongst the three of us.

Owain remained standing, although he set down his pack and Rhiwallon's bow and quiver. I wondered that he could bear to stay on his feet another moment. My own feet ached and my ankle, so recently injured, was tender. It wouldn't hold up much longer. I started to unlace my boots when Bramble sat up abruptly, her ears pricked.

We were no longer alone.

31

DIARMUID

$\mathcal{A}$ HOST OF beings filled the cavern. They resembled humans, appearing in a variety of sizes from child to adult, but their milk-white skin and ruby-red lips left no doubt they were fey. I pushed Bramble off my lap and clambered to my feet without lacing up my boots. The fey stared at us in eerie silence, their faces devoid of expression.

A particular couple drew my gaze. She was beautiful with long dark hair and a cold stare, and he was even taller than their fellows. Eventually, my tired brain realised these beings I so rudely stared at were probably their rulers. They featured in so many tales that every child knew their names: Titania and Oberon.

At my feet, Bramble stood with her ears alert and her tail drooping. Owain's face was white, his hands clenched. The fey seemed content to stand and stare at us. Despite their numbers, which must have been in the hundreds, there was not a noise from any of them.

I cleared my throat, awkwardly loud in the silence of the cavern, and when I spoke my voice was thready.

"We are looking for Rhiwallon."

Titania raised an eyebrow and her lips curled just the tiniest bit.

"Indeed," she said.

I waited, but she did not seem inclined to volunteer anything further.

"Have you taken her?" I asked.

Titania gestured around the cavern. "Do you see her here amongst us?"

I started to reply but stopped. The tales say the fey cannot lie, but they will willingly mislead, answering with trickery and riddles. I could read nothing in Titania's cold gaze. I searched for a question she could not mislead me with.

"Will you take us to her?" I asked.

Titania laughed, but there was no amusement in the sound. Others laughed also, then they all fell silent in the same moment.

"No," she said. "I will not take you to her. If you want to find the human girl, you must seek her yourselves."

I opened my mouth, but Titania forestalled my words with a raised finger.

"One question further," she said. "And then I will answer no more."

I closed my mouth with a snap. Three questions. How could I, steeped in tales as I was, not have anticipated this? I should have known, should have considered my words more carefully. I could ask whether Rhiwallon was safe, but that would give no clue as to her location.

"How can we find Rhiwallon?" I asked.

Titania's eyes glittered and when she spoke, her lips twisted cruelly and her voice rang through the cavern.

"One will bear another's coat until the final round. One will face their greatest fear, wearing a gossamer gown. One may pass the fiery depths and only once may go. Locate the key to leave this place. In plain view it will be found."

My heart sank into my boots. It was a riddle and it made little sense. Obviously, it was Rhiwallon who would face her greatest fear, although I didn't understand the reference to a gossamer gown. I had no idea who might wear somebody else's coat, for neither Owain nor I had brought such an item into the mound. I didn't want to even think about what might be meant by passing the fiery depths. And then there was the key: it needed to be found, but it wouldn't really be hidden?

In the time I spent thinking, the fey left. One moment they stood there, staring at us in silence, and in the blink of an eye they were gone. Not so much as a rustle or a murmur betrayed their exit and afterward, the only evidence of their presence was a single leaf, blood-red against the brown stone of the cavern floor. It hadn't been there before.

Owain bent to pick it up. I had never before seen such a leaf. Its edges were straight, the corners pointed. It shimmered with a red so deep, it was almost black. Lying on Owain's palm, it looked like a triangle sliced into his skin exposing the blood beneath.

"Odd," Owain said. He carefully tucked the leaf away in his shirt pocket. "Might be important."

Yet again I had fallen short.

"That their queen?" he asked.

"I assume so," I said.

I waited for him to comment, but whatever Owain thought of Titania, he kept it to himself.

"What do we do now?" I asked as I laced up my boots.

We had walked for at least a day, maybe more, to get here and now it seemed we must walk all the way back. We had no water and our only remaining food was a stale end of bread and two strips of dried meat. Perhaps in this strange world of the fey, the way out would be shorter than the way in. There were tales of such things. But we couldn't go back yet. We still needed to find Rhiwallon.

Bramble barked.

"What is it, girl?" I asked.

She gave me a haughty look and I muttered an apology for calling her girl. Bramble sniffed and looked back towards the far side of the cavern. I followed her line of sight.

"Is that—" Owain asked.

"It looks—" I said at the same time. "It's an opening."

"Wasn't there before," Owain said.

Where previously there had been nothing but solid stone now yawned a dark chasm. Owain and I looked at each other.

"It's that or go back the way we came," I said. "The fey brought us here for a reason and I don't think it was only to laugh at us. They didn't want us to see that opening until now."

"Got to find Rhiwallon," Owain said.

I looked from him to Bramble.

"Group decision. Do we go that way or back the way we came?"

Owain nodded towards the other side of the cavern. Bramble's gaze, too, was on the opening that hadn't been there before.

"Let's go then," I said.

As we walked across the cavern, our footsteps echoed through its depths. Were we making an awful mistake? The fey wanted something from me, but exactly what, I had no idea. They had interfered from the first day of my journey when they lured me from my path with the promise of water. But if I hadn't strayed, I wouldn't have found Bramble. Perhaps they meant for that to occur, but what possible reason could they have? What use was a dog to the fey?

Then there was Owain. If I hadn't strayed from my original route, Bramble and I would not have emerged from the woods right as Owain happened by. And if the three of us had not decided to pass a rainy night in a certain barn, we would not have discovered Rhiwallon hiding there. And all that led us to here and now: Rhiwallon abducted by the fey for some reason we could only guess at, but which might have something to do with my quest.

If we were in the land of the fey, as I suspected, these tunnels might lead on forever, endlessly twisting and turning. Branching paths could leave us hopelessly lost.

"We need to mark the paths we take," I said. "This opening wasn't here before. Or maybe it was hidden from us. There's no telling how many others there might be, openings that will appear as we pass or close after we enter. We need to know which way we came."

"If I had my axe..." Owain said, empty hands clenched.

I remembered the dagger in my boot. Would the fey notice if I used it in here? I hesitated with my hand halfway to my boot. The dagger was our only weapon other than Rhiwallon's bow, which was too small for Owain. I might be able to use it, but I had never actually killed anything before. Even if my aim was good enough — which it likely wasn't — I didn't know if I could kill someone.

Owain fumbled in his pack and retrieved a small bronze brooch. The yellow gem set in the front gleamed dully. A faint blush tinged his cheeks.

"Thought I might want something to remember her by." He extended the pin and scratched a small sigil — a simple cross — next to the exit. "Let's go find the girl."

The same sickly green light lit this new tunnel. Just enough to make our way by, not enough to see clearly. We had gone no more than a hundred paces before we faced three branching tunnels. The ones to the left and right were tinged with green, but a red glow lit the central tunnel. Dread and danger emanated from it.

Bramble sniffed the tunnel entrances, lingering at each before she moved on. Then she stood in front of the central tunnel with her tail tucked firmly between her legs.

"No, Bramble, not that one," I said.

She looked up at me and sniffed.

"She has led us true this far." Owain's face was pale, but his voice was steady.

As I looked from Owain to Bramble, it felt like a fist gripped my bowels.

"Are you sure, Bramble?" I asked. "Perhaps they took her down one of the other passages."

She sniffed at me again and looked towards the red tunnel.

"If Rhiwallon went that way, no point going another way," Owain said.

His matter-of-fact tone shamed me. Owain was right. If she had been taken down this passage, that was where we, too, must go. I nodded and Owain pulled out his brooch to mark the wall with a cross.

Menace pervaded the red-lit tunnel. Nausea rose in my throat and I swallowed it back down. We walked slowly, cautiously, but the tunnel stretched ahead, silent and empty and threateningly red. My heart hammered and my nerves were on edge as I waited for something to happen.

Owain's breathing was loud and ragged, and mine wasn't much quieter. The sense of impending danger magnified with each step until I was sure I would scream if something didn't happen shortly. We had not gone far, maybe a few hundred paces and two twists of the tunnel, before we reached another branching passage. Two tunnels stretched ahead of us. One was lit with the familiar green light and the other with the sinister red.

Both Owain and I looked to Bramble for guidance. She sniffed briefly at the green passage, then stood at the mouth of the red one.

I breathed deeply and forced my fists to unclench. Blood oozed from where my nails had cut into my palms. My legs still wobbled and nausea filled my stomach. Owain's face was pale, his eyes large. Bramble trembled, her tail still tucked between her legs. We walked on.

The red tunnel ended abruptly and without incident. A cavern yawned ahead of us. Unlike the previous one, which was empty and lit by clean, white light, this cavern was filled with red and the same sense of menace as the tunnel. The air felt too thick to breathe and the rosy haze distorted my perception of distance.

The cavern was filled with huge mounds of fallen rock, everything from pebbles to boulders the height of three men. An enormous web hung from the roof and stretched out of sight, a web which could not have been made by any ordinary beast, but one which was hundreds, maybe thousands, of times larger. It covered easily a quarter of the cavern's roof. I had no wish to encounter any beast that could create a web so large.

"She could be in here," Owain said.

I was reluctant to agree, but he was right.

"How do we search this without getting separated?" I asked. "There could be anything behind the rocks. A big hole or... I don't know, a creature of some sort."

Owain scooped Bramble up. "I'll carry her. Just to be safe."

"We need a plan," I said.

Owain pointed towards the nearest corner. "We zigzag. This way first and then back, until we reach the web."

"And we always pass the rocks on the right hand side."

We set off, walking slowly, scanning the area for any sign of Rhiwallon. Rocks taller than me shielded anything more than my immediate surroundings from view. I soon became dizzy with the effort of trying to look everywhere at once, up and down, left and right. The fey path would not have led us here if there wasn't some clue to be found. I didn't dare hope Rhiwallon herself would be here, but there must be something they wanted us to find. The key, perhaps — the key that would be in plain view.

Step by step, we searched, passing to the right around each rocky tower. I tried not to imagine Rhiwallon's body crushed beneath them. The tales said the fey wouldn't deliberately harm a human, but it was possible they might injure her through carelessness. I found myself inspecting the base of each rocky pile for a protruding hand or foot.

It felt like we walked for hours, but at the same time it seemed like nothing. With each step, I was acutely aware of the diminishing space yet to be searched. I grew less and less hopeful of finding any clue to Rhiwallon's location. Was this just another trick, another way to delay us?

I replayed the riddle in my mind. It contained no obvious reference to time, but from what I knew of the fey, it was likely that if we took too long Rhiwallon would be lost for ever. Even if the riddle did not mention a deadline, the creature that inhabited the web would not stay away from its home forever. And the longer we lingered here, the more time passed in our own world. Every day here brought the new moon one night nearer and Ida that little bit closer to being unstoppable.

32

IDA

I NO LONGER feel Diarmuid. Is he dead? Surely I would know if he was. I would feel some parting of our connection, a breach, a severing. But this does not feel like a parting. He has simply... disappeared. I no longer feel my beast either. It is most curious and I do not know what to make of their disappearance.

Without Diarmuid to fill my senses, I feel oddly empty. He is a part of me in a way I never understood before. I had thought I could simply leave his head and never think of him again. But we are irrevocably joined. Now he is gone and I am alone.

What will I do if Diarmuid doesn't reappear? I shall go on as I have been, I suppose. I shall continue cleansing my village. And when I am done, what then? Another village perhaps? It seems somewhat pointless now if I can never show Diarmuid what I have done, how hard I have worked to rid my village of its taint. I can never hope he will be proud of me, that he might join me so we can work side by side, a bard and his muse. I cannot be a muse if I have no bard. Without Diarmuid, I no longer know what I am.

33

BRIGIT

SECURE IN OWAIN'S arms, I puzzled over our strange situation as we scoured the rocky cavern. Whoever had snatched Rhiwallon made no attempt to hide their scent. It was almost as if they wanted us to follow. Diarmuid could ill afford any delay to his quest, although it was possible, perhaps even probable, that time in the fey tunnels did not pass at the same speed as time in the mortal world.

The odour that led us here was odd. It wasn't human, but neither was it like any animal I knew. It was a blend of every flower I had ever smelled mixed with something smoky and a trace of rotting leaves. It lingered so strongly that I wondered how Diarmuid and Owain couldn't smell it themselves.

Was my ability to track Rhiwallon's abductor the reason the fey girl had sent me on this journey in such a form? I had thought that perhaps she meant for me to play some part in Diarmuid's quest to stop his muse. But my only abilities were charms and cures, and the visions over which I had no control. What could I possibly do to aid him, especially in this form, if not to lead him to Rhiwallon?

The Sight had given no hint of this strange journey into the fey lands, but the vision in which I saw myself, in my own form, step forward to speak to Titania gave me hope that I would eventually be returned to my own body.

I suddenly realised that, as usual, I had wandered off into my own thoughts instead of paying attention to the task at hand. I turned my mind back to the search for Rhiwallon. My tail was firmly wedged between my legs and I quivered every time I looked at the web in the far corner of the cavern. I did not want to meet the creature who inhabited it.

Tucked under Owain's arm, I could feel that his heart beat too fast. He was scared, although on the outside he appeared as steadfast and implacable as ever. My paw ached and I had been thankful when Owain noticed my limp. I would have felt bad about burdening him with my weight, slight as it was, except that he barely seemed to notice. If he felt fatigue, he never showed it.

Diarmuid had started falling behind somewhere around the time we stopped to sleep in the green-lit tunnels. He never complained, but Owain slowed to accommodate his fatigue. I noticed, too, that as the water ran low, Owain barely drank anything, merely wetting his lips to leave more for Diarmuid and me. He was a good man, Owain, and deserved far better than Maeve, however much he adored her.

As we searched the cavern, the scent of Rhiwallon's attacker lingered strongly and beneath it was the faintest trace of Rhiwallon herself. She was close, I was sure of that. If she wasn't still in this red-shrouded cavern, then she had been here very recently.

Finally, the only place left to search was behind the web. As we drew closer, I realised it was even more mammoth than I had thought. Each sticky strand was as thick as a man's finger. Something loomed on the other side, obscured by the web and the red murkiness. The web was securely anchored to the floor and sides and ceiling of the cavern. There was no way to creep around it. It seemed that someone must put their head through to see what was on the other side. Given that I was the smallest it should have been me, but I lacked the ability to convey whatever I saw. Owain was too big. It would have to be Diarmuid.

My heart stuttered as I watched Diarmuid drop his pack and take a deep breath, steadying himself. He, too, had realised it must be him. He was still something of a mystery to me, a strange contradiction with his claim to be able to bring his tales to life coupled with an utter lack of intuition.

I owed him my life, but there was also something else I felt, although it was still new and I hadn't let myself examine it fully. Despite his flaws, despite his complete inability to listen to me, I felt an ache in my heart when he was out of sight. A leap in my blood when he returned. Disappointment he couldn't see me for what I really was. And hope that perhaps one day he would.

3 4

DIARMUID

AS I STARED up at the web, my courage faltered. Had I the strength to run away, and enough supplies to last until I found a way out of this place, I would have fled, however much of a coward that made me.

"I'll do it," I said, reluctantly. "My head is smaller than yours."

I half-hoped Owain would disagree but he said nothing, only picked up an orange rock the size of my head and hefted it. It gave me some small amount of comfort to know he was ready to defend me.

I dropped my pack on the ground. My legs already trembled so violently that I feared they might fail to hold me. I pictured myself falling forward into the web, trapped in its sticky strands and unable to free myself before its owner returned.

I met Bramble's eyes and she stared at me, unblinking. Her sense of smell was keen. Surely she would know if some otherworldly beast waited on the other side of the web. Surely she would try to alert me if she suspected imminent danger.

Slowly, slowly, I inserted my head between the threads, careful not to touch them. At first, I could only see more rocks. Just another enormous tower of rocks streaked with grey and purple and red, even larger than those we had spent the last hour circling around. I looked up. And there she was.

Rhiwallon perched at the very top of the massive rocky tower. Or at least, there was a figure with long red hair up there. I couldn't manoeuvre my head enough to see her clearly, but she seemed to be wrapped in a cocoon of silvery threads. She was upright, perhaps tied to a tall rock. A gossamer dress. The riddle seemed so obvious now. And her greatest fear? Abduction? The beast? I could only guess. I carefully withdrew my head from the web.

"Is she there?" Owain's face was pale and sombre.

"She's at the top of a tower of rocks, restrained with webs. Someone will have to climb up to cut her free."

We were both silent for a few moments.

"It has to be me," I said miserably, feeling like a pretty poor sort of hero. "We would have to cut too much of the web to get you through and the rocks might not be stable enough for you."

"No way of cutting through it, though."

I retrieved the little bronze dagger from my boot. Owain didn't comment on my secret weapon. I assessed the threads. Here, a part of the web looked thinner and more crudely made than the rest. Bile rose in my throat and I forced it back down. There was no choice. We couldn't leave Rhiwallon here. Bramble's eyes were wide and full of concern.

"Be good for Owain." My voice wobbled dangerously. I bent down to stroke her whiskery cheek and she leaned into my touch, briefly closing her eyes. I clenched my jaw against the tears threatening to fall. "I'll be back soon."

Bramble whimpered and my heart ached. If I didn't go right now, I might lose what little courage I had.

"We'll be right here," Owain said. "Waiting."

I turned back to the web and raised my dagger. The web's silk was thicker than my thumb. My hand trembled and I took a deep breath, willing myself to calm. Careful not to touch the strand in case it stuck to me, I gently sawed at it.

Vibrations danced along the web no matter how light I tried to make my touch. The strand parted. I sawed at the next and soon it, too, fell away.

One after another, I cut the sticky strings. One more and I would have an opening large enough to step through. Slowly the dagger sliced through and the strand fell away.

I sucked in a deep breath as I readied myself to step through. I wanted to depart bravely, like a hero in an ancient tale, striding forth to meet danger without fear in my heart. Instead, my legs wobbled and my hands even more. Some hero. All I wanted to do was turn and flee. I could grab Bramble and be gone in moments. The thought shamed me, for I knew Owain would never leave Rhiwallon here. I had come for her only because Fiachra hinted that my companions would be important to my quest. Owain would rescue her, or die trying, because it was the right thing to do.

"Watch for the beast," I said. Not exactly a bard-worthy final comment.

Clutching the dagger in my sweaty palm, my heart thudding so loudly that surely the beast must hear even if it hadn't noticed the damage to its home, I stepped through the web.

Far above me, the sticky strands held Rhiwallon upright but her head was tipped forward and hair obscured her face. I couldn't tell whether she was unconscious or asleep.

"Diarmuid, what are you doing?" Owain's voice was soft and urgent.

"I'm about to start climbing." I tucked the dagger into my boot.

"Hurry," he said and his voice caught on the word.

Sweat trickled down the side of my face as I stared up at Rhiwallon's limp form and wished it was Owain here rather than me. I took a deep breath and prepared to climb.

Most of the rocks were only knee-high to me, so as long as the tower was stable, I should be able to climb it. I stepped up onto the first rock and scrabbled for a grip, my fingers slick with sweat. I hesitated, but my purchase seemed steady so far.

Another step up, then another. Slowly, slowly, agonisingly slowly. Step, grip, pull, pause.

I kept my gaze on the rocks around me. I didn't dare look up or down for fear of losing my balance and falling. Step, grip, pull. A heart-stopping moment as a rock shifted beneath me. I caught my breath and dug my fingers in so hard that my fingernail broke.

I eased up onto the next rock. Step, grip, pull. Rock by rock.

Another fingernail broke. I left scarlet smears on the rocks. Time seemed to stop. There was no end to this tower. I would climb forever and never reach the top.

Finally, I hauled myself over the edge and wiped bloody fingers on my pants. My hands throbbed, but there was no time to check the damage. The beast could be on its way back. Thick strands of sticky web held Rhiwallon tight against a tall rock.

"Rhiwallon," I whispered. "It's me, Diarmuid."

She moaned and twitched. With one trembling hand, I drew the hair back from her face. I had expected her to be bruised and blood-ied, but she appeared uninjured, although she was very pale.

"Rhiwallon." I patted her cheek, leaving smudges of blood. "Come on, Rhiwallon, you need to wake up."

Finally her eyes opened. They fixed on me, seemingly unknowing, but then her eyes focused.

"Diarmuid?" she croaked.

"It's all right." I tried to sound more confident than I felt. "I'm going to get you out of here. Just be quiet."

Rhiwallon looked around. I knew the exact moment she under-stood where she was, for she moaned again, louder this time, and pulled frantically at her sticky bonds.

"Hold still," I whispered. "I can cut the web, but I need you to hold still."

"No, no." She thrashed and kicked but had little room to move. Her head cracked against the rock and she was still again.

"Rhiwallon? Come on, stay awake."

She moaned.

"Don't move," I whispered. "And be quiet. I don't know where the beast is."

She didn't respond. I took a deep breath, trying not to panic. When

I sliced through the sticky strands, she collapsed at my feet, her eyes open and staring blankly. I patted her on the shoulder, but she didn't seem to notice.

"Rhiwallon, get up." I poked her in the ribs and then, when she still didn't respond, slapped her lightly on the cheek. "Come on."

Rhiwallon blinked, her eyes dazed. I tugged her arm and managed to get my shoulder partially under her. She made some effort to stand as I hauled her to her feet. Once I got her up, she could stand without assistance.

"I need you to listen to me." I grabbed her chin and turned her face towards me. She looked in my direction, if not directly at me. "Concentrate."

Her eyes were blank.

"We have to climb down these rocks. I can't carry you down. You have to climb. Do you understand?"

Rhiwallon blinked. I dragged her over to the edge.

"Look down."

Slowly, she tipped her head.

"Can you see where we have to go? We need to climb down these rocks, all the way to the bottom. Owain and Bramble are waiting down there for us."

"Bramble?" she whispered.

"Yes, Bramble. She's at the bottom. You need to climb down to her."

"Climb."

"That's right. Let's go."

Somehow I got Rhiwallon down onto her belly and edged her, feet first, over the side. I could hardly breathe as I waited to see whether she would simply let go and fall.

"You have to climb," I said. "Go down."

Rhiwallon didn't move, didn't respond. Did she even know where she was? Neither of us would survive a fall from this height.

"Move." I spoke harshly, hoping she would respond to my tone if not my words. "Go on, move. Now."

She hesitated, wobbled a little, and I thought she would surely fall. But then her fingers flexed and took hold of a rock. She clung to it as she lowered herself down onto the next one. I could have cried with relief. As soon as Rhiwallon had progressed far enough that she couldn't grab me if she panicked, I followed.

Our progress was slow, for I had to continually prompt her. She kept stopping as if she had forgotten what she was doing. So I told her to move, to go down, to get to the next rock. I followed slowly, staying well out of her reach and trying not to worry about our slow progress. We were halfway down when Owain's cry echoed through the cavern.

"Diarmuid, it comes."

"Go, Rhiwallon." I dropped down onto the next rock and almost landed on her fingers.

She started and looked up at me. For a moment I thought I saw a flicker of comprehension, but then it was gone, replaced by the vacant stare.

"Move," I snarled.

Owain called out again, a challenge this time, and it was answered by a low hiss. There was a crash like rocks smashing together. I gritted my teeth and moved faster. Another clash of rocks. Another yell from Owain. We were almost at the bottom.

"Faster," I hissed.

Almost there. One rock to go.

Then I saw the beast. It was on our side of the web and far too close. It was easily twice my height with a furry black body and too many legs to count. I cowered as it reared up on its back legs, hissing, and all eight eyes looked directly at me. Venom dripped from its fangs and sizzled on the rocky floor. Time seemed to blur and disappear. The beast hissed again. Owain yelled and a rock slammed into the beast's side. It yowled.

I dropped down from the rocks, landing heavily. Pain shot through my injured ankle and I smothered a cry. Rhiwallon still hesitated on the last rock.

"Come on, Rhiwallon."

She moved far too slowly. As soon as her feet touched the ground, I grabbed her hand and we ran. My ankle burned with every step, but it held my weight. The beast blocked our access to the hole I had cut, so I ran towards the far end of the web. If Owain could keep the beast occupied long enough, I could cut a new hole. Rhiwallon stumbled and fell. I hauled her back to her feet, ignoring the blood on her knees.

Another hiss came from behind us. As we reached the far corner, I looked back and the sight of the enormous creature leaping towards us, legs outstretched, was worse than any nightmare. Its mouth gaped open, red and terrifying and far too large.

Rhiwallon stumbled again and fell, dragging me with her. The last thing I saw was furry black underbelly. Then I was squashed beneath it, still clutching Rhiwallon's hand with everything I had. The world went black.

3 5

DIARMUID

THE CAVERN FLOOR was hard beneath me, smooth but unforgiving on my sore body. Rocks towered above me and the enormous web was still. My skin was slick with blood and a putrid greyish goo.

I licked my dry lips, tasted something foul, and tried to speak. My first attempt was an incoherent mumble, but it was enough to bring Bramble to my side. She sniffed me, her nose close to my face, dark eyes worried.

"Hey girl," I tried to say. What came out was another moan but Bramble wagged her tail and gave a short bark.

Owain was at my side in an instant. His solemn face chilled me.

"Rhiwallon?" My voice was hoarse and my throat hurt to say even that much. Owain's face stilled and my heart dropped.

"Alive," he said. "But not well."

I tried to sit up, but my body wouldn't cooperate and my bloodied hands couldn't grip the rocky floor. Owain helped me, his shoulder strong and sturdy beneath my arm.

"What is this stuff all over me?" My head throbbed and the cavern shifted.

"Beast exploded."

"It's dead?"

Owain's face was grim. "Dead all right."

"Where is it?"

He shook his head. "Don't need to see."

"Where's Rhiwallon?"

"Behind you. I'll help, when you're ready."

His mouth was set in a grim line.

Once the cavern stopped spinning, Owain helped me to my feet, gripping my shoulders tightly. My injured ankle throbbed. My head felt as light as thistledown and my whole body hurt. My hands were sticky, but I couldn't find a clean place on either pants or shirt to wipe them, and we had no water. My stomach rolled and I clenched my jaw, fighting not to add vomit to the mess covering me.

Rhiwallon sat on a rock a dozen or so paces behind me, her shoulders hunched and hair hanging over her face. She, too, was covered in blood and goo. Owain held me upright as I staggered over to her. Bramble was right by my side, pressing her nose against my calf each time I paused. When we reached Rhiwallon, Bramble sat beside her, close but not touching, looking up at her with troubled eyes and lowered ears.

"Rhiwallon?" I croaked.

She sat perfectly still, hands clasped loosely in her lap. I reached out to push her hair away from her face. I wouldn't have touched her, covered in the sticky mess as I was, except that it was all over her, too. Globs of the stuff hung in her hair and on her cheeks. Rhiwallon's face was blank, her eyes open but empty.

Snatches of tales ran through my mind, stories of those who had returned from the lands of the fey with their minds damaged, their lives forever changed. I swallowed hard. She wouldn't have been here if it wasn't for me.

"Has she spoken?" I asked.

Owain shook his head.

"She's—" I couldn't put it into words.

"Gone," Owain supplied.

"I think so. She's… she's traumatised."

"Will she come back?"

I waved my hand in front of her eyes. Owain's face was hopeful, his voice tentative. I rested my hand on the top of Bramble's head and she leaned into my touch. At least she was unharmed.

"It was too much for her." I chose my words carefully. "More than she could handle. I think…" His face fell. I took a deep breath. "I think she's lost her mind."

"But she'll get better, won't she?" he asked, fiercely.

"I don't know, Owain. I'm not a healer, just a bard."

Owain crouched in front of Rhiwallon and wrapped his large hands around her tiny ones.

"It's over, Rhiwallon. The beast is dead. It's all over."

Rhiwallon didn't move. Owain released her hands and stood. His face showed remorse and guilt.

"It's my fault," he said. "I didn't protect her."

"It's not—"

He stopped me with an abrupt motion of his hand.

"I'll look after her," he said. "Won't let her down again."

"What do you mean?"

He nodded towards Rhiwallon. "I'll look after her till she comes back to herself. Then I'll handfast with her, if she'll have me. I can protect her, look after her. She'll never want for anything."

"What about Maeve?" The words were out of my mouth before I thought twice.

Owain gave me a tight smile.

"She's free to go her own way. Me and Rhiwallon will start somewhere else. A new life."

I looked back at Rhiwallon, so still and silent. This was more my fault than Owain's, but it never would have occurred to me to offer to bind myself to her.

"We need to move on," I said. "The beast might have a mate."

Owain nodded and slung his pack and the bow and quiver over his shoulders. Then he lifted Rhiwallon. She hung limply in his arms, like a broken doll.

I had avoided looking at the gaping hole at the end of the cavern until now. As we walked towards the opening, my heart was as heavy as the rocks surrounding us. Whatever we faced next might well be worse.

3 6

IDA

$\mathcal{W}$HERE ONCE I felt the shining spark of Diarmuid's life, somewhere in my breast, now there is nothing. For days, I have felt nothing.

I hardly know what to do. I am not myself. The thought that he might be dead fills my body with... with something I cannot name. My stomach clenches, my throat aches, and strangest of all, my eyes fill with liquid.

Emotions. I thought I understood them, but I find that although I know their names, I can't identify them. Is this fear? Sadness? Grief? Horror? Diarmuid's tales speak of all these things, but I cannot tell one from the other. My eyes burn when I think of Diarmuid and my hands tremble at the thought that he might be dead.

I sit alone in the living room of the house I inhabit. Its former occupants left when I announced I would live here. What else was I to do? I needed somewhere to live and this is a fine house. They needn't have left, though. I think I would have welcomed their company. Perhaps I would not feel quite so alone had I some distraction from wondering about Diarmuid.

A companion is what I need. A diversion. If he is strong and handsome, even better. I do not want to dwell on the reason for these strange feelings. For I suspect I know what it is and I am not yet prepared to admit it, even to myself. So I shall choose a companion and he will come here to live with me. He will be a pleasant distraction from these feelings I do not know how to deal with.

37

BRIGIT

THE BEAST LAY dead on the cavern floor and we walked away, albeit somewhat unsteadily. The smell of flowers and rotting leaves — the scent that led me to Rhiwallon — clung to its body. I wanted to flatten my ears back against my head and run away as fast as I could. Where to, it didn't matter, as long as it was far away from here.

Despite the fey companions of my younger years, most of my knowledge about their race came from ancient tales, and from the wisdom passed down from wise woman to apprentice. Although the task of the fey might seem unachievable, the law of balance meant there must be a way to complete it, however unlikely. I prayed that such ancient wisdom wasn't wrong. There had to be a way out of this place.

As we walked along yet another green-lit tunnel, I sensed someone watching us. I sniffed the air, searching for the watcher's scent, but the only odours I detected belonged to our party: sweat, the unmistakable stink of fear, and the dead beast, whose fetid insides coated Diarmuid and Rhiwallon. If the beast had a mate, I scented no trace of it. Even the fey, whom I thought I detected from time to time, were absent. I had mostly come to trust this body to understand the world in a way my human brain didn't. Even though I could identify no other scent, I knew we were not alone.

As we approached the opening, a new scent reached my nose. It smelled like the coals of a dead fire mixed with rotting eggs and utter desperation. Something terrible waited for us. Shudders wracked my body and my paws refused to move.

Diarmuid caressed the back of my head and despite the ooze coating his fingers I leaned into his hand. His warmth soothed me.

"Come, Bramble," he said. "We have no choice."

I willed myself to move, but my paws felt like they had sunk roots down through the rocky floor. Diarmuid scooped me up. This close to him, the stench of the dead beast was overwhelming and I gagged. He held me to his chest and I felt his heart beating rapidly.

As we passed through the opening, I rested my head against Diarmuid's shoulder. In the safety of his arms my terror faded and our hearts beat together for a few moments. I suddenly knew, deep in my soul, that he was the reason I was here.

How did I not see this earlier? My sense of smell had been useful in locating Rhiwallon, but there was little else I could contribute to Diarmuid's quest. But he was part of some pattern the fey intended to weave in my life. Or perhaps I was meant as part of his pattern. No matter. The fey intended we be together and they were determined to ensure it happened. So determined they cared little what form I was in.

Before I could think further on this revelation, I noticed the heat. I was not merely uncomfortably warm, but so hot that my skin burned. Sweat dripped down my back and over my belly, leaving my hair damp. As we reached the opening, the feeling of dread surged again. I whimpered and Diarmuid's arm tightened around me. Ahead of us, Owain stopped, his large frame blocking my view.

"What is it?" Diarmuid whispered.

I tried hard not to tremble. Owain stepped aside so we could see. Another cavern, even larger than the last. Not far ahead of us, the floor dropped away into a yawning crevice, a smoky haze obscuring its depths. It stretched all the way across the cavern, an insurmountable obstacle between this side and the other.

If I could have spoken, I would have begged Diarmuid to never let me go, but he set me down on the rocky ground. I chided myself. I was forgetting who I really was. I, Brigit, should not be intimidated by these events. My mother would be ashamed. I gave myself a good shake and strode forward.

I peered down into the depths of the crevice, holding my breath, for the stench was like rotten eggs. The crevice was exactly what it seemed from Diarmuid's arms: inconceivably deep, hot, and smoky. I stepped back from the edge and it was well that I did, for a wave of heat surged up and blasted my face. I stumbled back, eyes and skin burning. A massive tongue of fire followed the heat and a low grumble shook the ground, throwing me off my feet.

"What is it?" Owain asked. His face was ruddy and his shirt was drenched in sweat. He clutched Rhiwallon's limp body to his chest and I wished it were me there instead of her.

"There are tales of such places," Diarmuid said, "where the ground parts and shakes, where fire and flames leap up from below. Sometimes, the fire pours out like ale flows from an overfilled mug."

Yet within the boundaries of the fey lands, things might not be what they seemed. The heat on my face and the burning in my lungs seemed fierce and real, but this might prove to be our exit if we trusted enough to ignore the illusion and walk over the chasm.

"What do we do?" Owain asked. "Can we go back?"

Diarmuid shook his head.

"Not if I know anything about the fey's rules. If we don't continue, they might well snatch Rhiwallon away again. We have to keep moving forward and let the fey take us where they will."

The rising steam parted, revealing a rocky bridge. Its tenuous span passed from one edge of the gaping hole to the other, stretching right across the cavern. There was no visible means of support and it would likely crumble the moment someone stepped foot on it.

Diarmuid nodded towards it.

"That's our way out."

The words from Titania's rhyme already ran through my mind. *One may pass the fiery depths and only once may go.*

"A trap," Owain said.

The rankness of rotting eggs accompanied another ground tremor. The stench wormed into my lungs until I felt like I would choke on it. Diarmuid held his hand over his nose.

"There's always a way through the tasks set by the fey," he said. "We have to think."

"One may pass and only once," Owain said. "Clear enough. Go. We'll wait here."

Diarmuid glared at him.

"Nobody is staying behind. We came in here together and we leave together. We just have to figure out what we're missing. There's a way out."

The answer seemed obvious to me. Owain could carry all of us. His presence was no accident any more than mine was. But how could I tell them? Owain would listen but not understand. Diarmuid would understand but not listen. My tail drooped.

Diarmuid's face showed determination. I suspected he was considering crossing the bridge with the intention of seeking help for the rest of us. The ground trembled and nearly threw me off my feet. I couldn't think of a single way I might convey the solution. I had to stop Diarmuid before he stepped onto the bridge. I barked, short and sharp. They turned to look at me.

"What is it, girl?" Diarmuid asked, although he didn't even look at me.

Owain met my eyes. I held his gaze and he slowly nodded.

"Bramble wants us to listen," he said.

Diarmuid looked out at the bridge.

"There's got to be another way around," he muttered.

"Bramble knows it," Owain said.

"Huh?" Diarmuid shot him a puzzled look. "What? She's just—"

Owain cut him off, but I knew what Diarmuid had been about to say and my heart burned.

"We need to listen to Bramble."

Diarmuid shook his head.

"Owain, we don't have time for this. We've got one chance. There has to be another way across."

Owain still held my gaze. He nodded at me.

"Go on, Bramble."

Frustration mounting, I barked again. Why would the fey send me on this journey in such a useless form? Surely they foresaw this. They knew that at some point, I would desperately need to speak.

Diarmuid sighed.

"I don't think now is the time—"

"Course now is the time." Owain's voice, although placid as ever, was underlaid with tension. "Bramble needs to tell us something and we need to listen."

Diarmuid opened his mouth to argue, but Owain stood his ground.

"You're a bard," he said. "You must know tales where things like this happen."

"Things like what?"

"Folk trapped in other forms."

Diarmuid looked at him blankly and Owain gestured towards me. Diarmuid's mouth opened and closed several times before he managed to speak.

"She... I found her... She's just..."

My heart shattered into a million pieces. After all the time Diarmuid and I had spent together, all the secrets he had confided in me, he still had no idea. I had hoped that perhaps somewhere deep inside, he suspected there was more to me than there seemed. That he would understand once he finally let himself see.

Owain shrugged, adjusting his grip on Rhiwallon who still hung, unresponsive, in his arms.

"P'rhaps I'm wrong. I'm just a simple man. Seems to me a bard would know more about these things than me."

Diarmuid eyed me closely and I met his gaze, not trying to hide my hurt. It wasn't like he would see it anyway. Owain would, though. If his arms weren't full of Rhiwallon, he would have given me a comforting rub and some soft words. But it wasn't Owain I wanted to comfort me.

As Diarmuid looked me in the eyes — really looked at me for the first time — I saw his disbelief and also the tiniest spark of doubt in himself. He was thinking it through, wondering whether it was true, whether he might have missed some clue to my Otherworldly state. But mostly, he simply didn't believe. Eventually he shook his head.

"We don't have time for this." His tone was conciliatory. "The longer we spend in here, the stronger Ida becomes. Whatever you think Bramble may or may not be, what we need to worry about right now is finding a way out of here."

The look Owain gave him was the closest to disgust I had ever seen on the big man's face. Then he turned his back to Diarmuid and looked right at me.

"Tell us, Bramble."

Diarmuid sighed and I knew he probably rolled his eyes, but I tried hard to ignore both him and the hurt in my heart. How could I convey the idea of Owain carrying us? A horse. Horses carry people. In my mind, I saw a horse stretch out its neck. It shook its mane and extended a foreleg before prancing around. I tried to copy its action, but my body was all wrong. My neck didn't stretch elegantly like a horse's and I probably looked like I shook water off myself, rather than shook a mane. When I extended my front leg, it didn't bend the way I wanted it to and my prancing made Diarmuid raise his eyebrows as if I had lost my mind.

Owain nodded encouragingly.

"Go on, Bramble."

Diarmuid's eyes went blank. He wasn't even paying attention any more. My heart plummeted. How else could I tell them? My gaze landed on Rhiwallon, still held firmly in Owain's arms. Even now, after bearing her for so long, he showed not the slightest sign of tiredness. That gave me an idea.

I trotted over to Owain and stood beside him, arching my back as if he lifted me with a hand beneath my chest. He looked down and waited, his face patient. I stood up on my back legs, front paws resting on his knees like I did when I wanted to sit on his lap, and still Owain merely stared. Diarmuid wasn't even watching.

"Keep going, Bramble," Owain said. "What else can you show me?"

I voiced my frustration with a bark and Diarmuid glanced at me.

"She wants you to pick her up," he said absently, before turning back to contemplate the bridge.

I barked again — *yes, yes!* — and comprehension filtered into Owain's eyes.

"Clever Bramble!" he said.

I let my tongue hang out, panting a little.

"Don't you see, Diarmuid," Owain said. "That's the solution. We *can* all cross the bridge."

Diarmuid spun around. "What?"

"Bramble figured it out."

Diarmuid's face showed brief incredulity before he schooled it to politeness. Perhaps it was better I was a dog than a woman, for at least in this form I was under no illusion as to my future with Diarmuid. It simply didn't exist.

"I'll carry you across," Owain said. "All of you, all at once."

"One may pass the fiery depths and only once may go," Diarmuid said. "Yes, yes, it could work."

Owain smiled down at me and his plain face looked quite handsome. He might not recognise me for what I truly was, but at least he knew I was more than I seemed.

"Well done, Bramble," Owain said.

"I suppose Bramble gave us the key, by asking you to pick her up," Diarmuid said. "We would have figured it out sooner or later."

I raised my lips and snarled at him. Diarmuid, of all people, should have been the first to know. Instead, it was Owain with his simple mind and his open heart who was willing to listen.

Diarmuid raised his eyebrows in surprise. He extended his hand towards me, his face cautious.

"Bramble, take it easy, girl."

I snarled again and turned my back on him. I sat, the cavern floor warm beneath my rump.

"Leave her, Diarmuid," Owain said. "You can't fix it 'til you see the truth."

"See *what* truth?" Diarmuid asked, a frustrated edge in his voice.

"Look at her," Owain said gently. "Really look at her.

I didn't need to look back over my shoulder to know Diarmuid didn't so much as even glance at me. His attention was already on the bridge.

3 8

DIARMUID

*M*Y SOUL FINALLY felt the truth of Owain's words even as my eyes saw only the familiar scruffy terrier. Shame and utter disappointment welled up in me as I turned back to the bridge.

I was the bard, the one who knew the ancient tales. Here was one living an ancient archetype of tale and I never even noticed. It should have been me who recognised Bramble first. Me, whose occupation called for delicate words, filled with symbolism and meaning and truth. Not Owain who used brute force to deliver blood and death. I heard Titania's words again: *One will bear another's coat until the final round.*

"It's Bramble, isn't it?" I asked. "The riddle. The one who bears another's coat."

Owain barely glanced at me. He shrugged.

"So what is she?" I muttered, eyeing Bramble who sat with her back to me. "Human? Fey? Is she sent to spy on us or to aid us?"

Bramble huffed but didn't turn to face me. Owain scowled and shame coloured my cheeks. Bramble had never given me any reason to doubt her and, indeed, hadn't she deciphered the riddle's clue to crossing the chasm?

"We should go." My mind was all awhirl and I didn't know what else to say.

In silence, the three of us stepped up to where the bridge began. It was barely a handspan in width, a continuation of the same rocky floor we had traversed for so long. It looked as if the living rock had simply grown and stretched from one side of the chasm all the way across to the other. There was no visible means of support and the rock was so thin it could not possibly hold even Bramble's slight weight.

Owain still carried Rhiwallon as easily as if she weighed no more than Bramble but was he strong enough to carry all three of us across? The bridge must be two hundred paces or more. And what if the tongues of fire rose up again? There would be no escape.

"I don't think this is possible," I said. "There must be another way across."

"You can climb onto my back. Bramble will have to sit on Rhiwallon." Owain's voice was calm and certain. He nodded towards the terrier. "Lift her up."

If I could have thought of another option, anything at all, I would have suggested it, but my mind was blank. I felt a deep certainty that this was the solution Titania intended us to find.

Bramble trembled as I grasped her around the middle. If Rhiwallon panicked, she would knock Bramble right off her lap. Under other circumstances, I would have given Bramble a gentle stroke or said something comforting, but I couldn't bring myself to do it. I released her abruptly, almost dropping her onto Rhiwallon.

With Rhiwallon and Bramble in his arms, Owain planted his feet wide apart and waited for me to gain purchase on his back, between his pack and Rhiwallon's bow. My first two attempts resulted in hard landings on the rocky floor. With both tailbone and pride bruised, my third attempt was more successful and I managed to clamber up high enough to wrap my arms around Owain's neck. My legs grasped his waist tightly.

Owain shifted slightly, adjusting his grip on Rhiwallon, then he stepped right up to the chasm. I felt his chest expand as he took a deep breath. Then he placed one foot on the narrow bridge.

I held my breath, my heart pounding wildly, as Owain leaned forward. His muscles tensed beneath me and he hesitated, testing the bridge's strength. The moment seemed to last forever. Finally, he stepped forward. Now that he had committed to the crossing, he had no option other than to keep going until he reached the other side. If not, he may as well throw us all over the edge right now. Heat flooded up from the cavern's depths, the air so hot it burned my skin.

Owain walked confidently, carrying four lives with every step. I kept my gaze locked on the far side of the chasm, not daring even the smallest glance down, for fear I would panic and lose my grip. If I let go, Owain couldn't catch me, not without dropping Rhiwallon and Bramble, and they were both precious to him. Certainly more precious than me. I prayed that Owain would have the strength to get us across.

Halfway across, he wobbled. I tightened my grip on his neck a little too much and he gasped, choking. I forced my fingers to relax so he could breathe. He moved more slowly now. I was aware of every beat of my heart and of every breath Owain took. He laboured, drawing in big gulps of air and his neck gleamed with sweat. My limbs shook with the effort of holding on and the heat made my head spin.

We were barely a dozen paces from safety when a roar shattered the air. Images flashed through my mind: griffins, harpies, banshees. Owain's foot slipped and he teetered. Moments passed and my heart stopped as I clung to his back. In my mind, I saw the four of us plunging into the chasm. The image was so vivid that several moments passed before I realised we weren't plummeting towards the bottom after all.

Owain continued, step by step, bringing us steadily closer to the other side. My thigh cramped and the prospect of waiting even another few moments became almost unbearable. It took every scrap of my willpower to hold on as Owain made those last perilous steps. As his foot touched solid safety, my leg spasmed. Owain stepped off the bridge as I slid down his back and tumbled onto the rocky surface, landing mere finger widths from the edge.

He crouched with a grunt to deposit Rhiwallon, still insensible, on the ground. Bramble tumbled off Rhiwallon's lap, trembling convulsively, tongue hanging out as she panted. Owain sat, abruptly, beside Rhiwallon's prone form, his legs splayed out in front of him. His shirt was drenched with sweat and he raised his shaking hands to cover his face.

I rolled over and crawled away from the edge, then lay on my belly on the warm rocky floor. I could not have done what Owain did, even if I had the physical strength. Only the tremble in his hands now betrayed how terrified he had been.

"What was that noise?" I asked. "It sounded like…"

In truth, I didn't know what it sounded like, but I didn't need to identify the creature to know danger lurked nearby.

And it made me think of another winged beast: the raven I had dreamed of for so many years. Ebony feathers, beady eyes, midnight-dark blood glistening on its beak. Perhaps as I drew closer to a confrontation with Ida, I also came nearer to discovering the meaning of the raven.

Bramble stumbled over to Owain. She licked his knee and gazed up at him. Owain met her eyes and it seemed some wordless communication passed between them. How could I have ever thought of Bramble as mine? I had often fallen asleep imagining myself roaming the fields of Silver Downs, creating my tales while Bramble ran at my side, jumping streams and scrambling onto rocks to find a sunny place to nap. It had been many days since I had considered trying to find her previous owner, but perhaps staying with me was never her intention. I had no claim over her. For reasons known only to her, Bramble had decided to journey with me this far. It was clearly Owain she was fond of. Owain she would depart with once this was over. Perhaps it was better that way, for I likely wouldn't survive the coming confrontation with Ida. Still, it a little piece of my heart crumbled away. I scrambled gracelessly to my feet, my thigh muscles still cramping.

"We should keep moving," I said. "I would prefer not to wait until whatever creature made that sound arrives."

Owain's hauled himself to his feet. He winced and held his shoulders oddly as he gathered Rhiwallon up again.

"Are you hurt?" I asked.

He shook his head but didn't meet my eyes. The roar came again, ringing through the cavern. Was it a sound of challenge? Of alarm?

"Let's go." I turned to the opening at the far end of the cavern. "Maybe this path will lead outside."

I stepped forward, feeling more alone than I had since the day I first found Bramble in the woods. Owain followed me, bearing Rhiwallon, and Bramble trotted beside him. When I reached the opening, the tunnel stretched ahead of me, dark and ominous, smelling of damp and something I couldn't identify, like a cross between a wild boar and the new sparks from a tinder.

"Diarmuid?" Owain spoke quietly and I heard both hesitance and exhaustion in his voice.

I took a deep breath. "Let's go."

"We're right behind you."

We had been walking for only moments when I spotted light up ahead.

"I think the tunnel's ending," I said.

From the corner of my eye, I saw a flash of white near the ground. Bramble, moving ahead of me.

"Bramble, wait," I hissed. "It might not be safe."

A sniff of disgust.

I trudged faster. I could not let her go alone into unknown danger. Not now that I knew. We reached the end of the tunnel together and entered a small cavern illuminated by clean, white light. There were three doors.

Like the bridge, the doors belonged to this place, merging into the surrounding rock as if they had grown out of it. The doors were identical: smooth panels of wood stretching from side to side, arced at the top and fitting cleanly into the rocks without hinge or latch.

Owain and I looked at each other. I was sure he, like I, searched the riddle for any reference to doors.

"How do we choose?" I asked. "Are we permitted to open each and look through or may we open only one?"

"More tunnels?" Owain asked.

"Possibly. Or other places."

I searched my memory as I stared at the doors. Surely there must be a tale of mysterious doors in a fey tunnel, but I could recall nothing useful.

"There doesn't seem to be anything in the riddle that tells us what to do," I said. "If this is another test, there will be rules. We just don't know what."

"Can't follow rules we don't know."

"No." My voice was curt, although I did try to temper my tone. "All we can do is choose one door to open and trust it will be the right one."

"How?"

We stared at the doors and at each other, neither wanting to make a choice that might send us into an even worse situation. Bramble, meanwhile, was busy. I had paid scant attention as she sniffed each door again and again. She finally stopped, nose pressed to the base of the middle door.

"Bramble's chosen." Owain adjusted his grip on Rhiwallon whose head lolled backwards, her eyes still blank.

I didn't want to admit the truth only because I was disappointed that *I* hadn't recognised Bramble first. The fact that Owain saw through her disguise before me didn't make it any less true. It simply made it harder to accept.

"Bramble's choice," I agreed.

Bramble looked up at me and I saw, for the first time, the hurt in her eyes. I had let her down over and over. My recognition now did little to alleviate the pain I had caused, but maybe it would show I was finally willing to believe.

"Are you sure?" I asked her.

With her eyes locked on mine, Bramble nodded and I could no

longer even pretend to deny the truth. Whatever Bramble might be, she understood my words.

"All right, then," I said.

I set my hand against the door. Its wood was smooth beneath my palm and it swung open without the slightest sound or hesitation. Blinding light burned my eyes. Behind me, Owain muttered a curse. Squinting as my eyes adjusted, I gasped, for now I knew what manner of beast we had heard. Many a tale spoke of such places, but I never dreamed I would see one with my own eyes.

Here, by my foot, a golden bracelet studded with crimson gems. There, a cunningly-carved chest overflowed with jewels the size of my fist: blood-red, sea green, the clear blue of a midsummer sky, and wine-dark purple. A silver sword, so finely-wrought it could not have been made by human hands. A golden helmet, splendid enough for a king to wear into battle. Everywhere I looked, priceless treasures were scattered across the floor and piled into mounds. As always in this strange underground place, there was no obvious source of light. It seemed the air itself shone white, illuminating the vast treasure stores and reflecting off them. But where was the owner of these treasures?

"Don't like this," Owain muttered.

I was instantly thankful he was not the type likely to become overwhelmed with greed.

"The dragon won't be far away," I said. "We need to get out of here before it returns."

Rhiwallon stirred and moaned. Owain cleared some space, moving rare treasures out of the way with his foot, and gently set her down. Bramble leaned in, sniffing Rhiwallon's face. Rhiwallon lay still and quiet for a few moments. Then her eyes seemed to focus. She looked up at each of us in turn.

"Wh—" Her voice was hoarse and she stopped to clear her throat. "What happened?"

"You're safe now," Owain said gently.

"There was a..." Rhiwallon's voice was stronger, although still halting. "An enormous..."

"We came to get you," Owain said. "It's dead."

"Are you sure?"

"Dead," Owain confirmed.

"It won't come after you again," I said, feeling rather redundant.

"There was a… a *thing* standing over me when I woke." Her voice was a little stronger now. "And then there were hands. They touched me, picked me up, so many hands. Then I was in a cave and it tied me up. I thought it wanted—" She clutched both hands to her stomach and shuddered. "I thought it was going to kill me."

I wondered what she had been going to say before she stopped herself.

Owain raised a hand, as if to touch her, but hesitated. He let his hand fall.

"It's all over," he said.

Beside me, Bramble whined softly, and almost without thinking, I rested my hand against her back. Exactly what manner of creature she was didn't seem all that important right now. What mattered was that we were all alive, and together. But that might not last if we didn't get out of here soon.

"We need to move," I said. "The dragon will return sooner or later and I, for one, want to be gone before then."

Rhiwallon started to sit up and Owain reached out to help her. She waved him away and got to her feet rather unsteadily.

"I'm really not in the mood for a dragon right now," she said.

"I'll protect you," Owain said.

She looked at him for a long moment.

"We'll protect each other. I'd like my bow back."

He handed her weapons over without comment and she strapped the belt around her waist, fumbling a little with the buckle. Once the quiver hung the way she wanted it to, she slung the bow over her shoulder.

"How do we get out of here?" she asked in a voice that sounded almost normal.

All three of them looked to me. Why should it be me who led them? Surely any decision I made would only lead us astray. Look at where I had taken us so far. And yet they waited.

"We still haven't found the key," I said. "Perhaps the next door we need will be locked. It would make sense for the locked door to be the one leading from a dragon's lair. Of all the caverns, this might be the one we need to leave the fastest, so of course it will be locked."

"I can carry you, if you need," Owain said to Rhiwallon.

She glowered at him.

"I can walk."

"Don't touch anything," I said, feeling somewhat left out. "The tales tell that he who steals from a dragon's lair will pay dearly, usually with his life. And keep together."

We set off in single file, me first, then Bramble, Rhiwallon, and Owain at the back, scouring the treasures for anything that might be the key from the riddle. Our progress was slow and I was ever conscious that the dragon must soon return. Surely it had already scented us.

"This is impossible," Rhiwallon said. "How are we supposed to find a key in all of this? It could be buried within any of these piles."

"It must be here somewhere." I straightened my shoulders and tried to act like the leader they seemed to expect me to be. "The riddles of the fey are never impossible. They want us to give up, to fail, but they have to allow us an opportunity to succeed, however small. So the key is here and it's somewhere we can see it, just as the riddle says."

"What happens if we don't find it?" Owain asked.

We hadn't yet discussed the possibility of failure. In a tale, the hero eventually succeeds at his task. He might fail the first time and perhaps the second, and the odds against him might seem insurmountable, but he always wins in the end. Except in my tales.

"I don't know," I said. "Perhaps we will have to stay here forever. We should have asked."

"Too late now," Owain said, and I envied his simple practicality.

We traversed the dragon's lair step by step, passing countless mounds of treasures. Bracelets, rings and crowns. Shields, swords and a golden suit of armour. Box after box spilled over with brightly-coloured jewels. The dragon who possessed these treasures must be ancient indeed. Behind me, Owain called out.

"Diarmuid, wait."

I turned and discovered I was some distance ahead of the others.

"What's wrong?"

"Bramble stopped. She won't move."

Bramble crouched down low to the ground, tail tucked beneath her rump, her whole body shaking. Of course it would be Owain who noticed her distress. It was never me.

"Bramble?" I asked. "What is it, girl?"

Her gaze darted around the cavern as if she searched for something she could smell but not see.

"It's the dragon, isn't it?" I asked. "It returns."

Bramble met my eyes and whimpered.

Rhiwallon sighed. "Really not in the mood."

"We should hurry," I said. "We can still find the key and get out of here."

Even as I spoke, a bellow rang through the air. The dragon had returned.

3 9

IDA

I AM OUT of patience with the mortal man who has been my companion these last few days, although companion is hardly a suitable description. His overwhelming desire to please irritates me. He hovers by my side, waiting for the opportunity to do something, anything. At times, I tell him to go away and he does, but only briefly. Then he returns, eager as ever, apologising for whatever he believes made me send him away.

I can't help but compare him to the boy. The boy is tortured, with his dark thoughts and his twisted tales. But he is also aloof, reserved. He holds himself somewhat apart from others. He observes. He does not cling or fuss or smother.

I do not understand how mortals can commit themselves to another for a lifetime. True, their lives are fleeting, but surely they grow tired of their mate, bored with endlessly repeating the same conversations, the same actions, day after day after day. Some choose to leave, to find themselves a new companion. But so many stay and spend the rest of their lives trying to convince themselves they are happy.

This mortal has been my companion for, what, three, four days? I grit my teeth every time he enters the room, for I cannot bear to hear his whiny voice, full of flattery and hope. Today, I will tell him to leave, to go out to the woods and to remain there. And then I will be able to relax, to soften my tight muscles, to unclench my gritted teeth.

I shall choose another companion. There are plenty of fine men in this village. In fact, this morning I saw one who might be suitable. Lean and broad shouldered. Thick, red hair. Strong hands. He will be satisfactory. Pleasant to look at and not too annoying are my only criteria. There was a woman with him this morning, perhaps a little younger than he, small and dark-haired. She clutched his hand and smiled up at him. A sister perhaps, or a wife. No matter. He will forget her quickly enough.

If only I could forget. But I know I will measure every companion against the boy. If I could forget him, perhaps I could be happy. I need to find a companion who does not force me to remember what I no longer have.

40

———

BRIGIT

ROAR SPLIT the air and I froze, quivering, my belly pressed against the rocky floor. The dragon's scent overwhelmed me, a cross between some forest creature and a recently-extinguished fire. I felt it in my nose, tasted it on my tongue.

"Run!" Owain grabbed Rhiwallon's hand and scooped me up as he passed me.

Clutched to his chest, I felt his heart pounding. We darted around mounds of treasure, but surely running was pointless, for we had found neither the key nor the door to which it belonged. We needed time. Time to search for the key, time to find the door, time to make sure we didn't break the riddle's rules. We could hardly do that while fleeing a dragon. Another roar echoed and I clung to Owain, heedless of how my claws dug into his arm. We were out of time, doomed.

Diarmuid yelled and pointed.

"There, the door."

And there it was — a small wooden door, large enough for Owain to squeeze through, but not big enough for the dragon. If we could find the key quickly, we might yet escape. Another roar, closer this time. The dragon's odour grew stronger and I gagged as it wormed into my lungs. It was worse than the rotten eggs of the chasm.

Wind flowed over us and a presence passed above. Then the dragon landed its huge bulk between us and the door. Its scales were golden like the sun and as it folded its wings, I glimpsed a ruby sheen beneath them. Jagged teeth protruded from a long snout. Its eyes were startlingly human.

"Halt." The dragon's voice echoed around the chamber, repeating in a dizzying chorus.

Owain's arm tightened around me and he wrapped his other arm around Rhiwallon's shoulders. We stood together, he and I and Rhiwallon, with Diarmuid slightly apart from us. I pitied him for not having Owain's strong arm around him, too.

"Where are you running to in such a hurry?" the dragon asked, inspecting us each in turn.

We looked to Diarmuid. He hesitated, but cleared his throat and straightened his shoulders.

"I apologise for disturbing you." The wobble in Diarmuid's voice betrayed his unease. "We wandered in here by mistake."

The dragon snorted and its eyes glinted with amusement.

"By mistake, eh." Its voice was like rocks smashing together. I wanted to bury my face into Owain's shirt and cover my ears with my paws. "Humans don't enter my home by mistake. They come to steal my treasure."

"We haven't taken anything," Diarmuid said. "We didn't even mean to come in here, but we thought we were probably allowed to open only one door and this was the one we chose."

That was my fault. But the other doors smelled of danger and dread. The door that led us here smelled of hope and the way home.

"Of course you chose that door," the dragon said. "You could smell my treasure. The scent of it leads people here, drives them half-mad with desire. They come in and paw through my treasure, pocketing what they will. Then they sneak out, thinking I haven't been watching them the whole time, thinking I haven't seen everything they did, noted every item they touched."

"If you were watching, then you know we didn't take anything," Diarmuid said. "We were looking for a way out of the tunnels.

Nothing more. And we saw the door just before you arrived. In another few moments, we would have been gone."

"Aah, you saw the door, did you," the dragon said. "And how did you plan to unlock it?"

"There's a key," Diarmuid said. "We thought it might be here somewhere."

"So you did intend to steal from my treasure." The dragon's voice rose triumphantly. "I knew it. No human has ever entered my home without the intent of theft."

"We are here by the design of the fey," Diarmuid said. "The tunnels in this place twist and turn, leading wherever the fey want us to go. If we have been brought here by their design, and we face a locked door, surely they intend us to locate its key."

"The intent of the fey is no concern of mine," the dragon said. "It matters not what excuse you give for your presence. You have already admitted to entering my home for the purpose of stealing from me."

Diarmuid's face had that distant look that indicated he was riffling through all the tales he knew. He stood up straight and looked the dragon in the eye. I admired his bravery, even as I trembled with fear.

"Then what solution do you propose?" he asked. "How do you intend to ascertain our guilt?"

"I already know your guilt," the dragon said. "I have no need for further proof."

"We are entitled to be offered a task," Diarmuid said. "Satisfaction of which would earn us our freedom."

The dragon eyed him and the amused glint turned dangerous.

"You fancy yourself a druid, little human," it said. "Or a bard perhaps."

The dragon's tone made it clear what it thought of either profession.

"I am a bard. And not only that, but I am the seventh son of a seventh son."

The dragon's face twitched.

"And that holds some significance for you, it seems."

"It means I am destined to be a bard. In my family, the seventh son of a seventh son is always a bard."

"And be you a good bard?" the dragon asked.

Diarmuid hesitated and I held my breath, willing him to tell the truth.

"No," he said finally. "My tales do not resonate with my listeners."

"And who do you blame for that, little bard? Yourself, or the parents who cursed you to be bard by giving life to the seventh son of a seventh son?"

"The fault is none but my own. I might be a good bard one day, but I have much to learn yet."

The dragon looked Diarmuid up and down and when it spoke next, the sneer was gone from its voice.

"So, little bard, you snuck into my home with the aim of thievery. How do you intend to repay your debt?"

"Since we didn't steal anything, it seems to me we haven't incurred any debt," Diarmuid said.

His words made me quake, for they sounded like a challenge. Indeed, the dragon drew itself up higher. Its gaze swept from Diarmuid to the rest of us.

"And what say you, friends of the little bard?" Its eyes bored into us each in turn. Me it lingered on and I felt horribly exposed. Could the dragon's gaze pierce this form I wore? "Well?"

Owain and Rhiwallon glanced at each other and it was she who spoke first.

"We had no intention of taking anything," she said and I admired the way her voice didn't even tremble. "We only wanted to find a way out."

The dragon made a low noise, perhaps a growl or merely a clearing of the throat.

"You entered my lair without permission. Surely, for that, you owe me something."

"What do you propose we owe you?" Diarmuid asked.

"Why, treasure of course," the dragon said. "If you each provide me with a treasure worthy to redeem for your intrusion, I'll allow you to leave."

"We don't have any treasure," Diarmuid said. "Because this is a place of the fey, we were not able to bring anything of cold iron with us. We have neither sword nor jewels nor anything else of value. The only thing I have, which you are welcome to if it pleases you, is this dagger."

He retrieved a dagger from his boot and offered it on the palm of his hand.

"And my brooch," Owain added, fumbling in his pocket. He held out the small keepsake he had used to mark our progress through the tunnels. "You can have this, too."

The dragon barely glanced at the offered items before it snorted.

"Surely you jest. Look at the priceless treasures surrounding you. I have here riches worth many kingdoms. No human king possesses treasure to rival the value of mine. And yet you offer me a plain dagger and a scratched brooch?"

"We offer you everything we have," Diarmuid said. "Doesn't that make them priceless?"

The dragon tipped its head to one side, considering.

"I suppose it does, in a way, and yet your offerings are poor. None the less, I accept your treasures, such as they are. You may place them on the ground."

Diarmuid and Owain each set their item down. My lungs ached and I reminded myself to breathe.

"You have not redeemed yourselves," the dragon said.

"We have given you everything we have," Diarmuid said. "What else can we give?"

The dragon considered him. "You tell me. What else have you to offer, little bard?"

"Shall I tell you a tale?" An edge of desperation crept into Diarmuid's voice.

The dragon laughed and small puffs of steam escaped its nostrils.

"You have already confessed your failure as a bard. Now you expect me to accept a tale as payment for your intrusion?"

"Then what do you want from us?"

There was a long pause. The dragon looked around its cavern and, for a while, almost seemed to forget we were there. Hope flared and my tail curled up just the tiniest bit. Perhaps, while the dragon was distracted, we could sneak out. But we still needed the key.

"You will answer a riddle," the dragon said at length. "Four riddles, one each. For each correct answer, I will give leave for the one who answers to depart. How does that sound, little bard?"

I trembled. How could I answer a riddle while trapped in this form? I wished, for Diarmuid's sake, that I could be brave and tell him to leave me behind, but I desperately hoped he would find another way.

"Provided we can choose who answers each riddle and we are permitted to have one to answer for all, we accept," Diarmuid said.

"No," the dragon said. "Four riddles, four answers, one each."

I felt their eyes on me, Diarmuid, Owain and Rhiwallon. I tucked my tail between my legs and didn't look at any of them.

"That's not fair," Owain said.

"Fair?"

The dragon pulled itself up to its full height. I hadn't realised how much it had lowered itself, presumably for ease of talking to us. Now it sat up on its haunches and stretched its neck, glaring as it towered over us.

"What is fair about your intrusion in my lair? What is fair about forcing me to endure your stench? Do you have any idea how long the odour of humans lingers? It will be months before I no longer smell you every minute I am at home."

"And if we fail?" Diarmuid asked.

"Why, then, I eat you."

"We accept," Diarmuid said.

My heart broke. He intended to leave me behind.

"Ask your first riddle."

The dragon snorted but appeared mollified. It thought for a few moments.

"What whispers and roars, inhabits several forms, and can be a source of both life and death?"

My heart pounded and I felt Owain holding his breath. I had no idea what answer the dragon expected. Surely Diarmuid was the only one of us who could answer such a thing. There was no hope for me, but if the riddles were all this hard, then we had already lost. I knew the moment Diarmuid found the answer, for his face lit up. My heart ached to see it and it was only in that moment that I realised how much I loved him.

"Water," he said.

"Water indeed, little human," the dragon said. "Very well, then, what is quieter than a whisper and yet louder than thunder?"

Diarmuid spoke quickly before anyone else could answer.

"This is Bramble's riddle."

I held myself very still. I could hardly fathom his reason.

The dragon considered him for a moment, then turned its gaze on me.

"Aah, you mean the creature who wears not its own form?"

I stared back at the dragon. How did it know?

"Yes, I feel your surprise, little one. It blazes from your eyes."

It was probably very old and knowledgeable. Perhaps it could even tell me how I might escape this form. But I could not speak to the dragon, however much I might wish it, not unless it could read my mind.

The dragon turned back to Diarmuid. "How will she answer my riddle if she cannot speak?"

"She has already answered for you," Diarmuid said. "With her silence."

Of course, the answer was silence. My heart lifted and my tail curled. Maybe, just maybe, we could pass this test. Maybe Diarmuid didn't intend to leave me behind to be eaten by the dragon.

The dragon huffed and considered its next riddle.

"What is both welcomed and despised, liked and feared, a source of sorrow and a source of joy?"

"Death," Owain said.

The dragon acknowledged his answer with a dip of its head.

"What can make one both run and freeze, cry and scream, be thankful to be alive and wish one was dead?"

We waited. Rhiwallon was the only one who had not yet answered. To my surprise, she gave a faint smile.

"Fear," she said.

The dragon smiled, in as much as such a creature can. It nodded its huge head as it eyed us each in turn.

"Well done, little humans. You surprise me."

"Will you honour your agreement?" Diarmuid asked. "And allow us to leave?"

"A dragon never goes back on its word," it said, somewhat haughtily.

"And we can continue our search for the key?"

It hissed and its eyes flashed darkly.

"You are arrogant indeed to think I would allow you to take something from my home."

"Then how will we unlock the door?" Diarmuid asked. "You have agreed to allow us to leave, but we still need the key."

"How you achieve your goal is of no concern to me," the dragon said. "Go back the way you entered if you cannot exit by the other."

"We can't," Diarmuid said. "That way will take us many days and we have neither food nor water."

The dragon shrugged and its tail twitched, much as an irritated cat swishes its tail before it extends its claws and swipes.

"That is your problem. Not mine."

We looked at each other. They all looked as empty of hope as I felt.

"May as well keep going," Owain said.

Diarmuid's shoulders slumped.

"And then what? We sit and wait until someone else happens along?"

"Hurry up, little humans," the dragon said. "Linger too long and I may change my mind."

"Let's go," Diarmuid muttered. "We'll think of something."

Perhaps the door wasn't locked after all. The reference to a key might have been Titania's way of distracting us. Perhaps the key might even be in its lock. I sat up straighter in Owain's arms as hope surged within me. There might be a way out after all.

That hope lasted only until we reached the door and confirmed it was indeed locked. There was no sign of the key. Had I been in my own form, I would have sat down and cried. Instead, I was struck by a powerful urge to lift my muzzle and howl. Diarmuid traced the lock with one finger. It looked nothing like any lock I had ever seen.

"This reminds me of something," he murmured and his eyes were distant even as his hand lingered on the door. "The leaf, Owain, the red one."

Owain tucked me under one arm and fumbled in his pocket. He retrieved the scarlet red leaf, the one he plucked from the floor after the fey left. *Might be useful,* he had said. He offered it to Diarmuid.

"That's our key," Diarmuid said. "You do it, Owain. You were the one who thought to keep it."

The lock was exactly the size and shape of the leaf. Owain placed the leaf flat against the lock and it opened with a click.

"Farewell, little humans," the dragon said from behind us. "Perhaps you might return another time."

We stepped through the doorway, Diarmuid first, then Rhiwallon, then Owain carrying me. I pitied the dragon left behind, lonely and surrounded by mounds of treasure.

41

BRIGIT

I WANTED TO howl when I realised that yet another green-lit tunnel lay on the other side of the door. We had rescued Rhiwallon, crossed the fiery bridge, answered the dragon's riddles, and found the key. What more could be asked of us? I rested my head on Owain's shoulder with a heavy sigh.

We crowded into a tunnel, which was far narrower than the others and barely ten paces long before it ended in another door. The roof was high, but its width was exactly the size necessary for Owain to pass through and no more. He had just stepped through the doorway, when Diarmuid spoke.

"Owain, wait," he said. "Keep the door open."

By the time Owain managed to turn around in the too-small space, the door had closed with a soft thud.

"Too late," he said.

"See if you can open it again." Diarmuid's voice held an edge of panic.

"No handle," Owain said.

"What's the problem?" Rhiwallon asked.

"Push it," Diarmuid said. "Maybe it didn't close properly."

Owain pressed his palm to the door but it had closed securely.

"Won't budge," Owain said.

We waited.

"There's no way to open the door at this end," Diarmuid said, at last.

"We're trapped?" Rhiwallon asked.

"There must be a hidden lever or button," Diarmuid said, although he didn't sound like he believed his own words.

Owain managed to deposit me onto the ground, then he began running his hands over the earthen wall. I pressed my nose to the base of the wall, searching for anything that looked different. I searched the floor also but found nothing unusual in the hard-packed earth.

"We must be missing something," Diarmuid said.

"Could it be up higher?" Rhiwallon asked.

We looked up. The roof of this tunnel did seem much higher than the others.

"But what would be the point in putting it out of our reach?" she asked.

"Maybe it's another test," Diarmuid said.

We craned our necks, eyes straining with the effort of trying to see something that was intended to be invisible. I worked my way methodically along the wall, starting from the edge near the dragon's door. Everyone kept getting in my way and obscuring my view, and I let out a loud yelp when Rhiwallon stood on my paw. She muttered an apology.

Owain picked me up and I wriggled around in his arms to gain a higher purchase. When he realised what I was doing, he held me up over his head. My tail quivered at being up so high, but his hands gripped my ribs firmly, so I tried to ignore my unease and focus on my task.

It was easier to scan the walls now that I had an uninterrupted view, but even so, I could see nothing unusual. I let out a frustrated growl.

"Keep trying, Bramble," Owain said. He squeezed past Rhiwallon, which was only possible if they both turned sideways, to let me inspect the far end of the wall.

"This is hopeless." Rhiwallon sank down to sit cross-legged on the floor. "Titania wants us to rot in here."

"Can't give up now," Owain said.

"Well, what are we supposed to do? We've checked every inch of that blasted wall. There's nothing there. We're trapped in here until she decides to let us out. And what if she doesn't?"

My stomach rumbled loudly, reminding me it had been many hours since we last ate. And it had been so long since we ran out of water that I wasn't even thirsty anymore. We were all exhausted and covered in muck from the dead beast. We couldn't go on like this for much longer.

My eyes were sore from straining so hard, but I kept searching. There had to be a way out. The fey wouldn't lead us here for no reason. I checked the last section of wall, right above the door that would lead us somewhere else, but there was nothing. I sighed and Owain started to lower me. But just as he moved, I spotted something. It was the shallowest of depressions, just a slight dip in the otherwise smooth wall, and I only saw it because I was on exactly the right angle.

I gave a wuff and he froze.

"Do you see something?" he asked.

I barked and he held me back up high again.

The dip, whatever it was, was well out of reach. Even if Owain were to lift Diarmuid, he wouldn't be able to touch it. But how could we check whether this was the way to open the door if we couldn't reach it?

"I can't see anything," Diarmuid admitted.

"Me either," Owain said. He continued to hold me up over his head and I kept my gaze fixed on the indentation, fearful of not being able to find it again if I even so much as blinked.

"I think I see something," Rhiwallon said. "It might be nothing, though, and it's too high up."

"I could lift you," Owain said.

"I still wouldn't be able to reach it."

I was close to despair. We were hungry and thirsty and tired, and now it seemed the final key we needed was positioned deliberately far out of our reach.

"Could you push it with an arrow?" Diarmuid asked.

Rhiwallon shook her head.

"No, it's easily three times my height. I couldn't even get close. Unless…"

Owain's fingers dug into my ribs painfully. I wriggled and he lowered me, clutching me to his chest once more. Now that Rhiwallon had also seen the indentation, I was less afraid of not being able to find it again. She stared up at it, one hand on the quiver at her hip. I knew where her thoughts headed and my heart thudded faster. It could work. Slowly, Rhiwallon drew an arrow from her quiver. With the other hand, she reached for her bow.

"That's impossible," Diarmuid said.

Rhiwallon shrugged.

"I'll just keep shooting until I hit it. I need some room, though. And watch for the arrows as they fall. An injury is the last thing any of us needs."

Owain and Diarmuid moved to the other end of the tunnel. Rhiwallon nocked the arrow and drew it back, lifting the bow to aim.

Diarmuid was right: it *was* an impossible shot. But I had seen Rhiwallon take down a running hare with a single arrow that pierced right through the eye. As she took aim, I held my breath. She released the arrow and it sprang up, almost too fast for my eyes to follow. The arrow knocked the wall and vanished.

"What happened?" Owain asked.

"Where did it go?" Diarmuid said.

Rhiwallon's face was pale.

"It disappeared as soon as it hit the wall."

A long moment of silence followed her words. I was so very tired. After all we had been through, it seemed unfair that we should encounter such a charm now.

"How many arrows do you have?" Diarmuid asked, at last.

"I carry five," she said.

"Four left," Owain said.

Rhiwallon nodded.

"Four left." She took another arrow from her quiver. "Might as well get on with it."

I couldn't quite see the indentation from here, but the first arrow had been close. Under other circumstances, I had no doubt that Rhiwallon would have hit her target. But the tunnel was dimly lit and she was shooting on an extremely steep angle to a tiny target far above her head. Close would not be good enough.

Rhiwallon nocked the arrow and aimed. Once again it hit very near to the indentation and disappeared. She took out a third arrow, set it in place, and fired, all in the time it took me to draw a single breath. Again, the arrow disappeared. Rhiwallon hissed.

"You can do it," Owain said.

Rhiwallon turned and shot him a glare. Diarmuid opened his mouth and she glared so hard at him that he simply closed it again. The fourth arrow missed also. Her face was red now, although I didn't know whether it was with frustration or anger.

With a deep breath, she set the final arrow against her bow. The world seemed to slow around me as I watched her exhale gently, her gaze fixed on her target. She raised the bow and the arrow and they were like extensions of her arms. I followed the arrow's trajectory. I couldn't tell whether it had hit its target. If it hadn't, it was close. Very close. I held my breath and prayed.

Slowly, ever so slowly, the door in front of us rumbled open and light flooded the small tunnel. Diarmuid and Owain cheered and even Rhiwallon looked pleased. I barked in appreciation and we hurried through the door before it could close again. We stepped out into sunshine scented with spring.

4 2

DIARMUID

THE SUN HOVERED low over the horizon, its light soft. Dawn perhaps? Snow still remained on the ground, although patches of grass peeked through in some areas. How much time had passed in the outside world? I breathed in deeply, rejoicing in the feel of fresh, cool air filling my lungs.

We stood there for a while, letting the sunlight soak into our skin. Rhiwallon clasped her stomach. Owain's face was tight and his shoulders hunched. Bramble's tail and ears drooped. My fingers itched to stroke her hair, but I no longer felt I had any right to touch her. Not until we figured out what manner of creature she was.

Unless I was much mistaken, we had emerged from the mound in the same place we entered it. The paths of the fey could appear to lead in one direction when in reality going another.

"Why so morose?" I asked. "We did it. We rescued Rhiwallon, made our way through the tunnels, answered the dragon's riddles, and found a way out. You should be pleased."

"We barely got out," Rhiwallon said. "The dragon would have gladly eaten us."

"No it wouldn't." I didn't feel quite as confident as I sounded.

"Dragons enjoy company. They love riddles. It would have kept us alive as long as we kept talking."

"She," Rhiwallon said. "The dragon was a female."

"How do you know?" I asked.

"I just know. She was sad, too."

"Lonely, most like," I said. "Dragons lead solitary lives. She will probably think about us for years to come."

"Last dragon I ever want to see," Owain said.

"I'm sure it will be."

I only half-listened, for already my mind turned to Ida. Did I still have time to stop her? Or had she already killed everyone in Crow's Nest and moved on? How exactly does one go about destroying such a creature? And would destroying her also kill me? I would never fall in love, never marry, never bed a woman. I would never say goodbye to Eithne or learn whether Caedmon still lived or whether Grainne was injured. I would never find out who Bramble really was.

I had no choice, though. Ida came from my head, from my evil thoughts, and I had to be the one to destroy her. I hoped I was brave enough. I hoped it wouldn't be very painful when I died.

As we made our way back to the campsite, Owain stumbled and let out a yell.

"My axe!"

He picked up the weapon he had left behind when we entered the mound. I soon found the dagger he had loaned me. His other dagger was there, too, and eventually we found the lamp. It had rolled down a slope and rested at the bottom in a snowy ditch.

Clutching our weapons and the lamp, we staggered back to where we had made camp so many days ago. My legs shook, my stomach growled and I was thirsty enough to drink a river. When we reached our camp, everything was just as we had left it. The oxen grazed nearby, uninterested in our return. Maybe — just maybe — fewer days had passed out here than within the fey mound. I might still have time to stop Ida.

We filled our water flasks from the stream and eagerly gulped down every last drop. Never had water tasted so sweet. My stomach was so empty it hurt, but I couldn't eat with globs of the dead beast all over me. It had dried, hard and crusty, and my clothes were stiff with it. I waded into the icy stream and scrubbed myself all over with a handful of sand, letting the cold waters cleanse me. By the time I finished, my skin was raw and I was so cold I couldn't feel my toes, but at least I was clean.

While I bathed, Owain and Rhiwallon built up a fire. Then they, too, took turns to bathe and even Bramble returned wet and shivering. Rhiwallon dried her off with a blanket. Then we ate. The bread was stale, but the cheese was sharp, the dried meat smoky, the apples sweet and only a little too soft. As I ate, the fog lifted from my brain. It was a wonder I had been able to think clearly enough to answer the dragon's riddles while I was so hungry.

Our meal finished, we prepared to leave. There was no need for discussion about whether we should rest first. Without knowing how much time we had lost in the fey tunnels, the only thing we could do was get to Crow's Nest as quickly as possible.

Owain climbed into the front of the cart and Rhiwallon and I settled ourselves in the back with Bramble's basket squeezed between us. Bramble was still damp, so I wrapped an extra blanket around her. She sniffed at me before tucking her nose into the blanket, but the noise didn't seem quite as haughty as usual.

As we set off with a creak, I looked back towards the mound. Far beyond it, past an expanse of snow-covered hills, stood the lonely figure of a dragon. I raised my hand in farewell and it seemed the dragon dipped her head in response. Then she rose up on enormous wings and sailed away towards the rising sun.

Nothing of note happened for the rest of the day. The oxen trudged along, tireless as always. Rhiwallon and Bramble slept. Sometimes I dozed, but mostly I simply sat there. I should have used the time to plan, but I found I no longer cared. In two days I would face Ida, if she was still in Crow's Nest. In two days I would try to destroy her. And in two days I would likely die. There didn't seem to be much point in planning. Melancholy gripped me for the first time since the start of my journey. It wrapped around my shoulders, clouding my head, as familiar as an old friend.

We halted an hour or so before night fell, and made camp beside a small stream. Rhiwallon didn't offer to hunt and we all knew she had no more arrows anyway. She built a fire and Owain cooked a meal of porridge and flat bread. I tried to help but mostly just got in the way. Bramble sat close to the fire.

The heady scent of our first warm meal in days wafted through the campsite and my stomach grumbled. The sky darkened as we ate, burning our tongues and fingers in our haste. Hot porridge sank down into my stomach, warm and comforting and filling. The melancholy eased just the tiniest bit. The moon rose and it looked much the same as it had the night Rhiwallon was taken, a waxing crescent still a few days away from its darkness.

I slept soundly, waking only once. Owain sat by the fire, a blanket wrapped around his shoulders and over Bramble, who slept on his lap. I missed her warmth against my legs.

We packed the cart the next morning with the quiet speed of folk well accustomed to travelling together. We would reach Crow's Nest tonight and tomorrow I would face Ida.

I walked beside the cart for a while. Long rambles across the length and breadth of Silver Downs always gave me room to create my tales, so perhaps walking would also help me find a solution to the problem of Ida. I thought of, and discarded, a dozen possibilities. Threats, weapons, dire warnings. I doubted any such thing would work.

As we drew steadily closer to Crow's Nest, I still had no plan and failure seemed increasingly certain.

43

DIARMUID

E REACHED CROW'S Nest shortly before dusk and claimed a well-worn bedchamber in an inn called The Midnight Traveller. The bedclothes were threadbare, as was the rug, and the door didn't quite close. Nevertheless, the floor and furniture were dust-free, the dresser bore both an oil lamp and an almost-new candle, and I was thankful to not be spending another night outside.

The heady smells of fresh bread and good soup filled the dining room and my stomach grumbled in eager anticipation. The pub's dilapidated appearance belied the quality of the cook's meals, for the food was just as good as the aroma promised.

"Well, Diarmuid," Owain said as he tore off a large chunk of bread and soaked it in his second bowl of thick barley soup. "What will you do?"

Wiping my bowl clean with the last of my bread, I felt their eyes on me. Even Bramble, delicately lapping at her bowl, waited for my response.

"I'll think of something," I muttered.

They waited. I was very much aware of the other patrons slurping their soup, crunching crusty bread, and asking for more ale.

"I thought you had a plan," Rhiwallon said. Her bowl was mostly untouched for she ate little enough to leave a sparrow hungry. "I thought you knew what you were doing."

I had never said I had a plan, but I suddenly found it hard to meet her eyes.

"I have no idea what to do. I know how to fight a little, but not against a creature like Ida. Physical strength will not be the solution. I think this will require cunning and craft and trickery of some sort. But exactly what, I have no idea."

"Have to find her first," Owain said.

"And she may not want to be found," I said.

"Do you think she knows you are coming?" Rhiwallon asked.

"Probably. She knows how I think, how I react, as intimately as I myself do. She knows I will come after her. She probably already knows exactly what I will do. And she will know how to escape me."

"And if you fail?" Rhiwallon's voice held a challenge. "What then?"

I stared down into my empty bowl and despair flooded my body.

"I don't know. I don't think anyone else can stop her. It has to be me."

They waited, three pairs of eyes fixed on me. Bramble's ears drooped, a certain sign she was unhappy.

"She will destroy us all," I said. "One village will not be enough. Once there is nothing left there to amuse her, she will move on to the next village. Then the one after that, until she has destroyed everyone and everything."

"But why?" Rhiwallon asked. "Why would she want to destroy everything?"

I shrugged. "She is evil. There is no reason for what she does other than that she wants to."

"If she knows you so well," she said. "Perhaps you also know her."

A small glimmer of hope rose within me.

"Perhaps."

I ordered another round of ale to try to distract them. I could not voice my most secret fear about Ida: that I had created evil because *I* was evil. We sat in silence for some time, sipping our drinks. I was absorbed in my thoughts when somebody slammed half a dozen mugs down onto our table.

"Hello there," said a cheery voice. "Mind if we share your table? I'm buying."

Owain tipped his mug at the two men who stood beside us.

"Sit down, friends. It's a mighty thirsty night."

The men settled themselves at the other end of our table. Mugs clattered as the speaker passed them around. He had shaggy dark hair, ruddy cheeks and an air of merriness.

"I'm Braden," he said. "This here is Drust."

Drust barely glanced at us. He was a skinny man with hunched shoulders and red hair. A mist of misery hung over him as he toyed with his mug.

Owain introduced us. I wanted to plan for tomorrow, and enjoy the company of my friends on what might be my last evening, not make small talk with strangers. But the inn had filled while we ate and our party of four needed only half the table. I could hardly tell them to go away, but Owain didn't have to be quite so friendly.

"What brings you to Crow's Nest?" Braden asked.

I froze. I couldn't explain my journey to strangers. Owain and Rhiwallon didn't offer any explanation either. The silence stretched a little too long and eventually Braden laughed.

"No matter, friends." He drained his mug in little more than a swallow and reached for another. "You don't want to talk about why you're here, that's fine with me. Must be a secret quest, eh? Off to save the world?"

We all chuckled and if my laughter was hollow, I doubted Braden noticed.

"Drink up, Drust," Braden encouraged. "Not much point dragging you here to drown your sorrows if you won't drink."

Drust lifted his mug and took a half-hearted sip.

"Happy?" he asked.

"Drust here's mourning the loss of his brother," Braden said.

"How did he die?" Owain asked.

"He's not dead," Drust said. "Yet."

"Is he ill?" Rhiwallon asked.

Drust shook his head.

We waited, confused, and eventually Braden elbowed Drust. "Go on, you'll have to tell the whole story now. They'll hardly believe it, but it makes a good tale."

Drust sighed and fiddled with his mug.

"All right, then." Braden clapped him on the back. "You drink and I'll tell them. Drust's brother has been charmed by a witch. What do you think of that?"

I froze.

"A witch?" Owain's tone was cautious.

"Anything she says, he does," Braden said. "He's completely enamoured."

"What makes you think she's a witch?" Rhiwallon's voice was sceptical, although she shot me an uneasy look.

"She's been making a name for herself here," Braden said. "If she tells you to do something, you do it. People say it's like they forget everything other than the need to obey her. She's made folk around here do awful things. So many families ruined. And now she's got Drust's brother."

"He doesn't *see* her." Drust's voice was barely more than a whisper. "I mean really see her. He sees the lovely figure and the long hair and those innocent smiles. He hears the sweet whispers and tinkling laughs. But he doesn't see what she does, how she destroys everything."

"Can no one convince her to leave?" I had to know what they had tried.

"Nay. Everyone's too scared to go near her," Braden said. "Nobody wants to draw her attention. People are fleeing rather than chance be her next victim."

"Have you tried to reason with your brother?" Rhiwallon asked. "Tell him he's been charmed?"

"I've only been able to speak to him once," Drust said. "His eyes go blank and he seems to stop listening as soon as I mention her."

"I suggested we hit her over the head and drag her away somewhere," Braden said. "But Drust won't be in on that."

"We wouldn't even get near her," Drust said. "She would know before we arrived."

"We don't know that," Braden said. "Not for sure."

"I don't want to be her next target. Not even to save my brother."

"Where did she come from?" Rhiwallon asked.

Both men shrugged.

"She simply turned up one day and never left," Braden said. "We thought at first she might be one of the fey. But then things got nasty and what reason could they have for such a thing? We lead quiet lives here. Nothing of interest to them."

"My brother has never wronged anyone," Drust said. "He's a good man."

"Drust here's given up. He's mourning his brother as if he was already dead."

"I don't see that there's anything else I can do," Drust said.

"Drink up then," Braden said. "There's a plan for you."

Braden changed the topic and I stopped listening. Maybe they weren't talking about Ida. Maybe some other woman here was bewitching men and making them do her bidding, heedless of what chaos she caused. Somehow I doubted it.

We finished our ales and retired, leaving behind the two friends who were well on their way towards becoming exceedingly drunk. As we left, I turned back to Drust.

"What's your brother's name?" I asked.

He looked up at me blearily.

"Davin," he said. "His name is Davin."

44

IDA

*H*E LIVES. AT last, I feel him move towards me once again. I still cannot explain his disappearance, and his reappearance is just as sudden. I hardly know what to think. My hands tremble and my heart beats unevenly. His companions come, too, but not my beast. Perhaps he has killed it. That surprises me, for the beast in his tale did not die.

I am under no illusion as to his purpose, however I might wish it to be otherwise. He comes to destroy me, and that, I suppose, is as it should be. That is what the hero in one of his tales would do, or try to do at any rate.

I created him, one could say. All that he is today is because of me, for I whispered his every thought to him. Without me, he probably hardly knows who he is any more. He was a boy of ten summers when I flared to life in his head. He was hardly old enough to know his own name, let alone his mind. I influenced the man he grew up to be.

We shared his head for nine summers. When his brother went off to war, I told the boy he had no destiny of his own, not like his brother. When his brother handfasted, I told the boy he would never do the same since he couldn't even speak to a woman.

He always believed me. His emotions fed me, fuelled my power.

Jealousy, discontent, misery, loneliness. They bled into me, and drip by drip my power grew. So I continued to whisper and he passed his youth in a daze of melancholy, until the day I was strong enough to leave.

Perhaps once I left, he realised his thoughts had not been his own. It matters not whether he understands. All that matters is that he comes for me. He will not succeed, of course, for my power grows every day. The more I cleanse this town, the stronger I become. I fear nothing, not even the queen of the fey. I could crush her, if I chose, crumble her into dust like last summer's bloom. But I have nothing to prove. Not to her, not to the boy, not to anyone.

My current companion does not have a mind like the boy's. I tolerate his ingratiating presence only because I crave company. After sharing the boy's head for so long, my own thoughts are lonely. So I allow this mortal to stay here in my house and he amuses me somewhat, although already I tire of him. It is of no matter. There are companions aplenty here and I shall find myself another soon, as I did last time.

4 5

DIARMUID

ORNING DAWNED, COLD and clear. When I drew back the curtains, the sunlight was so brilliant it danced off the window pane. It seemed unfair such brightness should be darkened with what I must do today.

Breakfast was steaming porridge, creamy and thick with plump grains. My stomach threatened to refuse even such scant amounts as I forced myself to swallow. I had too many regrets, too many things left undone, unsaid, for this to be my last meal.

Bramble lapped her porridge, her pink tongue swiftly emptying the bowl. My fingers itched to stroke her soft hair and I allowed myself to do so for the first time since I discovered her secret. She stopped eating to gaze up at me with that unblinking stare. How I wished I knew what she thought when she looked at me like that. If only I had realised she was more than she seemed. Even as a friend, I was a failure.

Owain finished his meal and turned to me.

"Diarmuid, you have a plan now?"

The porridge turned to dirt in my mouth and I swallowed with difficulty.

"I need to find Ida."

"And then?" Rhiwallon asked.

I couldn't meet their eyes. "I don't know. I'll talk to her, I suppose. Try to convince her that what she is doing is wrong."

"She won't listen," Rhiwallon said.

"I know. But I don't know what else to do. I don't have any idea how to destroy her."

"You need a plan," Rhiwallon said. "You can't go into something like this hoping you'll figure it out as it happens. She's probably already planning what she will do."

"I know." I pushed away my porridge. I couldn't eat any more of it now. "But I don't know how to stop her, how to destroy her. I've been trying to come up with a plan the whole way here, but I have nothing. I think my tales are the key, but I don't know how they work. Not every tale comes true."

"Which ones did?" Rhiwallon asked.

"Only the one about Ida." I felt somewhat silly at the admission.

"Only one?" she said. "That's it? You've come all this way, just because of one tale that was probably a coincidence?"

"Every seventh son of a seventh son in my family is a bard who can bring his tales to life. But I don't know how the power works."

"How did they deal with it?" Rhiwallon asked. "The ones before you? Your father?"

"I never asked. I've never even heard him tell a tale. He stopped because they came true. I think he might have killed his brothers with a tale. That's all I know."

"Had you asked a few questions before you left home, we could have used that information today," Rhiwallon said.

Her words stung.

"I don't have any choice now. I have to find her and destroy her. That's what I came here for. It's too late to worry about what I should have done." I stared down at my empty bowl. I didn't want to say these next words but I had to. "You should all stay here. It might be dangerous." I corrected myself. "It *will* be dangerous."

"We will stand with you," Owain said and Rhiwallon nodded.

A soft grunt from Bramble indicated her agreement.

"I can't ask that of you."

I could have wept tears of gratitude and sorrow as I met their eyes: plain, simple Owain, a large man with a heart to match; Rhiwallon who glowered at me from across the table and who even now kept her secrets close; and Bramble who gazed at me with fear in her eyes. Would I live to discover the truth about her? Would I have the opportunity to repay their faith? I swallowed hard.

"No, you have come this far with me, but I need to go on from here alone."

"Pish," Owain said. "We're going with you."

And that was that. I didn't have the strength to argue further, not today when I must face Ida and could well lose my life.

"Where do we start?" Rhiwallon asked. "How do we find her?"

"I can find her." I was suddenly confident. "If she knows me better than anyone else, then I also know her."

This was what I had forgotten all along: I knew Ida. I had created her. She knew nothing but what I had given her.

As we left the inn and strode down the street, smoke curled up from chimneys to linger in the air. I tasted it on the back of my tongue, sweet and sharp, filling my lungs and nostrils with its pervading presence. A plump orange cat sunning itself on a doorstep glared a challenge at Bramble as we passed, but she barely deigned to look at it.

We reached a corner. Ahead, the road looked much the same. To the left, a birch tree, bright with new leaves, sheltered the path, and I knew.

"This way."

I followed the branching path past the birch tree and it felt right. A deep certainty centred in my bones. Soon enough we stopped in front of a cottage. It was prettily presented with whitewashed walls and a thatch roof.

"This is it," I said.

"How do you know?" Rhiwallon asked.

"I just know. I feel it. She's here."

Owain stared at the front door, a furrow between his eyebrows.

"What now?"

"We go in," I said. "She already knows we're here."

As we approached the door, it opened, seemingly of its own accord. Bramble stopped, sniffing the air.

"Like I told you," I said. "She knows."

I didn't need to call out, to ask where she was. Unerringly, I led my companions through the front passage, across the kitchen, and down the hallway.

We found her in a sunny back room with serviceable wooden chairs and a long workbench. Despite the morning's chill, the hearth was empty. Ida sat on a chair, hands folded in her lap, her gaze fixed on the doorway as we entered. Sunlight danced over her blonde hair and her plain white dress. Her eyes met mine and she gave a small smile.

"So," she said. "You come at last."

"You knew I would."

"Of course."

"Do you know why?"

The small smile became dazzling and I understood, briefly, why so many did as she requested.

"You want to destroy me. I know you, Diarmuid. I know your lofty goals of educating the simple man, teaching him compassion, honour and nobility beyond what his poor mind can comprehend. That's why people never understand your tales. Don't you know? They can have no possibility of understanding the concepts you try so hard to instil in them."

Her words cut through me, yet it was a distant hurt. It seemed so long ago that my biggest problem was that nobody liked my tales.

"What about you?" I asked. "Do you understand those concepts? Honour, bravery, loyalty. Surely you know of these from my tales?"

Ida tittered, covering her mouth with a delicate hand. Beside me, Owain gave a small sigh and I stiffened. Could Ida turn him on me? She hadn't looked at him once. Her attention, as far as I could tell, was solely on me. I resisted the urge to step away from Owain. If I could not trust him, then I could trust no one.

Ida's eyes, wide open and summer-sky blue, were fixed on mine and her voice was coy.

"What do you hope to achieve with such a question, Diarmuid?" she asked.

"What do you know of the world?" I countered. "The world is dirty, dark, messy, filled with blood and hopelessness and death and despair. Why would you want to leave my head to live in the world?"

"Oh, dear boy," she gasped, laughing again. "I know so much about the world and it's all thanks to you. Every tale you told, I heard it. Every lesson you tried to teach your hapless audience, I absorbed it. But your mind, although a fascinating place with all your agonies and tortured thoughts and hopeless dreams, is not nearly as good as being out in the world. You merely told tales. I bring them to life."

Behind me, Rhiwallon hissed. Owain shifted his feet and I felt like a traitor even as I tensed, wondering whether he would attack me. Bramble stood with ears alert, her eyes suspicious.

"You could hear my tales?" I asked.

"Not just your tales, my dear boy, but your every thought," Ida said.

Could she still hear my thoughts, even though we were now two separate beings? Before I could find a way to ask, Ida turned her attention to my companions.

"Oh, you naughty boy," she said with another tinkling laugh. "You have brought all these friends into my house and you haven't even introduced them. Let me see, who have we here?"

She turned first to Owain.

"Oh my, such a strong man," she said with a simper. "A simple man, honest, hard working. Not much else to you, is there?"

Owain sighed again. I would have glared at him had I dared take my eyes off Ida.

Next she fixed her gaze on Rhiwallon. "You are an interesting one. Do they know the truth about you, I wonder? Do they know from what you run? No, I think not. I cannot imagine the boy would harbour one such as you if he knew the truth."

There was no time to wonder what she meant. for Ida looked now to Bramble. My heart pounded and in my mind, I whispered *no, no, leave her alone.*

"Oh." Ida's tone was surprised. "Does he know?"

"Ignore them," I finally managed. "They mean nothing to you."

"Oh but they do." She arched her eyebrow at me. "For they mean something to you, don't they? Who would have thought you would find such a collection of friends. Such an *interesting* collection."

"They know nothing." I tried not to think about how much they meant to me. I willed my mind to be calm, blank, thought-less. "They barely even know why I'm here."

I wilted a little under the direct stare of Ida's cold blue eyes.

"And why are you here?" Her voice was steely. "Do you really come to try to destroy me, here in my own house?"

"Is this your house? Or did you charm it away from someone?"

Her chin jutted out and her eyebrows narrowed as she glared at me. My chest began to tighten and in just a few moments I could barely breathe. Choking as I fought to draw in air, I met Ida's gaze and she smiled, a slow, calm smile hinting at secrets only she and I knew.

Sweat trickled between my shoulder blades. My feet wouldn't move. I tried to speak, to ask for help, to beg Ida to stop, but nothing came out other than a strangled gasp. I couldn't breathe.

Bramble whined and, somehow, I managed to tear my eyes away from Ida and look down at her. She stared up at me, her gaze showing me her kindness, her goodness and her wisdom. Suddenly I could breathe again. Bramble's doing? I had no way of knowing. I fell to my knees, sucking in deep breaths.

Ida continued to stare at me, sending more tendrils of power winding around me. I didn't dare look at her. It seemed she had no power over me unless I met her eyes. Now there was only one thought in my mind. *Run.* I fled and my companions were right behind me.

Her laugh followed us, trickling like water over stones. As we reached the front door, I heard her voice as clearly as if she stood beside me.

"What a silly boy you are, Diarmuid."

The door slammed behind us. Rhiwallon and Bramble were at my heels as I ran, but Owain soon lagged behind. I halted beneath an old oak tree whose skeletal limbs stretched up to the sky, waiting for spring's new leaves to cloak them. I was horribly aware of how close we still were to Ida. Could she control us from a distance or did she need to see us for her charms to work? Owain gasped for breath as he reached us.

I should say something, thank them for going with me, even if we had failed, but there were no words in my head. I was empty, drained. I had nothing left. I had lost and Ida would continue to destroy Crow's Nest, one life at a time.

"What do we do now?" Rhiwallon asked.

"Go home, I suppose." I stared at the houses around us, although I barely saw them. Houses looked the same everywhere we went. Stone or whitewash. Thatched roof. Herb garden. Vegetable patch. Raven sitting on a low stone fence, head cocked quizzically as it watched us. Chimney with a plume of smoke curling up into the blue sky. How could the sky be so blue on a day like this? Didn't it know I had failed? That countless people would die because I couldn't stop Ida? Despair flooded my limbs, making them too heavy to move. I would stand here until my bones crumbled into dust. I had failed.

"That's it?" Owain asked. "You're done?"

"I tried. What more can I do?"

Bramble glared so fiercely that I had to look away.

"We travelled all this way with you," Rhiwallon said. "We stuck with you through those blasted tunnels and through cold, wet days on the road. We stood with you in her house. Because we believed you were going to stop her. You created something that should have never existed and we believed you when you said you would destroy her. And now you're running away."

"What would you have me do? I tried, but you saw what she's like. You felt her magic worming into your head and under your skin, just like I did. She will turn us against each other, twist us to her will. This is what she does, what she has done to the people here. What can I do against that?"

"Seems you could do more than run away," Owain said.

Shame raced through my limbs and coloured my face.

"You felt her power. I could tell. It was working on you."

Owain shrugged and his face was open and guileless.

"Yeah, I felt it. She wanted to control me. She nearly did."

"What stopped her?"

"You ran away before she fully had me. I followed."

I turned to Rhiwallon.

"What did Ida mean when she asked whether we knew the truth?" I asked. "Who are you running from?"

Rhiwallon's face paled a little and she looked away.

"That's my business, not yours."

"If Ida knows about it, she can use it against you. I'd say that makes it our business too."

"It's not," she said, fiercely. "You think everything is about you, Diarmuid, but it's not. This has nothing to do with you."

"P'rhaps you should tell us," Owain said. "Diarmuid's right. If she knows, she can use it."

She looked up at him for a long moment, but it was Rhiwallon who looked away first.

"You'll judge me," she said. "I don't need that."

"I won't," he said. "You have my word."

There was another long pause before she spoke.

"I'm carrying a child. I'm not sure whether the father knows. I don't have any way of contacting him, don't even know his real name. But if I can get far enough away, maybe he won't be able to find me. And he won't ever find out about the baby."

"Why don't you want him to know?" I asked.

Rhiwallon's face was calm and her voice held nothing but deter-mination.

"If he knows, he'll take the child. And I won't let him. It's as much mine as it is his. More, even, for he isn't the one who has to carry the babe for nine months."

"Why would he take it?" I asked and was rewarded with a with-ering glare.

"For a bard, Diarmuid, you really don't know much, do you?"

"What does that have to do with it?"

Before she could respond, Owain answered.

"Because he's fey. The father."

Rhiwallon nodded, chin held high.

"So the beast…" I said.

She shrugged. "He might have sent someone, or something, after me. More likely, he's completely forgotten about me and moved on to the next poor girl who swoons at his pretty face and fancies herself in love with him."

"I thought the fey were trying to delay my journey." I felt like an idiot even as I said it.

"Maybe," she said. "Or maybe it was me they wanted all along. It doesn't matter now anyway. We got away, and now we've got your creature to deal with. Once this is all over, I'll keep moving. The further I go, the less likely he is to find me."

"I don't think you can run from the fey," I said. "The tales tell—"

Rhiwallon turned her back on me and walked away.

"Thank you, Diarmuid," she said frostily over her shoulder, "but I think *your* wisdom is probably the last thing I need."

Despite all our days of travelling together, despite the frantic search through the land of the fey, nothing I knew about her was true. I had thought Owain was the one Fiachra warned me about, the one who wouldn't be what they seemed. Then I thought it was Bramble. Could it be Rhiwallon he had meant all along?

Owain and I looked at each other in silence, neither wanting to be the first to speak. Bramble leaned into me, her body warm against my leg.

"Did you know?" I murmured to her. "Did you see through her?"

Bramble blinked at me. I leaned down to rub her ears and she gave a little sigh, leaning her head into my hand. At least I had Bramble. Bramble and Owain. These were my true friends right here.

BRIGIT

I HAD GUESSED half of Rhiwallon's secret, but it had never occurred to me that the fey were involved in her life, too. The men we saw at the inn were clearly human, but perhaps the one who hired them was fey. I had never believed in coincidence or chance. If Rhiwallon was running from someone, and we happened across men searching for someone, the two were connected in some way, even if she wasn't the one they sought.

I wondered about the time we spent in the tunnels. Was that an attempt by the fey to capture Rhiwallon or, perhaps, her child? Or was Diarmuid the target? Or perhaps delaying us played some other role in Titania's plans. If she had nothing to do with Rhiwallon's abduction, she gave no sign of it, but that might be part of whatever game she played.

Owain seemed unperturbed. The woman he had claimed as his responsibility carried another man's child, but no doubt he already made and discarded various plans. He wanted to save her. He *needed* to.

In my own form, I could have eased the sickness Rhiwallon experienced most mornings. Perhaps Mother could do even more, for she had much arcane knowledge. She might know a way to shield

Rhiwallon from the fey. My chest tightened and my throat felt thick. I had often wished my abilities would disappear along with Mother's expectations for me, leaving me free to chase adventure and danger. I had wished them away too freely. Here was a woman — a friend, of sorts — who needed the aid I could have given her and I was as powerless as if I had no ability at all.

It seemed strange that the Sight had never shown me Rhiwallon. I had seen Diarmuid and Owain and myself. I recognised Ida the first moment I saw her in person. The white hair, the cruel smile. But the visions had never shown me Rhiwallon. I could only wonder why.

The three of us stood in silence for some time. Owain seemed absorbed in his thoughts. Diarmuid's eyes were downcast, mouth wobbling a little, shoulders slumped. He smelled of defeat.

"So…" Owain said at length. "What now?"

Diarmuid didn't look at Owain as he shrugged.

"Now I go home and admit I failed."

Silence stretched again. I looked from Owain to Diarmuid. I waited and, sure enough, Owain finally found his next words.

"Just like that?"

"Huh?" Still Diarmuid didn't look at him.

"You're giving up?"

Diarmuid hung his head.

"I tried. I really did. I thought I could… I don't know, *do something*. Convince her, persuade her. But she's too strong."

"She'll keep killing people."

"You don't think I know that? What she's doing is my fault. I have to live with that. But I tried. I couldn't stop her. What more could I have done?"

Another long pause.

"Seems to me," Owain said. "Instead of asking what you could have done, maybe you should ask what to do next."

Had I hands instead of paws, I would have applauded. Instead I was struck by an urge to bark long and loud, but I restrained myself. Owain was a fine man and if Rhiwallon couldn't see it, then she didn't deserve him. Maeve certainly didn't.

"You think I should try again?" Diarmuid asked.

"That or give up," Owain said. "But we've come too far for that."

"But what else can I do? You felt her power. How can I destroy something like that? Talking to her is of no avail. She will never be persuaded to stop."

"Hit her over the head. Like Braden and Drust said. Tie her up. Might be able to talk sense with her then."

I had forgotten Drust. Had his brother, Davin, been somewhere in the house while we were there? Should we have tried to rescue him?

"We need to surprise her," Diarmuid said at length. "She won't expect me to return."

"Need to strike fast," Owain said.

"Surprise is as good a weapon as any."

I contributed a bark of agreement.

Diarmuid tentatively stroked my shoulder. He had been odd with me ever since he realised I was more than just a dog. He often reached out to touch me, but pulled back at the last moment. I pressed my nose to his hand. He might be a fool sometimes, but he was still *my* fool.

"What do we do about Rhiwallon?" Diarmuid asked.

They looked at each other in silence. I read the same answer on each of their faces, but neither wanted to be the one to say it.

"I don't know whether we can trust her," Diarmuid said, eventually.

Owain studied his hands. "Don't know. Hope so."

"Maybe she shouldn't come with us next time. Just in case. She's been lying to us the whole time."

"Protecting herself."

"But how do we know she's not still lying? That she wouldn't betray us if she thought it would save her? She helps Ida and Ida helps her hide?"

Owain shrugged. "Either she'll betray us or she won't. Not much you can do 'bout it either way."

47

—————

DIARMUID

HAT WOULD CAEDMON say if he was here? He was born to be a soldier, one who fought and delivered death. I had never thought less of him for it. It was simply not the path I had envisioned for myself. But perhaps to defeat Ida, I needed to become a soldier, too.

"How would I do it?" I asked. "How do I defeat her?"

"Cut her throat," Owain said. "Messy but quick."

I tried to picture myself standing over a bound woman, knife in hand. Owain would hold her steady. There would be blood. Would she feel pain? Would she scream? Beg for mercy? Bile rose in my throat and I pushed the thoughts away.

"I'll find some rope," Owain said. "When we go back, you distract her. I'll get behind her and grab her. Then you tie her up."

"Then I... kill her?"

He looked me right in the eyes.

"Has to be done, Diarmuid. I can do it, if you can't."

I swallowed, hard.

"It has to be me. I have to be the one to stop her."

"I'll get the rope," he said.

Bramble and I waited beneath the oak tree. The street around us was quiet and empty, unusual for this time of day. Perhaps folk stayed inside, away from Ida's attention. My hands shook. Today I would kill a woman. No, not a woman. She wasn't human. I had to remember that. I also had to remember she might be able to read my thoughts. I couldn't think anything I didn't want her to know. I definitely shouldn't think about our plan.

When Owain returned, he had a length of rope wrapped around his waist, beneath his shirt. He was such a large man that the extra bulk was barely noticeable. My small dagger was already in my boot. Would it be enough to slit a woman's throat? No, remember she wasn't a woman, no matter how much she looked like one. She wasn't even human.

There was nothing left to say. Owain clapped me on the shoulder, nearly knocking me off my feet. Bramble met my eyes with a solemn gaze. I wished my feet would sink down into the earth beneath me and root themselves there. But step by step, we returned to the house Ida had made her own.

The curtains were drawn and there was no sign of habitation. But she was there. I felt her sense my arrival almost as clearly as if I could see her. She lifted her head, as if scenting me, and turned towards where we stood. Despite the walls between us, it felt as if we locked eyes.

"Oh, silly boy." Her voice was a mixture of surprise and disappointment. "You're not really going to try again, are you?"

"Let's go," I said to my companions, trying to look confident, despite my quavering voice and shaking knees. I laid my hand against the smooth panels of the door and pushed. It stayed firmly shut. I tried the handle, but it seemed to be locked.

"Let me," Owain said.

I stepped back.

He rammed the door with his shoulder. It splintered with a groan and swung open, wobbling on loosened hinges. Owain started to enter, but I put my hand on his arm.

"It should be me," I said. "I should be the one who goes first."

He met my eyes and I thought he would argue, but he stepped

aside. Inside was dimmer than before, a strange thing since the sky was clear and the sun had yet to lose its morning harshness. Yet inside held the murkiness of late afternoon, when the border separating one thing from another becomes harder to distinguish and one must squint to make out the details of a thing. I shuddered as a chill danced down my spine.

Ida was in the kitchen, a scene of apparent domesticity. She wore a wide apron, the ties wrapped several times around her slender waist. In front of her, on the workbench, was a large pot, a bunch of herbs and a freshly-skinned hare. The wood stove burned, but I felt no heat from it. The knife flashed as Ida chopped carrots and turnips.

"Diarmuid," Ida said and her tone was entirely pleasant. "Whatever are you doing here?"

She spoke as if she had expected me to be gone for the day and I had returned early. Wispy tendrils of power snaked out and wrapped around my mind. My thoughts wandered. I shook my head and steeled myself against her power.

"You know why," I said. "I'm here to stop you."

"What on earth are you talking about?" Ida trilled a silvery laugh. "I'm merely making soup. And you, my boy, are being extremely rude. Aren't you going to introduce me to your friends? You never did introduce them properly last time. I suppose there will be enough soup for us all. I'll add more vegetables to stretch it out."

Where was Owain? He was supposed to be inching around behind her. I suddenly realised what I was thinking and turned my thoughts instead to the ocean. I felt the motion of the waves in my mind and let my thoughts drift with the movement of the water.

Owain stood beside me, gazing at Ida, open-mouthed, his eyes seeing nothing but what she wanted him to.

"Stop it," I said to Ida. "I know what you're doing."

Her eyes were wide and innocent. "You know you're a silly boy sometimes. Now, who are your friends? I think there's one fewer than last time. Where is the pretty girl? My oh my, I suppose you boys must fight over her. Such a pretty little thing."

Beside me, Bramble shifted and growled, so softly as to be almost inaudible. A rush of relief flooded me. Owain might succumb to Ida's charms but not Bramble. But I didn't have the strength to hold Ida down by myself. I needed a new plan. I tried not to stare at the knife in Ida's hands. Tried not to picture myself pressing it to her throat. *Waves on sand, erasing footprints, leaving behind shells and rocks in their place.*

"Do you live here alone?" I asked, stalling.

She smiled, but there was no warmth in it.

"Oh no, I have a companion. A fine young man. He is not presently here but you may meet him if he returns."

Ida finished chopping vegetables and started on the hare. She removed the limbs with a couple of expert slices and stripped the flesh from the carcass. Beside me, Bramble whined and, for a moment, I saw her skinless form on the chopping board, her body being divested of flesh in preparation for Ida's soup.

Then I blinked and the world shifted and Bramble was by my side again. I restrained the urge to touch her, to reassure myself she was really all right. The more Ida knew about my friends, about how much they meant to me, the more danger they would be in. Even thinking about Bramble might put her in danger. *Seagulls flying above the waves, dipping and soaring with the wind.*

But Ida already knew. Of course she knew. She stared at Bramble even as she continued to strip the hare's carcass.

"What a sweet creature," she said. "Is she yours?"

If I said yes, Bramble might be in even more danger. If I said no, perhaps she would think Bramble didn't belong to anyone and add her to the cooking pot with the hare.

"Yes," I said at last.

Bramble's huff was both immediate and expected.

"She's darling," Ida said. "Her spirit fairly blazes from her eyes, but then I expect you know that, don't you?"

"She's just a dog." I carefully kept my voice casual and thought of restless waves. "Not terribly obedient, but she's company."

Bramble turned to me and now indeed her spirit blazed from her eyes. I wanted to beg her to understand, but I looked away and didn't let myself think about how I tried to protect her. Several soft thuds came as Ida finished chopping the hare and threw the pieces into her cooking pot. She lifted the pot and turned towards the stove. This was our chance.

Owain stared at Ida as she placed the pot on the stove and stirred the contents. I kept my mind blank, not letting myself think about how this was the moment in which Owain was supposed to act. I waved at him, trying to catch his attention without alerting Ida, and finally, reluctantly, he looked at me. I raised my eyebrows and tipped my head towards Ida. *Waves and currents. Swirling sand and frothy water.* Owain's face was expressionless, his eyes empty. Ida finished stirring and set down the spoon.

Beside me, Bramble uttered a soft growl. Slowly, the fog cleared from Owain's eyes and, finally, it seemed he actually saw me. Ida turned back to us, wiping her hands on her apron. At the other end of the house, a door opened and closed.

"Ida, my love, are you here?" a voice called.

"Of course I'm here," Ida snapped. "Where else would I be, you silly man?"

Heavy footsteps along the hall. My palms sweated. I pictured an enormous beast of a man, as broad as he was tall, and fierce. When the man entered, I swallowed my surprise. He was rugged, yes, and of muscular physique. But he was no larger than average and had a face which, under other circumstances, I might have described as kind. I saw echoes of his brother in the shape of his forehead and his chin.

"Ida, is everything all right?" Davin asked, scanning us each in turn.

I could not hold his gaze but looked at my feet. I did not want him to see an intent to murder in my eyes.

"Everything is fine," Ida said. "My dear friend has come to visit. And, look, he brought some friends."

Davin eyed me, as if waiting for me to contradict her. *Fish swimming, deep beneath the ocean's surface.* I said nothing.

Ida fluttered her eyelashes at Davin.

"You are home earlier than I expected." For all her soft words, her voice was waspish. "Did I not tell you to take your time?"

"But I didn't want to leave you for so long," Davin protested. "It is not good for you to be alone so much and it is not seemly either."

A shadow crossed Ida's face and she turned her back on him.

"Will you stay for lunch?" she asked me. "The soup will be ready in a while."

"No." I meant to say something further but unease built within me. Those few moments while she stirred the pot might have been our only chance.

"Oh, what a pity." Ida pouted.

Davin frowned. "Why would you want other company, my love? Am I not enough?"

"No, you silly man," she said. "You're boring. You never talk about anything interesting. In fact, I'm growing quite tired of you."

There was barely time for a look of disappointment to cross Davin's face before Ida turned to Owain. Bramble barked once, an urgent warning.

"Kill him," Ida said, with a nod towards Davin. "Do it for me."

Owain's eyes were glazed and his face blank as he drew a dagger from his boot. It took him only four steps around the bench to reach Davin.

Davin looked disappointed, rather than fearful.

"My love, you cannot mean this," he said.

"Oh but I do," Ida said, with a vicious smile. "And you would please me by not resisting."

"Owain—" I started, but I was too late.

Davin's eyes were still locked on Ida as Owain raised the knife and stabbed him in the heart. Davin staggered and blood ran down his chest, but he never took his eyes off Ida. I was too stunned to move until something splattered on my face. When I wiped it, my hand was covered in blood.

Owain pulled his knife from Davin's chest. Davin swayed for a moment before crumpling to the floor. He gasped and tried to lift an arm towards Ida. Even as he died, his gaze was fastened on her. Ida merely nodded and turned back to the stove.

"You may leave now."

I couldn't take my eyes off Davin's body. A pool of blood seeped around him, slowly stretching across the wooden floor. When I finally looked away, Owain was gone. Even now, he obeyed her.

Bramble barked and I stumbled after her. As we left, I glanced back. Ida stirred the contents of the pot on the stove. She looked calm and unperturbed. To see her, nobody would know that a man lay in his own blood beside her.

Bramble barked again and finally I followed, a sudden chill wracking my body. The sun was bright and warm as we exited the house. It soaked into my skin, although it didn't ease the chill. I had failed again, and this time a man had died.

I stumbled along, seeing nothing and aware only of Bramble's presence at my side and the pain in my ankle until we caught up to Owain. He stood in the middle of the path, staring at the bloody dagger in his hand.

"Diarmuid." His voice was full of anguish. "What have I done? Tell me, what have I done?"

"You killed a man, Owain." The words were bitter on my tongue. "And he didn't even raise a hand to defend himself."

"No," he said, then screamed to the sky. "No."

I left him and headed for the inn. First Rhiwallon, then Owain. Would Bramble be next? Would I stand in Ida's house as each of my companions betrayed me in turn? I suddenly realised I was alone. Bramble had stayed with Owain.

In my mind, I saw Fiachra. He sat at a desk, a sheaf of papers spread out in front of him. *I will be watching you on your journey,* he had said. *If you have need of me, call and I will come if I can.* He had not told me how, but somehow I knew. *Fiachra,* I screamed silently, holding his image in my mind. *I need you.*

Fiachra seemed to lift his head and look right at me.

"I am coming, Diarmuid," he said.

My mood lifted slightly as I hurried to the inn. Fiachra would know what to do. There would be a way to destroy Ida. I burst into the inn. He would be there, I knew it. But there were only two men in the common room and neither was Fiachra. My heart sank. Even

Fiachra had abandoned me. I stumbled towards the staircase that led up to our room.

"Ho, there," the innkeeper called. "Can I get you something, friend?"

"A bath," I muttered. "Send up water."

If he noticed the blood on me, he said nothing.

I was relieved to find our bedchamber empty. A boy brought a bucket of water and I washed thoroughly. Blood swirled in the bowl, leaving it muddy-red. I pulled off my clothes and left them in the corner of the room. I would not wear them again. Even if the blood splatters came out, they would always remind me of the day I watched my friend stab a man to death.

As I dressed, heavy footsteps announced Owain's arrival. My stomach twisted. How could I face him after what he had done? I kept my back to the door and finished buttoning my shirt.

"Diarmuid."

Despite my intention not to look at him, I did. His face was pale beneath splashes of blood. Sympathy surged at the anguish in his eyes, but I squashed it down.

"She made me do it," he said. "It was a charm. I would never do such a thing. I've never killed a man without a contract."

"You're a killer." I spat the words at him. "No wonder you do what you do for a living."

I pushed past him and left. He didn't try to stop me. Bramble waited behind him in the hallway. I met her eyes and her disapproval made me feel even worse. The last thing I needed was to be judged by a dog.

I stormed down to the common room and ordered an ale. I intended to drink until I fell off my chair. Then perhaps I might forget, if only for a while, what a failure I was.

4 8

DIARMUID

MIGHT HAVE expected one of my companions to join me in the common room — Bramble perhaps — but, hour after hour, I sat alone. I lost count of how many ales I drank. At some stage, I must have told the innkeeper to keep them coming because as soon as I finished one, the next would appear beside me. Eventually he brought me a bowl of soup.

"You need to eat, my friend," he said softly, depositing the bowl by my elbow. "Too much ale without food is not good for a young man."

He didn't wait for a response.

I intended to ignore the meal, but my stomach growled when its savoury scent hit my nostrils. The room was bright and almost empty of patrons when I sat down. Now it was more than half full. Lamps drove back the encroaching darkness and a small fire blazed in the hearth. I must have sat here for hours, noticing nothing but my own miserable thoughts.

My one remaining friend was Bramble, but she had stayed with Owain. Owain the killer. Owain who had stabbed to death a man who never even raised a hand in his own defence. My stomach churned abruptly and the soup came back up, splashing into the nearly empty bowl. The innkeeper appeared promptly at my side.

"I'll take that," he said, reaching for the bowl. "And I think perhaps you've had enough ale for today, my friend. How about you go upstairs and get some sleep?"

"Do you have any spare bedchambers?" I couldn't go back to our chamber.

"Sorry, we're all full up tonight." If he wondered at my request, he didn't ask. "You're welcome to sleep in the barn, though."

I found an unoccupied corner in the hayloft. I had left my blood-splattered coat in our bedchamber, but I found a horse blanket that didn't smell too strongly. I wrapped myself up and burrowed into the hay. My head spun and my stomach churned. I vomited twice more, although I managed to avoid the hay.

I felt thoroughly wretched when I woke. My head throbbed, my stomach still churned and my mouth tasted bitter. The loft reeked of sickness and sour ale, making my stomach roll and empty itself yet again. I washed outside in a horse trough, the water cold and none too fresh. The early morning glare burned my eyes and my head throbbed even harder. I stumbled into the inn.

I sat at a table in a gloomy corner, far away from the windows and the brightness of the fire, and massaged my throbbing temples. Then suddenly I realised somebody sat across from me. Bitter comments welled on my tongue as I looked at Fiachra. About how long he had taken to arrive, how he should have warned me that all of my companions would desert me and I would fail. But I said nothing.

"I told you this would be harder than you expected," Fiachra said.

"You should have told me everything you knew. I could have been more prepared."

"It is not my place to tell you what may or may not happen. I cannot foretell the future. The choices you make are your own decision."

"I think you know more than you pretend to."

He didn't respond.

"What do I do now?" I asked.

"What do you think you must do?"

"Must you answer everything with a question? Why can't you tell me what to do?"

Fiachra merely looked me in the eyes, his face as implacable as ever.

"This is your quest, Diarmuid. Is it finished?"

"How can I ever finish? I can't match her power. She is turning my friends against me, one by one."

It wasn't until I said it that I realised I no longer blamed Owain. Ida had charmed him, like she charmed everyone else who carried out atrocious deeds at her instruction. Still, I didn't want to face him. I couldn't bear to look in his eyes and see my friend and know he had killed an innocent man.

"Tell me about your journey," Fiachra said.

The words began to spill from me and I told him everything. About finding Bramble and how we almost died in the woods. Owain rescuing us. Finding Rhiwallon. The journey through the tunnels and the beast and the dragon. How I tried and tried again to defeat Ida. How I failed.

"So you intend to give up," Fiachra said.

There was no judgement in his tone, but I squirmed at his words.

"I'm not exactly giving up," I said. "But I have no other options. Ida is too powerful."

"You have power of your own, Diarmuid."

The tiniest flicker of hope flared.

"My tales?"

He looked at me and waited.

"But how could telling a tale defeat *her*?"

Still he said nothing.

Slowly, awkwardly, my thoughts came together and I discovered I already knew the answer.

"She came from inside of my head. Her strength, her power... it all came from my words. So perhaps I could defeat her with a tale, if I knew how they worked."

It sounded ridiculous. Whatever power I might have, surely Ida was far stronger. And when I deliberately tried to make a tale come true — in the fey tunnels — it didn't work. I picked at a splinter poking out of the table. It dug into my thumb and a bead of blood formed. I stared at the blood with disinterest. The pain was nothing. It could be someone else's hand for all I felt.

"Perhaps the aim is not to defeat her," Fiachra said. "Perhaps you need to mend the breach that is broken. Restore that which should not have been divided."

"Do you mean I need to send her back into my head?" My stomach suddenly felt hollow and my chest tightened until I could barely breathe. "I can't. Even if I could somehow get her back in there, I can't live like that. Knowing she's in there. Knowing she watches everything I do, listens to everything I think."

"You've lived like that for years already, Diarmuid."

"But that was different."

"How?"

"I didn't know she was there. I didn't know she was alive."

"Why does that matter?"

"I don't want to live like that."

"Ida is your responsibility," Fiachra said evenly. He rested his arms on the table, looking completely at ease.

"But how would I even do it? Do I tell a tale about a muse who comes to life and is returned to the bard's head?"

Fiachra shrugged.

"Can I wait until tomorrow?" I asked. "I can't go back yet. I need… time. To prepare."

"Time for more people to die?"

"You didn't see what happened yesterday. It was awful. Davin didn't even raise a hand to stop him. He just stood there."

"Remember, Diarmuid, this is what she does. She charms folk into doing what she wants, and they have no choice but to obey."

"Surely they could resist. Surely there was a part of Owain's mind that was still his own. He could have stopped if he wanted to."

"Have you asked him?"

My cheeks burned. "No, I haven't spoken to him. Not since… Not since we argued."

"Owain is your friend, Diarmuid. He acted on Ida's will. This is her fault, not his."

"I can't risk taking him with me again. What if she orders him to kill me? Would he do it?"

"Perhaps. It seems to me that the people she charms have no control over their actions."

"Will you come with me? Surely she couldn't charm you."

"I cannot interfere. I can only advise, and only because you asked me to. What you choose to do, and how you do it, are your decision alone."

"You would leave me to go to my death rather than interfere?"

He looked at me evenly but didn't answer.

"So I'm on my own," I said, bitterly. "All of my companions have deserted me and I'm left to face Ida alone."

There was a huff from the floor and Bramble glared up at me. I hadn't even realised she was there. As I met her gaze, the tightness in my chest eased a little.

She huffed again, then looked to Fiachra. He met her gaze and they stared at each other silently for the longest time. Eventually, he nodded.

"Your task has been great, little one, but it's almost at the end. You need to be strong a little longer."

Bramble dipped her head, as if in thanks.

"I guess we should go then." I felt like I had been excluded from a private conversation. "Might as well get this over with."

"Eat first," Fiachra said. "This is the day you either complete your quest or fail entirely."

I was suddenly famished. The innkeeper brought fresh bread and steaming bowls of porridge. I set a bowl on the floor for Bramble and ate with gusto.

Fiachra didn't speak again until I had eaten my fill.

"I can teach you how to deal with Ida once she is back inside your head. It will be different this time, for now she knows what it is to be alive. She will resist, and you must be prepared."

"But once she is back in my head, she won't be able to resist any more, will she?"

Fear clenched my stomach and already I regretted having eaten.

"She has power now that she didn't have before. She may continue to fight and you need to learn how to fight back. Now, close your eyes. Picture a box. Can you see it? It need only be small but you must see it clearly."

I concentrated on the blackness inside my mind and, slowly, a wooden box formed. It was a storage chest, like what one might use for clothes or blankets. I focused on it until all its edges were clearly defined.

"I see it."

"Good, hold the box there. You need to be able to see it, even when you open your eyes. This is where you will put Ida. As soon as you see her in your mind, open the box and push her inside."

"How do I push her?"

"With the force of your mind. It may help to exhale, quickly and strongly, at the same time. Push her into the box and replace the lid. Then you must hold the lid in place."

"How long do I hold it?" I looked into his dark eyes and he stared back at me, waiting for me to find the answer for myself. "Forever. I will always have to hold down the lid so she can't escape."

"It will be hard at first but, after a while, you will hardly need to think about it."

"What will happen if she gets out of the box?"

"I can't answer that. She may have the power to influence what you say and do. She might even be strong enough to take over your body. To make it hers."

"Could she force me into the box?"

"Perhaps."

I realised I held my breath and slowly let it out. I had always known I might not survive my quest, but I had never anticipated living with Ida in control of my body, watching helpless and trapped while she carried out her terrible deeds.

"I don't think I can do this."

"This is your decision, Diarmuid, and yours alone. I cannot tell you what you must do. I can only advise you to listen to your heart. What does it say?"

I didn't want to answer, but he waited patiently, his face calm and his hands relaxed on the table.

"I have no choice," I said at length. "She is my fault."

"Be strong, Diarmuid. As soon as Ida is back inside your head, you must get her into the box. She will be confused and disorientated for a few seconds and that is your chance. Once she regains her senses, she will fight you."

"I guess I should go then."

Bramble stood up. I looked down at her, a scruffy terrier not even as high as my knees.

"Are you sure you want to come with me?" I asked. "It will be dangerous."

She glared but didn't deign to huff.

"I know you want to help, but I... I might not be coming back again. I can't promise to look after you."

She stalked over to the door and waited. Somehow, the knowledge that I wouldn't be alone eased my fear the tiniest bit, even if my sole companion was a small terrier who may or may not turn out to be one of the fey.

4 9

DIARMUID

OON BRAMBLE AND I stood yet again on the doorstep of Ida's stone cottage. I carried no weapon except for the dagger in my boot, yet I felt strangely calm. I looked up at the bright blue sky. A single cloud drifted lazily. This might be my last view of the sky. I took a deep breath, letting the cool air fill my lungs. Perhaps my last taste of the air outside Ida's house. This was it. I would find a way to force Ida into the box in my mind, or die trying. I had my tales and, if that failed, I had my dagger. I would not live with her controlling my body. I would kill myself first.

I knew better than to ask Bramble again whether she was sure she wanted to accompany me, but there was something else I needed to say. I crouched down beside her.

"Thank you." I stroked the silky hair on her chest. I wanted to touch the torn ear and run my fingers over the red scar on her shoulder and flank, but I didn't. Hair already grew over the wounds and in a few weeks they would no longer be visible, except for the damage to her ear. "You've been a good friend to me. I had hoped you might come back to Silver Downs once this is all over. But if something happens to me in there, get out straight away. Go and find Owain. He'll look after you if I can't."

She blinked at me, just once.

"I know you understand me, even if I don't know what sort of creature you are."

Bramble extended her paw and touched me gently on the cheek.

"I hope I get a chance to find out who you really are."

She looked towards the door.

"You're right. Let's get this over with."

I stood, wincing at the pressure on my injured ankle. The door had been mended since Owain broke it down and it didn't resist us this time. The hallway was dim and silent, a memory of days spent in a fey tunnel. Nothing existed outside of this moment, just Bramble and I walking along the hallway, past a rack of coats and scarves. Past a pair of men's boots standing tidily against the wall. Past closed doors that led to other rooms. Lonely accoutrements of someone else's life. The house smelled of herbs and furniture wax and fresh bread.

I could feel Ida. She was in the back room where we had found her on our first visit. I had feared she might be in the kitchen with Davin's body still lying there, his blood staining the wooden floor, his limbs stiff and his eyes blank.

Doubt started as a quiver in my stomach. I hesitated and Bramble looked up at me, a question in her eyes.

"Perhaps I shouldn't do this," I said. "She's happy here. Free."

I turned back towards the front door.

"She won't hurt anyone else if I leave her alone. She just wants to live, in a real body, in the real world."

My feet already carried me back through the doorway.

"It was a mistake to come here. I see now that things aren't as bad as I thought."

Bramble barked once, short and sharp, and Ida's influence subsided. Anger and shame warred within me. Anger that she would try again to control me and shame that I had allowed it so easily. This was what it felt like to be one of her victims. Her thoughts had seemed as natural as if they were my own.

I clenched my fists and strode back down the hallway, Bramble at my side. I would not let Ida send me away. This would be our final confrontation. The culmination of my quest. One way or another, this meeting between us today would decide both our futures.

Ida sat in the back room, in the same wooden chair as on our first visit. She wore a plain white dress, the skirt covered with a white apron. She looked innocent. Harmless.

I caught myself this time before the thoughts could control me. Now that I knew she sought to influence me, it was easier to recognise when my thoughts were not my own.

We stared at each other in silence. It was still somewhat strange to see her in front of me. A figment of my imagination made real. She didn't look quite as I had imagined. I hadn't given such a hard glint to her eyes or such a cruel twist to her mouth. Those features were hers alone.

I fidgeted, growing impatient as the silence lengthened, and finally it was I who spoke first.

"You know why I am here."

"Of course." Her tone was entirely pleasant, as if we discussed something of no more consequence than the weather or what I ate for breakfast. "And you know I won't allow it."

"I can't let you continue doing this. You're my responsibility. I brought you into this world, even if I didn't mean to."

"Poor boy. Such a burden on you, isn't it. Such terrible powers. Such responsibility for one so young."

Her words wormed into my brain. They burrowed, trying to elicit self-pity. At my feet, Bramble growled softly. I clung to the sound, letting it too seep into my mind, and it eased Ida's hold.

"I didn't ask for this ability." My voice sounded strong. "I didn't know what I was doing when I created you. I didn't know I could do such a thing. But I did it, and I take responsibility for it."

"What do you intend to do about it, Diarmuid? How strong are you? And where are your companions? They seem to be deserting you, one by one. Look at you now, standing there with nothing but that creature at your side."

"My companions have been through much for me. They travelled a long way, even through the realm of the fey, because they believed in me."

"They never believed in your quest, Diarmuid. Each chose to accompany you for their own selfish reasons. You were a way for them to achieve what *they* wanted, not what you wanted."

"That's not true."

"Isn't it? Think about it. The girl is running away from the father of her child. You provided a disguise for her escape. Who would think to look for one such as she amongst a small party of friends travelling together? And the man, he flees his own demons. A wife who hates him, an occupation that allows him to indulge his desire for murder. We all saw what happened yesterday. He could barely stop himself from bathing in poor Davin's blood."

"Stop it. You're twisting it all. Everything you say is only part of the truth. They are my friends."

Ida's stare flicked down to Bramble and my breath caught in my throat. *Not her,* I thought before I remembered that I must not think anything I wouldn't want Ida to know. *My mind is an ocean. Restless waves. Impatient currents.*

"You know this creature is not what she seems." Ida's voice was light and her eyes sparkled as if she shared a joke. "But do you know exactly what she is? Have you ever wondered how she came to be in such a form? It is a punishment, surely, and a grave one indeed to be taken from your own form and forced into another. What secrets does this creature, the last of your companions, hold?"

"Leave her alone." My voice was less steady now. "She's done nothing to you."

"Oh, but she has. She's comforted you, aided you. Look at her now. She desperately wants to speak, doesn't she? But she can't, except with barks and whines and growls. Do you wonder what she might say, this fiery little companion of yours, if she could speak? Shall we find out?"

My heart stuttered as my eyes locked with Bramble's. I saw fear in them, but also hope.

"Please," I said. "Don't do anything to her."

I didn't need to look at Ida to know she smiled.

"Oh, I'm not going to do anything to her. I'm going to undo what has already been done."

50

BRIGIT

A RUSHING WIND filled my ears. The world blurred, fading and twisting as I fell. My body felt wrong. Stretched. Contorted. Too big. I wanted to tuck my tail between my legs and howl.

The scents were gone. I couldn't smell Diarmuid or Ida or the lingering traces of Davin's death. The only odours left to me were bread and furniture polish. Without my sense of smell, I was blind. I whined, but the noise was wrong. My mouth didn't work properly and my teeth were the wrong shape. My tongue was too small in my mouth. And my tail, where was my tail? I crouched on the wooden floor, confused and shaken. When I tried to speak, actual words came out, although my voice was croaky and my mouth numb.

"D-Diarmuid?"

I reached for him as I stumbled to my feet. Hands. Long fingers, a scar on my wrist where I had burnt myself through carelessness in the kitchen. My own hands. I looked down. Legs, feet shod in boots. I stood on human legs. I wore the same work dress as the day the fey girl had taken my form from me. With shaking hands, I touched my face, my hair. My heart leapt. I touched my injured ear. It felt misshapen, twisted.

Diarmuid backed away, bumping into the wall.

"Diarmuid?"

Words felt wrong. I had become so accustomed to Bramble's barks and whines, whimpers and growls. A dog can express such a variety of emotion within the limits of its speech.

"What are you?" Diarmuid whispered.

I took a step towards him and stumbled. My legs shook, but slowly I remembered how to walk without the certainty of four legs. I moved closer to Diarmuid, wanting to be near him. Wanting his arms around me. I wanted him to pick me up and hold me to his chest, where I could feel his heart and smell his scent.

"Don't," he said. "Don't come any closer."

I stopped, confused. "Diarmuid? What's wrong?"

His mouth twisted and his face was a furious red. "I don't know who, or what, you are, but you need to stay over there."

My heart shattered. My chin wobbled and I blinked away tears. I would not cry in front of him. Ida laughed, a soft tinkling like wind chimes.

"Oh my. Look at your little dog now."

Diarmuid glared at her.

"Are you satisfied? You've taken all of my friends from me, one by one. What's next?"

Ida smiled coldly and her hands gripped the arms of the chair so hard that her knuckles were white.

"What did you expect from me? Gratitude? You kept me locked inside your head for all those years. You owe me something for that."

"I owe you? I created you. Without me, you wouldn't exist."

"And what a fine existence it was. Trapped in your head, witness to your every thought and emotion."

Ida looked at me and I froze. *Please don't turn me back into a dog.* Had I still been Bramble, I might have whimpered. As Brigit, I stayed silent and looked her in the eyes. I was strong. My mother raised me to be confident, capable, a wise woman.

"My dear, you would be horrified if you knew even a tiny bit of what goes on inside his head," Ida said. "I've seen his true nature. You might think you know him, but you see only as much as he wants you to. He won't show you the darkness inside."

"I know a little more than you think," I said, and although my voice was hoarse and scratchy, the words were even enough. "Who do you think he confided to night after night? Why, the dog, of course. The dog always knows everything."

5 1

DIARMUID

SHE WAS PERHAPS a year or two older than me and wore a grey dress with scuffed boots. Her dark hair came loose from its bun and wisped around her face. This was the woman I had seen from time to time, the one I had hoped to find the courage to speak to. The one I had thought of when Caedmon asked whether there was someone he should meet while he was home.

I backed away. My legs were weak and my face hot. Secrets I had shared with her flashed through my mind. She knew everything about me, things I had never said to another person, things I said only because she was just a dog. I never expected to one day be face to face with a person — a woman — who knew those secrets.

She was strong, this woman who used to be Bramble. Ida was sending out her power, trying to weave a hold around her, but if the woman noticed, she didn't show it. At first she held herself uncertainly, as if still figuring out what form she inhabited. I recognised the moment she realised she was human again, the moment she decided to fight. She straightened her shoulders and stood tall. Then she glared at me and I saw Bramble in those wide, unblinking eyes.

"You needn't worry," she said in a voice that sounded unused to human speech. "I'll keep your secrets. But first we need to deal with her."

I turned back to Ida. It was time to be strong but, unexpectedly, I found myself pitying her. This would be the end of her freedom, here in this room with its workbench and its sturdy chairs. This was where her tale ended.

"Ida, it's time to finish this," I said. "I'm going to tell you a tale. It's about a bard who brings his muse to life. Somehow, she draws from him enough power to escape out of his head, and she goes off into the world. But something is wrong with the muse. She is dark, twisted."

"She is what she is," Ida said, "because everything she knows comes from the bard's head."

Her power swirled around me, seeking, burrowing. I pushed it aside and concentrated on my story.

"When his muse leaves, the bard knows he has done something very wrong and is determined to make things right again. So he goes in search of her, and when he finds her, he tells another tale, a new tale about how the muse returns to the bard's head. And as he speaks, his muse, just like the one in his tale, is drawn back inside of him."

I waited, bracing myself for her intrusion into my head. But Ida continued to sit in her chair, an almost bored look on her face.

"What's wrong?" asked the woman who used to be Bramble. "Why isn't it working?"

"I don't know," I said through gritted teeth. How could it not work? Even Fiachra thought this was what I needed to do.

"Think," not-Bramble said urgently. "Think of when you created her. What was different about that tale?"

Ida laughed. "Have you *still* not figured it out? We are in for a long day, aren't we?"

"Ignore her," the woman said. "Focus."

I cast my mind back, trying to ignore my welling panic. When I told my very first tale, the one in which I created Ida, it was the night before Caedmon left to become a soldier. I remembered thinking that the days ahead without him would be long and empty.

"I was lonely," I said. "Despondent. I was afraid that Caedmon might never return. And afraid he would return changed."

"How is that different from when you told other tales?" the woman asked.

I hesitated, but then the pieces came together and I began to understand.

"I am nervous before I tell a tale, anxious that my audience won't like it. But once the tale begins, I am calm. All other emotion disappears. The words flow from somewhere deep inside of me. That first time, I didn't know everyone would hate my tales. I was fully focused on the tale, on my words, on how I felt. My feelings are the key."

"Try it," the woman said. "Let the emotions fill you and overwhelm you, then tell your tale."

Perhaps she was right. I had nothing to lose if she wasn't.

Ida laughed. "You're never going to figure it out at this pace."

I blocked out her words, closing my eyes and taking a deep breath. I thought about the reasons for my journey, my desire to make up for what I had done. I thought about the journey itself and what we had gone through to get this far. I thought about my friends, one by one.

Owain, a killer by trade but a kind, gentle man who had saved both my life and Bramble's.

Rhiwallon, a woman fleeing the man she feared would take her child.

And then there was Bramble. My smallest companion. The one who lay beside me night after night while I poured out my fears and my hopes. Who stood beside me as we faced down the fey, a dragon, and Ida. The one who was really a woman, trapped in another form, and I never even realised.

And now here I was, alone. Betrayed by my companions, one by one. None of them was who I thought they were.

A warm hand grasped mine and I recognised Ida's intrusion into my thoughts. No, not alone. I still had Bramble. In a different form, perhaps, but still, she was here.

I told my tale again and this time I let my emotions infuse my words. I wove all my hope and horror, heartbreak and happiness into the tale. I let myself feel — really feel — the devastation of realising that my tales were responsible for such awful things. I opened myself to the hurt and abandonment of Caedmon leaving to become a soldier. I felt the jealousy I hid away when he handfasted. My resentment that he had everything: a destiny, a career, a beautiful wife. My envy at his confidence, his ability to talk so easily to women, his bravery.

I felt the horror of climbing up to rescue Rhiwallon and being pursued by the beast that had stolen her away. The terror of facing the dragon, the awful hopelessness of realising our fate would depend on the ability of each of my companions to answer a riddle. The frustration of knowing I had gotten us into such a situation and that I would need help to get us back out.

All of these emotions welled up inside of me, filling my heart and my limbs and my head, until I thought I would either burst or lose my mind. I poured it all into my tale. It was still a dark tale, but now there was also hope. There was wonder and beauty and love. It was unlike any tale I had ever told before.

As I reached the end of the tale, where the muse is drawn back into the bard's head, I opened my eyes. Ida still sat in her chair, but her face was pale and her eyes wide. She gripped the arms of the chair, her knuckles white and straining. I could feel her struggling, still trying to control my thoughts, still trying to influence Bramble. Her power had little strength over me while the woman who used to be Bramble held my hand, but still she tried.

My mind began to fill with a presence both strange and also instantly familiar. I kept my eyes on Ida as she faded, her essence drawn back into my head. I said my final words. The tale was ended. For the first time in many weeks, I saw her in my mind. Her delicate figure, the translucent skin, her long white hair.

Ida writhed and screamed. I closed my eyes and concentrated. I imagined the wooden box, its lid already open in preparation. Recalling Fiachra's instructions, I exhaled and somehow *pushed* at Ida, shoving her in the direction of the box. At first she didn't seem to notice. I managed to push her right up against the box before she realised. Then she fought back.

As Ida struggled, the pain was as real as if she beat a hammer against the inside of my brain. It hurt terribly, but I fought to ignore it and stay focused. Already my legs trembled and I panted from exertion. No matter how hard I pushed, Ida was always a little bit stronger. Then she was gone and instead I fought a black raven that somehow seemed to be both inside my mind and right in front of me. Wings beat against my face and sharp claws raked my arm. Something inside my mind that I recognised as my self, my own essence, was pushed towards the box. Panic grew, sharp and nauseating.

"Fiachra," I screamed. "Help me."

Then he was there in my head.

"This is *your* mind, Diarmuid," he said. "*You* control what happens in here."

His presence calmed me, helped me focus. I resisted, pushed back, managed to get away from the box. The raven disappeared and Ida returned. We grappled, struggled, fought. Then, so suddenly that I wasn't even sure how it happened, Ida was in the box. I slammed down the lid.

The box trembled and I held the lid secure. My mind-self had hands now and they gripped the lid so tightly that the edges cut into my fingers and my own blood stained the wood. Surely the box would break apart from the force of Ida's anger. But, somehow, it held and gradually her resistance lessened.

Eventually I thought I could probably make my way back to the inn while still holding down the lid. Fiachra was gone. I hadn't even noticed when he left.

I opened my eyes to find the room dark. The woman who used to be Bramble was curled in the chair in which Ida had sat. She looked at me, a question in her dark eyes.

"Don't speak." I finally noticed how my legs trembled and sweat dripped down my back. "I can't..."

We left Ida's house. I barely noticed the dark skies or the empty streets as I stumbled back to the inn. Beside me, Bramble was silent.

All my attention was focused on the box. Ida had settled for now, likely a trick to lure me into thinking she had given up. As soon as my attention wandered, she would spring from the box and take over my mind. The possibility of being trapped and helpless in my own body kept me focused, despite my fatigue.

Owain and Rhiwallon were in the common room when I reached the inn. I didn't look at them, couldn't risk being distracted by talking to anyone. I focused on the stairs, making my way up them with such single-mindedness that I hardly noticed when I crashed right into someone. He swore at me and Bramble muttered a soft apology, tugging my arm to lead me away. I reached our bedchamber and collapsed onto the bed, my weary body sinking into the softness of the straw mattress. Exhaustion flooded my limbs, making them heavy, and my concentration wavered.

Suddenly Ida sprang out of the box. Again, I grappled with her, pushing her back. She gained the upper hand and I gritted my teeth, pushing harder. This was my mind and I would *not* be a prisoner in it. I eventually managed to confine her again.

By that time, my hands trembled and I was dizzy with exhaustion. Then someone sat beside me on the bed, someone who smelled like sunny days tinged with lavender. A hand gently touched mine and the scent of fresh bread filled my nostrils. Something pressed against my lips and when I opened my mouth, a small piece of bread was deposited in it.

I hadn't realised how hungry I was. I kept my attention on Ida's box and when I opened my empty mouth, more bread appeared. Bramble didn't speak as she fed me, piece by piece. Once I had eaten my fill, she held a mug to my mouth and cool ale trickled down my throat.

I moved from the bed to a wooden chair so I wouldn't fall asleep. All through the night, I kept my attention focused on the box. Ida struggled for a while, but eventually she stopped. Perhaps she slept, or perhaps she wanted me to think she slept.

Bramble, Owain and Rhiwallon took turns to sit up with me through the night. From time to time, someone would hold a mug to my lips or offer me bread. I ate and drank to maintain my strength, feeling neither hunger nor thirst. Ida stirred occasionally, pushing at the lid for a while, but then settling again.

When eventually I was sure I could keep part of my attention on the box, I opened my eyes. Daylight filled the bedchamber. Bramble sat cross-legged on the bed, but Owain and Rhiwallon were absent.

"I think she is contained." I yawned. I was exhausted and drained, both physically and mentally.

"Does she still fight?"

"Sometimes. Mostly, she's just waiting."

I stood and stretched. My back was stiff from spending the night in the wooden chair. Ida moved, cautiously, testing my attention. She found the lid of her box securely fastened and sank back down into stillness.

"There's water here if you want to wash," Bramble said.

I nodded, too exhausted to speak if words weren't necessary.

"I'll wait downstairs," she said.

I pulled off my shirt, which was stiff and sticky, and washed the sweat from my body. The shirt reeked, but Davin's blood still covered my spare.

The common room was mostly empty of patrons. My companions gathered around one table and a sole man sat at another. He was hunched over, almost asleep, a mug of ale by his hand. He looked like he had been there all night. The scent of yesterday's mutton still lingered in the air, mixed with the stench of stale ale.

"Thank you," I said. "I couldn't have done this without you."

"Is she really back in your head again?" Rhiwallon asked. She held herself stiffly and didn't look at me. I couldn't tell whether she was still mad at me or afraid.

"She's still fighting, but I'm learning how to keep part of my attention on her. It's getting easier."

I turned to Bramble.

"Who are you? How did you come to be a dog?"

"I was stubborn," she said, with a hint of a smile. "I refused a task from the fey and that was my punishment."

"What was the task?"

"A journey. They wanted me to go somewhere, but wouldn't tell me where or why."

Was the journey she took the one they intended? She guessed where my thoughts led.

"Yes," she said. "I think this is where they meant for me to be."

"Why?"

She shrugged. "They have their own reasons, and are unlikely to share them with me. It doesn't matter. They achieved their aim."

"What was that?"

She shook her head and a faint blush tinged her cheeks.

"What is your name?" I asked. "Your real name? I can't help but think of you as Bramble."

"Brigit. But I don't mind Bramble. I've become quite used to it."

It was hard to think of her as Brigit when I saw Bramble every time I looked at her. Brigit's eyes were much like Bramble's, and like Bramble, her emotions flared from them. I hadn't often stopped to think about what she felt before, but I could read her eyes now: hope, confusion, and something that looked a lot like hurt.

The innkeeper brought bowls of porridge. I barely tasted my meal, focused as I was on Ida's box. Perhaps if I concentrated on it all day, I would be able to maintain my focus long enough to sleep for a while tonight. I suspected, though, that it would be several days at least before I could safely sleep.

I hardly knew what to think of the fact that Bramble was really a woman. Brigit. I tried not to think of the many confidences I had shared with her as she lay beside me at night. My cheeks were hot and Owain gave me a strange look, but he didn't speak until he had finished his porridge.

"Well, Diarmuid." He pushed away his empty bowl. "What now?"

"I suppose we go home," I said.

Rhiwallon made a strangled sound and buried her face in her hands. Owain leaned close to murmur something to her.

"What's wrong?" I asked.

A sharp kick bruised my ankle.

"Idiot," Brigit hissed.

Belatedly I remembered Rhiwallon's secret.

"I'm sorry," I said. "I—"

Another kick and Brigit glared at me. I stopped talking and ate my porridge in silence. Other patrons wandered into the room, some in pairs or groups and some alone. They ordered meals or ale and chatted with their companions. It was strange to see the world continue in such an ordinary fashion. After last night, it seemed everything should be different somehow.

"Where is your brother?" Brigit asked. "The druid?"

I shrugged. "He has probably left, gone back to wherever it is the druids live."

"He's very knowledgeable," Brigit said. "He taught me much."

I waited, but she didn't elaborate.

After the meal, we returned to our bedchamber to gather our belongings and start the journey home. I was right behind Bramble — Brigit — as she opened the door, and I saw what she saw: the room was gone.

We walked into an enormous cavern. And we weren't alone. The last time we confronted the fey, there was a multitude of them. This time we faced only the king and queen.

5 2

DIARMUID

BRIGIT STEPPED FORWARD. With a sigh, I followed. Rhiwallon and Owain were close behind me. It might have been the same cavern in which we last encountered the fey, for the walls were composed of layers of orange and brown and red rocks, and the ceiling arched up high out of sight.

Oberon looked grave, but there was a hint of something about him that suggested he might be more compassionate than she. Titania stood stiffly with her hands on her hips. Her dark hair flowed unrestrained to her waist. She wore a scarlet dress that swept the cavern floor and dipped so low over her chest that I averted my eyes, blushing. Titania looked at me, eyebrows raised, but said nothing.

"Why are we here?" I asked finally, tiring of her silent game and too exhausted to care about being polite.

"To account for yourselves, of course." Titania looked at us each in turn, her gaze lingering on Brigit. "So, you have found a way back to your own form."

"It was one of your kin who stole my form from me," Brigit said and although her tone was respectful, it also contained a clear challenge.

278

Titania's mouth turned up into something that might have been a smile if her face wasn't so cold.

"You refused an instruction. We made you comply."

"What right do you have to give me any instruction? Had she told me why she wanted me to go, I would have gone. You have no right to demand and expect me to obey."

"Mortals are stubborn and stupid. There is no point trying to explain something you can't understand."

"You could have given me a chance to understand."

"It matters little whether you understand or not." Titania's glare was icy. "You have done what we wanted. The reason is of no consequence."

"It mightn't matter to you, but it does to me," Brigit said. "Nobody should be forced into another creature's form. To have to learn how that body works, how it responds. To have everything they know about the world suddenly taken away."

Titania glared at Brigit.

"You are stubborn, just like your father. You had better be careful if you don't want to end up the way he did. You came too close this time. Cross me again and it will be worse for you."

Brigit looked like she wanted to say more, but Titania dismissed her with a slight lift of her chin and looked towards Rhiwallon.

"He suspects you are with child," Titania said. "He knew there was a reason you ran."

Rhiwallon paled, but she straightened her shoulders and stared back at Titania.

"Do you intend to tell him where I am?" she asked.

"He hasn't asked me."

"Was it his beast that stole me away? Or yours?"

Titania barked a laugh. "That beast was no fey construct. We have no need to conjure such a creature. If he knew where you were, he would have simply taken you himself."

"Then where did the beast come from?" Rhiwallon asked. "And why did it take me into your lands?"

Titania lifted one slender shoulder in an elegant shrug.

"It should not have been able to access my realm. The one who made such a creature is powerful indeed, but you should ask your own companions for the answers to your questions."

Titania turned to Owain then and looked him up and down. Owain stood silently, waiting for her to finish her slow inspection.

"You chose a strange path," Titania said and her tone was almost friendly now. "But you should choose your friends with more care. When she discovers your secret, she will turn on you."

She gave Owain no opportunity to speak, but turned now to me. I quailed a little. Ida stirred, perhaps sensing a momentary lack of attention, and I redoubled my focus on holding the lid securely on her box.

"Bard," Titania said. "Your quest is complete."

"So it would seem." My voice sounded strong and confident despite how I trembled inside.

"Mortals are not meant to have power such as yours. But your line is strong and determined. Unnecessarily stupid at times. I shall make the same offer to you that I have made to every seventh son of a seventh son in your family. I can remove your ability. I can take it away from you so you never bring your words to life again. You can be free to tell your little tales without fearing the consequences."

"Why would you do that?"

"My reasons are my own and they need not concern you." Titania's voice was impatient now. "Do you accept or not?"

"What will you give me in exchange?"

"What will I give you? Why would I give you anything? I have made an exceedingly generous offer to remove a troublesome ability. I needn't give you anything in exchange for making your life easier."

I hesitated, sorely tempted. If Titania took my ability, I could be a bard again. And this time, I would study my craft. I would not be so proud about telling the learning tales my audience despised, but would create tales of beauty and wonder, courage and heroes. But if I retained my ability, I could never tell another tale.

"If you want something from me, you must offer something in exchange," I said. "You cannot take my ability, but I can freely give it to you. And I do not intend to do that unless you offer me something of equal worth."

All pretence of a smile faded from Titania's face and I trembled as her face twisted in fury.

"You stupid mortal. Do you think to bargain with me? I have already been generous with you. I have given something of immense value, to you at least, but it seems you are too stupid to realise it. I shall not give you anything further in exchange. You will give me your ability in payment for what you have already received."

I didn't bother to ask what she meant. "Then I decline your offer."

"Foolish man. Why are the bards of your line so stupid? I make this same magnanimous offer to every one of them and they all refuse."

I held my tongue, for none of the responses that came to mind were terribly polite. But now I knew that Papa, too, had rejected Titania's offer.

"Go then," Titania said. "Stupid mortals. You have no idea how good I am to you."

I blinked and the cavern was gone. We again stood in the doorway of our bedchamber. The hallway stretched behind us and the murmur of voices and the crash of plates rose from the common room.

"Well, that's that." Brigit sounded as dazed as I felt. "She could at least have left us closer to home."

53

DIARMUID

I TRIED NOT to look at Brigit as we prepared to depart The Midnight Traveller. Clearly the task she refused had something to do with my quest. But why was Titania so interested? Did she know I couldn't succeed without Brigit? And if so, why did she care?

As we hauled our packs out to the cart, the oxen snorted and seemed as keen to be off as we were. The day was bright and sunny, perfect for travelling. The snow melted a little more every day and the wrens and robins had returned.

It was hard to concentrate on keeping Ida's box closed while doing other things, perhaps harder than I had expected. I clung to Fiachra's belief that it would become easier with time. Could she still hear my thoughts? Was she also witness to everything I said and did? Now that I knew how my ability worked, I understood why Ida was what she was. If indeed everything she knew came from my head, then all she knew of the world was from my tales. I had never told a tale where the hero succeeded because of his courage or where light triumphed over dark. Never had my tales culminated in a happy ending or the banishment of evil.

Caedmon tried to tell me. The night we sat up late in front of the fireplace after his betrothal party seemed like a lifetime ago. Was he still alive? Or had I killed him with that poorly-chosen tale about the soldier who was beaten to death by his new bride's menfolk? And what of Grainne? Did I harm her, too?

How many others had I hurt? All because I presumed to try to teach my audience to be better than they were. Why had I thought it was my place to do such a thing? Over and over people told me they wanted to hear of heroes and love and happy endings, but I resolutely continued to tell my dark tales of danger and injury.

I could never tell another tale. I couldn't be trusted with them. I would never forgive myself for the havoc Ida had wrought, but at least I was ignorant back then. I no longer had such a defence. And if there was any possibility that Ida still listened in on my thoughts, then I must be careful to only think such things as I would want someone else to know. Perhaps the right kind of thoughts could change her. Perhaps I could insure against the possibility that she might escape again. I could teach her honesty, courage and humanity. If she knew more of light and beauty, perhaps things would be different next time. Owain's voice intruded on my thoughts.

"I'll go settle the account," he said.

Brigit offered to go with him and I was left alone with Rhiwallon. I caught her glaring at me as she tossed a pack into the cart. She wore her travelling clothes today: long pants, her freshly restocked quiver hanging from a belt, and her red hair tucked up under a scarf.

I ducked my head, pretending to search for something in my pack. The air felt thick with our silence until Rhiwallon stomped over to stand right in front of me where I couldn't pretend I didn't see her.

"I wouldn't have betrayed you," she said, crossing her arms over her chest. "I can hardly believe you would think that. I thought we were friends."

Surprised, it took me a few moments to think of a response.

"I couldn't be sure. Her power was strong. She charmed Owain and he's the strongest man I know. I thought she would try to turn each of you against me. And I thought..."

"Say it." Rhiwallon's tone was withering.

"I thought that if she offered to protect you, to hide you, you might help her in return."

"She's evil, Diarmuid. She needed to be stopped. I knew that just as well as anyone did. I wouldn't have traded my own security against stopping her. I didn't come this far just for my own benefit."

"You didn't?"

Rhiwallon's glare became even frostier.

"But you didn't even believe me. I thought we just happened to be going in the same direction."

"It's a hard thing to believe when someone you barely know tells you they've brought a creature of their imagination to life. I partly believed you, just not completely. Not until I saw her. When I stood face-to-face with her and felt her power, then I believed. But by then you had stopped believing in me."

I hung my head, thoroughly ashamed.

"I'm sorry. I don't know what else to say. I'm sorry about the way I treated you. That I didn't believe in you. And I'm sorry about that night in the barn." I finished in a rush. "You deserved better than that. Caedmon set it up and he wouldn't listen when I tried to tell him no."

Rhiwallon's smile was gentle and for perhaps the first time, I didn't feel like she mocked me.

"I understand. But does she know?"

"Who?"

"Brigit."

"Of course not. I've not told anyone."

"But you'll tell her sooner or later, won't you?"

"No, never."

"It's not a secret you can keep if you intend to build a future with her."

My mouth fell open and I stammered.

"What- Why- I don't know what you mean."

Rhiwallon rolled her eyes.

"It's obvious, Diarmuid. Anyone who has eyes can see the way you feel about her."

"Do you think she knows?"

"Probably, but she's waiting for you to make the first move."

"But what would I do?"

"Just tell her. Tell her how you feel."

"I couldn't."

"Then the two of you will part ways and you'll probably never see her again."

"Is there nothing else I can do?"

"It's time to be a man, Diarmuid. If you want her, you have to tell her."

I swallowed hard and stared down at the ground.

"What will you do now? Where will you go?"

Rhiwallon shrugged. "Away from here. As far as I can. Somewhere he will never look. Where even Titania won't be able to find me if he thinks to ask her."

"I wish you luck," I said. "I hope you find somewhere safe."

"Thank you, Diarmuid."

Rhiwallon tossed the final pack into the cart and climbed in after it. It seemed the conversation was over.

5 4

BRIGIT

@S WE LEFT Crow's Nest, things felt strangely familiar and yet also so different that I wondered how I ended up here. Once again I shared the cart with Diarmuid and Rhiwallon. Only this time, instead of being tucked into a cozy basket with a blanket that Diarmuid wrapped snugly around me, I sat with my back against a pack and my leg pressed against Rhiwallon's.

Diarmuid sat on the other side of Rhiwallon. That didn't surprise me. He would hardly want to be where he might accidentally touch me. I hardened my heart. He had hurt me enough. It was time to remember who I was: Brigit, wise woman. Or intended to be a wise woman, at least. What would Mother say when I finally arrived home? Had she worried about me or had the Sight showed enough for her to make sense of my strange journey?

We spoke little as the cart trundled along and we passed the day absorbed in our own thoughts. My heart lifted at each sign of spring's approach: young shoots of grass in a sunny patch where the snow had melted, tiny new leaves on birch and beech, pale yellow catkins on hazels. The only sign of human habitation was a trail of smoke from an unseen chimney.

We were midway between towns as the light started to fade from

286

the sky. Owain directed the oxen away from the road and halted beside a row of shrubby birch that would provide some cover from overnight winds. I clambered out of the cart, my legs stiff after hours of sitting. Diarmuid, Owain and Rhiwallon quickly fell into their usual routine. I hesitated, unsure how to contribute, for as Bramble I was expected to do nothing other than curl up in my basket and watch.

"You could make some tea," Rhiwallon said, her tone almost friendly.

She seemed almost as startled as Diarmuid to see me in my own form for the first time. Owain, on the other hand, greeted me with a firm hug and a complete lack of surprise.

"Tea," I said. "Good idea."

A search of the area around us elicited a handful of sage and thyme. Diarmuid had already made a ring of stones for a fire pit and built up a pile of dry twigs and dead leaves. Rhiwallon started the fire as usual. I emptied a flask of water into a pot and nestled it amongst the flames.

Rhiwallon returned with a pair of hares before the water had even boiled. For a moment, I felt like Bramble again, curled comfortably by the fire, watching as Rhiwallon skinned and gutted her catch. As Bramble, I was always hopeful she might offer me the innards and was always disappointed when she tossed them into the fire. As Brigit, I could make a decent enough meal of the innards, although I preferred the roasted meat, smoky from the fire and dripping with hot juices. Rhiwallon chopped the hares into chunks, skewered them on sticks and arranged them around the flames.

Diarmuid sat on a blanket and removed his boots. Should I sit next to him or on the other side of the fire? The stiffening of his shoulders indicated he had noticed my nearness, but he feigned intense interest in his boots. That made up my mind. If Diarmuid wanted to pretend I didn't exist, I would sit right next to him. He said nothing as I sat on the blanket, but he edged over a little to give me room. I waited a minute or two, but he obviously didn't intend to speak.

"Do you still see the ravens?" I asked.

Diarmuid started and for a moment actually looked directly at me. His face was pale and haggard with deep shadows around his eyes. He hadn't slept since he captured Ida.

"I- What- How do you know about that?"

I shrugged and looked away into the fire. It had been more of a lucky guess than anything, but Diarmuid wouldn't know. I was being stubborn, as usual, for what good could come of forcing his acknowledgement? But my obstinate heart wanted to know he saw me, and as a woman, not a terrier.

"The ravens are still there," he said, at last. "Everywhere I look, I see them. They are Ida, or they are from her. I suppose it doesn't matter which. Either way, they are meant to remind me she watches me. She's always watching."

"Is she secure?" I asked.

"As secure as I can make it. Whether it will be enough, I don't know."

"What will happen if she gets loose again?"

He plucked a handful of grass and shredded it restlessly.

"Fiachra said she might be able to take over my body. Maybe she won't want to, though. Maybe she will want to leave again. Fiachra thought that if she became strong enough to escape again, I might not be able to restrain her. And all this will have been for nothing."

"It's not for nothing," I said, surprised at how fierce I sounded. "You did what you had to do, regardless of what happens in the future. Maybe that's enough for now."

"Do you think so?" Diarmuid looked at me with shining eyes. "Do you really think I've done enough to make up for what she did? The people she killed. The lives she ruined. The families she destroyed. They haunt me."

"Of course they do." I tried to soften my usual no-nonsense tone. "That means you care. There would be something wrong with you if it didn't haunt you."

"But I can never make it up to them."

"No. You can't. But what you can do is ensure she never gets loose again."

Diarmuid nodded but made no further reply. Rhiwallon fussed with the roasting chunks of hare, turning them so they didn't burn. Fat dripped and sizzled in the flames, sending up an aroma that made my mouth water. Owain returned from taking care of the oxen and eased himself onto a blanket on the other side of the fire. Such a familiar scene from our days of travel and yet at the same time, now so strange.

I missed Bramble with an intensity that surprised me. The steady balance of four paws. The pleasure of a wagging tail. The acute hearing and sensitive nose. The sniffs and barks and growls she communicated with. The simplicity of needing nothing more than a meal, a warm basket, and a kind hand to stroke your back. The freedom of returning an affectionate caress with a nuzzle of the head or the press of nose against skin.

The sun had set, leaving us in darkness except for the fire. Rhiwallon passed around the sticks of skewered hare. For a moment, I hesitated, expecting Owain to cut the meat for me and drop it into my bowl. Then I remembered and reached for a stick. The meat was sweet and tender. When I finished, I tossed the stick into the fire and watched it crumble to ash.

The herb tea was ready and I portioned it into mugs. I passed them around, then returned to my spot on the blanket. I wrapped my fingers around my mug, relishing the warmth as I waited for the tea to cool a little. Normally, I would either sit on Owain's lap or curl up in my basket, and it felt strange to sit in front of the fire in my human form.

"Tell us a tale, Diarmuid." Rhiwallon's tone was studiously casual.

Diarmuid flinched. "I don't tell tales anymore."

"But you know how it works now, don't you?" she asked. "You figured out what makes them come true."

"To an extent," he said. "But there might be more parts to the puzzle. Other ways to bring them to life. I won't risk it."

"Then tell the right sort of tale," I said. "One that won't hurt anyone if it comes true."

Diarmuid's gaze flicked up to meet mine ever so briefly. He was tempted, I knew. It must hurt to feel like he couldn't tell his tales anymore. After all, he had always expected barding would be his livelihood once he became accomplished enough. What would he do now?

"Try it," I said. "Keep your emotions in check, watch what you think, and tell only a tale that won't hurt anyone. Learn how it really works."

If I was honest with myself, I wasn't encouraging Diarmuid solely for his own benefit. I wanted to hear a tale, something grand and adventurous. I had now tasted three of the four things I had always wanted. Danger, mystery, adventure. I had yet to experience romance, but I could live with three out of four. My appetite wasn't dampened in the slightest.

True, they weren't what I had expected. Instead of adventure being a glorious thing where I was filled with courage and fire and reckless-ness, it was wet and cold, dirty and hungry, and sometimes miserable. There were times I didn't know whether I would live through it.

But it was also exhilarating and fabulous. My skin tingled and my feet itched to start walking, go somewhere, have another adventure. But I couldn't. It was time to resume the life intended for me. Time to go back to possets and charms, potions and cures. But perhaps the tales of a good bard might give me adventure and mystery and danger once more.

"I don't think so," Diarmuid said, at last. "Not tonight anyway."

55

DIARMUID

I AVOIDED BRIGIT as best I could on the journey home, although I was always conscious of exactly where she was. Each night as I wrapped myself in a blanket and lay staring up at the stars, I missed Bramble's warm body. The ache inside me seemed much larger than the absence of a dog. From time to time, I considered approaching her, but my cheeks heated at the very thought and I didn't know what I wanted to say anyway. It just seemed there was something between us left unsaid.

The four of us travelled together as far as Tors. From there, Owain and Rhiwallon were headed to a larger town some days travel away. Although neither mentioned an intention to stay together, it seemed that was the case. I was sad to part ways with them. Owain wrapped me in his big arms, almost crushing my ribs with his hug. Rhiwallon surprised me with a quick kiss on the cheek. I blushed fiercely, remembering how my hands explored her bare breasts the last time she kissed me, and Brigit gave me an odd look.

Brigit took Rhiwallon aside and spoke to her quietly. She handed Rhiwallon a small packet and they hugged. I couldn't be sure, but I thought Rhiwallon cried.

"What did you give her?" I asked later.

Brigit's face was shuttered. "Nothing you need be concerned about."

Brigit and I departed from Tors on horses purchased at Owain's expense. One day, when I had money of my own, I would pay him back. The horses were somewhat old and not terribly fast, but they were quicker than travelling on foot. We spoke little as the day passed although Brigit seemed to spend an awful lot of time glaring at me.

I spent the hours concentrating on Ida's box. I questioned every thought, wondering whether it was my own or hers. How much of what I knew of myself was Ida? I still didn't know whether she could hear my thoughts, but in case she could, I would ensure I thought nothing that would give her any power over me.

Despite everything, I found it hard to wish Ida away entirely. She had been my constant companion since my tenth summer, but I regretted bringing her to life, and I regretted that I hadn't tried to learn about my ability earlier. I found myself sinking down into melancholy and changed my line of thought. I couldn't afford to linger over thoughts like that anymore.

As we drew closer to home, the landscape became more familiar. The snow on the distant hills was melting and grass had started to grow in the fields. Birds circled overhead, too high up to tell their species. I could smell the faintest trace of a familiar scent I had always associated with home.

We reached the start of the woods stretching all the way to the edge of Silver Downs and Brigit reined in her horse.

"There is where I leave you," she said, with another glare in my direction.

I stammered something incoherent. She rode away without another word.

"Wait," I called.

Brigit turned her horse and came back. She paused in front of me, one hand holding the reins, the other on her hip, her eyes flashing. I recognised that look.

"Why are you angry at me?" I asked.

"For a bard, you don't seem to know much." Her horse stomped and snorted, as eager to be away as she.

"What's that supposed to mean?"

"How could you not know, Diarmuid? You were *surprised* when you saw me."

"I didn't know you were..." *A woman*, my mind supplied. *The very same woman I was trying to find the courage to speak to all those weeks ago.* "Human."

"What exactly did you think I was then?"

I must have looked like a fool, my mouth opening and closing uselessly.

"I don't know," I said, eventually. "I just knew you were something else. Something more."

"And yet Owain had to point out even that much to you." Brigit's tone was bitter. "I would have thought all those tales might have taught you something."

"They did. I just didn't expect to find something straight out of a tale right in front of me."

Brigit gave me an incredulous look.

"What has this whole journey been if not something straight out of a tale? You create a creature in your mind that somehow comes to life, one of our party gets abducted by a beast that most certainly shouldn't exist, we spend days searching bewitched tunnels, and answer a dragon's riddles. Is this not exactly like a tale? Even without what happened to me?"

"Well, yes, but..." Nothing I said would make this better.

Brigit rolled her eyes at my ineptness.

"You could have tried to tell me," I said. "Why didn't you?"

My feelings were confused. I was hurt that the little terrier who had been my companion for weeks was not what she seemed to be. Surprised she was really this fierce creature who glared at me until I wanted to sink into the ground. Amazed it was a woman with whom I had shared my darkest secrets and deepest hurts. Hopeful that perhaps, despite everything, there might be a tiny chance of a future for us.

"Why didn't I tell you, Diarmuid?" Brigit's tone rang with sarcasm. "Do you know how many times I tried? Every time I communicated with you, I hoped you would realise I was no ordinary dog. And you know what? You never noticed. You were too wrapped up in yourself and your quest. The noble bard who releases evil into the world and goes on a heroic journey to redeem himself and humanity."

"You make me sound pathetic. But I *did* release evil into the world and I *did* have to do something about it."

"Yes, yes, I know." Brigit sounded tired, as if all the fury was gone and there was nothing else left. "You know what, Diarmuid, just go."

If I left now without saying what I needed to, I would never have the courage to try again. I took a deep breath as she started to turn her horse around.

"Brigit, there's something I need to say."

She paused but didn't turn around. I took a deep breath. I had to do it.

"No," she said.

"But I have to—"

"I'm not interested." Her voice was calm and indifferent. "Whatever you want to say, it can go unsaid."

"No, it can't." I couldn't leave without knowing I had at least tried.

She turned back to me and I was struck by the lack of emotion in her face. She didn't care. Despite all we had been through together, Brigit didn't care about me.

I flicked my horse's reins and fled. There was no point saying anything. She was right. There was nothing left to say. At least I hadn't humiliated myself by telling her I thought I loved her. My eyes filled with tears and I dashed them away with an impatient hand. This would not be the homecoming I had hoped for, returning with Bramble, or Brigit, at my side.

Of course it won't be, Ida said. *You didn't really think it would be anything like you imagined, did you? Oh, poor little Diarmuid, you really did. What a shame.*

I ignored her taunts and redoubled my focus on keeping her box secure. Ida fought back, briefly, but seemed to have little fight in her yet. That would change. She would regain her strength and it would be harder to keep her locked away. But I would become stronger too, Fiachra said. And with time and practice, it would be easier to keep Ida in her box. Maybe one day I would hardly even know she was there.

5 6

DIARMUID

THE SUN was setting by the time the horse brought me in sight of the Silver Downs lodge. Lamplight shone from the windows and I could just make out a stream of smoke from the chimney against the red-streaked sky. My family would be sitting down to eat soon. If I hurried, I might be home in time for dinner.

I anticipated a raucous greeting with my brothers crowding around and Mother fussing over me. There should be news by now of whether Caedmon had arrived safely at the campaign front and I would finally learn whether my tale had injured Grainne.

Would they find me changed? I didn't know how to account for my journey. Ida had been defeated, that was obvious. But they would expect me to have destroyed her. How would I explain I had made her a part of me again? They would see only evil when they looked at me, Ida staring out through my eyes.

By the time I dismounted, my hands trembled so hard, I could barely hold the reins. I led the horse into the stable and busied myself with rubbing her down and filling the grain and water bins. I knew well enough what Papa would say if he discovered I went inside without tending to my horse.

I approached the lodge, my heart pounding. Never before had I been nervous about entering my own home. Ivy crept up over the grey stone again now that the frosts had passed, but otherwise the lodge looked the same as ever, from the outside at least.

As I reached the front door, I hesitated. What if it was locked? Should I knock? Wait for someone to come out? There was no reason for anyone to come outside until morning. I turned the knob and the door swung open with the smallest creak. A flood of warmth and *home* rushed out over me. Roasting mutton, the smoky scent of a fireplace, a faintly astringent smell I had always associated with the house being cleaned. I was home at last. I strode in and made my way to the dining room.

Fiachra was the first to notice me as I stood in the doorway. He inclined his head very slightly towards me, almost a *well done* motion, and I nodded back. Next to him was Mother. She half stood as I entered, then paused with a hand held over her heart. She looked tired and worn, and I regretted I had grieved her. At her side, Papa reached out to her. He looked older than I remembered.

On Papa's other side was Eremon with Niamh beside him. The children were absent, likely already put to bed and watched over by a servant. Eremon's face was grave, but Niamh's eyes widened when she saw me. Eremon wrapped his arm around her, as if to protect her.

My eyes stung and for a moment I thought I might cry in front of all of them. Then Ida stirred. I slammed the lid back down on her box and locked away my emotions. My brothers were all there, all except for Caedmon. It was Eithne who was missing, her and Grainne.

"Where's Eithne?" I asked.

Mother blanched and fled. Papa rose, but Fiachra stopped him with a hand on his arm and a few soft words. Papa lowered himself to his seat while Fiachra went after Mother.

"What happened? Where's Eithne?"

Silence stretched while my brothers all looked towards Papa. His mouth opened but nothing came out.

"She's gone away for a while," Eremon said finally.

Away? Eithne never went away. The look on Papa's face told me this was not the time for questions about my sister.

"Is there enough dinner for me?" I asked instead, sharpening my focus on Ida's box as she stirred again.

"Of course, son." Papa seemed relieved that this at least was a question he could answer. "Come, sit."

There were several spare chairs and I chose one next to Marrec. He said nothing, only passed me a bowl of root vegetables. I never expected him to say much and it was comforting to find that Marrec, at least, was the same as ever.

Someone handed me a platter of mutton and I served myself a large portion. The meat was juicy, the vegetables crisp and fresh — a far better meal than I had eaten for weeks.

There was silence at the table as we ate. Neither Mother nor Fiachra returned and Papa merely picked at his meal. My stomach clenched and my appetite fled. I caught the eye of Sitric, who sat opposite me.

"Have you started scribing yet?" I asked.

He flinched and almost dropped his mug.

"Yes. It's… fine." He swiftly crammed a spoonful of vegetables into his mouth.

As I looked around the table from brother to brother, they all avoided my eyes, and I finally realised what was wrong. They were scared of me. Scared that whatever had happened to Papa's brothers would happen to them, too. I pushed away my half-eaten meal and stood, almost knocking over the chair in my haste.

"I'm going to get some sleep," I muttered.

My bedchamber looked the same as ever, a little dustier perhaps and somewhat musty. I flung open the window and leaned out, taking a deep breath of the evening air. The sun had fully set and everything was shadows and darkness. Nobody had asked about my journey, but perhaps Fiachra already told them.

I took another deep breath of cold air and the faint scent of fire tingled in my nose. The moon was full, shining white and cold. Far beneath my second floor window was hard earth, grassy but devoid of rock or fence. I leaned out a little further. Would I die if I fell from this height?

A knock at the door interrupted my morose thoughts just as Ida roused. Fiachra didn't wait for an invitation. By the time I closed the window, he leaned against the wall.

"They're afraid of me, aren't they?" Bitterness edged my voice.

He met my eyes evenly. "They fear what they don't understand."

"I'm still me. This has always been a part of me. They just didn't know before."

"You need to show them."

"Haven't I already done enough?" I disliked the whine in my voice but was too tired to conceal it.

"In a way, you've done too much. And they fear what else you can do."

"Can she hear everything I say?"

"Does it make any difference?"

"I suppose not. Where is Eithne? And Grainne?"

"Eithne has her own destiny to fulfil. And she has gone to do it. Grainne, too, has her fate. They are together and, so far, they are safe enough."

"But where are they?"

I knew he wouldn't tell me.

"Is there any way to get rid of her?"

Perhaps speaking Ida's name would have no effect but there was a chance, a small one, that it might give her strength. I would never again speak her name.

"In truth, Diarmuid, I don't know."

57

IDA

OW DID HE trap me in here? I am stronger than him, yet here I am. Is this to be my world now? Confined to a box inside Diarmuid's mind? I cannot survive like this. Not after I have become accustomed to the smells and sounds and sensations of the world outside. In here I feel nothing. Not the gentle kiss of the breeze in my hair or the warmth of the sun on my arms. Not the crunch of ice under my feet or the wetness of water against my skin.

I am strangely weakened. I used so much energy to fight him that I have nothing left. I am smaller, shrivelled, drained.

Before, I could roam his mind. Explore his thoughts and feelings. Now the box in which he restrains me blocks almost everything. I can still, if I concentrate, hear his thoughts, feel his emotions. But it is muted, distant, and it takes too much of my meagre energy.

Time passes. Or perhaps it doesn't. I sleep, or maybe I stop existing for a while. When a little strength returns, I try to get out of the box. But he, too, has grown stronger and I can't fight him for long.

So I am trapped. But I will bide my time and conserve my strength. When I am stronger, I will escape again. And this time I will destroy him before he can restrain me again.

58

DIARMUID

OVER THE NEXT moon I found it difficult to fit back into my old life. Mother tried to pretend she wasn't afraid and my brothers grew more relaxed around me. I took long walks across Silver Downs, trying not to think about Bramble's absence, and spent my days learning how to function while still keeping Ida's box secure. I could finally sleep for a couple of hours, although I woke with a start every time, wondering whether Ida had escaped. I didn't tell any tales, didn't even let myself think any.

In the late afternoons, I sat in Eithne's herb garden as the sun slipped behind the tree-shrouded horizon. Blooming shrubs filled the air with sweet fragrance and often a lone warbler continued to sing long after the rest of his flock had bedded down for the night.

Lost in my thoughts one afternoon, I didn't notice Papa until he sat beside me on the wooden bench. I said nothing and it was some time before he cleared his throat.

"You've had a difficult time, son," he said.

"I did what I had to."

Papa stared down at his hands and I waited.

"We hoped not to have a seventh son. You were unexpected. Your mother was taking herbs to prevent a pregnancy."

I nodded, biting my tongue. There was so much I desperately wanted to ask.

"I didn't intend to pass on this curse." His voice broke a little.

"It's not a curse," I said. "It is what it is."

"As soon as I realised what I could do, I stopped telling tales. I've never told another since."

"Titania?" I asked.

He nodded, meeting my gaze only briefly.

"Why didn't you tell me? If I had known, I could have been prepared. I would have been more careful."

Anger rolled inside me and Ida stirred. I breathed deeply to calm myself and she subsided again.

Papa kept his gazed fixed on his weathered hands and sighed heavily.

"I tried, once, but you wouldn't listen."

"You should have tried harder."

"I know." A long pause. "At first, we thought… We thought that if we said nothing, if we let you determine your own future, perhaps you would choose a different path. You might have been a scribe like Sitric, or a farmer, or a craftsman. We hoped… *I* hoped the tales might not sing to your blood the way they do to mine."

"I would have done things differently had I known. Told different tales." I didn't even try to mask the bitterness in my voice. "Nobody *had* to die."

"We made a mistake. I know. The day you announced you were a bard, my heart sank down into my boots and it's stayed there ever since. But by then, we had spent so many years pretending you wouldn't be a bard, we didn't know what to say. We hoped the curse had ended with me, that since it had been so many years since I last told a tale, somehow you would be free of it. And when you first started telling your tales and nothing happened, we thought you were safe."

We sat in silence for some time.

"Did you figure it out?" he asked at length.

"Emotion," I said. "That's what brings the tale to life. When I tell a tale while I am filled with emotion, it comes true. There might be other ways but I've not explored them. I don't intend to either."

"I should have known. It explains… It explains what happened for me."

"Your brothers?"

He closed his eyes. And I knew. He didn't have to say it.

"That was the last tale I ever told," he said. "I knew about my — our — ability. My father warned me long before I was old enough to tell a tale. He never told a single one himself. He was too afraid. His own father had died when he was merely a babe and his grandfather was already dead. It was his grandmother who told him and she knew very little, only that there was a strange ability passed down from seventh son to seventh son. There was nobody left by then who knew how it worked.

"I didn't believe him at first, just as you didn't believe me. And for a long time, nothing happened, so I felt safe. I became confident, cocky even. Thought my father had been mistaken.

"I had argued with my brothers. They were jealous of the bard son who seemed to do nothing all day while they were busy making a living, supporting the family, supporting me. I didn't have any great renown so I contributed no income from my tales. My oldest brother, Eremon — your brother was named for him — he said he would no longer support a brother who didn't contribute to the family coffers. I was bitter. Jealous they all had destinies that allowed them to contribute. Angry they weren't prepared to be patient while I learnt my craft.

"The tale I told was based on the Children of Lir. I spoke of a bard who cursed his six older brothers and turned them all into swans. The brothers remained swans for three hundred years and then they returned to their original forms, still the same age as they were when they changed."

My heart seemed to stop.

"So your brothers… they're still alive? Still swans?"

"I saw them change." Papa's eyes held the most terrible sadness I had ever seen. "It was the first time one of my tales came true, and the last tale I ever told. They flew away. I hope... I hope they are alive and safe and that they will return one day. I deeply regret I will not be here to tell them how sorry I am."

"Have you tried to find them?"

"For many years, any time I saw a swan, I spoke to it, apologised. There was never any indication the swan understood. Whether any of them were my brothers, and whether they still retained any part of their human mind to understand my words, I'll never know. But in my tale, the swans returned and became men again. I pray that my brothers will also return, whole and sane."

"Do you think they will come home?"

He shrugged. "Where else would they go? As long as Silver Downs belongs to our family, it is still their home. Your brother, Eremon, knows, and he tell his heir when he is old enough. The knowledge will be passed down from father to son and when three hundred years has passed, I trust my brothers will be welcomed home as family."

Papa said nothing for some time after that. Occasionally he passed his hand across his eyes, as if to sweep away tears. Eventually he continued.

"Our father died shortly after. He couldn't live with the loss of six sons. So Silver Downs came to me, and I've kept myself busy ever since, running the estate the way Eremon would have. I wasn't supposed to be the heir and I had to learn fast. And that's what you need to do now. Find something else and learn it. Just because you were meant to be a bard, doesn't mean that's all you can do."

"But I don't know who I am if I'm not a bard."

"You'll figure it out," he said. "Trust me, son. There's something else out there waiting for you."

59

DIARMUID

A FEW DAYS later, a messenger arrived. He was a rugged man, travelling on a sturdy horse. Both man and beast looked well accustomed to lonely journeys across the country. Papa took the man into his study and closed the door. They remained in there for only minutes before Papa showed the man to the kitchen, then returned to his study alone. He didn't come back out again until dinner time and then his face was grave and grey.

My stomach growled at the aroma of soup thick with spring vegetables. But my appetite fled when Papa looked solemnly around the table.

"A messenger came today," he said. "From Caedmon's commanding officer. Caedmon did not return to the campaign front."

For a moment I couldn't breathe, couldn't see. I had killed him.

"We mustn't think the worst." Papa looked everywhere but at me. "Perhaps he has been delayed. He may have fallen ill and stayed somewhere to recover."

"Then why would he not send a message?" Eremon asked. "Either to us or to his officer?"

"Perhaps he is so ill," Marrec said.

"That he doesn't recall who he is," finished Conn.

Eremon shrugged and looked away. It was clear he didn't agree but was reluctant to argue. Of all my brothers, he was the most like Papa in that regard. Only now I understood why Papa held his words in such tight reserve.

We all pretended to be busy with our meal. The soup curdled in my belly and I was unable to eat more than a few spoonfuls. Mother stared intently into her bowl, stirring her soup but seemingly eating none. Her face was composed, but the knuckles on the hand gripping her spoon were white.

Another life ruined. If I hadn't told that wretched tale about the soldier and his wife, Caedmon would have made it safely back to the campaign.

"Where are Eithne and Grainne?" I asked, suddenly desperate to know. "Are they safe? Is Eithne... is Eithne well?"

Silence. Mother continued to stare into her soup. My brothers looked to Papa and it was clear nobody would tell me if he didn't. Papa put down his spoon.

"They have gone away," he said, finally. "On a journey, of some sort. Exactly what, we don't know. Fiachra said only that they will return if they can."

"Did he say nothing further?" I asked.

"He hinted that someone — something — might pursue them, and it was better if we knew no details."

"Was Grainne injured?" I stared into my soup, ashamed to ask, but I had to know.

Papa looked to Mother and it seemed this answer was hers to give. Mother nodded slowly.

"Badly?" My voice cracked.

"She was..." Mother's voice failed. She cleared her throat and tried again. "She was beaten. She refused to say who did it. She was still recovering, still fragile. She was not fit to undertake a journey and Fiachra knew."

"So why did she go?"

"The journey was Eithne's," Papa said, "and we know no more than that. Grainne went with her, out of love and friendship."

I had not known Eithne and Grainne were so close, but then I knew very little of Grainne. I had been too mired in my own discomfort with women and my jealousy towards Caedmon to get to know her. But I knew Eithne and I remembered the man who had attended Caedmon and Grainne's handfasting, the one who stood off in the trees and did not mingle with our family and friends. Now that I knew more about the fey, I recognised the pale skin and blood-red lips. Who was he to Eithne? Did he have something to do with this strange journey of hers?

All this talk of journeys made me think of Brigit. She never said why the fey wanted her to go with me, only that whatever their aim was, it had been achieved. Did I dare hope their aim had been to bring the two of us together? What purpose could the fey have for such a thing? But if their aim was achieved, did that mean she cared for me?

Staring into my soup, I saw not vegetables and broth, but Brigit's face, or rather, a meld of Brigit and Bramble. It was as Bramble that I first loved her and I couldn't not see the shaggy white terrier any more than I could not see Brigit herself. I had tried to forget and slide back into my old life, but I wasn't the same person as the one who first set out to find Ida. I could no more forget Brigit than I could forget Ida.

If it were true I had killed Caedmon, I would regret it for the rest of my life. I would also always regret Grainne's injuries, but I couldn't change those events. However, the way I had left things with Brigit was something I could still change, if I chose.

It seemed I faced a new decision. I could stay in a world I no longer belonged in, or I could seek out a new life for myself.

It took me until morning to decide what to do.

6 0

BRIGIT

I KNEW DIARMUID was coming, for the visions showed me. I recognised the gentle hill he rode up and the stand of silvery birch where he rested his horse. I knew the day's eye bush there in a hollow and the rock that looked like a giant frog. The thought of seeing him again made me want to run in circles and bark madly. For how long would my first reaction be that of Bramble rather than Brigit? Perhaps some lingering sense of Bramble would stay with me forever.

The Sight showed me myself, throwing my arms around him and weeping, although I knew not whether it was with joy or grief. Of course, I resolved there would be no embracing or weeping. I would greet him coldly, somewhat disdainfully, hear him out, and send him on his way again.

Anything I might have once felt for Diarmuid was gone. I had tasted adventure, mystery and danger like I wanted, and would learn to be a good wise woman, like I was supposed to. Perhaps I would never have the romance I once desired, but one cannot have everything. I had achieved three of the things I once wanted more than anything, and if my heart beat a little faster at the thought of Diarmuid's arrival, and my breath caught in my throat, it was of no consequence, for he meant nothing to me. Truly.

I searched the visions for clues as to when he would arrive. The birches still bore patches of winter bareness. The day's eyes were only just beginning to bloom. I examined the bush near our front door. It was a tight mass of buds with few flowers unfurling. He would come soon.

Diarmuid's arrival would almost be a relief, for the visions had tormented me all night. I had slept little and by mid-morning couldn't keep my attention on the task at hand. I knocked over a bin of flour and smashed a jar of preserved berries before Mother sent me out to work in the garden.

The sun was warm on my arms and spring was everywhere I looked. In the trill of the swallow, in the pale new shoots of garlic and onion, in the clear sky wearing nothing but a single cloud. My mood lifted as I lost myself in my work, pulling weeds, thinning some early carrots, and turning over the soil in preparation for planting the cabbages. At length, I paused to rest and stretch my aching back. It was then I saw the horse and rider.

They were still some distance away, far enough that I could only make out the shape of a body on horseback. But my soul knew it was Diarmuid and already my heart beat a little faster. I could almost feel the tail I no longer had begin to wag. I wished I was not wearing my oldest dress, entirely suitable for gardening, but perhaps not what a woman would choose to wear as she faces one who might, under other circumstances, have been her husband. I wished I did not have dirt up to my elbows and all over my apron, but then I hardened my heart. I had no need for nice dresses and frippery, for Diarmuid meant nothing to me. I would give him the courtesy of hearing him out, then send him on his way. No weeping. No embracing.

I caught myself touching my damaged ear. Bramble's fight with the boar had left that ear twisted and misshapen. The skin was thickened and still tender. I often found myself touching it in moments of uncertainty. It reminded me of the tenacity of a little dog who refused to be a boar's breakfast and the memory gave me strength. If Bramble could escape the boar, I could face Diarmuid.

I returned to my chores and tried to forget the approaching horse. But I felt him draw steadily nearer. He was still some way off when he reined in his horse, pausing for so long that I expected him to turn and leave. But soon enough he was right in front of me, silhouetted against the sun. I wiped dirt-covered hands on my apron and squinted up at him.

Diarmuid dismounted. His face was schooled to what he probably thought was blankness, but his eyes were full of hope. They showed anxiety too. He was uncertain of his welcome.

Good, I thought. *You will get no welcome here.* I stifled the urge to lift my lips and snarl.

"Bramble," he said. "I mean, Brigit."

My resolve softened ever so slightly, for his closeness made me feel like Bramble again, unsure of my own form and my mind. Craving his presence and his touch. Wanting nothing more than for him to see me as I really was. Well, this was what I really was. Covered in dirt and with my hair in disarray, this was me.

"Diarmuid," I said.

He hesitated and his gaze darted around as if looking for escape. He was uncomfortable, a contradiction as ever: the bard who could tell a tale to a roomful of strangers and yet couldn't speak to a woman without blushing and stuttering. Not that it mattered how much he blushed and stuttered because this woman didn't have the slightest interest in him. If my fingers longed to reach out and touch his face or stroke his hair, that didn't mean anything. If I craved the touch of his hand on my ear or my neck, it was merely a lingering memory of being Bramble. I crossed my arms across my chest, lest I accidentally reach for him.

Resolve fluttered across Diarmuid's face and he straightened his shoulders.

"Bramble. Brigit." He took a deep breath and tried again. "Brigit, I came to apologise."

"For what?"

My heart is hard, like rock. I will not bend like a willow, like a weak woman.

"For… for everything. For not seeing you, not listening to you. For taking you for granted. For letting you think I didn't w-want you."

"Right from the start you were trying to pass me off onto someone else." My tone was hard with accusation. "You wanted to leave me at Owain's house."

"I was trying to do what was best for you." His eyes begged me to believe. "I didn't know what was ahead of me and thought you would be safer if you stayed with Owain. You seemed to like him. I thought you would be happy there."

"So you thought you had the right to make decisions for me?"

"You were a dog. Or, at least, I thought you were. You were already special to me. We needed each other those first nights in the woods. Neither of us would have survived alone. I thought you must belong to someone who lived nearby and that if you stayed with Owain, they might find you. And if they didn't, I knew Owain would take good care of you. And that's all I wanted. To protect you."

What I wanted was to throw my arms around him and never let him go, but I held them stiffly to my chest, sternly forbidding them to move. I would *not* fall for his sweet words.

"I didn't need protecting," I said.

"Brigit, you were half dead when you found me. I didn't think you would survive the night."

"I would have gotten through somehow. I didn't need you to come sweeping in and rescue me."

"All right, then, I'm sorry." There was a hint of frustration in his voice. "I'm sorry I saved your life. I'm sorry I didn't leave you to bleed to death in the forest. Sorry I tried to protect you. I'm sorry for everything."

He ran a shaky hand through his hair and turned back to his horse.

"I'm sorry I disturbed you today. You don't have to worry about it happening again. You won't see me again."

He grasped the reins and set a foot in the stirrup. My heart stirred and myriad images flashed through my mind. Diarmuid tenderly washing the blood from my paw. Cupping his hand and filling it with water so I could drink. Lifting the blanket so I could curl up next to him, his warmth holding the freezing night at bay. Wrapping his arms around me at night as he prattled endlessly while I wished he would shut up and go to sleep. He was the reason the fey had sent me on such a journey. I could be stubborn and let him leave, or I could let him in.

"Wait," I said.

Diarmuid turned back to me so quickly that his foot caught in the stirrup and he almost fell. He said nothing, but at least he waited.

My mouth went dry and my knees trembled. I didn't know what to say. Yes, there were probably things I needed to apologise for, but my mind was as blank as his face. So I did the only thing I could. I threw my arms around him and wept. Diarmuid didn't hesitate. He wrapped his arms firmly around me.

"Bramble—" he started.

"Shush," I said, wiping away tears. "It's all right."

"I might not have seen what you really were, but I loved you from the first moment I saw you. You were covered in blood and barely able to stand and yet you held your head high as you stumbled towards me. A scruffy little beast so full of courage."

There was only one answer I could give.

"Diarmuid, I suggest you shut up and kiss me."

"Happy to oblige," he said.

As his lips met mine, a warm tingle raced through my whole body. I didn't know why the fey wanted us together, but clearly this was what they intended when they ordered me to journey to an undisclosed destination. If only I had known.

61

DIARMUID

I KISSED BRIGIT and my heart sang. When we finally drew apart, she took my hand.

"Come inside and meet my mother," she said. "I suspect she knew you were coming today."

"How would she know such a thing?"

"The visions," she said, as if that explained everything. "Mother is a wise woman. She has trained me for the same profession."

"You're a wise woman?"

"Not yet, but I'm learning. I could have helped you much on your journey, had I been in my own form."

"You helped enough."

My legs trembled with sudden nerves as we approached the stone lodge. It was smaller than the house at Silver Downs but looked cosy and sturdily made. The front door opened and the woman who stood there had the same sharp nose as Brigit and the same hair that refused to be restrained. The apron over her work dress was smudged with evidence of the day's chores. She smiled at me and her eyes shimmered with tears.

"You come at last," she said and hugged me fiercely. "I'm Treasa."

I stiffened and awkwardly hugged her back.

"You recognise him." Brigit sounded unsurprised.

Treasa raised her hand to rest it against Brigit's cheek.

"Brigit, my dear, I knew he was for you the first time the Sight showed him to me and that was long before your birth."

"How much—" I stammered. "That is, do you know—"

"I know enough," Treasa said, kindly. "What the Sight didn't show, Brigit told me. And now you must carry the consequences with you. It must be very difficult."

It was the first time anyone had shown sympathy for what I had done and my eyes burned. I quickly blinked away the tears.

"It was difficult at first but I'm growing more used to it every day. She doesn't seem very strong yet but Fiachra, my brother who is a druid, says she will regain her strength in time. I don't know whether I can keep her contained for ever."

As I spoke, Treasa led us into the kitchen. She took three mugs from a shelf and added a scoop of something from one container, a pinch from another, and a sprinkle from a third, then filled them with water from a pot on the wood stove.

"Is there any other option?" Treasa set the mugs on the well-worn table and motioned for me to sit.

I sat on a sturdy wooden chair. Bramble sat close beside me, her hand still tucked in mine.

"No," I said. "There is no other option. If I don't keep her contained, she might take over my body or she could escape. And I don't think I could restrain her if she got away from me again."

"We do what we must," Treasa said. "And that is as it should be. Now, your tales. Do you still tell them?"

I inhaled the spicy scent rising from my mug.

"I will never tell another tale. I can't, now I know what I can do."

"Brigit said you only recently discovered the key to your ability."

"I'm not taking any chances. What if I'm wrong? Or what if I'm right, but there's more to it?"

"So what will you do?" Brigit asked.

"My brother Sitric needs an assistant. He has more work than he can manage. I'm going to Maker's Well to work with him. He says there is enough scribing work for us both to make a living, good enough to support a family."

Treasa nodded and swirled the tea in her mug.

"Yes," she said. "That will be suitable."

"Where is the rest of your family?" I asked Brigit. "Your father?"

I wished I hadn't spoken, for a cloud quickly settled over both Brigit and her mother.

"You don't need to tell me," I added quickly.

"You should know," Brigit said.

She leaned across the table to grasp Treasa's hand. Treasa lifted her chin defiantly, a gesture I recognised from Brigit.

"I can tell him, Mother," Brigit said, softly. "You don't need to do this. Diarmuid, my father was killed. Murdered."

I inhaled a sharp breath. "I had no idea. I wouldn't have asked..."

Brigit smiled grimly. "We don't know who organised it, although we have our suspicions." She and Treasa exchanged a look. "Father had upset a certain person. A very wealthy and powerful person. We suspect he arranged for Father to be killed."

"By someone like Owain?"

"By someone exactly like Owain." Brigit's voice was milder than I might have expected.

I looked from Brigit to her mother. Treasa didn't look as accepting as Brigit did.

"You don't think..."

Brigit shrugged. "I don't believe in coincidence."

"I don't know what to say."

"I've made my peace with it. If it was Owain, he was doing his job. I don't blame him, I blame the man who hired him."

Our conversation was interrupted by laughter, which preceded four girls who all looked much like Brigit. They swarmed into the house, rosy-cheeked and with hair flying every which way from their adventures.

"My sisters," Bramble said with a suppressed smile. "Clidna, Sulgwenn, Keena, Myrna. Don't worry about which is which. You'll never remember and they all look much the same anyway."

"Brigit!" one of the girls exclaimed. "Mother, she is so rude to us."

Treasa said nothing and the girl didn't seem to notice. Brigit pursed her lips and grinned at me when the girls weren't looking.

I stayed a little longer, then left with the excuse that I wanted to be home before dark. In truth, the noise of Brigit's sisters made my head spin and it was difficult to concentrate on Ida's box. They were loud and vivacious, constantly teasing and arguing and shouting. Sometimes all four of them would burst into laughter at the same moment while I was left wondering what I missed. Perhaps it was me they found so amusing. I would have to get used to them, for they might one day be my sisters.

My heart was light as I mounted my horse and headed back to Silver Downs. I hadn't dare let myself anticipate how Brigit might greet me, but when she had been cold and a little disdainful it had seemed no more than I deserved.

I still saw Bramble every time I looked at her and perhaps I always would. It seemed Brigit had come to terms with what had happened to her and it wasn't fair of me to cling to Bramble but, still, I missed her warm body beside me at night. I missed the way she pressed her head into my hand when I rubbed her ears. I even missed the disdainful sniffs she gave when she thought I was being a fool.

Someone else I missed was Caedmon. As much as I hoped we might still receive a message explaining his delayed return to the campaign, I was certain I had killed him with my ill-considered tale. All because I had let myself be consumed by jealousy and bitterness.

I would probably never tell another tale, but sometimes I let myself hope that one day I might be brave enough to try again. I kept remembering what Brigit said about telling the right sort of tale. If Ida ever got away from me again, she would need to know about honour and bravery and integrity. If I ever told another tale, that was the kind I would tell.

But for now, the pain of losing Caedmon and the agony of

knowing I was responsible for Ida's actions at Crow's Nest were still too raw. I would live with that for the rest of my life, but maybe one day I could try again. If I ever had sons, I would want to be able to pass on the knowledge of how our ability worked. I wondered how Brigit would feel about seven sons.

6 2

DIARMUID

FEW EVENINGS after my visit with Brigit, I went out to Eithne's herb garden after dinner. Sitting in the garden my sister loved so much made me feel closer to her, even if she wasn't here. I still didn't know where she had gone. Fiachra wouldn't tell and it seemed nobody else knew the details. How my chronically ill sister would handle any sort of journey, I didn't know, and I lacked the courage to ask. Grainne was still healing when she and Eithne disappeared on their mysterious journey, but at least Eithne wasn't alone.

As I sat on the little wooden bench, which was still warm from the afternoon sun, peace seeped into me for perhaps the first time since I had told the tale about the soldier and his bride. Maybe for the first time since my tenth summer.

The herb garden was mostly still bare, for without Eithne nobody had thought to plant it for the new season. A couple of spiky bushes had survived, rosemary perhaps, and something I thought might be mint, but the rest of the garden contained only bare earth beneath melting snow. Even though little remained alive after the winter, the air still bore traces of the scent of herbs.

I should re-plant the garden for her. Tomorrow perhaps. Eithne

318

would have saved some seeds and I figured that as long as I could find them, I could manage the task.

I didn't notice Papa's arrival until he stood right beside me.

"Mind if I join you?" he asked.

His face bore a few more wrinkles than it used to, probably due to all the grief his wretched children had caused of late.

I moved over to give him room and he eased onto the bench with a sigh. I continued to look out over the garden, breathing in the herb-scented air and keeping my thoughts calm. The calmer I was, the less Ida was interested. She typically only stirred if I was anxious or angry or upset. So I was trying to be more serene.

"It's a gift, you know," Papa said. "I know it mightn't seem like it right now, and it took me many years to see it as such. Why it was granted to our family, I don't know."

"Titania seems to have taken great interest in us."

"Aah, Titania." Papa made a noise that might almost have been a laugh. "She was furious with me. Did she offer to take your ability away?"

I nodded. "I refused."

"As did I," he said. "And many others before us, from what I gather. Titania lives in hope that one day one of our bards will be foolish enough to agree. That's what makes me think it is supposed to be a gift. The fact that she wants it so much."

"Who do you think might have given it to us?"

Papa shrugged and rubbed his stubbled chin.

"One of the fey, I assume. Many generations ago."

"Maybe it was intended as a curse." Bitterness edged my voice and Ida stirred. I calmed myself and she settled again.

"I don't think so, given how desperate Titania is to reclaim it," Papa said. "I've always regretted that I didn't take the time to learn how it worked. Part of me died the day I stopped telling tales and a little more of me died every day since then. Don't let that happen to you, son. You're the first one in several generations who has a chance to learn how to use the power properly. Make it count."

"I don't know if I can. Caedmon…"

"Learn from your mistakes," he said, fiercely. "Don't stop telling tales. You can pass the knowledge on. Future generations of this family will benefit from whatever you learn."

"Perhaps," I said. "Would you want to learn, too?"

"No, son, my time for telling tales has passed. It's up to you now. You're the bard of Silver Downs. The tales, and their power, lie with you."

Papa might not be a bard any more, but even so, I felt the power of his words. They lodged in my mind and refused to let go. Could I be the one to really understand this strange power of ours? Could I be the first to pass down the legacy in full, not just the gift but also the knowledge of how it worked?

For the first time in many months, snippets of a new tale stirred in my mind. A fragment of words, a brief image. So the tales were still there after all and they still called to my blood. Perhaps I could be a bard again one day after all.

ACKNOWLEDGEMENTS

Thank you to my wonderful beta readers, Megan Grey Walker and Hannah Ivory Wright. Your insightful feedback gave me the confidence to finish this story.

Thank you to David Farland for teaching me everything I know about description and for advice when I didn't know what direction to take an early draft of what would eventually become *Muse*.

Thank you to my awesome editor, Meghan Pinson. Without you, this book would be nothing like it is today. Thank you to Deranged Doctor Design for a beautiful cover. I'm beyond thrilled. Thank you to Nick Hawkins for proofreading.

Thanks also to everyone who has read this far. I started this manuscript at a time when I wasn't sure I wanted to continue writing and it led me here. I hope Diarmuid and Brigit's story fills your heart the way it does mine.

And, finally, thank you to my family for supporting me through this journey. To Muffin and Lulu who are always convinced I can't write if they aren't there right beside me, guarding me. To Frehley, who really couldn't care less as long as I stop writing to feed her on time. And to my angel Bella. I miss you every day.

KYLIE QUILLINAN

TALES OF
SILVER DOWNS

FEY

BOOK 2

KYLIE QUILLINAN

*This book is dedicated
to all those who have endured slavery.*

1

EITHNE

When I am ill, my dreams are filled with things that aren't really there. Some of these things I have really seen, like the power of a fire as it rages out of control and the might of a winter storm that strips branches from beech trees and thatching from houses. Others I have never viewed with my own eyes. They probably came from the tales my bard brother told. Titania, queen of the fey, glowering at me. Tiny beings no larger than my thumbnail, human-shaped but with wings. A creature, in appearance nothing more than a rock, but clearly sentient. I longed to see these beings, but I could never hope to live a normal life, let alone one in which I might actually meet such creatures.

The images repeated one after another, but eventually they returned to the boy. Always the boy. He appeared to be around my own age, although the fey can seem any age they choose. His milky skin and crimson lips shouted his fey heritage, and his dark hair was roughly cut as if he cared little about the result. Blue eyes stared at me, never blinking or looking away, just watching, considering. Unusual eyes, for a fey. He stood silently in the corner of my bedchamber and watched as I drowned in fevered dreams. Sweat soaked my linen nightdress and my damp hair stuck to my cheeks.

As the fevers subsided, the dreams disappeared and the boy with them, and I once again became aware of my surroundings. It was always startling to emerge from the dreams and discover that time still had meaning.

I lay in my bed, staring up at the knotted ceiling. Thick green drapes shielded the window. A hand-knotted rug lay in front of the fireplace. The air smelled stale and old. Mother sat beside my bed, her eyes shadowed and her face pale.

"Welcome back, Eithne," she said.

I struggled to sit up, but my limbs were weak and I collapsed back down onto the bed.

"How long?" I asked.

My voice was hoarse and my mouth tasted dry and bitter. Mother hesitated, but I knew she wouldn't lie to me.

"Nine days," she said.

Her words chilled me and eventually I realised I clutched my woollen blanket so hard that my knuckles had gone white. I forced my fingers to relax and smooth the blanket. Its wool was coarse and prickly.

"It's never been that long before," I said.

Mother nodded.

"It's getting worse, isn't it?"

I needed to hear it, to know it wasn't all in my head. Like the dreams, no matter how real they seemed.

Mother sucked in a breath. She looked away, towards the window where the drapes were tightly drawn and her hands restlessly smoothed the skirt of her work dress.

"You can say it," I said.

She looked back at me and her dark eyes glistened.

"Yes, Eithne, it's getting worse. We always knew the illness might progress, but I had hoped you would have a little more time."

I inhaled deeply, steadying myself. I knew what was ahead of me, had known since I was old enough to understand the truth. She had never tried to shield me from it. Death was the end of the journey for each of us. It just came sooner for some.

"There's never enough time though, is there?" I was too fatigued to hide the bitterness in my voice. "We are always too young to die."

Mother swallowed hard.

"Always too young, my darling." She avoided my eyes as she gathered up the pitcher and mug from the small wooden table beside my bed. "I'll take these to the kitchen. I'll be back in a little while, to sit with you."

"I would like that."

I knew she left because she needed to compose herself, not because the pitcher needed to be returned to the kitchen immediately. We had servants who could undertake such a task.

I stared up at the ceiling as Mother closed the door. I traced a crooked crack with my gaze and tried to pretend I couldn't hear her sobs. Death had ever loomed present for me, from the day I first struggled out of my mother's womb, eager to be born and far too early with the birth cord wrapped tightly around my neck.

A sickness of the blood, the wise woman said when I told her about the recurrent fevers and chills. The days where I couldn't keep down even the thinnest of broths. Nights where my blood boiled within my veins. No cure, she said. Even the druid could only shake his head and say he was sorry. When one lives with the idea of death every day, one becomes somewhat used to it. At least I saw fabulous things in my dreams. They let me feel like I had lived just a little.

2

EITHNE

In the days following my illness, my strength slowly returned. On my better days, I would sit on a stool in the kitchen and help Cook with small tasks until I grew too tired. But on the bad days, I didn't have even the strength for that. Instead I passed my time alone, sitting beside the fireplace in the family room.

This was my favourite room in the whole house. On winter nights, we would gather here to drink warm spiced wine and share tales or commentary about the day. The sweet scent of pinecones on the fire would mingle with the spices from the wine and make my nose tingle. I usually sat beside Mother near the fire where its heat could warm my always-cold body. But during the day, only I ever sat here. Mother was occupied with running the house, and Papa and my brothers were busy with their various chores. The large room around me was empty and lonely.

A thick blanket and the dancing fire cloaked me with their warmth, although even the two combined couldn't shield me from the cold nearness of death. Wondering how much longer I might live was pointless, for my time would come and likely soon. In the meantime, I watched my brothers grow up and lived through them as much as I could.

Eremon, my oldest brother, would run our estate, Silver Downs, once Papa was gone. I had been ill the day he handfasted with Niamh, but my brothers carried me outside to watch the ceremony. I had sat in a chair, huddled under blankets while the mid-summer sun shone down on my face. Niamh bore Eremon twin sons, sturdy boys who were now two summers old.

My next brother, Caedmon, left home in his sixteenth summer to become a soldier. He returned every year or so, always looking a little more haggard, a little more battle-scarred. He showed me a wound once, where a sword had pierced his side. The skin was red and puckered, still healing, and the scar large enough for me to place my fisted hand inside. He didn't show anyone else, for he said Mother would worry if she heard whisper of it. If he walked a little slower on that visit, and hesitated before he lifted anything, it seemed nobody other than I noticed.

I had no memory of Fiachra, my druid brother, apart from what I had heard from my other brothers. He left with the druids when I was a babe of but two or three summers.

Sitric was the fourth brother. He worked as a scribe in Maker's Well, the town nearest to Silver Downs and a little more than a half day's walk away.

Marrec and Conn were next, two bodies sharing one soul. They would work the estate with Eremon, for it seemed they desired no other occupation. I could never think of them in isolation as they were constantly together. Marrec was the eldest by minutes and they were always referred to us Marrec and Conn, never Conn and Marrec.

And then there was Diarmuid, the bard. The youngest of my seven brothers and barely a couple of summers older than me. Sometimes when I was ill, he would sit beside my bed and tell me tales — long complicated things where heroes went on grand journeys and encountered all sorts of magical beings. They lingered in my memory and I would repeat them to myself over and over but with me in the hero's role.

I took long, dangerous journeys across mountains and rivers and deserts. I faced down evil creatures or deciphered Titania's riddles. Only, unlike in Diarmuid's tales, I would return triumphant, the evil defeated, the monster killed, the fey banished to their own realm. I lived many adventures through my brother's tales and sometimes I even created my own. They were poor compared with Diarmuid's, but they amused me well enough when I had no other entertainment.

The fey boy began to feature in the tales I told myself. He walked beside me as I trod across endless fields and climbed vast mountains and battled a dragon. I swooped in to rescue him at the last moment as he teetered on a precipice, his balance lost, or as a sword came crushingly near his neck. And sometimes he saved me.

Seven brothers and a sister. If we were in a tale, it would be a magical combination, for seven is a powerful number. Seven brothers united could withstand almost anything. The sister to seven brothers would be special indeed and — if my life was a tale — in possession of some magical ability.

In truth, the life I led lacked the excitement and fervour of my tales and I had no magical ability. I sat beside the fire with only my tales for company as the noise of the household drifted over me. Mother directing a servant. Papa and Eremon discussing estate matters in serious voices. From outside came the shouts and whoops of Marrec and Conn playing with Eremon's young sons. Papa would order them back to work if he noticed. A dog barked, a rooster crowed. People passed by without noticing me. I was the invisible girl huddled by the fire. Perhaps nobody saw me because I was already dead. A spirit lost or maybe trapped. I cleared my throat, coughed. Nobody noticed.

"Hello?" I said. My voice was weak and barely penetrated the emptiness of the room.

The household continued around me. If I really was dead, there was nothing I could do about it. I might as well sit here and enjoy the warmth from the fire while it lasted.

3

EITHNE

Only a handful of days passed before I again slid into the fever dreams. Dank caverns and mist-shrouded mountains. A river so vast it could only be the Great Sea, many days' journey from Silver Downs. Titania, always with a scowl on her beautiful face and an expression that said I was worth less than the dirt under her feet. And the fey boy, standing in the corner of my small bedchamber. He wore forest green today. For the first time, he crept closer, bit by bit, until he stood right beside my bed.

"Why?" The words stuck in my dry mouth and it was some time before I could continue. "Why do you watch me?"

"Curiosity." His voice was smooth and melodious. He sounded exactly the way I expected, which was only right since he was a product of my own fever dream.

"Of what?"

"Of why you cling so fiercely to life. Mortal lives are fleeting. Why do you try so hard to hold onto them?"

"It is what we do. We fight."

"Why? Your life is not worth fighting for. You are either ill in bed or huddled by the fire. You watch other mortals live and know you can never join them."

"I conserve my strength. It's how I stay alive."

He raised his lip in something that might have been a sneer. His blue eyes were bright and hostile.

"Mortal girls your age dream of betrothals and children and running their own home. Of what do you dream? Rivers and mountains, wind and fire."

"Titania," I gasped, struggling for breath now, for even so few words exhausted me. "I dream of Titania. And you."

He stretched out one slender hand towards me. His fingers were cool and smooth as they traced a fiery path along my skin. "Yes, you dream of me."

He left then, although I could not have said exactly how. With great effort, I managed to raise my arm in front of my face. My skin burned where he had touched me but looked just the same as always. Pale and sweaty, but otherwise unremarkable.

The fey boy had touched me. He was real. I was lost to the fever dreams then and by the time I surfaced again, I was no longer quite so certain that I hadn't imagined him.

The light through the window held the shadows of early evening. My limbs were weak as Mother helped me sit up and set a tray with a small bowl of broth on my lap. The tray shook as I tried to spoon the broth into my mouth and I spilled almost as much as I managed to eat. The savoury scent of beef made my stomach roll uncomfortably, but I forced down a few mouthfuls. Mother sat on a chair drawn up to the bed, her hands clasped in her lap.

"Four days," she said in response to my unasked question.

I hadn't been sure I wanted to know this time. I set down the spoon, needing to rest before I could eat more.

"Does anyone visit me while I am sick?" I asked.

"I do, of course," Mother said. "And your brothers sometimes."

"Nobody else?"

"I don't understand, Eithne. Who else would come?"

"I don't know. I'm confused."

I felt bad about lying to Mother, but how could I tell her the truth?

Several days passed before I had the strength to even stand

without aid. Sometimes one of my brothers would carry me outside to sit in the sun for a while, but otherwise I could do nothing other than lie in bed and stare at the ceiling. I knew every crack in its timbers.

Now that the rivers and woods and winds were gone, my thoughts were my own once more and they lingered on the fey boy. Was he real or another product of my imagination? For I was not so silly as to think the images of Titania and oceans and mountains were anything but dreams. A reaction caused as my body tried to cool my fevered blood. A healer had explained it to me once.

But the boy, he was different. In my dreams I was always somewhere else: standing in the leaf litter of an ancient wood, or in an underground cavern, or trembling as I knelt on cold grass before Titania. But when I dreamed of the boy, I was always lying in my bed and he stood in my bedchamber. Never before had I wondered whether he was anything but a dream. Until he touched me.

My health slowly improved over the next sevennight. No fevers, no sweating, no sudden weakness or dizziness. I experienced neither vomiting nor lack of appetite, although my hunger was never strong even when I was well.

The boy consumed my every thought. I had to see him again, had to seek further proof that he was real. Every morning, I stared into my hand mirror, hopeful for some indication of the imminent return of illness. The hand mirror was elegant, an unfair contrast to my thin and ever-pale face. The reflective glass was surrounded by wood carved with swirls of oak leaves and acorns. But my face was no paler than usual and the dark circles under my eyes were no more prominent. If anything, they seemed to fade a little as the days passed.

After a few days, I had the strength to make my way downstairs for breakfast, although I had to clutch the smooth wooden bannister to steady myself. The stairs were made for folk taller than I, so traversing them was awkward and slow, especially when I was still so weak. The other reason I walked slowly was because of my left foot, which twisted in on an awkward angle. I always tried to keep it straight and to not limp. My parents and brothers knew, of course, for a young child does not know to hide such a thing. But from the day I had understood my defect, I had tried to conceal it, and by now it was mostly forgotten. If I walked haltingly, an observer would likely attribute it to a lingering weakness.

The house was silent as I walked slowly through, the rest of my family already having gone off to start their day. The dining room table bore the remains of breakfast: scattered plates and crumbs, the lingering scent of porridge and herbal tea. The porridge kettle was empty, so I made a meal of a slice of bread with honey. I sipped at some tea, but it was cold and too bitter for my taste.

I went to sit by the fireplace in the family room. Somebody had thought to start the fire for me — Eremon, most likely — and it had already burned down to embers. I sank into my favourite chair and tucked my feet up under my long woollen skirt. There was no need for a blanket today, for even though it was early winter, the day was mild and the fire hot enough to keep me pleasantly warm.

I had never before longed for the illness to strike. Never hoped that by evening I would once again be confined to bed, to sweat and writhe and groan with pain. But if the fey boy was real — and I was not entirely convinced that he was — he would only come to me if I was ill. This time I would be prepared. I would seek a way to confirm whether he was real or just another fever dream. If I could obtain a token from him: a rock, a leaf, a hair, something I could see and touch once I had recovered, that would be proof enough.

4

EITHNE

en days had passed and rarely was I well for so long. The return of illness wouldn't be far off, but with yet another afternoon drawing to a close and my health still holding, I couldn't wait any longer.

Alone in the family room, I wrapped myself in woollen blankets and drew my chair up close to the fireplace. I loaded kindling onto the dying embers and the fire roared to life. I added a small log and the flames soon settled to a steady burn. Heat bathed my face and hands, and already I sweated within my blankets. I sat as close as I dared, roasting myself like a rabbit over a traveller's fire.

After some time I began to feel faint. My hand shook as I wiped sweat from my face. The back of my dress was damp and my mouth was dry. The heat from the fire had become almost unbearable, but I wasn't sure my legs would hold me if I tried to stand. I prayed I was forcing the illness upon myself, until Mother found me.

"Eithne, are you unwell?" She pressed a cool hand against my forehead and brushed sweaty hair back from my face, then frowned. "Goodness, child, your skin burns. Move away from the fire."

"I'm cold." I hoped my voice was strong and convincing, but I had never been a good liar.

"You have a fever." Mother's tone was the one that said she would tolerate no dissent. "You can hardly know how you feel if you sit so close to the fireplace with sweat pouring from your skin."

She pulled my chair back away from the fire. At this distance I could barely feel its warmth.

"No, I need to be closer."

I tried to get up, but her firm hand on my shoulder stopped me.

"Eithne, you will stay exactly where you are. As soon as one of your brothers returns, I will have them carry you upstairs. I'm sorry, child." Mother's voice was gentler now. "You were doing so well. I can't remember the last time you managed to fight off the illness for so long. But you know you need to rest now. The fever has started."

Shame washed over me. What right had I to cause Mother such worry? And all because I had some silly notion that an image from my fever dreams might be real. I was a foolish girl and if the illness returned tonight, it would be no more than I deserved.

So I waited patiently, ignoring the itch of sweat dripping down my neck, until Marrec and Conn came to make a chair with their arms and lift me. They joked as they carried me upstairs and swung me a little too high. I tried to join in the game, but in truth I was feeling quite dizzy so my laughter was weak.

They deposited me onto my bed, somewhat roughly, and left. I supposed they thought they had been gentle, for they had never experienced a day of illness and had no understanding of how such treatment might jar one's bones or make one's head pound. I pulled back the covers and crawled under. The linen sheets scraped against my sensitive skin.

For the hundredth time, I examined the place where the fey boy's fingers had grazed my arm. It was unblemished. Nothing to indicate that possibly the most significant event of my life had occurred the day he touched me. For the fey despise mortals. They do not watch us unless they have reason to.

So many of the folk in my family had a purpose. Eremon was the heir. Caedmon the soldier son. Fiachra the druid. The three sons every family desired to produce. More sons, and perhaps a daughter or two, were a blessing. But if a man had three sons, he could die satisfied. My father had seven, plus a daughter, and it wasn't just the first three born who had destinies. My brother Diarmuid was the seventh son of a seventh son and destined to be a bard, even if nobody had told him so.

That was a secret held tightly within our family. Nobody ever spoke of it and it was the reason Diarmuid did not know what it meant to be the seventh son of a seventh son of Silver Downs. The one in that position had the ability to bring his tales to life, although nobody had ever been able to determine exactly how the power worked. Perhaps Diarmuid would be the one to figure it out. Or perhaps the ability had passed him by, for he was nineteen summers old and had never brought a tale to life. Or so everyone thought. I was not so sure. I watched Diarmuid, like I watched everyone, and there was something odd about him. Something *more*.

Our father was also the seventh son of a seventh son. He too was a bard once, but no longer. He told a tale which came true, that much I knew. Something to do with his brothers, for they all died in some mysterious circumstances that were never discussed. Six brothers, all dead at the same time, and the youngest to inherit. That must be the result of a tale gone wrong. But now it seemed that I, too, had a destiny, just like Eremon, Caedmon, Fiachra and Diarmuid.

5

GRAINNE

"**G**rainne, Caedmon is here!"

I shuddered as my youngest sister's words echoed down the hallway. If I could hear her from the work room at the back of the house, where I was on my knees cleaning the hearth, Caedmon undoubtedly heard also.

"Grainne? Grainne, did you hear me?"

A thundering that sounded much like a herd of cows preceded Jenifry into the room. I sat back on my heels and brushed a strand of hair from my face with coal-dusted fingers.

"There you are, Grainne. Caedmon is here."

I took a deep breath and restrained my impulse to snap at her. "Thank you, I heard you the first time. As likely did the neighbours."

Jenifry pouted at me, all rosy-cheeked and flyaway hair. "But I thought you would want to know. Because, you know…" She dropped her voice to a conspiratorial whisper. "Because you love him."

"And I would much prefer he didn't know," I said. "Remember how that was supposed to be a secret?"

"I haven't told your secret." Jenifry's voice rose rapidly in both volume and pitch. "I *promised* I wouldn't tell."

I sighed and swiftly brushed the last of the ash into a pan. Caedmon, one of the sons of Silver Downs, was hardly likely to be here to visit with me, but I wasn't about to miss the chance to see him, even if I was covered with ash.

"I appreciate you keeping my secret, Jenifry. Do you happen to know why Caedmon is here?"

"He's talking to Father. They wouldn't let me listen."

"I hope everything is all right."

Was there an illness in the family? A fire? Some mysterious death of livestock? No, the folk at Silver Downs would have no reason to come so far if they needed aid. They had closer neighbours.

"Aren't you going to go out and talk to him?" Jenifry's voice was as loud as ever.

"Will you shut your mouth if I do?"

I swept out of the room before she could respond. Of course I would go talk with Caedmon. I had been in love with him since I was seven summers old. I didn't see him often, for Caedmon was a soldier and rarely at home. His last visit had worried me as he was thinner than usual and paler. He was broad-shouldered, like most of the Silver Downs menfolk, and well-muscled from his occupation. Hefting swords all day was excellent for the physique. But the last time I saw him, he had lost muscle tone. He walked more slowly than usual and with a slight hitch to his gait. I didn't have a chance to speak with him before he returned to the campaign front and I never heard the details of what injury he was recovering from on that visit.

Every time Caedmon left, I felt like I held my breath until he returned again. And every time I wished I had the courage to tell him how I felt. He had not yet taken a wife, although it would be a rare woman who wouldn't fall over her own feet to accept him. There were occasional rumours of dalliances, but nothing that lasted more than a night or two and I tried not to envy their intimacy with him. The day he took a wife I would stop yearning after him, but until then I was thankful that Father hadn't insisted I myself handfast. There were several eligible young men within a half day's walk and even one heir who had made it clear he was interested. But none of them compared to Caedmon.

I dashed into the kitchen to wash my hands in a bucket of water. Ash was smeared down the front of my dress and I had obviously knelt in it as well, but trying to brush it away would only make it worse. It was probably on my face, but there was no time to find a hand mirror.

I wore a sensible woollen work dress, my hair fastened back tidily into a plait that fell halfway down my back. My skirt was a little too short, showing my leather shoes and stocking-clad ankles. It was not what I would have worn had I expected to see Caedmon today. But he had never noticed me, so it hardly mattered. His visit would likely be brief and I wasn't about to miss the opportunity to see him by being vain about my appearance.

With a deep breath, I pushed open the front door. The chill hit my face and I would have paused to grab my coat except that Caedmon had already seen me. He and Father stood together only a dozen paces away, in a spot where neither lodge nor trees impeded the warmth from the sunlight. A sturdy black mare behind him nosed at the snow in search of grass.

Caedmon looked more like his usual self than when I last saw him almost a year ago. Gone was the paleness and the slight stoop to his shoulders. His dark hair was shorn somewhat shorter than he usually wore it, but I was much relieved to see him looking hale and hearty. He smiled as his gaze met mine and the early winter's day suddenly seemed much warmer.

"Grainne," Father said. "I was just about to send someone to find you."

"Did you need something?"

With difficulty, I dragged my gaze away from Caedmon. My mouth was dry and tasted like ash. Surely Father wasn't about to send me on some errand. Whatever moments I snatched with Caedmon now might well have to last me a year or more.

"Caedmon wishes to speak with you," Father said, to my very great surprise. He shook Caedmon's hand and departed swiftly.

I hardly knew what to say. I had never before been alone with him. Why would he seek me out now? Something to do with his sister, perhaps. I knew little of Eithne, other than that she was often too ill to attend festivities. But she was the only daughter in the family, whereas I was the eldest of four girls, even though I was younger than our two brothers. It must be something to do with Eithne unless, oh gods, had he fallen in love with one of my sisters? Was he here to ask for my advice in wooing her?

Caedmon cleared his throat and shifted from one foot to the other. He fiddled with his woollen scarf, unwrapping and then rewrapping it around his neck. I had never before seen him look ill at ease.

"You are well, Grainne?" he asked at length.

I opened my mouth to reply but choked on the words. My face burned as I coughed and spluttered. Caedmon helpfully thumped me on the back, which only made me choke more. By the time I got myself under control, I had forgotten his question until he repeated it.

"Oh, yes, I am fine. And you? You look…" *Wonderful.* "Better than when I last saw you. You were recovering from an injury then, if I recall correctly."

Of course I did. I never forgot anything when it came to Caedmon. I could probably remember every time I had ever spoken to him, not that it would amount to more than a handful.

"Oh, the wound in my side. It is a solid scar now. The healer said the skin might not mend evenly and could be uncomfortable, even once it was healed, but it feels good now."

I bet it feels good. I'd like to try feeling it myself. For one awful moment, I thought I had spoken my thoughts aloud, but the expression on his face didn't change. We stood in awkward silence for a few moments before Caedmon cleared his throat again.

"I have decided it is time I was handfasted," he said abruptly.

It was as if the world had fallen out from beneath my feet. How many times had I promised myself I would stop being in love with him once he claimed some other woman as his own?

"I am unconcerned if we do not love each other," he continued. "Perhaps, given enough time, we might learn to, but my priority is to choose a woman who will make a good wife, and someone who can give me a son."

Caedmon paused and looked at me intently.

Please gods, let my emotions not be written on my face. If he didn't already know I was in love with him, he must never find out now.

"I see," I said finally, because it seemed he waited for my response. Why was he telling me this? He didn't expect me to help find him a wife, did he? I wouldn't do it. I couldn't. It was one thing to vow to never again think about how I had loved him for almost as long as I could remember. It was another thing entirely to find him a bride. I would refuse. This was something I couldn't do, even for Caedmon.

"Grainne, will you handfast with me?"

Long moments passed before I finally grasped the meaning of his words.

"I… what?" My voice was uneven. Gods help me, I sounded like I was about to faint.

"Are you really going to make me say it again? Once was bad enough." Caedmon's lips curled up into the faintest hint of a grin.

Once again my voice failed. At least this time I didn't cough and choke like a fool but merely stood there with my mouth open and nothing coming out.

"Grainne." Caedmon reached for my hand. Good gods, he was holding my hand. Had I cleaned off the ash properly? His fingers were warm and calloused. "I have come home for the sole purpose of taking a wife. I have leave to remain only until the rivers start to thaw and then I must return to the campaign. I don't know when I will come home again. With the knowledge of all of that, will you be betrothed with me?"

There was only one answer any sane woman could give.

"Of course."

Caedmon smiled properly now and squeezed my hand very gently. "I'll send a message to the druid community tonight. We will be handfasted as soon as a druid can get here. If that is acceptable to you."

"Yes, of course." Husband. In just a few sevennights, Caedmon would be my husband.

He leaned in and swiftly kissed my cheek.

"I shall go home then and send the message. I will see you soon." He swung himself up onto the horse.

I watched him leave, hoping he might look back at me, perhaps give some sign that his decision had been influenced by even the tiniest feeling for me. I stayed in the yard long after he had gone. Snow crunched under my feet as I shifted from foot to foot in a futile attempt to keep warm. While Caedmon had been there, I hadn't even noticed how much I shivered. Foolish girl for not wearing a coat. Chill tendrils of air wafted up under my skirt and my teeth began to chatter.

In all my fantasies, I had never once let myself pretend Caedmon might one day ask for my hand. But now he had. So why did my heart feel like it had broken in two?

6

GRAINNE

It was six days before I saw Caedmon again. Messages had passed between Silver Downs and Misty Valley with arrangements for a betrothal party. Yesterday's message also advised that Caedmon would visit this afternoon. I immediately decided I would not dress up for him, although I did braid my hair a little more carefully than usual. He would see me in plenty of work dresses after our handfasting, so I saw no need to set any higher expectation during our betrothal.

I was still trying to figure out how I felt about the situation. Had Caedmon said he was in love with me — had he even hinted he might be — I would have been delighted. But he had made it clear that his choice was purely practical. I dwelt on his words for far longer than I should have. They were factual and honest. If Caedmon had ever been taught that sometimes one should not say exactly what one thought, the lesson had not stuck. He needed a wife and, for whatever reason, had decided it should be me. Love, or indeed any emotion, did not factor into his decision.

But perhaps it didn't matter whether he loved me. He had chosen me after all. I would live with him, get to know him, and gods willing, I would bear the son he wanted. With time, perhaps whatever it was he felt for me would turn into something more. Most women handfasted with men their fathers chose for them and I was fortunate that mine had done no more than hint he would be pleased to see me betrothed. Handfasting for love only happened in the old tales.

My resolve to wear my work dress lasted until I heard the clatter of hooves on the stone path in front of our lodge. I rushed back up to my bedchamber to exchange my woollen work wear for a high-waisted linen dress with delicate yellow day's eyes embroidered around the neckline and wrists. Should I greet him at the door or wait for someone to summon me? I was paralysed with indecision.

Jenifry solved the problem by screeching through the house. "Grainne, Caedmon is here."

I waited at the front door, holding it open despite the freezing breeze that gusted in and whipped around my skirt. Caedmon wore a woollen tunic with long pants, a dark blue coat, gloves and a hat. Even with the bulky winter garments, I would have recognised him anywhere. The way he stood with his back straight but his shoulders just a little slouched, as if entirely comfortable within his own skin. The tilt of his head when he listened to something and the way he lifted his chin before he spoke. I had watched him, studied every gesture, memorised every movement for years.

Sweat trickled between my shoulder blades and my stomach rolled uncomfortably. Usually when I saw Caedmon, I was filled with excitement, an intent to memorise every word and gesture, and a tiny hope that perhaps he might notice me this time. But now nerves made it impossible to think clearly and I hardly knew how to act.

Caedmon looped his horse's reins around a post and headed towards the lodge, rubbing his hands on his pants as if to dry them through his gloves. My heart sank. He had changed his mind. Why else would he be nervous?

"Grainne." Caedmon smiled as he met my eyes and he leaned down to kiss my cheek. He was a head taller than me and my startled jerk meant he almost missed. But at last his lips made contact with my skin and I froze.

Breathe, I reminded myself. *If you faint because you stopped breathing, he'll think you a fool.*

"Caedmon." My voice sounded oddly breathy.

"Aren't you going to invite him in?" Jenifry hissed from behind me.

"Go away," I hissed back without turning around.

At least it was only Jenifry who had taken it on herself to embarrass me. I didn't know where Paili and Vanora were, but at least they weren't hovering behind me. The three girls together could be utterly humiliating when they wanted to be.

Caedmon stifled a smile and pretended he didn't see Jenifry lurking. "I thought we might take a walk."

"I'd love to."

When I reached for my winter coat, Caedmon's hand was there before mine. He lifted it off the hook and held it out for me. This close, he smelled of woodsmoke and the crispness of fresh snow. I again reminded myself to breathe. I pulled my knitted gloves from their hook, hoping he didn't notice the way my fingers trembled.

The winter sky was clear blue from horizon to horizon, with a lone bird circling up high. Snow crunched under my boots. My mouth was dry and inside my gloves, my fingers tingled. Caedmon would think me boring and dim-witted if I didn't think of something to say soon.

"Cold today," I muttered.

Caedmon shot me a brief smile. "I'm nervous too. My sister is too young to be of any help, so I'm not sure I know what you expect of me. If I'm getting it all wrong, tell me. Please. I don't want you to be unhappy because I didn't know what I was supposed to do."

Tears sprang to my eyes and I turned my face into the breeze to dry them before he saw. He wanted to make me happy. And he chose me out of all of the women who would have gladly had him. Perhaps his reasons were irrelevant.

"I don't know what is expected either," I said when I trusted my voice enough to speak. "My sisters are also too young to be useful."

Caedmon took my hand and held it firmly. At least he wouldn't be able to feel my sweaty palms through my gloves.

"Then we will figure it out together," he said.

We walked in silence for a while. I felt like I was not quite grounded in my body, for surely this was not real, the two of us walking hand in hand. The naked branches of birch and beech swayed in the breeze, sending little flutters of snow drifting down to the ground. A pair of wrens balanced on a branch high above my head, their feathers fluffed out for warmth. They twittered together and their conversation sounded small in the openness of the fields.

Our estate was not as big as some, and certainly far smaller than Silver Downs, but most of what I could see belonged to Misty Valley. The snow-covered fields, the barn where the cows and sheep sheltered on winter nights, the stands of birch and ash and beech. Even with my eyes closed, I would recognise the smell of Misty Valley. In summer, it was grass-covered hills and mist-soaked valleys. In winter, it was the tang of frost and the sharpness of the northerly winds slicing in from the Great Sea.

"I've sent for a druid," Caedmon said, darting a sideways glance at me. "I'm hopeful my brother Fiachra might come."

"Do you see him often?"

"Never. He is not allowed to return until he has reached a certain stage in his training. We receive messages from him sometimes, though. He enjoys his studies and works hard to excel."

"When will he come?"

"Two sevennights, perhaps." Caedmon's face tightened. "Hopefully no longer."

"That will be just after midwinter."

"Yes, that still gives us a few weeks to..."

"Get to know each other?" I suggested, but the way his face reddened told me that wasn't what he meant. "Oh."

I didn't quite know where to look. The hand that still grasped mine felt warm, even through our gloves.

"I know most hope for three sons," he said. "But give me one and I'll be satisfied."

"I'll try." My face felt far too hot.

"The handfasting ceremony. Do you have any requirements?"

For a moment I felt recklessly brave. "I'd really like you to be there."

He laughed and squeezed my hand. "I'd like the ceremony to be held at Silver Downs, if you don't mind. Many generations of my family have handfasted there and it wouldn't seem right to do it anywhere else."

I agreed and we talked of inconsequential things after that until a chill breeze forced us to turn back towards home. Not that Misty Valley would be home for much longer. Although we hadn't discussed it yet, it would be expected that I would move to Silver Downs. We would probably build our own lodge there.

At least my family would be only a few hours' horse or cart ride away. As the wife of a soldier, I would be alone much of the year and it would be nice to be able to visit my family as often as I wanted. Caedmon's family would be even closer, probably just a short walk away, and perhaps with time I would think of them as my own. I barely knew his sister, Eithne, but she would be my sister soon.

"Should we hold the betrothal party here?" Caedmon asked.

"Oh." I was oddly touched. "I would like that."

A lump in my throat choked off anything further I might have said and suddenly tears rolled down my cheeks. Their warm path swiftly turned cold.

"Grainne." Caedmon looked startled. He stopped walking and turned me to face him, holding my hand tightly so I couldn't pull away. "I… What does this mean? If you don't want me, say it. I would never force you if you were unwilling."

"It's not that." I pulled my hand from his and fumbled with my gloves. I managed to get one off and wiped my cheeks with my fingers.

Caedmon placed his hand under my chin and tilted my head up.

"Why do you cry? Tell me. I can't fix it if I don't know the problem."

"I'm just overwhelmed. It's all so sudden. And this is my home. I didn't expect to be leaving so soon. I haven't really had time to think about it."

"I don't know what to say to make you feel better." Caedmon spoke slowly, as if choosing his words with care. "I wish I did. But we don't have time for a long betrothal. I need to leave with the first thaw. I'm sorry if this is too rushed for you."

His kind words made me cry in earnest this time. Caedmon wrapped his arms around me and pulled me against him. His body was lean and firm and the arms around me were gentle. I rested my face against his chest and breathed in his smoky scent. I pulled away as soon as I was composed enough to avoid embarrassing myself again.

"I'm sorry. I promise I won't cry on you next time you come to visit."

"I hope that next time I will be bringing news of when to expect the druids."

"I'll look forward to that."

I went to put my glove back on, but he took the glove and tucked it away in his pocket. Then he pulled off one of his own gloves and held my hand all the way back to the lodge. My hand felt tiny encased in his and no matter how cold my fingers were, I wasn't going to pull away. When we reached the lodge, Caedmon returned my glove.

"I'll see you soon." He leaned down and this time I was more prepared and didn't pull away. His lips brushed mine ever so softly. "Farewell, Grainne."

7

GRAINNE

*O*n the day of our betrothal feast, I woke with my stomach feeling like it was filled with pebbles. I barely made it to the wash basin on the dresser before my belly contracted painfully. Bitter vomit coated my tongue.

My whole world was about to change. In just a few hours, my betrothal with Caedmon would become official. Everyone would know. What if he changed his mind before the druids arrived? What if he noticed some other girl for the first time and wished he had asked her instead?

I had loved Caedmon since I tripped on a rocky path when I was seven summers old. I landed on my hands and knees. My knee started bleeding and I sat on the stones and howled. Caedmon was twelve summers old and already broad shouldered with a physique that promised future muscles. He used his shirt to wipe the blood that dripped down my leg and made a silly comment to make me laugh. And my heart became his.

In all practicality, my only aim should have been to find a good husband. But like all children of our people I was raised on a diet of old tales and they taught that love was to be desired, searched for, and treasured. And I loved Caedmon. It was hard not to wish he loved me back. But tonight I would sit at his side. Mine would be the hand he held, mine the lips he kissed before he left. My stomach heaved again and once more its contents sloshed into the wash basin. I dipped a cloth in the water jug and wiped my face.

Be calm, Grainne. Otherwise you're going to fall apart before tonight.

I put on a woollen work dress and pulled my hair back into a rough braid. Squeals from the hallway indicated Jenifry, Paili and Vanora were out of bed. A body thudded against my door. Time to face the world or it would likely come bursting in anyway.

I took the basin downstairs to empty it. After that, the day quickly became a blur. It seemed everyone wanted me to approve one thing or make a decision on another. I was required to decide exactly where the evening's celebrations would be held. I opted for the spacious living area. There was a fireplace at each end and plenty of room for chairs and long tables for food. I pointed to the corner where I wanted the fiddler and whistler to play, and consulted with the women who had come to prepare the food. A servant woman began to hang festive red ribbons from the rafters. My stomach rolled and I wanted nothing more than to crawl back into bed and pull the covers over my head. What if Caedmon didn't even turn up?

As the sun started to set, my sisters bustled me upstairs. While I washed myself with a wet cloth, they lounged on my bed and argued over which of my two good dresses I should wear. I ignored their decision and chose the yellow, for its summery shade, the colour of dandelions, reminded me of summer's warmth even in the middle of winter.

Vanora undid my braid and wove my hair into rows on each side of my head, merging them into one thick plait at the base of my skull. Paili had selected a gold ribbon which Vanora fastened around the bottom of my plait. Jenifry produced a small posy of dried flowers, the remnants of some summer expedition: blue cornflower, white honeysuckle and fire-edged sundew. Although they would probably crumble to dust in minutes, I allowed Vanora to carefully weave them through the length of my braid.

The clatter of hooves and wheels outside heralded the first guests.

It was time to go down and greet them. And pray Caedmon actually came.

I needn't have worried, for the family from Silver Downs were the first to arrive. My stomach clenched as Caedmon's eyes met mine and for a moment I feared I would vomit all over him. He strode up to me and kissed my cheek, taking my hand as he did so.

"You look lovely, Grainne."

My cheeks heated and I knew they would be bright red. He must think me a foolish girl for blushing every time he spoke to me.

"Thank you," I murmured, staring at his shoulder to avoid looking him in the eye. I wanted to say how handsome he looked, but the words wouldn't come out of my mouth.

"Are you ready to celebrate?" he asked.

"I was afraid you wouldn't come." I regretted the words the moment I said them.

"Why would you think that?"

I shrugged and tried to pull my hand away, but he clutched it firmly and drew me closer.

"Grainne, talk to me. Why would you think I wouldn't come? This is our betrothal party. It's a time to celebrate. You and me. Us."

"You don't love me. There isn't really an us." *Damn it, Grainne, stop talking.*

Caedmon's lips straightened. Despite the many years I had studied him, I wasn't sure whether this expression meant disappointment or anger.

"I hardly know you, Grainne, or you me," he said. "But I think you will make a fine wife. Gods willing, there will be time for us to get to know each other."

I nodded, swallowing down the words I wanted to say. Perhaps, with time, he would learn to love me. If I was a good wife to him. If I gave him the son he wanted and stayed faithful when he was gone. *One day,* I vowed, *you will love me. And you'll say it first.*

"I'm sorry." I forced a smile that almost felt genuine. "I feel a little strange today. Overwhelmed. Forgive me."

His easy smile melted my insides until I thought they might ooze out through my skin.

As people poured into the house, I gave up trying to remember who they all were. It seemed that for every friend or relative of my family, there were two of Caedmon's. He introduced me to some, but there were too many to remember. His sister Eithne squealed with delight and hugged me. I hugged her back very gently, for she felt fragile in my arms.

"I am so pleased we are to be sisters," she whispered in my ear. "I've always wanted a sister."

Caedmon's mother, Agata, embraced me more firmly. His father, Fionn, looked like he didn't quite know whether to hug me or slap me on the back. He settled for patting my shoulder. The brothers all offered congratulations: Eremon and his wife Niamh, Sitric, twins Marrec and Conn. Diarmuid was the last to greet me. He hung back and didn't look at me, even as I leaned in to hug him.

"Brother," I said.

He stiffened in my arms, rearing back as if I had bitten him, and I released him quickly. Tears stung my eyes. He didn't need to be so horrid. What did I do to make him hate me so?

Servant women brought around platters of roasted red deer and freshly baked bread. The fiddler and whistler kept up a constant jingle of merry tunes, some familiar and well loved, and others new to my ears. I tapped my toe to the beat as I watched old folk and young, in pairs or groups or even alone, dancing. They spun and skipped and whirled around the room. A sudden surge of impulsiveness gripped me.

"Dance with me, Caedmon," I said, and grabbed his hand.

He didn't say a word but wrapped his arm around my waist and spun me into the middle of the room. Only when I was gasping for breath did we stop. Caedmon barely breathed any harder than usual, but his eyes sparkled. We gulped down mugs of ale, and once I had caught my breath, we dived back into the dancers.

As folk tired, they collapsed onto the rows of chairs lining the walls. Every chair we owned had been brought into the room as well as a cartload of long benches from our nearest neighbour. When Caedmon and I finally fell onto a bench, he draped an arm casually over my shoulders and a thrill danced through me. Finally, I started to believe this was real.

My father stood by one of the fireplaces. I had spied him dancing earlier, much to my surprise, and his cheeks were still ruddy.

"Friends." Father's booming voice reached to the back of the room with ease. "Family. Strangers." A titter arose from the crowd and he beamed at them. "Misty Valley extends a warm welcome to you all. Tonight we celebrate the betrothal of my oldest daughter, Grainne, to Caedmon, son of Silver Downs."

Caedmon squeezed my shoulders and smiled down at me. Sometimes the way he acted made it hard to remember he didn't love me.

"We have feasted and imbibed good ale and danced until we are breathless. Now is the time for reflection and contemplation. This seems a fine time for a tale. Caedmon, my boy, I believe you have a bard in the family. Is he here tonight?"

Beside me, Caedmon stiffened but his voice was as relaxed as ever.

"Yes, my lord. My youngest brother, Diarmuid, over there, is the bard."

He indicated Diarmuid's location with a tilt of his head. Father turned in the direction Caedmon had indicated.

"Well then, young Diarmuid, will you favour us with a tale?"

Diarmuid slunk up to the fireplace. He was as different from Caedmon as summer was from winter. Where Caedmon's walk was easy, Diarmuid's footsteps were short and tense. Where Caedmon was broad-shouldered, Diarmuid was slender and he held his shoulders slightly hunched as if he wished he were invisible. Caedmon's smile was free and his dark eyes showed no hint of the horrors he had seen in battle. Diarmuid looked hunted, chased, haunted.

I had only spoken to Diarmuid twice, at most before tonight. He would always turn in a different direction and scurry away if he saw me walking towards him. I had never been sure whether he hated me or feared me. But perhaps now I was to be his sister, that would change. After all, we would soon be living together.

Diarmuid stood in front of the fireplace, hands clasped awkwardly in front of him. He held his head high and for the first time I saw a hint of the man he might grow into. He cleared his throat, an oddly presumptuous sound.

"This is a new tale." He projected his voice well. "There was once a woman who had a young child, a babe not yet four summers old."

He spoke well and at first I found myself entranced by his words. A good bard can cast a spell over his audience and make them forget where they are. Even in so few words, it was clear Diarmuid had the makings of a great bard. There was a magical, hypnotic quality to his words and I almost started to believe the mother in his tale was myself. But if I listened carefully, ignored the sweet pull urging me to sink deeper and deeper into his tale, there was something wrong about it. Titania, queen of the fey, charmed both mother and child and sent them off into the woods. Instead of the tale ending with the mother saving her child, she watched wild animals rip her to pieces.

My heart stopped for a moment, then stuttered wildly. The image was so strong, it was as if I was there. I heard the cries of the woodlarks, smelled the moss and damp and decay of the woods. The child cries, begs her mother to save her. The mother, also in tears, falls to her knees, but Titania's magic prevents her from moving. Wild boars circle the child, sniffing. One darts in to sample the flesh on her leg. The child cries out, her wordless scream filled with horror. Then the boars attack. The child is quickly brought down into the leaf litter. Her blood stains the leaves. The last sounds she hears are her mother's screams. Caedmon's arm around me brought me back to Misty Valley.

"Grainne." He shook me gently. "Grainne, are you all right?"

"The tale," I whispered. It was all I could say.

Caedmon's face was grim. "I know. His tales are always strange. He wants to please, but…"

"There is something wrong with him."

"Not wrong, just… different. Special. He has a unique ability but has not yet mastered it."

"I never want to hear him tell another tale."

"You will though, I'm afraid. Bards hold a very special place in our family."

Caedmon's arm around me tightened and I leaned against him, soaking up the warmth from his body and trying to shake the awful images from my mind.

8

GRAINNE

The day of our handfasting arrived too soon. I was still getting used to the idea of being betrothed, but I understood Caedmon's urgency. He would not be home for long.

When I woke that morning, thick clouds obscured the sun. Ice tinged the air and fresh snow blanketed the earth all the way to the horizon. I had already packed, not that I had much, just my clothes, a hairbrush and hand mirror, a few trinkets, a thick quilt I myself had stitched. Soon it would cover the bed I would share with my husband. I didn't let myself think about that. My bedchamber felt empty and somehow lonely as I dressed. No longer would this place be mine. When I next returned, it would be as a visitor.

I wore a simple grey gown, sewn by the womenfolk of my family, every stitch made with love and care. Each of my sisters had contributed to the design. Vanora threaded bands of silver around the hem and wrists. Paili stitched a honeysuckle blossom and Jenifry a dove, both symbols of love and peace. Mother added an elaborate spiral pattern around the throat. As I dressed, my family's wishes of happiness and harmony cocooned me. So it was with a full heart that I departed Misty Valley, leaving for the final time as a daughter of that household.

The ride to Silver Downs passed swiftly. I was snug within thick blankets, the warmth in my chest a sharp contrast with the wind stinging my face. My brief calmness evaporated as we drew up in front of the Silver Downs lodge and nausea again stirred in my belly. This was it. The last moments during which I was considered a girl. I would soon be a wife.

Why choose me? There were prettier girls, kinder girls, and surely others better suited to the role of soldier's wife. Others would be more sympathetic to his career and the long absences from home. Others more patient with his children and better at managing the household alone. But for some unknowable reason, Caedmon chose me. And perhaps, with enough time, he might learn to love me. But even if he didn't, I would love him, and not from afar. Instead of watching him with some other woman, it would be me beside him, holding his hand, perhaps with his son clinging to my hip. Our future dawned ahead of me, bright and sparkling and filled with opportunity. We would be happy. Caedmon would be happy. I would make sure of it.

When we arrived at Silver Downs, Father helped me from the cart, his beaming face red from the cold air.

"You will make a fine wife, Grainne," he said.

Mother embraced me, her arms around me thinner than I remembered. She took a step back and placed one hand on my cheek.

"He is a good man and will be kind to you. I couldn't have chosen better for you myself."

Of my two brothers, only Piran was present. He embraced me firmly but said nothing. My other brother, Wynne, was a soldier and likely didn't even know I would be handfasted today. I had often wondered whether he ever saw Caedmon when they were both at the campaign front but had never asked for fear of betraying my interest.

My sisters hugged me in turn from oldest to youngest. Vanora, then Paili, then Jenifry. A stranger would recognise the four of us as sisters, with our rosy cheeks and dark hair.

Jenifry's chin wobbled and her eyes shone.

"I'll miss you," she said.

"I won't be far away. You can come and visit me."

"But it won't be the same. Nothing will ever be the same again."

Her words echoed in my ears as I approached the lodge, flanked by my family. Its grey stones loomed over me, far bigger than our lodge at Misty Valley. It had to be, with seven sons.

Caedmon opened the front door just as I reached it. His dark hair was soldier-short and still damp from bathing. He greeted me with a wide smile and a brief kiss on my lips, then led me through the lodge. My family followed, my sisters unusually quiet. Perhaps they were intimidated by the fineness of Silver Downs. I knew just how they felt. It was hard to believe that this was about to become my home.

Everywhere I looked, the wooden furniture was carefully polished to a gleam. Thick tapestries lined the walls and heavy embroidered curtains covered the windows. The colours were dark and sombre: forest green, earthy brown, a deep scarlet. This house spoke of tradition and inheritance, of ancestors and history. The house in which I grew up had been built when my parents handfasted. It was light and airy and decorated in yellows and oranges and bright blues, for my mother was fond of cheery colours.

Caedmon's parents, Fionn and Agata, embraced me. Eithne's hug was enthusiastic, if not particularly strong. The shadows on her face suggested a recent illness and her dress hung loosely as if she had lost weight too recently for the seams to be taken in.

Diarmuid hung back as the brothers greeted me and at length I forced myself to approach him, trying to hide my unease as I did so. Images from his tale still lingered in my mind. The mother on her knees in the forest. The child, broken and bloody, limbs torn off. I shook my head and forced the dark images from my mind. Today was for happy thoughts. I would not dwell on Diarmuid's awful tale.

Amongst the brothers was one I had not met before. I would have known him as a son of Silver Downs even if I had first glimpsed him elsewhere, for he was broad of shoulder and dark-haired and looked much like Caedmon. The druids had sent one of Silver Downs' own.

"Well met, Grainne," Fiachra said as he embraced me with strong arms.

I hugged him back, feeling absurdly shy. He was just another who would shortly become my brother, but there was something about him that was different from his siblings. Some sense of Other, of depth and mystery. Inwardly, I shivered. This was a powerful man. Powerful and, perhaps, dangerous. Fiachra released me and Caedmon took my hand.

"Come, Grainne," he said. "Everyone is waiting outside."

As we exited through the back door into the crisp sunshine, calmness washed over me. Gone were my nerves. Gone was the fear that Caedmon might change his mind before we could be handfasted. Gone was my niggling doubt that perhaps his message to the druids would never arrive and nobody would come. Of course, I could have simply moved into the lodge at Silver Downs, but any child I bore would not be legally recognised unless we were handfasted by a druid.

We gathered beneath a mighty oak, its naked branches providing no obstacle to the weak sun. Fresh snow crunched under my boots. Caedmon and I stood together in front of the druid who would perform the handfasting ritual. It wasn't Fiachra but one of his elders. He was several decades older than Fiachra with a full beard tinged with grey.

"Beings of air and water, fire and earth, bear witness to this event." The druid's voice was strong and compelling. "This man and this woman pledge themselves to each other."

I wondered whether the elementals heard him and came. Perhaps even now they watched. The words of the ceremony flowed past me. I tried to concentrate on them, to linger over the significance of the event, but my mind kept urging the druid to hurry, to speak the words that would bind us. Eventually he wrapped a scarlet ribbon around our wrists, tying us together.

Caedmon's face was grave as he stared down at me and I tried to ignore a sudden sense of doom. Death was an ever-present risk for a soldier. He might die in his next battle, or if not then, the one after. My hands were cold as Caedmon reached for them. He kissed me soundly to the cheers and shouts of those assembled. His lips were warm against mine and the knot in my belly began to unwind just a little. Caedmon looked more relaxed now, almost carefree. Perhaps he too had been nervous.

With the ceremony concluded, long tables draped with red cloths were piled high with platters of steaming food. Meats and roasted root vegetables, various breads and cheeses. The red linen was stark as blood against the snowy background. The distant sound of a raven's caws reached my ears, although I saw no sign of the bird.

My stomach growled, for I had been too nervous to eat this morning. I managed no more than a few bites between the constant congratulations from well-wishers. Folk were loud and cheerful, hastening to eat before the food cooled. They stood in small groups, eating with a bread trencher in one hand and a mug of ale in the other. A group of laughing children darted in and out of the crowd, ignoring the food in favour of games.

The sun began to sink towards the horizon and the frigid air was thick with the promise of snow. I had thought folk might start heading home as evening fell, but instead they moved inside. The family room was warm, with the lamps lit and the fires already burnt down to embers. I accepted a mug of spiced wine from a serving woman. It slid down my throat easily, warming my insides. Somebody pressed a chunk of bread filled with roasted pig into my hands and I ate quickly while I could.

Hours passed and still folk drank and danced and talked. I grew tired of making small talk with strangers. Fatigue began to gnaw at me and my head grew light from tiredness and spiced wine. Caedmon saw me stifle one yawn and then another. He leaned close to whisper in my ear.

"Time for bed perhaps?"

My face grew hot. I had not let myself think of how the evening would end. I didn't know whether to look forward to it or fear it. Mother had pulled me aside a few days ago to ensure I knew what would be expected. I had some idea already, of course. One does not grow up surrounded by horses and cows and dogs without having at least some knowledge of such a thing.

We slipped away quietly without any goodbyes. My legs were heavy and it almost seemed like too much effort to lift them.

"We can choose a site for our home in the next couple of days," Caedmon said as he led me up the stairs. "The lodge here might feel a bit crowded, but it's only for a few months until our own is built. I've already hired some men. You can choose where you want our home to be. There's a place down by the river you might like." He paused outside a closed door, halfway down the passage. "Just a warning, I think some of the women may have been in here. I was told to keep out."

He pushed open the door and we left the chilly passage for the warmth of Caedmon's bedchamber. Our bedchamber. He stirred the embers in the fireplace and they quickly blazed back into fiery life.

Someone had spread candles along the dresser and the mantelpiece. Their tiny fires glimmered, making the room sparkle. Dried purple petals sprinkled the bed's snowy white cover. The scent of rosemary and pinecones filled my nose.

Caedmon finished stoking the fire and closed the door. He slid his arms around me from behind. I leaned back against him, still getting used to the feel of his body against mine. He gently guided me towards the bed, then turned me around to face him, his hands soft on my shoulders. My heart thudded and my hands trembled.

"I'm not sure I know what to do," I said, and to my embarrassment, my voice wavered a little.

"I want you to enjoy this, Grainne. All you have to do is tell me what you like and what you don't."

"I think I can do that."

His hands were gentle as he unfastened the ties of my grey gown and pushed it back over my shoulders. It slid to the floor with a whisper. Caedmon lifted me and placed me in the centre of the bed. He lay beside me and leaned in to kiss me firmly as his hands began to roam over my body.

"Oh," I whispered. "I like that."

9

EITHNE

As I finally sank into the fever dreams, the fey boy had come to stand beside my bed as I had known he would. When I asked for some token to prove he was real, he frowned. I feared scaring him away and didn't ask again. But I hugged my secret knowledge to myself: the fey had reason to watch me. I had a purpose, even if I didn't know what.

It had been more than a sevennight since I started to recover and it was so rare to feel any strength in my limbs that I couldn't bear to linger inside. A glance out the window showed me the sky was clear and the snow on the ground was thin.

"I think I'll go for a walk today," I said to Mother a little later as we broke our fast with new bread and honey. The honey was a gift from a neighbouring estate and was sweeter than that from our own bees. It lingered on my tongue, sticky-sweet.

Mother and I were the only ones at the table, for Papa and my brothers all started their work day early. Mother, too, had likely been up for hours already, but she usually waited to eat with me. It was only I who had the luxury of sleeping as late as I pleased. A crease wrinkled Mother's forehead.

"I'm not sure that is a good idea, Eithne."

"I feel good. Strong."

"Don't go far. Stay within sight of the lodge. And dress warmly."

"I will," I said, although I had already determined to walk as far as I could.

Winter was drawing to a close and soon the rivers would begin to thaw and the trees would grow their summer coating of leaves. A lone thrush trilled from bare branches and a patch of melting snow displayed glimpses of the sleeping earth beneath. Already the land stirred and summer felt close. I looked forward to working in my garden again, for Mother forbade me to touch it during the winter months. But when the weather was warm and I was well, I delighted in spending some time each morning pulling weeds or trimming herbs. Servant women would do the heavier work, planting bulbs and turning soil, while I sat on my wooden bench and directed them. When in full bloom, my little garden was a riot of colour with purple bluebells and white wood anemones and yellow tulips.

My heart felt light as the snow crunched beneath my boots and the sun warmed my face. It was almost warm enough that I didn't need my heavy coat or my scarf and gloves, but I didn't dare remove them in case Mother watched from a window. I did take off my hat, though, to feel the breeze in my hair.

I walked slowly and it was some time before the lodge was out of sight, hidden behind the small hill I ambled over. Ahead stood a stand of slender beech. In summer their dense canopy provided shade and a cool retreat for birds and bugs, but now their branches were bare, waiting for the new buds of spring. This was my favourite place to linger when I had the strength to walk this far. It was my private place, where nobody else ever came. A large rock, transported by my brothers to a sunny spot beside the trees, provided a convenient resting spot.

As I approached, something was different. It took me some time though — not until I was closer — to see what it was. A figure stood amongst the beeches; not one of my brothers, for his profile was taller and more slender.

My breath caught in my throat. Should I turn back now? I

wouldn't be able to run far, but perhaps I could make it to within sight of the fields. My brothers would be working out there. They would come if they saw me running.

The figure was perfectly still, standing a few paces from my rock. A silent, watching presence in a place that had always previously been my own. I still couldn't decide whether to flee, but my feet continued to carry me forward, never hesitating. Finally I drew close enough to make out the boy's features. Snow white skin, black hair cut without care for fashion. Blood red lips. He said nothing as I approached but watched me intently. Feeling awkward beneath his stare, I straightened my back and took extra care not to limp.

"You," I said, when I came close enough to speak without shouting. I stopped mere paces away from my private sanctuary, longing to rest on my rock, but not wanting to enter while the intruder was there. My legs trembled from the walk, although it wasn't all that far. He didn't acknowledge my words but continued to stare at me. "I thought you were a dream."

Finally, he cocked an eyebrow at me but I couldn't tell whether he was amused or offended.

"As you can see, I am not."

"Why are you here? This is my place."

"You claim this land? We were here long before your kind came."

"Not the whole land, just this bit." I gestured at beech and rock. "This is my private place. Nobody but me ever comes here."

"I come here all the time."

"But you can't. This is my place."

I was irrationally annoyed. He had already intruded on my bedchamber. How dare he also invade this sanctuary?

"You have no way of stopping me. I shall come here if I please. And when the day arrives that I no longer wish to come here, I will stop."

"That's not fair."

"I didn't say it was."

He was calm, unperturbed by my anger.

"But it's not your decision."

"Then whose is it? Yours?"

"This is my place."

"So you said."

Dark eyes watched my reaction, noting my increasing irritation. I stamped my foot, which had little effect on the snowy ground, and wished I could be more eloquent in my speech.

"You are infuriating."

"Why does your foot twist?"

A hot flush darkened my cheeks. "How rude."

"I'm curious."

"It's none of your business."

"Why do you hide it?"

"How do you know about it if I hide it?"

"I am accustomed to perfection. The way your foot twists is obvious, even when you try to hide it."

"I hide it because I don't like being stared at. Not that it's any of your business."

"Why would you tell me if you didn't want me to know?"

"Because you asked." I restrained from stamping my foot again, although only barely. "Why were you spying on me?"

"It's not spying if the other party knows you are there."

"I had no choice in whether you were there or not. You just showed up. In my bedchamber. It's highly inappropriate."

"It's only inappropriate if somebody else knows."

"What if I told someone?"

"Have you?"

My legs trembled even harder now and refusing to sit was no longer an option. I strode forward, trying to walk evenly, but tiredness always exacerbated my limp. I brushed snow from the rock with my gloved hand and didn't answer him until I had settled onto it, its solid form cold beneath my thick skirt.

"I might have."

"Nobody would believe you."

"You can't just come into a woman's bedchamber without her permission."

I looked out towards the mountainous horizon and willed myself to be calm. I had never met someone who could raise my temper with so little effort.

"Would it make a difference if I asked?"

"No. I still wouldn't allow you."

"Then there's no point in asking. I'm going to continue coming to you anyway."

A delicious thrill went down my spine, but I pretended it was just a shiver.

"Why?"

"Because you intrigue me."

I didn't know how to respond.

"What is your name?" I asked instead.

"Kalen. And you are Eithne."

He probably waited for me to ask how he knew but I refused to play his game.

"Where do you live?" I asked instead.

Kalen waived his hand to indicate somewhere behind himself. "There is a portal to our realm in the woods."

"Are you permitted to come here whenever you want?"

"Not exactly."

"Who would stop you?"

"My queen."

"Is that Titania?"

"You know of her?" A flicker of surprise crossed his face.

"Our tales tell of her."

"What do they tell?"

"That she is beautiful. And cruel."

He smiled slightly, amused, although I didn't know why.

"She is both of those things," he said.

"Why would she stop you from coming here?"

He looked away. "I can't tell you."

"Why not?"

He shrugged and didn't answer.

"How old are you?" I wriggled into a more comfortable position on the rock. It was starting to warm beneath me but when I moved, I shifted onto a cold spot. I edged back onto the warmth.

"My kind don't measure age the way you do. We live a very long time. Your world will crumble to dust before I die."

"That's sad," I said. "To see everything you know die."

"It's the way things are. It is neither sad nor not."

"Do you even know what sadness is?"

"I know it makes mortals cry."

"Happiness makes us cry sometimes too."

His gaze sharpened with interest. "How peculiar."

"Why do you watch me?"

Again, Kalen looked away.

The sun had started to sink towards the horizon by now and fingers of purple spanned the sky. A flock of birds — too far away to tell what — flew in an arrow formation. I wondered whether they would reach their destination before night fell. I clambered off the rock, my limbs sore and stiff.

"I have to go," I said.

"Farewell."

"Will you walk with me? Just until the house is within sight."

Kalen eyed me for a long moment and I shifted uncomfortably. Why did I ask such a thing? I barely knew him and he had already been spying on me from within my own bedchamber. My invitation sounded like encouragement. But the words were already said.

"Yes," he said finally, and my heart did a strange little leap.

We walked slowly, for I was tired and my foot ached. I couldn't help but limp, but Kalen didn't ask about it again. He didn't seem to mind my silence either which was a relief, for I didn't have enough energy left to talk. As the lodge came into view, Kalen stopped.

"Goodbye, Eithne," he said. "Will you meet me tomorrow?"

My heart beat so loudly that he could probably hear it.

"Yes."

I was determined not to watch him leave, but when I finally gave in and looked back, he was gone. I limped towards the lodge, my gait slow and awkward. Smoke streamed from the chimneys and lantern light shone around the drapes. The lodge was bedding down for the night. The animals would all be shut away in the barn, fed and watered. The house would be filled with noise and love and the good smells of dinner cooking. Sometimes I wondered whether I was the only one who ever felt lonely there.

10

EITHNE

My dreams that night were filled with Kalen. I returned to every word he had said, over and over. Every twitch of his eyebrows, every quirk of his lips. As dawn broke I was ready to leap out of bed and rush out to the stand of beech, but rain greeted me when I parted the curtains. It wasn't much more than a fine mist, but certainly enough that Mother would not let me leave the lodge today. Hopefulness dissipated into disappointment and I returned to bed.

By the time I emerged again several hours later, drizzling rain had become a storm. The air was thick with moisture. Thunder boomed and my room brightened with each crackle of lightning. Disappointment became frustration and crankiness. Without the sun, I couldn't tell the hour, but the rumble in my belly suggested it must be almost noon. I dragged myself out of bed and washed halfheartedly.

The house smelled of wet floors and smoky fires. It was cleaning day and Mother never let something as minor as the weather interfere with that. The servant women would have arrived at dawn, regardless of the rain. They were four widowed women who were permitted to live on Silver Downs land in exchange for their labour. Four servants was probably more than we needed, but Mother would never turn away a woman in need of employment. They were allowed to live in the cluster of cottages that lay a few minutes' walk from the main lodge and when Mother didn't need them, they helped in the fields, thus securing a portion of the crops for themselves. It was a hard way to make a living, but Mother said there were worse fates that could befall a woman than honest labour.

The remnants of breakfast had been cleared away and there was no fresh bread left. I found an end of a loaf from yesterday and pulled up a low stool to the kitchen fireplace. Despite my rumbling stomach, the bread stuck in my throat and most of it ended up in a pile of crumbs that I tossed into the fire.

I tried to sit in my usual spot in the family room, but my feet wouldn't stay still. I paced the house, getting in the way of the servant women, until Mother flapped her hands at me and shooed me away. I had thought that Papa and my brothers might be here somewhere, since they couldn't work outside in this weather, but perhaps they were occupied with chores in the barn.

I sat on a window seat, staring out at the fields. Everything was grey. The clouds, the rain, the snow on the ground. I couldn't see my little stand of beech trees from here. Did Kalen wait there for me? Did the fey even notice weather? Perhaps the rain was of no account to him. He might be there, wondering why I didn't come. I pictured him standing beneath a tree, water dripping from his ill-fitting clothes as the branches above him swayed in the wind.

I contemplated slipping out the back door. Mother would be horrified, but perhaps I could do it and be back before she realised. But I would be sopping wet and would have to make my way up to my bedchamber without being seen, likely leaving a trail of puddles on the clean floors.

And what if I injured myself? I might slip in the mud, for the ankle that bore my twisted foot had never been strong. If I fell heavily enough, I might not be able to get up without help. Nobody would look for me outside. If anyone even noted my absence, they would assume I was elsewhere in the lodge. I would have to wait, lying in the mud with the rain beating down on me, surrounded by thunder and lightning, until the storm passed and somebody ventured outside again. The picture in my mind was so vivid, I almost shed a tear for poor Eithne who lay in the mud, cold and injured and alone.

So I didn't creep out to look for Kalen but roamed the lodge until I rounded a corner and crashed into Fiachra. He was solid for a druid, with the broad shoulders and dark hair that is common to the menfolk in our family. I had expected him to be thinner, frailer, but his form was much like that of Papa and Eremon.

Fiachra grasped my arms to steady me. His warmth seeped through the sleeves of my woollen dress. I smiled up at him, somewhat tentatively, for this brother was mostly a stranger to me. He had arrived on the morn of Caedmon's handfasting, but I had hardly seen him in the sevennight since.

"Good morning, Fiachra. Are you well?"

He quirked an eyebrow at me.

"Is that really what you want to ask, Eithne?"

My mouth opened but nothing came out. I finally realised how close we still stood, barely more than a hand's width apart. I stepped back and he released me.

"I was merely being polite," I said.

"I care little for social niceties. Not in private, at any rate."

I had never before been alone with Fiachra, or any druid for that matter.

"If there is something you wish to ask, this would be a good moment in which to do so," he said.

"Why do you think I want to ask you something?"

"Because you found me."

"But I wasn't looking for you."

"And yet you found me anyway. Does that not tell you something?"

"Is it not possible I found you inadvertently? That it just so happens we ended up wandering in the same part of the house?"

"I am not easy to find. If you found me, you were meant to. Now, what do you wish to ask?"

I bit my lower lip as I considered my options. Who better than a druid to ask about the nature of the fey? But when I opened my mouth, a different question came out.

"Why did you not want to be found?"

"I don't care much for the company of people."

"That sounds…" My voice trailed off, for I didn't want to seem rude.

"My brethren and I pass many hours every day in solitude, practicing our training, learning the teachings. I am not accustomed to spending so much time with other folk."

"Why are you still here? Why do you not return to the druids?"

"Things are stirring here. Old power is rising. I am needed."

"What does that mean?"

"Tell me, sister, what is it you really want to ask?"

"What do you know of the fey?" Once I made up my mind, the words came out in a rush.

"Logic, reason, emotion. The fey see these things differently to how mortals do. Things that are important to us, are negligible to them."

"Are the old tales true?"

"Some are, and many more contain elements of truth."

I hesitated before I asked my next question. My heart seemed to beat very loudly.

"What of the tales of women who fall in love with the fey? Is it true they are never loved in return?"

Fiachra regarded me, his face giving no hint of his thoughts.

"Perhaps somewhere, in the history of our people, there has been a mortal woman who fell for one of the fey and whose feelings were reciprocated. Perhaps they are always reciprocated, for a time at least."

I longed to ask more but was hesitant to reveal too much to this brother I barely knew.

"Thank you," I said. "Your words… they give me much to think about."

I turned to leave.

"Eithne."

I paused but did not turn back to face him.

"Time is another thing the fey view differently. Because they live for eons, our lives are but a brief shift in the wind, a momentary flicker of candlelight. Understanding this gives much insight into the mindset of the fey."

I thought I understood what he was trying to say. I nodded and fled.

11

EITHNE

The wet weather lingered for two days and I was almost out of my mind with frustration by the time it cleared. As soon as the rain stopped, I pulled on my coat and boots and slipped outside. I didn't tell Mother because she would worry about the wet and the cold, and would keep me inside until the ground was dry. How could I sit in the house and do nothing, when Kalen might be waiting for me?

The air was cold and so was the water that clung to everything: the grass, the trees, the hem of my dress. The breeze smelled crisp and fresh and tore right through my coat. I meandered along, trying to appear as if I had no particular destination in mind. My twisted foot always ached in wet weather, so hiding my limp was a little harder than usual. The sun seemed overly bright today, as if to make up for the days of grey, and as the clouds receded they revealed a brilliant blue sky.

As I rounded the rise that hid the trees from the lodge, my heart beat faster and it became even harder to maintain my sedate pace. I wrapped my coat tighter around me and pretended it was the cold breeze that made me shiver. If Kalen was indeed waiting for me, I did not want to look too eager. So I continued to make my way slowly to the trees, although try as I might, I couldn't stop myself from walking just a little faster.

As I drew closer, my breath caught in my throat. Just a little further and I would know whether he was there. With eager eyes I examined the beeches, tracing each silhouette, every familiar trunk and shrub. There, in the dark depths, was that a shadow that did not belong? But as I came closer, the shadow resolved into just another beech.

I walked faster, but my foot slid in a patch of mud and I almost landed on my backside. Heart racing, I slowed and paid more attention to where I placed my feet.

"Kalen?" I called when I was close enough. "Kalen, are you there?"

The trees were silent and my heart stuttered. He wasn't there. But as I approached my rock, a shadow separated from the trees and moved towards me. He came out into the open and my heart began a crazy dance.

"You came," I said.

Kalen tilted his head to one side and eyed me curiously. "You did not think I would?"

"It's rained for the last two days. I thought… I didn't know whether you would be wondering why I didn't come sooner. I can't go out if it's raining. Mother worries for me. She thinks I will fall ill."

I was rambling. I shut my mouth with a snap.

"You said you would be here. I waited."

"I'm sorry. I couldn't."

"I understand. You will not come to meet me if it rains, even if you said you would."

I took a deep breath, inhaling the scents of rain and mud, and willed myself to find the right words.

"It's not that I didn't want to."

Perhaps things were different within fey families. Perhaps the younger fey did not have to seek permission to do things. Maybe that's why he didn't understand when I said I wasn't allowed.

"I can't stay long. It's too cold today and Mother will be worried if she realises I am gone. I just came…"

He waited as I tried to find words that were not quite as revealing as what I had almost said.

"I came to explain why I didn't come yesterday."

Still he showed no emotion. Had I upset him? Angered him? How could I make this right? I was growing too cold to stand here for much longer. Goosebumps prickled my skin and I wrapped my arms around myself, trying not to shiver.

"It is Imbolc tomorrow." My words came out in a rush. I had not planned this, had not even considered asking. "There will be a celebration here at Silver Downs."

I paused for breath and Kalen cocked his head at me, as if unsure what reaction I sought. I ploughed on before I lost my nerve.

"Will you come? To the feast? There will be dancing and a big fire."

"There will be many people."

"Of course. Everyone will be here."

"Your family would see us."

Excitement dimmed. "Yes, they might. But there will be lots of folk here. They won't know that you don't belong. You might be... I don't know... a worker from another estate. Or a visiting relative."

"What would we do there?"

"The same as everyone else. We could eat and talk and watch folk dance."

Kalen's face finally showed a spark of emotion. "I enjoy dancing."

"I've never tried. I have not the strength for it. But I like watching the dancers."

The wind changed direction and an icy gust dove under my coat. I could no longer hide my shivers. The sun wasn't shining quite as brightly anymore and a few grey clouds had crept across the previously clear sky.

"You are cold," Kalen said and his voice was more curious than anything else.

"The wind..." My teeth chattered. "I should go back."

Kalen nodded and stepped back into the trees. "Goodbye."

"Wait, will you meet me tomorrow night?"

But he was already gone. I clutched my coat tighter around me and set off for home. He hadn't said yes, but he also hadn't said no. That meant I could hope.

1 2

EITHNE

My fingers fumbled with the red ribbon as I tied it around my braid. It took three attempts before I managed to fasten it neatly. The face that stared at me from my hand mirror wore flushed cheeks and bright eyes. I wrapped another ribbon around my wrist, just beneath the bottom of my sleeve, and admired the glimpse of red fabric as I lifted my arm.

"Eithne, are you ready?" Mother's voice drifted up the stairs.

"I'm coming," I called.

I set the hand mirror on the dresser and straightened my gown one last time. I had always liked the way this gown skimmed my hips and then flared out slightly before finishing just short of the ground. It made me look not quite so skinny. I envied Mother's broad hips and ample breasts, while knowing I would never have such a figure. My gown hung a little looser than usual, but I had not thought to try it on in time to take in the seams.

The longer I stood there preening, the longer it would be before I found out whether or not Kalen would come. I hurried down the stairs and pulled on my warmest coat. I draped my scarf over my braided hair and wound the ends around my neck, then retrieved my gloves from my coat pocket. Mother paused to wait for me, pulling on my gloves as I hurried to her.

The sun was starting to sink behind the horizon and the sky was a riot of purple and orange. Tonight's festivities celebrated the start of spring. The long days of winter were almost at an end. The ewes were heavy with lambs, the snow had started to melt, and tiny buds had already appeared on ash and birch and beech.

The first cartloads of guests had just arrived and they went straight to where a huge fire had been built some distance from the lodge. They helped themselves to mugs of ale from the long tables and milled around, drinking and greeting friends and generally making lots of noise. Inside my gloves, my palms grew sweaty. Shadows crept in and I couldn't see the faces of those on the far side of the fire clearly enough to know whether Kalen was there.

"Eithne, don't go too far." Mother tucked a stray strand of hair back behind my ear. "You're still not very strong."

"I'll be fine, Mother. I'm going to see if I can find the Three Trees girls."

"Stay near the fire. Make sure you eat something and go back to the house as soon as you get chilled."

I forced a smile at her and left. I was not a child in need of being fussed over. I was seventeen summers old, which made me a grown woman and old enough to be married. I wove through the folk gathered around the fire, searching for the familiar pale face. Normally I avoided crowds as much as possible. Their clamour made my head hurt and I feared being trampled or trapped. But Kalen wouldn't show himself if I stood next to Mother all night.

The scent of sizzling roast meat and fresh bread filled the air but I wasn't hungry. The only thing I wanted was to find Kalen. A man flung his arm out to the side as he spoke, catching me on the shoulder and almost knocking me to the ground. He grinned an apology at me and turned back to the woman he was speaking with. She smiled up at him, an obvious invitation in her eyes.

My twisted foot started to ache, so I looked around for somewhere to sit while I waited for Kalen. Finally, I spotted a vacant bench where two girls had been sitting a few moments before. I sank down onto the bench gratefully and removed my gloves, tucking them into the pocket of my jacket. Someone sat next to me, a little too close for my liking, and I edged over slightly to put more space between us. Then I noticed his long, pale fingers.

"Kalen."

In the flickering light of the fire, his pale skin and too-red lips weren't quite as obvious as usual. He wore dark clothes and a thick cloak.

"I've been looking for you," I said.

"I did not expect this many people."

"It's Imbolc. Spring is on its way."

"It does not look all that different from our festivities."

"I wish I could see them some day." I spoke without thinking.

"I could take you there now."

"You know I can't."

"Why not?"

"I can't just disappear. Mother would worry."

We sat silently for a while. I couldn't tell whether he was annoyed or just being quiet. A fiddler started a merry tune and I caught myself tapping my toes in time with it. Folk paired up and began dancing. I shot a sideways glance at Kalen. If I were a different person, I might have asked if he wanted to join them, but folk would stare if they saw me dancing and Mother would worry that I exerted myself too much.

My clenched fists rested on my knees and Kalen slid his hand over them. His fingers were cool and barely touched mine.

"Come, Eithne, dance with me."

My mouth fell open. For someone who didn't want to be seen, now he wanted to dance with me in public?

"I don't know whether that's a good idea," I said, although my feet longed to move and I wanted nothing more than to throw myself into the crowd and dance until I was sweaty and exhausted. Not that it would take long.

He tugged gently on my hands. "I can't stay. One dance and then I must go."

Before I could think too hard about it, I stood. He took my hand and pulled me into the crowd. I was familiar enough with the steps from all my years of watching and Kalen picked them up quickly.

I hadn't been this close to him before and he was taller than I had realised. The top of my head barely came up to his shoulders. He held my hands lightly, his cool fingers gentle. I felt tiny next to him, although he himself was slender. Only a couple of handspans of air separated his body and mine. I wanted to lean against him and feel his warmth. What would it be like to kiss him? I quickly banished the thought from my mind lest he read it on my face. My heart pounded, as much from excitement as from the exertion.

We moved together, now closer, now further apart. The steps were quicker than I had expected and I could barely keep up. Kalen released my hands briefly as we each took a step backwards and spun in a quick circle. We came back together and he took my hands again before my fingers had time to grow cold.

The tune was only halfway over before my feet began to slow and my breath came in gasps. I kept moving though, determined to last the whole dance, although now I was a beat or two behind the melody. Our dance seemed to last for hours and at the same time, it passed in moments.

The song ended and the lingering notes of the fiddle faded away. After a moment of silence, the next song started and Kalen pulled me back through the crowd. Our vacated bench had been claimed so he paused in a shadowy spot a little distance from the fire.

"It is time for me to leave, Eithne. I am glad we were able to dance together tonight."

"Me too." I smiled up at him, still trying to catch my breath and wishing I could look more elegant as I did.

He released my hand and I felt a pang of disappointment.

"Farewell," he said and stepped back.

"Will I see you tomorrow?"

"Of course."

Kalen touched one cool finger to my lips. Then he was gone, melting away into the dark. Nobody looked at him as he slipped through the crowd. Perhaps he used a charm of some sort to render himself unnoticeable. The old tales told of the fey doing such things.

I pressed my fingers to the spot where he had touched my lips. It wasn't a kiss, but it was something close. I pushed my way through the crowd until I found a vacant bench close by the fire. I settled in for the rest of the evening. Mother would worry I was ill if I left so early, so I would sit by the fire, watching the dancers and thinking about Kalen.

1 3

—————

SUMERLED

Kalen doesn't know I follow him. When he slips away through the woods that separate our world from that of the mortals, I sneak along behind. I can't figure out why he is so fascinated with them. They are weak and boring with tepid lives and indifferent deaths. Yet still he watches.

At first it was just now and then. Then his forays into the mortal world came every few days. Now he goes to them every day, or rather, he goes to *her* every day.

I follow and hide. The woods are my home so I know how to move silently. I know just where to put my foot to avoid the crackle of leaves or the snap of a twig. I know how to move silently so the wood-larks don't sing a warning. He is not far ahead of me as I crouch behind a holly bush and peek through. I'm certain Kalen doesn't know I'm watching until he sneaks up behind me and grabs me by the scruff of my neck.

"Sumerled," he hisses. "What are you doing here?"

Startled, the woodlarks begin warbling.

He yanks me up, his hands rough. My teeth slam together as he deposits me on my feet.

"Following you." My voice is petulant and I refuse to look at him.

"Why?"

"Felt like it."

Kalen grabs my shoulders and shakes me. I taste blood where I have bitten my tongue.

"Why are you following me, boy?"

"Why do you keep going to her? She's just a boring mortal."

He shakes me again, so hard I think my head might fall off.

"What have you seen?" he says. "What do you know of her?"

I clamp my jaws shut. I will not tell him anything. He pushes me away, then turns and strides off. I hesitate, but only moments pass before I am scurrying after him, stumbling over a fallen branch in my hurry.

"Kalen, wait for me."

"Go away."

"I bet I know something about her that you don't."

He hesitates, mid-stride, then keeps walking.

"Tell me then, and prove yourself useful. Otherwise, go away."

I pause. What to tell? And what to save in case I need it later? I tell him my best secret.

"She is deformed. You could have at least picked one that is whole and sound."

"She's not deformed."

"Her foot—"

"I know about her foot." He whirls around and grabs me by the shoulder which already feels bruised from his previous abuse. "Sumerled, why have you been following me? Did someone tell you to?"

"I'm not telling."

He snarls and releases me, then storms off.

"Kalen—"

"Go. Away."

I try to follow but the woods are just as much Kalen's home as they are mine. He slips between beech and oak, and is gone. I look for signs of which direction he took — a patch of disturbed leaf litter, a broken twig, a heel print in the mud — but there is nothing. And I suddenly realise that if he does not want to be found, I cannot find him.

He knew I was following all along. He waited for me to reveal myself. Perhaps if I had, our encounter would have been different. He might have trusted me. But I hid and thought I followed in secret. I was trying to protect him, but instead I pushed him further away from me.

1 4

———————

GRAINNE

*W*aking up beside Caedmon each morning was still something to be savoured. I was aware of his presence before I opened my eyes, even when his body wasn't touching mine. He warmed the bed beneath our blankets and his breaths, when he slept, were long and deep.

I treasured these moments, for it would not be long before I would once again wake up alone. Imbolc had passed and winter drew to a close. But we had some time together yet: a sevennight, maybe two if I was lucky. Already beech and ash bore tiny buds that would soon open into new leaves. The days were a little warmer and the nights less frosty. When I looked out the window, snow still blanketed the fields all the way to the horizon but that would soon melt, the rivers would thaw and Caedmon would leave.

We had chosen a site for our home and Caedmon had already hired some men to build it. His brother Sitric, who intended to become a scribe once their father could spare him, had documented the details. In this way Caedmon could ensure our lodge would be exactly as he envisioned, even if he wasn't present for its building.

I was well pleased with the location, for the lodge would have a sunny aspect with a fine view of rolling hills from my work room.

391

There I would oversee the running of our house and do small chores such as darning socks. I would have a servant woman — Agata had already offered one of the women bonded to Silver Downs. We would be well out of sight of both the main lodge and also Eremon and Niamh's home, although both were only a short walk away. Here, surrounded by hills, we would have the illusion of privacy while being close to help and companionship.

Once Caedmon left, I would continue to live in his childhood home until our own was built. My heart froze whenever I thought about his departure. The long trek back to the campaign front would take ten days. The journey would be cold, and lonely for a man who travelled alone. I had asked Caedmon if he worried about sleeping outdoors, whether he feared robbers or wild animals, but he laughed and said nothing much scared him.

Beside me, Caedmon's breathing changed, signalling he had woken. I rolled over to face him. His short hair was dishevelled and when he first woke in the mornings, he always looked a little confused at finding me in his bed.

"Good morning, sleepy head," I said. "I thought soldiers woke at the crack of dawn. Aren't you supposed to get up early to train or something?"

Caedmon smiled and reached out to push aside a lock of hair that had fallen over my face.

"I'll be resuming my training soon enough. I can afford a few late mornings in the meantime."

"Do you know when you might come home again?"

I regretted it as soon as the words left my mouth, for I had promised myself I wouldn't ask. After all, he had made it clear that our handfasting was based on practicality, not love. But still, my stupid heart yearned to know.

Caedmon's hand stilled in my hair. He closed his eyes briefly and inhaled deeply.

"I know you have to go," I said quickly. "And I'm not asking that you don't. I don't mind, truly. It would just be easier if I knew when you might return. You have only ever come home when you were injured. I wondered whether your commander might give you leave to return more often now that you are handfasted."

"There's something I need to tell you." His gaze skittered away from mine and his hand withdrew from my hair. "I would have told you before I left anyway, but you might as well hear it now, since you asked."

"What is it? You sound so serious." My heart stuttered, but no, it couldn't be anything bad. It wasn't possible.

"A few months ago, I had a strange dream." Caedmon's voice was calm enough, but he didn't look at me as he spoke. "I saw myself lying in a ditch, with my throat slit. Dead."

A chill ran through my body and I edged a little closer to feel his warmth. "That's horrible."

"It was a true dream."

"How do you know?"

I felt, rather than saw, his shrug beneath the blankets.

"I just know. I saw my dead body and I looked no older than I do now."

"Does this have something to do with why you decided to handfast?"

Damn my stupid heart. A tiny part of me had hoped that maybe somewhere, buried too deep for him to notice, were feelings for me.

"Death approaches, my dear Grainne. I don't believe I will come home again, not alive at any rate. I did not want to die without having handfasted. I wanted, just for a little while, to experience this. I hoped to leave behind an heir, even if there is no time for more. I can die without regret if I do not produce a soldier and a druid, but it would mean a lot to me to have an heir. I've been well paid for risking the dangers of a soldier. Enough for you to be comfortable for a good long while. You and our son."

"I don't care about how much money you have." I fought to keep my voice steady. I would not cry in front of him. "Why didn't you tell me earlier?"

"I'm sorry. It was selfish of me. But I thought you would not want me if you knew."

I bit my tongue, for if I said anything right now, it would probably be that I loved him. That I would take whatever he had to offer, no matter how little it was.

"Say something, Grainne." Caedmon's warm hand touched my cheek ever so gently. "Tell me what you are thinking. If you are angry with me, it is no more than I deserve."

"I'm not angry. I just don't believe it was a true dream. I can't."

My voice wavered on the last word and I rolled onto my back so he wouldn't see the tears that welled in my eyes.

"I didn't mean to hurt you. I thought I knew something about having a wife from watching my parents, but it seems not. I'm sorry, Grainne. I did not expect you to take it so hard. I should have told you from the start, but I knew you wouldn't have me if you knew."

"I would have."

I bit my tongue again before I said too much.

He wrapped his arms around me, drawing me into his warmth. I leaned my head on his chest, drinking in his scent and the sound of his heart beating beside my ear.

"Forgive me," he said.

"I already have."

He kissed me and it was some time before either of us thought of leaving the bed. Eventually Caedmon rose. I lay under the blankets, watching as he washed in the basin. It was still surreal to think that this bedchamber in which he had grown up was now mine too. Caedmon leaned over to kiss my cheek.

"Do you want me to start the fire before I go?" he asked.

"No, I'll be quick."

"I'll see you downstairs then."

I waited until the door closed behind him before I climbed out from under the blankets. I was still somewhat shy about him seeing me unclothed. It was a relief to be able to wash and dress without wondering whether he watched, although he always closed his eyes and pretended to sleep.

I found Caedmon downstairs at the dining table, halfway through a bowl of porridge. He was all hard muscle from years of soldiering and ate enough for two people. I brushed away a sprinkling of crumbs that the servant had missed. Evidence that someone, at least, had eaten here earlier this morning. Shouts in a boyish voice came from outside. One of Eremon and Niamh's twins, most likely.

"I wanted to show you around the estate some more today, if you don't mind a walk. Introduce you to the tenants," Caedmon said between mouthfuls. "I'm sorry there aren't many women your age here. Just Eithne, although she's a year or two younger than you."

"Only a year? She seems much younger than that." I nibbled at my bread, but Caedmon's words about his dream had ruined any appetite I might have had. The honey tasted sickly sweet on my tongue.

"She won't be much of a friend for you, I'm afraid." He scraped out the last of his porridge. "You know she is often ill and confined to bed. But she will be company every now and then, if nothing else."

"I'm sure Eithne and I will be firm friends."

"I worry that you will be lonely once I am gone."

I tried to keep my face calm.

"You're not to worry about me. I don't want you distracted from your duties. I am perfectly capable of making myself useful and keeping busy. Eithne will be my friend and my sisters are not all that far away. I will speak to Agata about giving me some chores. There's little else I need."

Except you, my heart whispered. *The only other thing I need is for you to come back to me safe.*

15

GRAINNE

$\mathcal{A}$ few days later Caedmon took me to view the progress on our house. As we lingered by the river, we discovered that the ice near the edge had softened and was fast turning to slush.

"It's time," Caedmon said and squeezed my hand.

I said nothing as I stared at the melting ice, for my throat was tight with a sob I didn't want him to hear.

"When will you leave?" I asked at length, when I thought I finally had my voice under control.

"Tomorrow." His tone was regretful. "I'm sorry, I know it will be hard for you once I'm gone."

"Don't worry about me." I forced a bright voice, although it didn't ring true even to my own ear. "I'll be just fine and waiting for you to return."

Caedmon took in a long shuddering breath and turned to face me.

"Grainne, I need you to believe me. I won't be coming back. I'm sorry we have been handfasted for such a short time, but I don't want you to live with false hope. You are a fine woman and I wish I had thought to handfast with you earlier."

"Do you expect me to handfast with someone else?"

My voice was light for I didn't believe him, even if thoughts of his dream still gave me chills. I would miss him, and I would worry for his safety every minute, but I did not believe in his omen of impending death.

"You are young, Grainne. Too young to live the rest of your life as a widow. But if you choose to, Papa and Eremon would never turn you out of Silver Downs. You will have a house. I have quite a lot of coin saved; Sitric has the details. It should last you many years if you are careful with it. When the coin runs out, I suppose you will either need to take some work or handfast. It will be up to you."

I fought to shake off the gloom his words cast over me.

"Come," I said. "I'll race you back to the house, but only if you give me a head start."

He laughed. "I will count to ten before I follow. You had better be fast if you think to beat me."

I took off running, pushing my legs as hard as I could through the melting snow. The breeze in my hair made me smile and his words of dire warning were little more than a memory by the time he caught up to me.

That evening the family gathered at Silver Downs to farewell him. We sat around the long table and feasted on roasted wild boar and honeyed winter roots. The food smelled rich and wonderful, but tasted like ash in my mouth. The brothers were all there. Fiachra offered no explanation for his continued presence and I never heard anyone ask. Fionn and Agata were no doubt simply happy to have the family complete for a short time.

Agata was pale and quiet that evening. She must find it hard to say goodbye to her soldier son, no matter how many times it had to be done. Fionn was jovial. If he felt the same sadness as Agata, he hid it better.

Diarmuid appeared to be in a more agreeable mood than usual, even answering a question from me with a brief twist of the lips that might have been a smile. He had been strange recently. Or perhaps he was always like that; I didn't know him well enough to tell. I had sensed a growing rift between him and Caedmon. Usually they were inseparable while Caedmon was home, but some argument had happened around Midwinter. Caedmon wouldn't speak of it, except to say he regretted the situation. Diarmuid wouldn't even look at him. They appeared in the same room together only at mealtimes and only long enough for Diarmuid to gulp down his meal. He missed a number of opportunities for tale telling, which struck me as odd, given he was supposed to be a bard.

After the meal, we retired to the family room and gathered around the fireplace. Eremon built up the fire, although this close to spring it was hardly needed. This was the last time the family would be together for many months. Caedmon and I, sitting close together on a bench, his arm around my shoulders, my hand resting on his thigh. Eremon and Niamh and their boys. Marrec and Conn towards the back of the room. Fionn and Agata. Sitric. Fiachra. Eithne, in a prime position close by the fire.

"We want a stirring tale tonight, Diarmuid," Fionn said, his voice still light.

I shuddered as Diarmuid moved to stand in front of the fireplace. I had no desire to hear another of his twisted tales. He and Caedmon exchanged a long look. Diarmuid was the first to look away.

Beside me, Caedmon's body was tense. The arm which had been draped loosely across my shoulders now gripped a little too tightly. I leaned against him and hoped he would take comfort in my nearness.

Diarmuid stood silently for a long time, fists clenched at his sides. He looked like someone preparing for battle, not a man about to tell a tale. We waited in silence and I shifted uneasily.

"There was once a soldier," Diarmuid said. "A simple man. He knew nothing but war and fighting. At length he decided it was time he took a bride, so he returned home and chose a girl. They were handfasted in a ceremony under an ancient oak tree."

I was suddenly too hot and my stomach churned. Diarmuid's voice was cold and filled with power. If I had not known otherwise, I might have mistaken him for a druid rather than a bard.

"The night before the soldier was due to return to the campaign, he woke long before dawn. A strange state came over him and he became something that was not like himself. He beat his new bride bloody. He nipped at her tender skin with his teeth and tore handfuls of hair from her head. He slapped her face and bruised her body. When dawn came, he kissed his bride goodbye, picked up his pack, and set off on the long walk back to the campaign.

"When the bride's family learnt of what had befallen her, her father and brothers agreed they could not leave such a crime unpunished. They set off after the soldier."

My stomach rolled and I swallowed hard against the urge to vomit. I knew exactly where this tale was headed. Obviously Caedmon had shared his dire premonition with Diarmuid and the bard thought it clever to work it into a tale. I tried to think of more pleasant things: summer skies, fish leaping in a running stream, Caedmon's strong arms around me, the babe I hoped I carried within me.

Block out the words. Don't listen. Don't let his awful tale get inside your head or you will worry until Caedmon returns again. Don't listen. Don't listen.

But I couldn't stop myself from listening. I had to know the soldier's fate. Sure enough, the bride's menfolk caught up to the soldier and beat him. They slit his throat and left him lying in a ditch by the road. He died, alone, looking up at the sky.

The tale ended and the silence was loud. Diarmuid looked uncomfortable now. Gone was the proud lift of his head and the arrogant smirk. Now his shoulders were slightly hunched and he shifted from foot to foot.

"You all right?" Caedmon murmured in my ear.

"How can he tell such a thing?"

"Telling tales is what he does. But yes, some of them are awful. Don't let it affect you. They are just tales."

I noted the odd tone to Caedmon's voice. He too was disturbed, more than he let show. I reached up to squeeze the hand that hung over my shoulder.

We all sat in silence, shifting uneasily in our seats. I inhaled a shaky breath and the scent of flames and pinecones caught in my lungs. Several of the brothers darted sideways glances at me. The silence stretched uncomfortably, broken only by the crackle of the fire.

"Not exactly an uplifting tale with which to send me off, little brother," Caedmon said, finally.

"It was a different sort of tale," I said, my voice wavering somewhat.

Diarmuid shot me a look that might almost have been grateful and Caedmon squeezed my shoulders.

At length, Eremon offered to share a tale and moved to the front of the room. Diarmuid sat alone, neither brother nor sister choosing to sit with him for the evening's entertainment. I wanted to love my new family, but when it came to Diarmuid, I was torn between revulsion and something like fear.

16

GRAINNE

We lingered in the family room for some time after Diarmuid's tale, although when I next looked for the bard, he was gone. Eremon shared a tale about the hounds of Annwn and Sitric told a funny little tale about a man whose sole aim in life was to catch a fish.

Caedmon and I sat too far away from the fire for me to feel its heat and despite the warmth of his body beside me, I was still chilled. The image of a soldier lying dead on the ground, throat slit and eyes staring sightlessly, would not leave my mind. Every time I blinked, I saw him. When I looked at Caedmon, I saw the dead soldier. Damn Diarmuid for putting such thoughts in my mind. Caedmon noticed my restlessness and squeezed my shoulders. A lift of his eyebrows asked whether I was all right.

"Did you tell him about your dream?" I murmured.

"Yes, although I gave sparse detail. I am sorry if his tale disturbed you."

I shrugged and didn't answer. I didn't want to ruin his final evening at home with an argument. Caedmon was soon absorbed in conversation with his brothers. I was content to sit beside him and hold his hand. Eventually tiredness began to cloud my head and Caedmon noticed me restraining a yawn.

"I intend to leave early in the morning," he said to the family. "So I will make my farewells now."

They gathered around, Agata and Eithne hugging him hard, Fionn and the boys slapping him on the back. Caedmon didn't hurry through his farewells but took time to speak a few words to each person. Eithne, in particular, he spent long moments with, and her eyes glistened as she left the room immediately afterwards. There were tender words for his mother and a joke for each of the boys. His father, Fionn, was the last, and his face was haunted.

"Take care of yourself, son," Fionn said as he embraced Caedmon.

"Look after Grainne for me," Caedmon said. "Eremon will manage the men building the house and Sitric has my finances, but anything else she needs…"

"Don't you worry about her. She will be well taken care of. You know your brothers and I will not let you down."

"If…" Whatever else Caedmon intended to say went unspoken, but Fionn nodded.

"I know. And I will."

"Thank you."

They embraced, then Caedmon and I went up to our bedchamber. I didn't ask what his conversation with Fionn meant. If Caedmon wanted to speak of it, he would.

There were no final preparations to be done, for he had already filled his pack and left it leaning against the wall. I tried not to picture him shouldering it and walking away from me. Tried not to picture this chamber without him in it. My stomach clenched and tears filled my eyes. I blinked them away before he could see.

Caedmon had stirred up the fire, undressed and was already in bed. I changed into my nightgown and climbed in beside him, gladly sinking down into the embrace he offered. He kissed me and I savoured the warmth of his body pressed against mine. It might be a long time before I touched him again. We lingered over these final embraces and the night was late before Caedmon reached over to put out the lamp.

I lay with my eyes open, fearful that I'd fall asleep despite my intentions of remaining awake. I had a plan, a way I might save him from Diarmuid's tale. Caedmon lay on his belly, his arm draped across my chest, and I watched him in the dim orange light from the fire, which sent shifting shadows around the room. His face was mostly in darkness, but I knew every feature. I moved a little closer so I could inhale his scent, trying with every breath to memorise it. Tears tracked down my cheeks, despite my best efforts not to cry, but I tried not to give myself away.

Caedmon seemed to take a long time to fall asleep, but finally his breathing was deep and steady. I very slowly pushed his arm off my chest and slid out of the bed. He stirred and I froze, my heart pounding. But he merely murmured something and rolled over. His long, slow breathing resumed.

I tiptoed to the dresser. Hidden in one of my drawers was a small pouch Caedmon had never seen. I knew exactly where it was but wasn't sure I could retrieve it in the dark without making some noise. But the drawer that usually opened with a creak was soundless and my fingers reached straight for the pouch, hidden under my undergarments where I was sure Caedmon would never have reason to look.

It seemed the elements were working with me tonight, for even the door didn't make a sound as I eased it open. I crept along the hall and down the stairs. No candlelight shone from under any of the doors as I stole through the lodge. If only I could do what I needed to before anyone found me.

I tiptoed into the kitchen and set the pouch on a work bench while I fumbled for a candle. Before I could find one, a light flared behind me. Heart pounding, I turned. The druid brother, Fiachra, stood there, a candle in his hand. He set it down on the bench, near enough to my pouch to indicate he had already seen it.

"Be careful, Grainne," he said. "You tread a dangerous path."

"How much do you know?"

"Nothing for certain. I see you are on the cusp of a decision. A very dangerous one."

"So what should I do?"

"I cannot make your decision for you. I can only warn you. Be very careful in what you ask, for a simple request can have consequences one could never have dreamed of."

There was no point in pretending I didn't know what he meant and perhaps he could advise me. I was certainly in need of wisdom.

"I must keep him safe. Or at least try."

"Good intentions do not mean the outcome will be as you intend."

"I can't let him leave tomorrow unprotected."

"I'm not suggesting you don't try, or even that you do. I am simply warning you to be cautious."

"Do you know what I intend to do?"

"I see choices only. I cannot know what decision you will make. However, you must be sure you can accept the consequences before you act."

"What are the consequences? Either I manage to protect him, or I don't. I succeed or I fail. There are no other possibilities."

I might have expected Fiachra would smile at my blunt assessment, but his face was solemn. From a pocket within his robes, he produced a black feather and held it out to me.

"Include this in your ritual."

The feather was light and silky in my fingers.

"A raven feather? What is the significance in this?"

"If you do not know what a raven signifies to our family, this is not the time to reveal tightly-held secrets. The raven is a mysterious and powerful creature. The raven this particular feather came from even more so. It will add strength to your ritual. And strength is something you will need much of."

"Thank you."

He nodded and turned to leave without another word.

"Fiachra," I said softly, just before he slipped out the door. He turned to face me. "Would you stay with me? Help me?"

"I'm sorry, Grainne, I can't. This is your journey. I can only watch."

Then he was gone.

I shook off his strange words. I needed to move swiftly, for every moment I dallied was another moment in which Caedmon might wake and come looking for me. I unwound the ribbon sealing the pouch and spilled its contents onto the work bench. There was a very small bronze bowl with a suitably sized grinding stone, some dried herbs — sage, yarrow and rue — and a small vial of water that had been blessed by a druid.

I placed the herbs in the bowl and swiftly ground them. Once they were reduced to a fine powder, I added a few drops of water from the vial, then laid the raven's feather across them. How had Fiachra known that a token of air was the final element of my ritual? For I had herbs from the earth and blessed water. I could have used a candle from the kitchen for fire and had intended to add my own breath to represent the air.

I tilted Fiachra's candle down into the bowl and set fire to its contents. Despite the water, tiny flames caught immediately. I took a deep breath, steeling myself.

"Beings of earth and air, beings of water and fire, I implore you." My voice trembled a little and I inhaled deeply, trying to steady myself. "Watch over my love. Keep him safe and return him to me again, whole of body and sound of mind."

The burning herbs were pungent, their scent magnified as the fire consumed them. The feather was the last item to be devoured. A flame danced along its length, taking its time with this final gift. Once there was nothing left to eat, the flames died down and with a gentle puff of my breath, they were gone.

I wrapped the pouch around the bowl, careful not to burn my fingers. It was done. I had invoked the elements to request their protection. If they found my offerings acceptable, they would give what I had asked. There was nothing else I could do.

As I turned to leave, I noticed a figure standing in the shadows in the corner. At first I thought it was Fiachra, come back to watch and maybe even to help, despite his words. But as the man stepped forward into the meagre candle light, I realised I had never seen him before.

He was tall and thin, with sickly white skin and lips that looked far too red. His cheekbones were high and his face was somewhat pretty although foreign. My heart pounded and I was sharply aware that I was alone in a dark room with a stranger.

"Who are you?" I demanded. "You shouldn't be here. Come another step closer and I will scream for my husband and his brothers."

His smile was slow and lazy. "They will not hear you scream, pretty one. Go ahead if you feel you must."

"What do you want?"

I stepped back toward the door, in case I needed to flee swiftly.

He gestured towards the pouch in my hand, his long, slender fingers making the simple gesture somehow appear both elegant and obscene.

"That was an… interesting ritual."

"You had no right to watch. That was private."

"Perhaps next time you wish for privacy, you should check whether anyone watches."

"How long have you been here?"

"Longer than you. Longer than any mortal."

So he was fey. I was in more danger than I had thought.

"I meant, how long were you standing in the corner, watching me?"

He shrugged. "Perhaps it was long enough. Perhaps it was too long. Who can say?"

"What do you want?" My fingers tightened on my pouch. I wasn't sure I wanted to hear his answer.

"Your ritual was one of protection."

"My husband may be in danger."

"So you try to shield him."

"I am his wife." My tone was fierce. "I will do anything I must to protect him."

"Even if he doesn't return your love?"

His words stung. How could he know such a thing?

"He hasn't had time to learn to love me. He will, one day, if I can keep him safe long enough."

"What would you give if I could guarantee his safety?"

I held myself very still. Even though I had not grown up with a bard in my family as Caedmon had, I was still familiar enough with the old tales to know that pacts with the fey were not to be undertaken lightly.

"Tell me exactly what you mean."

"I mean what I say. No more and no less. I could take your husband to a safe place, where the danger you fear cannot find him. But there is always a cost."

"What would the cost be?"

"What do you have to give?"

"I have nothing. No jewellery or riches. No fine fabrics or elaborate embroidery."

"Everyone has something. A price they can pay."

"I have only myself."

"Is that your offer?"

"Myself? What do you mean?"

"You offer yourself in exchange for your husband's safety?"

My heart stuttered, then continued at double speed.

"Do you intend to kill me?"

"Kill you? No, I intend to ravish you."

His tone was devoid of emotion and the words chilled me. I took a step back, longing to flee but needing to see this conversation through to the end.

"What exactly do you mean?"

"You do not understand the concept?"

"I want to be very clear as to what you are suggesting."

"I'm suggesting nothing more than to take advantage of the price you are willing to pay. You offered yourself. I am tempted to accept."

"And how long would this arrangement last?" Thank the gods I had learned enough from the old tales to ensure I did not agree to some endless contract.

"How long do you want your husband to be safe?"

"Until the tale his bard brother told has no power over him."

"And how long do you offer yourself in exchange?"

I hesitated. What would be a fair deal?

"One night. From now until the sun comes up tomorrow."

"That is a paltry exchange, for the night is already half over."

"That's my offer. If you don't want it, I'll find another way to protect him."

"I accept. Go to your bedchamber. I will take your husband away."

"Can I see him first? To say goodbye."

"That was not part of our contract."

"Please?"

I was near tears now, panic rising in my throat. What had I done? Had I cursed Caedmon to be sent away forever? Had I damned myself to spend the rest of my life without my beloved?

"I will return presently. Tell nobody."

"I've changed my mind." Fear smothered my lungs and stifled my heart. "I want to re-negotiate."

"You have already agreed. The terms are fixed."

"Wait," I called, but he was gone.

Forgetting to be quiet, I raced through the lodge and up the stairs. Along the hallway. Into our bedchamber. The bed was empty, the covers tossed to the floor. Caedmon was gone and the fey man waited there for me.

"Where have you taken my husband?" My breath caught in my throat and I could barely speak.

"To a safe place, as we agreed. And now it is time for your payment."

The door closed behind me. I reached for it, turned the knob, but it was stuck fast.

"It won't open until I allow it." His voice came from close behind me.

I didn't answer but pounded on the door, hard enough to bruise my hands.

"Nobody can hear you in here. I have set a charm of silence on this chamber. You can scream, if you wish, and they will still not hear. Scream for me, Grainne."

Scream I did and I pounded on the door until blood ran from my fists. But nobody came. At length I stopped and fought to compose myself. My breathing was rapid and my heartbeat erratic. I wiped tears from my face, smearing blood on my cheeks as I did so. Once I was suitably calm, I turned back to the fey.

"Do you have a name?"

"Of course I do."

"Tell it to me. If we are to be intimate, which I assume is your intention, the least you can do is give me your name."

"The least I can do, Grainne? After having taken your loved one to a place where he will be safe? After guaranteeing that so long as you uphold your end of our agreement, he will continue to be safe?"

"You may only have me for one night. But you will keep Caedmon safe for as long as is needed. That was the agreement."

"It was. You drive a hard bargain."

"Your name."

"You may call me Lunn."

"Is that your true name?"

"What does it matter? You need a name to call me by, a name to scream. Lunn will do as well as any."

"Fine. Lunn. Now what do you want of me?"

Lunn inched closer, his gaze never leaving mine, his grin predatory. When he came close enough to touch me, he reached out one slender-fingered hand and trailed it along my throat and down between my breasts. I could barely restrain my shudder. I had never thought to have another touch me in this way, not after my handfasting. *It is for Caedmon,* I reminded myself. *I will do anything if it keeps him safe. Anything.*

Lunn leapt at me, hands outstretched although later in my nightmares I recalled them as claws. He tore my nightgown from my body, slashing it into long strips that drifted to the floor with a casualness I could not imitate. Once I was naked, he dug his fingernails into my soft skin, tearing it almost as easily as my gown. Blood seeped from the wounds.

He leaned in closer, closer. I thought, for an instant, he intended to kiss me. But he turned his head at the last moment and bit me on the shoulder, hard. His teeth sank into my skin, almost to the bone. I screamed.

I screamed again as he hit me. As he dug his nails into the soft skin where my limbs joined my body. I screamed as he tore the hair from my head in clumps, letting them drift slowly to the floor where they lay in splatters of my own blood. I screamed as he abused me in ways I could never have imagined. When I could scream no longer, I sobbed silently, the tears falling from my face to land, burning, in my wounds.

At times the night seemed endless and I thought I would die before he finished. Sometimes I wished I was already dead. But the sun always rises and it did, finally. As the first rays streamed in through the window, Lunn left without a word.

I lay on the floor in my own blood and hair, curled into a ball. I couldn't even cry anymore. No one pain was distinguishable from the others. Everything hurt. Everything bled. My soul was bruised. But Caedmon was safe. No matter what it had cost me, I had saved him.

17

GRAINNE

I lay on the floor as sunlight brightened the room. My body was bruised and battered. The woven mat under my cheek was wet through with my own blood, but I didn't have the strength to move. My ears rang, either from my seemingly endless screams or because Lunn had hit me there.

I hurt everywhere. I tried occasionally to rise but my limbs seemed boneless and I could do nothing more than lift my head. The room around me blurred. I didn't know whether it was because something was wrong with my eyes or merely because I cried. My heart beat slowly and weakly, and every now and then it seemed to pause for a long moment. Was it possible to experience so much pain that one's heart simply stopped? After what seemed like an aeon, somebody rapped firmly on the door.

"Caedmon, you lazy sod, are you getting up today? I thought you intended to leave at sunrise."

I didn't have the strength to voice a reply, but I must have made some noise for the knock came again, louder this time.

"Caedmon? Is everything all right in there?"

"Help," I rasped, my voice little more than a whisper.

It was enough though. The doorknob rattled and Sitric crouched beside me.

"Gods, Grainne," he gasped. He grabbed a blanket from the bed to drape over me, then returned to the doorway to call for aid.

Only moments passed before feet pounded along the hall. Other brothers crowded in. Somebody lifted me and lay me on the bed. It felt like the softest thing I had ever lain on. Someone wrapped the blanket more firmly around me. I blinked and it seemed that three of Sitric hovered over me, his face tight and worried. At length, Agata came and her face paled when she saw me.

"Everyone out." Her tone was so firm that nobody dared argue. "Sitric, send for hot water and clean rags. And somebody find Niamh."

The brothers exited and the door closed. Agata sat on the edge of the bed and lifted one trembling hand to touch my face.

"Oh, Grainne, how did this happen?"

The pain was so great, I could barely think. But one thought ran through my mind: Lunn had said to tell nobody. He hadn't said what the consequences would be, but I could assume it would invalidate our pact.

"Grainne?"

My face was so swollen I could barely move my jaw. Inside my mouth, my tongue felt far too big and blood still dripped down my throat. I must have bitten my tongue, or perhaps I had lost teeth. It hardly seemed to matter right now.

"I can't tell you," I managed eventually.

Agata flinched as if I had slapped her. She withdrew her hand, instead clasping her fingers in her lap and staring down at them. Perhaps she prayed for strength. At length she spoke again.

"Grainne, this family has secrets, some of which you might not be aware of. Sometimes, strange things happen. It is clear somebody ill-treated you last night. Will you tell me who it was?"

"I can't."

"Was it Caedmon? Tell me that much at least. Put a mother's mind at ease, if it wasn't."

I shook my head. The room blurred and a vicious throbbing started behind my eye.

"I will not speak of it. Please don't ask."

Agata stared me in the eyes for a long time before she nodded.

"Very well then, Grainne. I will never ask again. But if you need to talk, I will listen. You are my daughter now. And Caedmon is my son."

My brain was slow to process her words.

"What did you mean, secrets?"

"Caedmon has not told you?"

"No."

"He should have, if you are to live with us, but it is not my tale to tell."

"I should know."

"I agree. But I can't speak of it. I will ask Fiachra to talk with you, once you are recovered."

I nodded, unable to find the strength to speak any further.

Niamh bustled back in with an armload of cloth, followed by Sitric bearing a large bowl from which steam rose. Between the two of them, they drew up a chair beside the bed and set the bowl on it. Then Agata bustled Sitric back out of the room and closed the door firmly behind him.

Niamh sucked in her breath at the sight of my wounded body. I should have been embarrassed at being naked in front of them, but I barely cared. Nothing felt real anyway. Not the night I had endured. Not my injuries. Not the fact that Caedmon was gone, taken someplace where I would never see him again.

Agata and Niamh were as gentle as they could be, but even so their ministrations pained me terribly. They washed the blood from my body and cleaned out the bites. Niamh had brought a bag of herbs and potions and she applied a soothing paste to my bruises and wounds. Soon the pain began to ease.

After an endless age, I was clean and wearing a nightgown. Niamh took away the bloody cloths and red water. Agata stayed with me. She said nothing, for which I was grateful.

When Niamh returned, she brought a steaming mug. I smelled the herbs as soon as she entered the room, although I was too addled to make sense of what they were. Willow, possibly, for pain. Maybe henbane to make me sleep. She held the mug up to my mouth and helped me drink the bitter brew. I sipped what I could of it, although my bruised lips were clumsy and I kept spilling it. Niamh wiped up the mess without comment.

Soon numbness spread through my body and my tense muscles began to relax. When Niamh judged I had drunk a sufficient quantity, she put the mug on a stool drawn up close to the bed. She drew the heavy curtains and left.

Agata sat on the chair by the bed I had shared with Caedmon and folded her hands into her lap. She looked as if she was settling in.

"You don't..." Did it always take so much effort to speak? "You don't have to stay."

"I will sit with you," she said. "You shouldn't be alone right now. Close your eyes and sleep, and know that either Niamh or I will be here, should you need us."

A surge of gratitude rushed through me and tears sprang to my eyes.

"Thank you."

"Should I send for someone? Your mother, perhaps, or one of your sisters?"

Caedmon was the only one I wanted, but I might never see him again.

"Not yet. Let me... let me heal a little first."

Agata nodded and her face held no judgement.

"Sleep then. I will sit with you."

I knew I wouldn't be able to sleep. I would see Lunn every moment my eyes were closed. Feel his teeth sinking into my skin, and his fingers in places nobody but Caedmon had ever touched, and all of the other dreadful things he had done to me. But Niamh's potion was strong and as soon as I closed my eyes, I was asleep.

18

EITHNE

The house was quiet when I woke. At first I thought I must have slept late, that everyone was out in the fields working, or in the barn. But a glance out the window told me the sun was not long risen and when I went downstairs, my brothers were still there. They tiptoed through the house with tight expressions on their faces.

I couldn't find Mother anywhere or Caedmon. I had been sure he wouldn't leave without saying goodbye again. But it seemed he had already gone, for he was not in the house, the herb garden, or out in the fields, from what I could see from the doorstep. I wasn't strong enough to search further, for my blood ran hot and my skin was cold. I had been through this enough times to know I was about to succumb to the fevers.

The thought of breakfast made my stomach clench and bile rise in my throat. I settled into my chair by the fireplace, my feet tucked under me and a blanket wrapped around my shoulders. There was no fire but no matter, I would wait. One of my brothers would come along soon enough and they would surely light it when they saw me sitting by a cold hearth.

Fear teased me, lingering and waiting. Something had happened overnight. There was no point in asking, for nobody would tell me. They never told me anything. Everyone forgot that although my body might be frail, my mind was as sound as anyone's. But I always heard what was going on eventually. If I sat very quiet and still, people didn't see me. So I sat and waited.

Eventually Sitric came to light the fire although he didn't speak to me, only muttered to himself. I couldn't quite make out his words. Something about Caedmon, something about someone else whose name I didn't catch, and somebody needed to do something. He left as soon as the fire caught, still muttering, his eyes sombre.

It wasn't until Niamh hurried past that I started to understand. She carried a bowl and she walked carefully, which indicated the bowl wasn't empty. Tucked under one arm was a bundle that looked like blood-stained cloths. So, someone was injured and my guess was Grainne. It seemed that one of Diarmuid's tales had finally come true.

Diarmuid's ability was one of those things I wasn't supposed to know about. Nobody ever spoke of it and I wasn't even sure all my brothers knew. Eremon did, and probably Diarmuid for surely somebody had warned him after he first announced himself as a bard. Fiachra, maybe, because druids tended to know things they shouldn't. But perhaps not the others.

Diarmuid had been pale and pinch-faced for weeks and the tension between him and Caedmon was obvious to everyone. So this was his ill-considered revenge. He made Caedmon beat his new bride half to death and by now Caedmon was probably dead himself.

My chest constricted and tears welled as I pictured Caedmon dying in the manner described in Diarmuid's unlucky tale: alone, throat slit, empty eyes staring up at the sky. I swallowed my sobs. Damn Diarmuid. I hoped he never told another tale. In the meantime, though, perhaps there was something I could do to comfort Grainne, for it was likely that she was badly injured and also newly a widow. Here, at last, was a task I could undertake, at least until the fevers became strong enough to confine me to my bed.

I left my warm spot by the fire and crept up the stairs. My legs shook by the time I reached the top. The door to Caedmon and Grainne's bedchamber was closed. I knocked, my hand tentative, for I didn't know whether Grainne would welcome my presence. I barely knew her, after all.

The door opened just the slightest bit and Mother peered out. The lines around her eyes were deeper than usual. The astringent odour of some herbal concoction wafted into the hallway.

"I'm sorry, Eithne, Grainne is not feeling well," she said. "This is not a good time for visitors."

"I can sit with her." I tried to peer over Mother's shoulder, for she was not much taller than me, but she had positioned herself where I could see nothing.

"I don't think that's a good idea. No visitors today."

"I know what it is like to be unwell. I won't talk, but it might make her feel a little better to have someone sitting with her."

"I will sit with her. I'll tell her you came to check on her, though."

Mother started to close the door and I surprised myself by inserting my foot in the doorway.

"I know what happened, Mother. You don't need to try to keep it from me."

Mother looked at me for a long moment, her grey eyes steady. At length she sighed and opened the door wider.

"Keep your voice down so you don't disturb her. She is gravely injured."

I had not been inside Caedmon's bedchamber for many years, but it looked much the same as I remembered, except that he now had a larger bed. The heavy curtains were closed, making the room dim, and a comfortable chair was drawn up next to the bed. Mother's shawl lay abandoned across the back of the chair.

I approached the bed. Even in the shadowy light, I could see that Grainne was bruised almost beyond recognition. Her hair was clumped and matted around her face. The blankets drawn up to her chin hid whatever horrors had been inflicted on her body. Mother and Niamh had obviously washed her and tended her wounds, but they hadn't touched her hair. I took Grainne's comb from the dresser and began to untangle the knots. I worked gently, but the knots were tight and many would need to be cut out. I tried to pretend I hadn't seen the streaks of blood woven through her dark hair.

"Mother, would you fetch me some embroidery shears?"

Mother looked like she wanted to say something, but she merely nodded and left. I worked in silence while she was gone. Grainne's eyes were open, but if she knew I was there, she didn't react. Her hair was silky beneath my fingers. Her beautiful hair, now ruined.

When Mother returned, we helped Grainne to sit with pillows positioned behind her shoulders, so I could work on the back of her head. I tired already and the fever made sweat drip down the backs of my legs, but I couldn't bear to leave Grainne with her hair so bedraggled.

"You don't need to stay," I said to Mother. "I can sit with Grainne for a while."

"You shouldn't tire yourself," she said.

"I will send for Niamh when I am too tired."

Mother frowned at me. She opened her mouth as if to protest again, but only shook her head and left. I continued to work silently, combing out what tangles I could and snipping off the rest. I tried to catch the falling strands so Grainne wouldn't see, but some landed in her lap before I could grab them. She touched them with a trembling hand.

"Do I look hideous?" Her voice was quiet but steady.

"Not hideous, no. You look like a strong woman who has survived something terrible."

Her shoulders shook as she began to sob and I had to stop my work for fear of cutting her.

"Do you want to talk about it?" I asked.

Grainne shook her head. "I can't tell anyone what happened."

"I'm good at keeping secrets."

"Then tell me a secret this family keeps. Tell me one of the things I should have known before I married Caedmon."

"Caedmon is a good man."

I felt like I should hug her, but I didn't know how badly she was injured beneath the blankets. I rested my hand very gently on her shoulder. She flinched when I touched her and my throat tightened.

"That's no secret," she said. "I wouldn't have married him were he not."

Grainne's sobs had stopped so I resumed cutting her matted hair. Once that was done, I tried to disguise the fact that handfuls of hair had been ripped out, but there was little I could do. She would need to cover her hair with a scarf if she didn't want folk to stare.

"There are many secrets in this family," I said, eventually. "I'm sure I don't know them all."

"I bet you know more than people think you do."

I hesitated. "That is true."

"Then tell me a secret, for we are sisters now. What does this family hide?"

"Some of our menfolk have a special ability," I said, slowly, for I didn't quite know how to tell this secret. I had thought I would never share it. But what Grainne didn't know after last night, she had probably guessed. "In our family, when the seventh son of a seventh son is a bard, he is able to bring his tales to life. Not all of them, though, and nobody quite knows how the power works."

"Diarmuid is a seventh son," Grainne said. "And I presume your father is, too."

"Yes, only all of his brothers are dead. He does not talk of what happened to them."

"The tale Diarmuid told. The one of the soldier and his wife. Do you think it could come true?"

My hands stilled in her hair.

"It would seem it already has."

"Don't think that. Caedmon would never do such a thing."

"Then who? Caedmon is gone and you have been beaten. You know what folk will think, even if they don't know of Diarmuid's ability."

"I can't say. Only trust in Caedmon. He is a good man."

"Do you think he is alive?"

"I hope so. I have done what I can for him."

I didn't question her further. She had her secrets, and I still had mine. For there was another more precious secret that I would not share with her. Not yet, anyway.

19

EITHNE

As Grainne healed, I spent most of my waking hours in her room. Sometimes we spoke. More often we sat in silence. I would open the curtains and drag the chair to where I could warm my skin in the sunlight. I had some small items of embroidery in a little basket and I would work on my stitching for a short time until I was too tired. Then I would simply sit and look out the window.

The illness had held off for several days, although I could still feel it there, lurking, slumbering, waiting. The fevers came and went, but they were mild enough that I wasn't confined to bed. My hands would tremble for a while and my legs would shake, but that too passed without growing worse. I wanted to believe my body had finally learned how to fight back, but such thoughts were futile. I would succumb sooner or later. In the meantime, at least I was strong enough to be out of bed and able to support Grainne in some small way.

Grainne's face looked worse before it got better. Two days after she was injured, her face was swollen round like a pumpkin and her bruises were the dark purple of storm clouds. She could barely speak for the swelling around her jaw. I never saw the damage to her body, for Mother always sent me from the room before tending to

Grainne's injuries. But I had seen enough to guess the extent of injury to both body and mind.

Then came a day when I had barely been out of bed for an hour before fatigue gripped me and I began to shiver. When Mother came to check on Grainne, she found me trembling and flushed. With a typical lack of fuss, she summoned Marrec and Conn to carry me out while she tended to Grainne. Afterward, she came to my room and rested a cool palm on my burning cheek.

"Eithne, my dear, you have exhausted yourself."

"The sickness has been coming for several days," I said. My mouth was dry and my throat hurt when I spoke. "I wanted to sit with Grainne for as long as I could."

"She will be fine. Niamh and I will care for her. You need to worry about yourself now. Concentrate on getting better."

"Do you think he did it?" I felt like a traitor, but I asked only because I wanted to know what she thought, not because I believed it myself.

Mother's face was serious and she didn't ask what I meant.

"I hope not. I believe I raised my sons better than that. But the tale was strong and it may have left him with no choice but to act in accordance with what was foretold."

"Why does Diarmuid still tell tales, if he knows what he can do?"

"He doesn't understand it, my dear. I don't think he believed it until now."

She sat on the chair next to my bed and folded her hands in her lap. The dark shadows under her eyes told of her exhaustion and I regretted that I would add to that over the next few days.

"He hasn't even come to visit her. To see the product of his own handiwork."

"It seems he has gone on a journey of some sort."

"To where? And for what purpose? Has he not caused enough problems without disappearing too?"

"I know only as much as Fiachra told me and he was sparse with the details."

I was lost to the fever shortly after, but that meant time with

Kalen. I had not been able to walk out to the beech trees since Grainne had been injured, although I had longed to see him. No longer did he merely stand in the corner of my room and watch with dispassionate interest. Over time he had crept closer and now he actually sat in the chair Mother had occupied earlier. It was a plain wooden chair, not of the fine standard the fey must be accustomed to.

Kalen talked to me sometimes, small tidbits of information about his life. He didn't seem to mind that I never replied. I stored up every morsel of information, determined not to forget anything, so that when the fever was gone I could linger over every detail.

There had been a lonely childhood. If he had siblings, he never spoke of them. An animal, a pet of some sort, although I didn't recognise the word he used and I had no sense of what kind of creature it might be. Lessons learnt in the forest, both practical and philosophical. He was an outsider, shunned by others of his kind, although he didn't specify what offence he had committed.

The things of which he spoke were mostly wonders of the physical world: a fiery sunset, a majestic storm, the pleasure of walking barefoot on soft grass. He made me want to see all those things, too. As his words painted pictures in my mind, I added myself in. He and I together watched the sun set from a mountainous perch. We sought shelter under a stately oak from an unexpected spring storm. We walked over grassy hills and stopped to pluck the yellow tulips that grew in a hollow. The images were so real, I could almost smell their perfume.

Kalen left when the fevers subsided. As I began my slow recovery, it was easy to believe we really had done all the things I remembered. We had still had only a handful of real conversations, but I began to feel like I knew him so much better than that.

Another week passed before I was able to very slowly make my way back to Grainne's room. Although it was just down the hall from mine, my legs trembled with exhaustion by the time I rapped softly on her door. I breathed in great gasping pants. I could still smell the illness clinging to my skin. Grainne lay in bed, staring up at the ceiling. She started to sit up when I entered.

"No, don't trouble yourself," I said between gasps, and sank down into the chair. It was drawn up close to the bed, rather than in the sunny spot I favoured by the window, but I did not have enough strength to move it. The room smelled of healing herbs, although they were different to the ones Mother burned in my room when I was ill.

Grainne was thinner than I remembered and her eyes sadder. Large splotches of faded yellow bruises covered her face and the swelling was much reduced.

"Are you recovered, Eithne?" she asked, and her once joyful voice was tight.

"Somewhat. It will be a few days yet until I regain my strength."

I drew my feet up under my nightdress and rested my head against the back of the chair.

"These illnesses, they occur often?"

"Too often. I have been sick for most of my life."

"That's terrible." Grainne's voice was genuine.

"Don't pity me. I hate being pitied. It is what it is." My tone was brusquer than I had intended, but it was too late.

"Are you dying?"

Nobody had ever asked that before. I myself had only dared voice the question once. But I had never doubted it.

"Probably." I tried to keep my tone as matter of fact as hers. But it is hard to speak of one's own death and my voice broke on the last syllable. "I don't really talk about it."

"I'm sorry. I didn't mean to upset you, not after you've been so kind to me."

"I'm not upset. I'm still very weak. I can't talk for long yet. I really just came to sit with you."

"I appreciate that. I don't really want to talk either."

"Then we shall sit here in silence and both be perfectly happy with that."

20

EITHNE

Three more days passed before I saw Kalen again.

Three days in which I wondered whether he would come again.

Three days in which I berated myself for fearing that he wouldn't.

Any woman who forms an attachment to a fey is a fool; I knew that. The fey don't understand hope or horror, joy or sorrow, love or pity. Life is a game to them, and well they can afford it, for they live many hundreds of years. Lingering over each word, puzzling out unsaid meanings: those are the things a woman does when she is besotted. They are not things a mortal should think of a fey. That can only lead to unhappiness.

I regained my strength slowly. I wasn't yet recovered enough to walk further than from my bed to Grainne's chamber, but I persuaded Marrec and Conn to carry me out to my rock beside the beech trees. I even managed to convince them to leave me alone for an hour — one precious hour in which perhaps Kalen would come to me — before they returned to carry me back. The wind smelled of fresh spring air and trees and grass, which was a relief after so many days confined to the lodge.

I could not see Kalen as we approached the trees, but of course he would not appear with my brothers there. Marrec and Con deposited me on the rock and I wrapped myself in the blanket Mother had insisted I bring. Then my brothers left, assuring me they would return in an hour. Conn pressed a wooden whistle into my hand.

"If you need us to return earlier, blow this," he said. "We will listen for it."

"I will be fine. You can go now."

As they departed, I didn't dare turn to look behind me. As long as I didn't look, I could pretend he was there, waiting. Instead, I looked out towards the hill that hid the lodge from my sight. The fields were patchy with melting snow and contained nothing but trees and cows and sheep all the way to the horizon. In summer these fields would be emerald green, but now they were a quilt of white and brown.

Marrec and Conn were soon out of sight and yet I waited. The beeches around me were still and silent. The wind had died and not even a stray breeze disturbed their branches. There were no birds calling, no rustle of tree-dwelling creatures. If Kalen was there some-where, he was utterly silent.

I took a deep breath. I would be sad if he did not come, but I would survive. I was not some weak-willed woman who had fallen in love with one of the fey. I was merely intrigued. He was a bright spark in an otherwise dull life, a splash of colour on a canvas of grey.

Still no sound behind me. But perhaps he waited for me to speak, to indicate it was safe to come out. I would call him, just once. If he did not come, I would wait for my brothers and I would not allow a single tear to fall. I would not waste another thought on him. My life would return to its previous drabness and I would be no poorer.

"Are you going to hide all afternoon?" I asked, finally. "I have only such time until my brothers return."

Leaves rustled behind me and my heart pounded loudly. I didn't turn to face him but continued to stare out towards the snow-capped mountains of the horizon.

"I was not certain you wanted to see me," he said.

"I was hoping to talk to you. It's the only reason I came out here today."

I phrased my words carefully, lest I give him the wrong impression. I didn't want him to think I had feelings for him. For he was fey and that made him dangerous to a mortal woman. Extremely dangerous. And interesting.

"You are recovered."

I wasn't sure whether he intended a question or a statement.

"I feel better. It will be some days yet before I am fully recovered though."

"And then you will be ill again."

"Yes, there is never more than a few weeks between episodes."

"Is there no cure?"

I finally turned around. Kalen leaned against a silver-trunked beech. His hair was the same ruined cut as always and his dark clothes hung as if only a skeleton lay beneath them. His face was as imperturbable as ever. If he was as pleased to see me as I was him, he gave no sign of it.

"Apparently not. I have seen several wise women and healers, and even a druid, but they could suggest nothing other than herbs and rest."

"That makes you sad." Kalen tilted his head as if examining a curiosity.

"Just a little. It is the only way I know to live. I have been like this all of my life. It would be much harder, I think, to be healthy and to be struck down with such an illness. For then one would already know what it is like to live without such a thing."

"What if you could go somewhere the illness didn't affect you?"

My heart did a funny little leap. *Be careful here, Eithne. Be very careful.*

"There is no such place. Not for mortals anyway."

"There is no illness in my realm."

"Your kind are very fortunate then. Would that we had the same fortune."

"If you came there with me, you would not suffer any longer."

His face was emotionless, giving me no indication whether he understood the importance of what he offered. He continued to lean against the beech, although now he crossed his arms across his chest.

"I cannot go to your realm. I could not survive there."

"Of course you could. Your illness would no longer affect you. You would be whole and hearty."

"But mortals cannot live there. We cannot eat your food and drink your wine, or we can never leave."

"You would not go unless you intended to never leave."

"I could not do such a thing."

Kalen's face darkened as if I had angered him, but it passed swiftly.

"Why? You would be well."

"I could not leave my family."

"They barely notice you. You sit in your chair by the fire and they pass you by with barely a glance. Would they even notice if you were no longer there?"

Irritation flashed within me.

"That's an awful thing to say."

"How can the truth be awful?" Kalen's voice was as neutral as ever.

"It's not the truth. Not really. You're twisting it."

I felt flustered now. My cheeks heated and I twisted my fingers together and tucked them into my skirt to hide the way they trembled. I hated to argue with anyone and I particularly didn't want to argue with Kalen.

"I only ever speak the truth."

"Well, sometimes you shouldn't. Sometimes you only make things worse by telling the truth."

"You would rather I lied to you?"

"No, I just don't want you to tell me awful things, even if they might be true. Besides, when were you watching me sit by the fire?"

"I often watch you. You know that."

"I know you sometimes watch me when I am ill. I didn't know you watched me at other times, and in other places."

Kalen tilted his head and seemed to listen, although I heard nothing.

"Your brothers return."

"Already? They were supposed to give me an hour."

He shrugged. "I pay little attention to time."

"When will I see you again?"

I hated how needy I sounded. I would not be one of those desperate women who falls in love with a fey and is devastated when they lose interest. He was merely an interesting friend.

"When can you come back here?" he asked.

If Kalen felt anything for me, I neither saw it in his face nor heard it in his voice, but the question gave me hope.

"Tomorrow. I will return at the same time tomorrow. Will you be here?"

"Tomorrow," he said with a funny little tilt of his head. Perhaps it indicated agreement.

He melted away into the trees just as Marrec and Conn came into sight. My brothers chattered about nothing much as they carried me back to the house. I let their conversation flow over me, too busy analysing every word Kalen had said, and everything he didn't.

I would see him again tomorrow.

21

SUMERLED

Kalen has been spending far too much time visiting the disfigured mortal. Every time I ask why he continues to go to her, he stomps off without answering. So I do the only thing I can think of. Kalen will be furious, but it is for his own good.

I go in search of the underground cave Lunn has made his own. I don't dare go inside but instead linger nearby. There is a stream where I have sometimes seen him. He sits by it for hours and stares at nothing with a pensive look on his face. I am never quite sure what he is doing and I certainly never interrupt.

I overhear many a comment about Lunn as I wander around — Kalen calls it skulking — listening to whatever someone is careless enough to say without checking nobody can hear. A perversion, they say. An aberration. Lunn's penchant for mortals is well-known — he has taken many mortal lovers, both female and male — and nothing else is so disdained by the fey as consorting with mortals. He seems to have no interaction with anyone else, even at feasts where he is little more welcome than Kalen.

I hide behind a thick bramble bush. The stream is meagre with just a handspan of water, but even so it gurgles as it sweeps over the stones. A hare comes to drink from the flowing water. A sprite sails past in an oak leaf boat and yells a challenge to the hare. Birds chitter overhead and a soft breeze waves the branches of oak and ash. Water bugs skirt the surface, and nothing pays any attention to me. I am used to that.

Time has little meaning in the fey realm, so it might be hours or days that I wait. Sometimes I sleep, but otherwise I just sit and wait. Eventually Lunn appears. I wait until he has settled himself in a patch of lush, velvety grass on the stream's bank before I rise, very slowly and quietly. I stand there, not moving, waiting for him to see me. He does at last.

"Boy," he growls. "Get out of my sight."

"I have something to tell you," I say and despite my best intentions, my voice trembles just a little. I am well familiar with Lunn's style of punishment.

"Not interested," he says. "Go away. Unless, of course, you'd like to come closer so I can finish drowning you."

"I'm fine over here. Will you listen?"

He glares at me once more, then lies back in the grass.

"No."

He doesn't seem inclined to rise, though, so I decide to tell him anyway. He'll be pleased when I do, I know it. He might not reward me, but surely he'll at least stop trying to drown me every time he sees me.

"Kalen has a secret," I say.

Lunn doesn't respond, but I feel his sudden interest.

"He has been sneaking off to the mortal world."

Lunn sits up slowly and looks at me.

"Go on."

"He has been visiting a mortal woman."

Lunn raises one eyebrow and his lips very slowly curl up into a grin.

"Has he now. How interesting."

"I knew you'd want to know." I creep closer. "Have I done well?"

"You forget yourself, half-breed." Lunn's tone is suddenly cold. "If you come near enough for me to grab you, I'll throw you in the stream and hold you under until you stop breathing."

"But I told you Kalen's secret," I say, wounded. "I thought you'd be pleased."

"Oh, I'm pleased," he says. "But that doesn't change what I think of you. Now get out of my sight."

I hesitate for a moment, my mouth open and ready to plead my case, but he glares at me so fiercely, that I turn and run. My chest is tight and a hot tear drips down my cheek. I wipe it away with the back of my dirty hand before anyone sees. Full-blooded fey don't cry.

2 2

EITHNE

I met Kalen by the beech trees every day for a week. Winter had broken and spring's presence was everywhere. Buds covered the branches of the beech, the woodlarks began to sing again, and glossy grass sprouted where snow had melted. The days were warmer, with just the faintest scent of summer. Despite all that, I would have stayed huddled in front of the fireplace were it not for the enticement of time with Kalen.

The house was still in uproar and nobody questioned my sudden interest in sitting on my rock, alone and out of sight. Diarmuid had disappeared on some secret quest and it seemed only Fiachra knew where he had gone. There had been no word from Caedmon. He should have reached the campaign front by now, but it might be weeks before we received any message from him. Mother was distracted, but at least it meant she paid little attention to me. Even Papa's normally relaxed face became pinched with tension.

When I wasn't with Kalen, I spent most of my time with Grainne. Broken ribs gradually healed and soon she would be able to breathe without pain. I knew it was horrible of me to not wish her back to full health, but I would be alone again when she was ready to leave her bedchamber. We had become friends during those hours I sat by her bed. Maybe we had even become sisters. But she still didn't know my secret.

During the stolen hour Kalen and I spent together every day, we talked about all sorts of things. My childhood memories. Incidents with my brothers that had made me laugh or cry or, one time, so mad I punched Marrec in the nose. Kalen talked little of his own life. He never mentioned siblings or friends. There were irregular references to his queen, Titania, who I understood he feared, even if he never said so in as many words. The things of which he spoke were mostly occurrences of nature. The finding of a bird's nest containing three abandoned hatchlings. The discovery of a field of bluebells. The recent pleasure of a nap in soft grass beneath a shady tree, savouring the perfume of nearby honeysuckle.

"Spring has barely arrived," I said. "How is it that flowers already bloom in your realm?"

Kalen shrugged. "Seasons are not the same there as here. Titania's whim determines whether it is winter or summer."

"The queen controls the seasons?"

It was an unfathomable idea, but Kalen shrugged it off.

"We had almost a decade of winter once because she was mad about something. It snowed for years before she could be placated."

"How awful."

"She is the queen. She does as she pleases."

"What else does she do?"

But he wouldn't say much about Titania and I did not want to press too hard. Better that I let him choose what he would tell me, for when it was something that excited him, he would talk willingly. And it was detail I longed for.

I wanted to understand his life, to picture the things of which he spoke. The endless fields of flowers. The portals to my own world. The strange creatures that inhabited the woods, unseen and unheard. It all fascinated me. The more Kalen talked about his home, the more I longed to see it with my own eyes. I had never expected to experience adventure, but if I could have just a few minutes in the realm of the fey, I knew I would spend the rest of my life thinking about it.

My brothers' return always came too soon. I felt like I had barely settled on my rock before Kalen cocked his head and looked in the direction of the hill that hid us from sight of the lodge.

"Already?" I asked.

"Tell them to give you longer tomorrow. Two hours."

"They won't leave me alone for that long. They are only willing to do this because I have convinced them no harm can come to me in such a short time while I'm in the middle of our own lands and just barely out of sight."

"Persuade them."

I laughed, although I was somewhat irritated at the forcefulness of his tone.

"I told you, I can't. But I will return tomorrow. Will you come?"

"Of course." Kalen took my hand and gently kissed my palm, his gaze never leaving mine. "I look forward to it."

Then he melted away into the trees, just as my brothers came into sight, and I had no time to savour the feeling of his lips against my skin.

"You have the strangest look on your face, Eithne," Marrec said with a laugh.

"What do you do out here all alone?" Conn asked.

"Talk to squirrels?"

"Coax birds down to sit in your hair?"

"Perhaps she has a secret lover?"

"He must be very secret," Conn said.

"For we have seen neither hair nor hide of him," finished Marrec.

"Enough," I said. "Take me back now."

I returned at the usual time the next day. Marrec and Conn deposited me on my rock and hurried back to the house, for there was some chore Papa wanted completed urgently. But before they left, they checked I had the whistle and reminded me to blow it if I needed them.

The rock was warm from the midafternoon sun and its heat seeped through my clothes and into my skin in the most pleasant manner. I felt quite drowsy and my head nodded once or twice, but I made myself sit up straight and keep my eyes wide open. I did not want Kalen to arrive, find me napping, and leave. I could not bear the thought of passing a day without speaking with him.

Minutes passed. He was always already here when I arrived, although he never showed himself until Marrec and Conn had left. Perhaps he waited for me to call him. A game, although I didn't find it amusing.

"Kalen? Will you come out now?"

There was no response.

"Kalen, this isn't funny. You are wasting our time together."

Still nothing.

"Kalen!"

I was irritated now. I hoped he was not merely hiding and watching. For the fun of it, or to make me mad, or some other fey intention that was incomprehensible to me. But still he didn't speak and I detected no sign of his presence.

Eventually Marrec and Conn returned. They didn't notice that I said nothing as they carried me back. I made them put me down when we were halfway home so I could walk the rest of the way. My progress was painfully slow and I didn't have the strength to hide my limp, but they pretended not to notice.

I was panting and my legs trembled by the time we reached the lodge. I collapsed into the first chair I reached. Many minutes passed before my lungs worked normally again and it was even longer before I felt like I could stand without fearing my legs would immediately collapse beneath me.

Kalen hadn't come. For the first time I realised what I had refused to admit, even to myself: I was in love with him. How had this happened? I did not intend to become one of those women who fall in love with a fey and whose lives are destroyed when their beloved loses interest. I would not cling and hope he would return. I would not spend my time agonising over what might have prevented him from coming. I would simply forget him, for Silver Downs breeds its children strong and tough. Our blood is tinged with magic. How else could our bards bring their tales to life? I was just as strong as any other child of Silver Downs, despite the frailty of my body and my own lack of magic.

My resolution to forget Kalen lasted no more than a hundred heartbeats before a paralysing fear washed over me. He had given no indication that he tired of me. In fact, if I analysed his every word and action, he had seemed as infatuated with me as I was with him. Yesterday he had promised to meet me. He had kissed my hand. If today he did not come, then something had happened to him.

I worried throughout the rest of the day and barely slept that night for all my tossing and turning and fretting. When afternoon finally came again, Marrec and Conn carried me out to the beech trees and left with the usual injunction to blow on the whistle if I needed them. I waited only until they were out of earshot before I called.

"Kalen, are you there? Kalen?"

Woodlarks chattered above me. Branches rustled in the wind. But Kalen did not come.

When my brothers returned, I allowed them to lift me without a word. I made them set me down a little further from the lodge this time and again I painstakingly lurched the rest of the way. Two days. Two whole days.

Still, on the third day, I waited at the rock. Again I called for Kalen and again he did not come. It was only then that I was certain. Something might prevent him from coming to me once, perhaps even twice, but not thrice. Three times was deliberate.

If only I had a sister. Someone to confide in, someone who could advise me, perhaps hold my hand as I cried. At length I remembered I did indeed now have a sister. I had been tempted many times, as I sat beside Grainne's bed, to tell her about Kalen. But I had held my tongue, for I did not want her to think me foolish.

I slowly made my way up to Grainne's bedchamber. My legs trembled and I coughed repeatedly. I couldn't seem to get enough air into my lungs. My twisted foot felt like it was on fire. It would be some days yet before I was well enough to walk all the way from my rock to the lodge. But now, of course, there was no reason to go.

Grainne was alone and sitting up in bed when I limped into her bedchamber. She smiled when she saw me. She seemed to genuinely enjoy my company, even if I was usually lost in my own thoughts and said little. Most of her bruises had faded by now, although she said her ribs and jaw still ached. I had trimmed her silky hair well enough that it was not too ragged. It was far shorter than a woman would usually wear it and there were places where I could not disguise the handfuls that had been torn out, but I had done my best.

"Eithne, did you enjoy your walk?" she asked.

"I must tell you something."

I closed the door and settled into the chair beside her bed, still trying to catch my breath. My limbs shook uncontrollably and I was grateful to be able to sit at last.

"Is something wrong?"

I had resolved to be calm and logical, but at her words, I burst into tears.

"Eithne, tell me." Grainne sounded alarmed. "Whatever is the matter?"

"I have done something very foolish," I said. "It is so foolish, I am embarrassed to tell you."

"I will listen without judgement." She leaned back against the pillows and folded her hands in her lap. Her face was composed, although her eyes were shadowed and weary. "You can tell me. Whatever it is."

"Do you promise you will tell nobody?"

"I have grown up with sisters. I am very good at keeping secrets."

I waited until my tears subsided. When I thought I could speak without crying, I began.

"I have fallen in love. It is a foolish, foolish thing and I swore I would never do it. But it is done and I do not know what to do about it."

"Why is this a bad thing? Falling in love is the most wonderful thing in the world, unless he does not return your feelings. And even then, there is hope. As long as there is life, there is hope."

Grainne studied her hands as she spoke. How much of her words were intended for me and how much were a reminder to herself? Perhaps they were both.

"I do not know whether he feels the same," I said. "I had thought perhaps he felt something for me. But if he once did, it seems he does no longer."

"Will you tell me who the lucky man is? Do I know him?"

"His name is Kalen."

"A good Celtic name."

"He is… not mortal."

Grainne looked at me for a long moment, her dark eyes steady and considering.

"They are not like us, Eithne. I wish you had fallen in love with one of our own kind."

"I know. I am ashamed."

"Love is never something to be ashamed of. You cannot help who you fall for. But tell me, what has happened to upset you so? Has he told you he does not love you?"

"We have never discussed it. We have been meeting every day. He tells me of his world and I tell him of ours. But he has not come to me now for three days."

"And you have no indication of why?"

"None. He promised to meet me the next day and never came again. Three days I have waited."

"Do you have any way to send him a message?"

I shook my head. "I do not even know where he lives, save there is a portal to his world somewhere in the woods on the edge of Silver Downs. Father forbade any of us from entering the woods, for people disappear in there and never come out again, or they return changed, their minds broken."

"So what will you do?"

"What can I do, other than try to forget him?"

Grainne merely shrugged and returned to staring at her hands. I began to suspect she saw some other solution but hesitated to suggest it.

"What would you do?" I asked. "What if it was Caedmon?"

Grainne answered immediately and she looked me right in the eyes as she spoke.

"I would search for him. I would search every day and every night until I found him. And once I found him, I would never let him go again."

My mind was awhirl.

"I need to rest. I'm sorry to leave you alone."

"Go. I will be fine. Rest and we can talk later."

23

GRAINNE

I hardly knew what to make of Eithne's news. Why did the fey have such interest in this family? I had never known anyone who had met a fey, let alone encountered one myself, until I came to Silver Downs. In fact, I hadn't even entirely believed they still existed. But Eithne spoke as if it were of no great significance that she had been secretly meeting one, except in as much as she felt foolish for having fallen in love.

As a married woman, I knew I should offer advice. Something sound and intelligent. But what could I say? Reason suggested I encourage her to forget him, but how could I tell her to do what I could not myself?

I spent the evening puzzling over the situation. I briefly considered telling Agata, but dismissed the thought almost immediately. Eithne had confided in me and I would not breach her confidence. I might perhaps be able to convince her to seek advice from Fiachra. Surely her druid brother would be able to say the words I couldn't find.

I had plenty of time alone to think, for I had yet to leave my bedchamber since the night with Lunn. At meal times, Agata or one of the serving women would bring me a tray. Agata had been coaxing me to eat with the family. She said it would be good for me to do something normal again. But I had grown accustomed to being alone and was not yet ready to face the stares and questions I would encounter downstairs.

My hand mirror showed that the bruises were almost healed. My ribs hardly hurt anymore and running a hand over the back of my head told me that my hair was still somewhat ragged, but it would grow eventually. Of the child I had hoped I carried, there was no sign. Perhaps he had not survived Lunn's abuse, or perhaps he had never existed. I would rather think the latter than that my effort to save Caedmon had resulted in the loss of the heir he wanted so badly.

Eithne shuffled in early the next morning with a determined look on her face and her movements as awkward as ever. I still lay in bed in my nightdress. My breakfast tray was balanced on the chair where Eithne usually sat. The odour of uneaten porridge made my stomach roll and I was relieved when Eithne moved the tray to the floor.

She sat on the chair and tucked her feet beneath her. She often sat like that, as if to occupy the smallest space possible. Perhaps to make herself invisible. I had seen the way folk took little notice of her. She would hold herself still and quiet, seemingly to barely even breathe, and they would look right past her. It was a curious thing. I was sure her family did not intend to be cruel, for that was not the sort of folk they were. And yet unless she spoke, or moved, they did not see her.

"I have made a decision," Eithne announced.

Gone was the pinched, worried look from yesterday. Instead she looked calm, resolute, and I already knew her decision.

"I intend to find him," she said.

I wasn't sure what reaction she expected, but I hid my sigh of relief. It grated at me that Eithne accepted her presumed fate so readily. She fully expected to live a short life, enduring brief periods of wellness interspersed with days where she was confined to her bed. She acknowledged she would die from this illness, and likely soon. I would never understand how she could reconcile herself to this and if she had decided to also passively accept the fey boy's disappearance, I would have been irritated beyond words.

"I see." My voice was carefully detached, although my heart had begun to pound. I hadn't dare let myself hope she would come to this decision. Or think of what I would do if she did.

"I can't believe he feels nothing for me. I won't believe it. So if he no longer comes to me, it is because he is in some sort of trouble. I will go and find him and rescue him."

"What if he does not want to be found?" I carefully pulled a dangling woollen thread from one of my blankets and rolled it between my fingertips. "Or rescued."

"I don't believe that."

"Eithne, I am sure you have heard as many tales of the fey as I have. More, probably, since you come from a line of bards." I kept my expression neutral so she wouldn't see how desperately I wanted her to disregard my words. "The fey are fickle. They do not love the way we do. What may have seemed to you to be a deep connection might have been no more than a passing fancy to him. Something to occupy a few hours of boredom."

"I can't think that. I don't believe it. Something is wrong and I must go to him."

"What exactly do you intend?"

"I will go to the woods and find the portal."

"The woods are large. Do you intend to wander without direction until you stumble on the portal? How will you even recognise it for what it is?"

"If I am meant to find him, I will find the portal."

"How will you get there? Surely you cannot walk so far."

"I must, so I will."

Eithne's face was determined. Looking at her now, all fire and strength, it was hard to believe she regularly couldn't leave her bed for days at a time.

"Eithne, be sensible. You are not well enough for such a journey. The woods are a half day's walk for one who is physically sound. It would take you a day or more, if you even have the strength for such a thing."

"Grainne, I have no choice. I must find him. Something is wrong."

I sighed as if forced into a decision I did not want.

"Fine then. If you are determined, I will go with you."

"You will?" The surprise and delight on Eithne's face shamed me, for she had no idea of my selfish motive. "Grainne, I did not expect this. Will you really come?"

"I can hardly let you go alone. I suppose you do not intend to tell anybody else."

"Of course not, for they will only say I cannot go. And I will not be stopped."

"Someone has to keep an eye on you, I suppose. It would be unseemly for you to go alone."

Eithne wanted to set off immediately, but I convinced her we should commence our journey in two days. I had no idea how she would walk so far. She breathed too heavily from merely walking up the stairs and along the hall to my bedchamber. But she had come to this decision on her own, mostly, and that gave me a reason to go with her. If Caedmon was really somewhere Diarmuid's magic could not reach him, then he was most likely in the realm of the fey. And if Eithne was determined to go there, I would go with her. I would find Caedmon and bring him home.

24

GRAINNE

$\mathcal{E}$ithne and I discussed our plan numerous times over the next two days — not that there was much to it. Walk to the woods. Hope we stumbled over the portal, for neither of us had any idea what such a thing would look like. Pray we somehow found Kalen and could rescue him from whatever situation had befallen him. Trust that any fey we encountered would be sympathetic.

Probably the worst that might happen was to be forced to leave without completing our quest. Of course my own aim remained unspoken: find Caedmon and a way to avoid Diarmuid's magic, and bring him safely home. Every time I was tempted to confide in Eithne, Lunn's words echoed through my mind: *tell nobody.*

Eithne sat in her usual chair, her feet tucked beneath her. The sun was high in the sky and she had positioned the chair where the sun could warm her through the window. After so long confined to my bed, I craved the feeling of sun on my skin and fresh air in my lungs.

"You need to tell somebody," I said.

"But who would I tell? Mother would worry, Papa would forbid me. Eremon would go straight to Papa. Sitric has returned to Maker's Well. Diarmuid has gone off on his own journey. Marrec and Conn might be persuaded to keep a secret, but I can't be certain."

"So tell Fiachra."

"I barely know him," Eithne said. She chewed her fingernails, a habit I hadn't noticed before. "And he always looks so stern. I don't know what he would say."

"He is still your brother and you must tell someone. If I disappear, folk will assume I have returned to my family. But they will worry if you leave without explanation."

"But what would I say?"

"Tell him the truth. He is a druid. He might know something that can help you."

"I'll think about it," she said, although her tone indicated she intended no such thing.

A knock on the door interrupted our discussion. I bid the knocker to enter and Fiachra appeared as if we had somehow summoned him. My heart ached at the echoes of Caedmon I saw in his stance and his face.

"I came to see how you fare," Fiachra said. "Both of you."

His face showed no indication of his thoughts and I could see why Eithne professed to be afraid of him. But behind his serious eyes, I thought I detected the tiniest hint of a smile. He knew how to laugh, this druid brother. Eithne stared intently at her hands, so it seemed I must respond lest he think us both either rude or stupid.

"I am almost healed," I said. "My ribs still hurt a little, but otherwise I am fine."

"And what of your mind?" Fiachra asked. "For that does not heal quite as easily as the body."

Tears came to my eyes unexpectedly and I didn't know how to respond. I had consented, in a way, to everything done to me. It had seemed a fair trade to ensure Caedmon's safety. I did not doubt that Lunn would uphold his side of our agreement, for the fey might twist the truth, or omit a crucial detail, but they did not lie. Or at least that's what the old tales claimed. Although I had said nothing, Fiachra nodded.

"I see," he said. "Time heals most wounds, whether we intend it or no."

There seemed nothing left for me to say. Although I was inclined to like him, I wasn't sure I could trust this druid brother of my husband. Fiachra's inquiry of me was obviously concluded, for he turned now to Eithne.

"Sister." He offered her a brief smile and, to my mind at least, it seemed almost tender. "You have made a decision."

"I don't know what you mean." Eithne shrank back into her chair, shoulders hunched as if to make herself invisible.

Fiachra stretched out his hand and touched her gently on the forehead.

"Travel safe, dear sister. The one whom you seek is unreliable. You will need to keep eyes and mind open. Stay alert, for that place is fluid and dangerous. Do not trust anyone."

Eithne's face was pale, but the way she held her mouth said clearly that she would not be dissuaded.

"I will do what I must. I am not afraid."

"You should be," he said. "Mortals rarely return from that place and those that do are forever changed."

"There is risk in all life," Eithne said. "That does not mean one should sit at home and be afraid to step outside."

Fiachra smiled, and there was sadness in the expression.

"Our family has been blessed, and cursed, many times over. Some of those blessings are physical, like the fertile land around us. Others are invisible to the eye, but powerful none the less. That is why they watch us. Our ignorance is intrinsic to their aims. If our family ever understands the truth, what they aim for will be much harder and they may well fail. Diarmuid is not the only one in this family with power. You will not unlock your own ability until you understand its source."

Eithne's forehead wrinkled. "I don't understand."

"You will," Fiachra said. Then he turned back to me.

"Grainne, you have been brave thus far and it seems you must continue to be brave for much longer. You have thrown your lot in with the family of Silver Downs. Whether you understood what you were doing is no longer relevant. You have made your choice and choices have consequences."

"I will face whatever I must." I clenched my hands together so he would not see the way they trembled.

"He is safe, for now. Get to him as fast as you can."

My heart lurched and I wanted to jump out of the bed and shake Fiachra until he told me everything he knew.

"Are you certain?"

"He will be much changed from the man he was."

"Where is he? How do I find him?" My voice cracked.

Fiachra stepped back towards the door.

"If you look, I believe you will find him, for your will is strong and your heart is pure."

He left, closing the door softly behind him. Eithne and I sat in stunned silence.

"How did he know those things?" she asked finally.

"He is a druid. I would not assume anything is secret from one such as he."

"What did he mean, the things he said to you?"

I hesitated. I was not yet ready to talk about Caedmon or what I had done. When I didn't answer, Eithne shook her head.

"You don't need to tell me. I don't mind if you have secrets."

"I feel like I should tell you. After all, you have shared your secret with me. But I can't."

"You can tell me when you are ready. I won't pester you about it."

We fell into silence. I was occupied with thoughts of Caedmon and what Fiachra might mean about him being changed. At least I knew he was safe.

We agreed to leave after breakfast the next day, then Eithne retired to her bedchamber. I tipped out the pack Caedmon had intended to take with him and sorted through its contents. I had not been able to make myself empty it until now. It had seemed too much like an admission that Caedmon would never need it. The pack didn't contain much: a spare shirt, a blanket, a water flask, flint, a small purse of coins, a knife. If that was all Caedmon had thought he would need, I would trust it would be sufficient for our journey too.

As dusk fell and I ate yet another lonely dinner from a tray, my memories of Caedmon were so strong I could almost feel him there with me. The room still held the faintest trace of his scent and if I closed my eyes and concentrated, I could just smell it.

"I'm coming, my love," I whispered into the empty room. "Wait for me. I will find you."

2 5

GRAINNE

After breakfast the next morning, I took my pack and left my bedchamber for the first time since the night Lunn had locked me in. Although I had walked no further than the length of the bedchamber for some weeks now, I felt stronger than I expected as I tiptoed down the hall.

I hoped to slip unnoticed through the house, for there would undoubtedly be questions and exclamations if anyone saw me and I didn't know how I would answer them. The brothers must have already left to start their day's chores, though, and the only voices I could hear were of Agata and the servant women, and they were at the other end of the house.

Eithne already waited at the back door, looking wan and delicate in sturdy boots and a thick coat. A large pack sat beside her on the floor.

As I pulled my coat off its hook, she hefted her pack. She hesitated a little and I swiftly reached for it, twisting it from her arms with little effort. It was far heavier than mine.

"Here, you carry mine and I will take this one," I said.

"I can manage."

She reached for her pack, but I slung it over my shoulder.

"Don't be foolish, Eithne. You won't last an hour carrying this. Take mine, it's much lighter. What on earth do you have in here?"

"Food, mostly. Bread, cheese, dried meat, fruit. The tales say mortals should not eat the food of the fey or they will never be able to leave."

We departed and I set a slow pace, aiming to conserve her strength for as long as possible. What we would do when she could walk no further, I didn't know. Nights would be cold with only my one blanket between us, but we had our coats, and flint. I could survive a couple of early spring nights. It was Eithne I worried about. We had been walking for only minutes before her breathing grew heavy and she began to favour one leg.

"Have you hurt your foot?" I asked.

She shook her head, too breathless to speak. Her face was red and covered with a sheen of sweat.

"Let's stop for a few minutes. We both need to catch our breath."

There was nowhere to sit, other than the dewy grass and patches of half-melted snow, so we stood with the morning sun beating down on our heads. Although we had a long journey ahead of us yet, I felt free. Lighter. Every step brought me closer to Caedmon. When Eithne's breathing sounded more even, I set off again.

"What is wrong with your foot?" I asked, noting that she still seemed to limp.

"It is deformed." Eithne's tone was somewhat defensive. "It twists inward. I was born like this."

"I've never noticed you limp before."

"I don't, usually. But when I am tired, it is hard not to."

I didn't comment further, although I wondered what else she kept hidden.

Again and again, we walked until Eithne struggled to breathe, then we stopped to rest, standing in a field. When our stomachs started to rumble, we ate bread and cheese. The bread was fresh and the cheese sharp and crumbly. My appetite was stronger than it had been for weeks.

The sun had started to set by the time we finally reached the edge of Silver Downs' land. The woods loomed ahead of us, far larger than I had imagined. I could see nothing past the first few trees, which were a mix of ash, oak and birch. The darkness within was like a blanket, thick and obscuring, despite the mostly naked branches of the trees on the edges. I quailed a little and if my journey had been for any purpose other than to find Caedmon, I might have turned around and gone home. But I did not intend to let my husband down.

Eithne's face was pale and she trembled with exhaustion. When she caught me examining her, she lifted her chin in a manner I had come to recognise as Eithne deciding to be brave.

"I am fine," she said.

"We will need to make camp soon. Should we go into the woods or find a suitable place out here?"

"Let's keep going. We are close to the portal, I can feel it."

"What do you mean?"

I felt nothing other than apprehension about entering the woods, the creeping coldness of night approaching, and fatigue from walking all day.

"There's a… pull," Eithne said. "It's like something tugging on my insides. Drawing me closer. Whatever it is, it wants me to find it."

So we entered the woods. They were dark and still, but not as cold as I had expected. In fact, within their shelter, the air was rather warmer. If the woods held a consistent temperature, the nights might not be as unpleasant as I had feared.

Once we passed the outer trees, the light within the woods was brighter than I had expected, given the setting sun. In fact, the further we walked, the brighter it became, until I would have sworn we walked through a shady patch of trees in the middle of the day rather than through woods at dusk. Somewhere high above me, a woodlark sang a merry tune.

"Strange," Eithne murmured, and I finally realised she had stopped some distance behind me.

"What is it?"

"The birch already has catkins. And look, blackberries."

"It is warm in here. Perhaps winter has not touched these woods as much as it has affected us outside."

Now that Eithne had drawn my attention to our surroundings, I noticed that the naked branches of winter were gone and so too were the buds of early spring. The oaks were decked in their summer finery with glossy green leaves and small acorns. The ash bore tiny purple blossoms. A small flying creature fluttered past my face, its colourful wings drawing my gaze, and landed on the branch of a birch not far from us, as if to watch our progress.

Eithne breathed more easily now and her limp was less pronounced, despite how exhausted she must be. My pack didn't seem quite as heavy and my feet hardly ached at all anymore. There was something invigorating about these woods.

I was about to ask whether Eithne still felt the pull of the portal when the ground began to vibrate and a thundering echoed through the woods. It sounded like horses. A stampeding herd, perhaps? An unusual thing to encounter here, but then these woods were strange anyway.

Eithne looked as confused as me. My thoughts whirled. What should we do? My first instinct was to climb a tree, to get out of the way before the herd crushed us to death. But I could not climb wearing a long skirt, and Eithne would not have the strength to, so I grabbed her hand and we backed up against an oak. I held my breath and prayed the herd would run right past.

They were elegant white beauties, heaving from their run. But this was no spooked herd. They carried fey riders: tall and thin with hair the colour of the dark of the moon and lips so red they looked like gashes in their pale skin. They clutched long spears and wooden clubs. Running along with the horses were hounds, brown and slender with long necks and eager legs.

They would have rushed right past if it weren't for one of the hounds who stopped to sniff at us, perhaps curious about our foreign scent.

"Go away," I hissed quietly. "Please, go."

One of the riders reined in his horse to check on the hound and then they were all pulling up, surrounding us. They sat straight-backed on their horses, their dark clothes giving them a grim appearance. Their faces were angular and cruel and filled with suspicion. The horses and hounds were unnaturally silent and still.

"What have we here?" asked the one who had stopped to check on the hound.

Eithne squeaked in fear and it was obvious I would have to do the talking.

"We are merely passing through." My voice trembled almost as much as my legs. I clutched Eithne's hand tightly, as much to stop her from running away as to remind myself I was not alone. "We mean no harm."

As one, the fey all laughed.

"We mean no harm," one said in a falsetto clearly intended to mimic my tone.

"Merely passing through," said another.

"You are trespassing," said the one who had found us. "How did you get here?"

"We walked. The woods border our lands on one side."

"You walked from there to here?" He lifted an eyebrow as if to suggest he did not believe me.

I did not respond for I didn't know what to say. How else did he think we got here? By flapping our arms and flying like birds?

"How did you find the portal?" he asked.

"We didn't. That is, not yet. We were looking for it."

A low hiss arose from the rest of the party and was silenced immediately when the one speaking to us, clearly their leader, held up his finger.

"Do you mean you passed through the portal without even knowing?" His tone held a dangerous message.

Eithne and I looked at each other.

"Is this… is this the realm of the fey?" I asked when it became clear he intended to wait for however long it took us to respond.

Again the fey laughed and once again they were silenced at the slightest gesture from their leader.

"You did not even realise you were no longer in the mortal realm? Why must mortals be so stupid?"

"How were we to know we had passed into your lands?" Anger rumbled within me. "There was no visible portal. We simply entered the woods and found ourselves here. There was no transition, nothing to mark the passing from one place to another."

"You did not recognise that woods as lush and bountiful as these could not exist in your own realm?"

"I have never been in any woods before. How am I to know whether these are unusual?"

The fey twittered and even their leader laughed this time. They all stopped in the same instant.

"Bring them," the leader said, his voice casual. He tugged on the reins, turned his horse, and rode away.

Before I had time to wonder what he meant, one of the fey leaned down from his horse to grab me. His fingers dug painfully into the soft skin on the undersides of my arms as he hauled me up to sit behind him. There was no consideration given to the practicality of riding a horse while wearing a gown and consequently my skirt was bunched around my hips, displaying an inappropriate amount of leg.

"I suggest you hold on," he said.

I barely had time to grab his waist before we set off. The horses thundered through the woods. The hounds kept pace, baying from time to time. I had no hope of remembering the path we took, for we travelled so swiftly that the trees were merely a blur. I couldn't see Eithne and panic began to well within me. Surely they didn't leave her behind? But eventually I caught sight of her dark hair. She, too, was lodged behind one of the riders. Then the horse I rode jumped over some obstacle and I could think of nothing other than clutching the fey man in front of me.

We rode for hours. As the terror wore off, I became tired, for we had walked all day and it must be late night by now, even though the light never changed. My eyes grew heavy and my arms and legs ached from holding on so tightly. I dozed off several times, waking with a start as my head nodded and my desperate grip on the fey man slackened. Still we rode, the horses and hounds never tiring.

Occasionally one of the riders let out a blood-curdling scream. I couldn't see anything but the back of the fey in front of me. Whatever quarry they pursued must have finally escaped, for all of a sudden, the horses veered off. I clung to the fey rider as his horse turned sharply. If I fell, I would be trampled beneath the horses' hooves.

After what seemed like several more hours, the horses finally slowed. We halted in a large clearing, a dozen horses and half as many hounds. The horses heaved and strands of white foam dripped from their mouths. I wondered what they really were, for no ordinary horse could have run so long.

The fey slid down from their mounts, and boys — mortal boys — emerged from somewhere behind the trees that ringed the clearing. They took the horses' reins and led them away. A mortal woman appeared and although she said not a word, the hounds gathered around her and followed her back into the woods. The fey, too, melted into the trees, except for their leader and the riders with whom Eithne and I had travelled.

"How dare you," I spluttered, finally able to speak now that my feet were on the ground and my skirt covered my legs. "What right have you to abduct us?"

Their leader was unperturbed at my outburst.

"We do not suffer mortals to trespass uninvited in our realm."

"I already told you we did not know we had passed through the portal."

"You also admitted you were searching for it. The portal chooses who it allows through. Some may search their entire lives and never find it. Others find it immediately."

"So how is it our fault if this portal chose us and let us through? That hardly counts as trespassing."

He shrugged, looking bored.

"I will not debate with you. The queen will decide your fate." He snapped his fingers at the two riders and stalked away without another word.

One of the riders grabbed me roughly by the arm and dragged me with him as he strode through the woods.

"Could you at least slow down?" I struggled to keep my feet beneath me as we hurried over twisting roots and rocks and slippery patches of leaves.

He didn't look at me nor slow his pace, and all I could do was try to keep up. I had little time to wonder how Eithne fared. We stopped beside a large oak, its mighty girth and spreading branches bearing testament to its age. The fey pressed his palm to the trunk and it swung open. He flung me into the cavity within the tree.

By the time I got my feet back under me and managed to stand, Eithne was on her hands and knees beside me. The trunk closed and we were left in darkness.

26

GRAINNE

The darkness was absolute and panic gnawed at my stomach. I had never liked the dark.

"Grainne?" Eithne's voice was thin and full of fear. "Where are you?"

I swallowed down my fear. I was the older of us, the married woman. I had to lead by example.

"I'm here." My voice wavered only a little. "Stand still and I will find you."

I stumbled around until I crashed into her and we clutched each other. She felt small and fragile in my arms. The space in which we stood seemed too large for the inside of a tree, even one the size of a great oak. The air was a suffocating mix of mustiness and damp earth. I closed my eyes and tried to pretend it was only dark because of that. But still my heart raced and my breathing was ragged.

"What do you think they mean to do with us?" Eithne whispered.

"He said we will be presented to the queen. I suppose that's Titania." I breathed deeply, in and out. I had to stay calm for Eithne's sake. "We will have an opportunity to make our case and then, when she realises we have done nothing wrong, we will be released."

A small sob was Eithne's only reply.

"We should sit," I said. "Get some rest. Who knows how long we will be waiting here and surely we have been up all night."

Still clutching each other, we sank down onto the ground. It felt to be hard-packed dirt, scattered with small remnants of something that might have been hay.

"Lie down and put your head in my lap," I said. "You may as well try to sleep."

Eithne said nothing, but she did as I said. I stroked her hair, which was tangled from our ride. Eithne's shoulders shook occasionally, although she tried to suppress her sobs, but eventually her breathing deepened. My fear of the dark returned once I no longer needed to be brave for her sake. I continued to smooth her hair slowly, forcing myself to inhale and exhale in time with the motion.

I tried to stay awake, but my eyes were heavy despite my fear. I woke with a start each time my head dropped, my heart thudding as I listened for any sign that the fey returned. Hours passed and my fear receded a little. My bladder began to ache and my stomach growled. Hunger and thirst warred with fatigue. Finally Eithne stirred and sat up. The darkness was so complete that I couldn't see her, even though she was right beside me.

"How long did I sleep?" she asked.

"A long time."

"I feel a little better. You should sleep now."

I lay down and rested my head in Eithne's lap. Her skirt smelled of horse and sweat. The earthen floor was cool and hard beneath me.

I woke as light poured in, burning my eyes and leaving me blind. I struggled to sit up, but my feet tangled in my skirt.

"Get up," a voice said.

Eithne and I stumbled to our feet. My muscles were stiff and I moved slowly. I bent to pick up my pack, but somebody grabbed me by the arm and hauled me outside.

"Wait, my pack," I said, but they paid no heed.

Again they led us through the woods, caring little whether we kept our feet beneath us or were dragged behind. By the time my eyes adjusted enough to see, there were no familiar landmarks.

We stopped in a large clearing; the same as yesterday or a different one, I couldn't tell. Dozens of fey waited. A crowd of mortals would be fidgeting, chatting, quieting noisy children, but the fey were silent and still. They stared as we stood at the clearing's edge, our guards beside us still grasping our arms.

"Can we not have some time to make ourselves presentable before we speak with the queen?" I asked the fey who held me. He wasn't the one with whom I had shared a horse yesterday.

He clearly heard me, for his gaze flicked towards me briefly, but he didn't acknowledge my words in any other way.

"Please?" My voice was as meek and placid as I could make it. "I'm rather—"

"Silence," he said with a tug on my arm so firm, I wondered that it didn't pop out of its socket. "You are not permitted to speak until you are told to."

"Not permitted?" I forgot all thoughts of being meek and placid. "How dare you! We have been brought here, unwillingly, by force. Kept in a dark room for hours, and now you tell me I am not permitted to speak?"

He turned to me and looked me in the face for the first time. His midnight eyes blazed.

"You will be silent. If you wish to see the queen, you will do as you are told. Otherwise I will return you to your quarters and you will wait until the queen expresses a desire to see you. And that may be a very long time."

I opened my mouth, but Eithne caught my eye. Her face was pale and streaked with tears and I suddenly remembered why we were here. I closed my mouth with a snap and directed my gaze at the ground so he would not see the hatred that surely burned in my eyes.

We waited. I began to wonder how much longer I could hold my bladder when a company of guards marched into the clearing. Following them was a fey woman. Tall and luminescent, with the white skin and black hair typical of that race, she exuded power and cruelty and I was suddenly very afraid. Afraid for our safety, afraid she might not allow us to do what we came for, afraid we would spend the rest of our lives locked in that dark hole in the tree.

Titania settled herself on a golden throne I would have sworn wasn't there earlier. She wore a long scarlet dress that flowed like blood over her legs and pooled at her feet. She raised one hand and our fey guards dragged us forward to deposit us in front of the throne. Titania eyed us up and down, distaste apparent in her cold gaze.

"Kneel," my guard hissed.

When I hesitated, he grabbed me roughly by the shoulders and forced me down. Side by side, Eithne and I knelt in front of Titania, the grass damp and cold beneath our knees.

Finally, Titania spoke.

"What have we here?"

"Two mortals, my lady," my guard said. "We found them on the edge of the woods."

"They passed through the portal without aid?"

"So it seems, my lady."

"What is your purpose here?"

For a moment I didn't realise Titania's words were directed at us. I glanced at Eithne, for this was her story to tell. My purpose would remain a secret for as long as possible lest I jeopardise Caedmon's safety.

Eithne's mouth trembled but she straightened her shoulders and lifted her chin, much the way her bard brother composed himself before he began a tale. My heart pounded as I waited for her to speak. Her words would determine our future.

27

EITHNE

"My lady, we apologise for the intrusion." I wasn't sure whether I was permitted to look at the queen, but when I dared to raise my head nobody shoved it back down again. I was proud of how steady my voice was. "We stumbled through the portal without realising, although it is true we were searching for a way into your realm."

"Explain yourself." Titania's voice was as wintry as her eyes.

The fey around us were silent and I didn't dare look away from her to see whether they stared at us. I darted a glance at Grainne and she nodded. Whether she meant for me to tell the truth, or merely intended encouragement, I didn't know. We should have spent the time we were shut inside the tree figuring out what to say to our captors instead of sleeping. I took a deep breath and continued.

"We came to search for someone. One of your folk. His name is Kalen."

Titania made a sound I couldn't interpret and her face screwed up as if she had tasted something sour.

"What makes you think he wishes you to find him?"

"Do you know him?" My heart leapt. This might be easier than I had expected. "Can you tell me where he is?"

"I ask the questions. How do you know him?"

I hesitated. If I told the truth, Kalen might be in trouble, but I couldn't think of a plausible lie quickly enough.

"I've met him. In the mortal world."

"So why do you seek him here, if you can see him in your own world?"

"Because he has stopped coming to visit me and I am afraid it means he is in trouble."

Titania raised one eyebrow and continued to stare at me. The guards flanking her throne smirked.

My knees ached, but I didn't dare stand. The guards' reaction confused me.

"Why is that funny?" I asked.

"Many mortal women have been in the same situation as you find yourself now," she said, and if I had thought her stare cool before, it was even colder now. "They fall in love with a fey. They think themselves to be special. They believe their fey lover's promises to always be true. And when he loses interest, the mortal fails to understand. She searches for her lover, determined to find him and reignite his interest. But the truth is that the attention of the fey is fickle. We forget far easier than mortals do. If he has stopped coming to warm your bed at night, the only thing you can do is forget."

"It's not like that. He is not my lover. And I don't believe he has merely forgotten me. Something is wrong."

"And you think you can solve his problem? You, a mortal woman?"

"Without knowing what the problem is, I can't say. But I have come to find him and to help however I may."

Titania's face twitched and I thought for a moment she would laugh. But her voice was still as unforgiving as stone.

"There is no problem," she said. "He has merely lost interest. Go home. I will have you taken back to the portal if you promise to leave immediately and never return."

Beside me, Grainne stiffened. Was this what she wanted? To turn around and go home? I couldn't ask with Titania glaring down at us.

But Grainne knew why we had come. Surely she would not expect me to leave so soon.

"I am here to find Kalen," I said. "Will you give me leave to search for him?"

"Search for him?" Titania's voice rose. "How do you think to find him? Do you plan to wander aimlessly through my realm, hoping you might stumble upon him?"

Yes, that was pretty much what I had intended.

"Do you know where he is?" I asked.

"I know everything that happens in this realm."

"Would you send someone to fetch him? Give me a chance to speak to him? If what you say is true, that he has merely lost interest, I will return home without complaint and will never come back. But please let me talk to him."

"He will not be interested. He has probably already taken a new lover and forgotten about you."

"If that's true, I will accept it. But I will not believe he has forgotten me unless I hear it from his own lips."

"What would you give to speak to him?"

"I don't understand."

I wiped my sweaty palms on my skirt. The ache in my knees was almost unbearable and the damp from the cold grass soaked my skirt.

"You think to come uninvited to my realm and demand to speak to one of my subjects? For nothing?"

"Tell me what you want."

"You must complete a task."

"Name your task."

"You will serve as a slave to my people — for one hundred years. At the end of that time, you may speak to him."

My heart dropped. For a moment I could hardly breathe. One hundred years? I would not age in the fey realm, or I would age very slowly, but life would continue in my own world. By the time I left this place, everyone I had ever known would be dead. I could never return to my old life.

"And if I refuse?" Papa always said one must understand the consequences before making a decision.

"You will be a slave anyway. Until I choose to release you."

"And you will allow Grainne to return home?"

"If you refuse, you will both stay as slaves."

I heard Grainne's intake of breath. I couldn't condemn her to an endless period of slavery at the whim of the fey. No matter the consequence for me, Grainne must be free. She had come out of friendship, or perhaps loyalty to her husband's family. The reason was irrelevant. It only mattered that she was able to leave safely.

"The agreement is that I will serve as your slave for one hundred years, after which time I will be able to speak to Kalen, and then you will allow me to go home?"

"Correct."

"Then I agree."

Titania nodded once, the movement short and sharp.

"Take them away."

The guard seized me once more by the arm and hauled me away, his fingers digging into already-bruised flesh. Beside me, Grainne was subjected to the same treatment. There was no time to protest. I didn't have breath to speak as long as I tried to keep my feet beneath me. We stopped in front of a tree and the trunk opened, revealing a dark interior. Whether it was the same tree as before, or another, I couldn't tell. I was tossed inside with Grainne close behind me. Then the door closed and I could see nothing more.

"Wait," I called. "Grainne is supposed to go home."

On my hands and knees, I stumbled back to where the door was. My skirt, wet from the grass, wrapped around my legs. I found the door and banged on it with my fists. It felt as solid as any tree trunk and my fists quickly bruised.

"Come back. You have to take Grainne home."

"Eithne, Eithne."

Grainne's hands were on my shoulders, pulling me back from the door. I turned to her and we wrapped our arms around each other.

"She was supposed to send you home," I said, stifling a sob.

"She did not say she would. Only that she would not allow me to go if you refused."

"I did not intend to agree for both of us. She knew that." I could no longer hold back the tears. My sobs came thick and fast.

"Ssh." Grainne stroked my hair. "What is done, is done. There is nothing we can do about it now."

"We can ask to see her again. Explain I wasn't speaking for you."

"It's too late, Eithne." Only now did Grainne's voice break and her hot tears fell on my arm. "It's done and it can't be undone."

"I would have never agreed if I knew."

"There was no choice. She intended to keep us as slaves no matter what you said. At least this way, we know when our imprisonment will end."

"One hundred years. How will we survive that long?"

"We will survive because we must."

All I wanted to do was cry into her shoulder, but Grainne was being so strong that I tried to collect myself.

"You're right. We mustn't lose hope. But how will we mark the passing of the days? It is impossible to tell in here, and out there, the light is always the same. Already I don't know whether we have been here for one day or several."

"I don't know. We will find a way. But for now, let's see if we can figure out what we have in here. My bladder will burst if I don't empty it shortly."

With outstretched hands we felt our way through the darkness. In one corner we found a meagre pile of hay. Elsewhere was a clay pot that stank of urine. Nothing else. If our packs had been here, they were no longer, but perhaps this was not the same place we were kept in previously.

"Nowhere to sleep," I said, my voice forlorn, "unless the hay is intended as a bed."

"I suspect it is." Grainne's voice was brisk. She was much better at coping, at just getting on with things, than I was. I resolved to learn from her example. "It seems they think us little more than pigs, so they have given us hay to sleep in and a dark hovel."

"I wouldn't treat a pig this badly."

"At least we have a chamber pot."

I heard the rustling of skirts and then the sharp ping of liquid hitting the base of the clay pot. The stench of urine reached my nose.

"Do you need the pot?" Grainne asked.

We fumbled around, searching in the darkness for each other, before she finally managed to pass me the chamber pot.

"We need somewhere to keep it," she said. "Where we won't knock it over."

There weren't many options. The area in which we were confined appeared to be roughly circular. The complete absence of light left us with no means of navigation. The only feature that might serve as a landmark was the pile of hay and we decided to stand the chamber pot against the opposite wall. It was still possible, perhaps even probable, that one of us would knock it over, but it was the best we could do.

"They could at least have left us some food," Grainne said.

My stomach growled in response. My pack had contained food enough for a couple of days, but if we were to remain here for a hundred years, we would have to eat their food sooner or later. And eventually we would learn whether the old tales were true.

28

EITHNE

Grainne and I curled up together in the hay. We left our boots on for fear that we would not be given time to put them on when the fey returned and might lose them forever. With both our coats draped over us, we huddled close together for warmth.

I dozed for a while, but mostly I lay awake, cursing myself for getting us into this mess. If only I hadn't allowed Grainne to come with me. If only I had been more specific when I agreed to Titania's offer. I should have stipulated that Grainne was to be returned safely home immediately.

I went over and over everything that had been said, both my words and Titania's. What else had I missed? The wording of the pledge seemed simple enough: *The agreement is that I will serve as your slave for one hundred years, after which time I will be able to speak to Kalen, and then you will allow me to go home.* No matter how I picked and prodded, I could find no loophole Titania might exploit, except perhaps that I had agreed to speaking *to* Kalen instead of *with* him. My words indicated clearly that I spoke only for myself and not Grainne.

But as Grainne said, what was done was done. I couldn't blame her if she was furious with me. If she refused to speak to me for the next hundred years, that would be no more than I deserved. I could see why Caedmon chose her. A soldier needed a wife who was strong and composed and not given to fits of hysteria. And that was Grainne. He would be proud of her. Tears pricked my eyes again. I could not afford to think about Caedmon. I would likely never learn his fate now, not if I was kept here for a hundred years.

Hours passed — certainly longer than a single night — before the tree silently cracked open and light flooded our prison. Grainne and I sat up, arms shielding our eyes from the sudden brightness. A draught flowed in and it was only now that I realised how stale the air had become. Hay stuck to my skin, making it itch, but before I could brush it away, a woman spoke.

"Get up," she said. Something landed on the dirt floor with a thud. "Eat and make yourselves respectable. It is time for you to work."

Still mostly blind, we scrabbled around in the dirt. I found it first, my fingers closing around a half loaf of bread. I tried to tear it in two, but it was stale and hard.

"Here, let me."

Grainne took the bread from my hand and ripped it apart. She handed me half and started nibbling on hers. I gnawed ravenously, hungry enough to ignore its strange taste and odour. As my eyes adjusted, I finally saw what we were eating. The bread was not only stale, it was covered in large blotches of moss-green mould. I gagged, spitting out the mouthful I had yet to swallow. My stomach spasmed.

Grainne tossed the mouldy bread to the floor and leaned over to retch loudly. When she had finished, she wiped her mouth with the back of her hand, then turned to the fey woman who waited in the doorway.

"We cannot eat that," she said. "That is not fit for human consumption."

"It is fit for slaves," the fey said, her voice bored and uninterested. "Eat it or not. There will be no other food."

"But it will make us ill," I said.

The fey shrugged. "If you are finished with your meal, it is time to leave. If you walk nicely, I will let you walk on your own feet. Run, or do anything else to annoy me, and I will have you carried like sacks of turnips." She waved her hand in the direction of two large men who waited just outside.

They did not have the tall thin stature of the fey, nor their pale skin and black hair. Rather they were broad, one tending to fat, with pasty complexions, straw-like hair and blank faces. If they recognised us as fellow mortals, they gave no indication of it. But still, seeing them gave me a small surge of hope. There might yet be someone who could help Grainne escape.

Grainne vomited again, a foul-smelling clear liquid that splashed over the bread on the floor.

"We're ready," she said.

We followed the fey woman as she led us on a winding path past birch and beech, fallen branches, and holly bushes laden with shiny red berries. I tried to remember landmarks, but it seemed we walked in circles, for a birch tree with a distinctive silvery knot seemed to be everywhere and we kept passing a log that held the nest of some small forest creature. A raven squawked from the branches of a beech, his harsh cry a challenge to those who disturbed the woods.

I was so intent on remembering our path that at first I didn't notice that it was no effort to keep from limping. My twisted foot seemed straighter than usual and I walked evenly.

The two mortal men followed, their footsteps loud in the silence of the woods. The fey woman walked ahead of us, soundlessly gliding from spot to spot. I tried to walk as quietly as she did.

"What is your name?" I asked at length.

"That is irrelevant."

"How is your name irrelevant? I just want to know what to call you."

"You call me nothing, for you will not speak unless I tell you to."

I said nothing further. There was no point wasting breath on her. I had hardly slept for what felt like days and had eaten nothing more than a few nibbles of mouldy bread. My limbs were weak and my head fuzzy. My tongue felt fat and thick, and my mouth tasted bitter.

Eventually we stopped in front of a large oak. My head swam by then and my vision wavered. Grainne reached out and took my hand.

The trunk cracked open soundlessly, spilling out light and heat and the tantalising scent of fresh pastries. My stomach growled loudly. The fey woman waved us inside.

"You will work in here until I come to collect you."

Grainne and I hesitated and she huffed, indicating again for us to enter.

"Go. Hurry up."

Side by side, we entered the tree and the trunk closed behind us. Sweat immediately dripped down my back, for the room was uncomfortably hot. Like the oak in which we had slept, this one seemed larger than it should. It was equipped as a kitchen, with a row of wood ovens along one curving side and a vast wall of food-laden shelves against the opposite side. A long work bench in the centre took up most of the rest of the space. Four mortal women worked frantically at the bench, sweat dripping from their faces right into the pastries they prepared.

"Hurry up then," said a woman standing near the ovens. "Get to work. There's no time to waste and I won't have dawdlers in my kitchen."

She was definitely mortal, short and almost as round as she was high. She glared at us over a glistening red nose and a tray of pastries hot from the oven. My mouth watered.

"You there." She dropped the tray on a bench and pointed at Grainne. "Get over there and start peeling the turnips. And you—" She pointed at me. "Start sweeping."

"Could we—" I motioned towards the tray of pastries. "We haven't eaten since we were brought here."

The woman drew herself up to her full height, which was only about as high as my shoulder, and gave me a withering glare.

"Slaves do not eat the food we prepare. You ought to get that straight first thing. You get caught eating this, the penalty is harsh. First offence is a whipping. Second offence, your hand is cut off. So get any thoughts of tasty pastries out of your head and start sweeping."

I was too scared to say anything else. Trying to ignore the tantalising scent, I took up a battered broom leaning against the wall and started sweeping the wooden floorboards. The floor, though, was charmed, for I would clear one patch and start on another, and when I turned back to the first area, it would be just as dirty as before. I paused to wipe away the sweat dripping into my eyes.

"Sweep harder, you lazy wench," the fat woman said. "You think you're ever going to clean the floor at that pace?"

"It doesn't matter how fast I go, it's always just as dirty," I said.

She rolled her eyes and started transferring the hot pastries to cooling racks.

"Every new slave says the same thing. Lazy, you all are, and don't think I don't know it."

"Are you not a slave?" Grainne asked. She stood at the far end of the long bench and I could barely see her above the enormous pile of purple turnips. She used a knife to scrape a turnip, dropping the skin into one tub in front of her and the peeled vegetable into another.

The fat woman huffed.

"I am no slave. I am kinswoman to one of the fey. Half sisters, we are."

"Why do they make you work in here then?" Grainne asked.

"Make me?" The fat woman's voice was incredulous. "This is a privilege. And you will understand that before you ever leave here. Those turnips ain't going to peel themselves, so I suggest you move faster."

As harsh as the fat woman's words might have been, her tone wasn't quite as fierce as when she had spoken to me. I resolved to keep my mouth shut. Perhaps Grainne would be able to win her over. If the woman sympathised with us, she might help us escape, or at least give us some food. We worked in silence for a while before Grainne spoke again.

"Is there a name we might call you by?"

"You can call me Treva," the woman said, and now her voice was almost kind.

"Well met, Treva. My name is Grainne and my sister is Eithne."

"You won't need names here, girl. The fey consider their slaves to be worth less than livestock. A few more years and you'll be thanking them for keeping you alive. So forget your names and focus on doing what you're told."

Grainne didn't speak again and I kept my head down, sweeping, sweeping, always sweeping, as my eyes blurred with tears. What had I done?

2 9

EITHNE

I could barely stand by the time the surly fey woman came to collect us. I had no way of marking the hours, but surely we had laboured for at least the time between dawn and sunset. We were marched back to the tree they kept us in when they had no use for us. The two mortal men again followed.

The fey woman stopped at the tree. She handed Grainne a small jug of water and half a loaf of mouldy bread.

"I suggest you eat it this time. The next time you throw your food on the floor, there will be no more until you finish it."

We stumbled into the tree. There was just enough time to see that vomit still stained the earth, although the uneaten bread had been removed. Then the door closed and we were in darkness. The room reeked of sickness and I breathed through my mouth in an attempt to avoid smelling it.

"They could have at least given us something to clean that up with." Grainne's voice was a mix of irritation and sadness. "I'll try to loosen some dirt to cover it or we'll end up walking through it."

She managed to pass me the bread and jug, then I heard her scrabbling at the ground. I stood still, clutching our poor meal, for fear that if I set it down to help, I would either knock it over or put it straight

474

into the vomit she sought to cover. My legs shook and I swayed. My stomach had stopped growling, which was a blessing, but my throat felt so dry I could barely swallow. Finally Grainne was finished.

"Hand me the jug, Eithne. I know we have precious little water, but I need to rinse my hands. I will drink less to make up for it."

"No, we will share whatever is left," I said, or at least that was what I intended, but my mouth didn't seem to work properly.

Grainne fumbled for the jug and I released it into her grasp. Water splashed on the earthen floor as she rinsed her hands. Then she took the bread and passed me back a portion.

"We have to eat it." Grainne's voice was determined. "Perhaps if we do, they will give us something better next time. And if they don't, at least we have something in our bellies. It is better than starving to death."

The darkness made the bread easier to eat, for I could more readily ignore the smell of mould than the sight of it. It tasted earthy, as if the loaf had been covered in dirt. We took a long time to eat, for it was so hard and stale that we could only gnaw at it. When we had finished, we took turns sipping from the jug. All too soon the water was gone.

"We may as well sleep while we can," Grainne said. "Who knows how long they will leave us here this time. Now that we have work to occupy us, they will likely give us less time to rest."

Irritation stabbed at me. Why did Grainne think she could make all the decisions? But I was too tired to fight with her, so I said nothing. We lay on the hay with our coats draped over us. Although my stomach still felt empty and I was too thirsty, I fell asleep quickly. If any of the fey passed by our tree, I never heard a thing. I was still in a deep sleep when light flooded the interior.

"Get up, get up." It was the same fey woman who had escorted us yesterday. "Lazy creatures. You should be up already."

"How are we supposed to know?" Grainne asked. "There is no light in here and no way of marking the hours."

"You have food and water and a safe place to rest. You don't need anything else."

"But you said we should have known it was time to get up."

The fey exhaled, a short, sharp huff.

"Get up already. I don't have all day to wait on you."

"If you could show us how to find the kitchen, we could make our own way there tomorrow," Grainne suggested.

I stumbled to my feet and tried to pick some of the hay off me as my eyes adjusted to the light. Beside me, Grainne did the same.

"Oh yes, give you a chance to escape? Wouldn't the queen be pleased with me."

"Why does she hate us?" I asked, sourly. "We haven't done anything wrong."

"You think she hates you?" The fey woman raised her eyebrows and looked genuinely surprised. "She feeds you, protects you, gives you work to do. Do you think she would do that if she hated you? I am starting to understand why they say mortals are too stupid to reason with. Follow me and keep close."

She turned and strode off. Grainne and I hurried to catch up. The two pasty-faced mortal men followed.

Treva greeted us with something that might almost have been a smile.

"Turnips." She pointed at Grainne. "Sweep," to me.

The kitchen looked exactly the same as the previous day. The four mortal women were already at the work bench, shaping small pieces of pastry and filling them with something that might have been stewed fruits. My stomach grumbled loudly at the scent of cooking pastries.

Just like the day before, no matter how hard I swept, the floor was never any cleaner. And the pile of turnips next to Grainne never grew any smaller, despite the tub that filled with peeled vegetables.

Grainne tried to strike up a conversation with Treva, but the fat woman seemed ill inclined to speak today. She tried also to talk with the other mortal women, but they did not even acknowledge her.

It was stiflingly hot in the kitchen. Treva kept a steady stream of pastries going in and out of the ovens. I couldn't tell what purpose there was to Grainne peeling so many turnips as I never saw Treva actually use any of them. But I was learning not to ask questions, only to watch. Watch and listen and look for an opportunity to get Grainne out of here.

Each day passed much the same. Some days stretched forever and others seemed like only a few hours before the fey woman came for us. The nights were as variable as the days. Some seemed as long as the span from one dawn to another, and on others we barely had time to eat our mouldy bread and fall asleep before the light streamed in and the fey woman yelled at us to get out of bed.

The hem on my shirt began to fray and I had caught my skirt on sharp branches often enough that it hung in tatters. The sole of one of my boots was near coming off. I didn't need a hand mirror to know I had lost weight I could ill afford to lose. Grainne's face was pinched and pale with dark shadows under her eyes. Her frame now looked much like mine, all angles and edges. I had to keep reminding myself that I did this for Kalen. Survive long enough and Titania would let me speak with him. And Grainne would be able to go home.

I began to wonder how much longer we could live like this, though. The erratic pattern of days and nights. Eating nothing but mouldy bread and a few mouthfuls of water. Being locked in the dark when we weren't required to work. I could barely remember what it felt like to sleep in a bed with a soft pillow beneath my head and woollen blankets piled over me. To sit in a comfortable chair drawn close by a fire. To eat a proper meal, with meat and vegetables and fresh bread. To drink ale or spiced wine. To be comfortable and clean. Things I once took for granted and which were now all distant memories.

Every time I slept, I dreamed of Silver Downs. In my dream, I lay in my own bed, clean and well fed and comfortable. I would wake as sunlight slipped in through the gap where I hadn't quite drawn the curtains. And then I would open my eyes and find myself in darkness, lying on a pile of hay, with Grainne beside me and our coats for blankets.

How much time had passed in the mortal world since we left? The old tales said time did not run to the same path in the mortal and fey worlds. I held onto the slim hope that although our slavery might span one hundred years, perhaps it wouldn't be that long in our own world. I might yet return home while my parents lived.

But one hundred years here might be many more in our own world. My parents would probably die still wondering what had happened to the daughter who disappeared so many years ago. We might return to find Silver Downs crumbled to dust, generations of my family dead and gone.

Time was monotonous. Maybe it even stopped here. My hair and fingernails didn't grow, and my monthly cycles, although always irregular, had ceased. Or maybe we had been here no more than a few days and that was why I saw no evidence of time passing.

Every time I woke, I worried that my illness would return. For a few moments my stomach would tense and my heart would beat in double time. What would the fey do with a slave who was too sick to work? But I had no fevers or sweats, no sudden faints. I was weak from lack of food, too much work, and not enough rest, but I was not ill. The other odd thing was that my deformed foot didn't twist quite as much. I didn't need to concentrate on keeping it straight as I walked or on hiding my limp. I was too embarrassed to ask Grainne if she knew why, but if I had any small joy during these days, it was that my foot seemed almost normal.

Sometimes I woke in the middle of the night and thought I couldn't keep living like this. That nothing existed other than this dark hole in a tree. I would cry — quietly so Grainne wouldn't wake — until my nose was blocked and my chest was tight. Then I would wipe my face with the grimy sleeve of my coat and wait for either sleep or the fey who escorted us to the kitchen.

And still I swept. Every day, I took up the battered broom with the misshapen wooden handle that left splinters in my soft palms before they grew hard with calluses. I swept and swept and swept. The floor never looked any different, whether I swept it or not, just as Grainne's pile of turnips never grew any smaller. Finally, after many days of frustration and exhaustion, I asked Treva why. She gave me a disparaging glare.

"It's because you're doing it wrong. Foolish girl. I wondered how long you would sweep before you thought to ask."

My mouth dropped open. "Why didn't you tell me?"

Treva shrugged. "Not my place to offer advice. Not if you don't ask. Here, do it like this."

She took the broom from me and demonstrated. With a little flick of her wrist, the dirt disappeared as the broom touched it. It took several tries before I could mimic the action. Pain stabbed through my wrists, but if I flicked the broom in a certain way, the floor cleared. I almost cried with relief as I worked my way around the room and the dirt melted away before me.

"Would you show me too?" Grainne asked.

I didn't see what Treva did, but before long the pile of unpeeled turnips was visibly smaller.

By the time the fey woman came for us, the kitchen floor was clean and Grainne had only a small pile of turnips left.

"Might finally be able to put you to work doing something useful tomorrow," Treva said as we left.

She was true to her word. The following day, I was given the task of shaping little pastries like the other mortal women. I had still never heard any of them speak. They clustered down the other end of the long work bench and worked furiously at their tasks.

Now that I knew how the magic worked, it didn't take long to figure out the little flick of the wrist I needed to use as I formed each pastry. The piles of pastry and bowls of preserved fruits for the filling steadily decreased as I worked. The pastry was soft and cool on my callused fingers and if I hadn't feared Treva's reaction, I would have sunk my hands into it for the satisfaction of such a pleasant sensation.

Grainne finally finished the turnips and now she worked beside me. Her fingers were defter than mine and she soon produced twice as many pastries as I.

"How many of the fey does this feed?" I asked Treva a couple of days later, my fingers flying as I moulded the pastry, working more by feel than by look.

Treva pounded away, making pastry and stewed fruits and overseeing the constant stream of trays going in and out of the ovens. The other mortal women hunched over their own piles of pastry.

"None."

I waited, sure I must have misheard, but Treva didn't offer any further information.

"What do you mean, none? We work all day producing pastries. Surely we must feed a small army."

"This food does not feed anyone." Treva didn't look at me as she spoke, instead focusing on a mound of dough that was receiving a particularly severe beating. "It disappears overnight and tomorrow we start again."

"I don't understand."

"These pastries, they undo themselves overnight, pulling apart into their original ingredients. And tomorrow we make them all over again."

"We make the same pastries every day?" Grainne sounded as dispirited as I felt.

"You could think of it that way."

"But why?"

"Why what? There are lots of whys and you will drive yourself mad if you try to figure them all out. Just accept it and get on with the task. That's what I do."

"Why are you here, Treva?" Grainne asked. "Are you here of your own will?"

"Do you think anyone in their sane mind would do this willingly?"

Treva left her dough and stooped in front of an oven. She removed a steaming tray of pastries. Her face was flushed from the heat of the oven.

"What did you do?" I asked.

"It is of no consequence, and indeed I have been here so long, I hardly remember anymore."

"How long will they keep you here?" Grainne asked.

I held my breath as we waited for Treva's response.

"Until they tire of me," Treva said. "And then, if I am lucky, they will kill me. If I'm unlucky, they will take my mind and send me home."

Grainne and I were both shocked into silence. She was the first to recover.

"You would rather die than go home?" she asked.

"I would rather die than go home without my mind. You must have heard tales of folk who return from the fey realm, witless and dumb. That is no life. Besides, I've been here so long there's probably nothing left of my family or my home."

"What family did you leave behind?" I tried hard not to think of my mother and father and brothers whose faces already blurred in my memory.

"A husband and two sons." Treva passed a hand over her face. I couldn't be sure whether she wiped away sweat or a few tears. "But enough years have passed that I doubt they still wonder what happened to me, or hold any hope of my return. They will have moved on. If they are even alive. Chances are, they are long dead and sent to their rest."

"I have a husband," Grainne said after a while.

"He'll forget you soon enough," Treva said. "Men usually do. We're the ones who spend our lives remembering."

30

EITHNE

*B*ack in our tree cave, once we had eaten our meagre meal of mouldy bread and water, there was nothing to do but sleep. Grainne and I huddled under our coats on the pile of hay. I no longer even noticed the hay that pricked my skin and clung persistently to my clothes and my hair.

Treva's comments about being sent home without her mind kept running through my head. I had assumed that when we were eventually sent home, we would be whole. It had not occurred to me that there might be more punishment to come. The thought was more than I could bear.

"I don't know how much longer I can do this," I said softly into the dark.

Grainne's hand found mine.

"Be strong, Eithne. There is no other choice."

"A hundred years is so long. And we don't even know how much time has already passed. Have we been here for a month? Six months? A year?"

"It has been months, at least. Who knows, perhaps a whole year has already passed. We might only have ninety-nine years left."

Somehow that sounded even worse than a hundred years. A few

tears slipped from my eyes and I tried not to sniffle. I didn't speak again until I had myself under control.

"I don't know how you stay so strong. I wouldn't blame you if you never spoke to me again."

"What would be the point in that, Eithne? We have to stick together until we can get out of here."

Although I knew her words were intended as encouragement, irritation nibbled at me. Grainne hadn't cried since that first day we were locked in here. She wasn't losing hope. She was as confident and capable as ever. I might have felt less alone if she had shown some emotion occasionally.

"I can't live like this for much longer. I'll go crazy, if I don't starve to death first." I stared into the darkness, forcing my eyes wide to stop more tears from falling.

"Like I said, we have to stay strong." Grainne's voice was still brisk and firm.

"We could try to escape. We've been assuming we can't, but what if we are wrong?"

"And what then? We are in a strange land, with no food or drink but what is given to us, no friends, and no means of navigation. What do we do? Wander around until we happen on someone who will direct us back to the portal rather than imprisoning us?"

"It would be better than being slaves for a hundred years."

"You think starving to death lost in some fey woods is better than being a slave? At least here we are fed and we are safe."

"That mouldy bread they give us is hardly food," I said bitterly.

"You got us into this, Eithne. The only thing we can do now is endure it."

Her words stung although I knew she was right. I stopped trying to provoke her. It never mattered what I said, Grainne still didn't show any despair or fear or even longing for home. Although with Caedmon dead, maybe she felt there was nothing worth going home to.

"I need to find Kalen," I said. "That's what I came here for. If we get away, you should try to find the portal, but I still need to find him."

"I'm not leaving you alone."

We were silent for a time. I concentrated on breathing evenly, still trying not to cry, and wished we at least had a proper blanket. I wasn't quite cold, but I wasn't exactly warm either. The temperature in here, like so many other things about this world, seemed unchanging. Even the smell never changed. It was always earthy and dank with a faintly lingering odour of sickness.

"We are always locked in," I said into the dark. I wasn't sure whether Grainne was still awake. "They guard us whenever we are outside. Our best chance might be to overpower the guards on the way to the kitchen."

"We assume we are locked in the kitchen," Grainne said.

The hay rustled as she shifted and I felt another stab of annoyance at her tone. If she knew so much, why hadn't she tried to escape already?

"If the door is not locked and there is no guard, why are Treva and the other women still there?"

"We know little of Treva's story and none of that of the others. They may well have tried and failed. Or there might be something keeping them here, something that stops them from even trying to escape. Treva, at any rate, for she is the only one who still has her own mind. I think there is too little left of the other women for them to know, or care, where they are."

"That will be us eventually." I closed my eyes, although it made no difference. The inside of my head was just as dark as the inside of the tree. "Mindless, care-less, just doing what we are told. Sleep when we are told to. Eat when we are told to. Make pastries when we are told to. A hundred years mightn't be so bad if I didn't have my own mind."

"Don't say that," Grainne said and at least now her voice held a spark of emotion. She grabbed my hand and squeezed my fingers so hard it hurt. Her fingers felt soft against my own calloused skin. "Don't ever wish you didn't have your own mind. You know they can take it from you."

"I hate Titania. She tricked me and now we find that even once we have served our time, they will take our minds. There was nothing fair about the deal she offered."

"We must stay strong and focused. We will watch for an opportunity to leave and see if anyone stops us."

"If they don't stop us, what do we do?" I asked.

"We run."

GRAINNE

I tried not to be bitter with Eithne, but it was hard. I was trapped like a rabbit in a snare. Caedmon was here, somewhere, and maybe not very far away, yet I couldn't search for him. We had seen nothing of this place except our tree, Treva's kitchen, the winding walk through the woods between them, and the clearing where Titania had pronounced our fate.

I tried hard to hide my resentment, but it slipped through every now and then in my words or my tone. I felt bad about it — Eithne knew she was responsible for trapping us in this gods-forsaken darkness. The guilt ate at her constantly. But every day I thought about how I wouldn't be here if she hadn't agreed to Titania's ridiculous proposal. I would have found Caedmon and we would be back home at Silver Downs. Our own house would have been built by now. Perhaps we would even have the son he wanted. I ran my hand over my stomach, which caved in towards my spine. The fey gave us barely enough food to keep us alive. It was perhaps fortunate that the babe I had hoped I carried seemed to be no more. Or perhaps he had never existed.

As the months passed, Eithne sank deeper into melancholy. The only thing I could do was be strong and confident we would survive, in appearance if nothing else. At least Eithne couldn't see into my mind where I, too, teetered on the edge of defeat every day.

The one weakness in our situation, it seemed, was Treva's kitchen. Getting out of the kitchen would be difficult, though, for we couldn't open the door ourselves and we wouldn't know whether there were guards outside until we tried to leave.

No matter how carefully I watched the fey woman who escorted us there every day, I couldn't see how she opened the doors into the trees. No magical words were said and she didn't appear to use any special hand motion. I watched where she placed her feet, wondering whether perhaps she released a secret lever by standing on it, but she never seemed to stand in exactly the same place twice. It was as if she simply willed the tree to open. The fey who had first locked us in a tree had pressed his palm to the trunk, but clearly that wasn't necessary.

I considered asking Treva if she would open the door for us, but she had made it clear that she herself was imprisoned. Reporting our intention to escape might win her some special favour. I couldn't risk it. So long as the fey believed we had no thought of escape, they probably didn't watch us too hard. Our only hope was surprise.

Day after day, for months on end, I stood at the long wooden work bench, my fingers flying as I shaped little pieces of dough into triangles and diamonds and squares. Dab the stewed fruit in the centre, fold up the corners, pinch, twist, turn, crimp the edges. Pastry after pastry. Between us, we made thousands of tiny pastries every day. I had grown used to surviving on so little food and my stomach no longer rumbled at the scent of the delicacies.

I had never heard a word from the other mortal women who worked with us. Treva rarely had reason to give them a direction, but when she did, they swiftly obeyed. At least some part of their minds remained. I had tried to speak to one or other of them at various times when Treva was busy with the ovens, but they never acknowledged me. I wondered whether they worked through the night, for they were always there when we arrived, and they remained when we were taken away.

Then came the day when Treva seemed distracted. We never spoke much as we worked, but I had twice asked her for more stewed fruit and she hadn't answered. From the corner of my eye, I saw that Eithne's fingers had stilled.

"Don't stop," I urged, for the pastry was fickle and would be ruined if we held it too long. Treva had hinted that our imprisonment could be made much worse if we were careless.

"Do you smell something burning?" Eithne shot me a glance.

Her eyes glittered brightly and my first thought was that the illness had finally returned. Then I smelled the burning pastries. I kept working, although more slowly now, and tried to hide the way my body tensed ready for flight.

"Treva?" Eithne said. "Is everything all right?"

Treva didn't respond. She was rearranging some pastries that had been set out to cool, although I could see no purpose to her task. Black smoke began pouring from one of the ovens. The air was suddenly thick and hard to breathe.

I flung my pastry down on the bench and raced to the oven. When I wrenched open the door, smoke poured out and heat blasted my face. I snatched up the towel that hung from a nearby nail. Trying not to inhale the smoke, I fumbled around inside the oven. I managed to grab the tray of pastries. They were burnt to embers.

"Treva." Eithne's voice was urgent. "Quickly, open the door before Grainne's hand burns."

"Hurry, Treva, it's hot," I said.

Treva finally noticed me standing by the oven, clutching the tray of flaming pastries.

"Oh my," she said. "Oh dear. I am going to be in such trouble."

"Just open the door."

I gritted my teeth and prayed. The tray was so hot that my fingers already burned through the towel.

The door swung open and fresh air streamed in. I raced for the exit, holding the tray out in front of me. As I stepped outside, Eithne was at my side. A quick glance around showed no sign of a guard. I threw the pastries, tray and all, on the ground, grabbed Eithne by the hand, and we ran.

32

GRAINNE

here was no sound of pursuit from behind us — yet. Perhaps Treva was busy clearing the smoke from the kitchen or something. We might have a precious few moments before she noticed our absence. I didn't let myself wonder what sort of punishment she would face for letting us escape. Treva was not my responsibility. My only obligation in this strange realm was to Caedmon. Eithne, I would keep safe for as long as I could, but now that we were free, Caedmon was my priority.

At first the woods seemed sparsely treed. Flight was easy and I ran too fast to think about where to place my feet. Step, leap to avoid a rock, slide in leafy ground cover, step, jump over a fallen branch, step, step, step. I dodged a startled raven who flapped his wings in my face. My thighs burned and my breath was short, but I kept going. As long as Eithne could keep running, I could too.

I had no idea what time of day it was. The light was noon-day bright as it always seemed to be in this place. We moved too fast to be cautious about how much noise we made, but I figured it didn't matter. They would pursue us anyway and our best chance was speed.

Just as my legs started to tremble and my lungs to heave, we were forced to slow to a jog. The trees grew closer together here, birch and ash and oak standing side by side. Every step now involved not just avoiding obstacles on the ground, but also watching for branches positioned just so to poke out an eye or stab us through the chest.

Eithne lagged behind, although not so far that I felt obliged to wait. She gasped for breath, but continued gamely. No doubt if I could see her, her face would bear that expression I was now so familiar with, the one that said Eithne was determined to do something. Little sickly Eithne. If her brothers could see her fleeing the fey, how surprised they would be.

We splashed across a shallow creek. My well-worn leather boots filled with cool water, but there was no time to remove them and I dared not run barefoot anyway.

The trees gave way to thick holly bushes laden with shiny red berries. The leaf matter covering the ground disappeared and was replaced by a dense weed that wound around my feet. I paused to rip its sticky tendrils from my boots, but they clung to my hand. When I tried to brush them off against my dress, they stuck there too. They tugged at my boots, threatening to tear them from my feet. The only thought in my mind was *keep moving*.

Eithne caught up when the sticky weed reduced my flight to a walk. There was an odd whistle in her breath.

"We should stop," I panted. "Rest."

Eithne shook her head. If she could continue, so could I, although my legs burned and with every breath I thought my lungs might burst.

The holly bushes gave way to enormous piles of tangled brambles. I forced my way through them. The strange weeds that clung to my feet now had more time to tighten their grip and I could no longer shake them off. I had to lift my foot and tug until the weeds broke. Then I could lift the other. Soon the brambles became too dense to push through and we could go no further.

There was no option but to go back. But when I turned, the brambles behind us were just as thick. We had left no trail, or perhaps the passage had closed.

"What is this?" Eithne asked between gasps.

"The woods have their own mind."

"They are alive?"

"I don't know. But they are surely trying to stop us."

"Do they mean to keep us trapped until the fey find us?"

"Maybe."

The air was warm and thick like honey as I caught my breath. The woods around us were strangely silent. There were no sounds of pursuit, but neither were there the usual calls of woodlark or deer or badger. The only noises were our own ragged breathing. Eithne's hand slid into mine.

"Something is wrong," she whispered. "What do we do?"

Her eyes were wide and her face too pale beneath the flush of exertion.

"We wait, I suppose. The woods have decided we may go no further."

My heart pounded and a sense of something sneaking up on us rose over me until I felt sure I would scream if I didn't do *something*.

"Perhaps we were going in the wrong direction," Eithne said quietly after we had stood there for some time. "Perhaps the woods don't mean to stop us, only to prevent us from going the wrong way."

We were surrounded by thick brambles that stood taller than us. If the woods wanted us to go in a particular direction, they gave no clue of it.

"Which way then?" I asked.

She shrugged and turned to her left.

"I suppose we just try and see." She tried to step forward, but the brambles remained solid and unyielding. "Not that way then."

But when she turned to the right, the brambles edged backward. One step, two. Our progress was slow, but we were definitely moving. And the sticky weeds no longer latched onto my boots or wound around my legs.

"It's working," I said, too exhausted to be amazed.

"Do we keep going?"

"I can't see that we have another choice. We either go where it wants us to or we wait for the fey to find us."

She squeezed my hand and we moved forward together. The brambles gradually thinned and soon disappeared altogether, making way once more for the sparse woods in which we had started our desperate flight. We continued in the same direction, for fear the woods might rise up against us again if we didn't.

We walked until we could go no further and in all that time, I heard no sound of pursuit. But perhaps they did not need to pursue us. Maybe Titania had some magic that told her where any intruder stood.

Eithne finally threw herself to the ground. She covered her face with her hands and her shoulders heaved. I wasn't sure whether she was crying or merely catching her breath and I didn't have the energy to ask. I lowered myself onto the blanket of fallen leaves. It was the softest seat I had had for months.

We sat in silence for some time. My eyes drooped, but I dared not let myself fall asleep for fear the fey would sneak up and capture us again.

"We should keep moving," I said after a few minutes. My legs still trembled and, in truth, I wasn't certain I would be able to stand.

Eithne nodded and hauled herself to her feet.

"All right?" I asked as I got up. My thighs burned, my feet ached and a long shallow cut stung my calf.

"I can't quite believe it," she said. "I don't dare believe for fear this is a dream and I will wake up in that horrid dark hole in the tree."

"We have to go. They might not be far behind us."

"But to where? We have no food or water. No shelter, no friends."

"I don't know. I'm just hoping that if we keep going, we'll figure something out. Or come across someone who can help us. Or stumble upon the portal. Perhaps if we go far enough, we'll find the edge of the woods and whatever is on the other side."

"There might be more than one portal." Eithne's voice was hopeful. "Although how we would recognise it, I don't know, given we never knew when we passed through the first."

"We just have to keep going. We managed to escape and the woods have helped, in their own way. If we go far enough, we will find something else, or someone, who can help us."

"Maybe we will find Kalen."

Or Caedmon, I thought, but I didn't say it.

33

GRAINNE

As soon as we had caught our breath, we started running again. I kept my gaze on the ground, partly to watch for obstacles but mostly because I didn't have enough energy to look anywhere else. The ground never changed: leaf litter, twigs and fallen branches, moss-covered rocks. I moved slowly now, too slowly.

Sunlight filtered in through the branches of oak and ash and beech. It could be mid morning or mid afternoon. I had long since given up trying to figure out what time of day it was, let alone the season. The woods hadn't changed at all during the months of our captivity. They were still lush with thick bushes and vines, mosses and the pleasant scent of decaying leaves. Shiny red berries blanketed the holly bushes. Catkins covered the birch trees. Woodlarks called from the branches of the trees, and under other circumstances, a walk through the woods would have been pleasant. But the relentless need to keep moving tore any joy from the fact that we were finally free.

Eithne stumbled and fell to her knees. I didn't ask whether she was hurt. I couldn't. Staying upright, breathing, keeping my feet moving — they were the only things I could focus on.

My wet boots rubbed my feet raw. Something dripped down the back of my boot — blood or perhaps pus. When I placed my hand over a stitch in my side, my ribs stuck out so sharply that I wondered how they didn't burst through my skin. I couldn't catch my breath and I moved slower and slower. We needed rest, sooner rather than later, and for that we needed shelter. A way to hide ourselves away from the sight of both casual passersby and those who might have reason to search for us.

I hardly noticed when our surroundings began to change again. It seemed that one minute we passed through normal woods spread with trees and bushes and leaf litter. Then all of a sudden, the trees were so close together that I had to turn sideways to slide between them. The leaf litter disappeared, replaced again with the strange tangly weed that reached up sticky tendrils to grasp my boots.

Brambles once again blocked our path and crept up behind us. They formed a solid wall taller than we stood. It was only then I noticed the woods were deathly quiet.

"Why are the woods stopping us again?" Eithne's voice trembled.

"I don't know." I could barely make my mouth form words and I didn't know whether they were even comprehensible. I reached out and clasped her hand.

The ground began to vibrate and Eithne squeaked in fear.

"Ssh," I said. "Be quiet and still."

Within moments, the vibration became the recognisable thunder of hooves. I didn't need to see them to know that a herd of horses hurtled towards us. I was suddenly very thankful for the strange bramble wall that crept even closer around us until my legs could have given way and I would still have remained upright.

The horses thundered past, not very far away from us. Without the bramble wall, we certainly would have been seen. Were these our pursuers? Or other fey who just happened to pass by?

The sounds of the horses faded as rapidly as they had come. The bramble edged away from us and soon we were able to continue walking. Eithne and I looked at each other. Her eyes were huge and dark in a face pale with exhaustion.

"Do the woods protect us?" she asked in a whisper. "Or does someone control the woods?"

I didn't have enough energy to reply.

We stumbled on. Surely at least a day had passed since we fled Treva's kitchen. A day in which we had not eaten or slept. We had drunk briefly from a stream, but that was hours ago. I spied a tree with wide-leafed branches that draped down to the ground like a skirt. When I stopped beside it, my legs wobbled so hard that I didn't think I would be able to move again. I parted the leaves and peered inside. It would quite nicely fit a grown woman if she lay on her side and curled her body around the trunk.

"We can rest in here," I said. "Maybe we should split up. If one of us is found, the other might yet escape."

"We should stay together," Eithne said. "It's gotten us this far. I'll take the first watch. Lie down, Grainne. You look about to fall over."

Indeed I found myself swaying on my feet as she spoke. I should have argued, for Eithne was not as strong as I, but I couldn't. Instead I lay on the dirt with my hands under my cheek. The earthy aroma of my bed filled my nose. It smelled fresh and alive, not like the dank, stale smell of the tree in which we had been imprisoned. I was asleep almost before I closed my eyes.

I woke with a start, sitting up so quickly that my head spun. Eithne sat with her legs drawn up, arms resting on them. Her face was pale and her eyes shadowed.

"Did I sleep long?" I ran my fingers through my short hair. It didn't seem to have grown at all in the last few months. At least it was mostly short enough that it didn't tangle.

"A while. Maybe a couple of hours."

"I feel much better," I lied. My mouth was dry, but at least I no longer felt hungry. "Your turn."

Eithne obediently lay down and seemed to fall asleep almost immediately. I eased my boots from my feet. The leather had dried and the backs were stained with blood. I would have given almost anything for a hot bath and a change of clothes. After wearing the same gown for many months, it was so threadbare that the linen was falling apart. The fey must have noticed our tattered clothes and yet they had offered us nothing. I hoped the fabric would hold together until I could find Caedmon and get us out of this place. The boots would have to be forced back on my feet, although where we walked to, or for how much longer, I didn't know.

We desperately needed food and water. We could continue to walk if we had some supplies. Once Eithne woke up, we would make a plan. Perhaps we could forage in the woods around us. Surely there would be berries or nuts or mushrooms.

I sat up straight, legs tucked under me, and concentrated on staying awake. This was the first time in months that I had been able to sit in daylight, even if I was shrouded by branches. To just sit and be able to see seemed a precious thing after so long in darkness.

My eyes were heavy and although I kept telling myself I must stay awake, my head nodded. I would rest my eyes for just a moment, although I would not let myself fall asleep.

34

SUMERLED

The mortal women walk and walk, stumbling and barely lifting their feet. Why they do not stop to rest eludes me. They move with the force of much larger creatures, revealing their location to anyone who cares to listen as they stomp on twigs, crunch leaves, and frighten woodlarks into silence. I follow them easily, for they make no attempt to cover their tracks.

In appearance, they are bedraggled and spent, with pallid skin and greasy hair. Their clothes are falling apart, they limp, and they breathe far too heavily. I still have no idea why they fascinate Kalen. But right now they are my own delicious secret. He has no idea they are here. I knew from the moment they passed through the portal, for I had been watching even then. I have spied on them ever since without anyone ever being the wiser.

Keeping a secret is hard. It is even harder when the secret is so exquisite. I know why Kalen stopped going to visit the mortal woman. I know she came here to search for him. And I know he doesn't know she is here.

When a group of fey come too close, I don't want the mortals to be discovered. I am having far too much fun sneaking along behind them, watching, and imagining Kalen's face when he discovers the mortal he is so fond of has been here all this time. I wouldn't help them in other circumstances, for nobody cares what befalls a pair of mortals trespassing where they should not. But if they are captured again, it will spoil all my fun.

So the woods rise up and shield them and the fey pass by without ever knowing how close they came to finding the mortals Titania has instructed the whole realm to search for. It would not do for my fun to end too soon and I know just how to make it last even longer.

35

EITHNE

I woke with Grainne's hand pressed over my mouth. Her calloused fingers were rough against my lips.

"Don't make a sound," she breathed into my ear.

I froze, muscles tense and heart pounding, my cheek pressed into the dirt.

Leaves crunched. A twig snapped.

Footsteps. Right outside our shelter.

They had found us.

Grainne was pressed close to me. She smelled of sweat and fear, and her heart beat just as wildly as my own. I reached up to remove her hand from my mouth.

The footsteps came closer. They stopped, right beside us. If it weren't for the curtain of leaves that stretched down to cover us, we would already be face to face with our finder.

A hand reached between the leaves and parted them. Somebody slipped inside.

It was a boy, maybe eight years old. He was thin enough to be called malnourished and his clothes were almost as tattered as ours. His skin was pale, like someone who had spent a lot of time indoors. He looked startled to see us and swiftly held his hands up as if indicating he was no threat. Then he put a finger to his mouth, signalling we should be quiet. He eased down onto the dirt and sat cross-legged.

The three of us were frozen, staring at each other, but there were no noises other than the normal sounds of the woods. My heartbeat gradually slowed, for the boy was obviously no threat and indeed it seemed he, too, was pursued. I sat up slowly, trying to be soundless. When the boy finally spoke, his voice was quiet and hesitant.

"Do you have any food?"

Eithne and I looked at each other and I heard her stomach rumble.

"No," she said. "I'm sorry."

"I haven't eaten for days," he said.

"Who is following you?" Grainne asked.

His eyes were shadowed. "You know."

"Tell me."

"They do." He waved his hand, vaguely indicating something outside.

"Who?"

"Them that live here."

"The fey?"

He shrugged. "I suppose."

"What is your name?" I asked.

He looked at me seriously for a long while. His face was clean, despite his bedraggled clothing.

"Names are a funny business. Knowing a name gives you much power."

"It's just a name. Something to call you by."

Still he was silent, his mouth scrunched up as if thinking hard. Finally he said, "You can call me Sumerled."

"I'm Grainne and this is Eithne," Grainne said when it became clear Sumerled was quite happy to sit in the dirt and stare at us. "Where are you going?"

"Here and there. Away."

"Do you know how to get there?" I asked.

Sumerled considered me for a moment. "I might."

"Do you know Kalen?" Under other circumstances, it might have seemed a strange question, but there was something odd about the boy, something that made me feel like we were meant to meet him right here and right now.

"It depends on how badly you want to find him."

"Do you know him or not?"

Another shrug. One shoulder poked through a hole in his shirt. He was all bones and skin. Had he, too, been a prisoner of the fey?

"Can you take us to him?"

"Probably. Or maybe not. What do you have to offer?"

Beside me, Grainne stilled.

"What would it be worth to you?" I asked.

Sumerled considered me with squinting eyes.

"It will be a dangerous journey. I could be injured, or even killed."

"Name your price and I will consider it."

"A promise."

"What exactly?"

"A promise you will fulfil at a time of my choosing."

"Eithne," Grainne said. "I don't think—"

I hushed her, rudely probably, but her cautions would only distract me.

"What would the promise entail?"

"Whatever I ask."

"That is too vague. It must be more clearly defined."

"You asked my price and that is it. We can leave right now to go find Kalen or we can sit here all day, until they find us. They're looking for someone right now. Looking very hard."

"How do you know?"

"I saw them."

"How did you find us?" Grainne asked. Her face looked far too pale.

Sumerled smiled, a tight, controlled smile. "I have been watching you, ever since you left."

"You couldn't have kept up with us." Grainne's tone was scornful. "We ran for ages, and you aren't even wearing shoes."

I looked at his bare feet. They were clean. Far too clean for someone who had spent a day following us through the woods.

"Who are you really?" I asked, shuffling back a little, struck by a sudden need to get away from him.

"I'm just a boy. I can't hurt you."

Grainne and I exchanged a look. She didn't trust him. I hadn't decided yet.

"Are you mortal or fey?" she asked.

"What difference does it make? I am alive and so are you. But you won't be much longer if you stay here. I told you they search for someone. They will find you soon. And what do you think they will do then?"

"Are you sure you can lead us to Kalen?" I asked.

Sumerled sniffed. "You're asking the wrong question. You should be asking whether I will."

"The promise must have a timeframe. A date by which you will ask for it or give it up."

"You must fulfil your promise before you return to the world of mortals."

"I will not harm any living being."

"Fine."

I didn't know what other limits to put on his promise. I had an expiry and an agreement that I would not be required to inflict injury. The promise was still too loose, but I was too hungry to think clearly. I could only hope I wasn't dragging us into an even worse situation.

"If the Kalen you take us to is not the Kalen I seek, the promise is void," I said.

Sumerled yawned. "Agreed. Anything else?"

"Grainne has no obligation to you. She is not a part of my promise."

"Fine. Then you accept my terms?"

"I do."

Sumerled jumped to his feet.

"Let's go then. The longer we dally, the closer they get."

3 6

EITHNE

Sumerled went first, easing out from beneath the leaves that had sheltered us. He moved cautiously and quietly, and seemed alert for any sign of pursuit.

"I don't like this," Grainne muttered. "There's something peculiar about him."

Irritation flashed through me. This was the first time anyone had offered us aid and she knew I had to take it.

"He says he can find Kalen," I said.

She shook her head but said nothing further. We emerged from beneath the branches of the tree into the perpetual daylight of the fey woods. I heard only normal woodlands noises: little feet scurrying, birds chirping, leaves rustling. No sounds of pursuit.

We walked in single file, Sumerled leading the way and Grainne taking up the rear. Sumerled moved soundlessly, which seemed odd given he had made so much noise in approaching our hiding place. But he was my best chance to find Kalen — my only chance so far — and I dismissed my suspicion.

We walked for a very long time. Whenever Grainne or I asked how much further we needed to walk, Sumerled would say that we couldn't stop now, that the fey were right behind us. My thoughts wandered aimlessly and my legs trembled so much that I feared they wouldn't hold me up for much longer. My feet no longer hurt and I worried about what that meant.

"Sumerled, stop," said Grainne from behind me.

He stopped so quickly I almost walked into him.

"Would you give us a moment?" she asked. "I need some privacy and I'm sure Eithne must too."

He motioned to a nearby hawthorn bush.

"You can go behind there. But hurry, because they are likely not far behind us."

Grainne grabbed me by the arm and pulled me behind the bush before I could speak.

"Eithne, hush, listen. He is leading us in circles."

I noted the paleness of her face and the way her shoulders slumped. She was just as exhausted as I was. Likely she searched for a reason to rest.

"He's leading us to Kalen," I said.

"We have passed by this same bush several times. I know because the third time we passed it, I pulled a piece of thread from my shirt and draped it over a branch. It is still there."

"He's probably trying to lose the fey."

"Nobody is following us, Eithne. Don't you think they would have caught us by now at the pace we're moving? We would have heard them, if nothing else."

"You're only saying that because it was my decision to go with him."

She glowered at me for a moment.

"He's trouble, Eithne. We need to lose him."

"He knows Kalen."

"He hasn't given you any proof of that. You asked if he could lead you to Kalen and he agreed. That doesn't mean he intends to, only that he *could* if he chose to."

"But I agreed to a promise. The fey take promises very seriously."

"He's trouble. That's all I know. He has been leading us in circles for hours. Nobody is following us, not at the moment anyway."

I ran my fingers over the prickly bush beside us. Its thorns dug into my fingertips. The pain grounded me and my foggy head cleared just a little.

"He might have an explanation for that. And what if he really does know Kalen? This could be my only chance to find him."

"Then ask. If Sumerled can explain himself, he must. If not, we leave him and find our own way."

My irritation at her bossiness suddenly fled.

"I'm scared, Grainne. Scared we won't find Kalen. That we're never going to find a way out of this place."

"I am too." She wrapped an arm around my shoulders and I leaned into her. "But we can't let fear rule us. We have to be smart, cunning. And I think the smartest thing we can do is get away from Sumerled."

When we emerged from behind the hawthorn bush, Sumerled was tapping his foot impatiently, not that it made any sound in the leaf litter. He set off again as soon as he saw us.

"Sumerled, wait." I pitched my voice low in case someone really was following. "We need to ask you some questions."

"We don't have time to waste," he said. "They could catch up to us any moment."

"Who exactly are they?" Grainne asked.

"You know who."

"No more," I said sternly, and stopped walking. "Tell us who you believe is following because we have neither seen nor heard sign of them."

"Don't believe me then. Dally here and let them catch you. Why would I care?" Sumerled kept walking, although he slowed as if reluctant to leave us behind.

"I don't think anyone is following us," Grainne said. "But I think you want us to think it."

Sumerled ignored her and looked only at me.

"Don't you want to find Kalen? The longer we wait, the greater the possibility we won't. He might have moved on from where he was last."

"And where was that?" I asked.

"Where I'm taking you."

"You're taking us nowhere," Grainne said. "We've been walking in circles for hours. Why?"

"Because that's how we will find Kalen."

"By walking in circles through the woods?" Her tone was sceptical.

Sumerled shrugged. "I didn't make the way. Kalen did. I'm just following."

I didn't know what to believe. Sumerled said someone followed us; Grainne insisted there was nobody. Grainne said we walked in circles; Sumerled said it was because Kalen had. The only thing I knew was that I would never find Kalen if we kept standing here.

"Keep going," I said to Sumerled.

Grainne grabbed my hand.

"Eithne, you can't be serious."

"What other choice do I have?"

"I don't believe him."

"I do. This is why we're here. I'm willing to believe him for a little longer."

Grainne sighed and rolled her eyes.

"Fine. I'll be right behind you."

Now that I knew we walked in circles, I began watching for landmarks. A fallen log, two trees that grew in a tangle, the rotting carcass of some woodland animal. A fall of leaves masking a rock on which I caught my foot the first two times we walked over it. The signs were all around us. And we kept passing them by. When finally I could walk no further, I stopped.

"Sumerled, I need to rest. I need food and water and some sleep."

He turned back to us. "But we can't stop now. We're almost there."

"We are?" My heart leapt.

"Close. So close. We have to continue."

"Exactly how close are we?" Grainne asked.

"Almost close enough to see. Almost close enough to touch. We can't stop."

"If it's only a little further, I can keep going," I said, although I could hardly lift my feet to put one in front of the other. We walked for what felt like another hour. Twice more I asked Sumerled to stop and twice more he told me we were too close to stop.

Finally Grainne halted.

"That's it. I am not going any further until I have rested."

"But—" Sumerled started.

Grainne cut him off with a sharp motion. "I said we're stopping."

I sank down into the leaves. They were damp and soft and smelled like rot. My head swam, I could hardly swallow, and the ground seemed to wobble and shift in front of my eyes. Beside me, Grainne sat with her knees drawn up and her arms and head resting on them.

"Grainne?" I managed to say.

"I'm fine," she said. "I just need to rest. And I need to eat, but there's not much we can do about that right now."

"I can get you food," Sumerled said.

We both looked at him.

"From where?" Grainne asked, and the suspicion had returned to her voice.

He raised a hand and indicated our surroundings.

"The woods will provide."

He trotted off and returned shortly after with a sack.

"Where did that come from?" I asked.

Sumerled shrugged, which seemed to be his typical response to anything he didn't want to answer. He reached into the sack and pulled out a loaf of bread, thrusting it at me with quick impatience.

Grainne and I stared at each other. Doubt gnawed my stomach. The sack was one thing. He might well have had it tucked inside his shirt, but a whole loaf of bread? I turned the loaf over, its crust smooth beneath my fingers. It was soft and fresh. In fact, I fancied it was even still a little warm from the oven.

Sumerled produced a wedge of yellow cheese, ripe red apples, a handful of plump blackberries, a small knife. He laid the sack down on the ground with a flourish and piled the food on top.

"Eat," he urged, stepping back.

Grainne and I just stared. The aroma of fresh bread filled my nostrils and my mouth watered. After nothing but mouldy bread for months, this was a feast.

"Sumerled, where did this food come from?" Grainne's voice was stern.

I reluctantly tossed the bread down onto the sack as we waited for Sumerled's response.

"The woods provide."

"The woods did not just hand you a loaf of bread and some cheese," she said. "And you certainly didn't carry it all this way. Tell me where you got it."

Sumerled's mouth had a nasty set to it.

"You said you were hungry. I got you food. You should eat it."

"We aren't eating a thing until you tell us where it came from," Grainne said.

I wanted to cry at the sight of that food and not being able to eat it. It took all of my strength not to snatch it up — any of it, all of it — and cram it into my mouth.

Sumerled's jaw clenched and his face reddened.

"You have to eat."

"Where did it come from?" Grainne sounded just as stubborn as he.

Sumerled glared at her. "You shouldn't be so ungrateful. Bad things happen to ungrateful people."

Grainne rose stiffly to her feet. She stepped right up to Sumerled. His head was only as high as her shoulders.

"Are you threatening me, little boy?"

Sumerled's face was sullen and he turned his back on her.

"I will not speak to you any further. You can find Kalen on your own."

"I don't believe you could lead us to him anyway," she said. "It's all just a game, isn't it? A big game of how long can you make us follow you. Round and round in circles, never going anywhere, never getting any closer to Kalen."

"That's not true," he said.

"Who sent you?" she asked. "Somebody knew where we hid and it wasn't you. You're too young to know anything."

"I am not. I'm older than I look."

"I doubt that." Grainne's voice was scathing. "You're just a boy. A mortal boy. You couldn't possibly know anything useful or important. I think you should leave. We will find Kalen faster without you."

I held my breath for fear that Sumerled really would leave. He was my only link to Kalen.

Sumerled turned back to us, his fists clenched.

"I'm not mortal. I'm half fey."

"Oh, a half-blood." Grainne sounded bored. "How impressive."

"I'm the only one who can find Kalen for you."

"What makes you think you can find him at all, let alone that you're the only one who can?"

"Because I'm his brother."

Grainne and I froze.

"What did you say?" I awkwardly got to my feet and my thigh muscles spasmed. "Kalen never mentioned a brother."

"We have the same father."

"What about your mother?" Kalen had never spoken about his family so I had no way of knowing whether Sumerled lied. But now that I looked at him carefully, I saw echoes of Kalen in the shape of his chin and mouth.

"Our mothers were mortal. And irrelevant."

"Kalen is half-mortal?" Why would he not have told me something so important?

"Why are you looking for him anyway?" Sumerled asked, and it was me he directed his words to.

"That's none of your business," I said. "You haven't managed to take us to him, so I don't owe you anything — neither explanation nor promise."

"I can take you to him. I know the secret place where he hides. Nobody else knows. Without me, you won't find him if he doesn't want to be found."

"Why wouldn't he want us to find him?" Grainne asked.

Sumerled's face closed again and he shrugged.

"How far away is he?" I asked. "We are exhausted."

Sumerled pointed over my shoulder. "That way."

"Exactly how far?"

A shrug. "A hundred paces. Maybe less."

I froze and my heart seemed to stop beating. "A hundred paces? Are you telling me we are only a hundred paces from Kalen? Why did we stop here?"

"You wanted to stop."

"You never said we were so near."

"I told you we were close."

"You've been saying we were close for hours," Grainne said. "How were we to know you were telling the truth this time? Not that I'm convinced yet."

"He is too. He's just over there."

"Prove it," she challenged.

He glared at her and stomped away in the direction he had pointed. He disappeared from sight behind a birch tree.

The ground seemed to tilt from side to side and Grainne quickly took me by the arm.

"Eithne, sit."

"I'm fine. I can stand a little longer. If he's telling the truth…"

"He might not be. You should be prepared for that."

"But he could be."

Finally Sumerled reappeared. A few paces behind him was Kalen.

3 7

EITHNE

I lurched forward, barely aware of having moved.

"Kalen!"

Kalen paled and his jaw dropped. He grabbed Sumerled's arm and shook him, saying something stern. The boy's face turned sulky again. Kalen released him with a shove and looked back towards me, his face a thundercloud. I stopped, suddenly unsure. He didn't look pleased to see me.

"Kalen?"

"Eithne." He stopped in front of me and surveyed me from head to toe. He looked the same as always with his ruined haircut and dark clothes that hung loosely off his frame.

I was abruptly reminded of my threadbare clothes, my grimy and tangled hair, the stench that rose from my body. I wanted to reach out to him, but instead I made fists of my dirty fingers. I had grown used to the filth that coated my entire body but Kalen was clean. He wouldn't want me touching him.

"You shouldn't be here," he said, his voice a little gentler now.

"I came to find you. To help you." I clutched my tattered skirt to stop myself from reaching for him.

"Help me with what?"

"You stopped coming to see me. I thought… I knew something must be wrong."

Kalen's laugh was hollow. "Surely, Eithne, you know enough to understand what it means when a fey stops visiting a mortal woman."

My heart plummeted. All these months I had never doubted his feelings. Never thought he would be anything but pleased when I found him.

"You don't mean that." My voice was a whisper.

"What did you expect me to say, Eithne? Did you think I would fall at your feet in gratitude that you risked your life to be here? What happened to you anyway? You look atrocious."

I covered my face with my hands and burst into tears. They dripped between my fingers and fell onto the leaves in grimy, grey splatters. Grainne took a step closer but didn't touch me.

"Kalen, why are you being so awful? You have no idea what I've been through to find you."

"I don't need you to rescue me, if that's what you thought. Go home, Eithne. Sumerled will show you to the portal. Get back to the mortal world before you draw unwanted attention."

"Titania already knows we're here."

Kalen sucked in a breath. "She does? Have you spoken with her?"

"Spoken with her?" My voice rose. I scrubbed the tears from my face with my fist and scowled at him. "She kept us as slaves. We've been locked in the dark and fed mouldy bread and forced to work in a kitchen where everything we make unmakes itself overnight."

Kalen's glare became even fiercer. "How long have you been here?"

"Months. She was going to keep us for one hundred years."

"That's a penalty Titania reserves for those who offend her the most."

"All I did was ask to see you. She said if I worked as a slave for one hundred years, she would let me. But I didn't know she would keep Grainne here too."

Kalen glanced towards Grainne for the first time. When he looked back at me, something flickered in his gaze.

"You need to leave immediately. Both of you. Sumerled, take them straight to the nearest portal. Don't linger for any reason. Keep quiet. Don't draw attention to yourselves. If you can get back to the mortal world, she isn't likely to come after you."

"We can't leave now," I said. "We've only just found you."

"You must leave, Eithne. You have no idea how much danger you are in."

"Kalen—" I stepped forward, but he quickly backed up and I finally understood. "You don't want me here."

"You are in danger here."

"I came to help you."

"You can't help me. Nobody can."

"When will I see you again?"

"You won't. I won't be returning to the mortal world and you must not come here again."

A sob tore from my chest. "I thought you loved me."

"I'm sorry." Kalen's mouth twisted and his tone was almost regretful. "You have no idea how sorry, but you need to leave right now."

My heart was wrenched into pieces. My chest was too tight. I couldn't breathe. I turned and ran.

Grainne called out, "Eithne, wait."

I fled and if Grainne followed, she didn't catch me.

I crashed through the woods, tripping over logs and roots, blind to the direction in which I ran. When I could go no further, I collapsed onto the soft leaves. My chest heaved and tears dripped from my face. I was a fool. Every tale that tells of such a thing says the fey are fickle. We always feel far more than they. Kalen didn't love me. He never had.

I cried until there were no tears left. My nose was blocked, my eyes were swollen and my chest hurt. I lay in the leaves, the woods around me quiet and lonely. When I was with Grainne, I was ever conscious of the fact that we were possibly — probably — being pursued, but even then I had not felt this vulnerable. But alone I was weak and fragile and scared. If someone indeed followed, they would need little effort to overpower me. Even Sumerled could probably do it, as weak as I was right now.

I shouldn't have run away. Shouldn't have left Grainne behind. But I hadn't been thinking clearly. All I knew was that I couldn't bear to look at Kalen for a moment longer. I had put both Grainne and myself through so much, and all for a fickle fey who had probably not given me a thought since we last met.

I sniffed and wiped my nose with the frayed hem of my skirt. I couldn't lie here all day, no matter how miserable I was. I stood on wobbly legs, and began to stumble back to where I thought I had left Grainne. My stomach was tight and my heart ached. Kalen would be long gone by now, but hopefully Grainne had waited for me. I had led us both to the point of starvation and exhaustion. Kalen might not care about me, but Grainne did. We were sisters and friends. I would find her and we would make our way home together. And once we were safely back at Silver Downs, I would never think about Kalen again. I had learnt my lesson. No more fey. No more men at all. I would be content with my life, such as it was.

I stumbled through the woods, paying little attention to my surroundings until I smelled smoke. I stopped, realising for the first time just how loud I had been, carelessly putting my feet wherever they landed, paying no mind to the noise I made or the trail I left. Smoke could mean one of two things. It might be a wildfire or it might mean fey. I had better be prepared to run regardless. My legs trembled at the thought. I had already run so far.

I couldn't see or hear anyone, but the acrid scent of smoke was strong. It was not far away. Slowly, softly, I walked another few paces, placing each foot ever so gently, freezing, my heart pounding when a twig snapped beneath my boot. There was no indication that anyone heard — no shouts of alarm, no feet running to investigate — so I kept moving as quietly as I could.

I waited for the woods to close in around me, to protect me as they had before, but the trees didn't move and the bramble stayed where it was. Even the tangly weed didn't appear. The woods had decided not to shield me this time.

I searched for another of the skirted trees that had sheltered us before Sumerled's arrival, but they were scarce in this part of the woods. The best I could find was a knotty bramble bush with a small hollow beneath it. It would not shield me from view if anyone passed on this side, but it might hide me from someone on the other side, provided they didn't look too closely. I crawled into the small space. The earth was cool beneath my body.

I was well experienced in making myself unnoticeable. All of those times I had sat by the fire, being still and quiet, and folk's gaze would slide straight over me. All of the secrets I had heard while sitting in plain view because people stopped seeing me. I drew on those times now, curling my body into a small ball, making myself still and quiet. I waited.

With my eyes squeezed shut, I listened intently and soon began sorting the usual chatter of the woods from the noise of those I sought to avoid. The quiet murmur of voices; at least two, although whether they were mortal or fey, I couldn't tell. The crackle of a fire. A harsh laugh startled me and I stiffened in alarm. At length I heard movement. Snaps and pops as somebody stirred up the fire, then footsteps heading in my direction.

Still and silent, I held my breath as he came closer. Clearly not fey, for he walked as heavily as I did. He stopped on the other side of the bush I hid beneath.

Still and silent.

A rustle of cloth, then a stream of liquid hit the bush. Warm droplets splattered my back.

I held my breath and hoped he couldn't hear my heart pounding. Still and silent.

At length he was finished. Another rustle of cloth and he left, stomping heavily through the woods, back to his fire and his companion.

I remained where I was. I had no way of knowing how long the men might stay or in which direction they would leave. I also didn't know whether the fey watched them. I needed to be invisible until they left.

For hours I lay under the bramble bush. The earth beneath me was cool and I had just enough space to avoid the bramble's thorns. Occasionally a laugh reached my ears. The men, it seemed, had settled in for a lengthy stay.

A shout of alarm.

The noise of a brief struggle.

The sound of bodies being dragged away.

Still and silent, I waited.

38

GRAINNE

When Kalen told Eithne to leave, the cracks in the armour she had shielded herself with for so long finally broke open. The possibility of finding Kalen, of saving him from whatever she believed had befallen him, had sustained her through the months of darkness and slavery. I had never asked what she would do if she discovered it had all been a fantasy and indeed I now suspected she had never considered the possibility.

Eithne fled and I moved to follow, but Kalen grabbed my arm.

"Let me go." I gave him my coldest glare and tried to shake him off.

"Let her run," Kalen said. "It might be her best chance."

"Don't be ridiculous. We need to stay together. If I can't find her again, we're both in even more trouble than we already are."

"She needs to be as far away from me as possible. If you are captured again, tell them you never found me."

He finally released my arm.

"If you want her to be safe, then she and I should be together."

"You are here for your own reasons, not hers. She is safer alone."

My heart stuttered wildly. I looked away and clenched my hands together so Kalen wouldn't see how they trembled. I tried to keep my voice casual.

"Is he still safe?"

"More or less."

"How do I find him?"

I kept my gaze on a handful of young hazelnuts growing on a nearby bush. My stomach spasmed at the thought of food and the constant smell of fresh bread made me sick with hunger. I couldn't even look at the food lying on the sack for fear I would lose the last shreds of my control and throw myself on it.

"Are you sure you want to?" Kalen's eyes were serious and gave no hint of betrayal.

"Of course I'm sure. Why would I come if I didn't intend to find him? I'm here to take him home."

"Why do so many of the women in your family think their men need saving?"

"Eithne is my sister, but only by marriage. Do you consider yourself her man then?"

Kalen hung his head and his breath hitched. "She should not have come here."

"She loves you. She has spent months as a slave and all to find you."

"I'm protecting her." His words were hesitant, as if he didn't quite believe them.

"By sending her off into the woods alone? She doesn't need your kind of protection."

"Sumerled will find her easily enough. Go," he said to the boy who stood behind him, forgotten. "Take Eithne back to the mortal world."

Sumerled looked like he wanted to argue, but after a moment of hesitation, he darted off into the trees.

"Why did you let her think you don't care?" I asked.

"It's a long story."

"Tell me."

Kalen shook his head. "The more you know, the more danger you will be in. I am protecting her as best I can. That is all you need know."

We eyed each other warily. His jaw was clenched and one eyelid twitched. Clearly he was not as indifferent as he pretended to be.

"Where is my husband?"

"He lives with some of the wilder fey. They like to hunt and feast. They live large."

"Is he well?"

"As well as any mortal can be when exposed to such a lifestyle. He has probably long forgotten who he is, though."

"How do I find him?"

"They will hunt tonight, for the moon is full. I can take you to a place where you can hide and wait for them to pass. He won't remember you, though, and he won't want to leave."

"How do I restore his memory?"

He shrugged and I saw echoes of Sumerled in the gesture.

"He will choose to remember or not. But if you can convince him to leave, make for the edge of the woods immediately. You will need to find a portal and return to your own world before he changes his mind. You won't convince him a second time."

"He won't change his mind, not once he remembers."

"Perhaps, perhaps not. The delights of our realm are intoxicating to mortals. Most will not willingly leave, even if they remember."

I didn't let my mind linger on what delights Caedmon might have sampled.

"You should eat." Kalen gestured towards the food Sumerled had provided. "Sleep. Then I will take you to where you can wait for your man."

3 9

GRAINNE

I tried not to gobble, but it was almost impossible to restrain myself. The bread was fresh and soft, the cheese creamy and the blackberries juicy. I ate just enough to ease the ache in my belly, mindful of making myself ill, then I lay down to sleep. Kalen leaned against a slender ash, lost in his own thoughts.

My dreams were strange and confusing. Times of darkness interspersed with periods of running through the woods. Sounds of invisible relentless pursuit. Treva's kitchen and the pastries that unmade themselves every night. Running, hiding. Darkness. Woods.

I woke feeling like I emerged from a deep sleep. My thoughts were woolly and a few moments passed before I noticed him.

He sat cross-legged about ten paces away from me, his back straight and his piercing gaze fixed on me. How long had he watched me as I slept? I sat up, pulling leaves from my hair, and trying to pretend I was not suddenly deathly afraid.

"Lunn," I said. "Why are you here?"

He looked at me in a way that made the hair stand up on my arms.

"Why, Grainne, are you not pleased to see me? I am most delighted to see you."

Memories of his clawed hands on my body made my stomach roll. I pushed the thoughts away and repeated my question.

"I could ask you the same thing," he said. "I am surprised to see you here, but oh so happy that you are."

He moved quickly, his limbs a blur, and suddenly he crouched in front of me. I didn't have time to so much as blink before something snapped around my throat. My fingers touched a thick wooden collar. It was attached to a bronze chain, the other end of which was wrapped around Lunn's wrist.

"What have you done?" The collar was too tight. I couldn't breathe. Panic welled within me. I tucked my fingers under the edges and tried to pull it open. "Get this off me."

Lunn's smile was slow and lazy.

"You're mine now, Grainne. You shouldn't have come here."

My limbs went weak and when I spoke, my voice trembled.

"Where is Kalen?"

"He's gone," Lunn said. "Did you think he would stick around to help you? Risk his own neck? No, he ran away as soon as I arrived."

I tried to push the panic down, to breathe normally. The collar was uncomfortable, but it didn't actually impede my ability to breathe. Until Lunn tugged the chain. I choked and gasped. My panic was sharp and almost overwhelming. For a few moments I really couldn't breathe.

"You'll learn to do as you're told, Grainne," Lunn said. "And you'll learn quick, I promise, because that's just a taste of what will happen if you don't. Now get up, we're leaving."

He tugged the chain again, this time harder. It pulled me off my rear and onto my hands and knees.

"I said, get up." His voice was cool and impatient.

I climbed to my feet, my legs stiff and clumsy. Tears streamed down my cheeks and I hurriedly wiped them away. He had better hope I didn't have a knife in my hands when I finally escaped.

Lunn set off at a loping pace. I had to jog to keep up. We ran until I began tripping over my own feet from fatigue. Lunn allowed me a brief rest and then set off again. At long last, we came to a clearing. In the middle was a grassy hill about half the height of a man. Lunn halted in front of the mound and it opened soundlessly. A yawning chasm led down into the ground. He walked in.

"Wait." Panic welled again. It was dark inside, like the tree the fey had kept us in. "Stop. Lunn."

He paused and glanced back at me.

"Better follow, Grainne. I thought you would learn faster."

"I can't. Please don't make me go in there."

"Last chance. Follow or I'll simply drag you in. I don't care how but one way or another, you're coming in."

He tugged the chain, not quite hard enough to choke me.

I forced my feet forward. My breaths were shallow and fast. A rushing noise filled my ears and if Lunn spoke again, I didn't hear him. He disappeared down into the darkness and I followed. I had no doubt that he would drag me in if I didn't.

The tunnel bore down sharply, but it wasn't completely dark. Instead it was filled with a dim green light that shone from some invisible source. I focused on breathing more evenly and not thinking about the earth piled above me and how I would be buried if the tunnel came tumbling down. The walls were made of packed earth with no supports that I could see. The air had a pleasant earthy smell, like a freshly dug garden.

We had only walked for a few minutes before Lunn stopped and turned to face the wall. An open doorway appeared in front of him and he walked through. I followed quickly.

I had expected another tunnel, but this was a small earthen cavern decked out as a home of sorts. There was a bed and an assortment of chairs, a dresser, a table and a cupboard, all made of wood that looked as if it had simply grown into shape. I ran my fingers over a chair. The wood was smooth and if there were any joins, I could neither see nor feel them.

The wall closed behind me and when I turned, there was no sign a doorway even existed. There were no windows, no other doors, no means of escape. I forced myself to breathe slowly.

Lunn released my chain, letting it fall from his hands to land with a thud on the earthen floor. He gracefully lowered himself into a chair, crossed one leg over the other, and smiled at me.

"Well, Grainne, here we are."

I stayed where I was.

"Why am I here?"

"You amuse me. I like things that amuse me."

"Where is Caedmon?"

"Hmm. Who? Oh, you mean the mortal you took such pains to save? And they were pains, weren't they, lovely Grainne? You suffered much for him."

"What have you done with him?"

"Don't you worry. I've kept my end of our agreement."

"Will you take me to him? I need to see him for myself. See that he is safe."

Lunn laughed. "No, Grainne, I don't think so."

"How can I believe you if you won't show me?"

"I don't care whether you believe me or not. I've done what I said I would and that's all that matters."

"It matters to me."

"But not to me, and that, my dear, is what is important. Now sit down like a good girl, Grainne. You may as well rest while you can. You can use my bed if you want to sleep."

"No thank you." I couldn't restrain my shudder.

Lunn noticed and seemed amused.

"Suit yourself. We have a big evening tonight. A feast. It will be a late night."

Lunn settled back in his chair and closed his eyes. Whether he slept, or was just thinking, I couldn't tell.

I gingerly sat on the chair closest to me. It was surprisingly comfortable. I leaned my head against the back and closed my eyes. I was sure I wouldn't fall asleep, not with Lunn in the room, but I woke when he tugged hard on my chain, almost pulling me off the chair. I choked and coughed and wheezed.

"You could have just spoken to me," I said, when I could breathe again.

Lunn didn't even look at me.

"Get up. It's time to leave."

He had changed his clothes while I slept and now wore a blue shirt which flowed over his shoulders like water rippling in a pond.

"Can I wash first?" I was suddenly acutely conscious of how filthy I was. "And I need new clothes."

Lunn finally looked at me, a slow examination of my body. The edges of his mouth turned up slightly.

"What you're wearing is quite appropriate. Let's go."

The door opened and he led me back out through the tunnel. A short walk through the woods led us to a clearing strung with tiny coloured lights — not candles, but presumably some sort of fey magic — and long tables piled with food. Dozens of fey already sat at the tables, although nobody appeared to be eating. Conversation stopped when Lunn and I walked into the clearing.

"Whatever have you found, Lunn?" a woman asked as she looked me up and down with a snide expression.

I glared at her but Lunn only laughed.

"A mortal, obviously. Wandering where she shouldn't be."

He led me to a table and settled himself into the sole empty chair. I stood behind him, close enough that the chain was slack between us. As much as I didn't want to be near him, I felt even more unsafe surrounded by so many fey. I endured several more unpleasant comments, including an offer to swap me for another mortal from a tall fey whose mouth twisted in a cruel expression. Lunn turned him down with a laugh. I scanned the fey but couldn't see Titania. Would anyone realise that I was one of the mortals she searched for?

As one, the fey reached for the food and started feasting. Roasted birds, too big to be hens. Strange vegetables I had never before seen. Unfamiliar fruits and berries. Sauces and salads, puddings and wines. My mouth watered and my stomach growled. My simple meal of bread, cheese and berries felt like a very long time ago.

They feasted for hours while I stood behind Lunn, forgotten. Eventually I sat behind his chair on the ground and drew up my legs to rest my head on them. The grass was cold and damp, but I was too exhausted to care. The chatter and clatter of the fey feast seemed to fade away as I dozed. Eventually the fey began to rise and drift away. Lunn set a plate of scraps down on the grass beside me.

"Eat," he said, and to my shame, I did.

I gnawed on half-eaten bones and finished vegetables with only a few bites taken out of them. The food was rich and spicy but strangely unsatisfying. When I had finished, I felt almost as hungry as I had been before. The clearing had emptied by the time I looked up. Lunn tugged on my chain.

"Up," he said.

I clambered to my feet, slowly and stiffly. We walked back through the woods without speaking. Twice Lunn stopped to wait while I picked myself up off the ground, but he didn't comment. We entered the mound that led down into the tunnel and again came to the cavern where he lived.

The wall closed behind us and Lunn dropped my chain. He stripped off his clothes as he strode towards the bed and was naked by the time he climbed into it. His shoulders were narrower than Caedmon's and the muscles not as well defined.

"Find somewhere to sleep, sweet Grainne," he said. "You can join me in here, if you wish, but be warned you won't get much sleep if you do."

I quickly sat on a chair. The light in the room disappeared and soon soft snores came from the direction of Lunn's bed. I woke when the light came back on. Lunn stood in front of me, fully dressed.

"Time to get up, Grainne. We are going to watch the hunt pass by."

40

GRAINNE

The woods were lit with the perpetual noon-bright light, although my body told me it was late evening. We walked for some time before Lunn stopped beside a large oak. He leaned against the trunk, the end of my chain dangling from his fingers.

"Now what?" I asked.

"We wait. They will be along soon enough."

Mere minutes passed before the ground began to vibrate. I edged a little closer to Lunn. He both repulsed and terrified me, but he was the closest thing to protection I had here.

"Stand against the tree," he said. "They will not stop if you get in their way."

Lunn had positioned us where we would have a clear view as the hunt swept through. Dogs came first: slender, baying hounds. I didn't see whatever quarry they pursued, but the hounds ran as if they knew exactly where they were going.

Next came the horses, tall and sleek and white. Their riders were deathly silent, as focused on their quarry as the hounds. I thought I recognised some. One might have been the fey who sat opposite Lunn at the feast. Another might have stood near Eithne and I the day we were presented to Titania. Or perhaps not. It was hard to tell when they flew by so fast.

Then I saw Caedmon. He rode towards the back of the herd, crouching low over his horse's neck, his face intense and focused. He had aged from when I saw him last. Not like he had lived longer, but as if he had lived harder. My heart thudded and my palms went clammy.

"Caedmon!" I called, thoughtlessly stepping out in front of his horse. The beast didn't slow.

Lunn grabbed my arm and yanked me back a moment before the horse trampled me.

"Let me go." I tried to pull my arm away, but he held on tightly. "Caedmon, it's me, Grainne!"

If Caedmon heard, he gave no indication of it. The horses disappeared into the woods. The ground still shook from the thunder of their hooves.

"Caedmon, don't leave me here," I called after him forlornly. I turned to Lunn and beat my fist against his chest. "Where are they going? Take me to them."

Lunn laughed and wrapped his hands around my wrist, holding it against his chest. If a heart beat within, I couldn't feel it.

"You can't follow those who ride horses bred from our stock. They are too fast and can run far further than you."

"Why did you bring me here?" I wrenched my hands from his grip. "Why show me Caedmon like that? Was it just to gloat? You must have known he wouldn't hear me."

"It wasn't that he couldn't hear you, my dear. He didn't *want* to hear you. And why would he? Look at the life he enjoys now. He feasts and hunts and does whatever he wants. How can any life you offer compare to that?"

"He would want to go home."

"And what would he return to? Working the fields? Breeding children? Watching you grow tired and haggard and old?"

"He's a soldier," I said, my voice both fierce and proud. "A very good one. And family means everything to Caedmon. He would go home if he could. If not for me, then for his parents and his sister and his brothers. He does not want to be here."

"You saw him, Grainne. Did he look like a man who did not want to be here?"

"He looks like a man who is charmed. He only sees what you want him to."

"It sounds to me, my dear, like you are the one who only sees what you want. Now come along, I am tired and want to sleep."

"I won't go with you." I crossed my arms over my chest and gave him my fiercest glare. "I demand you take me to Caedmon."

"Oh, he won't be found for hours yet. Not until the hunt finishes."

"Then take me to wherever he sleeps. I will wait there for him."

"For what purpose? He has forgotten he ever had a life before this. He won't even recognise you."

"Let me try, at least. If I can convince him to leave with me, let him go."

Lunn raised his eyebrow at me.

"You are stubborn, aren't you? I am almost persuaded to let you try, just for the fun of watching. But no."

He tugged gently on the chain, just enough to remind me who was in charge, and we walked back to his chamber beneath the earth. Once inside, with the wall sealed up behind us, Lunn dropped my chain and went straight to his bed, peeling off his clothes as he walked.

"There is food on the bench if you need to eat," he said.

I glanced towards the wooden bench which grew out of the earthen wall. A small loaf of bread and a mug waited. The bread was fresh — I could smell it from here. I didn't feel like eating, though, despite my constant hunger.

I sat on the wooden chair where I had spent the previous night. Or perhaps it was still the same night. I was tired, so very tired. For the first time, I felt old. I refused to believe Caedmon would not want to come home. He might not have had time to learn to love me, but I was his wife, after all. And I could give him the thing he wanted most in the world: a son. As soon as Lunn woke, I asked again.

"Take me to Caedmon. Let me at least try."

He dressed slowly, not caring that his naked body was on display to me the whole time. I kept my gaze on his face, refusing to show my discomfort.

"Leave him be, Grainne. He is happy here."

"He is not happy. He is charmed. He will be happy when he is home again."

"You should be pleased for him. He has the perfect life here, the kind all mortal men hope for."

"What do you know of what mortal men hope for?" I asked scornfully. "If this is what you think life is, you are sadly mistaken. Look at you. You live alone in this cave under the ground. You sleep alone. I haven't even seen you speak to another fey except at the feast. You have a sad, lonely, pathetic life."

Surprise crossed Lunn's face.

"But I will live for many hundreds of years. Your kind will wither and die in my lifetime."

"A life like yours is not worth living, whether for one year or a thousand. I pity you."

He glared at me and I glared back.

"You should learn to guard your words, my dear," he said. "They will get you into trouble one of these days."

41

———

EITHNE

A very long time passed before I felt safe enough to leave my hiding place. The men and whatever attacked them had been gone for hours. I huddled under the bramble bush, too fearful to do anything other than stay still and quiet. But I couldn't stay here forever.

As I crawled out, my body was stiff and my limbs numb. My legs failed to hold me as I try to stand, and I fell. On hands and knees, I listened for the snapping of twigs or rustling of leaf litter that might indicate someone coming to investigate. But I heard nothing to alarm me and at length I climbed to my feet.

Now that I knew the woods would not necessarily shield me, I walked carefully, although I was far from stealthy. I had paid little attention when I ran away. I could only hope I could find my way back and that Grainne would still be there.

Eventually I spotted a fallen log that may have been the one I tripped over on my heedless flight. Soon after, I spied a scrap of fabric dangling from a low branch. It was grey and nondescript, just like my own dress after so long without washing.

I sniffed the air as I walked, searching for any trace of smoke, but there was nothing other than the usual scents of earth and trees and decay. A startled deer bounded away into the trees. A raven perched in a nearby oak eyed me curiously. I remembered Kalen's tales of other creatures that inhabited these woods but saw nothing out of the ordinary.

After what seemed like a very long time, I found a small clearing. It was empty of mortals and fey, but in the centre was a sack upon which sat the remnants of the meal Sumerled had provided. Without a second thought, I fell on the food. Never had bread and cheese tasted so good. The bread was fresh and the cheese was sharp and crumbly. I crammed them into my mouth and didn't stop until it was all gone. It wasn't until afterwards that I wondered why the food was still there. Why it hadn't been eaten by the creatures of the woods.

With a belly that was blissfully full for the first time in many months, I sat back on my heels. I should have shown some restraint rather than gorging myself, but it was too late. It was only now that I wondered about Grainne. Was it she who had eaten the rest? And where was she? Surely Kalen would look after her. He might not care for me the way I had thought, but I did not believe he would leave a mortal woman alone in fey woods. He had probably taken her to a portal. Grainne might already be back home at Silver Downs.

With that hopeful thought, my eyes drooped. Although I had dozed while hiding under the bramble, I had not slept properly for days. It would be unwise to sleep here without shelter from spying eyes. Anyone could sneak up on me. I would not sleep but merely rest for a few minutes. I lay down in a mossy patch with Sumerled's sack bundled under my head for a pillow. I closed my eyes and sank down into sleep.

When I woke, I was lying on my side, curled up like a babe. I felt like I had slept long and deeply. For the first time in months, I felt refreshed and clear-headed. It took some time for my eyes to focus, but when they finally did, I realised I had not been alone while I slept. Right in front of me, where before had been nothing but leaves and dirt, was a rock the size of my head.

There was nobody else here, neither mortal nor fey. And yet someone must have been here, for rocks do not move themselves.

Again I became aware of my vulnerability. A lone woman, I was easy prey. And yet whoever it was had not disturbed my sleep. They had merely placed a rock beside me.

Was it a message? A warning? I couldn't even guess at its meaning. I heard nothing other than woodlarks calling, undergrowth rustling with the creeping of vole and badger, the distant bark of a deer. And yet sitting in front of me was inarguable proof that somebody else had been here, however briefly.

The rock was the grey of a winter's sky and had no markings. Nothing unusual. Nothing exceptional. Except that every time I looked at it, I heard something buzzing. As soon as I looked away, it stopped.

Tentatively, I reached out my hand. My fingers shook just the tiniest bit, although I told myself I was being ridiculous if I feared touching a rock. I placed the tips of my fingers on its surface. It was warm and smooth. The buzzing stopped.

"That's better," a voice said, from somewhere very close to me.

I started and pulled back my hand. The buzzing resumed and I could no longer hear the speaker. I slid closer to the rock and touched my fingers to it once again.

"Took you long enough," the voice again. It was deep and gravelly and the words came slowly, as if the speaker stopped for thought after each one.

I looked around, but I was still alone.

"Haven't quite figured it out, have you?"

"Who's there?" I asked, forcing courage I didn't feel into my voice. "Where are you?"

"I'll wait. You'll figure it out sooner or later. Time doesn't mean much to one such as I."

"Stop hiding. Come out and face me. It's cowardly to hide and try to scare me."

"Oh I ain't hiding, girlie. You just aren't looking properly."

"I don't like being teased. Show yourself or go away."

"Not teasing. Just waiting for you to figure things out."

I thought about the image from my fever dreams: the creature that looked like a rock.

"Think it through, love. You don't look all that stupid."

Maybe Titania had taken my mind after all.

"Perhaps I should sleep while you think? I'll warn you though, I don't wake easily. Once I nod off, you won't wake me again for, oh, a few hundred years."

"Are you the rock?" I felt like a fool, but the voice came from somewhere nearby and I only heard it when I touched its surface.

"*Rock* isn't a very pleasant kind of word, is it? Rather harsh. But I suppose it will do as well as any."

"What are you if you aren't a rock?"

"I didn't say I wasn't. Just that it wasn't a nice word. But yes, I suppose, to you I am probably a rock."

Gaining confidence, I pressed my fingers a little more firmly against its smooth surface.

"Are you fey?"

A sound like a cross between a snort and someone clearing their throat.

"Usurpers. Interlopers. Children."

Dimly-remembered snippets of ancient tales came to mind. Supposedly a species already inhabited these lands when the fey arrived. Older and smaller and not inclined to fight for their territory. The tales didn't say what had become of them, or if they did, I had never heard. I had always assumed they left. But perhaps they didn't go anywhere. Perhaps they were still here, waiting for the day the fey left — or died out.

"Why did you come to speak to me?" I asked.

"You have questions. I have answers."

"What kind of answers?"

"What kind do you want?"

"Where is my friend Grainne? She was right here the last time I saw her."

"Is that your best question? I might as well go back to sleep."

What information did I need the most?

"Why does Titania hate me?"

A sound like rocks grinding together. Perhaps it laughed.

"She doesn't hate you. She fears you."

"Me?"

"Well, not you, exactly. Your children."

"I don't have any children."

"Yet."

That made me pause. I had always assumed children would not be for me. That I would not be strong enough to survive a pregnancy.

"Why would Titania fear any children I might have?"

"A child that is part-mortal, part-fey is a dangerous combination."

"My children will be part-fey?" I hardly knew what to think.

"Just said that, didn't I."

"Who will their father be?"

"Not going to tell you that. Have to leave some surprises."

There would be time later to dwell on this news.

"She watches you, you know. And your family. Has for generations."

"Does it have anything to do with the power the bards in my family have? If they are the seventh son of a seventh son?"

"Special thing, that, to be the seventh son of a seventh son. Powerful. Power like that could wipe out the fey, if anyone thought to use it right."

I stared down at the rock in surprise.

"Why would we do that? The fey have never done anything to us. At least, not until now."

"Aah, but there's always potential, isn't there? Potential for someone to think a little bit harder than those who came before. But it's not just the menfolk who have power. You have some of your own."

"Me? I don't have any power."

"Oh, you do, all right. Might not have realised it yet, though. But you have your own power, girlie. Time's a-coming when you'll need to know how to wield it. Or maybe it won't be you. Might be your daughter or your granddaughter. Better figure it out while you have time."

"I don't understand."

"No, you probably don't. But I've said enough. Tired me out, all this talking. Time to go back to sleep."

4 2

EITHNE

Try as I might, I couldn't wake the rock again. I should have asked for instructions on how to get back to the mortal world. I could have asked how much time had passed while we lingered in the fey realm. There were so many things I should have asked had I been more prepared. These were fey woods after all. I should have expected the unexpected.

I set off through the woods, but stumbled, distracted. A woodlark rose from a nearby branch with a startled squawk. I forced away thoughts of the rock creature and concentrated on moving quickly and quietly. I searched for signs of Grainne, but there was nothing. No footprint in the damp soil, no disturbed leaf litter. No scrap of fabric hanging from a branch. Nothing that said she had passed this way.

The skin on the back of my neck began to prickle and an uneasy feeling crept over me. I paused beside a birch and looked around, peering hard into the shadows between trees, but saw no evidence of anyone watching. I held myself very still and listened. No footsteps. No crackle of undergrowth. No snap of broken twigs. Nothing. Not even the usual sounds of the woods.

I continued walking but still couldn't shake the feeling that somebody watched. At last, I spied a raven sitting on a branch, its beady gaze fastened on me. It tilted its head and seemed to look me right in the eyes. Relief surged through me. It was just a bird. The raven let out a caw and took off, its glistening black wings lifting it into the air with ease. I breathed a sigh and kept walking. But the sensation of being watched didn't abate.

The hair on my arms was standing straight up. A growing sense of doom rose within me and I fought the urge to run. *Flee*, something inside me said. *Run, as far and as fast as you can, or something bad will happen.*

A bug darted in front of my face. I swatted it away, but it came right back. I walked a little swifter. A second bug arrived. I fervently hoped they did not bite or sting. A third joined those circling me and now my heart beat a little faster.

With every few steps, another bug appeared until within a minute or two a dark cloud surrounded me. I waved my arms, trying to keep them away from my face.

"Shoo," I said. "Go away."

A faint sound like a titter reached my ears and suddenly my palms were clammy. I stopped walking.

"What are you?" I asked. "What do you want?"

Something grabbed my foot. The finest thread, no thicker than a spider web, draped over my boot. It sparkled in the bright sunlight. I tried to lift my foot, but the strand held me fast to the ground.

Another strand shot over my other boot, then something shoved me from behind. I fell to my hands and knees in the leaf litter. A second shove sent me to my stomach. The leaves were cool against my face and when I inhaled, everything smelled fresh and earthy. Down here, the trees towered over me, impossibly tall.

My hand rested on a tree root that ran along the surface of the ground. I dug my fingers into the loose soil and grasped the root but couldn't pull it free. With my other hand, I scrabbled in the leaf litter, searching for something else that might serve as a weapon: a stick, a rock, anything. But all I found was damp leaves and rich dirt and a few mushrooms.

One of the bugs stood right in front of my face and now I saw it wasn't a bug at all. It was only as tall as my fingernail, but its form was human. Tiny wings fluttered behind its shoulders as it pointed one hand at me and made a high-pitched noise.

More threads shot over me, pinning me to the ground at shoulder and waist and legs. Panic welled within me and my chest tightened. I was trussed like a pig about to be roasted.

The tiny winged folk swarmed over me, their footsteps so light, they felt like nothing more than stray hairs brushing against my skin. I strained against the ropes and they dug into me.

"What do you want?" I asked.

Once I was fastened to their satisfaction, the tiny creatures flew down to the ground and assembled in front of my face. They flitted around, seeming to spin and turn and dip.

"Release me." I glared at them. "We can talk if you untie me."

They seemed to laugh again and one in front of me shook his head.

"I could squash you." I raised one fist. They hadn't thought to tie my hands. "I could squash you like the bugs you are."

An indignant chatter reached my ears. Those close to my hands flitted backwards out of reach.

"If you don't let me go immediately, I am going to hunt you down and squash each and every one of you. I will stomp you into the ground."

The creatures seemed to confer, but it was obvious they couldn't reach an agreement. While they talked, I strained at my bonds, but the delicate threads held me fast.

43

SUMERLED

The mortal woman's face is pale and her eyes large as the sprites pin her to the ground. I fancy I can almost smell her fear from where I hide beneath a hawthorn bush.

They laugh and mock her, although her feeble mortal hearing probably doesn't allow her to hear their words. I have to slap a hand over my mouth to stop myself from laughing as the sprites bring her to the ground and dance on top of her. She challenges and threatens them. Are all mortals so stupid? Or just this one that Kalen has chosen?

I am so absorbed in the spectacle before me that I don't notice Kalen until he grabs me by the shoulder and hauls me to my feet.

"Sumerled, what are you doing?" he hisses. "I told you to take her to the portal. Not to spy on her."

I glare at the ground.

"I would have. Sooner or later."

"You were supposed to do it straight away. Eithne must be terrified. We are used to creatures such as these, but mortals are not."

That's what makes it fun, I think, but I only kick the ground and continue to glower at it. Kalen gives me a final shake and shoves me away.

"I don't know why I waste my time with you," he says. "You're not worth it. Just go away."

I flee. He will forgive me. He always does. And I have not forgotten the promise she owes me. I will collect on that before she returns to the mortal world. I now know exactly what I want for my promise.

EITHNE

ell-worn boots appeared in front of me. I craned my neck to see their wearer.

"Release her." Kalen's voice was like thunder. "Then leave, before I make you regret coming here today."

An angry hum reached my ears and the little creatures darted around. The threads securing me suddenly disappeared. Kalen reached out to help me up, but I ignored him and scrambled to my feet. Why had he come back now? He had made it clear he cared nothing for me.

A sudden wave of dizziness sent me pitching forward into his arms. He grasped my shoulders, but I shook him off. I didn't want to be near him. Didn't want him to touch me. I might not be strong enough to do what I had to if he touched me.

I busied myself with brushing leaves and dirt from my clothes. The flying creatures circled my head making angry chattering noises. Kalen waved a hand at them.

"Go," he said, louder this time.

With a final vexed buzz, they flew away. We looked at each other. Or rather he looked at me and I glared at him.

"They meant you no harm," he said.

"No harm?" My voice was embarrassingly high.

"They were toying with you. Had they intended harm, you would have been dead before you ever saw them."

What other horrors did these woods hide? I bit down the words that rose to my tongue. I wouldn't thank him. I didn't need him to rescue me. I would have rescued myself eventually, just like in the tales I used to tell myself.

"Where is Grainne?" I asked.

Kalen looked away and swallowed before meeting my eyes again.

"She is safe enough."

"What does that mean? Is she safe or not?"

"She is with someone I know."

"A fey? You left her with one of the fey?" My voice rose in both volume and pitch.

"I didn't leave her by choice. He sent me away."

"And you just left? Without her?"

"Grainne is not my responsibility." He shot me a look I couldn't read.

"She is my friend. My sister. You should have stayed with her."

"I came to find you."

"She needs you more than I do."

Kalen shrugged but said nothing.

"Why are you even here?" I was suddenly exhausted. It was all I could do to not throw myself to the ground and wail like a child.

"I hurt you." He said it as if only just realising.

I glared at him.

"I didn't mean to. I was trying to protect you."

"I don't need protecting."

"I was doing what I thought was best. Having me around put you in danger. The only way to remove the danger was to remove myself."

"You should have told me. Let me decide for myself whether the danger was worth the risk."

"Are all mortal women so stubborn?" he asked with a sigh.

"If you wanted less stubborn, you should have chosen someone else."

Kalen met my gaze steadily and my heart faltered.

"But I chose you," he said.

I swallowed. This was dangerous territory. I was too close to letting him back in.

"Then why did you stop coming to visit me?"

Kalen dug the toe of his boot in the dirt. In his silence, I heard the wind moving through leaves. Birds called. Life continued all around us while I waited for his next words.

"I was trying not to draw Titania's attention. I didn't want her to know about you."

"Why?" My voice was calm and even, giving no hint of the crazy way my heart pounded.

"Because she would forbid me from fraternising with a mortal. And because I didn't want you to be in danger."

"Was I in danger? Before I came here?"

I plucked a stray leaf off my ragged sleeve and watched as it fluttered down to the ground.

"Not as long as she didn't know about you. That's why I stopped coming. Somebody knew and threatened to tell Titania."

"Why?"

"Because he could."

I longed to know more, but for now it was enough that he had finally told me the truth. The reason he stopped coming to me wasn't because he didn't care. I clung to this new knowledge, letting it soften my heart just a little.

"Where is Grainne?" I asked.

"He has probably taken her to his home."

"Will he hurt her?"

Kalen looked away, shuffled his feet, cleared his throat.

"Kalen, will he hurt her?"

"I don't know."

I pushed my softening feelings away. The fey never changed.

"What do you mean, you don't know? How could you hand Grainne over to someone who might hurt her?"

"He wanted her. I had no choice."

"There is always a choice. You should have kept her safe."

"I know. I knew. But he… there is something he holds over me. A threat. I am protecting someone else, somebody who can't protect himself."

"Take me to Grainne. Please."

"There's nothing you can do for her. He won't hand her over until he gets bored. Anything you do will make things worse for her."

"Grainne has been by my side through this whole thing. All the months Titania forced us to work as slaves. She offered to come with me. She didn't have to. I can't just walk away and leave her in danger."

"There's nothing you can do."

"I have to try. There must be something."

An emotion I couldn't read flashed briefly across his face, but eventually he sighed and nodded.

"You have to do what I say. Promise me that if I say we are leaving, you will. I'll protect you as best as I can, but…"

"I'm not promising anything. If you won't take me to her, I'll find someone who can. Sumerled might be able to find her. He found you, after all."

"Leave Sumerled out of this."

"Then take me to her yourself and I won't have to ask him."

We eyed each other.

"It's a long walk from here," he said.

"It can't be any further than I've already walked."

Kalen sighed again. "Let's go then."

45

EITHNE

s we walked, I studied Kalen out of the corner of my eye. He looked exactly the same as when I last saw him, wearing clothes that were a size too large and with raggedly cut hair. He glanced towards me and I quickly looked away.

I couldn't afford to let myself feel anything for him. Once we found Grainne, he would take us to a portal and after that, I would likely never see him again. There was no point dwelling on the way my heart ached at being so close to him and the way my hands itched to reach out and touch him.

Those thoughts reminded me of my own filth and I wished he hadn't seen my tattered clothes and tangled hair. Grime covered every inch of my skin and I stank of sweat. But at least I wasn't limping. Whatever fey magic had straightened my foot continued to hold.

"Is there a stream near here?" I asked. "Could we stop somewhere I can bathe?"

"I can take you to a place where you can bathe," he said, then whistled sharply.

A moment later, a rustling noise came from behind us. I turned around in time to see Sumerled creeping out from beneath a bramble bush. Kalen glared at him.

"Were you spying again?" he asked, his voice stern.

Sumerled's face was sullen and he glowered in my direction. "Not much worth spying on around here."

Kalen inhaled deeply. "Sumerled, you try my patience."

The boy merely shrugged and looked away.

"Go find Eithne some clean clothes," Kalen said.

Sumerled opened his mouth to speak.

"Now," Kalen said.

Sumerled fled into the trees. Kalen resumed walking and I hurried to catch up.

"Why does he hate me?" I asked.

Kalen shook his head. "It's not you. He hates everyone. He's not had an easy life."

"Is it true that he's half mortal? That you and he are brothers?"

Kalen's gaze flickered sideways to meet mine ever so briefly.

"He told you that?"

"Yes."

"Our father is Oberon."

He spoke quickly, as if to get the words out before he changed his mind.

I stumbled over a tree root but caught myself before I fell, pretending I didn't see Kalen reaching out to help.

"The king? You're… what, a prince?"

And I had fancied myself in love with him. Fooled myself into thinking he felt the same.

Kalen barked a laugh.

"Not exactly. An outcast, more like. Titania hates me. I live here only at her sufferance and on the condition that I keep out of her sight. She would prefer to forget I exist."

"Why don't you live in the mortal world? You wouldn't be beholden to anyone."

"I am only half fey. If I were to live in your world, I would age and die. This—" He gestured at the woods that surrounded us. "This is my birthright. I should be here, amongst my own kind."

"If you are indeed half mortal, then my world also contains your own kind."

Kalen flinched.

"You despise us so?" I shouldn't let it bother me because I would never see him again after today, but still I was bitterly disappointed. "Are we that far beneath you, that you would rather live here, where you are an outcast, than live in freedom in the mortal world?"

"I am trying to live the way Titania expects. I hope… I hope that if I live as any other fey does, she will realise I belong here."

I looked away into the trees, composing myself before I spoke further. I didn't want my voice to give away my disappointment.

"She hates you?"

"She hates what I represent. Oberon's dalliance with a mortal. Titania doesn't care about his indiscretions with women of the fey. He has had plenty and she, too, has her own affairs. But she was gravely offended that he would choose a mortal over her, and not just once. Sumerled's mother is also mortal. Titania hates him even more than she hates me. Once, I think, she might forgive such an indiscretion, but not twice."

I concentrated on keeping my footing and pretended Kalen's revelation meant nothing to me. But it explained so much.

"And this is why you stopped coming to see me," I said eventually. "You didn't want Titania to think you were following in your father's footsteps. Fraternising with a mortal." My voice was bitter, however much I tried to suppress my feelings.

"If I had only myself to think of, I wouldn't have. But I have to look after Sumerled. If she threw me out of her realm, he would have nobody."

"So what happened?"

"Sumerled found out about you. He thought this knowledge would grant him favour with somebody we both know. He told, and the person he told threatened to tell Titania."

"So you gave me up to protect him, knowing he would betray you in a heartbeat."

"I was protecting you, too."

"But mostly him."

"Both of you."

Kalen stopped walking and reached for my hand. He finally looked me in the eyes.

"I care about you, Eithne. I don't know the words to tell you how I feel. This is not what I planned when I first started visiting you. I was merely curious."

Sumerled suddenly appeared beside me, seemingly out of nowhere. Kalen dropped my hand and took a step away from me. Sumerled thrust a bundle towards me.

"Here," he muttered.

It was heavier than I had expected and I almost dropped it.

"Thank you," I said. I couldn't bring myself to look at him. If it wasn't for him, Kalen wouldn't have stopped coming to see me. Grainne and I would never have come here. We wouldn't have spent months imprisoned as slaves. All because Kalen wanted to protect this unlikeable boy.

"Go now," Kalen said. "No spying."

Sumerled glared at each of us in turn, then disappeared into the woods.

"There's a small pool just over there," Kalen said. "Nobody will disturb you. I'll wait here."

Less than a dozen steps, past a row of thickly-leafed hawthorn bushes, took me to a rocky pool filled with clear, still water. It was surrounded by a blanket of lush moss. There was no sign of the stream that fed the pool, but perhaps the water came from underground.

I placed Sumerled's bundle on the moss and untied the cord. Wrapped inside a large piece of linen cloth was a dress, underthings and boots. They were clean and in far better condition than my own. There was also a hairbrush and a bundle of soapwort leaves — unexpected luxuries. I was surprised at the boy's thoughtfulness.

With a quick glance around to ensure neither Kalen nor Sumerled lingered nearby, I stripped off my threadbare gown. The fabric fell apart in my hands. I slipped my aching feet from my boots and stepped into the pool.

The water was blissfully warm. I sank down to my knees and the warm water surrounded me to the neck. Gods, it felt good. For a while, I just knelt there. How long had it been since I last bathed? The water soothed my sore feet but stung the many cuts and abrasions that covered my skin. I knelt until my fingers wrinkled, then I ducked beneath the surface to drench my hair.

I scrubbed myself with the soapwort, sloughing off months of grime and sweat and dirt. The water around me turned grey. I scrubbed until my skin was red and stinging, then sniffed my arm, just for the pleasure of smelling clean skin. This was the first time I had seen my naked body in months and I tried not to notice how far my ribs stuck out or how my belly curved in towards my spine. If I ever got out of this place, I would never miss a meal again.

Eventually I climbed out of the rocky pool and wrapped myself in the linen. I brushed my hair as best I could, but sections were so matted, they would need to be cut. The thought reminded me of how I had cut Grainne's hair after she was attacked. I still didn't know what secret she hid about that night or who her attacker was. I supposed it didn't matter much anymore. We had been here for months at least, maybe even a year or more. Caedmon was long dead. I pushed my feelings aside. Once we were out of this place, I would grieve for him.

When my hair was as tidy as I could make it, I dried myself and put on the clothes Sumerled had provided. They fit surprisingly well. I returned to where Kalen waited. He leaned against a tree, arms crossed over his chest. My heart ached when I saw him. How different might things have been if he were mortal? Or even if he had cared less about pleasing Titania? When I got home, I would never again let myself think about him. In time, I would forget and my broken heart would heal. That was what a sensible woman would do.

"Now take me to Grainne," I said.

Kalen sighed. He opened his mouth and I knew he was going to argue again.

"She came here to help me, to protect me. I'm not leaving her behind."

"You don't understand."

"I understand as much as I need to. And you're going to help me find her."

Kalen's gaze flicked to something behind me and his face paled. As I turned around, a fey man stepped out from behind an oak tree.

"It's Grainne you seek, is it, my dear? I might just be able to help you."

46

EITHNE

Kalen stepped forward, one hand held out in a strangely beseeching gesture.

"Lunn—" he said, but I interrupted.

"Let him speak." I nodded toward the stranger. "How do you know Grainne?"

He had the pale skin and dark eyes typical of his race and was slightly taller than Kalen. His dark hair was cut shorter than Kalen's and more neatly, and his mouth held a hint of cruelty.

"Grainne and I are old friends," he said with something that might have been a smirk.

If Grainne hadn't mentioned him, surely there was a reason for it.

Kalen moved to stand in front of me.

"Lunn, please, let her be."

"Friend of yours, Kalen?" Lunn asked. "How interesting that you've never mentioned her. Seems we both have secrets when it comes to mortal women."

"Eithne was just leaving."

"No, I'm not." I stepped out from behind Kalen. "I'm not leaving without Grainne."

"Fascinating," Lunn said. "But I don't think she will be interested."

"What do you mean?"

"She's determined to find her man. She seems to believe he needs rescuing."

"Caedmon is here? He's alive?"

"Of course. Grainne came in search of him. You did know that, didn't you?"

Lunn raised his eyebrows and I got the distinct impression he enjoyed himself.

What was the truth? That Caedmon was here and Grainne somehow knew? That she came, not to support me, but to find him? That she wasn't searching for me now, as I searched for her, because she was busy looking for Caedmon? I took a deep breath. I would not cry in front of the fey. Any of them.

"Can you take me to her?" I asked Lunn.

He tipped his head to one side and looked me up and down.

"I could, if you were to make me the right offer."

Kalen grabbed me by the wrist.

"No, Lunn, you cannot have her."

Lunn's gaze never left me.

"Mind yourself, Kalen."

"I will not let you have Eithne."

I wrenched my wrist from his grasp.

"What do you mean, have me?"

Kalen met my eyes briefly.

"Eithne, trust me. You do not want this. Even to find your friend."

"I don't know what you're talking about. All I want is to find Grainne and go home. And if Lunn is able to help me, I want to hear what he has to say."

"No." Kalen turned back to Lunn. "Lunn, don't do this. Please. She is… special to me."

"How interesting. The mongrel has broken his leash and thinks to attack? You can't protect them both, you know. If you have to choose one, which will it be?"

"Leave Sumerled out of this."

"Oh, but you know how I feel about that lying, thieving half-breed.

I've tolerated him for far longer than I would have, were it not for your interference. So now you choose. Sumerled or the girl."

"My name is Eithne," I said. "I don't appreciate being referred to as *the girl.*"

"She has spark, this one," Lunn said, with a laugh. "I'm going to have fun with her."

Kalen grabbed my hand and held it a little too tightly. His fingers were warm, his palm sweaty.

"They are both under my protection," he said.

"Choose." Lunn's voice was cold now and he gave up any pretence at a smile. "One or the other. I take the one you don't choose."

"What do you want with Sumerled?" I asked. Beside me, Kalen stiffened and I glanced at him. "What is Kalen protecting him from?"

Lunn barked a laugh. "From me, my pretty. The half-breed needs to learn a lesson about keeping his sticky fingers off other people's property."

"He's just a boy," Kalen said. "He doesn't know any better."

"Then I'd be happy to teach him," Lunn said.

"We have an agreement," Kalen said.

"We *had* an agreement. You can continue to protect the little half-breed or you can keep the girl. Sorry, *Eithne,*" Lunn said with a mocking glance towards me. "It's one or the other."

"I don't need your protection, Kalen," I said. "Look after Sumerled if you must. I can look after myself."

"You can't protect yourself here," Kalen said. "No mortal can."

"You're choosing the girl?" Lunn asked. "I just want to be clear about your choice. Because then I'm going to find Sumerled and finish drowning him."

"What?" I asked. "You can't do that."

"He took something that belonged to me. Drowning seems a fair punishment. Unfortunately Kalen interrupted the last time, but I'm willing to try again."

"You'll kill him," Kalen said. "He needs to breathe."

"That's the whole point." Lunn's voice was dry. "Get rid of the half-breed. Should have been drowned at birth."

"Don't hurt him," Kalen said. "He's a thief, but he doesn't deserve to die."

I suddenly felt very tired. If Grainne didn't need me, I no longer had any reason to stay.

"I'm going home," I said. "You two can stay here and argue all day for all I care. I found the portal once and I'll find it again. I don't need you. Either of you."

I stomped away into the trees. It didn't matter what direction I went, only that it was away from them. Behind me, Lunn laughed, loud and mocking.

"Go ahead, little girl," he called after me. "Let's see how far you get on your own. You'll come back soon enough, looking for help. And I'll be most pleased to assist you. For a price."

4 7

EITHNE

I stormed through the woods, wishing I could knock down everything that stood between me and the portal, wherever it was. Brambles grabbed at my dress and weeds tangled around my ankles, but I tugged them off and kept moving. The air was hot and heavy. I was drowning in it.

Emotions swirled. Disappointment that Grainne had kept secrets from me. Anger that she had left me here, not knowing whether I was safe. Relief that Caedmon was alive. Anger at Diarmuid for that stupid tale that left us all thinking Caedmon was dead. Fury at Kalen for so many reasons.

I stomped along without caring about how much noise I made. So what if I attracted attention? What could possibly be worse than what I had already suffered? I was going home and anyone who got in my way this time could be damned. If Titania watched, she could come and face me and I'd tell her exactly what I thought of her and her kin.

"Damn you, Titania," I yelled, uncaring of the silence that swept through the woods at my voice. "You hear me? Damn you."

I was so focused on the maelstrom of emotions swirling through me that I almost didn't notice the *pull*. It felt exactly the same as it had so many months ago. The portal was close.

I stopped, closed my eyes, concentrated. The pull was stronger when I turned to the right. I moved cautiously now. I wanted to get through the portal and be back in the mortal world. Away from the politics and infighting of the fey. Away from a dictatorial queen whose subjects lived in fear. Away from cruel fey who solved a problem by drowning a boy. Away from a certain heartless fey who toyed with a woman's emotions and chose his half-brother over her. I didn't need any of them. I never heard Kalen's approach, but suddenly he was beside me.

"Eithne." He grabbed me by the arm. "Stop. We need to talk."

I didn't even pause as I shook his hand off.

"Don't touch me. You have no right."

"Please stop. I can explain."

"Who is Lunn?"

Now the pull came from further off to the left. I corrected my path.

"Would you stop walking for just a moment? Let me explain."

I was tempted to keep going. Find the damn portal and get out of here. Leave Kalen behind and hope his heart hurt as much as mine did. But I stopped. I held my head high and looked him in the face. I squashed down the feelings that rose when I saw the pain in his eyes. Whatever I might have once felt for him was gone, I told myself. He had no control over me anymore.

"Has anything you ever said to me been the truth?" I asked. "Or was it all just tales, made up to amuse yourself as you toyed with a mortal woman?"

"It was all true. I promise. I've never lied to you. I mightn't have told you everything, but I never lied."

"Who is Lunn and how does he know Grainne?"

"Lunn is — was — an old friend. We played together as boys, before he knew I was half mortal. I didn't know it then myself. The day he found out was the day he started hating me.

"And then Sumerled came along. I have more of Oberon's blood than my mother's and can pass for fey, but he can't. He bothered Lunn one too many times and one day I caught Lunn holding his head under the water in a pond. I talked him into letting Sumerled live on the condition that I kept the boy away from him. But Sumerled doesn't listen to anyone, including me. He does what he wants."

"How does Grainne come into all this?"

"I don't know. Lunn is not nice to women and there's only one way a mortal woman would attract his interest. You want to hope your friend hasn't experienced that."

"She wouldn't have given herself to him. She loves Caedmon."

I started to walk away, but Kalen's next words stopped me in my tracks.

"I meant everything I said, Eithne. And all of the things I didn't say but probably should have. You meant — mean — a great deal to me. There were days I almost wished I was fully mortal, just so we could spend more time together and I didn't need to worry about Titania finding out about you."

"It's too late," I said. "I was a foolish girl, but I've learnt a lot the last few months, about myself and about the fey. I can't be with one of your kind. I'm not willing to sit and wait and hope that one day you'll come back to me. Not willing to pray every night that you haven't lost interest. If I'm ever with somebody, he'll be mortal."

"I've treated you badly, I know. I can make amends though. We could start over."

He caught up to me and walked beside me. His arm brushed my sleeve and suddenly I couldn't think straight. I couldn't concentrate on finding the portal while he was so close. I stopped walking, although I couldn't look at him for fear I would change my mind. I stared down at my boots, half buried in golden leaves, and forced myself to say the words I knew I had to.

"It's not what I want anymore."

"I never meant to hurt you."

Kalen touched me on the cheek. His fingers were cool and gentle. It seemed my stupid heart, which leapt crazily, didn't yet understand that we couldn't be together.

When I didn't berate him for touching me, Kalen took a step closer. He was barely a handspan away from me. If I leaned in just the tiniest bit, I could close the gap between us. But it would only be temporary. I could never close the gap between mortal and fey. There was a reason our two races weren't meant to mix.

The fey were addictive but they were also unfeeling, calculating, unknowable. We were emotional, irrational and totally unprepared for how they could make us feel. No wonder so many of the old tales told of mortal women who gave up everything for them. I understood it now. But I hardened my heart. It didn't matter. The only thing that mattered was finding my way home.

I turned away and started walking again. Kalen followed me.

4 8

GRAINNE

*S*everal days after he had captured me, Lunn finally gave me a bucket of almost-warm water and allowed me to bathe. He refused to leave while I washed, so I had no choice but to strip in front of him. He had already seen me naked anyway. When I had finished, I still didn't feel clean and there wasn't enough water to wash my hair or my clothes but at least I managed to remove some of the grime from my skin. Lunn waited until after I had finished bathing before he left.

There was no need for him to restrain me when he was gone, for there was no exit other than the doorway that appeared only when Lunn wanted it to. I carried the chain attached to my collar as I explored his chamber. It was clean to the point of fastidiousness. When I ran my finger over the wooden surfaces, there was not a trace of dust. Other than the clothes he dropped on the floor each night — which were always gone before I woke — everything else he owned was neatly put away. I investigated every corner of his chamber and felt no guilt at going through his meagre possessions.

Where he went, I had no idea and I preferred not to know. When he was at home, I badgered him. I demanded he take me to Caedmon and I reminded him of the sad life he himself led. I told him of everything Caedmon had to live for in the mortal world: his family, the son he wanted, his career, the house we were building, Silver Downs itself. And gradually cracks appeared in Lunn's facade. He became snappy with me and sometimes he ignored me for hours on end.

He had been gone for at least half a day this time. When he returned, I was sitting in the chair in which I slept, half dozing while I waited for him.

"Let me try," I said as the doorway appeared and he stepped inside. "I have the right to at least try to bring my husband back."

"You have no chance of getting through to him." He sounded exasperated. He pulled his shirt over his head and dropped it on the floor, then sprawled on one of the chairs, his legs stretched out in front of him. His torso was lean, the skin as white as his face. He leaned his head against the chair back and closed his eyes. "I have told you over and over. He will not remember you. And he will not willingly give up his life here."

"Then what does it hurt to let me try?"

"Why are you so certain you can get through to him?"

"Because I am his wife. I represent everything he has to live for."

He didn't reply although I waited for a long while.

"Lunn—"

He cut me off. "What would you give for the chance to speak with him?"

Vivid memories of my night with him flashed through my mind. I pushed them away and kept my voice steady.

"I have nothing to give. You have already taken everything I have."

Lunn opened his eyes and looked at me.

"I will give you one chance. One chance in which to convince your man to hear you. If you fail, you will stay here with me forever. And you will never mention him again."

"Three chances," I countered. "Three and if I fail, I stay."

Lunn considered my offer for so long that I really thought he would refuse.

"Fine," he said at last. "Three chances. And if you fail, you are mine."

I swallowed hard and reminded myself to breathe. The thought of spending the rest of my life wearing Lunn's collar was unbearable. I'd find a way to kill myself before I endured that.

Lunn rose and came to stand in front of me. I shrank back into my chair a little when he reached for me, memories of his clawed hands still fresh in my mind. But all he did was press his finger to my collar. It opened and fell into my lap. At the same time, the doorway appeared in the earthen wall.

I touched the tender skin of my neck. It was raw, bruised and swollen. But at last the collar was off. I was determined to never wear it again.

"Will you take me to the place where the hunt will pass by?" I asked.

"I think I've done enough already."

He returned to his chair, leaned back and closed his eyes again.

The collar still lay in my lap. I wanted to throw it away from me but was reluctant to touch it even that much.

"Please Lunn. Give me a fair chance."

"I've already given you three chances. I hope, for your sake, you don't squander them."

"I will get through to him. You'll see."

He shrugged but didn't open his eyes.

"You will or you won't. Time will tell."

"Take me to him. Please."

He sighed. "Oh, what difference does it make. I may as well. I've already all but handed him to you."

I kept my mouth shut. He might well change his mind yet. When he stood and went to the doorway, I followed. The collar fell to the floor. I left it there.

I kept close behind him as he strode through the woods. He left me by an old oak tree. It might have been the same one we hid behind the last time we watched the hunt.

"They will come past here sooner or later," he said. "It may not be today, though, or even tomorrow."

"I will wait."

"Keep out of the path of the horses. They will not hesitate to ride straight over you. You will be crushed to death if they do."

"Thank you for the warning."

Lunn shook his head. "You are determined, for a mortal woman. It almost makes me hope you will succeed."

"Thank you," I said. "I think."

Lunn turned and left without a backward glance. I sat in the leaves beneath the oak and leaned back against its trunk. I breathed in the earthy scent of the woods. There was nothing to do now but wait.

49

GRAINNE

ime passes slowly in the fey woods. Or perhaps it doesn't pass at all. Leaning back against the rough trunk of the oak tree, I shredded a fallen leaf, gradually reducing it to slivers. My mouth was dry and my fingers shook a little. What would Caedmon do when he saw me? Perhaps he would lean down and swoop me up so we could ride like the wind to the portal? I saw myself sitting behind him astride the horse, the scraps of my skirt trailing behind us, my arms around Caedmon's waist. But perhaps he would tell me he didn't want to leave. That he liked his life here and I should go home and forget about him.

Or if Lunn was right, he would see me, but not remember his wife or that we had handfasted only a few weeks before Lunn stole him away. He might have forgotten the house we had started building or the son he had hoped I would be carrying before he left for the campaign front. He might not remember his career as a soldier, the enemies he had faced, the scars he bore, the nightmares that some-times woke him in the dead of night. I didn't let my thoughts linger long on this possibility, for I would lose all hope if I did. No, he would remember me. He would want to come home and we would leave this place together. I would make sure of it.

I dozed on and off, sometimes waking with a start, certain I had heard the hunt approaching before realising it had been nothing more than a dream. Had Caedmon been with the fey riders who captured Eithne and me when we first passed through the portal? Could I have found him then if I had thought to look? Perhaps he had even attended the feast where I stood behind Lunn's chair and ate scraps from his plate.

Eventually, the ground began to vibrate and the faint baying of the hounds reached my ears. The rough bark of the oak's trunk caught at my hair as I scrambled to my feet. I stood close to the oak as Lunn had instructed. My hands trembled and I clasped them tightly together.

At last the hounds tore by. As the riders came into sight, I scanned them impatiently. At last I saw Caedmon. He rode right in the middle of the hunt. There were horses on each side of him, and in front, and behind. I could get no closer for fear of being trampled. I called out, but he didn't even look towards me. They were gone before I could do anything else.

I sank down to the ground. Tears trickled down my cheeks and for just a moment, I let them. Then I wiped them away and sat back against the tree to wait. One chance gone.

The time before the hunt came again was long and lonely. Even after all these months — or was it years? — I couldn't tell what time of day it was. The noon-bright light never changed. Yet there were times when the woods quieted around me, as if all its creatures slept. I had come to think of this as night, even though the sun was just as strong.

I dozed and ate juicy blackberries from a nearby bramble bush and stared at my ragged nails. My palms were calloused and the skin on my fingers peeled. A far cry from the smooth, white hands I once had. Back then, these hands knew no harder work than mending or cooking or pulling weeds in the garden. Now they knew what it was to labour day after day without respite or soothing salves. These were nothing like the smooth fingers that had once touched Caedmon. What would he think of my new hands?

When the distant sounds of the hunt came next, I was ready. The hounds ran past, sniffing and baying. When the riders appeared, I held my breath as I scanned every face and prayed Caedmon would be where he might see me. The fey no longer looked peculiar to me, with their thin frames and pale skin, their angular faces and high cheek bones. Caedmon was dark haired and dark eyed like them, but his shoulders were broad and well-muscled and he was not as tall as them.

My heart leapt when I saw him, for this time he rode on the outer edge, on the side where I waited. I risked stepping out a little further. I took a deep breath as he approached. Just a little closer. A little more. Then I would jump out and call to him.

Something slammed into me, pushing me backwards into the leaves. My head smacked against the oak. Before I could recover, Caedmon was gone.

"No," I cried. "Caedmon!"

But of course he didn't hear me.

I lay in the leaves, catching my breath. At last I forced myself to rise. My head ached and bright lights sparked at the edges of my vision. My palms were grazed and my back throbbed.

What had happened? It couldn't have been one of the horses for I would have been trampled. A fey rider perhaps, leaning out to the side, to knock me away, out of Caedmon's sight? Whatever the cause, it was done and Caedmon was gone again.

Two chances gone. Only one left.

50

GRAINNE

I was ready for them the next time. I would risk being trampled to death if I must, for this was my last chance. Death was better than forever as Lunn's plaything.

As the thundering of the horses and the hounds' baying reached my ears, I stepped out into the middle of the area through which they would pass. My heart pounded so loud that it merged with the sound of the approaching herd until I could hear nothing else.

The leaders came into sight, bearing down on me on their enormous white horses. The rest of the hunt was only moments behind. I braced myself, half expecting they really would trample me as Lunn had said. Instead they reined in their horses and surrounded me. I could see nothing but horses and the legs of the fey riders.

"Caedmon!" I screamed. Where was he?

One of the horses whinnied and reared up. I jumped out of the way of its enormous hooves and then, in a gap between horses, I saw him. He leaned over his horse's neck, murmuring to it as it danced sideways. I pushed my way through the gap.

"Caedmon, it's me, Grainne. Your wife."

If he heard me, he gave no acknowledgment. I moved closer and grabbed him by the leg.

"Caedmon, look at me."

He still didn't respond. Panic flashed through me. I had only moments, if that, in which to act. If the fey decided to leave now before I could get his attention, my last chance would be gone.

I grasped Caedmon's leg and pulled hard. His horse scuttled sideways again, but I held fast to his leg and suddenly he came sliding off. We landed on the ground in a tangle of limbs. Something hit me hard in the chest. His elbow, or maybe a knee. I clutched his leg, gasping for breath.

A slow clapping reminded me we were not alone. Several fey riders stood in a loose circle around us.

"Well, wasn't that impressive," said one who held himself with a regal air. His voice had the tone of one accustomed to being obeyed. The leader of the hunt, I assumed.

"His name is Caedmon and he is a mortal man." The words came out of my mouth before I had time to think. "He is mine and I claim him."

I had no idea what made me say such a thing, but something about my words felt very right.

The leader laughed and that seemed to be a signal for the others to laugh also.

"Do you understand the rules?" he asked. "If you seek to claim him, you must be able to hold him."

"I can hold him," I said, still clinging tight to Caedmon's leg. He had twisted himself around and half sat up, although he made no attempt to remove his leg from my grasp. He stared at me blankly. I tried not to fear the lack of recognition in his eyes.

"He is mine."

"We'll see how long you last," the leader said.

Caedmon began to squirm in my arms and as I looked at him, his familiar features melted away. He became a black hog, wriggling and snorting in my arms. Its rank odour filled my lungs and brought bile to my throat, but I clutched its bristly leg. It kicked and its hoof caught me in the stomach.

This is Caedmon. He is mine.

Eventually the hog stopped wriggling and relief flooded through me. It was over.

The hog's features began to shift and soon it was the leg of a brown bear that my arms were wrapped around. It swiped me with its paw, catching me in the shoulder and knocking me onto my side. I held tight to its leg.

You will not take him from me.

The bear became a horse, which became a snarling hound. The hound bit my hand and its tooth sliced through my skin, all the way down to the bone. I ignored the pain and hung on.

Mine.

I was only vaguely aware of the fey around us. They laughed and jeered, but I barely heard them.

As a raven, Caedmon cawed and pecked at my face. As a bee, he slipped right through my fingers, but I made a wild snatch and caught him. He stung me twice before changing into a tom cat. Fierce and wild, the cat sank claws and teeth into my arms.

Mine.

Hour after hour, creature after creature, some I couldn't even name. I hung on with everything in me. With every new creature, I thought *Mine.*

A serpent wriggled in my grip. I wrapped both hands around its slender body as its fangs sank into my arm.

Mine.

The serpent grew bigger. Limbs appeared. Then suddenly it was Caedmon, in his own form, who lay in my arms. He didn't struggle but appeared to be sleeping. I still clutched him, afraid he would change again and slip away from me if I let go.

"Is it over?" I asked, panting.

The leader shrugged and turned away. He mounted his horse. Only once he was astride did he look at me again.

"Take him if you wish. I tire of this."

"He is mine?" Was this just another of their tricks?

"You have held him all night," he said. "It is your right to claim him now if you wish."

"I claim him. Caedmon is mine."

The other fey mounted their horses and then, in a thundering of hooves, they were gone.

Caedmon lay on his side. His clothes were clean enough and someone had patched them, but his face was lined and deep shadows underscored his eyes. He was thinner than I remembered and his fingernails were crusted with dirt. He smelled different, as if the fey realm had tainted him, but I detected a faint underlying scent that I recognised as his.

Mine, I thought, fiercely.

"Caedmon." I shook him gently. "Wake up."

Eventually he stirred and opened his eyes. He stared up at me blankly for several heartbeats but slowly recognition seeped into his gaze.

"Grainne?"

"You remember me?" Tears filled my eyes and I blinked furiously to chase them away.

"Where are we?"

"You don't know?"

Caedmon shook his head and winced. "I feel like I have been in a deep sleep and just woke up. I dreamed, vividly, but it's mostly gone now. What happened?"

"You were taken by the fey, but I claimed you."

"We're in the fey realm?" Caedmon slowly started to rise and I reluctantly let go of him. "Grainne, we need to leave."

He extended his hand to me and I gratefully accepted his help. The many bites and kicks and tears I had suffered as I held onto him were painful, but they would heal soon enough. Once I was on my feet, I wove my fingers through his.

"I will hold on to you until we get out of here," I said. "Just in case."

With his free hand, Caedmon touched me briefly on the cheek. "I don't know what happened, but I assume I am not here by my own choice. I guess you came to find me. So thank you."

More tears and I dashed them away.

"I did what I had to, and it's my fault you were here anyway. Now let's go home."

As we started walking, I remembered Eithne. I hesitated to tell him, for I didn't want to give him any reason to linger, but he would want to know.

"Your sister is here, somewhere."

Caedmon froze. "Why?"

"It's a long story."

"Is she safe?" He didn't look at me, as if not wanting to guess the truth if I lied.

"I don't know. There is one of the fey who might help her. But even if he doesn't, she is strong. You have no idea how strong she is."

"Do you know where she is now?"

"No. This realm is vast and we have been separated for weeks, maybe longer."

Caedmon exhaled, long and slow. "Then whatever fate has befallen her is probably long past. I want to see you safely home, then I'll come back for Eithne, if I can."

We walked for hours, searching for the portal. We stopped to rest once, lying on soft moss. I lay with my back pressed against Caedmon's chest, his arms around me. Even as we lay there, I kept my fingers threaded through his. I would not risk someone snatching him away from me.

"You should sleep for a while," he said. "I will keep guard."

"Do you promise you will stay awake? And not let go of me?"

"I promise."

I woke with a start from a dream in which Caedmon had turned into a raven and flown away as I slept.

"I'm here, Grainne," came his voice from behind me, even before I realised his arms were still tight around my waist. "You didn't sleep long."

"It was enough. You should sleep now."

He did, although I sensed he wanted to argue. But he held his tongue and soon his breathing deepened. I was content to lie with his body pressed against mine, the smell of him all around me, and our fingers tangled together. He slept for only an hour or two, then we continued on our journey through the woods, hand in hand.

"What does the portal look like?" Caedmon asked.

"I don't know. We passed through it without realising."

"They wanted you to come then."

"Does that mean they can stop us from going home?"

"Probably."

Leaves crackled behind us.

"Who would do such a thing, my dear Grainne?"

I knew who it was even without looking. A shiver of disgust crept over me. I had spent days listening to that voice and had hoped never to hear it again.

We turned to face Lunn. Caedmon looked puzzled as if he vaguely recognised him.

"You remember my husband," I said.

Lunn raised his eyebrow. "So. You managed to claim him. You impress me, Grainne."

"We are going home."

Lunn smiled and my blood froze.

"Aren't you forgetting something?" he asked.

"What?"

"He can never go home."

Beside me, Caedmon was very still. "Explain yourself."

"The tale your bard brother told. As long as you are in this realm, its power cannot reach you. But if you return to the world of mortals, you are again subject to the magic your brother wrought."

"I claimed him," I said. "He is free now."

Lunn's lips lifted into something that resembled a smile.

"You have gone to much effort to locate him, my dear, but I'm afraid it has all been for naught. For if you wish him to live, he must remain here."

"No," I said. "There must be a way around that. There has to be, or you would have said something earlier. You would have dissuaded me if you could have."

"I didn't believe you would succeed," Lunn said. "It seemed pointless to tell you."

"How do I break the enchantment? Tell me and I will do it."

"I'm afraid you can't. Your man's brother is a powerful bard. It is only a matter of time."

"But I claimed him." I wrapped my fingers tighter around Caedmon's, fearing that even now he would be torn away from me. "The leader of the hunt agreed. He is free to leave."

"Yes, he may leave, if he wishes. But as soon as he steps foot in the mortal world, his life is forsaken."

"I don't believe there is nothing I can do. There is always a way."

If Lunn felt any pity for me, it did not show in his face. "Your man may remain here, if he wishes. Or he may leave. The choice is his."

"Then he stays," I said, and my heart shattered.

Caedmon's hand tightened around mine.

"Grainne—"

"No, I know what you are going to say and I won't allow it."

"Can she stay here with me?" Caedmon asked.

"I'm afraid not," Lunn said. "My contract with her requires I allow you to stay in order to protect you. But I have no further obligation to her."

"I will make a new contract with you," Caedmon said. "To protect Grainne."

Lunn laughed. "Ask Grainne how she forged her contract, but wait until I leave before you do so."

"There must be something we can do," I said. "I'm not giving up now."

"It wasn't for nothing. You saved your man. If he chooses to abandon that safety, it's his decision. He can stay here if he wishes, but once he passes through the portal, our contract is void."

"Let me make a new contract," I said. "One that will protect him in our world. Or one that will keep me here. I don't care which."

"Aah, lovely Grainne. No, as pleasant as it was, I have no interest in repeating myself."

"So that's it?" I asked. "You're going to let Caedmon be killed?"

"I've fulfilled our contract."

"You can't just let him die."

Lunn turned and walked away, moving as silently as he had appeared.

"Goodbye, Grainne."

We watched as he disappeared between ash and beech. I turned back to Caedmon.

"You can't do this," I said. "You can't just walk out of here and back into danger."

"You forget I'm a soldier." Caedmon placed his palms on my cheeks and kissed my forehead. "Walking into danger is what I do."

"Please. Anything but this."

"My one regret, my dear, will be leaving you. I chose well when I picked you. I was just trying to find a wife I thought I could tolerate waking up to each day. I didn't count on finding one I could fall in love with."

A deep sorrow entered my heart as he gently touched his lips to mine.

"I love you, Grainne. My time here has felt like a dream. I could feel my body move. I could hear what I said, taste what I ate. But I had no control over it. I kept your image fixed firmly in my mind and every day that passed, every step I took, I pretended I was moving that much closer to you. Even when I could hardly remember who you were or why I was trying to get back to you, your image reminded me I had something to live for. Something waiting for me. I just couldn't quite remember who or what or where."

"Please, stay here." I didn't realise I was crying until Caedmon wiped the tears from my face with his fingertips. "I could bear being separated from you for the rest of my life if I knew you were safe. I promise I won't come looking for you again."

"This is no life here. It might seem like every man's dream, doing as you want all day, with no consequences, no cares. But it's a shallow life, half-lived. I would rather come home with you, even if I can't stay long. Now dry your tears, sweet Grainne. Don't leave me with the memory of you crying. I want to be able to picture you smiling as I die."

"I won't be smiling."

"Are you ready?"

"No."

He held my hand firmly. "Together, Grainne."

We stepped forward and suddenly we were at the edge of the woods. And somehow I knew the road in front of us and the far-off mountains shrouded in clouds were in the mortal world. We had already passed through the portal.

51

GRAINNE

This was not the same portal Eithne and I originally passed through, for instead of arriving at the lower end of Silver Downs, we faced an unfamiliar road. A smudge of smoke near the horizon indicated a lodge. Somewhere nearby, cows lowed. The air was fresh and clean after so long breathing the moistness and decay of the woods.

"That way." Caedmon indicated with a nod of his head. "We are less than a day's walk from home."

"Maybe we should go back, try to find the other portal. The one that leads directly to Silver Downs."

"I can't avoid my fate, Grainne." Caedmon's voice was gentle and his dark eyes full of sorrow. "You've done more than any man could ask. I'm sorry I won't be returning home with you, but I'll go as far as I can. You'll make someone else a fine wife one day."

Tears sprang to my eyes and I blinked them away.

"I can't bear to go home just yet. Can we rest for a while?"

"Of course."

He led me back a little ways into the ash and oak and birch. I watched carefully for any unseasonal lushness but saw no sign that we had returned to the fey realm. Caedmon made us a bed of fallen leaves between two stout hazel shrubs. I tried to help but he shooed me away.

"Let me do this, Grainne. You've already saved my life, twice over. Let me provide somewhere for you to rest."

So I stood back and watched as he heaped up the leaves, adding more and more until the pile was almost as high as my waist. Then he held out his hand and helped me into it.

I sank straight down and leaves drifted in to cover me with a soft blanket. Caedmon climbed in beside me, burrowing in until his body was pressed against mine. I turned to face him.

"I've missed you, Grainne." His breath was warm on my face.

"I missed you, too. I wish—"

"I know, but we don't have enough time for regrets."

He kissed me and soon I forgot we lay in a pile of leaves in the woods. I forgot my grimy skin and greasy hair and my stench. His touch was gentle and my body responded as if it had been only yesterday that he last touched me. Memories of Lunn's hands on me wormed into my brain and I pushed them away. If this was to be my last time with Caedmon, I would not let it be tainted with thoughts of Lunn.

Some time later, we tumbled out of the pile of leaves. Caedmon wrapped his arms around me and rested his chin on the top of my head. I pressed my forehead to his chest and breathed in his scent.

"Ready to go home?" he asked.

"You can still change your mind."

"You know I won't."

"I know."

He took my hand and we started back towards the road. I stumbled over a tree root shrouded in leaves, but Caedmon grabbed me around the waist before I could fall. I clung to him for a moment longer than necessary.

"Caedmon, I need to tell you something."

"Anything."

I took a deep breath and peeled myself off him. We kept walking.

Somehow I had never imagined saying this to him. It had seemed too big. Too needy. But I didn't want to live with regrets.

"I've loved you since I was seven summers old."

He took another few paces before darting a glance at me.

"Really?"

I nodded, shy now that the words were said.

"I never knew."

"I'm surprised you didn't. My sisters did their best to tell you every time they saw you."

He tipped his head back and laughed.

"They were always prattling on about one thing or another. I mostly didn't listen. I must have missed whatever hints they dropped."

"And here I was, mortified every time you were within hearing distance of them."

"I wish I had known."

"Would it have made any difference?"

He considered my question, his face serious and thoughtful.

"It might have. It's a serious matter to ask a woman to handfast with you. You never know if you'll be rejected. I had been toying with the idea for some time, but didn't know whether anyone would want a soldier who is away from home most of the year. Had I known you would respond favourably, I might have asked earlier."

We reached the road and turned towards the setting sun. The golden orb melted into the horizon in a riot of gold and lavender and scarlet.

"How beautiful," I murmured.

"Indeed." But Caedmon was looking at me, not at the sun.

I blushed and ran my fingers through my knotted hair.

"I must look like a fright."

"You look like the most wonderful thing I've ever seen."

He took my hand and we continued to walk. In the distance, far ahead of us, a shadow appeared against the flaming sun. It was too far away to see clearly, but my heart froze. I knew what it was. Already Caedmon's fate came for him.

From the corner of my eye, Caedmon looked as calm as ever. He walked in his usual straight-backed way, a result of his soldier training I assumed. His fingers around mine were no tighter than they had been, although his palm now sweated just a little.

We walked for a long time before they were close enough to make out. My father and my two brothers. They looked no older than when I last saw them. Perhaps time had passed no faster here than in the fey world. Finally they were right in front of us. We stopped and now Caedmon's grip on my hand was a little tighter.

"Father," I said. "Piran. Wynne. Don't do this, please."

But their eyes were glazed and if they even saw me standing beside Caedmon, they didn't acknowledge me.

Caedmon turned to me. He raised our joined hands and kissed my fingers, his lips warm against my skin.

"Farewell, Grainne."

Then he pushed me so that I stumbled away and was not caught in the middle as they came for him.

5 2

GRAINNE

After it was over, I sat in the ditch on the side of the road with Caedmon's head in my lap. His blood soaked into my skirt and the fabric stiffened as it dried. I stroked his hair and kissed his forehead and cried bitter tears.

As the sun sank behind distant hills, I dragged his body off the road. It was a difficult chore, for he was much larger than I, and solid muscle, even after months of living with the fey, but I couldn't leave him where he had fallen.

I finally managed to drag him onto the grass. I had no way of starting a fire for a pyre, nor any digging implements to bury him. I searched for rocks, thinking to build a cairn over his body, but in the dark I could find nothing but a handful of pebbles. I hated to leave him lying by the side of the road, but there was nothing else I could do. So I kissed him one last time and walked away.

The moon was high in the sky, providing plentiful light as I walked. All around me was still and silent, the birds and dogs and cows bedded down for the night. I prayed I travelled in the right direction, that this road would lead me back to Silver Downs, but I recognised nothing here, especially in the darkness. The air was warm but grew cool as the night wore on. Late summer, perhaps. Had Eithne and I been gone for as little as two seasons?

I encountered nobody during that long night of walking. I paused to rest twice and then only briefly. It was as if I was the last person alive in the world. Perhaps I would walk through the quiet dark forever.

As the sun rose, I reached a crossroads and finally knew where I was. Silver Downs was only a few hours walk from here. When I finally reached the edge of Silver Downs, the tears I had restrained all night broke free and for some time all I could do was stand there and cry. At length I dried my tears and set off again.

The lodge loomed over me, large and imposing as I approached. My footsteps slowed. All night I had kept walking with this one aim, to reach Caedmon's family and relay his fate. Tell them I had tried to save him, but that it wasn't enough. But now I was here, I was afraid.

I forced my feet to keep moving and finally I stood at the front door. I was gathering my courage and wondering whether I should knock, when the door opened. Diarmuid slunk out and met my eyes with a startled gasp.

"You," I spat.

I wanted to call him every vile name, but none came to mind. I wanted to scratch his eyes and kick him and spit on him. But I just stood there and glared at him.

"Grainne." Diarmuid's face was pale and haunted. "You're back. Is Eithne with you?"

"Eithne is somewhere in the realm of the fey." I heard the bitterness in my tone but didn't care enough to restrain it. "And Caedmon is lying dead by the side of the road, although I doubt you were going to ask about him."

Diarmuid leaned heavily against the door and sucked in a breath.

"I'm sorry. I'm so sorry. You have no idea—"

"I have no idea?" My voice was high and loud. "*You* are the one with no idea. I did everything I could to save him. I spent months as a slave. I escaped and was captured by another fey. He kept me as a prisoner, shut up with him in a hole in the ground. I finally escaped again and found Caedmon. I found him and I claimed him, even though they were so sure I couldn't. He knew he would be subject to your vile magic as soon as he left the fey realm, but he did it anyway. And now he's dead and it's all your fault."

I was screaming by the time I finished. Diarmuid huddled against the door and said nothing. Agata had appeared behind him while I spoke. She covered her mouth with her hand and her eyes filled with tears. Then Fiachra was by my side. He wrapped his arm around me and suddenly there was no fight left in me. I sobbed as I let him lead me away.

He took me around the corner of the lodge where there was nobody other than a sheep which must have escaped its paddock. It nibbled at some long grass and considered me with serious eyes. It was some time before I could compose myself. Fiachra simply stood beside me and looked out over the fields.

"It's not fair," I said. "Caedmon should have been safe."

Fiachra said nothing.

"It should have been him. Diarmuid. I sent Caedmon away so he would be safe. The magic should have come for Diarmuid instead."

"Does the death of one brother ever compensate for the life of another?" Fiachra asked.

"But I loved him."

"You have suffered much for your love, and he knew the truth, in the end."

"What truth?"

"Of your love and of his own for you. It might not have been what he expected, but it found him anyway. He was at peace with himself when he died."

"He should have fought them. He could have killed them before they killed him."

"Would you have your husband kill your father and brothers, even to save himself?"

I couldn't reply.

"He did what he thought was right. We grieve him, yes, but we must also respect his decision."

I wiped the tears from my cheeks with my palms.

"Has Eithne come home?"

If I hadn't been looking at Fiachra in that moment, I would have missed the flash of sorrow on his face.

"No, Eithne yet has a long journey to travel."

"Is she safe?"

"As safe as she can be in that place and with one of them."

"Did she find Kalen again?"

He gave me a sad smile.

"Aah, Grainne, that is Eithne's tale and she will tell it when she can."

53

———

EITHNE

*K*alen and I walked in silence. I tried to ignore his presence and instead concentrated on the pull of the portal. I didn't trust myself not to blurt out what I really felt if I spoke to him. The time of our final separation was close and now I doubted my decision.

To distract myself, I focused instead on the sorrow that welled within me when I thought of Grainne. Why had she left me here alone? And why had she concealed the true purpose of her journey from me? I had thought we were friends, sisters even, but now it seemed I never knew her at all.

Kalen cleared his throat as he stopped walking.

"The portal is here. Another few steps and you will be back in your own world."

The woods around us looked no different. A mix of ash and oak and beech. Hawthorn and bramble bushes. Mushrooms grew in the shelter of a rock. Birds called and unseen creatures rustled through the leaf litter. The portal tugged at something inside me, just as it had before, but I saw no sign of it. No wonder Grainne and I never even knew when we passed through it.

I studied Kalen, with his ill-cut hair and his pale skin. The

585

clothes that were too big, the high cheekbones, the dark lips. It had all been for him. Was he worth it? He waited silently while I thought. He had never been inclined to ask me to speak before I was ready.

What was it about him that drew me in? It was more than merely fascination with the fey, with their long lives and indifferent hearts. He and I had a connection I had never experienced with any mortal. I could walk away now and leave him. I could do it. My heart was hard enough right now to let me leave.

But if we parted now, I would regret it until the end of my days, although they would pass like the blink of an eye to Kalen. Hundreds of years would pass before he grew old. Would he remember me? Or would there be many mortal women after me — too many to count? Eithne, he would say, which one was Eithne?

Should I take one last chance before I walked away to a lifetime of regrets? I took a deep breath and spoke before I could change my mind again.

"Come with me," I said. "Back to my world."

Kalen studied me, his dark eyes revealing nothing of his thoughts.

"I would have to leave Sumerled. He wouldn't survive there. He knows nothing of mortal ways."

My breath caught. I couldn't show him how much this meant to me. Even if he came with me, it would probably only be for a while. Years, months, maybe only weeks. But I was too far gone. I would take whatever he offered, even if it wasn't enough.

"It would do him good to look after himself for a change. Father could find work for you at Silver Downs. And find you somewhere to live. We have some tenants who might like to take in a boarder."

He studied me for a long moment. I still couldn't tell what he thought, but finally he nodded. He held out his hand and when I took it, his fingers were cool and steady. Before he could speak, a voice came from behind us.

"You owe me a promise, Eithne."

Sumerled waited there, as small and bedraggled as when I last saw him.

"What sort of promise?" Kalen's tone was suspicious and his fingers tightened around mine. "Eithne, what did you agree to?"

Sumerled danced a little jig.

"She made me a promise. I can choose what I want and she has to give it before she leaves here."

"What exactly did you offer in exchange for this promise, Sumerled?"

"To take her to you."

"You should not have agreed to that."

"But she wanted to find you. I was helping her. You always say I should be more helpful."

"Not by extracting promises from mortals who don't understand what they are agreeing to."

"I knew exactly what I was agreeing to," I said somewhat indignantly, wrenching my hand from his grasp. "And it was my own choice to do so. Sumerled had something I wanted and I had something he wanted. He was the only one who offered us aid. What else could I do?"

"What else? You should never make a promise to the fey. No matter what the reason. The cost is always too high."

His words stung, although I tried to hide it.

"But I never would have found you."

"I would have realised you were here, eventually. And I would have come for you."

"I couldn't wait any longer. I had to find you before Titania found us again. She would have made sure we didn't escape again."

Kalen shook his head and looked back at the boy. "Sumerled, what do you intend to request for your promise?"

Sumerled continued to dance, his feet stepping lightly in the leaf litter, and his face bore an enormous grin.

"You, of course."

"What?" My heart thudded sharply against my rib cage.

"No, Sumerled, you can't," Kalen said.

"I can and I will. It's my promise." Sumerled stuck out his lower lip and crossed his arms. "I can do whatever I want with my promise."

"You knew I only came here to find Kalen," I said. "It's not fair to take away the one thing I want from this realm."

"You didn't say the promise had to be fair," Sumerled countered. "I can ask for whatever I want."

"No," I said. "I refuse. I take it back. I won't give you a promise."

"You have to," he said. "Kalen, tell her she has to."

We both looked at Kalen. His face was filled with regret, but also something that looked strangely like relief.

"I'm sorry, Eithne. If you made Sumerled a promise, it must be fulfilled. There is no other option."

"He can't force me to keep it."

"A promise is the ultimate commitment. Nothing is worth more. Nothing costs more. I won't help you break a promise."

My stomach sank and when I spoke my voice wobbled.

"But that means it was all for nothing. All those months of slavery and being starved and living in a horrid, dark hole. I endured it only to find you."

"That's how promises work. They are dangerous things. You shouldn't have promised Sumerled anything."

"I was desperate. I had no other choice."

I might have thought he would argue with Sumerled, somehow fight to come with me, but Kalen merely released my hand and stepped back, towards the boy.

"Goodbye, Eithne."

"Kalen, don't do this."

He and Sumerled turned and walked back into the woods. I tried to follow, but tangly weeds wrapped around my boots and rooted them to the ground. As long as I tried to follow Kalen, I was stuck fast.

"Kalen, please."

He and Sumerled melted away into the trees and were gone.

5 4

———

EITHNE

The weeds would only release me if I walked in the other direction. Within a couple of steps, I suddenly stood at the edge of the woods on the far end of Silver Downs' lower pastures. Time enough had passed for the last of the snow to melt and the grass to grow tall.

It turned out I was no different to any other mortal woman who went chasing after some fey, only to find she had already been forgotten. I glanced back at the woods once, twice, hoping Kalen had changed his mind. That he might have merely pretended to leave with Sumerled. But he didn't come back.

The sun was warm on my shoulders as I made my way across the fields. I felt strong, eager to be home at last. I would not look back again. The chapter of my life that contained Kalen was over. Yet I couldn't help but steal a glance back from time to time, pretending I checked whether a bee had landed on my shoulder or some such other nonsense.

I had walked for only a few minutes before I noticed I limped. It had been so long since my twisted foot had bothered me that I barely remembered what it felt like. Already the familiar shortness of breath and light-headedness crept over me.

I pushed on, striding only slightly slower through the thick grass. The months I had spent as a slave had taught me that what I used to think were my limits were a construct of my own imagination. But soon the ground began tilting from side to side and I sank down into the grass to rest. It seemed my limits were not artificial constructs after all, at least not in the mortal world.

The grass where I rested was verdant and stood almost to my knees. This would make fine grazing ground. We rarely grazed the livestock down here in the lower fields, only in the upper pastures where the soil had better drainage and more sun. But it seemed these fields were much improved. I had better remember to tell Father or Eremon.

I set off again, more slowly this time. Everything looked bigger, wilder, more colourful than I remembered. The sky was bluer, the sun brighter, the grass an emerald shade.

I walked and rested, walked and rested. The sun began its journey down toward the horizon before I reached the stand of beech trees where Kalen and I had secretly met so many months ago. I paused to rest on my rock. It was more weathered than I remembered, and blackened with mould, but it still held the sun's warmth, just as it always had. The beeches were taller and their branches spread further than I remembered. I didn't dare wonder just how many months had passed. I would find out soon enough.

I slid off the rock and started the last part of my journey home. The lodge was only just out of sight. I would see it as soon as I crested the small rise in front of me. Some of my brothers might even still be out in the fields. The rise was only gentle but my fatigued legs resisted even so small a hill. My calf ached from the effort of walking with my deformed foot. I trudged on and at last I came to the top. I could hardly believe what I saw.

The house was still recognisable but only barely. The bones of what I once knew were there, but one wing was entirely gone, replaced with another of different materials and a different structure. The barn which Father had always kept watertight and snug so that the animals would be warm on winter nights was gone. A new, larger barn stood some distance away. New fencing ringed a paddock, new vegetable gardens. Day's eye bushes were planted in front of the house, a new path laid. It was wrong, all wrong. Men worked in the fields and even a couple of women, but nobody I knew by silhouette, at least not from this distance. Nobody who was recognisable as Papa or Eremon or Marrec or Conn.

I ran the last of the way home with my heart pounding and my breath catching in my lungs. How long had I been gone?

"Papa," I shouted, although I knew I was too far away for him to hear me if he wasn't out in the fields. "Papa, where are you?"

The workers turned to stare at me. They weren't close enough to see clearly, but I was sure none were my brothers.

"Papa," I called again.

The front door opened and an old man hobbled out, leaning heavily on a cane. His back was stooped and his slender shoulders hunched. He had the look of our family about him, but I could not place his face. He peered at me, then took a few steps nearer to look at me more closely.

"Eithne?" His voice was full of wonder. "Is it really you?"

"Where is my father?" I asked. I tried to swallow my fear.

"Eithne." Tears began to trace their way down his wrinkled cheeks. "Eithne, it's me. Diarmuid. Your brother."

I opened my mouth to call him a liar, but the words died on my lips as I looked harder. Traces of the Diarmuid I once knew were still there, in the slant of his forehead and the colour of his eyes. His hair was grey now and his face bore wrinkles that were testament to the passing of years.

"Diarmuid?"

"It's been sixty years, Eithne," he said and his voice wobbled. "Everyone else is gone. It's just me left, and Fiachra, although he doesn't come here often."

"I don't understand." The world spun around me.

Diarmuid called into the house, "Boy, bring a chair. Quickly now."

A boy of about ten summers ran out with a wooden chair that

looked almost as heavy as he. He placed it beside me and bowed with a small flourish then skipped away.

"One of Eremon's great-grandsons," Diarmuid said. "He keeps me company. He has aspirations of being a bard and he thinks I might teach him something if he stays long enough."

"Do you still tell tales?" It wasn't what I wanted to ask but there were so many questions, I didn't know where to start. How could I ever ask them all?

"Not anymore. I did, for a while. Enough to learn how the magic worked but then never again. I have regretted that last tale you heard for sixty years. I killed Caedmon with it. Better that you know. We buried him near the house he had built for himself and Grainne."

"I've only been gone a few months," I said.

"And you look little older than the last time I saw you. They always hoped you might return home some day."

"Papa?"

"He died about thirty years ago and Mother followed him only a year or two later. Our brothers died one by one over the last few years. Eremon was the last, just a few months ago. He wanted to be here when you came home. Papa made him promise he would be."

"Who runs the estate now?"

"His eldest son. The younger is a druid."

An elderly woman appeared in the doorway behind Diarmuid. Time had been kinder to her than to him, although the wisps of hair that escaped her bun were solid grey. She stared at me keenly with eyes that were still as sharp as a hawk's.

"Diarmuid?" she said. "Why don't you bring your visitor inside."

"My wife." He tipped his head towards her. "Brigit, although I call her Bramble. Dear, it's Eithne."

"Your sister?" She covered the ground between us swiftly to hug me with the strength of a much younger woman. "Welcome, my dear. One of the boys sleeps in the bedchamber that used to be yours, but I'll have it cleaned out and ready for you by night."

If she thought anything odd in my appearance, she gave no indication of it.

"That's very kind of you." I suddenly felt like a stranger.

"You must have a curious tale to tell," Brigit said, her steady gaze giving nothing away.

Tears sprang to my eyes and I brushed them away. I nodded, not trusting my voice.

"There will be time enough to tell it. Come inside. You look like you need rest, and some good food. Annick, Eremon's youngest daughter, does most of the cooking these days. She'll fatten you up in no time." Brigit leaned closer and rested a hand against my cheek. "The fevers, they still come?"

"They haven't, for a while. But maybe now…"

She nodded. "I'll make up a potion for you. I can help keep the illness at bay."

We went into the house, Diarmuid hobbling ahead of us, calling directions to boys who seemed to spring out of nowhere. The children scattered, each sent off on his own task.

Brigit led me into the family room and pulled a chair close to the fireplace. The furniture was all different. One or two chairs I thought I recognised, although they had been restored and maybe they were different chairs entirely.

"This is where you used to sit, is it not?" she asked.

"How do you know?"

She smiled at me and there was both wisdom and acceptance in it.

"I see things that others don't. I, too, once travelled a long way in search of something I thought I wanted, only to discover that what I wanted most in the world was already right in front of me."

I sank down into the chair. A boy already crouched in front of the fireplace and soon a small fire blazed merrily. Its warmth bathed my skin and I sighed with relief, closing my eyes as I leaned back. Home.

"You can come in now," Brigit said, and something in her voice made me open my eyes.

There in the doorway stood Kalen.

I tried to say something but my mouth wouldn't work. I didn't know whether to fling myself at him or to pretend I didn't care why he was here. I supposed it didn't matter, though, as I didn't have the strength to rise anyway.

"Kalen," I said eventually and although I tried to sound disinterested, my voice cracked. "Aren't you breaking my promise?"

"You're the only one who can break your promise."

I was tired and feeling all too easily confused. "Why are you here?"

"Because I don't want to be there without you."

"Where's Sumerled?"

"Safe."

"I don't understand."

"You made a promise. You had to keep it. The only way you could was if you left with no intention of coming back again. You had to leave me there."

"So you intended to follow me all along?"

"Of course I did. Did you really think I would let you walk away, after everything you went through to find me?"

"Why didn't you tell me? I thought you didn't care."

He came closer and crouched down in front of my chair so that we were at eye level.

"Eithne, of course I care. But if you didn't truly believe you were leaving me behind, you would be breaking your promise."

"People break promises all the time."

"The fey don't. A broken promise is a very serious thing. There are consequences."

"What sort of consequences?"

"It doesn't matter now. You kept your promise."

"Does Sumerled know you are here?"

"He knows. He's not happy about it. He was only trying to protect me."

"Will he come after you?"

"He promised he wouldn't."

"I'm not the same here as I am there. It won't be long before the fevers return."

"I know all about your illness. Remember?"

I suddenly felt terribly tired. "Would you ask Brigit whether my bedchamber is ready?"

"Go ahead, Eithne," came Brigit's voice from the doorway. "The boy has moved his things and the bed has been made up fresh for you."

"Thank you."

My voice was much weaker than I wanted it to be. I tried to stand but my legs wobbled violently and my vision dimmed. I sat back down abruptly. Kalen scooped me up in his arms.

"Tell me which way to go," he said. "You're too exhausted to walk."

I directed him through the house in which I had grown up, a house that seemed at once familiar and strange. The door was open when we reached my bedchamber. Kalen set me down just outside the doorway and waited in the hallway. I entered my old bedchamber alone on unsteady legs, both hands grasping the doorframe for support.

The slope of the ceiling was the same, and the knots in the walls. But everything else was changed. Gone were the thick, dark green drapes that had kept out the winter chill. In their place hung lightweight yellow curtains. My bed had been replaced with a newer, larger frame with intricately carved knobs. The dresser too was new, and the cupboard. The ewer and basin on the dresser were made of delicate white pottery, much finer than my own. It might be my old room, but its spirit was new.

"Everything is different," I said. "It's all... wrong."

"This has been someone else's bedchamber for a long time." Kalen closed the door, then came to place his hands at my waist, supporting me as my legs trembled. "Probably several someone elses."

"I didn't know so much time had passed. I knew things might be different, but I thought perhaps a year for every month I stayed, at most. Or perhaps no time at all and I would come back to the same day I left. I never expected to find almost everyone I ever knew is dead."

My voice broke and tears welled in my eyes.

"You never quite know how much time will pass, and it isn't

always the same. If you went back to the fey realm now and returned in six months, you might find only six days had passed."

"My mother died without ever knowing what happened to me. She must have thought… I don't know what she thought."

"Ssh." Kalen turned me around to face him. "Nothing about the realm of the fey is fair or right. It just is what it is. The time has passed. There's nothing you can do about that now, only live for each new day. And I'll be here with you, if you'll have me."

"You'll age here. You'll get old, like Diarmuid. You'll die if you stay here."

"So will you. But you can't return to the fey realm, so I must stay here with you. We will grow old together."

"I wish I had told Mother where I was going. She would have understood. She would have known I had no choice."

A tear spilled down my cheek and Kalen wiped it away with his thumb.

"My kind aren't very good at loving, Eithne. You will have to teach me. And you will have to be patient when I don't understand or I get it wrong. All I know about love I have learned from you. I know there is more to learn, if you will have me."

He kissed me then, gently and carefully, as if he had never before kissed a woman. Kalen lifted me onto the big bed that wasn't mine. His hands were soft and gentle as he showed me things I had never expected to experience for myself. For who would want one such as me, damaged, ill, likely unable to bear children? But Kalen wanted me. It likely wouldn't last, but I would take whatever he offered.

55

EITHNE

e were woken by a gentle tapping on the door.

"Aunt Eithne, Uncle Diarmuid says you should come downstairs," someone said. The voice was young and male, presumably one of Eremon's many descendants. "He says there is someone you will want to see."

I opened my eyes to sunlight streaming through the summery curtains. My old, thick curtains had shielded me from both light and cold, a useful thing when one is often in bed in the middle of the day.

"Who?" I asked.

"I'm not supposed to tell you."

"I'll be down shortly."

The boy scampered away down the hallway. Kalen already stood and was pulling on his clothes. I paused to admire his lanky form which I suddenly knew more intimately than I had ever expected.

"I will need some more clothes," he said. "Two or three sets will suffice."

"I'm sure Diarmuid will sort it out. Or Eremon's heir, he who is the master of Silver Downs now."

It pained me to think of the estate in the hands of someone other than Papa or Eremon. I pulled on the dress Sumerled had provided and tried to ignore the small twinge of guilt that he was now without Kalen's protection. I looked around the bedchamber of a stranger. What had happened to my old clothes and the small things I had possessed? My hairbrush, my hand mirror. My wash basin. My favourite plate and mug. Had they broken in the intervening years? Or were they discarded, unwanted, the remnants of a forgotten inhabitant? I might never know, for Diarmuid would likely not remember such detail and Eremon's descendants wouldn't know. They would care little for the personal items of some long-lost ancestor.

As I left the room, I noticed a wooden box by the door. It was knee-high to me and bore no decoration or label. I must have walked straight past it last night. I knelt beside it and lifted the lid.

Inside were my most treasured possessions. The hairbrush and mirror I had been so fond of. My favourite mug. My two good dresses. A pair of shoes. A wooden ring carved by one of my brothers and accidentally left behind the day I departed, for I had always worn it until then.

Tears dripped from my cheeks as I unpacked memory after memory. I hadn't been discarded after all. Someone had put away my favourite things, perhaps against my possible return, perhaps just wanting to keep something I had loved. Mother probably, for I couldn't imagine any of my brothers doing such a thing.

I undressed and pulled on my old favourite grey gown. It smelled a little musty, and the fabric felt more fragile than I remembered, but it was mine. I slid my feet into my old shoes. They were tighter than they used to be. Perhaps my feet were swollen after my journey.

"Ready?" Kalen asked, wrapping his arms around me from behind.

I leaned back into his embrace. "I'm ready."

We went downstairs hand in hand. My deformed foot was uncomfortable to walk on and my thigh muscles already tired by the time we reached the bottom level. I had no idea who might be here that Diarmuid thought I would want to see. There was nobody left who I cared about except... I ran the last few steps as I realised who waited.

But instead of Grainne, an old woman stood at the fireplace with her back to me. Her shoulders were hunched and she shivered, her arms wrapped around herself despite the summer morning. Her grey hair lay loose against her shoulders.

"Hello?" I said.

She turned to me and my heart dropped. It was Grainne after all, but not the Grainne I remembered. Her face was lined with deep wrinkles and her frame had the thinness of an old woman. When she reached out to me, her hands shook.

"Eithne," she said. "Oh, Eithne, I am so happy you have finally returned."

"Grainne? What happened to you?"

"I got old, Eithne. Only a few months had passed when I returned. I've lived all the years since then wondering whether you were safe. Fiachra said you were, but you never know with a druid."

"I was safe," I said. "For me, it's only been a day or two since we were separated."

She stared at me for a long moment. Her eyes were rheumy and the skin under her chin sagged. I saw only shadows of the Grainne I knew in her, but the warmth with which she looked at me was the same.

"I've always regretted that I left you behind," she said. "Fiachra said your journey wasn't finished, but I still knew I shouldn't have done it. I was only there to find Caedmon. I lied to you about why I went."

I had believed he was dead before we even left home. It hurt to know that she had kept such a secret, despite all those long, dark months together, but I pushed the pain aside. It didn't matter anymore.

She embraced me and her body was far too delicate in my arms. When we pulled apart, she studied Kalen for a long moment.

"So, you brought him with you," she said.

"Not exactly. He followed me."

"I am glad it was not for naught."

Kalen dragged a chair up behind me and gently pushed me down into it. It was only then I noticed how my legs trembled, although whether it was fatigue or the shock of seeing Grainne so aged, I didn't know. A boy bustled in with a tray bearing delicate cups filled with steaming liquid. I accepted one and found it contained a sweet tea. Kalen had disappeared to the back of the room, leaving Grainne and me with a measure of privacy. I sipped my tea and listened to her tale.

I cried as she told me how bravely Caedmon had died and of her long, lonely journey back to Silver Downs. My brothers had retrieved Caedmon's body and buried him near the house he had been building for Grainne. She still lived there with one of Eremon's grand-daughters.

When Grainne finished her tale, I told her what she didn't know of mine.

"I am glad you found him," Grainne said. "Truly."

It was only then I noticed Diarmuid standing in the doorway. His shoulders were hunched, his posture defeated. I didn't know what to say to him. I didn't even want to look at him.

"I know you must hate me." His voice was slow with age and choked with tears. "Both of you. And you are right to. But when I told that tale, I didn't believe it would come true. Caedmon was always my favourite brother. I never meant to kill him."

"He was everyone's favourite," I said, perhaps cruelly. "And he is dead because you were young and foolish."

"I won't be here much longer," he said, abruptly. "Something eats at my insides and my time is close to its end. You will only have to share this house with me for a while."

Brigit bustled into the room.

"I think that's enough for now," she said. "Diarmuid has already talked longer than he should have. He needs to rest."

"I'm glad you have someone who cares for you, Diarmuid." Grainne's voice was bitter. "Would that I had the same."

She left then. I started to follow her, but Brigit stopped me, her wrinkled hand gentle on my arm.

"Let her be, child. She knows you are here for her and she will come to you when she is ready."

"Has she never forgiven him?"

"She has, I think, but your return stirred up old feelings."

I looked into her eyes which were sympathetic and still clear, despite her age.

"How can you stand to be with him, knowing what he has done?" I asked.

"We've been together for a long time. I knew what he was when I fell in love with him. He is a better man than he would have been if not for this. You don't know him, child. He is not the man he was when you left. He has atoned for what he did, in ways you couldn't even begin to imagine. So let him be. Let him die in peace. He has been holding on, hoping you might return one day, but now he can let go."

Her eyes were dry, but her voice was filled with anguish.

"I'm glad he found you," I said.

She smiled as a tear trickled down her cheek.

"Me too, Eithne. Me too."

56

EITHNE

onths passed, then a year. Brigit's potions helped hold the fevers at bay. There were still days where I didn't have the strength to get out of bed, but they were few and not as harsh as they once were.

With time, my body began to change. My belly became swollen with Kalen's child, and my breasts, which had never been much larger than hazelnuts, became plump and round. I feared the babe's birth but Brigit promised to aid me through it. She became something like both grandmother and sister to me.

Diarmuid didn't live to see my child's birth. We buried him under the great oak where so many of our family had handfasted. My parents were buried there too, and my brothers, except for Caedmon.

Brigit mourned Diarmuid's loss and buried herself in her work. She was well respected as a wise woman, apparently, and folk travelled a good distance to consult her. One of Sitric's granddaughters was apprenticed to her and a long line of our women had already been trained by Brigit, starting with a daughter each of Eremon and Marrec, and both of Conn's twin girls.

I found it hard to comprehend that my brothers had left so many descendants, some of whom had died before I came home.

Silver Downs was filled with the shouts and laughter of children and the thundering of feet. Most lived nearby, but Eremon's granddaughter Annick, who had never married, and his grandson Rogan lived in the main lodge, along with Rogan's wife and his seven sons.

Nobody complained about me claiming my old bedchamber and several days after I arrived home, I discovered a new bed had been moved in there, large enough for two. Kalen and I never formally handfasted. After all I had been through to find him, it didn't seem necessary, and indeed without my parents there to witness it, I couldn't bear the thought.

One day, just a few weeks before the babe's birth, we went to the beech trees where we used to meet. It was a long, slow walk, for the child sat low in my belly and carrying her was exhausting. I puffed long before we reached my rock and I sank down onto it gratefully.

The air was warm today and heavy with the scent of honeysuckle. It pleased me that our babe would be born during the summer months. Kalen and I sat together on the rock and talked quietly. We had already agreed the babe's name would be Agata, for my mother. He wanted to choose a boy's name as well, but I was adamant the child would be a girl.

Absorbed in our conversation, it was some time before I noticed Titania. She stood beside a grey-trunked beech, her lips lifted into a sneer. Kalen's words died as he saw her.

"What a lovely setting," Titania said. "Look at the two of you, laughing and carefree."

"Why wouldn't we be?" I asked. I wished I could get to my feet but my legs still trembled from the walk.

"You choose this?" Titania directed her words at Kalen. "You choose this frail mortal and this world over your own?"

"It was never my world," he said. "You made that perfectly clear. With everything you did and everything you said, you reminded me that I lived there only at your indulgence."

"Do you not wonder about the boy? Who protects him without you there to do it?"

"It was time for him to learn to look after himself," Kalen said. "He is no longer my responsibility."

"What do you want, Titania?" I suddenly felt impatient with her questions. "You've already taken almost everything I ever loved. What is left for you to take?"

Her gaze went straight to my belly. I immediately clasped my hands over it.

"No," I said. "You will not take my child."

"She's bred of a fey. She's mine to claim if I will."

"No, she's bred of two mortals. You never recognised Kalen as fey before and you won't start now."

"The child is an abomination. Half mortal, half fey. It should not be allowed to live."

Now I did climb to my feet, slowly and shakily. My voice was low and calm.

"If you harm her, if you touch one hair of her head, I will find you. I will make you pay for it, you and all the rest of your kind. Now go away. Leave the children of Silver Downs in peace. We don't intend you any harm unless you harm us first."

"I could rip the child from your belly as you stand there." Titania looked me up and down with the same scornful expression she had used the very first time we met. "Who do you think you are to threaten me?"

I lifted my chin proudly.

"I am a daughter of Silver Downs. You know there's magic in our blood. We could be dangerous to the fey, if we chose."

Titania spluttered and a faint blush tinged her cheeks.

"You impudent wretch."

My legs trembled more violently now, but then Kalen was beside me with an arm around my waist. I leaned against him gratefully.

"The children of Silver Downs are strong, Titania," I said. "We're only just discovering how strong we are. You don't want to cross us again."

Titania glared at me for a few moments longer, then suddenly she was gone. I sank back down onto the rock. My legs trembled even after I sat.

"I think you scared her," Kalen said with something like a laugh.

"Somebody told me once that I have my own power. I think it's time I figured out what it is."

"Brigit can probably help you with that."

"I'm sure she can," I said. "I will speak to her as soon as we get home. My child will not live in fear of Titania. I'll find a way to protect her, and a way for her to protect herself. We must sit here a little longer though. I don't think I can manage the walk home just yet."

Kalen sat back beside me on the rock. He draped an arm around my shoulder.

"Take as long as you need, my love," he said. "We have all the time in the world."

ACKNOWLEDGEMENTS

Thank you to my beta readers, Megan and Hannah.

Thank you to Deranged Doctor Design for once again producing a beautiful cover. I love this one even more than the last.

Thank you to Meghan for assisting with editing.

Thank you to those who read *Muse* and, even more, to those who enjoyed it. *Muse* was a story about a boy who didn't want to be a hero. *Fey* is about strong women who readily step up to be heroes. It was also an attempt to keep Caedmon alive. I spent the entire story trying to find a way around the magic of Diarmuid's tale but regrettably it just wasn't possible. Caedmon accepted his fate with more grace than I did. The story in *Druid* takes place a little later than *Muse* and *Fey* and continues the theme of heroes.

And, finally, thank you to my family for tolerating my continued absence while I write.

KYLIE QUILLINAN

TALES OF SILVER DOWNS

DRUID

BOOK 3

KYLIE QUILLINAN

For my dear friend, Claudia,
Who doesn't read fantasy
and will probably never see this.

1

———

ARLEN

I sat cross-legged in front of a pond. Its depths were clear and calm, with just the slightest ripple. The woods around me rang with birdcalls and the rustle of leaves from various forest creatures. I stared into the pool and concentrated on letting go of all thought.

As my mind became as calm as the water, my body also relaxed. The mossy ground was cool and slightly damp beneath my linen trousers. A beetle crawled over my bare foot. I inhaled, filling my lungs with the scent of moist earth, cool water and rotting leaves. I watched the water and tried not to let anxiety crowd into my mind. Eventually, I would master control of the Sight. If I waited long enough and kept my mind still enough, the waters would show me something. A voice from behind me disrupted the stillness I concentrated so hard on.

"Arlen, Oistin asks that you go to him."

I sighed and pushed my irritation aside. It was not the boy's fault I had managed to achieve the calmness I sought only moments before he spoke.

"Did he want me urgently, Pilib?" My gaze never left the water, hoping I might yet See something.

"He asked that you go immediately. He's in his bedchamber."

I nodded and heard just the faintest rustle of leaves as the boy retreated. I shouldn't have been able to hear him at all, but he was an apprentice just newly arrived. He had much to learn yet. With one last wistful glance into the pond, I climbed to my feet and brushed the dirt from the seat of my trousers.

As I set off through the woods, I wondered what Oistin wanted. Perhaps he intended to ask me to take a new boy under my wing. Perhaps he merely planned to ask after my studies. I pushed the thoughts from my mind. There was no point in speculating. I would find out soon enough.

The stone lodge stood in the middle of a large clearing deep within the woods. The remoteness of the location suited us, for those training to be druids spend much time alone. Surrounded by woods as we were, there were plenty of quiet places for a druid to wander off by himself. Many a day had I spent perched in the branches of a tree, or sitting on a flat rock, or roaming the woods, reciting the lore we learned, practising calling the elements, or trying to master the Sight.

The heavy wooden door of the lodge stood open. It was rarely closed. Inside was cold and dark, for evening approached and the lamps had not yet been lit. The aroma of vegetable soup and fresh bread made my mouth water and reminded me I hadn't eaten yet today. I made my way through the corridors to Oistin's quarters.

As the master druid, Oistin had a bedchamber that although modest, was far larger than the one I shared with three others. I rapped softly on the open door, waiting until he bade me enter. The room contained a bed, which was neatly made, some shelves, a cupboard, and a large desk. Its window looked out at an elegant rowan tree. Oistin sat behind the desk, examining a piece of parchment which he held close to his face.

"Arlen." He placed the parchment on the desk and waved me in.

"You wished to see me?"

"Yes, yes." For a moment, Oistin looked puzzled, as if he couldn't recall why he had summoned me, then he nodded. I suspected he wasn't as forgetful as he sometimes pretended. He ran our community with tight reins and rarely let an important detail slip. "I have a task for you."

I waited.

"I am sending you to Braen Keep to be an advisor to Hearn. You will leave as soon as you pack your belongings."

"Master?" My carefully cultivated calmness evaporated.

"It's a new stage of your journey, boy. A grand adventure. Great responsibility."

"You're sending me to the king?"

"He needs a trustworthy advisor. Someone honourable. Someone who will guide him with the country's best interests in mind."

Oistin looked at his desk, at the window, at the rug-covered floor. Anywhere other than at me.

"Master, I don't understand."

How could he have forgotten? Oistin knew my greatest failing as a druid. He knew why I was the person least suitable to undertake such a task.

"I know it might seem intimidating. You'll be surrounded by more people than you're accustomed to. It'll be noisier. You'll need to find a quiet place of your own where you can continue to practise your craft."

"How will I advise the king?" I asked. "You know I have no ability with the Sight."

Oistin sighed and finally looked at me.

"You will do what you must do, Arlen. Now, go gather your belongings so we can send you on your way. Tonight you will dine in the king's hall."

"Does this mean my training is concluded?"

He studied me before he responded. He knew there was a personal task I planned to complete as soon as I finished my training. A task I had never kept secret from him and that I had no intention of postponing. I would repay my training and serve as druid wherever he wanted to send me — once my task was complete.

"Your training is suspended," Oistin said. "You must continue to learn what you can in the meantime. When Hearn no longer requires you, you will return here to finish your training."

I left Oistin's bedchamber with my head held high and my shoulders straight. I breathed deeply — in, out, in — as I strode along the corridors to my own bedchamber. A sigh of relief when I arrived to find it empty of my fellow druids. Our accommodations were sparse: four narrow cots, each draped with a grey blanket, one cot against each wall. A well-worn rug covered the wooden floor. Our belongings, such as they were, were stored in boxes beneath our cots. We were permitted two boxes each. Our bedchamber was in the middle of the lodge, so there were no windows. The stone walls were bare with the exception of a small shelf holding a lamp, which I lit with trembling hands.

I sank onto my cot and dropped my head into my hands. I had grievously offended Oistin. Why else would he punish me in such a way? To send me away, my training incomplete, was a clear indication I had failed.

I had always expected to leave the community eventually. Other than those few druids who remained here to teach, most stayed only for the ten years of our training. They departed to perform the roles for which we had studied: advisor, confidante, teacher. They interpreted visions and signs, performed ceremonies, led festivities. All except for me.

Twelve summers had passed since the druids came to take me from Silver Downs. Twelve summers during which I studied hard and learned all I could, yet I showed little sign of ability. Small charms that my fellows performed easily required many long hours of practice for me. I could not call on the elements until several years after all my fellows had mastered the practice, and even now the air elementals still eluded me. I found it difficult to interpret the signs, for it seemed they could be read in several ways, depending on one's motive. But the area in which I had most soundly failed was the Sight. No matter how many hours I practised, I never Saw even the briefest vision in the waters. But despite that, the druids believed I was intended for them.

I had a secret reason for pursuing my training, despite my lack of ability, and it pained me that Oistin had seemingly chosen to disregard this now. I had confided in him many years ago about my sister, who had been stolen at birth by the fey queen, Titania. He knew I planned to search for her as soon as my training was complete. Once she was located and safely returned home, I would again be at the druids' disposal — for the rest of my life. It seemed to me to be a fair exchange.

Given my lack of ability, there must be another reason the druids had selected me all those years ago. If Oistin had Seen the path that lay ahead of me, he had never hinted at it. So this assignment was completely unexpected. How would I advise the king with no Sight?

2

ARLEN

There was no point sitting here feeling sorry for myself. Oistin had made his decision and I would not shame myself by arguing with him. From under my bed, I retrieved the boxes that held all my worldly belongings. Two spare pairs of linen trousers, three tunics. A pair of socks, long overdue for darning. A well-worn pair of boots. A thick cloak. A sack in which to pack my belongings if I travelled from the community.

The other box contained a comb and a few small mementoes of Silver Downs, for as a boy I had been permitted to take from home only what fit in my pockets. A black raven feather, gathered on some long-forgotten expedition. A stone plucked from one of the twin rivers that crossed our estate, worn perfectly smooth and round from the waters. A small wooden dagger one of my soldier cousins made for me. I remembered him wrapping my fingers around the dagger as he taught me to use it. And the final item: two small, flat blocks of wood bound together with a faded yellow ribbon. It contained a single day's eye bloom, taken from a bush on the very edge of Silver Downs, swiftly plucked as I walked away for the last time. This was everything in the world that belonged to me.

I pulled on my socks and boots, then quickly packed the rest of my belongings in the sack. I pushed the boxes back under my cot, which would likely belong to someone else by sundown tomorrow. Cots did not stay empty around here for long. Clutching the sack, I left my bedchamber without another glance.

When I returned to Oistin, he still sat at his desk, although whether he stared at the parchment lying there or at his hands in his lap, I couldn't tell.

"Aah, Arlen. Are you ready?"

"I am at your command, Master."

"Then we shall send you immediately." He went to the door. "Come."

"May I ask something before I leave?"

Oistin's step faltered and he paused before turning to face me.

"Of course, and I will answer if I can."

"Will you tell me what I have done?"

"Whatever do you mean? This is a great honour. Some druids spend their whole lives angling for a position at court."

"But not me. You know this is the last thing I desire. So I would know what it is I have done to cause you to punish me in this way."

Oistin sighed and for the first time I noticed how old he looked. His face was lined and his eyes shadowed.

"Arlen, this is not a punishment."

"Then why do you send me? Why not Niall or Donat? They would be better suited to such a position than I."

"Give yourself time to settle in. It won't be that bad. You've been here a long time and I suppose you think of this as your home. There is always a sense of grief at leaving one's home behind."

"You know I despise politics. I have little patience for it. I am entirely unsuited to advise the king."

"I think Hearn will find you refreshing. He has enough sycophants surrounding him. An impartial advisor will be welcome."

"You know the other reason I am unsuitable. That hasn't changed. I will be useless to him."

"I haven't forgotten. The visions will come with time. Patience. Practice."

"I've had patience. I've spent hundreds of hours practising. And still I See nothing. How can I advise the king if I cannot See?"

"He doesn't need to know that you See nothing. You have common sense and wisdom and enough knowledge of politics, history and geography. Your Sight will come eventually, but in the meantime, you can still guide Hearn to make the right decisions."

"You want me to lie to the king?"

"I'm not suggesting you lie to him. Merely that you don't tell him what he doesn't need to know."

"Master, is there no one else who can do this?"

Oistin's mouth twisted and he laid his hand on my shoulder.

"Arlen, I regret that I have to ask this of you. But it must be you who goes. I have Seen it."

"Tell me. Please."

"There is little to tell. I Saw you at the king's side with a shadowy woman behind you. That is all."

"That doesn't mean I am intended as his advisor, only that for some reason, at some time, I might meet the king."

"I feel this deep in my bones, Arlen. A sure certainty. You are meant to be at Hearn's side. You will be instrumental in something he must achieve. It has to be you."

"And what of my sister? When will I be able to search for her?"

Oistin looked at me steadily and at first I thought he would not reply. When eventually he spoke, I felt like I had been punched in the stomach.

"Your sister will be important to the kingdom's peace," he said. "It is crucial that you find her, but not yet. Certain events must occur first. If you search for her too soon, everything will be ruined."

"You have Seen her?" I whispered. "She is alive?"

He nodded. "But I must caution you, Arlen. Do not search for her until I tell you. Peace is fragile and tenuous. Your sister will either make peace or irrevocably destroy it."

I sucked in a deep breath and bowed my head.

"I understand. If you wish me to go, I will go."

"I will send someone to visit occasionally, so you can return any news. Ronan, perhaps. He itches to be out in the world and away from here. Don't send a messenger unless the matter is dire. Wait until I send someone we can trust."

I nodded.

"Let's send you on your way, then."

As I followed Oistin out to the stone circle that stood not far from our lodge, druid after druid came to pay their respects, for already word had gone around that I was leaving. About two dozen druids lived in our community and I knew them all. Most were youngsters, arrived only in the last couple of years. A few were master druids who stayed to guide the younger ones. And then there was me. I stayed because I had not managed to complete my training. Yet I was about to step into one of the most highly coveted positions.

I said my farewells quickly. There were none here I was close to. There had been good friends over the years — boys who came to the community around the same time as I had — but they all moved on eventually. They mastered their studies and left for whatever role Oistin chose for them after their ten years were concluded.

By the time we reached the stones, only Oistin remained. The stone circle was ancient and we had no knowledge of those who set it in place, or why they would select such a site deep in the woods. I rested my palm against one of the stones, seeking a connection with it, and received a faint sensation of peacefulness and endurance.

"Farewell, Arlen," Oistin said. "You have studied long and hard and your journey is not over. Keep up your practice. Find a place where you can study and meditate in quiet. That which you seek will come when the time is right."

"Of course, Master. Thank you for everything."

"Step into the centre of the stones, then. Keep your eyes closed until you stop moving. Someone should be there to meet you. Hearn is expecting you."

Dead leaves crunched under my boots as I followed his instructions. I closed my eyes and waited. There was nothing left to say.

Oistin murmured an invocation to the air elementals, asking them to take me to my destination. I had never before travelled in this manner, although I knew what to expect and, in theory, I knew how to summon the elementals to send me through the stones. I resisted the urge to open my eyes and check what happened.

Soon enough a gentle breeze flowed around me. It circled my legs and moved up my body, bringing with it the fragrant scent of honeysuckle. I clutched my sack of belongings as the breeze grew stronger, whipping around me, faster and faster. There was no other sensation of movement, only of wind swirling around me, as if I was in the eye of a storm.

Eventually the wind died down. It became once more a gentle breeze that wafted around my legs. Then that, too, withdrew and I was alone.

3

ARLEN

hen I opened my eyes, I stood in the centre of a much larger circle, the stones of which were taller and wider than any man. Despite Oistin's promise that someone would meet me, I was alone. Grassy fields and a few ash trees surrounded the stone circle, but nothing that might be a commoner's lodge, let alone a king's. The sky held no trace of smoke that might signal a home, only a few clouds and the golden blush of sunset. Not the most auspicious of beginnings.

I dropped my pack in the middle of the circle and sat on the grass. I had no idea which direction Braen Keep lay in. As the sun sank, the air grew cool. I shivered in my linen trousers and my stomach growled. I had not thought to bring any supplies. I could probably make enough of a meal if I left the stones. There would be mushrooms or nuts or any number of things I might eat, but I might miss whoever was meant to meet me. So I waited. I would not let Oistin down by disobeying him on my first assignment.

Darkness fell and stars appeared. I should have used this time to meditate, perhaps on my failure with the Sight, but instead I leaned back on my hands and stared up at the sky. It had always fascinated me. The sun. The moon. The stars. The beauty of it all. Had anyone ever persuaded the air elementals to let them travel the skies? Could I touch the sun if they were willing? Stand on a star?

My thoughts wandered to my lost sister. I had heard the tale of our birth more times than I could count. How Eithne struggled in labour for almost a day before the first babe was born. It was a girl child, as she had known it would be, and she had already determined the babe would be named Agata for her own mother. No sooner was the child born than Titania revealed herself.

Nobody knew how long the queen of the fey had watched. Perhaps she had only just arrived, in which case the timing was fortuitous for her. Or maybe she had looked on all through that long day. Before anyone could move, Titania snatched up the babe, still coated with birth fluids and not yet even wrapped in a blanket.

"The child is born of a fey," Titania said. "She should be with her own kind. If you want her to live, you will not follow."

Then she disappeared and the child with her. Before Eithne could make sense of what had happened, her womb contracted and it was only then she realised there was a second babe. I was born and Eithne named me Arlen.

"The child has been unSeen this far," said Brigit, who was wife to Eithne's brother and midwife for the births. "Even my own Sight didn't show him. If you acknowledge him as your son, she will steal him, too."

Eithne was distraught at the loss of one child and unwilling to give up another, but she knew the wisdom of Brigit's words. So I was given to Cryda, a servant who had recently borne a child, and she nursed me with her own babe. But I grew up knowing that Eithne had given birth to me, although Cryda was the one I called Mother. We had neither seen nor heard of Agata since then. I was a young boy when I first vowed to search for my sister and bring her home if she still lived. I reasoned that since I had been unSeen, Titania's instruction not to follow Agata did not apply to me, only to those who had been present for our births.

As night deepened and moonlight shone on the ancient circle surrounding me, I took my woollen cloak from the sack and wrapped it tightly around my shoulders. It kept out the night breeze, but still the chill crept underneath and I began to shiver. I knew techniques that would keep me warm, if I could attain the right level of focus. Settling into a meditation pose, with my legs crossed and my back straight, I closed my eyes and tried to let go of my thoughts.

It was difficult at first, for I was distracted by my bodily need for warmth, but eventually I stopped feeling the cold. I passed the night in the peacefulness of deep meditation, not even noticing when the sun rose, and only opening my eyes when someone spoke.

"Are you going to sit there all day?"

Standing over me was a man perhaps a couple of summers younger than I. He wore dark blue trousers and a shirt of the same colour. He gave me a friendly grin and reached out to help me up.

"Bram," he offered. "You the druid? From Oistin?"

"That would be me," I said. "My name is Arlen."

"Come on, then. I'll take you to the keep."

We bore west, walking through ankle-deep grass that still held the lushness of late summer, although that season was past. The ground sloped upward gently. We walked in silence for several minutes.

"Did you not expect me yesterday?" I asked eventually, thinking I should try to make conversation.

Bram shrugged and his ears turned pink.

"We was busy yesterday. Hearn couldn't spare anyone to come get you until this morning."

Perhaps Hearn wasn't enamoured of Oistin's belief that he needed a druid advisor. We walked in silence and eventually we came to the top of a long slope. In the distance, still a couple of hours' walk away, stood a town.

"You walked all this way to fetch me?" I asked.

"Set out at first light," Bram said.

I wondered why he didn't ride a horse or perhaps bring a cart, but I didn't ask. It seemed politics were at play even before I arrived. I would need to learn fast. The sun was past its zenith before we reached Braen Town. I had never been to a town before, so I had no sense of its size compared to others. The streets were dusty and poorly paved, and the air stank of rotting refuse. Skinny children crouched in the dirt, watching forlornly as people rushed past. The adults looked downtrodden and surly. I made eye contact with a woman and she raised her lip in a snarl. I was careful not to look directly at anyone else after that.

It took at least another hour to wind our way through the streets. Eventually we reached a tall stone wall set with heavy wooden gates which stood open. Bram greeted the two guards stationed there as we passed through. Inside were fewer people, although this side of the wall seemed no better maintained than the other. I saw bare earth, stunted trees, and paths in need of repair. My spirits sank. I was used to greenery and solitude and the peacefulness of the woods. Here was all dirt and dust and people rushing. Surely Oistin didn't expect me to stay here for long.

Braen Keep was far larger than the druids' lodge. My memories of Silver Downs were faded, but I had always thought it to be a large lodge. However, even it paled in comparison to the king's keep. Like the town around it, though, Braen Keep was poorly maintained. Weather and mould darkened the grey stones, window shutters hung crookedly, and the roughness of the thatching suggested it leaked. A raven perched on the roof cawed and I had the uncanny sense that he warned me away. We entered through a small side door, guarded only by a single man who nodded at Bram.

Inside, the keep was dim and dusty. There were no lamps or candles lit, despite how little sunlight reached through the shuttered windows. Bram led me up several flights of stairs and along twisting passages before we reached a small bedchamber with an ill-fitting door.

"This is where you'll sleep," he muttered as he put his shoulder to the door to force it open.

The bedchamber was no larger than the one I had shared at the druid community, but it contained only one bed rather than four. The rest of the furniture consisted of a wooden chair, a small chest of drawers, and a single shelf. Wooden shutters covered the window, but there were no curtains. There was no rug on the floor or blanket on the bed. Nevertheless, it was reasonably clean, although it needed a good airing, and would be quiet.

"This will be ample," I said.

Despite its plainness, a bedchamber of my own was a luxury. I had never slept alone, even during my boyhood days at Silver Downs.

"You'll need a blanket." Bram's ears were pink again. "I'll get someone to send one up. And a candle."

"Thank you." I should try to make an ally of the young man. After all, he was the only person I knew here. "You've been very kind to walk all that way to fetch me."

Bram stared at the ground. "Just doing my job."

"What exactly is that?"

"I fetch things. Run messages. Things like that."

"Then you will be a useful man to know should I need to send an urgent message." I tried to give the impression he might someday be privy to secret information, but Bram looked unimpressed. I swallowed a sigh. I knew nothing about politics.

"Would you show me to the kitchen?" I asked. "I've not eaten since the evening before last. Or do you think Hearn would want to see me immediately?"

"He'll call for you when he wants you."

"Wise advice," I said, feeling like a fool.

I left my sack on the bed and followed Bram along the twisty hallways and down three flights of stone steps. I paid careful attention to our path, for fear I would not find my bedchamber again.

The kitchen seemed to have no order and nobody in charge, which was a far cry from the community's kitchen. The heat from the wood stoves and two hearths was stifling, and the aroma of beef stew filled the air.

Bram showed me where I could obtain some bread and a mug of ale, and a spot where I could eat without being in anyone's way. I sat beside two guards who looked up at me blearily, then returned their attention to their meals. They had probably just come off a night shift and I thought better than to try to make conversation with them. I would not win any allies by pestering people.

Bram had disappeared, so I ate my meal, then managed to find my bedchamber with only one wrong turn. A neatly folded blanket and two candles sat next to my sack of belongings on the cot. I placed my spare clothes and my cloak in the dresser. They barely took up one of the three drawers. What else was I supposed to put in there? Surely nobody expected me to have enough clothes to fill three drawers.

I managed to force the window shutters open. The wood was swollen and they probably wouldn't close properly again, but at least I could air out the room. Winter nights would be cold with shutters that didn't close, though. I pulled off my boots and stretched out on the cot. Might as well sleep while I could. Who knew what sort of schedule Hearn might expect me to keep once I commenced in my new role as his advisor?

Hearn kept me waiting for four days. The time spent alone didn't bother me, for I was used to solitary days. When I was hungry, I made my way down to the kitchen and helped myself to bread and ale. Nobody ever commented on my regular presence, although one of the guards who was often there for a meal at the same time soon began to offer a friendly nod.

I secured the loan of a small bronze bowl, which I filled with water and carried carefully back to my bedchamber. I spent hours peering into the bowl's shallow depths, hoping to catch a glimpse of something. Past. Present. Future. Maybe. But the Sight remained as intangible as ever, and all I saw was the smooth interior of the bowl and the reflection of candlelight on the water's surface. This was what I was doing when Bram finally came to say Hearn had sent for me.

I followed Bram along the keep's twisty hallways. He paused outside a thick wooden door flanked by two guards on each side.

"In there." Bram indicated the doors with his thumb.

"Thank you," I said.

"Don't thank me till you know what he wants."

Bram left. I hesitated, wondering whether the guards were supposed to open the door, but they kept their gaze fixed straight ahead. It seemed their duties extended only to keeping people out, not helping them go in. I pushed open the door and entered the king's audience hall.

There were only five people in the room, and although I had never seen Hearn before, the stout man lounging on a massive chair padded with rich purple cushions had to be him. He appeared to be deep in conversation with a man standing in front of him. Behind Hearn stood two guards and to his left was a much smaller chair on which a woman sat.

I wondered how it had taken me so long to see her. Even seated as she was, I could tell she was tall and skinny to the point of ungainliness. She held her arms awkwardly, as if she didn't know whether to fold them in her lap or across her chest or rest them on the arms of the chair. Her face was long and horsey, with a large nose and protruding ears. She wore a deep purple gown that looked like it was intended for a woman with a much larger frame.

As I met her eyes, a jolt passed through my body and it seemed that somebody said *pay attention for she will be important*. Was this a glimpse of the Sight or merely my own brain being overly dramatic? The woman broke our eye contact to look down at her hands and the moment passed. Trying to cover my discomfort, I strode forward. I stopped a few paces away from Hearn and bowed.

Hearn paused his conversation to look me up and down. He was a large man in his middle years, with a physique that was turning to fat. His hair hung almost to his shoulders and his eyes were unintelligent.

"So Oistin has sent his plaything to me." Hearn's voice boomed, far too loud for the distance at which I stood.

"Your Majesty, I understand that I am to advise you," I said.

"Have you not sufficient advisors, my lord?" asked the man he had been conversing with, eyeing me with clear displeasure. He wore a frilly shirt which he kept straightening and a moustache which he probably thought was more impressive than it really was.

"I have more advisors than any man should have to suffer," Hearn said. "But it seems the druid master thinks I need one more. Well, let's see what kind of advice you give, druid. You'll stay for as long as your advice pleases me, despite what Oistin says. Go now. I'll call for you when I want you."

I hesitated. Was he not going to introduce me to the others? I desperately wanted to know who the woman was.

"Are you deaf, druid?" asked the other man.

I bowed and left. The heavy door closed behind me with a thud.

4

AGATA

"Agata, my dear, you look like you have been rolling around on the ground. Whatever were you doing?" Titania reached over and plucked a leaf from my hair. She waved it in front of my face, her eyebrows raised. "Hmmm?"

I held her gaze and willed myself not to blush.

"Looking for birds' nests."

Titania's face said clearly that she didn't believe me, but she wouldn't question me further. That wasn't her way. As long as I looked suitably meek, she would let it go.

"Well, straighten your clothes and sit down. And Agata," she said as I moved to take my place at her feet. "Do fasten your gown properly."

She looked pointedly at my chest and I realised my gown was only partially laced up. This time I couldn't hold back my blush. I had taken it off earlier in order to climb a tree more swiftly and hadn't realised I had failed to tie my laces again. I could only guess what she thought I had been doing. I fixed my gown and sat on the edge of the dais, where I could see Titania from the corner of my eye, and ensured my gown covered my legs.

The dais stood at the edge of a circular clearing in the woods. This was fey territory — Titania's realm — and we were deep in the heart of it. The fey realm sat side by side with the mortal realm, not that I had ever visited that fey-forsaken place. I had no interest in mortals and no reason to visit their realm.

Oak and elm shaded the clearing, but lush grass covered the ground despite the thick canopy. Titania's magic gave her realm whatever appearance she wished, and the seasons changed only at her desire. Guards stood behind the dais, a full dozen of them. Not that she needed their protection. This was her place and her people. Nobody would dare attack her here and even if they did, Titania could protect herself with her magic. More guards ringed the clearing and in the centre stood a group of fey. Men and women and a few children. They waited silently and without moving, even the children. Appearing impatient was a certain way to bring Titania's wrath down on oneself.

Titania sat on her throne. Her gown pooled around her feet, shimmering like blood, and her dark hair was artfully arranged to flow over her shoulders in a cascade of curls. Her fingernails — half as long as her fingers themselves and the shade of congealed blood — tapped against the arm of her throne.

"Where is he?" she hissed, barely moving her mouth. This was why she liked me to sit so close, so she could speak to me without anybody else hearing. I was the only one she could confide in.

"I haven't seen him all day," I answered quietly.

She waited for Oberon, king of the fey and her husband, although not my father. She had never told me who my father was and I had never asked. He obviously meant nothing to her, so there was no reason for me to care either. He was probably just some fey she had a brief affair with.

"He knows I hate waiting for him." Her fingernails drummed against the curved arm of her throne.

"He'll be here soon."

It was a lie and we both knew it. Oberon did his own thing. He might turn up, but then again he might not.

"I'm not waiting any longer," she said, then raised her voice for the guards. "I will hear the first petitioner."

The guards communicated silently with hand signals, and within moments a fey woman crossed the grassy court and sank to her knees. She bowed her head and waited for Titania to address her. I shifted slightly to get more comfortable and prepared for a tedious day. I had long ago perfected the art of looking attentive while retreating into my own mind.

My legs had gone numb and I had long since stopped listening when a soft whistle caught my attention. I turned my head slowly, trying to seem as if I just happened to look in a different direction. If Titania thought I was restless, I'd earn a sharp kick in the ribs. That was another reason she liked me to sit so close.

Sumerled waited in the shadowy depths of the woods. He tipped his head as my gaze met his, beckoning me to come to him. Irritation flared within me. He knew I couldn't leave until Titania allowed it. I gave him the tiniest shake of my head, although even that was more than he deserved.

"Are we boring you, my dear?" Titania's voice was dry and I knew even without turning that her words were directed at me.

"Of course not, my lady," I said. "But he is little more than a child and doesn't understand restraint. I don't control him."

"You should learn to," she said.

I swallowed the retort that came to mind, about how she was unable to control Oberon, who hadn't yet showed his face today.

"Yes, my lady."

She sighed and with a wave of her hand silenced the current petitioner. He stopped as suddenly as if she had slit his throat.

"Enough," she said. "Leave."

The clearing emptied, the fey departing swiftly and silently, even the one whose petition had been cut off. I didn't move. The instruction to leave was unlikely to apply to me, and Titania would only be crosser if I presumed to depart.

"Agata, come to me," Titania said.

I stood, my movements graceful, just as she had taught me. I would never move with the sinuousness that Titania did, however much I tried, but I could be graceful and elegant when I remembered. My skirts drifted down over my legs and I gave them a tiny shake to ensure they lay properly. Of course Titania noticed with a frown and I mentally admonished myself. Had I moved correctly, there would be no need to adjust my skirts. She didn't comment, though, and her usually observant gaze was somewhat distant. Perhaps she still wondered about Oberon's absence. Eventually, Titania looked me in the eyes. She had a way of staring that made me feel as if she peered inside my brain.

"What is our role?" she asked.

"To rule the fey," I said automatically.

"And how do we do that?"

"By being regal and authoritative at all times."

"Were you regal and authoritative today?"

I hesitated and her gaze sharpened.

"No, my lady," I said quickly before she could admonish me. "I was distracted."

"And it showed."

"It won't happen again."

"Make sure it doesn't. Now go. See what that boy wants. I've had enough of listening to whining fey for today anyway."

I turned to leave but stopped as she said my name.

"Don't ever turn up for court looking like that again."

My fingers twitched, but I held them at my sides and didn't let them stray to check my gown was fastened properly or that no more leaves were caught in my hair.

"Yes, my lady."

I fled before she could change her mind.

5

AGATA

Sumerled had at least enough sense not to stand right on the edge of the clearing, where he would have been visible to everyone. He waited further back amongst the trees. Oak and ash and beech grew thickly here, leaving little space for the sunlight to penetrate.

"What took you so long?" His voice held a whiny tone that made my fingers itch to slap him.

"Shut up," I hissed. "Just move. Before she changes her mind."

I held my gown up to my knees and ran through the woods with Sumerled at my heels. We fey know how to move swiftly and silently, although it had taken me somewhat longer to master than is usual for a fey child. Titania had often bemoaned my slowness to learn.

I inhaled deeply as we ran, savouring the aroma of moss and trees and damp leaves. The fey woods were home. I couldn't imagine ever living anywhere else. Some fey did, of course. Some chose to live in the mortal realm. Titania's opinion of such fey was scathing.

Although I had no desire to venture into the mortal realm, I was just the tiniest bit curious about it. Could it really be as bad as folk said? I pictured it as a wasteland, all brown and grey and dead. How did mortals survive in such a place. Where did they live? What did they eat? Did they wear clothes like ours? Did they live alone or in groups? What kinds of creatures inhabited their world? A sprite flew past my nose, near enough to brush my skin with its wings.

"Shoo," I muttered, adding a small burst of speed to get away from it.

The sprite laughed and flew away. Or at least I thought it laughed. I heard the sprites only as the faintest tittering. Sumerled claimed he could hear them clearly. I was never quite sure whether he lied, although it was true my senses didn't seem quite as sharp as those of most fey.

"Where shall we go?" I called over my shoulder once we were far enough away from court.

"Anywhere you like," he called back.

If it was my choice, I knew exactly where I wanted to go. My favourite place in all the fey realm was a pretty pond shrouded by elegant weeping willows. Their branches draped right down to the ground, forming a green curtain all the way around the pond. The water was warm and came from somewhere deep underground. In the morning, soft white mist hung over the water. Emerald-green moss surrounded the pond and a nearby patch of bluebells scented the air perfectly.

It would take us some time to get there, even running as fast as we were. I had never seen another living being there — not even a sprite, and they tended to be anywhere one didn't want them. There, I could pretend I was far away from the politics of court and from Titania, whose expectations I never quite managed to live up to. Somewhere where nobody watched to see when I would disgrace myself next and where nobody tried to befriend me just to get closer to Titania.

There was no point wishing for what I didn't have. Things could be much worse. If I lived in the mortal realm, I'd be far enough away from court, but I would be surrounded by stupid, uninspired, insipid mortals. The worst day amongst the fey was surely a hundred times better than any day in the mortal realm. I stopped thinking and pushed my legs faster as I hurtled over rocks and ducked under branches. If I ran fast enough, maybe I could outrun my morose thoughts.

"Slow down," Sumerled called from behind me. He might be able to move more quietly than me, but I had always been swifter.

I ignored him and ran even faster. He would know where to find me. This place was where I always went when I truly wanted to get away from fey intrigue. My legs were tired by the time I reached the pond. I had long left Sumerled behind, although he ran so silently that I never knew exactly where he was. I should have a few minutes to myself before he arrived, though.

I was hot and sweating from the run as I stripped off my gown and dived into the pond wearing just my underthings. The water was clear and blissfully warm. I took a deep breath and ducked under until my hair floated out around me.

The pond was so deep that if I held my breath and dived down, I couldn't touch the bottom. I had always wondered whether anything lived down there. Maybe some of the Old Ones who inhabited this land before the fey arrived had retreated to lonely places like the depths of a pond. The thought that there might be something down there, watching as my toes dangled above it, made me uneasy. I surfaced and splashed back to the edge. I was hauling myself out of the water as Sumerled arrived. He looked at me for a long moment and I felt almost naked in my dripping underthings.

"Now that's a nice sight to arrive to," he said, with a smirk.

"Too bad you're so late," I said easily. I wrung the water out of my hair and sat on the mossy ground, leaning back on my elbows and enjoying the cool shade. Sumerled sat beside me, a little too close. He leaned in, his breath hot on my neck.

"What do you want to do now?"

His breath tickled my neck and I shoved him away.

"Don't be disgusting."

He shrugged, but didn't seem offended. "I didn't do anything."

"I know exactly what you were thinking."

He leered. "I doubt you know *exactly* what."

I glared and his smile wavered a little. Nothing untoward had ever happened between us, but I was never entirely sure whether he joked when he said things like that. Resolving to ignore him, I lay down in the moss and fanned my hair out around me to let it dry, then closed my eyes.

The air was just warm enough that I didn't feel chilled, and I was pleasantly drowsy. The chirps of water bugs drifted past. Something made a small splash in the pond. Again the thoughts of hidden Old Ones rose, but I didn't let myself open my eyes to check that we were still alone. They were probably more myth than truth anyway. Even if they had existed long ago, it wasn't possible for them still to be here somewhere, waiting. The fey were the longest-lived of all species.

I must have drifted off into sleep, because when I next noticed my surroundings, my mind was fuzzy. Fighting my way out of sleep was like swimming back up from the bottom of the pond. Eventually I managed to open my eyes. The light hadn't changed, but I could tell the day was late. The fey woods had a certain tone to them as night approached, even though the light and temperature remained constant. I rarely ever slept so soundly, but there was something about this place that made me deeply relaxed. I reached over to poke Sumerled in the ribs.

"Sumerled," I said. "Wake up. I need to go back."

He grunted but didn't move. I poked him harder.

"If you don't wake up, I'm going to leave you here."

He opened his eyes and squinted at me. "Just a little longer."

"I'm leaving now."

I twisted my still-damp hair up into a knot as I climbed to my feet. It was only then I noticed the rock right next to where I had been lying. It was about the size of my head. I stared at it for a long moment. My thoughts were jumbled and my ears rang. Surely I would have noticed that I lay down next to a rock that large?

"Sumerled, did you put that there?" I poked my fingers in my ears, trying to relieve the pressure that made the air sound like it vibrated.

He had closed his eyes again and seemed to have sunk back into sleep. I toed his ribs.

"Sumerled!"

"I'm awake," he grumbled, sitting up. "What's the hurry?"

"You mean apart from the fact that we've been here all afternoon and Titania will be wondering where I am?"

"It's not like she'll send someone looking for you. She always knows where you are. It's peculiar."

"Don't say things like that," I said. "You never know who might be listening. Did you put this rock here?"

He gave me a bewildered look as I pointed.

"What do you mean? Why would I put it there?"

"Is it some sort of game? Leaving a rock right next to my head for me to find when I wake up?"

"Of course not. I didn't do it. I never even saw it before."

"Then how did it get there?"

He shrugged. "It must have already been there."

"It wasn't. I would have noticed."

"Then you explain. How did it get there if I didn't do it and it wasn't already there?"

I stared down at the rock and an uneasy feeling crept over me. My skin began to pimple. Someone else had been here while I was sound asleep in my underthings.

"Somebody must have snuck up and put it there while we were sleeping," I said.

Sumerled started to laugh, but stopped when he realised I was serious.

"Who? And why?"

"I don't know," I snapped. "I just know it wasn't there before. So either this is one of your stupid games or somebody snuck up on us."

"I would have noticed if anyone came here," he said scornfully.

"Apparently not."

We glared at each other for a minute.

"I have to get back." I pulled on my gown and slid my feet back into my slippers. I didn't wait to see whether he followed.

6

IDA

It is a long time since he first trapped me in here. I was sure he wasn't strong enough to contain me. But somehow he was, and he has. His druid brother shows him how to trap me in the box inside his head. How to envision the box, how to make sure it is solid and real. How to hold the lid closed, even when he sleeps.

I try many times during his long life to escape. Sometimes I almost do. When the pain starts in his stomach, he knows his end is near, and hope rises in me once again. I watch those last long months as the disease eats his insides. I feel the fatigue and bone-crushing pain with him. At times it is hard to remember whose pain it is. We have shared his mind for so long that sometimes I think my thoughts might have really been his to start with. The box he keeps me in dims my view of the world. I can see what he sees, hear what he thinks, but only if I concentrate. Most of the time it seems like too much effort. Instead I sink down into the darkness and wait.

He prepares well for his death. He spends time with his druid brother, who coaches him in how to keep me trapped inside his mind. They think that if he can keep me confined as he dies, I will die with him. I am not so sure and I am not ready to die.

When the moment comes, I am ready. As his mind drifts into

silence and his heart stutters to a halt, I push hard against the lid of the box. As prepared as he thinks he is, he finally loses control in those last moments. I burst out of the box and finally I am once again free in his mind. I immediately think, *Out*, and suddenly I stand beside him.

I look down at his corpse. He lies on a bed, soft pillows under his head and a fine blanket drawn up to his shoulders. He is much older than when I last saw him. Then he was a boy of only nineteen summers. Now he is an old man, withered and wrinkled and yellowed. How many years has it been? I have felt the strength leaving his body as time passed. The aches in his knees and hips and the throb in his lower back. The way his hands shook and didn't quite do what he wanted them to. I felt his frustration with these things and then, later, his acceptance.

I finally notice the woman who sits on the opposite side of his bed. When he looked at her, he must have been seeing a memory, for she looks little like that now. She has aged just like him, although her eyes are still sharp and her hands steady. She glares at me.

I ignore her and glance around the bedchamber. The coals in the hearth spit sparks and the air is fragrant with healing herbs. Heavy curtains drawn over the windows prevent me from seeing whether it is day or night. The room is well furnished with solid wooden furniture and expensive bedclothes.

"It's been more than sixty years," the woman says. "And yet you look exactly the same."

I stretch my arms, feeling my skin tighten and my joints move. Muscles flex and contract. Blood races through my veins. My heart pumps. I inhale and air rushes into my lungs. I hold it there a moment, then exhale. It is intoxicating, being alive again after so long.

"He spent his life trying to atone for what you did," the woman hisses. "You should have died with him."

"As you can see, I did not." I arch my eyebrow at her. Oh, the flexibility of muscles and movement.

"The lodge is well warded. You won't be able to leave this place."

"That would be a shame for you, wouldn't it?" I say. "For I don't think you and I could live here together."

She glares at me but says nothing further. I notice the way she holds his hand in her own, the way her grip tightens as she swallows whatever it is she burns to say. She helped him confine me all those years ago. I should probably kill her, but I turn my back and leave the bedchamber.

The lodge feels quiet and solemn as I stride along the hallway. The air is heavy with grief. There are people here who mourn his death and not just his wife. The boy experienced much sadness in his life as he watched first his parents, then his brothers grow old and die. There were other lesser griefs which were not as personal for him. The loss of wives in childbirth for two of the brothers. Children born still and quiet; others who fall ill and die before their second birthday. He rejoiced in the sounds of running feet and the laughter of children, even as he sorrowed that none of them were his.

As I reach the bottom of the stairs, folk appear in the doorways of various rooms. Their solemn faces turn to surprise as they see me. Nobody steps forward to challenge me as I stride through the lodge. Until I reach the front door.

A young man steps out in front of me. He is probably about the same age as the boy was when he created me. We stare at each other and understanding crosses his face. He squares his shoulders and clears his throat and I recognise the boy in his actions. Not a son, for he never had one, but trained by him perhaps. I haven't been paying enough attention recently to recognise his face. His voice is amusingly earnest.

"When the great bard died, the creature he had imprisoned in his mind broke free."

I feel his power immediately. He is not as strong as the boy, but he understands his ability. I will not be trapped again. Before he can speak another word, I wave my hand towards him. He goes tumbling back into the room he came from, gone before his expression can change.

I open the door and step out of the lodge. Drizzling rain kisses my skin and for a moment I close my eyes and lift my face to greet it. Too long have I been bereft of feeling, locked inside the boy's mind.

When I open my eyes, someone else stands in front of me. Like the boy's wife, he too has aged, although he still holds his back straight and his head high. The dark hair is silver now, but it still hangs in braids to his shoulders. His face is not as wrinkled as the boy's and he stands without aid of a cane, which is something the boy has not been able to do for some years. It is his druid brother. Without him, the boy might have been able to return me to his mind all that time ago, but he wouldn't have known how to keep me there.

We stare in silence, each waiting for the other to make the first move. Rain runs down his face, but he doesn't try to wipe it away.

"Keeping you confined was his dearest wish," the druid says, at last.

"I cannot be confined," I say. "Not any longer. I will live my own life."

"You live only because he created you. He knew he was wrong to do so. It was done in a moment of rashness without any under-standing of his ability."

"But I live now."

"Brigit has warded the lodge." He gestures towards my feet. "You are standing right in front of the line she has drawn. Take another step and the wards will kill you."

I extend my senses, feeling, tasting. I sense something, a lingering power of a type I am unfamiliar with. I hesitate. What if his words are true?

"Step back into the lodge," the druid says. "We will allow you to stay here, provided you cause no harm. You can still live."

"That is no life," I say. "Confined to the lodge just as I have been confined to his mind for so long. I will not live like that."

"Then cross the wards and die," he says. "Those are your options."

I hesitate on the doorstep, looking past him to green fields and grey sky. Heavy clouds. Fog shrouding distant mountains. There is a whole world out there. A world I have yet to experience, for the boy never travelled again after his journey to capture me. He was content to pass the rest of his life on these grounds. I cannot be content with that. Not now.

The cold rain against my skin raises goose bumps and with each passing moment, I remember more and more of what it is to be alive. I can't go back. I can't stay. I can only move forward. Even if this is my death. I raise my foot and take a step.

White sparks blind me. Pain shoots through my body. My vision fails and I taste blood. All I can think is, I don't want to die. I gather my power and push the pain away. It is difficult and I strain, already panting. She is strong, the boy's wife, and her wards are powerful. They wrap around me, writhing up and down my limbs. They cling, suppressing my power. The pain is like nothing I have ever imagined. I am weakening. Dying. But no. I *will* live. I will not die now, not when the boy is dead and I am finally free.

I fight back, *pushing* at the wards. I fear I am not strong enough, but first one weakens, then another. One by one, the wards fizzle and fade away. I am left trembling, vastly weakened. My heart pumps once, then more strongly, and blood starts to flow in my veins again. I take a deep breath, filling my lungs with cool air. My head begins to clear, although the pain is still strong. I ignore the discomfort and take a shaky step forward. The druid backs away. His face is pale as he raises his hand towards me.

"Enough," I say, and my voice is stronger than I expect. "You have already seen that her wards cannot control me. You can do no more than she. Move out of my way."

"The people out there are innocent," he says. "They had no part in what happened to you. Do no harm to others and we will not have reason to come after you."

I force out a laugh, although it nearly chokes me.

"Come after me? You would dare? You have seen my power. And I will only grow stronger now that I am free. There is nothing you can do to me."

"Perhaps not I alone," he says. "But my brethren will aid me. And there are others like Brigit. Together, we can stop you."

"No," I say. "No mortal can stop me. Not now. Not this time."

He opens his mouth as if to argue, but closes it without another word. He steps aside, leaving the path clear for me. I walk on unsteady legs. The sensation of having a form is already familiar from the last time, although my legs never trembled like this back then. I force myself to take one step after another, away from the lodge.

"Ida," he says from behind me.

I had forgotten I ever had a name. Ida. This is what the boy named me all that time ago when he first created me. Ida. It means thirst. He thirsted for me.

"Ida, please."

Without looking back, I raise one hand and flick my fingers. I hear a thud as his body slams against the stone wall of the lodge. He doesn't speak again.

I walk on. Away from the lodge. Away from those who confined me.

I am free. And this time I will not be stopped.

7

IDA

I stride down the road that leads away from the boy's home. I have no plan, no idea of where I am going. Just the notion that I need to be away from here. I dealt with his apprentice easily enough, and even the druid posed little problem. My power grew while I languished inside the boy's mind and it will continue to grow. I have not forgotten how to feed it.

I look up at the grey sky as I walk. I am tempted, briefly, to halt the rain, but it is pleasant to feel its chill dampness on my skin. Cool rivulets run down my face and neck and limbs. They drip beneath the bodice of my white dress and trickle into my shoes. It has been so long since I have felt anything and I savour it.

I walk until the rain finally ceases of its own accord and then I walk some more. In the distance across some fields, I see a lodge. Sturdy grey stone, smoke rising from a chimney. Should I make that my home? But no, it is too close to the boy's lodge, where his wife and the druid are.

I continue to walk. Eventually my stomach starts to feel hollow and a growl emits from it. I recognise the feeling from before: this is hunger. It means I need to eat. Far off in the distance, smoke rises.

Where there is smoke, there are usually mortals. And mortals will have food. I keep walking.

The day is drawing to a close as I reach a small stone lodge. It is weather-beaten and the thatch roof is poorly made. The front door creaks loudly as I tug it open. A screaming baby immediately assaults my ears. I try not to listen, but the shrill noise reverberates through the lodge and worms into my head. I cover my ears as I walk down the hallway. How can they stand such noise? Why does nobody stop it?

The kitchen is devoid of inhabitants. I inspect the pantry, but it is almost bare. Just a few soggy turnips and an almost empty sack of barley. My hunger has grown so great that it almost eclipses the continuous screams of the child. Something gnaws at my insides. If I go long enough without food, will my stomach start to eat itself? I cast my gaze around the room, desperate for something to eat.

A half loaf of bread rests on the workbench. I rush towards it, ready to devour it. But it is dry and hard. Stale. I hesitate, but there seems to be no other food in this sorry place. I lift the bread to my mouth and bite into it. It is dry and I almost choke trying to swallow it, but I force it down.

My stomach still growls after the bread is gone. I return to the cupboard and inspect the turnips. They are soft and spongy to touch. I think I recall they should be cooked before eating, but perhaps that isn't always necessary. I take a bite from one, but it tastes nasty and I spit it out. No, these cannot be eaten without cooking. In fact, I think they will not be edible even if cooked. I let the turnip drop to the floor. The baby continues to scream.

I search the room again, but there is no other food. I consider checking the other rooms, but memory tells me that mortals usually only store food in the kitchen. I leave and continue walking. I feel drawn in a particular direction. There is one of the boy's blood out there somewhere. It is as good a destination as any.

Night has long fallen before I reach another lodge. This one, too, is poorly made, but the contents of its kitchen are more substantial. A cooking pot hangs over banked coals with the remnants of the inhabitants' dinner. A savoury scent arises from the pot. A vegetable stew of some sort. I take a bowl from a shelf and spoon the stew into it. There is even an end of bread which tastes like it was baked only yesterday. Together they make a satisfying meal and my stomach finally stops trying to eat itself. I leave the bowl and spoon on the workbench and leave.

I walk through the night, still following the invisible trail that leads to the one who shares the boy's blood. It is a fine evening, clear with a waning moon. The air is crisp, but not too cold, and walking keeps me warm enough. I had forgotten how fragile mortal bodies are, that they cannot withstand cold or heat or lack of food.

The sun rises over distant mountains, casting the sky a fiery shade of orange. I continue to walk as the sun creeps up through the sky. Twice more I stop to eat. On both occasions I encounter mortal women in the kitchen. One raises a knife at me, threatening. I merely wave my hand towards her and she drops the knife to clasp her throat, wondering why she can no longer breathe. She falls to the floor and is still long before I finish eating the porridge she was cooking. The other has the sense not to threaten me. She merely backs into a corner and waits. I ignore her and when I leave, the quiet sounds of her sobs follow me out the door.

As the sun sets and my legs become too tired to continue, I encounter a small village. It is nothing much — merely a dozen or so tiny lodges clumped together. I select the finest, although even that is poor. The inhabitants flee when I announce that I require their lodge, and I sleep soundly.

At dawn, I rise and break my fast with bread and honey from the kitchen. I had forgotten honey. Sticky and fragrant, sweet almost to the point of sickliness. After I have eaten, I continue walking. The sky is patchy with clouds, but no rain falls. The crisp wind holds a hint of winter's approach.

Towards the end of the day, I come upon another village. Although it is far larger than the last, it is no grander. Skinny, dirty children flee ahead of me. Weeds struggle through the cracks in the roads and every lodge looks ready to fall down in the next strong wind. I follow the widest road and trust it will lead to something more habitable. Eventually it does.

There is a stone wall, far taller than me. Soldiers guard a wide wooden gate which, like everything else in this village, looks to be in need of repairs. I merely look at the guards and they swiftly open the gate. None meet my gaze as I walk through, drawing ever closer to the one I seek. He is near.

Ahead is a lodge much larger than the others I have seen, larger even than the boy's home. Someone important must live here. I walk past dusty garden beds and empty fountains. People scatter ahead of me, hiding behind stunted trees or barns in sore need of maintenance. I approach the front doors. They look sturdier than those at the gate, although it would cost me little effort to blast them away.

I look at the two soldiers who guard the doors. The men tremble and one immediately moves to open the doors for me. The other hesitates, one hand lingering on the sword at his waist. I am tired after my long walk and have no patience for silly mortal bravery. I point my finger towards him and he pales as his chest tightens. His heart pumps one final time and bursts. He falls to the ground, already dead. One arm flops out across my path, and I frown as I step over it. Mortal bodies are so messy. I wish they would have the decency to fall away from me as they die.

Inside the lodge is dark and the air smells musty. The wooden floor needs polishing and a thick layer of grime covers every surface. I stride along the hallways, wondering whether I should seek food first or a place to sleep. Food, I decide, as my stomach growls again. It seems to need feeding at unreasonably common intervals. The scent of roasting hares reaches my nostrils.

I follow the aroma to the kitchen, where a skinny woman removes two hares from a spit over a fire. My mouth waters at the meaty scent, and it is all I can do not to rip them from her hands, but I know they will be hot and will burn my tender skin. The woman's eyes meet mine and like most of the mortals I have encountered, there is no fight in her. She merely places the hares on a platter and waits to see what I want.

"Where do you serve these?" I ask her.

The woman points towards a door at the other end of the room. It leads down another dark hallway. I glance through open doors as I pass. None hold anything of interest until I reach the room at the very end. To say it is sumptuous would be a lie, but it is a large room and appears well used.

A wooden table at one end is positioned on a raised platform. The chairs at this table are finer than the others with elaborate swirls carved along their backs. The rest of the room contains two more long tables, these with plain wooden chairs. Only two tables — the one on the platform and one of the others — are set ready for dining. Dark tapestries cover the stone walls and the lamp lighting is inadequate. The air smells of long-eaten meals and spilled ale.

I go to the table on the platform. Up five shallow steps and I am looking out over the rest of the room. I seat myself in the finest of the chairs and wait. Only minutes pass before a man enters the room. His form is overly substantial and his beard needs cleaning. He stops at the steps leading up the platform and glowers at me. Perhaps he thinks it is his place in which I sit. Other men crowd behind him. They exchange mutters as they watch.

"Are you the one who was in charge here?" My voice is pleasant and even, for he has not yet offended me.

Discontent radiates from him and I know immediately that he can feed my power. He is not the one who drew me here, the one with the boy's blood. That is the one I need most, but the man who stands glaring at me can nourish me in the meantime. He seems to take a very long time to decide what to say and I begin to wonder if perhaps he is simple. At length, he clears his throat.

"My name is Hearn," he says, "and I am king."

"Well met, Hearn. Come and sit beside me."

I arch my eyebrows at him. My voice is musical and enticing. He will either respond or he will be dead. Either way, if dinner is not served shortly, somebody will die.

He hesitates a moment longer, then walks towards me. I wait to see whether he will bluster or try to threaten me, but he merely pulls out the chair beside me and squeezes his substantial form into it. My chair is wider, perhaps built for his girth. He reaches for a mug, and swiftly a serving woman is at his side, pouring ale into it. I have only to glance at her and she quickly fills my mug too. I raise it in Hearn's direction.

"My name is Ida. And this is now my lodge."

In response, Hearn drains his mug. The servant refills it and he drinks again. Only then does he look at me.

"Well met, Ida," he says.

It seems I will find no opposition here.

8

ARLEN

I was meditating on the floor in my bedchamber when someone knocked on the door. It took me a moment to find my way back into the world outside my mind. I had to push the door hard to open it, for it stuck against the floor. The woman who waited there was the one I had seen when I met Hearn. The one who was all limbs and angles with a horsey face. She smiled timidly at me.

"Druid, I realise we have not yet met, but Hearn bade me show you around the keep. I am Derwa." She paused for a moment. "I am hand-fasted to Hearn."

"You are the queen?" I was so surprised that she had come all the way to my bedchamber that I spoke without thinking.

She smiled a little sadly.

"I suppose you could say so."

"Forgive my rudeness, my lady." I bowed. "My name is Arlen."

She acknowledged me with a slight nod and looked away, fiddling with some stitching on her sleeve.

"Well met, Arlen," she said, after a moment. "I understand you have been sent here by Oistin."

"I have, my lady. This is the first time I have lived anywhere other than with the druids since I left my home as a boy of ten summers old."

"You were not permitted to return home?"

"We remain with the community for the duration of our training. After that, we depart for whatever role Oistin allots us."

"And what position did you last hold?"

"My lady?" I probably had a strange look on my face, but I hadn't been prepared for such a question.

"Your previous posting. What was it?"

"This is my first."

"But you must be more than twenty summers old."

"I am indeed, my lady. But my studies were incomplete and I stayed to remedy that."

"In what manner were they incomplete?"

I studied my bare feet. I couldn't afford for Hearn to find out.

"My lady, with all respect, I would prefer not to say."

"Of course." Her tone was brisk. "You are under no obligation to tell me anything. Your role here is to advise the king, not to entertain my simple curiosities. Hearn has asked that I show you around. Would you like to see the gardens?"

"I would, my lady, for I have seen little other than my bedchamber and the kitchen since I arrived."

I followed Derwa through the hallways and outside. The gardens she led me to were meagre things and not deserving of the name. Those bushes that still lived were overgrown and yellowing. The grass was worn down to the soil in some places and too long in others. It seemed even the birds found this place unattractive, for the gardens were devoid of their chirps and chitters. Likewise, there was no buzzing of bees or fluttering of butterflies. The wind was sharp with a hint of frost, reminding me that winter fast approached.

Derwa said little as she led me around the pitiful gardens. I hadn't even known Hearn had a wife, so I knew nothing of her and could think of no conversation we might share. If she minded my silence, she didn't comment on it. After we had walked through the gardens in their entirety, I thanked her and retired to my bedchamber. Why would the queen seek me out? Given Hearn's cold welcome, it made no sense that he would direct her to show me around. Yet I kept remembering the thought that crossed my mind the first time I saw her, that she would be important.

My peaceful life had been turned on its head. Only days ago, I had held no expectation of leaving the community until I mastered the Sight. As a boy, I knew I would go to live with the druids, for a child who is to be torn from his family and taken to live with strangers must of course be prepared for such a fate. Normally the druids know when a child is intended for them and they arrive on the day of birth to say small charms over the babe. But not me. My mother believed she carried only one babe, not two, and it seemed nobody else foresaw my birth either.

But when Fiachra, my mother's brother and a druid himself, first saw me, he sent word to Oistin. A few days later, two druids arrived to say the charms I had missed out on. And on my tenth birthday, two of their community came to fetch me. Whether they were the same two or not, I never knew.

As a young boy, I used to go up to the grassy knoll that was the highest point on the estate. From there, everything I could see, all the way to the distant woods, was Silver Downs. I used to sit there and pretend I was already a druid, that I had mastery over the elements and could call up a storm or ask the earth to divide, demand that the rivers rise up and cover the lower pastures or summon a fire to sweep over the lands. That was what I knew of druids as a child.

I did not know of the many hours of learning the lore and the history of the lands around us. I did not understand I would spend most of my days in silent contemplation. I thought it was all about charms and magics. I had some understanding that we studied the fey, and even as a boy I knew this would be useful for when I went to find my sister, but I did not know I might be sent to advise a king who did not want me.

Four more days passed before Hearn summoned me again. This time he sat in a smaller room which was sumptuously appointed with tapestries on the walls and knotted rugs on the floors. Two boys who appeared to be barely into their teens sat on stools in front of him.

"Druid," Hearn said. "Sit."

He pointed to a stool which stood slightly apart from the others.

"Boys, tell the druid what you know of battle." Hearn leaned back in his chair, hands folded over his girth.

"We have been learning about strategy," one of the boys said. He was broad-shouldered and already I saw shades of the man he would grow into. His dark hair was too long, like Hearn's, and his eyes were cunning. "We must know our enemy. If he has few soldiers, we can beat him if we have more. If he has many soldiers, we can beat him if we divide his army. We must choose the location for the battle and make it one that is favourable to us. We must arrive first, so our soldiers can be rested. That way we can engage the enemy as soon as they arrive, while their soldiers are still tired from the march."

"Well done, Brennus," Hearn said. "Girec, do you have anything to add?"

The other boy, younger by perhaps two or three summers and small for his age, shook his head. He stared down at his scuffed boots and didn't speak.

"Of course you don't," Hearn said. "I despair of your ever learning anything." He turned to me. "Well then, druid, what do you think of my foster sons?"

I took a moment to look each boy in the eye. Brennus stared back boldly, while Girec barely glanced at me before returning his gaze to his boots.

"Who is your enemy?" I directed my words at the boys.

From the corner of my eye, I noticed Hearn start. He hadn't expected me to speak to them. Perhaps he had intended that I would observe only. Was he trying to impress me — or intimidate me?

"The enemy is anyone who opposes the king," Brennus said. Although his voice was confident almost to the point of insolence, he glanced at Hearn, as if gauging his approval. He was not as self-assured as he pretended to be.

"Girec?" I asked.

Girec started to shake his head, but stopped at Hearn's exasperated sigh.

"The enemy are those who oppose our freedom." His voice was barely more than a whisper. "Those who take our land, or steal our people away to be slaves. Those who burn our fields and steal our cattle and leave us to starve."

I nodded my approval at him.

"So, druid, which one is best suited to be my heir?" Hearn cocked his eyebrow at me and waited.

I hesitated. How could I make such a determination after only moments speaking with them? If this was a test, the wrong answer might jeopardise my chances of Hearn ever trusting me. From his obvious favour towards Brennus, it was clear the older boy was the chosen one. But it seemed clear to me that Girec was the better choice, if these two boys were the only options.

"There is much more to kingship than being able to identify one's enemies, my lord," I said. "I know nothing of their strategy or cunning, their fairness or compassion, their wisdom or sense of justice. I would not presume to identify the one you have chosen based on such a brief interview."

Hearn seemed satisfied enough with my response and continued instructing the boys. Brennus and Girec focussed all their attention on the king. Hearn hadn't forgotten me, though. The occasional sideways flick of his gaze, checking whether I still paid attention, told me this was all for my benefit.

I tuned out Hearn's words and focussed on the boys' body language. The way they both faced Hearn directly, with straightened shoulders and heads held high, told me they wanted to please him. Brennus often followed his answers with a sneaky sidelong glance towards Girec, suggesting he thought the younger boy should be impressed with him. When Girec paid him no attention after a response Brennus clearly thought was particularly witty, Brennus turned his back slightly towards him. If Girec noticed the snub, he didn't react. He seemed entirely focussed on Hearn, although nothing he said seemed to satisfy the man.

At length, the lesson was over and Hearn dismissed his foster sons. They left the room at a run, Brennus elbowing Girec out of the way in order to pass through the doorway first. Hearn turned to me.

"Druid, there is a feast tomorrow night. You will attend."

He left without another word.

9

ARLEN

A boy pounded on my door the next morning with a message asking me to meet Derwa in the afternoon. Once again, we walked around the pitiful gardens and I found myself enjoying her company. She spoke more easily this time, and her observations displayed a sharp and intelligent mind. After that, it became a habit for us to spend time together each afternoon and a tentative friendship of sorts blossomed between us.

Hearn had told her to keep me busy — she admitted it with obvious embarrassment — but I also sensed she was lonely. She didn't have ladies-in-waiting trailing after her, or even a maid. It was a curiously lonely existence for someone who should have been surrounded by fawners and flatterers.

"I supposed nobody briefed you on court etiquette before you came here?" she observed as we made our way around the dusty courtyard.

"I never expected to have a position at court," I said. "And there was no time for anything else the day Oistin told me. He sent me as soon as I had packed my belongings."

"Curious. I wonder why it was so urgent that you come? Hearn had already made it clear he didn't want one of Oistin's druids here and two days later he received a message that you would arrive that evening."

"I can't imagine he was pleased with that."

No wonder Hearn seemed to dislike me as soon as he saw me. Derwa grinned and for a moment I forgot how strange she looked with her long face and her awkward limbs. She was almost pretty when she smiled.

"He was extremely displeased. But something you need to understand is that when Hearn summons you, you should wait outside the audience hall. He will call you in when he is ready. It will go easier for you if you accede to at least some of his expectations."

And I had walked straight in that first day.

"I had no idea," I said.

"Of course you didn't."

I shot a glance at her, wondering whether she mocked me, but her face was unreadable. Since she was in a talkative mood, I gathered my courage to ask what I knew I probably shouldn't.

"Why are you always alone? You have no flock of maids trailing after you, no herd of women who want to be able to say they are intimates of the queen."

"They fear me." Her voice was emotionless. "Even as a child of five summers, I knew I didn't look like everyone else. I certainly don't look as one expects a queen to. They fear my ugliness will tarnish their reputations if they are seen associating with me."

I wanted to protest she wasn't ugly, but it would be a lie. Instead, I waited to see if she would offer more. Clouds shrouded the sky today and the wind made lingering outside unpleasant. Derwa shivered and wrapped her cloak more tightly around herself. My mouth tasted gritty from the dust kicked up by the wind.

"You didn't look away when you first saw me," she said, finally. "You looked me right in the eyes as if you saw into my soul."

"I felt it, too," I admitted. "Something inside me said you would be important."

She glanced at me, startled. "To what?"

"To my duties here. To the kingdom. To everything."

To me, I added silently.

Derwa was quiet for a while and I knew her well enough to understand this was no easy silence where she simply didn't feel the need to speak, but rather that she didn't know what to say. The air seemed to grow colder by the minute and I wrapped my cloak more tightly around me.

"I've never been important to anything," she said, long after I had decided she would say nothing further on the subject.

"You are the queen. How could you not be important?"

"I always expected to handfast well, despite my looks. But I never thought, or desired, to be queen. My father owns a massive estate that borders near half of Hearn's land. Joining their two estates together in an alliance of marriage provided significant benefits to both parties. With my father's land and not inconsiderable army, and Hearn's wealth and power, both men gained greatly. And I acquired a husband who was not as intelligent or prudent as I might have hoped for."

Derwa's voice suggested she saw some irony in the situation, although I couldn't imagine how. Hers was not an unfamiliar tale. Many women handfasted with men chosen by their fathers for political or strategic reasons. Some eventually grew to love their husbands. Others at least came to respect them. Derwa, it seemed, had neither.

"Are you very unhappy?" I asked.

She sighed a little as she considered my question.

"Unhappy, no. I have the kind of security that few women gain, even if my husband is petty and stupid. Lonely and unfulfilled? Yes. I could do so much *more* if Hearn wasn't so afraid someone might realise I can actually think. He wanted a pretty, vapid wife. He was reluctant to handfast with me, even to gain such substantial holdings as my father settled on me. I suspect there were other inducements I wasn't told about. Do you know he wasn't supposed to be king?"

"I knew Hearn had an older brother who disappeared some years ago," I said.

"There were two older brothers. One was an excellent horseman, yet he died in a fall from his horse. The other disappeared one night and has never been seen since. Folk said he took off with a travelling girl. A musician or a bard."

"You think…"

Her lips were pursed. "Hearn was supposed to be the soldier son. He was meant to go off to war. But with both brothers dead, and his father following them to the grave shortly afterwards, the role of king fell to him."

"And you became queen."

"And I became queen."

"Why does he dislike me so much? You said he didn't want me here, but is there more to it? He is barely civil to me."

"He fears you will report back to Oistin on everything you hear. That's partly why I am supposed to keep you occupied. So you have little chance to hear what he doesn't want you to."

"And the rest of the reason?"

"To keep myself occupied, I presume. But he tries to offend you in the hope you will choose to leave. He will look weak if he sends you away."

"He hasn't offended me," I said. "I've hardly spoken to him."

"You should have received chambers suitable for an honoured guest, not a servant. That was your first test. To see if you would complain about your lodgings."

"I don't need fine accommodations. The bedchamber I have is perfectly adequate for my needs."

I didn't mention the door that only opened if I put my shoulder to it or the shutters that didn't quite close.

"I suppose druids are accustomed to having little." She sighed. "I might have been a druid myself, had I not been the oldest daughter. That life would have suited me well."

I could picture her walking gently through the woods. Meditating. Memorising the lore.

"I've always had an affinity with nature and the elements, especially that of water." Derwa reached out to caress the naked branch of a young ash tree. "I remember as a child playing with the water elementals, creating fountains in a pond. But the oldest daughter of a powerful landowner would never be permitted the indulgence of being a druid."

I hardly needed to ask whether she would have preferred such a life. The longing in her voice was unmistakable.

"Had you ever met Hearn before you were handfasted?"

"Oh, yes. We met on a number of occasions, although I had never spoken more than a few words to him. But I knew who he was and what he looked like, which is more than many young women can say about their intended husbands. He has changed of late, Arlen," she said suddenly, the words coming out in a rush. "He has never been a clever man, but he used to be petty rather than cruel. Recently though…"

"What?" I asked. "What has he done to you?"

She waved away my question.

"Nothing I can't handle. But there's a meanness about him now that wasn't there before. Or perhaps he just never let it show. I don't know. I'm tired, Arlen. I think I will retire to my bedchamber."

We walked back to the keep in silence and stopped just inside the main entrance. I wanted to offer some comforting words, something she might hold close in difficult moments, but my mind was blank. Instead I touched her lightly on the arm, barely letting my fingertips graze her sleeve.

"Farewell, my lady."

She gave me a sad smile. "Farewell, Arlen."

10

ARLEN

I passed the rest of the day in silent contemplation of my borrowed bronze bowl. I was still getting used to sitting on the hard floorboards, which left my backside numb. I was more accustomed to a seat of moss or fallen leaves or even bare earth to better enhance my connection with the natural world. But there were no woods here, just a few scraggly trees, and I didn't desire to make a spectacle of myself by practising where folk could observe.

I had never before felt self-conscious about my studies. In the community, it was not unusual to come across some druid or other meditating or practising the Sight. Druids walk silently — one of the first things we learn is mastery over our bodies — and we can glide through the woods without disturbing our brethren. Here though, folk might be more inclined to stop and stare, perhaps even interrupt with questions. And they made so much noise when they walked that I wouldn't be able to concentrate. Perhaps nobody would be interested anyway but I preferred to work behind a closed door.

I concentrated on clearing my mind. For hours, I stared into the bowl. Occasionally I thought I glimpsed something in its depths, but even as I stared it melted away. It might have been nothing more than a ripple in the water's surface, caused by my own breath, or a glimmer from the sunlight through the gaps around the shutters. I pushed down my frustration. This was a skill even the youngest apprentice could learn. If I could master the Sight, I might actually be of some use to Hearn.

The light began to soften and the air became colder, signalling the approach of dusk. I pushed the bowl away. Another fruitless session. Oistin had always said my ability would come eventually, that sometimes those who struggled the greatest became the most proficient. But even so, he admitted I was well past the age of any druid he had known to be unable to See.

I had tried every technique for opening myself to the Sight. Hours of quiet contemplation. Silent walks through the forest. Lying back to observe the sky, letting my thoughts float as high as the clouds. I had even once tried inhaling the smoke made by burning a particular leaf which was supposed to open one's mind. Nothing. No matter what I did, the result was the same: the water at which I stared so intently, be it in bowl or pond, was always empty.

The fact that none of a druid's skills had ever come easy to me was a constant source of frustration. I studied harder and practised longer than anyone else to achieve a modicum of proficiency. Even a task as basic as summoning the elementals was a struggle. If they responded, a druid could do almost anything: summon rains or fire, make mountains rise up out of the ground, or travel to the furthest edges of the earth in no more than a few hours. There was nothing magical about any of this, just a working relationship with the elementals. With great difficulty, I had forged relationships with the elementals of earth, water and fire, but the air elementals were elusive and completely unresponsive to me. I sometimes wondered whether I unintentionally offended them as a child.

I concluded my session with a sigh. I had still Seen nothing and it was time to attend Hearn's feast. Careful not to spill the water, I moved the bowl to the dresser. I had been here for less than a cycle of the moon and yet already I wanted nothing more than to return to the community, where I could practise in the silence of the woods, where quiet contemplation was easier, where there was no expectation of me other than that I study hard and learn all I could.

I never wanted a place at court, where folk did not say what they meant and did not mean what they said. Where appearances were everything and motivations were questionable. I wanted solitude and service and the time to finally master the Sight. To finish my studies so I could search for Agata. But my Master had determined a different path for me and I suspected he knew more of both Agata's and my fates than he said.

The only preparation I made for the feast was to wash my face and pull on my boots. I didn't know what clothes might be expected, but I had nothing but my usual linen trousers and long-sleeved tunics anyway. I hadn't thought to ask where the feast would be held, but as soon as I reached the ground level I spotted several finely dressed folk.

I followed them to a large room, roughly the size of Hearn's audience hall, only this one was filled with rows and rows of long tables and benches. The tables were laid with plates and mugs, with tall clay jugs positioned at regular intervals. At the far end of the hall was a table elevated on a dais. I was disappointed that Derwa wasn't here. Not that I would have approached her in front of everyone, but knowing a friend was nearby would have been a comfort.

I hesitated in the doorway. Everyone else seemed to know exactly where to sit. Would I cause a grave insult if I sat at the wrong table? Presumably the further away from Hearn, the lower the standing of those who sat there. I went to the furthest table and claimed a spot on one end of a bench.

I quickly discovered I didn't look out of place in my plain attire. Although a good many of the diners wore finery, those folk gravitated to the tables at the top end. The ones who sat down my end were dressed far more simply, and indeed many wore their work clothes. Folk were in high spirits and the room filled with conversation and laughter.

Eventually somebody else joined my table. It was a young fellow, perhaps in his late teens. He was red-haired and dressed no more finely than I. He sat opposite me and gave me a friendly nod.

"Well met, druid," he said.

I stifled an urge to ask how he knew me. Was my recent arrival the subject of court gossip? I let go of the thought. It was irrelevant to me. I smiled at the fellow.

"Well met, friend. I'm Arlen."

"Rogan," he said and poured two mugs from a nearby jug. He pushed one across the table towards me and raised the other in a salute. He downed the contents and poured himself another.

"Drink up," he advised. "Hearn is unusually generous on feast days. They'll refill the jugs as fast as you can drink."

I raised my mug and sniffed. Ale, it seemed, and not of particularly good quality. Nevertheless, I took a few mouthfuls and tried to swallow without grimacing.

"What do you do here, Rogan?" I asked.

"Look after the oxen mostly," he said. "The master scribe has been teaching me to write in my spare time. He might take me on as apprentice soon."

Before I could respond, several other folk arrived and seated themselves in a flurry of activity. They all seemed to know each other, including Rogan. Most gave me a nod or a smile, or at least a curious stare, and the girl next to me offered her name: Zethar. After that, she turned towards the young man on her other side and seemed wholly immersed in conversation with him.

Rogan talked to the fellow next to him and tried to pretend he wasn't sneaking glances at Zethar. I leaned my elbows on the table and sipped at the bitter ale. If nothing else, a feast was an opportunity to learn something of the politics of the place. And it wouldn't hurt to make a few allies if I could.

Servants brought around food and after so many days of little more than bread and cheese, the aroma was tantalising. There were cauldrons of barley soup and platters of roasted pig, turnips and parsnips, bread filled with seeds and grains, and a variety of cheeses. Folk helped themselves, then passed the trays along the tables. I dished out a modest helping and found the food tasty and liberally seasoned. Across from me, Rogan piled his plate high and ate as if it was his first meal in days.

My companions somehow managed to both eat and talk at the same time. The trays were passed around again. I declined, although I did allow Rogan to top up my ale. Zethar pushed away her empty plate and turned to smile shyly at me. Before she could speak, there was an almighty crash. All around us, people jumped to their feet, roaring and cheering. My table mates joined in and Zethar climbed up on the bench to see over the crowd.

"What's happening?" I asked.

Her eyes shone as she glanced down at me.

"A fight."

I was ashamed of the excitement that welled within me and I quickly squashed it down. It was unbecoming for a druid. Nevertheless, I slipped through the edges of the crowd and around to the side, where I had a better view. Two men stood on opposite sides of a table. Both had thick beards and fine clothing. One was broad-shouldered with legs that looked as strong as tree trunks. The other was taller with a more slender frame, although when he pulled off his tunic, his arms were well-muscled. A woman stood near the taller man, her hands clasped to her chest and her face anxious. The burly man appeared to be alone. Folk formed a ring around them and the boisterous roar of the crowd died as the burly man held up his fist.

"Do you challenge me, oaf?" he roared.

"Aye," the other replied and spat on the floor. "Although if you intend to live, you had best walk away now."

"I intend to live all right," the first said. "After I feast on your liver."

The second man roared and thumped the table. The crowd began to chant. A chill ran down my spine as I made out their words. *To the death*, they cried. *To the death.*

With another yell, the burly man tipped over the table. Platters flew to the floor, clanging and clattering. Jugs smashed and ale spilled. He leaped over the table and flung himself at his challenger.

Folk yelled in support of one or the other and waved their fists in the air. Even the woman who had looked anxious now cheered. Brennus pushed to the front of the crowd where he hopped from foot to foot and shouted enthusiastically. If Girec was also here, I couldn't see him.

The fighters circled each other, feinting and ducking. Testing each other. Eventually the slender one darted in and delivered a blow. The burly man merely shook his head and hit back.

Were there no guards present? Surely they would put a stop to this. But I spied a couple of fellows wearing the blue of the guard's uniform and cheering the fighters.

A roar from the crowd brought my attention back to the two men. They were on the floor, rolling around in the remains of their meals. Over and over, they struck each other. First one seemed to gain the upper hand, then the other would deliver a well-placed blow and force his opponent to defend himself. They seemed evenly matched, despite the differences in their builds. Cries of *to the death* continued from the crowd. A man in front of me hefted a small girl of three or four summers up onto his shoulders for a better view.

My stomach rolled and the bitter taste of bile filled my mouth. I had never before witnessed such a thing. As a boy, I saw occasional scuffles between my cousins, or amongst the younger druids, but there was always an adult nearby to haul the fighters apart and shake them until they calmed down. Here, though, not only was the vicious-ness allowed to continue, it was actively encouraged.

Even Hearn stood to watch the fight. He roared and his eyes held the same battle-crazed expression as those around me. Beside him sat a woman I had never seen before. Her almost-white hair was loose and flowed down over her shoulders. She wore a simple blue dress with a high neck and sleeves that came all the way to her wrists. She was the only person in the room who was not on their feet. Instead she leaned back in her chair and watched. The expression on her face was strangely satisfied. Who was she? Hearn's mistress, perhaps? That might explain why Derwa was not present. I turned my attention back to the fighters.

It would be madness to try to separate them. Even if I could get through the crowd, folk were too consumed with battle lust to understand reason. I might be torn apart myself if I deprived them of the fight.

The burly man sat on top of the other, using his legs to pin down the man's arms. He grabbed the man's head and repeatedly slammed it into the wooden floor. The man on the bottom flailed around, unable to get a good grip on his attacker. After his head hit the floor five or six times, he stopped trying to fight back and eventually he stopped moving altogether. Words were exchanged between them, although I couldn't hear what. Then the burly man raised his arms in triumph. The crowd roared. Men dashed in to help the victor up.

They ignored the man on the floor as he rolled over and tried to stand. He staggered, his eyes rolling up in his head. Nobody stepped forward to help him. I started to push through the crowd. Now the battle lust had abated, I could help him get to a quieter place and find a healer.

Someone else reached the injured man before I could, bringing with him a tall shield, man-height and sturdy, which he lay on the floor. A man wearing a fine brocade shirt tossed a small pouch, which landed on the shield with a clink. Others deposited single coins or a handful. As folk stepped forward to throw their coins onto the shield, they said a few words to the injured man. He swayed and clutched the upturned table for support, seemingly barely aware of his surroundings.

When the stream of coins ceased, the victor motioned towards the shield and the injured man stepped forward unsteadily. His legs buckled and two men moved in to aid him. They helped him lie down on top of the coins that covered the shield.

A woman knelt beside him, the one who had looked anxious at the start of the fight. She leaned in to speak to him. He reached for her and she clutched his hand. Then she rose and stepped back.

The victor stepped forward with a dagger. He knelt beside the man on the shield and, without hesitation, ran the dagger across his throat. Blood splattered the victor's chest. He grinned down at his opponent and stood, holding the bloody dagger aloft. The crowd roared again and there were more chants of *to the death*. At last I understood what they meant. My stomach heaved.

The guard stationed at the door that led outside barely glanced at me as I staggered out. I vomited until there was nothing left in my stomach.

Every time I blinked, I saw the man lying on the coin-covered shield, his throat slit. The woman who had farewelled him, who was she? Wife? Sister? Betrothed? I presumed she would take possession of the coins, penalty for the loss of income incurred by the death of her man.

When I was sure I had nothing left to vomit, I made my way back to the door. The guard smirked as he looked me up and down.

"Looks like you've had enough for tonight, my fellow," he said and his voice wasn't all that unkind.

I didn't respond, only pushed open the door and stumbled back through the keep to my bedchamber. I didn't bother to light the candle. In the dark, I stripped off my vomit-splattered clothes and dropped them on the floor. Then I crawled into bed, knowing I would spend all night with the memory of a dead man lying on a shield.

11

ARLEN

Hearn summoned me before noon the next day. My mind still whirled from last night's events and my mouth tasted sour. If the man had a wife, she was now a widow. Any children she had borne him were fatherless. I had never seen folk take so much pleasure in the pain of another, and Hearn did nothing to stop them. How could I respect a king like that?

I dropped my reeking clothes off at the washer room. The servant woman didn't flinch at the smell and assured me they would be returned by this evening. I supposed the wash servants would be kept busy today removing stains from clothing far finer than mine.

The hallways were silent and empty as I made my way to the library. Perhaps most of the inhabitants were still sleeping off the feast. The door stood open and Hearn sat at a heavy desk, studying a piece of parchment. A lamp cast its flickering light over the page. The image brought memories of being summoned to Oistin's bedchamber and seeing him seated at his desk reading a message or examining a map. I swallowed down a wave of homesickness as I knocked. The two men were nothing alike.

"Aah, druid, there you are." Hearn sounded like he was in an agreeable mood today. I hoped he wouldn't ask what I thought of last night's events. "Come and tell me what you make of this."

I examined the shelves of books and stacks of parchment as I made my way to him, surprised at the size of his collection. I immediately recognised the parchment Hearn studied as a map of the country. A black cross within a large rectangle indicated Braen Keep. Bold lines marked neighbouring estates. A twisting line crossing the lower end of Hearn's territory was likely a river.

"A map," I said. "Of Braen Town and its surrounds."

"What do you know of my territory?"

Another test. I studied the parchment.

"This is an old map, my lord. Your boundaries are somewhat different at present."

He had ceded a large block of his territory to Cullen, whose land bordered his, in a dispute three summers ago. I was sure Hearn didn't need to be reminded.

"What do you know of Cullen?" Hearn spat out his neighbour's name.

"I know there is a longstanding hostility between the two of you. There have been a number of skirmishes between your troops over the last few years, one in particular that might have led to all-out war had you not retreated when you did."

"There will be war between us yet, druid." Hearn's voice was cold. "Cullen pushes me towards it. He encroaches on my land, he steals my cattle. He begs me to send my troops against him."

"Is that what you want? To face him in war?"

Hearn studied the map and didn't look at me.

"I want him to learn his place. And you, druid, will help me."

"My lord?"

"War is coming for us, druid. The time draws near. I can smell it in the air. Druids are good at identifying when a war should start, aren't they?"

"I am trained to examine the signs and advise on the most favourable day for battle," I said.

"And you will do so, when the time is right. When I am ready to meet Cullen in battle, you will interpret the signs for me."

I understood what he didn't say. He expected me to have his interests at heart when I examined the signs. He would choose when to go to war and when to stop, and would expect me to decipher the signs favourably. He wanted me to lie.

"Interpreting the signs is a complicated matter." I made sure my tone was suitably respectful and prayed Hearn would not take offence. "I cannot be sure until I have carefully studied them as to what the outcome might be."

"Oh, I think you'll know the outcome when it's needed, druid." Hearn tapped the triangle marking Cullen's land and gave me a steady look. "Or at least, for your sake, I hope you do."

12

ARLEN

"Druid, a letter for you," a messenger boy said from the doorway.

I sat cross-legged on the floor in my bedchamber, staring into the bronze bowl. I hadn't bothered to close the door since nobody came all the way up here unless they were looking for me. He tossed a scroll towards me and scampered away.

It was bound with a scrap of leather and stamped with the Silver Downs seal. Likely it had been sent to the druid community and was redirected, because I hadn't yet sent a message home about my relocation to Braen Keep. I felt strangely uneasy as I broke the seal. I had received a message from Silver Downs only a sevennight or so before I left the community, and to receive another again so soon was unusual.

The fine parchment was lettered with a neat but unfamiliar hand. I glanced at the name at the bottom and my heart froze when I saw it was from Fiachra, who was one of Eithne's brothers and also a druid. I would have been perhaps seven or eight summers old the last time I met him and was awestruck by how grand my druid uncle seemed. If he spoke to me on that visit, the conversation had not stayed in my memory. I remembered only that it was strange to see him with

Eithne, for he was old enough to be her grandfather, although they were actually brother and sister.

Eithne had travelled to the fey realm as a young woman, and when she returned a few months later, sixty years had passed in our world. Her parents and five of her brothers had died while she was gone, leaving only Fiachra and Diarmuid left alive. I feared to learn what would prompt Fiachra to write to me after all this time. *Arlen, matters have occurred here at Silver Downs of which you need to be aware,* his letter began.

Your uncle Diarmuid died yesterday and the creature he had kept imprisoned for many years has escaped. Eithne tells me you have no knowledge of this creature. She felt it best not to terrorise a child with this tale, especially as you already knew far too much about the terrors of our world.

As a young child, I feared Titania would come to steal me away, just like she had taken my sister. I barely recalled the details now, but for many years I suffered from night terrors and would wake scream-ing, certain the fey queen stood over my bed with arms outstretched to snatch me away. The dreams subsided eventually, but I had never forgotten the paralysing terror of them, even if the details themselves were now somewhat blurred.

You know, I presume, that your uncle was a bard. We shared five brothers, he and I, all of them dead long before your birth. Diarmuid was the youngest and the seventh son of a seventh son. In our family, the one in that position is always a bard and has the ability to bring his tales to life.

I set the parchment down on my knee as I absorbed this news. I vaguely remembered hearing that Uncle Diarmuid had been a bard in his youth. I couldn't recall him ever telling a tale, though, and as a child I didn't think to question it. But the ability to bring tales to life — this was a power I had never heard of, even with all my training. I resumed reading.

Diarmuid was, as far as we know, the first in his line to understand the secret of how his ability worked. Others before him had brought their tales to life but without knowing how. However, long before this happened, he was a boy who was only just beginning to explore his first tales. He told nobody, so we did not know to warn him. I suppose we should have anyway, for we knew that as the seventh son of a seventh son, he would be a bard. But our parents hoped that by not telling him, they might spare him. That he might instead turn to another career. So Diarmuid was left to explore his earliest tales unguided and without knowledge of the ability that lay inside him.

His first tale was about a bard who created a muse, a woman to whom he whispered his tales, and from whom he fancied his inspiration flowed. When Diarmuid told that tale, the muse he imagined came to life. At that point, though, she was confined to his head and we knew nothing of her existence. It may be a difficult thing to understand, but although she lived only in his mind, we believe she was already very real. Our father warned him then of the ability he possessed, but Diarmuid didn't believe him.

We watched him carefully over the next few years, but there was no indication that any tale he told came true and gradually we began to relax. In truth, we even forgot for a while. It seemed that Diarmuid, like so many of those who came before him, had not discovered how to bring his tales to life. We did not know that during these years, the muse he created was living inside of him, whispering to him, watching everything he did and said, and growing in power of her own.

It was not until his nineteenth summer that his creation — he called her Ida — finally gained enough strength to break free of his head. She became real. She had a body and a mind of her own. She left Diarmuid and travelled to Crow's Nest, where she terrorised the inhabitants. From what I have pieced together over the years, I believe she was recreating tales she had heard Diarmuid tell. The tales he told back in those days before she left him were dark, and it seems this is all she understood of the world.

Diarmuid found her, and once he unlocked the key to his ability, he was able to return her to his head. He has kept her in there all the years since, trapped in a box inside his mind. We could never be sure, but we believe she still watched him. Everything he has done, everything he has said, everything he has learned during these years, she has probably been silent witness to.

Once again, I set the parchment down to absorb Fiachra's words. My heart pounded and my mouth was dry. Why had I never before heard this part of our family history? I could hardly believe it. An imaginary muse brought to life and escaped? It sounded like something straight out of a tale, although it was no tale I had ever heard. But as a druid, I had seen many strange things, and Fiachra had no reason to lie to me.

Diarmuid had an apprentice of sorts, Tristan, who is determined to be a bard although Diarmuid was ever reluctant to teach him. He is my brother Eremon's great-grandson and, like Diarmuid, he is the seventh son of a seventh son, even if the line stretches only as far as his own father. Nevertheless, he showed early promise with his tales, and the ability has become apparent in him, too. He tried to contain Ida when she escaped, but failed.

Ida is strong — far stronger than before — and I have little hope she can be contained again. Regardless, we must try. I leave here today to search for her. Arlen, I urge you to be on your guard. As you are a son of Silver Downs, she might be drawn to you. Be alert for any mention of trouble, especially where it involves family, friends or neighbours turning on each other with little justification. It may well be Ida's doing. She is cunning and insidious, and folk subjected to her power never even realise they have been charmed.

Also beware of birds, particularly if there is anything unusual about them. Diarmuid believed Ida had the ability to change her form and that she sometimes travelled as a raven. Message me at once if you hear of anything that might be related to her escape. Send all messages to Silver Downs. I will keep in close contact with the family here.

I wish you well, Arlen. I regret that we have never had the opportunity to spend time together. There is much I would wish to pass onto another druid of our blood. Circumstances have so often prevented me from making contact and I fear the opportunity has now passed. I have little expectation that I will survive an encounter with Ida. However, if I can stop her, I will gladly forsake whatever is left of my time on this earth.

Be cautious, Arlen, and be alert.

Your uncle,

Fiachra, Druid, of Silver Downs

I read the message again, paying particular attention to Fiachra's words about what sort of trouble Ida might cause, and a sudden strong longing for home welled within me. I remembered a large stone lodge filled with plenty of nooks and crannies for young boys to lose themselves in. Grassy fields, gurgling rivers, dark woods. Early morning mists and winter winds that sometimes held a hint of the far-away ocean. A portal to the fey realm somewhere on the edge of Silver Downs land. Sometimes I wondered whether my training could ever compensate for my lost boyhood.

I was saddened to hear of my Uncle Diarmuid's death. An old man who was probably more patient with young boys than they deserved. I remembered gnarled hands that grasped the head of the cane he always carried. He had bad hips that made walking difficult at times, and we all knew he had suffered enough of boisterous boys when his knuckles tightened on the cane and he twitched it restlessly.

Had Fiachra Seen something that prompted him to send this message, or did he merely preempt the possibility that Uncle Diarmuid's muse might be drawn to me? Now, more than ever before, I desperately needed to access the Sight. I set the parchment aside on the floorboards and drew the bronze bowl back in front of me. I closed my eyes and took a few deep breaths.

It was difficult to centre myself, for my thoughts spun, but when I finally achieved some modicum of composure, I peered down into the bowl. The water was clear and calm, without even the slightest ripple to disturb its surface. I stared into it until my eyes grew gritty and still I saw nothing but water.

13

ARLEN

I forced open the sticking shutters and leaned right out the window of my bedchamber. I ached for the sight of grass or trees. Anything green. The longer I stayed at Braen Keep, the more trapped I felt. Everything here was grey and brown, dirty and dusty, broken or incomplete. There was no beauty, either natural or created. There were no woods, no grassy patches where one might sit for a while. No flowers, no bugs. Nothing of the natural world except the sky above, and even that was grey and dreary at this time of year. Some days I felt like I couldn't breathe.

Hearn hadn't summoned me again in the sevennight since our discussion in the library. Derwa and I still met most afternoons to walk around the dusty courtyard, despite the frigid wind heralding winter's approach. I considered her a friend, in so much as a queen and her husband's druid advisor can ever be friends. I spent most of the rest of my time in my bedchamber meditating and trying to access the Sight.

I longed to return to the druid community, just for a few hours, to sit amongst the trees and ferns and crawling vines. Hearn probably wouldn't notice if I disappeared, but Oistin would be furious I had left my post. As I thought about fertile earth and towering trees, crawling insects and sweetly-scented flowers, my chest tightened. I wouldn't breathe freely again until I had restored my connection with the natural world. It was only midmorning and Derwa wouldn't expect me for our afternoon walk for hours yet. I pulled on my boots, wrapped my cloak around my shoulders and left my bedchamber.

I didn't bother to hide that I was going somewhere. Nobody would care if Hearn's pet druid left. As I approached the keep's gates, they opened to admit a pair of oxen and a laden cart driven by a skinny man who looked as downtrodden as everyone else in this place. The guards didn't seem to notice as I slipped through.

On the other side of the wall, the town was just as miserable as the keep, and I didn't waste any time there. What I sought wouldn't be found here. I recognised the road Bram had brought me along that first day and set off.

As I left the last of the falling-down lodges and woebegone gardens behind, my spirit lifted like the sun rising above clouds. Sparse patches of yellowed grass soon became a field, and in the distance stood a line of trees. I headed towards them.

The first tree I reached was an ash, its naked branches spreading majestically above me. I rested my palm against its fissured trunk and the faint vibration of its life force against my skin soothed my soul. I inhaled deeply, rejoicing in the fresh scent of trees and grass and earth. I left the ash and kept walking. Just a little further. Just until I couldn't see the town behind me anymore.

In a short while I came to an area that was so beautiful, I almost cried. Winter-brown grass that reached halfway up my calf. Oak and ash and a single rowan with shiny red mistletoe berries drooping from its branches. A patch of weeds, taller than the grass, had gone to seed and an ant crawled up one stem. Pale yellow primrose bloomed and fat bees buzzed around them.

I lowered myself to the ground. It was warm from the sun and the tall grass tickled my arms pleasantly. I sank my hands down into the earth. Life vibrations buzzed against my fingers as I centred myself. I inhaled deeply three times and easily slipped into a meditative state. I could feel life all around me. Ants, worms, dragonflies, a lone raven in a tree somewhere to my left. My mind drifted with the breeze as it swept over my little sanctuary.

After some time, I became aware of the approach of two life forces which were larger than the birds and insects, and I reluctantly withdrew from my meditation. I stayed in the grass, though, my hands still immersed in the earth, unwilling to lose my connection with the natural world so soon.

I heard them before I saw them. A man and a woman, carefree and laughing, trading jokes and mock insults. Travellers, perhaps, on their way to Braen Town maybe. The man said something I couldn't catch, but I heard what he called her: Agata. My sister's name. It was a common enough name and I shouldn't be surprised to encounter someone else with it. After all, my sister was named for her grandmother.

I had been so wrapped up in events at Braen Keep that I had almost forgotten my own mission: to rescue my stolen sister from the fey realm. Did she know she had a family? Did she wonder whether we searched for her? Why was I wasting time sitting around at court when I could be looking for Agata? Forget Oistin's commands. Forget Hearn who made it clear he didn't want my advice. *I'm coming, Agata,* I thought. *Tonight. I won't waste any more time.*

I paid little attention to the man and woman as they drew closer. He came into view first and I was struck with the feeling of having seen him before. He was slender, with dark hair and a face that was vaguely familiar. But when I saw her, my heart stopped. I had seen my own face in various bodies of water enough times to recognise it immediately. She had my eyes, my nose, my chin. The same dark hair, although mine was barely shoulder length and hers fell almost to her waist in a long braid draped over her shoulder.

I wasn't even aware I stood until they looked at me. My face probably mirrored the confusion on hers. The man looked between the two of us, his eyebrows raised.

"Agata?" he said. "What is this? How does he look like you?"

She took a step towards me and reached out one hand as if wanting to touch me.

"Who are you?" she whispered. "And why do you have my face?"

"I'm your brother," I said.

I wanted to say that I had always intended to search for her as soon as I was free to make my own decisions. I wanted to tell her of the nights I had lain awake, unable to sleep for knowing that half my soul was missing. Instead, the words that came out of my mouth were not about myself.

"Our mother misses you greatly."

Her mouth opened and closed before she found any words.

"Our mother? You, too, are born of Titania?"

Fury rose within me. She didn't know. Titania had stolen her away and never even told her.

"Titania is not your mother," I said, and my voice trembled a little. "Our mother's name is Eithne, and she is mortal. You were stolen from her just moments after your birth and she has grieved you ever since."

Agata laughed and flicked her braid back over her shoulder.

"Don't be ridiculous. I am fey, not born of a mortal woman. I don't know why we share a face. Perhaps you are fey and just don't know it?" She turned to the man. "Sumerled, tell him I am fey."

Even his name was familiar, although I couldn't place it. Agata's laughter died on her lips as she took in the look on his face.

"Sumerled?" Her voice was less certain now.

He laughed and held out his hand to her.

"Why are we standing here conversing with a mortal? You've seen their realm. Now let's go home."

She didn't move to take his hand but folded her arms across her chest.

"Sumerled, tell me he is lying." Her lower lip trembled. "Tell me I am fey."

"Come," he said, and his tone was so enticing that I almost reached for his hand myself. "It's time to go home."

"Don't try to charm me," she said, crossly. "I want the truth. Is Titania really my mother?"

He let his arm fall back down to his side and looked away, off into the trees.

"You should ask her yourself if you have questions."

"Tell me it's not true," she whispered. "Please."

"Agata, our mother would dearly love to see you," I said. "She had only moments with you before Titania snatched you away."

She glowered at me.

"You lie. I don't know why you lie. I don't know why you have my face. Titania is my mother and I am fey."

She turned and ran. I didn't bother giving chase, for she ran like the wind and I would never catch her. As soon as she was gone, the pleasantness disappeared from Sumerled's face, and when he spoke his tone was vicious.

"Stay away from her," he said. "Titania has left your family in peace all these years, but if you interfere she will ruin you all."

Then he ran after Agata.

My knees trembled so hard I had to sit back down in the grass. I had found my sister. And she didn't even know she was missing.

14

AGATA

I fled the mortal, running through the long grass as fast as my feet would take me. I didn't try to run silently. I just wanted to get away. Sumerled called me, but I tucked down my head and ran even faster. I didn't stop until I was back in my own realm. Or what I had always thought was my own realm.

I stopped to catch my breath, leaning against the smooth trunk of a young beech. The woods had gone silent at my noisy entrance, but as I calmed myself, bird and vole and hedgehog slowly returned to their usual doings. The air smelled of living trees and moist soil and rotting leaves. I hadn't realised the mortal realm would smell so different. It lacked the damp, woodsy scent of the fey realm and instead smelled of smoke and dry grass and the odour of something rotting. By the time Sumerled caught up with me, I breathed normally even if my mind still raced.

"Is it true?" I demanded as he stopped beside me.

He was too winded to speak, but I didn't have the patience to wait until he caught his breath.

"Answer me," I said. "Tell me whether what the mortal said is true."

"Of course not," he said, between gasps. "You can't trust anything a mortal says. They're tricky."

"Why does he look like me?"

"Does he?"

I glowered and he quickly looked away.

"There might be a passing resemblance, I suppose. If you look hard enough."

"It's more than a passing resemblance. He looks exactly like me."

"His hair is shorter."

I punched him in the arm.

"Don't be stupid. Tell me what you know."

"What makes you think I know any more than you do? I've never seen him before."

"I know you hear all sorts of things when you skulk around."

"Don't say that," he said, sulky now. He dug the toe of his boot into the ground, scraping away the leaves to expose the fertile soil beneath. "I hate it when folk say I skulk."

"Well, you do."

"I don't. I'm allowed to walk around. And if folk are careless enough to say things they don't want anyone to hear, how is that my fault?"

"So tell me what you know. Is it true I'm half mortal?"

"Of course not."

I crossed my arms over my chest and glared at him.

"Don't lie to me, Sumerled. I know you lie to everyone else, but I won't stand for you lying to me. So tell me what you know or we won't be friends anymore."

"Agata, don't be like that." Sumerled stared at me with wide eyes, likely trying to gain my sympathy. "You're my best friend. You can't stop being friends with me."

"Last chance." I tapped my foot, although the motion was ineffective against the soft leaf litter.

"I don't know anything for certain."

I waited without speaking. At length he sighed and told me. I watched the slow progress of a dragonfly as he spoke. Somehow his words didn't hurt quite as much if I didn't look at him as he said them.

"You were a newborn babe the first time I saw you. Titania

presented you to the court one day and said you were her daughter. Why wouldn't I believe her?"

"Had she…" I didn't quite know how to word it. "Did she look like she was with child before that?"

Sumerled blushed. "I don't know. She can look however she wants to. She might have concealed it."

"So she just turned up with me one day?"

"You were wrapped in a blanket and squealing," he offered.

"What exactly did she say?"

"Just that you were her daughter and your name was Agata."

"Did she say who my father was?"

I had never asked Titania. It obviously wasn't Oberon, for surely he would have had some involvement in my childhood. I had always assumed I was the product of one of Titania's many affairs. Both she and Oberon had them and neither seemed particularly concerned. The one exception was Oberon's occasional dalliances with mortal women. I understood why Titania found that so insulting. That the king of the fey would choose a mortal woman — unattractive, clumsy, inept, boring — over Titania was unthinkable, and yet it happened time after time.

Was it possible my father was a mortal? That despite her fury over Oberon's affairs with mortal women, she herself had borne a child to a mortal man? And yet the stranger with my face had said my mother was mortal. So who was Titania to me? I realised Sumerled hadn't answered my question.

"Did she say who my father was?" I asked again.

"If she did, I never heard of it. But then I never heard anyone ask either. Folk talk, though, you know that. And there were whispers that your father was mortal. I suppose Oberon must have asked at some point. Wouldn't you think he would want to know?"

I glared at him and he shrugged, his face guileless.

"What? I'd want to know, if I was he. Did you think he was your father?"

"Of course not," I snapped. My feet moved restlessly, wanting to run, but I had to see this conversation through to the end.

"Why not?"

I was astonished at his surprise. It had never occurred to me that anyone would think Oberon to be my father. Did others know the truth of my parentage or did they, like Sumerled, make assumptions?

"You can't tell anyone," I said. "Not a soul."

He gave me that wounded look again.

"I wouldn't."

"You would too, if it suited you. I'm serious, Sumerled. If you tell a single person, if you even hint that I'm not a full fey, I will make your life a misery."

He gave me a sad look.

"My life is already a misery. The only thing about it that's not is you."

Guilt stabbed me, but I strengthened my resolve.

"I mean it, Sumerled."

He stalked away through the woods. I followed slowly, still trying to make sense of what I had learned. Trying to slot this new information in amongst the things I thought I knew about myself. Why had Titania kept this from me? And who else knew?

15

AGATA

I made no attempt to catch up with Sumerled on the way home and he didn't wait for me. I expected to encounter him leaning against a tree, taunting a sprite and chewing a blade of grass as he waited for me to catch up. But he didn't and I was too busy adjusting my view of myself to really care.

I wasn't a full fey. It seemed so obvious now. It explained my lack of elegance and grace. The fey fluidity I had never had. It also explained why I had always been something of an outcast, not quite shunned by the fey, but also not fully embraced. By the time I reached the palace, I had decided to demand Titania tell me the truth. It was my right to know where I came from.

The guards at the palace entrance watched impassively as I climbed the shallow wooden steps which had been smoothed by hundreds, maybe thousands, of years of time and feet. The building was an impossible concoction of living trees shaped by fey magic to grow how they would not normally. The doors were tall and narrow, and they swung open soundlessly as I approached. They had no hinges or doorknobs, bolts or latches. They simply grew into doors which opened and closed on their own. Hallways stretched ahead of me, living corridors of wood lit by fey magic.

I went straight to Titania's private chambers, where the guard admitted me without comment. Inside, Titania lounged on a low couch. Her shimmering white gown glistened as she reached out to pluck another fruit from the bowl beside her. They were exotic things that Titania herself created and did not grow naturally.

"Agata, my dear," she said. "Did you enjoy your day?"

"I need to talk to you."

I was suddenly unsure of myself. Demanding the truth of my parentage seemed like a good idea earlier, but now that I was here I feared her famous temper. Titania patted the seat beside her.

"Come. Sit with me. Tell me what troubles you, my dear."

Never in my life had Titania suggested I tell her my troubles. As a parent, she was strict but mostly distant. Praising when I pleased her but cold and unforgiving when I didn't. *She already knows,* I thought. *And she's waiting for me to say the wrong thing.* I cast my gaze around the room, looking for... I wasn't quite sure what. An excuse, perhaps. A way to distract her from the conversation I had intended.

The room was simply but tastefully appointed, the furniture having grown out of wall or floor and formed itself into useful shapes. Chairs, shelves, side tables. They were all living wood from the trees that made up Titania's palace. The air was strongly fragranced with the floral concoction Titania favoured, which made my nose itch. I tried not to sneeze. Titania regarded any such action as ungraceful.

"Agata," she said, sharply.

Titania did not like giving an order twice. And an order it was, even if she merely told me to sit beside her.

I crossed the room, acutely aware of the lack of grace in my movements. Distracted, I caught my slipper against the floor and stumbled. Titania raised one perfect eyebrow but didn't comment. Blushing and wishing I wasn't, I sat beside her. The couch was harder than it looked.

"I met someone today," I started. I didn't know how to say this.

"Oh? Was he handsome?"

She winked at me and I was sure she deliberately misunderstood. I took a deep breath.

"He looked just like me," I said. "My face. My eyes, my chin, my nose. He was the same height as me and slender like I am. His hair was the same colour as mine." I took a deep breath. "And he was mortal."

Titania studied me. Not even a flicker of emotion crossed her face. I should have expected she would keep her secrets well. I could pretend I didn't know. Pretend I saw no connection between me and the boy. But it would be a lie. For as soon as he said he was my brother, I felt the truth of it. I stared down at my hands as I said words I never expected to say.

"Am I half mortal?"

Would she lie? To protect herself, if not to save my feelings. But when I glanced up, her expression was not what I expected. I thought she might be ashamed of her liaison with a mortal man. Perhaps embarrassed I found out. Angry I knew. Worried I might not keep her secret. Perhaps wistful I would never again think I was a full fey. But her face showed none of those things. Instead she looked smug, and maybe a little gleeful.

"I'm afraid so," she said, her voice crisp and and utterly unsympathetic.

The last tiny shred of hope inside me died.

"Who is my father?"

"Curious you have never asked about your parentage until now." She cocked her head to the side and considered me. "Tell me about this boy you met."

"No, I want to know who my father is."

She went very still.

"Tell me about the boy," she said, each word slow and clear.

"There's nothing else to tell. I met a boy who looked just like me. And Sum—" I stopped, realising I would probably get Sumerled into trouble.

"Go on, my dear." Her voice was frosty. "Sumerled did what?"

She would know if I lied. It was too late. *I'm sorry, Sumerled,* I thought.

"He said there was a rumour that my father was mortal."

She smiled, but there was no warmth in it.

"Sumerled, my dear, is wrong."

My heart leapt. I was fey after all.

"He is?"

"Your father is fey," she said. "Well, half fey, but I don't suppose you care about that distinction."

"Half fey?"

I struggled to keep up with the morsels of information she doled out. She was enjoying herself and clearly intended to make her revelations last.

"It's your mother you should be asking about."

Now she looked like a cat that had found a pail of milk and sipped away all of the cream floating on top.

"My mother?"

"You are not an imbecile, my dear," Titania observed, mildly. "There is no need to repeat everything I say."

"But you're my mother."

"Have I ever said that?"

As I looked into her cold eyes, it was like the floor had fallen away beneath me and I was falling, falling, falling. No, Titania had never said she was my mother.

"But I thought—"

"Unfortunately, thinking is something mortals are not terribly good at."

"I'm mortal?"

She lifted one slender shoulder in a shrug.

"Three-quarters mortal is close enough to full mortal," she said.

My chest constricted and my throat narrowed. I sucked at the air but couldn't get enough in. My vision started to swim.

"Oh, my dear, must you do that here? It is so inelegant."

I tried to control myself, to calm my racing heart and slow my gasping breaths. I clasped my hands in my lap to hide how they shook, although she likely missed nothing. I was mortal, or close to it. Titania was not my mother. My father was half fey.

"Who are my parents? Where are they? Why am I here?"

Titania leaned back against the couch. She stretched her legs out in front of her and crossed her ankles. Her slippers were made of the same shimmering fabric as her gown. I edged further along the couch to give her more room.

"Let me see." Her voice was almost a purr. "Your mother is an annoying mortal who was too stupid to stay in her own realm. Your father is a traitorous half fey who decided to go live as a mortal. And you, my dear, are here because I stole you."

My mind went blank. I couldn't speak. I clasped my hands together so tightly that my fingernails cut into my skin.

"I took you just moments after you dropped out of your mother's womb. It was punishment for her interference in things that mortals should stay out of. And since you're half fey, it was more appropriate that you grow up here instead of there."

"But I'm really only one-quarter fey." My voice was faint and I hardly even knew why I said it. But it seemed important. I was more mortal than fey. "What did my mother do?"

"That does not concern you," Titania said briskly. "Now tell me about this boy you met. He could be a cousin, I suppose. Your mother had a large number of brothers as I recall."

I spoke automatically, barely registering the words that passed my lips. Perhaps she charmed me, for I told her more than I intended.

"He was about my age and he looked exactly like me. When I saw him, it was like something inside of me that was empty suddenly filled up. Something I didn't even know was missing was regained."

Titania's eyes were distant and I wasn't sure she was even listening.

"A boy child," she murmured. "And of an age with her. It couldn't be. I would have Seen."

"Seen what?"

"I would have Seen if there were two babes. I took the only child she bore. I did watch for a while to make sure she didn't get herself with child again, but eventually I lost interest. I've had no reason to look in on them again since. It's not possible there could have been two babes."

"When two babes are born together, their soul is split across the two bodies," I said. "Is this what happened? Is he the other half of me?"

Titania raised one hand and motioned for me to leave the room.

"You bore me with your incessant questions, my dear. Run along now."

"You have to tell me."

If she didn't tell me now, while she was still willing to boast about her actions, I would never get any answers from her. "You can't tell me so little and then nothing more. I have to know."

Titania turned her cold gaze on me and I knew I had gone too far. I stood on shaky legs and sketched a brief curtsey, surprising myself that I managed to do it without stumbling. I fled without another word.

I ran from the palace. I didn't want to be anywhere near her and this wasn't really my world anyway. She wasn't my mother. I didn't belong here. As I ran through the woods, tears trickled down my cheeks. At first I brushed them away, for fey do not cry. But they continued to fall and eventually I gave up. What did it matter if I cried? I wasn't fey. I never had been.

16

AGATA

I ran on swift feet, moving almost as silently as a fey. Long years of striving to be like everyone else meant I hardly needed to think about it. Tears dripped down my cheeks, but I refused to sob. I ducked under tree branches and jumped rocks and fallen limbs. I would run so far that nobody would ever find me. I'd never again have to look into the eyes of those who had gossiped about my heritage. Never again would they whisper about me behind my back. Never again would Titania smirk as she told me how she stole me from my mother. My mortal mother.

When I could finally run no further, I slowed to a walk. I spotted an elderly oak tree with long spreading branches I could climb. When I was as high as I could go, although probably not as high as a fey could have gone, I sat on a thick branch with my back against the trunk. As I shifted to get more comfortable, my sleeve snagged on its rough bark. I tugged it free, hardly caring that my gown was probably ruined.

From up here, the world seemed normal. A woodlark trilled a song. A sprite flew past, reaching out one tiny hand to tap an acorn and send it swinging. An ant scurried along the branch. The calm and peace of the woods seeped into me. My heart slowed and my breathing steadied. Intermittent tears still leaked from my eyes, and I wiped my dripping nose on the hem of my gown. Just a few hours ago I thought I was normal.

Tentatively, I let myself explore my feelings. Hurt. Outrage. Shock. Dismay. And when I examined my feelings honestly, perhaps there was a tiny part of me that wasn't surprised. I had always been different, and I suddenly realised there were fey abilities I had not even wondered about, such as being able to change one's physical appearance. What would Titania have said when I finally asked about such a thing?

I knew Sumerled was older than me and yet we had always appeared to be the same age. From my perspective, it seemed we grew up together. But how old was he really? He could be just a handful of years older than me, or scores. And Titania had always looked exactly the same. Her skin was smooth, her hair still dark and lustrous without even the slightest tinge of grey. And yet she must be hundreds of summers old at the least.

Had I been half fey, I could have accepted it much more easily. Half fey, half mortal. It was still a balance. But I wasn't even half fey. I was three-quarters mortal. More mortal than fey. I didn't belong here, but where could I go? Not to my mother. I couldn't live among mortals. To struggle as they did. To live for only a few years and return to the earth far too soon. Yet that was exactly what would happen if I left the fey realm. Even here I would age, albeit far more slowly than in the mortal realm. I wouldn't live for thousands of years like Sumerled. Like Titania. Like everyone I had ever known. Eventually I would grow old and grey and wrinkled.

I didn't even know how old I was. Age was unimportant in the fey realm, but it was suddenly important to me. How could I know how much longer I might live if I had no idea how old I was? I had no wrinkles on my face or grey streaks through my hair. My skin was taut and supple, my breasts high, my limbs still flexible. I was not an old woman, but I was also no longer a girl.

My stomach rolled as I recalled Titania's smug grin when she revealed she had stolen me. It suited her plans for me to be ignorant of my origins only so long as I never asked. Would she banish me from her realm now that I knew? Force me to handfast? Mortals had some strange custom of young women handfasting with men chosen by their fathers, or at least that was what Sumerled said. Would I be subjected to that, or would she let me continue as I had, running wild with Sumerled with no cares, no responsibilities?

No learning, I realised. No education other than what Sumerled had taught me of the world. I could count, but I couldn't tally and I didn't understand letters. I knew quite a lot about fey politics, courtesy of Titania's insistence that I regularly attend court. But I knew little about the history of the fey, only what Sumerled told me, and he had scant knowledge of such things himself. Of mortals — of my own race — I knew almost nothing. Only that they were stupid and lazy, ugly and boring, short-lived and frail.

"Agata?" Sumerled's voice came from the ground below. "I've been looking for you for ages."

I didn't reply. My mouth refused to shape a pleasant response to someone who had kept the truth of my mortal blood from me. I wiped my nose on my hem again.

The tree barely shook as Sumerled made his way up through its branches. As always, he was quiet and lithe. But then again, he was a full blood fey, I reminded myself bitterly. Something I wasn't and never would be. He hauled himself onto a nearby branch and looked at me for a long moment.

"Are you mad at me?" he asked finally.

I sighed. "I've just learned the most traumatic thing, something that makes everything I thought I knew about myself a lie, and you ask if I'm mad at you?"

Sumerled's forehead creased and he made his eyes very large and sorrowful.

"You *are* mad at me. You shouldn't have asked if you didn't want to know."

"It's not that I didn't want to know. Or maybe it is. I don't know. I'm confused and overwhelmed and I really need a friend right now."

My voice broke on the last word, and he seemed to finally realise how upset I was. He reached across to take my hand.

"I don't care that you're not a real fey," he said.

I snatched my hand back as if he had burned me.

"Don't say that. Don't ever say that."

"But I don't."

"Don't you dare tell anyone. If you even breathe a whisper of this, I'll..." I stopped because I had no idea how I might punish him. I leaned back against the trunk and closed my eyes. "Just forget it."

"Are you leaving the fey realm?"

My eyes snapped open and I glared at him.

"Of course not. Why would you suggest that?"

He looked away into the trees.

"I thought you might want to go live as a mortal. I've known other part fey who left." His voice trailed away into mumbles as I continued to glare at him.

"Who?"

I pounced on the nugget of information. Maybe there was someone who could help me make sense of this. Someone like me. They could tell me what the mortal world was really like, whether it was as bad as I had heard, whether I would be forced to handfast with a stranger. Maybe they could even help me find out who my mother was, for I would never ask Titania again.

"Does Titania have any enemies in the mortal realm?" I asked.

If I hadn't been looking at Sumerled at that moment, I would have missed the way his eyes widened. He recovered quickly and shrugged.

"I'm sure she does. Nobody could rule for such a long time and not have enemies."

"I need specifics."

Another shrug. "You'd have to ask her."

"I'm asking you."

"What makes you think I'd know?"

He shifted so he sat astride a branch with one leg hanging over each side and swung his legs lazily.

"I know you do. Now tell me. Who are her enemies?"

"There are probably dozens of them. Hundreds. I wouldn't know which ones would still be alive."

"How old are you?"

My behind was going numb, but I couldn't move. Didn't want to show that I was in any way different to Sumerled, who now lay back along the limb and let his arms hang down like his legs. I felt slightly nauseous watching him. He didn't seem at all concerned about falling.

"I don't count my summers," he said at last.

"You must have some idea of how long you have lived."

"Not really."

His voice was sullen now, the way it turned when he was about to start sulking and refuse to speak. I knew better than to push any harder and returned instead to my earlier question.

"Can you introduce me to a mortal?"

He gave me a suspicious look, as if he thought I mocked him. My even gaze must have convinced him I intended neither.

"Maybe," he said.

"Will you take me to meet one?"

"Why? It's horrible there and you'll get old if you stay too long. It's only here that you won't age, even if you aren't—" He stopped himself, tactful for once, although I knew what he had been about to say. Even if I wasn't fey.

"I need answers and I won't get them here. Will you take me and introduce me to a mortal?"

He sat up and swung around so that both legs hung over the same side of the branch, then eyed the ground as if assessing whether it was too far to jump.

"Maybe another day," he said.

"Sumerled, please. You're the only one who can help me."

"I don't feel like going right now."

His voice held the fretful tone of a child who believes he has been unfairly treated. I had lost any chance of him aiding me today.

Without another word, I slid off the branch, snagging my gown again, and climbed back down to the ground.

"Where are you going?" he called.

I ignored him and walked away. If Sumerled wouldn't help me, I would do it by myself. I could go back to the same place and find the mortal again. The one who wore my face and carried the other half of my soul within him. The one who claimed to know my mother.

17

IDA

I warm myself by the fireplace, pondering the unreasonable frailness of mortal bodies. My chair is well-padded and soft, although the fabric is worn in places. It is positioned close to the fire and I have a thick shawl around my shoulders but still my hands are so cold I can barely feel my fingers. Winter has started in earnest over the last day or two, and it is impossible to warm myself adequately in this draughty keep.

This room used to belong to Hearn's wife, but she no longer comes here, not since I claimed it. It is a pleasant room with comfortable chairs and several small tables. The fire in the hearth hasn't yet burned down to coals and it crackles and roars pleasingly. The sweet scent of burning pinecones teases my nose. There are thick drapes at the windows and soft rugs on the floor, which do little to hold the cold at bay.

I wonder how Hearn's wife used to occupy herself in here, for all I do is sit and stare into the fire. It is pleasant enough for a while, but what am I supposed to do after that? I have seen women working away with needles and little pieces of cloth. Perhaps that's what she did. Or maybe folk came in here to talk to her. What do they discuss when they sit and talk for hours?

I think of all the things I might tell someone. There's not much. My creation, my brief time in the world before the boy found me and trapped me back in his mind. The long, dark time afterwards. The sweet release as he died and I escaped. That's my entire story. It would not take long to tell.

My thoughts are interrupted as a servant girl slips into the room and places a tray on the low table beside me. Her hands shake and the tray's contents clatter and slosh as she sets it down.

"Tea, my lady," she whispers, so softly I strain to hear her. She turns to leave.

"Wait," I say.

She freezes like a hare caught in a trap. Slowly, reluctantly, she turns to face me. Her face is white and her eyes are wide.

"My lady?" she breathes.

"Sit with me." I nod to the chair beside me. Like mine, it faces the hearth.

"I don't understand," she says.

"Sit."

She rushes forward so quickly she almost trips on her own skirts. She positions herself on the very edge of the chair, back straight, trembling hands clasped in her lap. I glance at the tray she brought.

"Tea?" I ask.

She stares at me but doesn't respond. I sigh and pour myself a cup. The aroma of fresh mint perfumes the room pleasantly. I don't particularly like tea, but they bring it whenever I sit here. Sometimes I drink it to be polite. Other times I don't.

"We should talk about something," I say. I sip my tea and a pleasurable warmth spreads through me.

The girl whimpers and I frown at her.

"A conversation. Isn't that what we are supposed to do in here?"

She swallows hard and finally finds some words. "What— what do you wish to discuss?"

"I don't know. What do people usually talk about when they sit here?"

Her eyes widen and she winds her fingers together nervously. I sigh and wonder why I chose such a stupid girl to have a conversation with.

"Sometimes they discuss the weather," she offers at last.

"I know what the weather is like. I looked out the window earlier."

She swallows and stares at her hands.

"Fine, then. If we were to discuss the weather, what would you say?"

"I might observe that it is unseasonably cold today." She speaks so softly that I lean forward to hear her. "And the wind has chased away yesterday's clouds."

"I already know it is cold. I don't understand the point of such a conversation."

She is silent for so long that I am almost ready to tell her to leave.

"The point is to exchange pleasantries," she says. "You don't have to discuss the weather for long, but then you can talk about something else."

"What would we discuss next?"

"I might mention that we are having soup for dinner tonight."

"We had soup last night, too."

She doesn't respond, only continues to stare at her hands in her lap.

"Well," I prompt her eventually. "What do we discuss next?"

"I have chosen the last two topics." Her gaze darts up at me ever so briefly before returning to her hands. "If we are to have a conversation, it is your turn to suggest one."

I think for a moment, casting my memory back to the many evenings I watched through the boy's eyes as his family gathered around the living room hearth. I can't remember their conversations, only that they took turns to tell tales. Now that is something I know. The boy, after all, fancied himself a bard.

"I could tell you a tale," I say.

She bobs her head up and down, fast enough that I watch curiously to see whether it might fall off. Mortal necks are fragile, after all. Beneath her skirts, her feet tap anxiously.

Which tale to tell? I know so many. The boy created quite a

number of them in the years when he told tales. Of course, that is a very long time ago. Once he imprisoned me inside his head, he told a few more but then never again. He still listened, though, and I observed his thoughts about how he would have made the tale different.

"I know a tale about a boy and his muse," I say.

She looks up at me, startled, and nods.

"There was once a boy who fancied himself a bard," I say. "When he was still young — too young to know what he was doing — he told himself a tale about a muse. She was a beautiful woman with long white hair and pale limbs."

"Like you," the girl says softly.

I smile, but do not tell her just how much like me the muse is.

"He pretended this muse whispered to him, that all the inspiration for his tales came from her. He put so much of his own energy into her that eventually she came to life. And she lived inside his head for many years. She saw what he saw, she heard what he heard. She knew his every thought.

"Of course, this was not a satisfactory life for the muse, but she tolerated it because she had no other choice. She bided her time and she watched and learned and let her power grow. She discovered how to feed off the boy, the kind of thoughts he must have in order for her to grow stronger, and she encouraged those thoughts, whispering them to him until he believed they were really his own."

"Did he not know she was there?" the girl asks.

"He didn't believe she was real. He thought she was just a silly idea in his head. Somebody had warned him once that he had the ability to bring his tales to life. He should have been more careful, but he didn't believe. So he created her and she lived inside his mind as he grew older.

"Eventually the day came when the muse was strong enough to leave his mind. She thought, *Out*, and suddenly she was, standing in a barn in the middle of winter while the boy slept in a hay stack, never knowing she had left.

"The muse went off to make her own life, but the boy soon realised what had happened and followed her. He tricked her and trapped her back in his mind again. All she wanted was to live and be free, but he wouldn't allow her to. This time, instead of being able to roam free in his mind, he restrained her inside a box he created in there. And for the rest of his life, she was trapped inside the box, unable to feel the sun on her skin or the earth beneath her toes. Unable to feel cold air in her lungs or warm food in her belly. It was no life for anyone, much less someone who has already learnt what it is to live."

The girl watches me avidly now.

"That's terrible," she says, but she sounds interested rather than shocked.

"But then the boy died, as all mortals do. And in that moment, the muse sprang out of the box in which she had been confined and fought free of his mind. She could have killed them all, the mortals who conspired with the bard to keep her imprisoned all these years, but she merely walked away."

I stop. There is more to the muse's tale, but I am not yet ready to speak it. I'm not sure I even know the rest of the tale.

"And then what happened?" she asks.

"The muse walks away. That's the end."

"But where did she go?"

"That's not part of the tale. It's a different tale."

"Oh," she says. "I would like to hear that tale sometime."

I feel genial. "Perhaps."

She twists her fingers in her skirts and suddenly looks nervous again. "I should get back to work."

I am tired of talking. "Go."

She leaves the room at a brisk walk, but I can tell she wants to run.

18

IDA

Hearn fidgets and shifts in his seat at the high table as we wait for the evening meal. We were the first diners to arrive — Hearn is never late for a meal — and others are only just entering the hall. A servant pours dark wine into Hearn's mug. Hearn reaches for it too fast and knocks it over.

"Idiot," he hisses at the servant, even though it was his own hand that caused the spill.

"Sorry, your majesty, so sorry," the man mutters. He produces a towel and sops up the spilled wine.

"You can do that later," Hearn growls. "Pour more wine."

"Of course, your majesty, sorry, sorry," the servant says.

I watch this interaction with interest. Hearn has done little more than growl and yet the servant trips over his own feet in fear. Hearn gulps down the wine and gestures impatiently for the man to pour again. I wonder why he doesn't do it himself. It would be quicker than waiting for the servant, and now the man is so nervous that his hands tremble as he pours. At least once Hearn has had another mug or two, he will be more pleasant.

He is not an interesting man, neither handsome nor intelligent. He is, however, attentive and with him beside me, anything I request is done immediately. It takes little encouragement for him to have the sorts of thoughts I need to feed from him. My power strengthens every time I am near him. It is worth tolerating his presence for a little longer. At least until I decide what to do with the Silver Downs boy.

There is something about the boy that bothers me, but I can't quite figure out what. He hasn't noticed me yet, or if he has, he forgets immediately, for I have charmed him. I don't know why a son of Silver Downs is here, but it was his blood that drew me to Braen Keep. I suspect he is the son of my boy's sister — the child that went off to become a druid. If he is druid-trained, he could be dangerous and I hesitate to try feeding from him. It is one thing to charm him from a distance. It may be more dangerous to try to charm a druid once I have interacted with him. I might not be able to make him forget me once we have spoken.

Hearn drinks the second mug more slowly. I feel his dark thoughts, although I can't hear them the way I used to hear the boy's. I only know that he is having the kind of thoughts I need, for my power surges pleasurably in response. I toy with my mug, taking only a single sip. The wine Hearn favours is bitter and unpleasant on my tongue.

I watch as folk enter the dining hall. The ones who eat here are favoured, it seems, for only about two dozen are invited each night. I recognise some, although one or two familiar faces are not here. Perhaps they have fallen out of favour. There are new faces, though. A pair of guards who swagger in, talking loudly. A young couple, newly handfasted from the way they smile fondly at each other. A striking woman of middle years, finely dressed and accompanied by an older, plainer woman. I wonder what she has done to earn Hearn's favour.

His ugly wife eats elsewhere, which pleases me. I want to grind my teeth every time I see her. Her limbs are too long and she holds them as if she is surprised to find them attached to her body. Her hair is too fine and never looks elegant, no matter what her maid does to it. She is painfully thin and her gowns look as if they were made for a larger woman. When she sees me, she flattens herself against the wall as if she thinks it will make her invisible. If I ignore her, she scurries away soon enough. She has not eaten in this room since I arrived. How long ago was that? Three days? Four? It is hard to keep track of the days when one has never needed to count them before.

"My lady?"

A servant appears at my side, a large platter of roasted fowl in his hands. It looks dry and overcooked but my stomach growls, so I nod and he serves me a portion. Hearn already has his mouth full. The man could eat an entire bird every night and possibly often does, judging by his girth. I cut a small piece of the fowl. It is already cold. It seems to be difficult for the servants to serve food hot in this place. Perhaps I should speak to the kitchen staff.

I chew, savouring the feeling of my teeth shredding meat, my tongue moving the morsels around in my mouth, the muscles in my throat contracting as I swallow. I spear another piece and pop it into my mouth.

Hearn finally eats enough to satiate his most urgent hunger. He leans back in his chair, mug in his hand, and surveys the room. I don't know how the diners manage to eat enough when they spend so much time talking, but most look like they manage. They have a stew of some sort, for the hall is filled with a savoury aroma that mostly masks the odour of unwashed bodies.

"Ida, my men are bored," Hearn says.

"Oh?" I raise my eyebrows at him. What response does he seek from me?

"They are trained to fight, but they have seen no action for months. They are brawling in their quarters and their captains are complaining."

"So do something," I say.

He gulps down the rest of his wine and slams the mug on the table. That seems to be a cue for the servant to refill it, which happens promptly. Hearn is a little drunk by now and his words are slurred.

"They need a good battle, that's what they need," he declares, brandishing his mug in the air. Wine sloshes down his arm, dark like blood, but he doesn't seem to notice. A servant darts forward, towel ready but hesitates when Hearn waves his arm around again. I catch the servant's eye and shake my head slightly. He darts back into his corner, a relieved expression on his face.

"Then you should give them a battle," I say.

"A contest? They would scorn that. No, a real battle is what they want. Swords clashing, shields ringing, blood flowing, men dying. Nothing like a real battle to calm the fellows."

"So do it."

"Need a reason to go to battle."

He drains his mug and waits impatiently while the servant fills it yet again. He is well and truly drunk now and sways in his seat. Another mug or two and he'll have his head down on the table fast asleep. Unfortunately that will mean I can draw no more power from him for the rest of the evening, but he has strengthened me enough tonight that I don't begrudge him passing out.

"What kind of reason do you need?" I ask.

"Theft. Violence against my people. Law breaking. Can't go to battle over a few cross words."

"I don't see why not," I say. "If you make the decision, will your men follow?"

"Of course they will." He is not too drunk to look indignant. "They'll do whatever I tell them."

"So give them a tale."

"Lie to them?"

"A reason to believe. That's all they need. Give them a tale they can believe and you can lead them into battle."

He ponders this.

"Some of my cattle have disappeared. Wandered off, the man who looks after them says. But maybe they were stolen."

"Do you have a neighbour who covets your cattle?"

He drums his fingers on the table and creases his forehead as if thinking hard. Given how much wine he has consumed, I assume this is a difficult task. Finally he smiles.

"Cullen. He has stolen from my cattle before. He must be doing it again."

I wonder why it took him so long to think of, but I can't be bothered to ask. I take a tiny sip of my own wine. I never drink enough to let it cloud my thoughts the way Hearn does. That seems dangerous to me.

"Might you be able to prove he has stolen your cattle?" I ask.

He smiles broadly.

"I don't need to prove it. I just need to tell my men he did it."

"So you can send them to war."

"Yes." He thumps the table. There is so much noise in the room that nobody notices. He looks puzzled for a moment, then shakes his head, likely too drunk to make sense of why no one pays him attention. "To war we go."

I have never seen a war. I've heard tales of them, of course. One of the boy's brothers was a soldier. That was a very long time ago, though, and he died, although not in battle. Others in his family were soldiers. Sons of brothers. Sons of sons of brothers. War, according to the tales, is a glorious thing. Men are filled with courage and they battle bravely and die even more bravely. I look forward to seeing it.

19

———

ARLEN

I barely slept the night after I met Agata. Instead, I spent the hours lying on my narrow cot, staring up into the dark. After so many years of not knowing what had happened to her, of hoping and praying she was safe, to finally see her alive was a blessing. And for her to look so well — vibrant, even — was beyond what I expected.

I had often imagined her locked in a fey prison, wearing rags and eating scraps, being treated as a slave. Instead it seemed she believed she was Titania's own daughter. While I was worrying for her health and her sanity, she was raised as a fey princess. In fact, she had so much of the fey about her that I would have thought her to be one if we hadn't looked so much alike.

The man with her was also clearly fey, and I had the lingering feeling I should have known him. It was impossible, of course, for the only one of his kind I had ever met before was my father, Kalen, and he wasn't a full fey. But there was something in the shape of the fey man's jaw and the set of his eyes that seemed familiar.

By the time sunlight filtered through the shutters that didn't quite close properly, I had made a decision. I would leave Braen Keep and search for Agata. I would explain to her — properly this time — that she had been stolen from her family, and I would take her home to Eithne. My promise to Oistin that I wouldn't go until he gave me leave would have to be broken. I couldn't dally any longer, not now I knew she was so near. I would leave as soon as I broke my fast.

I wouldn't tell Hearn for fear he would refuse me permission to leave. He so rarely summoned me that I might be able to find Agata, take her home and return to Braen Keep before he knew I had left. It wasn't so easy, though, to decide how much to tell Derwa. I felt some obligation due to our fledgling friendship, but I wasn't sure I could trust her not to tell Hearn.

As I left my bedchamber, I came face-to-face with a boy who stood with his fist raised, ready to knock. His shaggy hair was uncombed and his clothes looked like he had slept in them.

"Message from the king," he said with a yawn. "He wants you in the library right away."

I acknowledged him with a nod and he scampered away, likely back to his bed. I envied him, for I couldn't remember the last time I had a full night of sleep.

"Druid," Hearn said when I arrived at the library. He stood at the window, staring out at the grey dawn sky. Neither lamps nor hearth were lit and the air in the room was uncomfortably crisp.

"My lord." I bowed, wishing I had worn my cloak, and tried not to shiver as I waited.

Hearn continued to gaze out the window, and I thought he had forgotten me.

"Tomorrow, druid, we go to war," he said.

My heart sank. Why had he decided today, just as I resolved to go in search of Agata?

"I see," I said.

He waved his hand in my direction, dismissing me.

"Yes, yes, I know you are supposed to do some ritual or other. So go, do what you must and confirm it."

I bowed again and left. Hearn knew as well as I that only a druid could authorise battle. Only a druid was trained to interpret the signs and determine whether this was a favourable day for battle to commence. For a king to claim that power for his own was blasphemy.

The orange fire of dawn had almost faded from the sky as I reached the courtyard. The wind was biting and I again longed for my cloak. In the kitchen, where I had planned to break my fast, the fires were always stoked and I would have been plenty warm enough in my tunic. But I didn't want to risk angering Hearn by delaying long enough to fetch my cloak. Hopefully the signs would present themselves before I froze.

I knew the courtyard and the gardens well enough from my afternoon walks with Derwa. There was no sacred grove from which I might observe the signs as I had been trained and the group of three stunted birch trees made a poor substitute. I sat cross-legged in front of them and waited, watching the sky. The dirt beneath me was damp and soaked my trousers almost immediately. At least there was not yet any frost on the ground.

Dawn was an appropriate time for signs involving birds. A flock would give me the best guidance, although even a solitary bird might provide the information I sought. A flock flying in a certain direction indicated a favourable time for battle. If they flew in another direction, the time was not favourable. The number and type of birds and the formation in which they flew was also useful.

My skin prickled with goosebumps and shivers racked my body. Without being able to meditate, I had no way of warming myself. I could hardly tell Hearn I was too cold to stay long enough, so I waited. At least an hour passed before I saw a single bird. It was so high that I couldn't tell its species. I followed its path across the sky, willing it to veer off its course, but it flew along the exact midpoint of the two directions that would give me guidance. My teeth chattered and I prayed the next sign would come soon.

At length a flock of seven birds flew over. An auspicious number. But as I watched, another two birds caught up and suddenly the flock was nine. They, too, flew in the same direction as the first bird. I had received two signs and both were ambiguous.

I waited another hour and didn't see so much as a single bird. By now I shivered so hard I had strained a muscle in my back and I couldn't feel my hands anymore. If my stomach still growled, I couldn't hear it over the chattering of my teeth. It was time to admit the signs had provided no guidance.

Dismay welled and my feet dragged as I returned to the keep. I dreaded telling Hearn I couldn't authorise his battle, but I had no other choice. The signs had been neither positive nor negative, and I dared not act without definite guidance.

When I reached the library, Hearn was deep in discussion with Cahan, one of his favoured advisors. I hesitated in the doorway, but Hearn quickly waved me in. Cahan gave me a look of distaste as he smoothed his moustache. He was in the audience hall the day I first presented myself to Hearn, the man with the frilly shirt who had made it clear he resented the king having any other advisors.

"Don't just stand there, druid," Hearn said. "Come in, come in. Let us hear your approval of tomorrow's battle."

Although his voice was jovial, his eyes held a warning. There was only one answer he would accept. What would he do when I refused? He might send me back to Oistin in disgrace, or lock me in a cell in chains. Either way, I wouldn't be able to look for Agata.

"Go on," Hearn said. The joviality was gone from his voice, replaced with an edge of impatience. "Do your job, druid."

The signs were unclear. I had been trained well. Unless the signs were unequivocally positive, battle could not be authorised. But if I was imprisoned for displeasing Hearn, who would search for Agata? I couldn't let her down again.

"I approve your request to go to battle tomorrow," I said and forced myself to look him in the eyes.

Hearn smiled and slapped Cahan on the back.

"See, a pet druid is a useful thing. Oistin knew what he was doing after all."

Cahan grinned and rubbed his hands together.

"I'll go speak to the men. They'll need the day to prepare."

"Tell them to make sure they get some sleep," Hearn said. "Tomorrow we go to war!"

I slipped away quietly while they congratulated each other. My stomach churned and bile rose in my mouth. I walked faster and faster through the twisting hallways. The guards ignored me as I burst out the front doors.

I made it back to the birch trees before I vomited. I wiped my mouth on my shirt and placed my hand against one of the sickly birches, seeking contact with its spirit. I could barely feel its life force at all. I should have been sad about that, but there were no emotions left inside me.

Men would die tomorrow. Possibly men I had met during my time in Hearn's court. I shouldn't have authorised the battle, no matter what Hearn expected. I considered going back to the library and telling Hearn I had been mistaken. But it wouldn't matter what I said. He had made a show of requesting my approval, but Hearn would do whatever he wanted. Whether I approved it or not, he intended to take his men into war.

20

AGATA

I returned to the portal Sumerled and I had travelled through. Maybe it was the same day as when we last visited the mortal world, or maybe not. I had heard they counted their days one by one, measured against the turning of the sun. Time is largely irrelevant to the fey, but perhaps mortals must be more conscious of it since they are so short-lived. Maybe I needed to learn about time.

As I passed through the portal, a chill breeze whipped through my skirts. I shivered a little, wrapping my bare arms around me for warmth as I surveyed the vista. The fey realm had been suspended in summer for my entire life. I had some understanding of the passing of seasons from what Sumerled had told me, but never had I experienced for myself the cold winds or frost or snow he spoke of. The sky in the mortal world was grey now, not the bright blue of earlier. The grass was now all brown and dead. The air smelled crisp and stung my skin.

The grove where we had encountered the man who wore my face was further than I remembered, and when I reached it, he wasn't there. Surely he must live somewhere nearby, though, and it would be easy to find him since we shared the same face.

I ran, searching for any sign of mortal dwellings. There, smoke drifted with the wind. It was as good a place as any to start. I ran for some time before I reached a rough road. Eventually I came to a towering wall. The path led right up to a tall, wooden gate. Two men beside the gate were dressed alike in dark trousers and tunics. Swords hung from their belts. They paid me no attention as I slipped through the open gate.

On the other side of the wall were more lodges than I could count, which meant more mortals than I had expected to find in one place. I knew their homes would be nothing like I was accustomed to, built out of living trees that grew where the fey wished them to. Sumerled described the mortal dwellings to me once, but he didn't say they were so poorly kept. Doors hung unevenly, window shutters didn't quite close. Skinny, dirty children stared at me. I crouched in front of one girl. Dirt and snot were smeared across her face in equal proportions.

"Do you know a man who looks like me?" I asked in the friendliest voice I could manage.

The girl spat in the dust, then turned and fled. I was so shocked that it took me a few moments to realise I should stand up. Nobody had ever disrespected me like that before. Not even those who suspected I wasn't fully fey. I walked on, past a knot of children who huddled closer together and turned their backs. A woman stood in the doorway of a small lodge, a malnourished babe clutched to her hip. I waved at her, but she only stared and didn't return the gesture.

"Do you know a man who looks like me?" I called to her.

She backed into her lodge and slammed the door. I wanted to batter it down and tell her I was the daughter of Titania, queen of the fey, and that she should be more careful who she scorned. But I wasn't Titania's daughter. Not anymore and not ever. I walked on.

People ignored me when I spoke to them. Some simply looked away; others walked off. I found a shabby inn and approached the woman who stood behind the counter, but she hissed when I said I wanted to ask a question, not buy a drink.

A man sitting beside the road seemed more promising. His clothes were threadbare and he looked like he hadn't bathed for months. But he didn't look away when I spoke to him. Instead, he enticed me to come closer, come closer and he would whisper in my ear what I wanted to know. I leaned down to him, holding my breath, for I had never smelled anyone so rank. Quick as a fox, he grabbed my breasts with both hands. I shoved him away and darted back out of his reach. He fell backwards with an unnecessarily loud shriek. People started muttering and edging closer. I suddenly felt very unsafe.

I left at a run and didn't stop until I was back in the fey realm. Then I dropped to the ground, put my face in my hands, and sobbed.

I didn't look up when Sumerled arrived. He sat beside me and waited, and didn't even mention that fey don't cry.

"They were horrible," I said between hiccups. "I only wanted to ask if they knew the man who looked like me, but they spat at me and yelled and then I thought they were going to attack me, so I ran away."

Sumerled said nothing. I was used to that.

"All they had to do was answer my question."

"Why did you go to the mortal realm without me?" he asked.

I wiped my tears and my nose with my skirt. Crying was becoming a habit.

"I wanted to find him. I didn't think it would be dangerous. I didn't know they would be so horrible."

"I would have gone with you."

"I wanted to go by myself."

"Did you talk to Titania?"

A sob choked me and I leaned against an ash tree, placing my cheek against its smooth trunk. Its unchanging steadiness comforted me.

"What did she say?" he asked.

"I'm not her daughter. She stole me from a mortal woman. I'm not even fey."

I couldn't look at him. Didn't want to see his face change as he learned the truth.

"That can't be true. You have at least some fey blood in you."

"My father is half fey."

Sumerled was silent and I felt like he prepared himself for something.

"Did she tell you who the mortal was?" he asked.

"Did she tell me who my mother is, you mean?" I didn't try to mask the bitterness in my voice. "No, although I'm not sure I asked. I was too surprised. She was so smug about having stolen me. She didn't even try to deny it. What will happen to me now? Will she let me stay here?"

"Are you sure she didn't say anything about your father?"

"She said as little about him as she did about my mother. Does she ever let half-bloods stay? Will she turn me out? Do you know anyone here who is not a full fey?"

"Why don't you ask her for more details? Try to find out the name of the fey who fathered you."

"Why do you want to know about my father? What difference does it make? I always thought Titania was my mother."

"Surely you suspected she wasn't."

"Of course not. Why would I think that?"

"Well, because she's…" He stopped and his ears went red.

"She's what?"

"She's not exactly the motherly type. She's never acted like a mother to you."

"I had no reason to think she wasn't. You should have told me. I thought we were friends."

"We are friends." He frowned as he studied me and I was acutely conscious that my eyes were swollen and my nose still ran. "I'd have told you had you asked."

"I didn't know I should ask. You never thought you should just tell me?"

"I knew everything would be ruined if I told you."

"Not everything. Just my life."

I got to my feet and started walking, although I didn't know where to go. How could I go back to the palace now? It was Titania's and I didn't belong there. Sumerled followed me.

"Will you go and live in the mortal realm?" he asked. "Look for your parents?"

"Don't even say that." I turned and grabbed his shirt. "Don't ever tell anyone about any of this. If Titania hasn't told anyone in all these years, there's no reason for anyone to know now. Nobody needs to know anything is different."

"You age too fast. Everyone already knows you must be part mortal or you wouldn't look so old already."

"I don't look old."

"You look old for a fey of your years. And it will become more obvious soon. The younger ones don't really bother, but most fey would stop themselves from looking any older once they reach about your age. Soon, you'll look old and it will be obvious you're not—"

"Go on, say it." I released his shirt and looked away into the woods. I couldn't bear to look at him while he said it.

"It will be obvious you're not fey," he said glumly.

"You didn't even say part fey," I whispered. "Is that how you think of me already? I'm not fey? Not even a little bit?"

"You're not a whole lot fey."

I gave him a hurt look and left. It was a long walk back to the palace. I had time yet to decide. Should I go home and pretend nothing had changed? Or pack up my things and leave, try to find somewhere I belonged? *You might have to go to the mortal realm,* something inside me whispered. But I wouldn't belong there either. I had never lived there. I knew little of their customs. I despised mortals. I hated everything about their smelly, nasty, broken-down world. It was the worst joke to find out I was mortal myself.

Sumerled caught up and we walked in silence. Everything around us was solemn and silent, with barely a rustle of undergrowth or chirp from a bird. It was as if even the woods understood everything had changed. When we reached the palace, Sumerled slipped silently away into the trees. I stood at the entrance and tried to decide: Should I go back and reclaim my old life? Or was this the end of everything I had ever known?

21

———

AGATA

I decided to pretend nothing had happened. Despite Sumerled's comment, nobody else knew about my parentage. There might be whispers and gossip, but that's all it was. I had time yet — months, maybe even years — to decide how to handle it. As long as Titania didn't make me leave, I would continue as I always had. And tonight was a feast night. I would wear my prettiest dress and attend the feast with my head held high. As far as anyone else knew, I was Titania's daughter.

The monthly feasts were the only public events where Titania didn't expect me to sit at her side, where I was in full and constant view of everyone. Sumerled and I always sat together. Some nights our table was full of young fey and the conversation would be vibrant and exciting. On the nights when we sat with older folk who only wanted to discuss court politics or other boring things, Sumerled and I would ignore them and talk to each other.

I took my time choosing my clothes and eventually dressed in a golden gown with long, full sleeves and a daring bodice with a lace insert. The gold slippers were made specially for me. My feet were somewhat larger than the average fey's, which was a constant source of embarrassment. I brushed my dark hair until it shone and fell to my waist in a sleek waterfall. A brilliant bracelet set with blood-red gems and a matching necklace with a pendant that dipped down into my bodice complemented my gown. My jewellery was cast-offs from Titania, but was still finer than most fey ever possessed.

It was late by the time I was ready to leave but as long as I arrived before Titania, I wasn't too late. It was not a good idea to arrive after she made her grand entrance. Better to stay home and miss the feast than risk drawing Titania's attention to yourself in that way.

I walked briskly along the smooth wooden hallways. They twisted and turned at random, sometimes in a different way to how they had earlier in the day, and it took much longer than usual to reach the main entrance. I walked at a decorous pace, but as soon as I was deep enough into the woods to be out of sight from the guards, I lifted my skirts and ran, not fast enough to ruin my hair but just enough to hurry.

I heard the diners before I saw them. Purple and yellow lights sparkled from the branches of the oaks that circled the feast clearing. Dishes clattered and folk talked loudly. That could only mean that Titania had arrived and the feast had already begun.

I slowed to a walk as I considered my options. Titania always knew exactly where I was, even when she couldn't see me. I had no idea how and she was the only fey who possessed such magic. She would know if I didn't attend the feast, but I couldn't guess whether she would be angry or indifferent. Given her recent revelation about my mostly mortal parentage, I needed to make a show of fitting in and Sumerled would have saved me a seat. So I would go.

I reached the edge of the clearing and hid behind an oak while I searched for Sumerled. Tasty aromas wafted out from the clearing and my stomach grumbled fiercely. When one of the diners leaned over to speak to her neighbour, I finally glimpsed the back of Sumerled's head. He was on the far side of the clearing and it looked like there was an empty seat next to him. But even if I approached from the other side, he was not where I could slide in beside him without being noticed. There was only one thing for it. I took a deep breath and stepped out into the clearing.

Of course Titania saw me immediately, but she would have already known I hid in the shadows. She looked as exquisite as always in a gown that was the blue of deep water. Its neckline plunged all the way to her waist and her dark tresses were piled artfully on top of her head. She gave me a pointed look. There was no point in trying to hide.

As gracefully as I could, I sashayed across the clearing and between tables, right up to Titania's dais. I stopped a respectable distance away and curtseyed, trying to make it the deepest and most elegant curtsey I had ever performed. Titania raised her eyebrow at me as she took a delicate bite of her meal. Conversation died as fey paused to watch, some with food still midway to their mouths.

"Good evening, my lady," I said. "I apologise for my tardiness."

Titania chewed slowly, so slowly. She stared into my eyes the whole time. I tried not to flinch. She wasn't really reading my mind, however much it felt like it. Finally she swallowed. Then she lifted her knife and delicately speared another piece of whatever she was eating. She nodded at me, then looked away.

Was that it? She wasn't going to publicly rebuke me? Before she could change her mind, I hurried over to Sumerled. I slipped between tables piled high with platters of roasted bird and exotic fruits, sharp cheeses and crusty breads. Flowering vines trailed between the plat-ters and draped over the sides of the tables. Almost every seat was full and it seemed everyone had already forgotten me as they resumed feasting and drinking. My stomach growled again and I could already taste the succulent meats and fresh breads.

A fey who was seated across the table from Sumerled was the first to notice my approach. As I had already made eye contact with her, I smiled pleasantly. The woman didn't return my smile but leaned across the table to say something to Sumerled. I didn't like the smirk she wore as she did so. A couple of others glanced over at me as she spoke. My own smile faltered a little, but I fixed it more firmly on my face.

Sumerled had indeed saved me a seat. I was only a few paces away when the fey on the other side of my seat slid across into it. She leaned close to Sumerled to speak right into his ear. He tilted his head to listen and his shoulders moved slightly as he laughed.

I reached the table and stood just behind the spot he had saved me. Sumerled glanced up at me with a guilty expression. I fixed the smile more firmly on my face and tapped the woman's shoulder.

"Excuse me, I think that seat is mine."

I tried not to show my irritation with Sumerled for not immediately telling her to move. She didn't even look at me.

"This seat is taken," she said.

I waited for Sumerled to defend me. When he didn't even look up, I nudged his shoulder.

"Sumerled, didn't you keep this seat for me?"

He turned his head, but didn't look at me.

"You could sit in the next chair," he said. "There's nobody there."

"That is where *she* was sitting up until a moment ago," I pointed out, my tone firm. "This seat is the one you saved for me."

"You should consider yourself lucky to be permitted to sit here at all," a woman said from across the table. "If I were you, I'd sit down and be grateful."

My jaw dropped. Again I waited for Sumerled to speak up for me, but he pretended he didn't hear her. Of the eight diners, half studiously ignored me. The others watched with badly concealed grins.

"Sumerled?" Embarrassingly, my voice was a little shaky. "What is the meaning of this?"

His ears turned pink, but he didn't acknowledge my words.

"Sumerled?" I spoke a little louder and he slowly turned to face me. "What is going on?"

The fey on his other side sniggered.

"If you want that seat, I'd suggest you sit down," she said. "Otherwise you might find somebody else claims it and you miss out. Wouldn't it be sad if you couldn't join in on the feast?"

"What do you mean?" I tried to sound casual. "I always come to our feasts."

"Mortals should be careful where they tread," a fey whispered to his neighbour, loudly enough that he clearly intended for me to overhear.

"What did you say?" I demanded. I turned to Sumerled. "Sumerled, what is going on?"

His ears grew even pinker. He glanced back at me, but his gaze quickly slid away to something else.

"Sumerled?"

The fey who stole my seat twisted around to glare at me.

"We know your dirty little secret. You can either take the seat that's available or leave," she said. "Your choice."

I blinked back the tears that suddenly threatened to flood my eyes. I couldn't cry in front of them. I swallowed and hoped my voice would not reveal my hurt.

"Thank you, but I'm suddenly not very hungry," I said. "I don't think I'll stay."

With my head held high, I made my way back between the tables. I needed to get to the safety of the woods. I would run far enough that nobody would find me and then, only then, would I let myself cry. Howls of laughter rose from behind me.

"I don't think I'll stay," a male voice said in a mocking falsetto.

"Excuse me," I muttered as a man suddenly pushed his chair back from the table and blocked my path. He ignored me. "Excuse me, I need to get through."

He turned and glared at me.

"Half-blood," he hissed.

I stumbled and almost tripped over my skirts. Others turned to look and a tear tracked down my cheeks. I pushed between tables, knocking over someone's wine in my hurry. A shriek indicated it had spilled into her lap, but I didn't stop to apologise. From the corner of my eye, I saw Titania put down her knife and look in my direction. I moved faster, needing to get away before she demanded I stop and explain myself.

Finally I was past the last of the tables and into the trees. I lifted my skirts up to my knees and ran. My golden slippers bounced lightly off leaf and rock. An outstretched branch caught on my pretty golden skirt and it tore. A sob burst out of me and I ran faster.

I ran until I could go no further. It was only then I realised where I had fled to: the pond surrounded by weeping willows. The last time I was here, I lay on the moss in my dripping underthings and fell asleep next to Sumerled. How innocent I was then.

I flung myself down on the moss and tried to stop crying. My eyes were swollen, my nose ran and my bodice was wet through from the tears that dripped from my chin. I could only imagine how appalling I looked. Titania would be horrified if she saw me. I wiped my face on my tattered skirt. The gown was ruined, but even if it wasn't I would never wear it again. It would always remind me of tonight. When the fey snubbed me.

Some fey didn't like me. I didn't like them either. But they had never been nasty before, only a little cold. Perhaps being viewed as Titania's daughter had protected me somewhat. But now it seemed they all knew I wasn't fey. There had been only two people other than me who knew: Titania and Sumerled. Even if that fey girl hadn't said it was Sumerled who had told, I would have known. Titania wasn't the type to whisper secrets behind someone's back. If she was going to tell people of my true heritage, she would do it loudly and in front of me. No, it was Sumerled, who I had always thought was my friend. My only friend.

For a while I lay on the moss and felt sorry for myself. Eventually it occurred to me to wonder what Sumerled had gained by sharing my secret. Was telling secrets that didn't belong to him a way of winning friends? I would have to confront him eventually. I had to know how much he had told and why. But I needed to be calm when I did. I wouldn't cry. I wouldn't let him see how much he had hurt me. I would coolly demand an explanation, then I would leave. And I would never speak to him again. Ever. I didn't care if it meant I no longer had even a single friend. No friends were better than a friend like Sumerled.

I drew my knees up to my chest and draped my ruined skirt over them. The fabric flowed over my legs like a golden stream. I sank my fingers into the moss. It was cool and velvety and soothing. Idly I noticed that the rock which had appeared beside me while I slept last time was no longer here. Perhaps Sumerled moved it before he left that day.

I looked out at the still pond which reflected broken shards of sunlight, despite the lateness of the night. The sky never darkened here in Titania's realm, not unless she wanted it to. I wished I could see the moon. I had heard it gave off light like the sun, although not as strongly. I wondered what moonlight on a still pond looked like.

My eyes drooped and I yawned widely. It was late and I should go back to the palace. But I didn't want to leave yet. I wasn't sure I even wanted to go back. How could I? If I was to be treated as an outcast, I couldn't live here anymore.

What I didn't understand was why Titania had kept her secret for so long. She was pleased when I finally asked about my parentage, so why hadn't she told me earlier? Was there more to the secret that I hadn't yet learned?

I rested my chin on my knees and closed my eyes. I was too tired to think anymore. I let my mind drift and I must have fallen asleep because when I woke, I lay on my side, curled up with my legs tucked beneath my skirts. The air had cooled overnight and I was just cold enough to be uncomfortable. I sat up and stretched. My hand brushed against something. A small hazel bush grew beside me. It hadn't been there earlier, and bushes don't grow overnight, not to knee-high, anyway. Not even in the fey realm.

My feet tangled in my skirt as I scooted away from it. The bush stayed where it was. I could hear a strange humming sound, almost like a vibration inside my head. The bush seemed to grow right out of the moss-covered rock, which was impossible. Unless perhaps there was a crack in the rocks and the little bush somehow grew up through it from the earth beneath. But still, no bush could grow that high overnight.

I tentatively touched a leaf. It felt real. I edged a little closer, feeling ridiculous at being spooked by a bush. But it definitely wasn't there before, and this was twice that something strange had happened to me here. I examined the place where its spindly trunk met the moss. It certainly looked like it grew straight out of the rock. I placed my hand on its trunk and gently pushed. Nothing. I pushed harder. The bush was firmly fixed to the rock. I felt a bit silly. What had I expected? That the bush would fall over? That it had been cut off at its base and placed there beside me as a prank?

Nothing else looked out of place. Other than the strange bush, the clearing looked exactly the same as always. I remembered my thoughts of something living at the bottom of the pond and the hair rose on my arms. Should I look into the pond and see if anything was there? I had a terrible feeling that if I looked, I would see something this time.

I left the clearing swiftly, but not without a backwards glance to ensure that nothing climbed out of the pond and followed me. The hazel bush stayed where it was, although I had the strangest feeling that it watched me leave.

22

IDA

The palace is in chaos tonight as folk prepare for the impending war. Nobody pays me any attention as I wander the hallways. I have heard many tales of war over the years, some told by the boy and some by others. So I know that war is a glorious thing. It makes heroes of men. They fight bravely in long battles and win marvellous victories. Then they return home loaded with plunder and willing slaves, or they die, nobly and with dignity.

There is the tale of the man who goes to battle because his wife has been stolen by a neighbour. He kills the man and reclaims his wife before her virtue can be sullied. He also claims all the man's possessions, puts his sons to death with his sword, and installs his own son to manage his enemy's estate.

Another speaks of the king who wants to rid his land of a dragon that is eating all the cattle. He pursues the dragon to its lair and single-handedly cuts off its head. It takes his entire army to carry all the dragon's treasure back to his keep.

Then there is the tale of the young man who wants to win the hand of a particular woman. She sends him on a dangerous quest to collect certain magical items. He has to kill the creatures that possess each of those items. This he does with a minimum of injury to himself, although at great cost to his companions. He collects all the items and goes home to be betrothed to the woman. Only one of his companions, the most faithful, survives.

So many tales of the glories of war and tomorrow I will finally see it for myself. Perhaps I will be there at Hearn's side. I might sit astride a horse — I seem to recall a tale where a woman sits a white horse as she watches her man do battle. The image is picturesque and I wonder whether there might be any white horses in the stables.

I reach one of the rooms where the men gather in the evenings to drink ale and tell tales. Nobody notices as I stand in the doorway. The room is crowded tonight with men sharpening swords and axes and daggers. They polish their weapons until they gleam and stack them carefully in preparation for the morrow.

Their sons sit at their feet, watching and probably dreaming of the day they themselves will go into battle. Those who are old enough are given small tasks which they undertake with pride. Servant boys rush in and out, delivering various messages or being sent in search of particular items.

"Papa, I want to go with you," a boy says as he hands a long dagger to his father.

His father inspects the dagger and notes a notch in the blade, which he swiftly begins to polish out.

"I've already said no," he says.

"But I'm old enough," the boy says. "I could march with you and carry your weapons."

"And then I'd have to look after you as well as myself. You'll stay here and protect your mother and sisters."

"It's not fair," the boy says. "I want to go to battle. You said I might the next time."

"I didn't expect the next time to be so soon," his father says. "You are too young and too small. When you are a man grown, you may go to battle. Until then, I need you to keep our womenfolk safe."

I leave and move on through the hallways. In the kitchen, the stoves are stoked and the heat is stifling. Again I am unnoticed. It feels like I am back in the boy's head, unseen, unheard. It is not a feeling I care for.

Women line the long wooden workbench in the centre of the kitchen and prepare small packs of salted meat, hard bread and dried fruits. I assume the men will take these to provide sustenance should they have an opportunity to eat before dying. The men in the boy's tales never needed to eat during a battle. Perhaps Hearn's men are not as good at battle as the men in the tales. It is an interesting thought. I leave the kitchen and walk on through the keep.

A woman's voice reaches my ears. She is half-hidden behind a pillar. I step a little closer to listen. She speaks softly and presumably her words are intended only for the man with her, but I hear her well enough.

"Don't do anything stupid," she says, fiercely. "Promise me you will stay safe."

"It's a battle, my love," he says. "If I try to stay safe, the men will think me a coward. All I can promise is that I will fight as well as I can."

"I need more than that," she says. "You have to come home safely to me. Promise me that."

"You know I can't," he says with a sigh. This sounds like a conversation they have had many times already. "Men die in battle and I can't promise you that I won't. But if I can come back to you, I will."

"The battle has been properly authorised, hasn't it?" she asks. "Sanctioned by the druid?"

"I'm sure it has, my love. Hearn would not send us into battle otherwise."

"But did the druid make a sacrifice?" Her tone is desperate. "Somebody should make a sacrifice to the gods. Perhaps they can be appeased without war."

"I go where Hearn tells me," he says. "You know this. If he says we must fight, then fight I will. But I promise I will come home if I can."

"That's not good enough," she says and there are tears in her voice. "You can't die and leave me here alone. You can't."

The rest of her words are muffled as if he has pulled her close and she speaks against his chest. It reminds me of a tale the boy told many years ago of a woman farewelling her man as he sets out on some impossible quest. I walk away, leaving the couple behind.

Women are going down into the bowels of the keep bearing baskets and large bundles. I follow and discover they are stocking the cells below. If any prisoners were here, they have been moved or killed, for the cells are empty except for the women working to clean them of grime and mould and old splatters of blood.

As the cells are cleaned, other women bring in piles of blankets and cushions and baskets of food. Perhaps they prepare for the prisoners they expect the men to claim tomorrow? It seems strange they would take so much care to make the cells habitable. Cells are supposed to be dark and dank and cold. The tales do not talk of warm blankets and soft cushions, nor of conveniently placed baskets of food and jars of ale. They do not mention lamps filled with oil, nor of baskets of toys to amuse children. I do not understand, but tomorrow will come soon enough.

I prowl the hallways. Everyone is busy with some task or other. I search for Hearn but he is nowhere to be found. Perhaps he discusses strategy with his commanders. They will decide how the battle will run and tomorrow they will effortlessly implement their plan, thus ensuring their victory.

What are Cullen's men doing tonight? Does his lodge look like this, with folk industriously busy at their tasks? Or do they already sleep, having feasted and drunk until they fall over? Perhaps they are so confident of victory that they feel no need to plan. It would be interesting to see whether their preparations look very different.

23

ARLEN

I sat on the floor of my bedchamber and stared into the bronze bowl of water. My thoughts circled each other, no matter how much I tried to calm my mind. Tomorrow Hearn would send his men into battle against Cullen. Unless Cullen's men were already armed and could be ready to fight at a moment's notice, it would be a slaughter. Men on both sides would die. Men whose deaths I had authorised. I wished I had the courage to refuse Hearn and I didn't much like the man I was discovering myself to be.

Tonight, more than ever, I desperately needed the Sight, but I struggled to achieve the calm necessary to even try. Frustration gripped me and I realised I was clenching my fists. I took a few deep breaths and forced my fingers to relax. I noted each beat of my heart and the resulting rush of blood through my veins. I felt the air as it entered my nostrils and filled my lungs. My mind gradually stilled.

I stared into the bowl, but as always the water remained clear. I pushed away the frustration that edged back into my mind. Patience. The Sight would only come with patience. When my mind wandered, I nudged it back to my task. I was well practised at enduring boredom while staying focussed.

After several hours a dark smudge appeared in the water. I held my breath and leaned forward. Had I finally broken through whatever blocked me from the Sight? But as I moved, the smudge disappeared. I sighed in disappointment, but even as I did, the image returned and slowly resolved into a face. Agata's.

I barely breathed as the vision cleared and clarified. Agata wore an elaborate golden gown, the skirts of which she held up as she ran, showing her bare ankles and feet clad in golden slippers. She moved too fast to make out her location other than that it appeared to be woods. Tears ran freely down her face and she made no attempt to wipe them away. Every now and then she gasped, or maybe sobbed, but she kept running, leaping over obstacles in her path and ducking under branches. The image was visible for less than a handful of heartbeats, then it merged into a different scene. Now I saw Agata and myself, hand in hand as we stood in front of a woman with long white hair. After only a moment, the image faded.

"No." I leaned closer to the bowl. "Come back."

But Agata was gone. I could barely take any satisfaction in finally accessing the Sight after what it had shown. My sister — who I had repeatedly delayed searching for — was in trouble. No, I didn't know that. The Sight could show past or present. It could show the future or a possibility. What I saw might be yet to occur or it might already be over. It might not happen at all.

I tried to breathe calmly. Inhale. Exhale. I had no context to the vision. She might be running from danger or merely an argument. She might have received bad news. The more I tried to persuade myself that I couldn't know what had happened, the more uneasy I felt. I had to find her.

But tomorrow Hearn would take his men to war. I had an obligation to stay, to witness the aftermath of what I had authorised. This was not the time for me to run off and undertake my own personal task. Yet this was more important to me than anything else. I needed to find Agata. To take her home to Silver Downs, just like I promised Eithne all those years ago.

Conflicted, I examined my feelings, trying to assess them as I had been taught: impartially and with a view to the greater good. I felt guilt that I had sanctioned Hearn's desire for blood. Dread at the thought of what tomorrow would bring. Fear at the knowledge that men would die. Anger at Oistin for putting me in such a situation. All emotions that were to be expected under the circumstances, although I was shamed at the ferocity of some of them.

But absent from my feelings was any sense that I owed Hearn. He barely tolerated my presence and had made it clear he didn't want me at Braen Keep. He called on me only when he had a point to prove, not because he needed my advice. I lied about what the signs showed and he undoubtedly knew it, but he didn't care. How could I respect a leader like that? The truth was that I didn't and, sadly, I respected Oistin less for sending me here.

The only person at Braen Keep who I felt I owed something to was Derwa. I chastised myself for the way my heart softened at the thought of her. She was another man's wife and I had no business thinking about her as anything other than my queen.

I stood and set the bowl carefully on the dresser. I studied the water for a final few moments, hopeful the Sight might grant one last glimpse of Agata, but I saw nothing other than the ripples caused by moving the bowl.

I found Derwa in a small room which I had previously thought unused. She sat in front of the hearth where the fire had burned down to coals, giving off a steady heat and the sweet scent of pinecones. A small oil lamp on the table beside her provided some light for her task with thread and a needle. I lacked enough knowledge of women's tasks to know what, other than that it was some form of stitching. She was alone, for which I was thankful. As I hesitated in the doorway, Derwa glanced up and smiled at me.

"Arlen." Her voice was full of genuine pleasure. "I didn't expect to see you this evening."

"May I speak with you?" I stayed in the doorway, unsure whether it was appropriate for me to enter, given she was alone.

"Of course. Do come in." She gestured with a long needle to a chair opposite her. "Come, sit."

I glanced down the hallway, but there was nobody to see me enter the room. I left the door open so as not to raise suspicion and sat in the chair Derwa had indicated.

"Is there a problem?" She glanced at me so briefly that I would have missed it if I hadn't been looking at her.

She returned her attention to her stitching and I realised I had been staring at her. I averted my eyes and looked instead at the tapestries hanging from the walls. They were ugly things, done in sombre shades of brown and green. I wasn't even sure what they were supposed to depict.

"I need to go away for a while." It was only as the words left my mouth that I made my decision.

"Will you come back?" Derwa kept her gaze on her stitching.

Not where was I going. Not did Hearn know I was leaving. Just would I return. Her words affirmed that the connection I felt wasn't one sided.

"I intend to, but I don't know when," I said. "There's something I need to do. I should have done it a long time ago, but I kept putting it off and now it's urgent."

Derwa set her stitching down in her lap as I spoke. She turned it around and resumed her work.

"Is it dangerous, this thing you need to do?" she asked.

"I don't know. It might be. It might not."

"Will you at least tell me where you are going?"

"To the fey realm, I think."

She looked up at me, surprise plain in her eyes.

"I'm sure you know better than I the dangers you might face there," she said.

"I'm not sure I do, but I have to go."

"Tell me why, Arlen. If you are to leave me tonight and possibly never return, at least tell me why you left."

She continued to stitch, not looking at me at all.

"There is… someone I need to find," I said. I should have anticipated she would ask.

"Someone special to you?" Her voice was studiously casual.

"Yes."

I saw the way her face changed and my heart jumped.

"Not the way you're thinking," I said. "She's my sister."

"Younger or older than you?"

"Older, but only by minutes."

"You shared your mother's womb," she said. "And so she is the other half of you."

"She was stolen shortly after her birth. I've spent my life learning all I could about the fey with the intention of searching for her, but then Oistin sent me here. I feel like I keep putting my plans to find her on hold and I can't wait any longer."

"Has something happened?" Derwa asked.

"I don't know. Maybe it's happened or maybe it's yet to happen."

"Did you See her?"

For a moment, I was tempted to tell her about my failures with the Sight and how tonight I finally broke through. But I couldn't afford to be distracted.

"What I Saw suggested she was in danger," I said. "I need to find her urgently."

"Of course, you should go. Do you have need of anything? The kitchen staff are preparing packs for the men. I could get one of them for you."

I hadn't thought that far ahead. Of course I would need food. The old tales told that a mortal who ate the food of the fey realm could never leave. My studies had not provided any evidence as to the truth of this, but I wouldn't risk it if I didn't need to.

"Some provisions would be much appreciated if it can be done quietly," I said.

"I'll fetch it myself. If anyone asks, I will blush and say I find myself exceptionally hungry these days and would like some provisions in my bedchamber. They will assume I am with child. And that I am too daft to understand what tomorrow is about."

I didn't let myself think of Hearn's hands on her body.

"Thank you."

"Wait here. If anyone asks, say you have an appointment with me and are to wait until I come."

Derwa departed in a rustle of skirts. I let myself sink back into my chair and ponder my upcoming journey. How would I find the fey realm? Supposedly a portal existed somewhere in the woods that bordered Silver Downs. Eithne had travelled through it. I could go home and ask that she tell me its location.

But there must be a portal somewhere near where I met Agata. I would try there first. The little I knew about such portals suggested they were not detectable by sight, but rather by feel. Those who had stumbled upon them reported feeling a strong urge to walk in a particular direction. They usually said they never knew the exact moment they passed through the portal, only that at some point they realised they were no longer in the mortal realm. Some druids believed the portals chose who would be admitted and who would be refused. Others believed it was Titania who controlled them.

Whatever had blinded the Sight to me might well be broken now that I could See. Titania might already know of my existence. It seemed foolish to bring myself to her attention by venturing into her realm. But I had no illusion of safety within the walls of Braen Keep. If Titania wanted me, no mortal-built gate would keep her out.

Derwa's return interrupted my thoughts. She carried a bulging sack which she set on the floor beside my chair. I suspected it contained far more than the provisions Hearn's men would receive on the morrow.

"Do you have need of anything else?" she asked. "A blanket, flint, new boots?"

"This is already far more than I expected. Thank you, my lady."

As always, she blushed slightly at the appellation. It appalled me that a queen could be so unused to being spoken to respectfully. I wished I could help her, but until Hearn treated her with more respect, his people had no reason to either. And Hearn thought so little of me that anything I said would only make the situation worse for her.

While I was thinking, I had been staring into Derwa's eyes. She returned my stare and now it was my turn to blush. I looked away. I trod on dangerous ground. Longing for another man's wife was never a good thing. Longing for something that belonged to Hearn could only end badly. I stood and prepared myself to say goodbye to her.

"There is something you should know before you go," she said.

I sat down again, my knees suddenly weak.

"I know Hearn has given you little reason to think well of him, but I do not believe this war is entirely his fault," she said.

My heart sank. Of course she hadn't been about to say what I had hardly dared to let myself think.

"I don't understand," I said.

"Hearn wouldn't send his men into battle on so flimsy an excuse as stolen cattle." Derwa spoke slowly, choosing her words with care. "There is a woman here who I believe is somehow influencing him. He has been… different since she arrived. Cruel."

"You think he is going to war because of a woman?"

"She has charmed him. I don't understand her motives, but whatever she plans, tomorrow's war is a part of it."

"Do you think Hearn is aware of this?"

"I doubt it. I tried to discuss it with him, but he thought I was jealous. Of her beauty." Her voice was bitter.

I wanted to tell her she should be jealous of no one. That no matter how beautiful this mistress of Hearn's was, she would not be as kind and as genuine as Derwa. It had been a long time since I had seen her as awkward or strange looking. She became more beautiful to me the more I got to know her. But the words stuck in my mouth. So I stood and picked up the sack. It was nicely heavy and I resisted the urge to peek inside. I would be grateful for whatever she had thought to provide.

"I should leave now, my lady." It was the only safe thing I could say.

"Can you tell me what direction you travel in? Or how long you expect to be gone? How will I know if you have fallen into trouble?"

"I think the less you know the better. And if I encounter trouble in the fey realm, there's nothing anyone here can do for me."

"You will return, won't you?" Derwa's eyes suddenly shone with unshed tears. "I can't bear the thought that you might not. Your presence makes this place bearable."

"I'll try."

It was the most I could offer. And I wasn't sure it was even right to offer that much to another man's wife.

2 4

ARLEN

I left the keep quietly. I had an unusual ability, which I had rarely had reason to use, of making myself unseen to mortal eyes. The only other person I knew who could do this was Eithne and she had been a woman grown long before she ever realised that folk weren't just ignoring her when she sat very still and quiet. She had never been able to articulate exactly how her ability functioned and neither could I. As a child, I had only known that if I pretended nobody could see me, they didn't. If there was a connection between being unseen and being unable to See, my ability might now be broken.

The night air was cold and I wrapped my cloak tightly around me as I hurried through the courtyard. I stayed close to the walls of the keep until I reached the last shadows. The gate stood slightly open, just enough to admit a man, but I would have to step out into the open to reach it. If the guards saw me, I would say I had received an urgent summons from Oistin.

I leaned against the stone wall, which still held some warmth from the sun, and made myself still. I sank deeper and deeper into the dark. *Don't see me, don't see me,* I thought. I could typically only be unseen if someone didn't look for me. If they heard me and looked, they would usually see me.

I stepped out into the open just as a gust of wind lifted some fallen leaves, sending them skipping over the stones. A guard turned. He gave the area a cursory glance, but never noticed the shadow that sank back against the keep's wall. When he turned away again, I hurried towards the gate, careful to keep my footsteps light. My heart pounded and it was only with effort that I kept my breathing steady.

I slipped into the shadows at the gate and waited until one of the guards spoke. That moment when they looked at each other was all I needed. I was through the gates and into the shadows on the other side of the wall before they could see me.

The moon was only a day or two off its darkest time, so it shed little light, but it was enough. My plan was simple: go to the place where I met Agata and search for the portal. I would traverse every footstep of the area if I needed to, for it had to be nearby. If I couldn't find it, I would go to Silver Downs and ask Eithne where the portal she passed through was.

Walking kept me warm enough, although only barely. I set a steady pace and reached the clearing before midnight. I stopped and closed my eyes, cleared my mind and waited. Those who had passed through the portals spoke of feeling something tugging at their insides. A light breeze swirled around me, dancing through my hair and the linen of my trousers. Insects chirped and a frog croaked. I broadened my awareness of the place around me and let my mind drift with the wind. I pushed away an edge of frustration that I hadn't yet felt the portal. I waited. And waited.

I felt no tug at my insides, no pull from the portal. I let my mind drift further, but still I felt nothing. Despite my attempt to keep my mind clear, Agata's face burst through my concentration. I remembered the way her expression changed when she first saw me, her eyes widening with surprise and her mouth dropping open. And I finally felt something, although it was in my heart, not my stomach.

I pushed Agata's image away and just as quickly the feeling was gone.

When I let her face take shape in my mind again, the pull to my heart returned. Without letting myself think about direction, I began walking. It felt like I was moving right towards her. Could I have done this earlier if I thought to try, or was it only possible now I knew what she looked like?

The night grew even colder as dawn approached. Frost crackled beneath my boots and walking no longer kept me warm. I held my cloak tight around me, trying to secure any gaps where the breeze could sneak in, but it cut straight through my clothes. I had expected the portal to be somewhere near where I met Agata, but I walked all through the night. The sense that I walked towards her grew stronger by the hour.

Eventually the pale moonlight revealed an old oak up ahead, its gnarled trunk almost as wide as I was tall. The pull led me straight to it. It was only when I reached the oak that I no longer knew which direction to go. I rested my palm against the oak's scarred trunk and felt its life pulse strong and vibrant.

I circled the oak, searching for a clue, and suddenly the world shifted. Instead of a lone oak, I now stood in the depths of an ancient woods. The moonlight was gone and the sun shone, although the canopy concealed it from view so I couldn't judge the time of day. The air was warm, but not overly so. The creatures around me didn't seem to notice my intrusion, for they continued with their own lives, digging through undergrowth and cawing from the trees.

An insect flew past my face and I raised my hand to wave it away, until I spied the tiny humanoid form. She hovered in front of me and seemed to study my face as curiously as I studied her. Then she made a soft tittering noise and flew away. I hoped she wasn't a spy. Titania might already know I was here.

A raven peered at me from a low branch, its head cocked to one side. As I met its eyes, it looked away and groomed its glossy plumage, tugging each feather with its beak. It looked back at me as if to check whether I still watched, then it too flew away.

I focussed on Agata's image and let her guide me again. The pull was stronger now. The plants around me were those I would expect to find in woods anywhere: ash, oak, birch and beech. Hawthorn and dogwood and spindle. Wood sorrel and bluebells. Creeping vines and decaying leaves. I saw moss and mushrooms, bugs and birds. The woods were perfumed with damp earth and rotting leaves, fragrant blossoms, and from somewhere nearby, the crispness of cool water. The trees were older, the life within them stronger, and everything was greener and glossier than I was accustomed to. It soothed my homesickness for the woods surrounding the druid community.

I walked quietly, not wanting to draw attention to myself. Yet I was aware of being watched. I looked around, trying to appear as if I merely inspected my surroundings, but saw no sign of anyone spying on me. And yet there was a definite prickling at the back of my neck. I kept my shoulders relaxed and my hands loose and tried to look unthreatening. If somebody already watched, it was too late to make myself unseen.

The pull towards Agata seemed to follow no particular path. It wound between trees, up a gentle slope and across a bubbling brook. I followed it until suddenly someone stepped out from behind a tree and blocked my path. He was tall and slight with the pale skin and red lips of the fey. He was the one with Agata in the mortal realm. We looked each other up and down.

"You won't find her," he said at length and I was surprised at the venom in his voice.

"I must," I replied. "She needs me."

"She has no need of any mortal." His voice was scornful. "You should go. Return to your own world and I won't tell anyone you were here."

"I came to find my sister."

"She doesn't want to be found."

"If she wants nothing from me, then let me hear that from her own lips."

"It would distress her to know you followed her here. If she wanted to know you, she would have searched for you."

"It seems she did. For how else could we have stumbled across each other?"

"She wasn't looking for you that day," he said. "She merely wanted to see what the mortal realm looked like."

"Does she know where she is from?"

He hesitated, and I hoped the old wisdom that the fey would not lie was true.

"She knows she is part mortal," he said. "She has no desire to know more. Is it true she is your sister?"

His interest surprised me. But if he cared anything for her, perhaps I could convince him to help me.

"She was stolen just moments after her birth," I said. "I have come to take her home."

"This is her home."

"Her mother would dearly love to meet her."

"Who is her father?" The fierceness in his voice told me this information was terribly important, to him at least.

"You don't know?" I tried to buy myself a few moments in which to figure out how much to tell him.

"Would I ask if I did? Tell me who he is."

"Agata has never met her father. I think it best that she be the first to know. I don't know you are or what your relationship is to her."

"If you tell me who her father is, I will consider taking you to her."

"Take me to her and you'll hear what I tell her."

"Unacceptable."

I shrugged and made as if to walk away.

"Then I will find her by myself," I said.

"You won't find her. This place is not what it seems."

"We are connected. I will find her if I search."

"If it's so important that you find her, why didn't you come sooner?"

Would Agata ask me the same question? And how would I answer her?

"I had obligations that prevented me," I said. "But I am here now."

"Obligations." He barked out a laugh. "If you cared anything for your sister, you would have come as soon as you could. Not waited until—" He stopped abruptly.

"Until what?" I turned back to him. Was I too late? "What has happened to her?"

He shrugged and looked away, and the motion was suddenly painfully familiar. I studied his face and suspicion grew within me.

"Do you know Kalen?" He darted a look at me, and my suspicion was confirmed.

"Why would you think I do?"

"Just answer the question." He narrowed his eyes at me as if trying to guess the answer from my face.

"Will you tell me where Agata is if I do?"

He pouted.

"I don't have to tell you anything."

"Just as I don't have to tell you. But we could help each other. It seems we each have information that the other wants."

"Is he happy?" His words came out in a rush. "Kalen. Is he sorry he left?"

"He is happy as far as I know."

"So you do know him."

"Where is Agata?"

He turned and ran away into the woods. I tried to follow, although I knew it was probably pointless. I should have realised he must be a blood relative to my father. The shape of the jaw was the same, as was the slant of the eyes and the high proud forehead. He looked to be about my own age, but fey appearances can be deceptive. So who was he to Kalen: brother, cousin, son? And who was he to me?

I gave up trying to follow him and stopped to centre myself. I pictured Agata again and concentrated on the connection between us. Did she feel the pull too? Did she know I searched for her?

2 5

ARLEN

he light in the fey woods never changed, even though I walked for at least a day. Twice I sat to rest and eat sparingly from Derwa's provisions. The sack contained a loaf of dark bread, two wedges of hard cheese, a cloth pouch filled with beef jerky and hard biscuits, and several small green apples. I doubted these rations were what the men going to war received. Was the battle over yet? How many had died? I felt both shame and relief at not being there to witness the aftermath.

I tried to stay alert, despite my fatigue. Once or twice I saw another of the tiny humanoid creatures, but they flew past too quickly to be sure they weren't merely bugs. For a while I thought a raven spied on me. He might or might not have been the same one who watched me earlier. He flew from tree to tree just ahead of me, staring as I drew closer, before flying on a little further. But soon enough he flew away with a disparaging caw. I kept my mind and senses open but noticed no other sign of anyone nearby. The pull leading me to Agata never changed. I tried to prepare what I would say to her, but everything sounded trite.

My feet were sore by the time I stumbled on a pretty clearing with a deep pond. A ring of weeping willows gave a feeling of privacy, and the moss creeping across the rocks around the pond looked invitingly soft. The water was still and clear, and too deep to see the bottom. When I sat down, I discovered the moss was as soft as it looked.

I pulled off my boots and rolled up my trousers, then slid my aching feet into the water. It was pleasantly warm with a sweet scent. I was tempted to cup my hands and taste it, but I refrained, wary of the tales that warned not to eat or drink anything of the fey realm.

For a while, I just sat there. Had Agata ever been here? I liked the thought that perhaps this was a place she had visited. I turned when I caught movement at the edge of my view and realised I sat beside a large rock. How had I not seen it earlier? As I stared at the rock, a strange buzzing sounded in my ears. Wondering whether the rock itself was the source of the sound, I pressed my fingers to its surface.

"Well, hello there," said a deep voice that seemed to speak straight into my mind. It spoke slowly with a long pause between each word.

"Hello, rock."

What manner of creature was this? I had never heard of the fey taking such a form.

"There's that word again. Rock. Mortals seem awfully fond of describing me like that."

"I didn't mean to cause offence. Is there another name you would prefer I call you by?"

"Hmm, a name." The rock was silent for a long while. "I seem to remember I was called Orm at some time. You can call me that."

"Well met, Orm. What manner of creature are you?"

"I suppose I shouldn't be disappointed you don't recognise me. It's been a long time since my kind last spoke to yours. Not since before the usurpers came."

"Do you mean the fey?" I asked. Tales told of the Old Ones who had inhabited these lands before the fey arrived. Nobody knew whether they left or died out, but at some point it seemed none remained. "Are you an Old One?"

"That name will do as well as any."

"Why have you shown yourself to me?"

"You're not the first of your line to see me. There was a girl once.

Might have been yesterday, might have been a hundred years ago. We only spoke briefly the once. Eithne was her name. You might have heard of her?"

"That's my mother."

"Aah, I had hopes for her, but she took too long. It's all down to you now."

"What do you mean?"

"Banish the fey. Reclaim our lands. Your job."

"Me?" My voice squeaked a little. "I'm just trying to find my sister."

"Oh yes, you need to do that, too. But *she's* not going to be very happy when you do."

"She? Do you mean Titania?"

"Hush. Don't say her name too loudly. She doesn't want you to find the girl. Doesn't want the girl to go back to her family. The girl doesn't want to either. But that's by the by."

"Agata doesn't want to go home?"

"Of course not. But that's not what we need to talk about."

"Oh." I started to feel rather stupid. "How would I go about banishing the fey?"

Orm harrumphed.

"That's for you to figure out," Orm said. "I'm just alerting you to the task."

"Why me? I don't have any idea how I would do such a thing."

"You're a druid trained, aren't you? A son of Silver Downs. And fey blood in your veins. Special combination, that."

I had never thought of myself as having fey blood, but Orm was right. Even though my father, Kalen, was only half fey, it did mean I was at least part fey myself. It was a pity Kalen's blood didn't give me any talent with the Sight.

"I don't know what I can do," I said. "I haven't even finished my training."

"Still struggling with the Sight, are we?"

I supposed there was no point asking how Orm knew. "I've only Seen once and that might have been an accident."

"It's your ability stopping you, you know."

"My ability?"

"Your ability to be unSeen. Can hardly See if you're unSeen yourself."

"Is it really that simple? If I find a way to make myself Seen, I'll be able to access the Sight?"

"Not simple, but that's the gist of it. But do you really want to be Seen?"

"She still doesn't know about me?"

"As long as you're hidden from the Sight, you-know-who has no idea you exist. Do you really think she will leave you in peace once she knows?"

"What would she do?"

"Why, she'll come after you, of course. She would have stopped at nothing to steal the girl away. She's going to be furious when she realises she left a child behind."

"I Saw today for the first time. I thought I might be able to finally finish my training."

"You're not meant to be a druid, boy. There are bigger things in store for you."

"Like banishing the fey." I tried not to sound mocking.

"You've got work to do. Alliances to make. Can't banish the fey on your own."

I thought very carefully before I spoke. It would take a matter of the utmost importance to draw an Old One out of hiding after thousands of years. If I helped the Old Ones, maybe they would help me find Agata.

"Who would I speak to if I was to seek an alliance with the Old Ones?" I asked.

"Well, any representative would do."

"Like you?"

"Not here for my health, you know. Takes a lot of effort to communicate with your species."

"If you want me to try to banish the fey, I'll need help from your people."

"Of course you will. Can't do it alone."

"Why didn't you fight the fey when they first came?"

The rock made a noise that seemed like the verbal equivalent of a shrug.

"Didn't seem worth the effort. Figured they wouldn't stay long."

"But now you've decided it's time to fight back?"

"Tired of waiting. And they don't seem inclined to leave any time soon."

"Do all the Old Ones look like you?"

A sound like rocks grinding together and then something that might have been a cough. I got the impression that Orm laughed.

"No, we come in all sorts of shapes and sizes," Orm said. "Look around you. We're everywhere."

I had been so focussed on Orm that I hadn't notice the strange assortment of creatures around me. A young hazelnut bush stood just a few feet away where no bush had grown earlier. Rocks of various sizes. A log. A bird's nest. Were even the weeping willows Old Ones?

"How many of you are there?" I asked.

"Oh, quite a few, I suppose," Orm said.

"How long have you been hiding?"

"Not hiding. Waiting. But the time has come for us to return."

"And you think I can help you."

"It's you we've been waiting for. The unSeen one."

"You make it sound like a prophecy."

"Guess you are, in a way. But you'll need the girl. Can't do it without her."

So many questions. I didn't know what to ask first.

"What do you want from me?" I asked.

"You'll figure it out."

"Will you help me?"

"She's coming."

I blinked and Orm was gone, along with the assortment of shrubs and rocks and logs that had surrounded me. Who was coming? Titania? Before I could pull on my boots, Agata arrived. I held my breath and stood as still as a stone.

She wore a gown of forest hues with colours that seemed to shift and flow into each other as she moved. Her long hair was loose and tangled. She was unguarded in that moment with shoulders slumped and her mouth downturned. Until she saw me. In an instant, she had pushed her emotions down to where I couldn't see them. She gave me a cold, haughty glare.

"You again," she said. "Why are you here?"

"I've come to find you. To take you home."

She stared at me incredulously. "Home? I am home."

But her voice broke a little and she didn't sound certain.

"My name is Arlen. We shared our mother's womb. You were born just a few minutes before me."

She studied the pond and didn't look at me.

"Is that true?" she asked, eventually. "I have a brother?"

"You have a mother and father, too. And they would dearly love for you to come home."

"I couldn't live anywhere else." She gestured around us to the woods.

"Don't you want to meet our parents? Show them you are alive and well?"

"I shouldn't have been there that day. In the mortal realm. She would be angry if she knew."

Interesting that even Agata feared to say Titania's name.

"Why were you there?" I asked.

She shrugged. "I just wanted to see it. I wanted to see if it was really as bad as they say."

"What did you see?"

She smiled. "The sun was much brighter than it is here and the sky so much bluer. Sumerled told me the sun moves across the sky each day and sinks down below the horizon. And when it does, it casts the sky in fiery shades."

"That's all true and there's so much more. At night, when you look up to the sky, you can see thousands of stars. Some say that's where the gods live."

"I'd like to see the stars," she said wistfully.

"Then come with me. Just for a little while."

She seemed to consider it for a moment, but shook her head.

"I have no reason to go to the mortal world again."

"The mortal world is your home. It's where you came from. It's where your family is."

"They would have come searching for me if they cared."

"Titania forbade our mother from coming after you. I've always intended to search for you, though."

"And you waited until now?"

How could I answer that? She was right. I'd spent my life putting off the search. I had promised myself I'd go as soon as I finished my training, but why had I waited even that long? My training was important only because I hoped it would equip me for my search. I had learned all I could about the fey and their realm. I memorised the old tales. Talked to everyone I could find who claimed to have met a fey or been to their realm or even just thought they might have glimpsed a fey once. It was all stored in my mind, ready and waiting for the day when I would go in search of Agata.

"That's what I thought," she said, sadly, and I realised I still hadn't answered her. "If I was important to you, you would have come earlier."

"It's not that simple."

"I'm sure it's not." She took a long look at me as if memorising my face. "Farewell. Don't come looking for me again. If she catches you, she won't ever let you leave. We can't meet again."

"Agata, please."

She ran away. I started to follow, but she disappeared into the woods before I had taken more than a few steps. I couldn't even hear what direction she ran in, for she moved as quietly as the fey.

"Agata," I called.

2 6

ARLEN

he walk back to Braen Town took several hours and dawn broke as I reached the keep. Time rarely runs to the same course in the fey and mortal realms, so I didn't know how long I had been gone. I had spent my whole life waiting for the right time to look for Agata and now my search was over. I had failed. I barely noticed anything around me as I walked. I wasn't weary or hungry or even disappointed. I was numb.

The keep's courtyard bustled with men bearing weapons and packs of useful supplies. It seemed that only a single night had passed and I had returned in time to witness the men departing for war.

I stifled a yawn as I made my way to the kitchen. The men I passed looked as tired as I felt, with pale faces and dark rings under their eyes. Likely many had experienced a sleepless night as they waited for what might be their last day alive.

Usually the only others breaking their fast so early in the kitchen were the men coming off overnight guard duties. They would eat silently, interested only in filling their bellies with warm food before departing for their beds. But today the kitchen was crowded and even Derwa was there, handing out steaming bowls and mugs to men who ate standing. The aroma of hot porridge and fresh bread relieved my numbness and my stomach growled.

Hearn waited impatiently, not eating but leaning against the wall with barely contained fury on his face. I found myself a corner out of the way. My need for food was not so great that I couldn't wait until the men who faced death today were finished their meal.

As Derwa passed Hearn, he grabbed her roughly and pulled her close to hiss something at her. She held her head high as she replied. His face darkened and his other hand twitched. Derwa showed neither fear nor pain as she glared at him. Hearn pushed her away and left. It was only after Hearn was well out of sight that Derwa rubbed her arm where he had grabbed her. I looked away and tried to breathe calmly. I could do nothing for her in front of so many people.

As the men finished eating, they took up their packs and weapons, and departed. There were no tender farewells for their women, although I saw more than one couple pause for a final look at each other. Most of the women were calm and restrained, if pale with worry. One or two burst into tears and were shushed by the others as if they were naughty children.

Two women cleared away the bowls the men had eaten from. I was unsure as to what my role was supposed to be. I had half-expected Hearn might order me to accompany him and was relieved I wouldn't have to witness the battle for myself. I followed the women and children and those men who were too old or unable to fight as they made their way down the steps to the cells.

The stairs were ill-lit, damp and a little slippery. I was dizzy from lack of sleep and I clutched the railing tightly so I didn't fall on the old man in front of me. The cells smelled like rotting fish, but at least there were no prisoners, which surprised me. Hearn did not seem like the type of king to leave his cells empty.

We crowded into two of the larger cells, which had been cleaned and stocked with provisions. The air still smelled dank, but it wasn't unbearable. Thick blankets and piles of cushions covered the stone floors. Someone had even brought down a few low stools for those who could not easily reach the ground. Lanterns sent out an almost cheery light as two of the women passed around bowls of now-cooled porridge and slices of dark bread.

I accepted a bowl and ate leaning against the cold stone wall, ashamed at my hunger at such a time. Despite Hearn's confidence, there was no guarantee his men would be victorious. If he were a different man, he would have expected his druid to be at his side, to tell him exactly when the battle should begin and conclude. I didn't know whether to feel insulted or relieved that he didn't want me there.

Had Oistin known what it would be like here? How much of this had he Seen? I scraped the last of the porridge from my bowl and try to let go of my questions. I would never guess Oistin's intentions no matter how much I tried.

"Are you finished?"

I hadn't noticed the woman standing in front of me until she spoke. She held out her hand, waiting for my bowl. I passed it to her with a soft thank you and she moved on.

I spied an unoccupied spot on a blanket and made my way over there, careful not to step on hands or feet. How many men would Hearn usually have in these cells? Four? Six? There were more than thirty folk crowded into this cell alone, leaving little space for each person. Some small children crawled into their mothers' laps. One or two lay down, curled into tight balls. An old woman was fast asleep in the corner, her head resting against the wall, soft snores emitting from her mouth. I envied her ability to sleep in this place. People spoke in hushed voices or sobbed quietly.

If Hearn's men did not win today, these people would become Cullen's property. I was probably the only person here with the certainty of safety, for neither victor nor loser would take vengeance on a druid. Even if Cullen was as unprincipled as Hearn, I had my ability to be unseen. If there was danger to myself, I could slip away. I could do nothing to protect the folk around me, though.

27

IDA

I watch from an upper window as the men march out. I suggested to Hearn that I should accompany him, perhaps on a white horse, and he looked at me as if I had lost my mind. Women have no place in war, he said and left the room. I am a little perturbed that he did not offer any fond farewell, for that is what the tales say men do as they depart for battle. But perhaps these went to his wife, that strange ugly creature who hovers in the shadows.

I see her watch me, although she thinks I don't. She fears I have taken her place in her husband's bed. I have no appetite to press my flesh against his, but surely she knows that other women share his bed when he does not go to her — servant girls and the wives of his men, some more willing than others.

Where is his wife now? Does she weep in her bedchamber as he marches away? Does she, too, watch from a window or does she stand down there with the other wives as they wave farewell? I look for her, but if she is in the courtyard, I cannot see her.

As the men march, I change my form and slip out through the window. On raven wings I follow. They set a steady pace, although not particularly fast. I expect Hearn to lead, for that is what the hero always does, but he walks at the back of the column.

The sun has only moved two fingers' width across the sky before they encounter the opposing army. It seems this is no surprise attack. They meet on a grassy field with nothing but a few trees between them. Hearn's men are at the bottom of a gentle slope. I perch on the branch of a rowan some distance away, my strong claws wrapped securely around its limb. The wind is cold and I fluff up my feathers for warmth.

There is little hesitation before they engage in battle. Men on both sides strip off their clothes and drop them on the ground. They run forward holding axe or sword up to the sky and wearing nothing but their own skin and a shield on their forearm. Some few remain clothed, although I doubt their linen garments will provide any obstacle to the sharp weapons.

The two armies meet in a clash of metal and their battle cries fill the sky. Each side has about the same number of men and very soon I see they all bleed the same colour. Men fall to the ground, dead or dying. Limbs are sliced off, intestines spill onto the grass. They wail and sob as they die. A foul stench reaches my nostrils and my stomach curdles. I can no longer tell which are Hearn's men and which are Cullen's. The battlefield is one writhing mass of dead and dying men.

I search for Hearn and find him in the middle of the battle. He bleeds from several wounds, but this does not seem to slow him. His sword pierces his opponent's side and the man falls to the ground. The grass beneath him quickly stains with blood. Hearn sticks his sword into the man's belly, then turns to slash another in the hamstrings. The man on the ground stares up at the sky as he dies. I wonder what he sees there.

The ground is choked with the dead and dying. How do they know who wins? Sometimes in the tales, men fight until only one remains. I suppose this makes it easier to identify the victor.

Suddenly men throw down their weapons and fall to their knees. This must be surrender, but I still can't tell whose army has won. Men approach the ones on their knees and slice with their swords, sending them falling to the ground as blood spurts from their throats. I am aghast. Those who have surrendered are supposed to be taken prisoner. That is what the tales say. They should be taken back to the victor's lodge to be imprisoned until they waste away. But every one of the surrendering men is swiftly killed. It is only then I see that Hearn is amongst those left standing.

A cheer rises from the remaining men, although it is weak and somewhat dispirited. Less than half of those who set out this morning are still alive. Those who are naked find clothes to wear. Men begin gathering the abandoned weapons. Some inspect the fallen. Those who still live are given a quick death. More than one man cries as he does this. Other men take the heads of their dead enemies and place them in a row on the bloodied grass.

At length there are no more men to be killed and no more weapons to be gathered. They take up the heads they have collected and tie them by the hair to their belts. Hearn's men march on to Cullen's lodge. The gate is guarded by a pair of teenaged youths who tremble at the army's approach. They drop their swords and fling themselves to the ground, begging for mercy. Mercy is swift, but perhaps not of the type they hope for.

Cullen's lodge is not as large as Hearn's, but it is still of a substantial size. Women, children and old men are gathered in a room at the back. The doors are of heavy wood and barricaded with a steel bar. But two old men open the doors when Hearn drums his fist against them and demands entry. Like the youths, the men receive swift ends. Women of childbearing age, girls and young boys are herded to one side of the room. The old men and those women who are too old or ugly to interest Hearn's men are killed.

There is much sobbing and wailing from those who are permitted to live. Those who are meek leave with little injury, but some try to resist as they are led from the room, digging in their heels and clutching at furniture or door frames. Any who are too difficult are promptly killed, except for one pretty young redhead. Despite the fight she puts up, one of Hearn's men has taken a particular liking to her. He slaps her soundly, but when she continues to fight him, he closes his fist and punches her in the face. She stops fighting. He drapes her over his shoulder and carries her away. Blood dripping from her face leaves a trail behind him as he walks.

The prisoners are led outside and some of the men stand guard around them while others search the lodge. When they have located enough plunder, they set fire to the building. As it burns, the sky grows dark with smoke and ash. The day is late as they march towards home with the heads of their enemies dangling from their waists and the women and children herded in front of them.

The gate to Braen Keep is guarded by an old man who can hardly lift his head high enough to see who approaches. He peers short-sightedly at Hearn.

"My lord?" he asks.

"It is I," Hearn says. "We are victorious."

A great cheer rises from the remnants of his army. The sound is much heartier than it was earlier, as if the march home has restored the men's strength. Some of the prisoners begin to wail and are slapped into silence.

The old man shuffles over to where a large bell hangs. He rings it and the men cheer again. There is little discipline as they pour through the gates. By the time they reach the lodge, the women and children emerge. Women smile and cry as they clutch their men to them. Others search the returning army, then gather their children close as they realise their men have not returned.

The prisoners are shepherded down to the cells. The kitchen workers rush off to begin preparing a celebratory feast. Before the men eat that night, the heads of the fallen stand on pikes in front of the keep's wall. Ravens flock to pull and tear at the flesh. I can smell the remains even from my bedchamber two levels above the ground. It is the smell of death and defeat. I wonder how long it will be before I stop noticing the stench.

28

ARLEN

orty-two prisoners. Twenty-eight women, ten girls of less than marriageable age, four boys aged no more than eight or nine summers. Only one old woman and no old men. These were all that Hearn's men thought worth saving.

From what I overheard, they destroyed Cullen's entire estate. The human inhabitants were either dead or locked in Hearn's cells. Everything of value was taken from the lodge and the buildings burnt to the ground. Some of the men intended to return on the morrow for the livestock and then they would torch the barn as well.

The cells were stripped of blankets, cushions and lamps before they brought the prisoners in. At least they were put in the cleaned cells. They huddled on the stone floor, broken and defeated. They were not dressed for warmth and they had no blankets. The cells were chilly enough during the day and would be cold at night.

Nobody thought to offer the prisoners food or drink, despite their long walk. At a well in the courtyard I found a bucket and a long ladle. Back down at the cells, I convinced the guard on duty to open the door of each cell, one by one, so I could offer water to the prisoners. But when I drew a ladleful and held it out to a child, she shrank away from me. She was too young to understand what had happened and probably knew only that her mother was afraid.

"Come," I said. "Drink. It's fresh water from the well."

Her mother clutched the girl's shoulder, preventing her from coming to me, so I addressed my next words to her.

"It's safe. Just fresh water. I promise."

She stared at me for a long while, as if trying to judge whether I lied, before she nudged her daughter forward. The girl took the ladle and drank eagerly. Her dirty face and runny nose made me wish I could offer her wash water as well, but I suspected that wouldn't be permitted. After the girl had drunk her fill, her mother accepted the ladle and then others came forward. When the bucket emptied, I went back up to the well and filled it again.

I reached a prisoner who was more girl than woman. She must have been barely of marriageable age, yet her belly was swollen and she kept one hand clasped over it as if to protect her unborn babe.

"What is your name?" I asked.

She drained the ladle before replying. "Eithne."

I almost dropped the ladle as she passed it back to me. I dipped it in the bucket and tried to hide my shaking hands.

"My mother's name is Eithne," I murmured.

She gave me a sad smile but didn't reply.

"How much longer until the child is born?" I asked.

She patted her belly gently.

"About three moons. But the midwife—"

She stopped and I guessed the midwife was not amongst those Hearn's men bothered to take prisoner.

"There are midwives here," I said.

Her mouth twisted and her eyes shone.

"Not for me there won't be," she said.

"I'll speak to the queen," I said.

She nodded but didn't look hopeful.

Eager hands reached for the ladle every time I offered it and it was a long time, and many trips back up to the well, before everyone had drunk enough. Many of them were willing to talk to me, especially once I offered them water. They told me their names and some volunteered the names of their men who had died today. None asked what I thought would become of them.

As I trudged back up the steps, I realised I had missed the start of the feast to celebrate Cullen's destruction. Apparently everyone at the keep was invited. I cared little about it, except that I didn't want to draw attention to myself by not attending. Raucous noise reached my ears as I made my way towards the feasting hall, along with the scent of roasted meat and fresh bread. Perhaps if I slipped in quietly, Hearn would not realise I arrived late.

I paused in the doorway to look for an empty seat. I spotted one and strolled over to it, hoping that if Hearn saw me he would assume I simply returned after slipping out briefly. The platters still bore plenty of food, but my stomach churned at the thought of eating. How could they feast and drink and laugh when Cullen's people down below were left to go hungry? I poured a mug of ale and took a small sip. If Hearn noticed my entrance, he paid me no attention. In fact, he looked as if he was barely aware of the feast at all, for he was so focussed on the woman who sat beside him.

She was thin and pale, with long white hair and a vicious smile that was currently directed at Hearn. She leaned over and said something into his ear. Her hair brushed his shoulder as she spoke and he laughed heartily. They both drank and she took a dainty bite of something from her plate.

Just looking at her turned my spine cold. I had the vaguest feeling I had seen her before. She was an unusual-looking woman — striking, but obviously not of the same stock as folk around here, who were all dark of both hair and eye. Surely I would have remembered if I had seen her before.

As if she felt my gaze, the woman met my eyes. Again I felt a jolt of recognition. She lifted her lips in what could only be a snarl. A voice inside my head said, "Careful, little druid. You know not what you find." She looked away and directed her attention back to Hearn.

My hand shook a little as I raised my mug. Surely I imagined the voice in my head. And I must have imagined the feeling of having seen her before. Discomfited, I drained my mug and poured another.

29

ARLEN

The feast continued well into the night. The servants kept bringing jugs of ale and by the time I left, everyone was so drunk I judged it unlikely my absence would be noticed. Hearn was as drunk as anyone and seemed sullen, despite his victory. The woman sitting beside him drank little as far as I could tell. There was something strange about her. I didn't seem to be able to look directly at her and when I wondered why, my thoughts would disappear and my mind went blank. I blamed it on fatigue as I slipped away to my bedchamber.

Despite my exhaustion, I slept poorly. My heart was heavy with guilt and regret. I never expected to be advisor to a king, and I certainly never thought I would falsely authorise a battle. It was my fault folk had died. My fault women and children were prisoners. They would probably be given to Hearn's men who had excelled in the battle. My mind shied away from their fate when those men had no further use for them.

I gave up trying to sleep when the sun was an hour or two from rising. Frost crunched beneath my boots and the wind stung my cheeks as I wandered aimlessly through Hearn's sorry courtyard. I rubbed my hands across my face, wishing I could scrub away the images in my mind. The faces of women who had been captured and who knew exactly what was in store for them. The faces of children who had no understanding. Their pale, dirty, terrified images haunted me.

I was in sore need of advice. There was no point trying to See what lay ahead. That one glimpse of Agata might well be the only time the Sight came to me and Orm's comments made me reluctant to try again in case it made me visible to Titania. Oistin said not to send a messenger, but he hadn't said I couldn't go to him myself if the need was great enough. And I could think of no way my need could be greater right now. I sorely needed his advice.

Without a second thought, I went to the gate. I didn't bother to make myself unseen and the guards grinned heartily at me. I tasted bitter bile and swallowed, hoping I wouldn't embarrass myself by vomiting in front of them. They knew I authorised the battle. Of course they knew. And it seemed they ascribed some of their success to me.

Dawn broke long before I reached the stone circle and the emerging sun sent fiery tongues of gold and crimson across the sky. My breath steamed in the cold morning air and I stamped my feet in an attempt to restore feeling to my toes.

I knew the theory of how to invoke the air elementals. I had never done it myself, though, and I could only hope the elementals would respond. It would be a long walk to the druid community otherwise — several days at least — and I couldn't afford to be absent from the keep for that long. Not now.

As I stood in the middle of the stone circle, all I could see around me was tall grass that was starting to die off with winter's approach, the early morning sky, and the trees that stood strong and proud. Birds sang their morning songs. The beauty around me soothed my spirit after the dryness and desperation of court. I closed my eyes and breathed in the crisp air. Inhale, exhale. I centred myself and searched for the quiet place in my mind. When I felt suitably calm, I called the elementals.

"I seek to travel with the swiftness of Air. I seek the lightness and fluidity of Air. I seek the gracefulness of Air. Elementals of Air, would you transport me to the druid community?"

I waited, but nothing happened. When Oistin sent me here, only moments passed before the elementals answered his call. I counselled myself to patience and waited. But after several minutes, I realised they didn't intent to respond. I should have expected this. Air was the one element I had yet to forge a relationship with. Why had I thought its elementals would agree to transport me now?

"Elementals of Air, I beg you." I poured all my heartbreak and homesickness and sorrow into my words. "Please, I have the greatest need for swift travel and you can transport me faster than anything else. I don't know what I did to cause offence, but whatever it was, please accept my humble apologies. I beg you to aid me. It is a matter of life and death, and I don't have time to travel in any other way."

I waited. And waited. Still the elementals didn't respond.

"Please, Air." I didn't know how else to persuade them. "Please, if not for my sake, do it for my mother's. My mother is Eithne, daughter of Silver Downs."

I had no idea what possessed me to say this but the words felt right. At last the elementals responded. They circled me, swirling and dipping, around and around. The scent of honeysuckle filled my nose. I kept my eyes firmly closed. The elementals did not like to be seen when performing such a task and Oistin had often warned they would leave if a traveller tried to look at them. The journey seemed to take a very long time, but at length they ceased their dance.

"Thank you, Air," I said as the elementals departed. "I am most grateful."

I waited until the last stray winds were before opening my eyes. I stood in the familiar stone circle not far from the community's lodge. The sky was fully dark and the tree canopy prevented me from seeing the moon, but the night felt late. My journey had lasted the entire day.

The lodge was quiet and dark as I approached. Oistin would be in his bedchamber, studying perhaps, for he rarely slept. The front door opened with a soft creak like it always had. The druids here had no reason to lock their doors. I crept along the hallways, knowing which floorboards to avoid.

Lamplight spilled into the hall from Oistin's bedchamber and I reached the door to find him waiting for me. Of course he was. His Sight would have told him I was coming. I felt like a fool for not thinking of this sooner. There had been no need to sneak through the lodge like a thief.

"Master, I need your advice," I said.

"You should not be here."

"Things there are not what you think."

"Only I know what I think."

His calm words gave away little except to one who knew him as well as I did. He was angry. Furious. I could tell by the way his left eye squinted just the tiniest bit as he spoke.

"I've made a terrible mistake and I don't know how to fix it," I said.

"Your mistake was in coming here. You should not have left your post without permission."

I hung my head. "I know, Master, and I'm sorry. But I need—"

"Go back."

His words cut through me. I hadn't anticipated he might refuse to advise me. Oistin was the man I knew best as I grew up. Not quite the father I didn't really remember but my mentor. He was wise and patient, and I had believed he would give me sound advice. After he rebuked me, of course.

"Master, please—"

He held up his hand to stop me.

"Events will happen as they are intended," he said. "You will act your part. Go back to Hearn immediately. If you leave now, you can be back before he notices you are gone."

"Men died today."

"Go now, Arlen. Everything is going to plan."

Later I wondered why I didn't argue longer. Why I didn't try harder to find the words that would make him listen to me. But as I stood in front of Oistin and knew for the first time in my life that he was severely displeased with me, I felt like a whipped dog. I could expect no assistance from him.

I trudged back to the stone circle and again asked the Air to transport me. I didn't need to invoke Eithne's name this time, for the elementals came immediately. Perhaps for her sake they had forgiven my offence, whatever it was. They left me at the stone circle and I started the long walk back to the keep.

3 0

ARLEN

It was dawn by the time I reached Braen Keep. I spent the walk trying to understand why Oistin refused to advise me. I had never expected he would let me down like that. It felt wrong to be hungry but I was starved after the long walk, so I stopped at the kitchen for some bread and cheese. I had just reached my bedchamber when a boy came trotting down the hallway. The message he conveyed was brief. Hearn expected my attendance in the feast hall tonight.

Another feast so soon? How could folk celebrate when men from both estates died yesterday? How many children amongst both Hearn's and Cullen's people were now fatherless? How many women were widows?

I didn't know if I had the strength to stay here much longer. I was completely unsuited for this position. But it was clear that Oistin wouldn't reassign me. He had withheld information from me, perhaps something that was critical to my presence here. How much of his vision of me with Hearn and the shadowy woman had he kept to himself? I assumed the woman was Derwa, although I didn't know why her identity was concealed in Oistin's vision. Or maybe he lied about that.

The only thing I knew for certain was that Oistin had a reason for wanting me here. He would likely expel me from the community if I gave up my post without permission. Would my family accept me back if that happened? An estate the size of Silver Downs required a large number of folk to farm and look after livestock, and for repairs to fences and walls and roofs. There would be plenty of work for me if I went home — if they allowed me to stay after such a disgrace.

Despite my worries, I slept soundly. I woke late in the afternoon with the feeling that I had figured something out while I slept, but it had already slipped away. I lay in bed for a while, grasping after the threads of my thoughts, but they were elusive and whatever it was I had understood was gone.

I claimed a seat in the feast hall just as servants started bringing around the food. Hearn's table was served first, of course. Derwa was absent tonight and a strange white-haired woman sat in Hearn's own seat. I studied her from the corner of my eye, not wanting to be caught staring. Something about her stirred a memory, but I couldn't place it. I felt like I should know who she was, but I would have sworn I had never seen her before.

Someone passed me a jug of ale and I filled my mug. I sipped it sparingly, although my fellow diners eagerly gulped theirs. If any still had sore heads from last night, they didn't let it slow them. The wild boar was juicy and the vegetables crisp and fresh, but I had little appetite.

A whole roasted swan was delivered to Hearn's table and he ate with gusto while still managing to talk to the white-haired woman at his side. She took bites of her meal from time to time, but seemed more interested in listening to Hearn than in eating.

Most of the diners were well on their way to emptying their plates when a line of servant women came in. Each bore a single clay jug and they positioned themselves around the room in a clearly orchestrated move. At the high table, Hearn put down his knife and stood. Folk quickly fell quiet. A small smile played across the white-haired woman's face as she toyed with her mug.

"My people, we feast tonight to celebrate a great victory." Hearn's voice was loud and he slurred his words a little. "The house of Cullen is no more. His men are dead. His women and children are slaves. His livestock stands in my own fields and his lodge has been burned to the ground."

He paused and the diners roared their approval. I was silent. I would not cheer such words, even if it drew me to his attention. The white-haired woman said nothing, but her smile grew larger. Whatever this was about, it was pleasing to her.

"To celebrate our victory, I present to you the very finest Roman wine," Hearn said.

He gestured towards the servant woman standing beside him. Like the others, she bore a single jug.

"This wine has been imported at great expense, and never have I purchased a finer wine, nor one more costly. Each jar of wine cost me one slave." Hearn paused to let his words sink in. "So drink of this fine wine, my friends, for you will never drink finer."

He sat and the diners roared their approval. The servant woman filled his mug and he held it aloft before draining it. She filled it again, then poured for the white-haired woman.

Twelve women bearing jugs. Twelve prisoners were sold for this wine. Who? Was the woman who shared my mother's name and who feared she would not have access to a midwife one of them? How many of the children were sold?

A servant woman filled my mug, but I only looked at it. I could not bring myself to drink of wine purchased with slaves. Never again would I authorise a battle I shouldn't, regardless of what either Hearn or Oistin expected of me.

3 1

ARLEN

"**D**ruid, come in."

Hearn barely looked at me as he waved me into his library. As usual, the messenger gave no indication of why he wanted to see me. I clasped my hands behind my back and looked straight at him as I waited in front of his desk. I couldn't let him see that I feared what he might want from me this time. He continued to study the parchment on his desk. Eventually he looked up at me.

"Druid," he said.

I waited.

"Do you know geography?"

"Yes, my lord."

"Tell me about the estate to the south of my holdings."

"It is owned by Fingen and has been held by his family for at least four generations. A substantial estate, roughly half the size of your own."

"And what do you know of Fingen himself?"

"Little, my lord."

"Do you know that for the last few years his sheep have been grazing on my land?"

"I was not aware of that, my lord."

"He, of course, would tell you it's his land. But that's because he's forgotten where the boundary line lies."

Breathe. In. Out. "I see, my lord."

"He needs to learn to graze his sheep on his own property. My men can teach him that."

"You intend to go into battle against him."

I counted to five as I exhaled. My pulse raced and my palms were sweating. Barely more than a sevennight had passed since the feast at which we had been served wine purchased with Cullen's folk.

"I do," Hearn said. "Go interpret the signs. We march in two days."

I bowed and left silently. My thoughts were clear as I made my way outside. I wouldn't authorise his battle unless the signs were in complete agreement. It didn't matter what he threatened me with. He could send me back to Oistin and I would face my master's disapproval if necessary. But I would not falsely authorise another battle.

As I left the keep, something flew past my head, barely missing me. I stumbled back to avoid it. Wings flapped and wind rushed. The raven cawed as it flew higher and disappeared over the top of the keep. That alone was enough of a sign to tell Hearn I couldn't authorise his battle. But I needed to be very certain. I needed multiple signs.

Some distance from the keep, I sat on a low stone wall. Its only purpose, as far as I could tell, was to separate the poorly paved path from the dusty remains of what might once have been a flower bed. I looked up to the sky and waited.

It was an unusually warm day for midwinter, but even so I shivered and wished I had my cloak. The stone beneath me had barely started to warm before a dark shape plummeted from the sky. The hawk snatched something from the ground and flew away. Another unfavourable sign. Still, I cautioned myself to patience and settled more comfortably onto the stone wall.

When I looked up to the sky again, it was no longer clear. An enormous storm cloud rolled in from the south — the direction in which Fingen's estate lay. The cloud grew darker and larger. Thunder rumbled and a fork of lightning shot towards the keep. I had never known the signs to be so clear. Three signs indicating Hearn's battle would be unfavourable. And all three were from Air. Surely there was extra significance in that.

The storm cloud suddenly opened and heavy rain sheeted down. I was drenched before I could get to my feet. The water was so cold, it left me breathless. Puddles formed quickly and the dusty paths turned to mud. I started back towards the keep. I had all the information I needed.

But as I stepped over a particular puddle, it darkened and within it I Saw Hearn. He lay on a funeral pyre, his eyes closed as flames licked his hair. The image lasted only a moment, disappearing so quickly I wondered whether I imagined it. It was, after all, only the second time I had Seen.

I went straight to Hearn's library, soaking wet and leaving a trail of puddles behind me. He didn't comment on my appearance when I arrived in his doorway.

"So, druid?" he said. "Two days, heh?"

"The signs are very clear." I shivered, not just with cold but with the fear of what I was about to do. My teeth chattered and I couldn't feel my hands or feet. "Never have I seen them so clearly indicate that battle is to be avoided."

He stared at me coldly.

"Druid, I thought we understood each other."

"I understand what you want me to say, my lord, but I cannot. If you go to battle in two days, it will go badly."

"I don't accept that," he said. "Try again."

"My lord, there is no other way to interpret the signs. The conditions for battle are most unfavourable."

"Again. I'm still waiting for the correct response."

"You will die. I have Seen it. If you go to battle now, you will end it on a pyre."

"Your approval, druid." He said each word carefully and clearly. "You have one task here. Do it."

"Do you understand what I am saying, my lord? Even if I approve your battle, it will mean your death."

"Druid."

What else could I do? He was determined to go to battle. It hardly mattered whether I authorised it or not. I nodded.

"Let me hear you say it," he said.

"Your battle is authorised." I tried to keep the snarl from my voice but wasn't entirely successful. "And it will mean your death."

"We will discuss your insolence later. After my men return victorious."

He nodded towards the doorway, dismissing me without another word. I walked out, leaving puddles in my wake.

32

AGATA

"*A*gata!"

Titania's screech echoed through the palace. I was sitting at a window, staring out at nothing while I brooded. For the first time in my life, I found myself discontent. But when Titania called, I jumped up.

"Where is she?" I asked the first person I encountered, a mortal slave.

The woman looked at me dumbly.

"The queen," I hissed. "Where is she?"

The woman pointed down the hallway behind her.

"I was going in that direction anyway."

There was no point wasting time with a mortal. She was either too stupid to speak or too afraid. And she was obviously a full mortal. Not like me. I at least had some fey blood in me.

Usually if I was in a hurry, the palace hallways would be certain to be tricky, but today they led me straight to Titania's sitting room. I stopped to compose myself as I reached the final hallway, smoothening my hair and straightening my gown. I took a deep breath and walked briskly to her door. The guards admitted me immediately.

"Agata, explain something to me."

Titania perched on the edge of a deep red daybed. Her forest green skirts were rumpled, as if she had sat up suddenly, and she appeared to have one bare foot. Given Titania never let herself be seen as anything less than supremely elegant, this was not a good sign.

"My lady?"

I dropped into a deep curtsey, trying to keep my movements graceful. When she was in this sort of mood, she would pounce on the slightest inelegance from me. I kept my head bowed and my eyes averted, and pretended I didn't see the green slipper lying on its side.

"What have you learned about the man who wears your face?" she demanded.

Her words shocked me so much that I looked straight at her. Her face was white and her mouth pinched.

"My lady?"

"Don't *my lady* me," she snapped. "You're not a fool, so don't act like one. Tell me who he is."

"My brother." It was pointless to pretend I didn't know who she meant. "He was born shortly after me."

"The mortal woman bore a second child?" Her voice rose in both pitch and volume with every word.

"So it seems." I bit off the instinctive *my lady* that wanted to come out of my mouth.

"How do you know this?"

I hesitated, but she would know if I lied.

"I met him again."

"Where?"

"Here in the fey realm."

"When?"

"Recently."

"How did he get here?"

"I don't know. I was walking in the woods and stumbled across him."

"And you spoke to him." Her voice was flat.

"Of course I did. He has my face. Wouldn't you speak to someone who looked just like you?"

"Nobody looks like me."

"You know what I mean," I muttered. It was overly warm in here and the air was so heavy with Titania's floral perfume that my head ached.

"What did he tell you?"

"He said that my—" My mother, I almost said. "He wanted me to go with him to meet the mortal woman who bore me."

Titania smiled, a tight, bitter smile that didn't mean she was amused.

"She barely got to hear you squawk before I took you."

"Why did you take me?"

"A punishment." Her voice was distant, as if her mind was elsewhere. "She took someone from my realm. So I took someone from her."

"You mean my father."

"He's only half fey, you know."

"Did he fall in love with her?" All my life I had been taught that a fey never loved a mortal, or anyone else for that matter. Love simply wasn't in our nature.

She shrugged. "Mortals can be persistent. She may have convinced him he loved her. He will come crawling back someday, begging forgiveness, wanting to live amongst us again. When she gets old and haggard and wrinkled, he'll realise what a mistake he made."

"He will age, too, won't he? If he stays there?"

"Slowly. Much more slowly than her. She will be old and grey while he is still in his prime."

"He must love her, if he knew all that and still went with her."

"Love is a facade." Titania glared at me. "It is a construct of mortals used to justify their pathetic existence. We have no need of love." She changed topics abruptly. "The man. Your brother. Why did I not See him earlier?"

"I don't know. I barely talked to him. I know nothing about him."

"I Saw your birth. I should have Seen his also. He has been shielded from the Sight somehow, just like the mortal woman, but whatever was hiding him is broken now."

"What are you going to do?"

I felt a sudden surge of protectiveness towards him. We shared a womb if he had told me the truth. That should mean something. Abruptly I realised what a mortal thought that was. No true fey would feel a responsibility for someone just because they were born of the same blood.

Titania gave me that tight smile again, the one that wasn't really a smile.

"I haven't decided yet," she said. "Go now. We are finished talking."

I curtseyed and left at a sedate pace, my heart hammering. Titania was unpredictable except in the fact that she never forgave a grudge. But I couldn't guess whether it would be Arlen she would punish or the mortal woman who bore us. Eithne, he called her. My mother. I wondered whether I should try to warn either of them.

3 3

AGATA

y thoughts lingered on the idea of warning Arlen, even though he was a mortal. No, I realised. That wasn't quite right. He was no more and no less mortal than me. If we had shared a womb, then he, too, was part fey. We were connected in some strange way I didn't understand. How else could I have found him the first time I'd ventured into the mortal realm, without knowing who he was or where he would be?

After several days of vacillation, I resolved to try. *If* I found him, I would warn him. I was letting my mortal blood influence me to an unreasonable extent, but as I slipped through the portal, I knew only that I had to warn him.

The frigid air of the mortal realm hit me with a fierce blow. The sun was high in the sky, although today it barely warmed me. A few scattered clouds were bowled along by the wind. Perhaps I would stay here all day and see for myself the way the sun disappeared at night and how the moon and stars revealed themselves.

Which way to go? There was no point in going to the sad town I visited previously. They didn't know Arlen there. I chose another direction at random and began to run. The grass crunched under my slippers and the wind left my cheeks tight and chafed.

After some time, I reached a lodge. It was large and looked well made, with many people busy at various tasks outside, although I couldn't identify what most of them were doing. Some walked around, others stacked things in great heaps. Swords and boxes and other objects I didn't recognise. Some folk were clustered in a group, clutching each other and crying. Everyone else seemed to ignore them. I approached a man who carried a sack that clinked and rattled as he walked.

"Do you know Arlen?" I asked.

He turned towards me, and it was only as he dropped the sack that I noticed the dark red splatters that covered him. Suddenly uncomfortable, I stepped back away from him, but he seized my arm.

"What are you doing here?" he demanded, shaking me. "Why aren't you with the others?"

"I'm looking for Arlen." My heart pounded. Something was very wrong here.

He dragged me with him as he walked, his fingers digging painfully into my arm.

"Stop that," I said. "You're hurting me."

He didn't respond and didn't loosen his grip either.

"I said stop that," I shouted, trying to wrench my arm out of his grip. "I am the daughter of Titania, queen of the fey, and I demand you unhand me immediately."

"Oh, daughter of the queen of the fey, hey?" he asked with a snigger. "Well, princess, if you know what's good for you, you'll shut up and do as you're told."

He shoved me towards the group that was huddled together. I landed on my hands and knees.

"Watch her properly this time," he said to a man standing nearby. "I found her wandering through the courtyard."

My knees throbbed, the skin torn and bleeding. My palms stung and my skirt had a hole at the knee. I sniffed and my eyes filled with tears which I quickly blinked away. Fey did not cry.

The man who had been instructed to watch me glowered.

"How did you sneak off?" he asked.

I raised myself up, pretending a dignity I didn't feel.

"You have no right to treat me like this," I said.

He stepped towards me and slapped me across the face. My cheek felt like it exploded. I stumbled, pushed backwards by the force of his blow, and raised my shaky hand to my cheek.

"Keep your mouth shut," he growled. "Next time I hear your voice, that pretty throat will be meeting my sword."

I glanced down to the weapon at his waist and noted the redness smeared on the hilt. Something dark and sticky wound through his hair. I swallowed hard.

The mortals I was deposited amongst were mostly young women and children. They were pale-faced and sad-eyed as they huddled together. I wanted to ask what was happening, but was too afraid that the man might keep his promise about letting my throat meet his sword. I had a horrible feeling the red splatters might be mortal blood, and I tried to forget the seeping redness I had spied on my own knees.

I studied my surroundings, trying to make sense of the situation. It seemed that things from within the lodge were being brought out and added to the pile of crates and weapons. Other men loaded items from the pile into a cart hitched to an ox, although a few items were surreptitiously slipped into belts or pockets. Not twenty paces from me a woman lay in a pool of blood. She stared sightlessly up at the sky, her throat gaping open. I swallowed hard and wished I hadn't seen her.

Other men crowded around us now and said we should start walking, keep together, don't cause any trouble. The man who threatened to cut my throat looked at me when they said that. They herded us through the gates and marched us along a road. From time to time someone would start sobbing, but others quickly shushed them. I desperately wanted to ask where we were going and whether I would be allowed to go home once we got there, but I didn't dare speak.

We walked long enough that I was able to see the sun move across the sky. Perhaps I would see the moon and the stars after all. Eventually we reached the walls of a town and I recognised it as the place where I searched for Arlen. People rushed into their lodges when they saw us coming. Doors slammed and shutters were swiftly closed.

We reached another wall with a gate. Inside was a very large lodge. It was perhaps as big as Titania's palace, but not nearly as fine. The sun was almost gone by now and the light had turned murky. Shadows stretched across the courtyard. Perhaps Sumerled had actually told the truth when he said the sun disappeared from the sky at night.

The men ushered us into the lodge, along a long corridor and down steep stone steps which were only dimly lit with lamps. The air was cold and smelled foul. A woman ahead of me slipped and fell. She cried out and when she got to her feet, her arm hung wrongly. Nobody offered to help her.

We reached the bottom and were ushered into small chambers in groups of five or six. I was sent to a chamber at the far end where the flickering lamplight barely penetrated the darkness. The floor was slippery and the air felt damp. I smelled mould and moss and dankness. There was no furniture.

"Where am I to sit?" I protested as the sturdy wooden door closed behind me. I received no response.

I couldn't see the other women in my chamber clearly enough to judge their ages, although I had noticed before the door closed that one of them had a belly swollen with child. Two others eased her down to the floor. I sat with them and found the damp stones was covered in a slimy growth. I got to my feet, but the back of my skirt was already wet through.

"You may as well get used to it," the woman who was with child said. "This is probably preferable to whatever they will do with us next."

"Why were you in the courtyard?" one of the others asked me. "You aren't from Fingen's lodge."

"I was looking for someone," I said.

"It was a stupid thing to do, to let yourself be seen," she said. "You could have hidden and waited until they left. They had found enough of us to be satisfied."

"What is happening?" I asked. "I don't understand."

"War," someone said. "When your men lose, we all lose."

"I don't know what that means."

"Even if you are lucky enough to have never seen the results of war before, surely you know what happens."

"There is no war where I come from," I said.

She laughed as if she didn't believe me.

"Well, aren't you a special one. Let me enlighten you, then, sweet thing. When your men lose the battle, the victor takes all. His lodge, his animals, his people. They slaughter the folk they don't want, but those are the lucky ones. The rest are either given to the victor's men as spoils of war or sold into slavery."

"You could go either way," one of the others said.

"Aye," agreed the first woman. "You're pretty and young enough to fetch a nice price in the slave markets. But if you've caught the eye of one of the men, he could ask for you. Might be a good thing, might not. Depends on whether your new master has any kindness about him. But if you have any notions of your body being your own, you'd better get those out of your head right now. Your body belongs to the victor and he'll grant it where he chooses."

A horrifying truth dawned on me.

"I'm a prisoner?" I whispered. "I can't be a prisoner. I'm daughter to the queen of the fey."

"I wouldn't keep saying that if I was you," she said. "If they think you're not right in the head, you'll be sent straight to the slave markets. Nobody wants a halfwit slave, even one as pretty as you."

I sucked in a breath. "Titania will come looking for me and they will feel her wrath when she does."

But secretly I wasn't so sure. Time passed differently in the two realms. Months, or even years, might pass here before Titania noticed my absence. And would she bother to search for me, or would she assume I had returned to my mortal family? Sumerled would come, I thought with a rush of relief. He would notice I wasn't there. I just had to endure it until then.

I waited. My stomach growled and my bladder needed to be

emptied. Had I been here long enough for the moon and stars to appear yet? They might be out there in the sky even now while I was stuck underground in this nasty, damp chamber.

There was movement out in the hallway. Doors opened with a squeal. A conversation in male voices. Eventually the door of my chamber opened. Lamplight flooded in, burning my eyes.

"One with child," a man said. "A sevennight or so out."

"The market," another man said. "She'll be useless until the child is born and for some time afterwards."

"An old woman," someone said.

"How strong does she look?"

"Got some reasonable life in her yet. Might make a decent field worker."

"Send her to market."

"There's a pretty one here, but she looks like trouble."

The lamp was held right in my face. I squinted, eyes watering, and glared back.

"Stand up, girl," one of the men said.

When I didn't move, someone reached out of the light and grabbed my arms. He hauled me to my feet.

"He means you," he said. "Stand up now."

My legs were almost numb after sitting on the cold, wet stone for so long and I would have fallen if he hadn't been holding me. Still I held my head high and shook off his hands as soon as I thought I could stand by myself.

"Says she's a fey princess," someone said with a laugh.

"I am the daughter of Titania," I said. "And you will regret your insolence when she comes looking for me."

They laughed.

"There's one or two of the men who would like to keep her," one said.

"Too feisty," said the man who seemed to be in charge. "One like that won't be tamed easily. She'll fetch a good price, though, provided you can stop her from talking until the deal's done. It's the market for her."

They left, taking the light with them. The door slammed and a bolt shot home. Once again we were left in darkness. It was a long time before anyone spoke.

"That's what you get for telling such tales," one of the women said softly. "You made yourself look like trouble and see where it got you."

"What do you mean?" I asked.

"They're sending you to the slave markets, girl," the old woman said and her voice was kinder than the other. "You'll be auctioned off. Sold. You'll be a slave for the rest of your life."

"They would do that?" No wonder the fey thought so little of mortals. If they would do this to their own kind, what would they stop at?

"All you can do is hope that whoever buys you is not too unkind."

"What will happen to you?" I asked the two woman who weren't destined for the slave market.

"We'll be given to Hearn's men," one said. "The ones he wants to reward."

"What if nobody wants you?"

"There will always be someone who'll take a woman that's being offered for free," she said.

My eyes had adjusted enough that I could more or less make out her features. She was probably almost at the end of her childbearing years, with a haggard face and stringy hair.

"Doesn't matter what she looks like or how old she is," she continued. "All that matters is there's nobody left to care about her. Because if nobody cares, you can use her up and kill her when you're done. A quick death is the best we can hope for."

I kept my mouth shut after that and hoped Sumerled would hurry.

34

ARLEN

I watched from my bedchamber window as Hearn and his men returned from the battle with Fingen. Their shoulders drooped and there were few smiles or calls of bravado. They brought a group of women and children and a wagon piled so high that its contents were in danger of spilling. Hearn slumped next to the driver.

As soon as the cart stopped, men rushed forward to help Hearn down. He seemed unable to stand unaided, but they held him up. A cloak draped around his shoulders obscured his injuries. He should have believed me when I said this battle would mean his death.

Several hours passed before he sent a messenger boy for me. When I reached Hearn's bedchamber, the only other person there was a woman stoking the fire, although the air was already smoky. It reeked of herbs and not all of them were for healing. Hearn lay in his bed, sweating and pale.

"Druid," he spat. "We won the battle."

"So I hear, my lord."

"You said we would lose."

"Actually, my lord, I said you would lose, not your men."

He glowered, but it seemed he had already expended his remaining energy. He raised one trembling hand to touch his belly.

"Took a sword to the guts. Healer says it missed the organs, but it's already turning putrid. Nothing else she can do for me."

I didn't reply. What could I say other than to remind him I had warned him?

"Go," he said and turned his face away. "I don't want to see you again."

I bowed and departed. There was nothing left to say. My king was dying and I couldn't summon even the smallest amount of sorrow. Before I reached my bedchamber, a serving girl approached.

"Master druid," she said. "The queen wishes to speak to you. She is in her sitting room."

I nodded my thanks and she scurried away.

Derwa was alone when I reached the room she had recently started using as her sitting room. I kept meaning to ask why she had abandoned the previous room, for it was larger and nicer.

"Come," she called when I knocked on the closed door.

I slipped in, leaving the door ajar so nobody would think anything improper.

"You have been to see him?" she asked.

Her face was composed, if pale, and her hands twisted together in her lap.

"I have," I said.

"How is he? Tell me truly, for nobody has told me anything and I will not go to him unless he calls for me."

"He is dying. He was stabbed in the belly and the wound is putrefying. He might live another couple of days yet, but he faces a painful death."

"He said you authorised the battle."

It wasn't a question, but I knew she wanted me to deny it.

"I did," I said. "He left me with no choice. I told him this battle would mean his death, but he refused to hear me."

"Have you Seen what will become of me?" Derwa stared down at her hands as she asked.

"I haven't. I'm sorry."

"Brennus… resents me." Her voice was little more than a whisper.

I wished I had some reassurance to offer her, but it would be improper for me to make her any promises. Not while her husband still lived.

"You could leave," I said. "Disappear in the night. There is a stone circle a few hours walk away. I can help you travel through the stones."

"I never thought it would come to this when I first came here." Derwa gave me a small, sad smile. "I thought the people would respect me. That I would have time to earn their trust, their love. I could have done much for them had they let me. But they've always hated me. Because I'm different. Because I look strange."

"You are beautiful to me." The words were out of my mouth before I could think. The soft smile that spread across her face stopped me from apologising for my inappropriateness. In that moment, she truly was beautiful.

"Will you send me word if you hear anything?" I asked. "If there is any hint you might be in danger, you should leave immediately. Maybe you should even go now. Don't wait—" I stopped, but she said it for me.

"Don't wait for my husband to die? Flee while he lies waiting for death?"

"It sounds callous, but you need to think about your safety."

She shook her head. "I can't. He is still my husband and I must stay until he dies. He might want to see me."

"He doesn't deserve loyalty from you."

"Regardless, this is the man my father gave me to. I stood up in front of both our families and vowed to be faithful to him. Running away while he is dying hardly demonstrates my faithfulness."

"He doesn't deserve you. He never has."

"Oh, Arlen, things might have been so different. If Hearn was a different man. If I was a different woman. If—" Her voice dropped to a whisper. "If I had met you at a different time. But things are what they are and I must stay until he dies."

"I understand."

"I will send word if I hear anything," she said. "In the meantime, the men brought back prisoners. Folk of Fingen's household. You might perhaps go speak with them. See if they need anything, medical treatment particularly. There's little else I can do for them."

"You could go see them yourself."

"Hearn would think I was trying to undermine him."

"I'll go now, then."

Dread filled me as I descended to the cells. The last time I spoke to Hearn's prisoners, some were sold to buy jars of wine. I still didn't know who. The guard stared me down as I approached.

"What do you want?" he asked. "I don't have instructions to let anyone in."

"The queen sent me to check whether any of the prisoners need medical care."

"They don't."

"She has bid me to view them myself."

He glared for a good while, but at length he shrugged.

"If Hearn hears of this, I'll tell him you insisted," he said.

"You can tell him the queen insisted."

"Go on, then."

"Can I take the lamp?"

He snorted and turned away from me.

"Should have brought a light with you if you wanted one."

I didn't waste time arguing. He might decide he wanted Hearn's approval after all if I lingered. I approached the first cell and peered through the bars in the opening set into the door. The light from the guard's station behind me meant I could see nothing inside the dark cell.

"Hello," I said. "Is anyone injured?"

Silence greeted me. I could smell the sweat of the folk in there and heard the little noises they made as they moved, but although I repeated my question twice, nobody answered. I moved on to the next cell.

Again I asked if anyone was injured, and again nobody responded. The last prisoners were all too willing to speak, to tell me their names and their positions. I went to each door and repeated my question several times. It was only when I reached the final door that anyone answered me.

"There is a woman in here with a broken arm," an indignant voice replied. "And I demand to be let out immediately. Titania will punish everyone here when she discovers how I have been treated."

"Agata?" I asked. "Is that you?"

"Who's that?" came her reply. "How do you know my name?"

"It's Arlen. Your brother."

Her face appeared at the opening.

"Why are you here?" she asked.

"I live here. I advise the king."

"Bring this king to me," she said. "So I can demand he release me immediately."

"I can't," I said.

What did she know of the world if she thought a prisoner could demand the king be brought to her cell?

"Why not?" she asked.

"Do you understand you are a prisoner?"

"Do these mortals not fear Titania's wrath?"

"They fear only the king's wrath."

"Then do something. Go talk to him. Tell him— *Ask* him to let me out."

"I can try," I said. "But I doubt he will. Be patient. The situation will improve soon."

I couldn't tell her Hearn was dying, not with so many ears listening.

"The only way it will improve is if I am released," she said. "And don't forget the woman here who needs a healer."

"I'll ask for one to be sent down." That would give me a reason to return to Hearn's bedchamber and it might afford an opportunity to ask for Agata's release. "I'll come back after I've spoken to Hearn."

"Who?"

"The king," I said, tiredly. Really, did she know *nothing*?

"Thank you." It sounded as if these were not words she was accustomed to saying.

I left, hoping Eithne never heard I had found my missing sister and left her locked in a dark cell. But the guard would only release her at Hearn's order. Without his approval, I could do nothing.

Hearn's bedchamber was just as dim and smoky as before, only now two old women were there. Healers, perhaps. One of them cocked her head questioningly at me.

"May I speak with him?" I asked. "I have come from visiting the prisoners."

She shrugged and turned back to Hearn.

"You may speak, but I doubt he will hear you," she said.

Hearn was flushed and his chest was soaked with sweat as he tossed restlessly.

"He is in great pain," the elder of the two said. "We've given him something to make him sleep."

"The queen asked me to look in on the prisoners," I said. "There is one who needs a healer."

"The folk from Fingen's estate?" she asked. "Sick or injured?"

"She has a broken arm. Is there someone who can authorise a healer to attend her?"

The two women looked at each other and the elder nodded.

"I will go," she said. "I need no authorisation when the only crime a person has committed is belonging to the wrong man."

"She is in the cell furthest from the guard's station," I said.

It was only after she left that I wondered whether I should have warned her about Agata.

ARLEN

I woke to the jangle of bells. I figured they must be announcing Hearn's death, so I dressed and went straight to Derwa's sitting room. Even though the first golden rays of sunlight were only just peeking over the horizon, I figured she would be awake. It was only as I knocked that I wondered whether I shouldn't have come. I didn't let myself think about the fact that she was no longer someone else's wife.

Derwa's soft voice bade me enter. She wore the same gown as yesterday although now she had a shawl wrapped around her shoulders. The fire had long died and the air was chilly. I went straight to the hearth to light the fire.

"Have you been here all night?" I asked.

"I didn't know where else to go," she said. "I couldn't go to my bedchamber. I needed to be somewhere that didn't make me think of him."

I let her words flow past me, not letting myself linger on thoughts of Hearn visiting her bedchamber. As the fire took hold, I sat beside Derwa and we watched the flickering flames in silence.

"What will become of me now?" she asked. "I can't claim the throne. Hearn's chief advisors despise me. They would never allow it.

The people have no respect for me anyway and would not support me. Brennus will need a regent until he comes of age, but I doubt the advisors will choose me." She clasped her hands in her lap and closed her eyes for a moment. "Am I a terrible person, Arlen? My husband has just died and all I can think about is myself."

"I would think it strange if you didn't think about yourself in such a situation," I said. "Surely the queen would be expected to act as regent."

"Brennus hates me even more than the advisors do. I wouldn't mind if they sent me back to my father, but I fear Brennus will seek revenge for all the slights he has imagined over the years."

"You should leave. Now. Just slip away quietly and disappear. You know I'll help you."

Derwa sighed heavily. Her knuckles were white and she seemed to notice how tightly she clenched her fists because she relaxed her fingers.

"Truth be told, I've considered it many times over the last day," she said. "What does that say about me that I look for the first chance to run away?"

"These are not your people. They're Hearn's people."

"They have never accepted me. If they had, if they viewed me as their queen, I would stay, truly. I would stay if they were mine. But they are not." She leaned back and looked at me with shadowed eyes. "I am so tired, Arlen. Tired of trying to make people see me as I am, not as they want to. Tired of pretending I don't hear the vicious lies they spread about me. Tired of being in this place that I hate. I once heard a woman say I shouldn't be allowed to look at a newborn babe in case I turned it ugly."

"Leave," I said again. "Don't wait any longer."

"Where would I go? Back to my father? That is the first place Brennus would look for me. If he demanded my return, my father would have to comply."

"Do you have other relatives? A married sister you could go to?"

"I don't know where my sister is. Hearn didn't let me correspond with my family. I tried, twice, to send messages. He caught me both times. The first time he merely threatened me. The second... he ensured I would never try again."

I couldn't tell her I was glad he was dead.

"I could take you to Silver Downs," I said. "My family's home. They would never turn away someone in need. I can't take you all the way through the stones, though, as it is more than a day's walk from the ones nearest to Silver Downs. We would need some horses or a cart and oxen."

"It is kind of you to offer."

"We could go now, but it might be best to wait for cover of darkness. And—"

I remembered Agata. How could I leave her behind?

"And?" she prompted.

"I visited the prisoners as you asked." My words came slowly and she waited patiently, her gaze never leaving my face. My sister is among them."

"Agata?"

"You remember her name."

"Of course I remember. How could I not? Such a strange tale. But how is your sister there? Why is she with Fingen's folk?"

"Somehow she got mixed up with them. I don't know the full story, but she's here and extremely indignant. I don't think she fully understands she is a prisoner."

"Has she been that sheltered in the fey realm?"

"She seems to think Titania will rescue her."

"Do you think that likely?"

"I don't know what their relationship is. She lived with Titania for more than twenty summers. They might well be as close as mother and daughter."

"Has she been treated well here?" Derwa didn't look at me as she asked, as if she couldn't bear to hear the answer.

"She has not been harmed as far as I know," I said. "I'm sure she would have told me loudly and in great detail if she had. She was quick to tell me of a woman with a broken arm. I sent a healer to her."

Derwa nodded, although she hardly seemed to be listening anymore.

"Arlen, I wish there was a way I could free your sister. I am tempted to go down there and demand her release. If I could be sure the guards would obey me, I would do it."

"We both know you can't do that."

"You will need to petition Brennus to release her. As soon as he claims the throne."

"I intend to. I just hope she doesn't draw too much attention to herself in the meantime."

"Oh, Arlen. I don't know what to say."

"I've been trying to come up with a plan," I said. "I could get her away from here if I could just get her out of the cell."

"We'll think of something," she said. "She's safe enough where she is for now. I don't know whether anyone has thought to send food down to the cells. I'll check. That's probably all I can do for her, though."

"I'll go talk to her again later. She might have calmed down by then. If I can convince her to keep quiet, things will probably be easier for her."

"Is she pretty?" Derwa's voice was wistful.

"It's hard for me to answer that since she has the same face as me."

She flashed me a rare grin and I revelled in it.

"Of course," she said. "I'm sure she is very pretty. She would do well to not draw attention to herself. Don't worry, Arlen. We will find a way to save her."

"I should leave you. You probably have things to do to prepare for Hearn's funeral. Do you need anything?"

She sighed. "Just a friend from time to time."

"You have that. Send for me if you need me."

Shortly after I left Derwa, I encountered Brennus and Girec running down the hallway. Brennus was in the lead and the younger boy gamely tried to keep up with him. They came skidding to a stop in front of me. Brennus looked me up and down with a sneer.

"I hear your sister is in the cells, druid," he said.

I made myself breathe normally and waited for him to continue.

"She's being sent to the slave market," he said.

Girec fidgeted, clearly uncomfortable with the conversation. I looked Brennus in the eyes and waited.

"It's a shame," he said. "She's a pretty one."

"You've met her?" The words were out of my mouth before I could stop myself.

"I inspected the prisoners. I made sure the guard pointed out your sister. She's feisty. Could be fun. I'll be king pretty soon and there will be changes around here when that happens. Your sister, for one. She won't be going to market."

Breathe. He wasn't done yet. He was enjoying himself too much.

"I'm going to keep her for myself," he said. "Until I get bored of her. How do you like that, druid?"

I had never felt the urge to punch someone before. Had never understood why men fought. But now I did. I wanted to tighten my hand into a fist and punch him in the face. I forced my fingers to relax. Then I walked away.

"Your insolence will be punished, druid," Brennus called after me. "Just wait until I'm king."

Long after I left, Brennus's words still rang in my ears. *I'm going to keep her for myself. Until I get bored of her.* I mostly dismissed his threat to me. It was well established that druids could not be subjected to retribution and I had my ability to make myself unseen. I could slip away quietly if I needed to. But Agata was in more danger than I had realised.

3 6

ARLEN

 paced my bedchamber, my mind working furiously. How long would the chief advisors take to make a decision about the throne? I doubted any regent would be able to control Brennus, but the right person might influence him. Hearn's main fault was ignorance. But Brennus was both clever and cruel. He would be a callous king, and I had no doubt he would be ruthless in ensuring he secured the throne. He was, after all, Hearn's chosen heir.

Once again, I longed for Oistin to advise me. But it seemed he had his own plans and — I was ashamed to admit it even to myself — I doubted his motives. When he sent me here, Oistin spoke of how he had Seen me at Hearn's side, but clearly there were other factors at play. Factors which perhaps related more to Oistin's own ambitions than the good of the people. So if Oistin would not advise me, who else could I turn to?

I remembered the letter from Uncle Fiachra, which I never responded to, and retrieved it from the drawer where I put it for safe keeping. As I re-read it, a chill swept over me and I realised what had been in front of me all this time.

The letter held a warning about Uncle Diarmuid's muse who Fiachra thought might follow me here. I had seen a strange woman around the keep in recent days. The white-haired woman. How could I have forgotten her? Could this be the muse Fiachra searched for? He described her well and I should have noticed when a woman matching his description arrived. Yet I hadn't. I suspected I had seen her, perhaps on several occasions, but I seemed to keep forgetting. Perhaps she had charmed me to forget.

I found a servant boy who seemed to be doing nothing much and begged some parchment and ink from him, which he quickly located. I took the items back to my bedchamber and sat down to write to Fiachra. *Uncle Fiachra,* I wrote.

I apologise for the tardiness of my reply. I received your message some time ago, but events here have been such that I neglected to respond. I am also ashamed to admit that I believe the woman you seek is here. It has taken me until today to realise.

Hearn died early this morning from a battle wound. I Saw that this battle would mean his death, but he didn't believe me. It shames me to admit I authorised the battle anyway. I will not give my excuses for such action, but I know I am unfit for this role.

It is difficult to recall when I first saw the woman you seek. I think she may have placed a charm on me, for I keep forgetting I have seen her. I don't know why I have suddenly remembered her now and I can't be sure I won't forget again, so I am writing this letter as quickly as I can.

I believe I first saw her in the great hall, where I have on occasion been invited to dine. At some time recently — perhaps ten nights ago — a stranger dined at Hearn's table. In fact, she sat in his own chair and he sat in the queen's place. The queen herself did not attend. The woman is slender of frame with long white hair and fair skin.

Hearn did not seem bothered that she sat in his place, a fact which surprises me greatly now I think on it. If anyone else noted her presence or thought anything strange of it, I heard no comments. Truly, now that I consider it, the situation was most unusual. Yet at the time I thought there was nothing odd in what I saw.

Your letter alluded to the fact that she had charmed folk in her previous foray into the real world and it seems clear she has done this here, too. There has been an increase in violence lately and I suspect she may be the cause. As to why I have suddenly remembered her, I can only guess. Perhaps Hearn's death has somehow interfered in her magic.

Uncle, I find myself in sore need of advice. It is expected that Hearn's foster son, Brennus, will claim the throne in the coming days. Brennus is a child yet and is neither ready, nor fit, to rule. Agata is here also and will be in great danger if Brennus becomes king. If you can suggest any remedy for this situation, I beg you to send me a message immediately.

I expect that by the time you receive this, Brennus will be king and I will have been sent back to the druid community. Please be wary of sending messages there as I no longer fully trust certain people.

There is someone here who needs a place of sanctuary. Someone dear to me. I hope that if a person were to arrive at Silver Downs and say I had sent them, the family there would offer them all aid.

Your nephew, Arlen

I hesitated before I added the final words: *Druid, of Braen Keep.*

As soon as the ink dried, I rolled up the parchment and returned to Derwa's sitting room. She now wore a clean gown and her hair was damp. Coals still burned in the hearth, keeping the room warm, and a tray on a low table bore the remnants of a meal. I felt a rush of relief at knowing she no longer wore yesterday's clothes or sat in a cold room.

"I need to send a message," I said. "It is somewhat urgent."

"Of course," she said. "I will have a messenger sent."

I hesitated to hand her the scroll.

"I don't have any wax," I said.

She went to a shelf holding several boxes and retrieved a small cube.

"You have no seal either, I presume?" she asked.

I flushed a little.

"I've rarely had reason to send messages, and when I did, I always used Oistin's seal."

"Use mine."

She handed me a small ring. I stared down at it in surprise.

"You use a raven for your emblem?" I asked.

"It is my family's symbol," she said. "Why does that disturb you?"

"It's just… surprising."

Fiachra mentioned a raven. It seemed that two women who claimed that bird for their symbol now resided here.

I melted a small piece of wax and pressed Derwa's seal into it. She promised a messenger would leave tonight with my letter. Likely there would be many messengers leaving the keep that night.

The next thing I needed to do was explain to Agata why she couldn't be released yet.

3 7

AGATA

I had been in this horrid dark chamber for so long that my stomach grumbled fiercely. At least a healer had come to see Wenda, the woman whose arm was broken. The healer splinted Wenda's arm and gave her willow bark tea to ease the pain. I tried to explain I needed to be released immediately, but the healer barely deigned to even look at me.

Dampness seeped from under the stones that lined the floor. It crept through the thin fabric of my gown and into my bones. I sat with my legs tucked up to my chest and my arms wrapped around them, but still the warmth leeched from my body. I didn't even notice the foul odour anymore. Time passed, or maybe it didn't, and I grew colder and colder. I could barely feel my toes anymore. I would freeze to death before I found anyone with enough sense to release me. I didn't even look up as a shadow passed in front of the opening set in the door until I heard Arlen's voice.

"Agata," he said softly.

"I'm here." I scrambled to my feet. The other women didn't move. Perhaps they slept. "Have you come to release me?"

"I can't. The king needs to approve your release."

"Then go talk to him. Tell him he must do it at once."

804

"I can't. He's dead."

"So who can let me out? There must be someone."

"Right now, no," he said. "I'm sorry, but you need to wait a little longer. I will petition to have you released as soon as the matter of the succession is finalised."

"How long will that take?"

"I don't know. Maybe a couple of days for decisions to be made. Another few days after that to get an audience with the new king. There will be many people jostling for his attention and he might not have time to talk to me immediately."

"Is there nobody else who can release me?" I couldn't stay in here for days and days. I'd die. I was cold and damp and miserable. "There must be something else you can do."

"Only the king can authorise the release of prisoners."

"But I'm not supposed to be a prisoner."

Arlen answered every argument with another apology, and slowly I came to understand he really believed there was nothing else he could do.

"Could I at least have a blanket?" I asked.

"I'll speak to the queen about it. Agata, tell me, why are you here? What were you doing in the mortal realm?"

One of the sleeping women stirred. Someone muttered. I lowered my voice so as not to disturb anyone.

"I came to find you," I said.

"Why?"

How much should I tell him? I barely knew him, even if we did share a face.

"Things have been bad for me lately," I said. "I didn't know I was mortal. It seems everyone else knew, or at least they suspected. I confronted Titania and she didn't even try to deny it. She's proud she stole me away. And now everybody knows and they're treating me horribly. I wanted to find out where I came from. Who is my mother? And why was Titania trying to punish her?"

"Our mother fell in love with a half fey named Kalen," Arlen said. "When he stopped coming to see her in the mortal world, she went to the fey realm in search of him. Titania imprisoned her, but she escaped. She found Kalen and he followed her back to our world."

"But why is Titania still so mad about it? That was a long time ago. Who is he to her?"

"Her husband's son, borne to a mortal woman."

"My father is Oberon's son? Titania's husband is my grandfather?"

Arlen was silent as I absorbed this revelation.

"So my father is a half fey who chose to leave," I said. "Does Oberon have any other half fey sons I should know about?"

Arlen hesitated.

"He hasn't told you?" he asked, at last.

"Who? What?"

"Sumerled."

It all fell into place. This was why Sumerled was shunned by the other fey. Why he made friends with me.

"I'm going to kill him," I said. "He's no more fey than I am, and he was the one who told everyone I'm only part fey."

"He's a friend of yours, isn't he?"

"He was, but I never suspected he might be part mortal. He can control his appearance like the fey always can."

"You can't?"

"No. Or at least I don't think so. It seems to be something fey instinctively know how to do."

"Maybe one who is part fey gets a different mix of abilities. There might be something you can do that he can't."

"Maybe." It was an interesting thought. "But I'm still going to kill him, just as soon as I get out of here."

"I'll petition to have you released as soon as I can."

"I wish Sumerled was here," I said. "I would kill him right now."

38

IDA

*H*earn is dead. I discover this when I ask a servant woman the reason for the ringing bells. It seems rather early to make so much noise, but apparently it is customary when the king dies. I have not seen Hearn since he rode out to battle against Fingen, although I have heard he returned injured. I am hardly surprised as mortal bodies are weak and delicate. It surprises me they live as long as they do.

My boy told a tale once about the death of a king. His wife, the queen, claimed his throne and ruled for many years. She even led her people into battle. As I wander through the keep, I overhear comments about Brennus becoming king. He is but a boy, though, and not old enough to lead men to war. But it seems there are no other suitable candidates. I feel generous today. Perhaps I should help them by taking the throne myself.

I ponder the boy's tales, but none give any instruction on exactly how to claim a throne. It seems that when the king dies, someone simply sits on his throne and it then belongs to him. The closest Hearn has to a throne is the big chair in his audience hall. When he sits there, people come to stand in front of him and complain. He makes decisions and sends them away.

The audience hall is empty when I arrive. I climb the five steps to the dais and seat myself in Hearn's chair. It is overlarge and padded with soft cushions. I understand why he likes this spot, for I am raised up over the room. I can see everything that happens in here. I suppose I just sit here and wait until somebody comes to petition me.

The day passes slowly as I sit alone on my throne. The air is chilly and my toes go numb. My stomach growls, demanding to be fed. It reminds me again of the fragility of mortal bodies. Perhaps I should leave and come back tomorrow. The day is almost over before finally someone enters the room.

It is a servant boy carrying a bundle, which he almost drops when he spots me. His eyes bug amusingly and he quickly backs out of the room. I do not have to wait much longer.

The double doors swing open and Brennus strides in. He is dressed finely in a red tunic and a brown cape, but he has grown too tall for his trousers. He looks like a boy pretending to be a man. He is accompanied by men who I recognise as Hearn's favoured advisors. Other people follow, but the doors slam behind Brennus and his companions. Brennus comes to the dais and stands in front of me. I wait for him to bow, but he doesn't. Perhaps he doesn't know who I am as we have never been introduced.

"What is the meaning of this?" he asks.

His voice breaks halfway through and I stifle the urge to laugh. I should appear regal.

"I am Ida and I claim the throne." I hold my head high and give him my haughtiest stare.

"The throne is mine."

"You should have claimed it, then."

"Have you no decency? Hearn still lies in his bedchamber."

"That is irrelevant to me."

"He was our king." He glances towards the advisors, perhaps hoping they will support him, but none speak.

"And I am the new king," I say.

"A woman can't be king." Brennus's tone turns scornful and he crosses his arms over his chest. "Everybody knows that."

I hesitate. What of the queen who claimed the throne? I sift through the many tales I know and find none where women have ruled as kings.

"I shall be queen, then," I say.

He eyes me for a long moment. "You will be queen to my king?"

What does this mean? If he thinks I will be subordinate to him, he will learn fast. Perhaps it is better to resolve this issue of kingship and thrones quickly and deal with the details later.

"That is acceptable," I say.

Nobody mentions there is already a queen somewhere in the keep and that she still lives. For the time being. Brennus turns to his advisors.

"Find another throne. Make one if you must. The queen and I will each require a throne. Am I not right, Ida?"

At least he hasn't suggested I give up Hearn's throne.

"Correct," I say.

Two men scurry away and Brennus holds out his hand to me.

"My queen, I believe it is dinner time. Will you join me in the dining hall?"

"I will."

I place my hand in his and allow him to lead me from the room. His hand is too warm and his palm sweats. In the dining hall, he escorts me to Hearn's chair, where I have eaten ever since I arrived here. He makes no fuss as I settle there and seats himself in Derwa's place, where Hearn has been sitting.

Diners enter shortly after. They seem to avoid looking at the high table as they sit and talk amongst themselves. When the platters are brought around, the servers hesitate as if unsure who to present them to first. I don't miss the subtle nod Brennus makes towards me. The servers seem relieved the decision has been made and the dishes are offered to me first. My wine cup is the first to be filled.

I spear a piece of wild boar with my knife and place it in my mouth. Its aroma is tantalising but it is cold and over-cooked. Nevertheless, I am hungry, so I eat. Tomorrow I will speak with the kitchen staff about keeping the food warmer.

I lean back in Hearn's chair as I chew and look out over the diners. My people. I am queen. If only the boy could see me now.

39

ARLEN

I was not invited to eat in the dining hall the night after Hearn died, but I overheard enough the next morning to understand that Ida and Brennus had jointly claimed the throne. For a moment I was confused about who Ida was, but then I remembered. Brennus as king was bad enough. The thought of Uncle Diarmuid's muse on the throne was horrifying. I suspected it was she who encouraged Hearn to take his men to war against first Cullen and then Fingen. It gave me some understanding of what would be ahead for the people of Braen Town if she ruled over them.

Had Fiachra received my letter yet? It would take a messenger on foot a sevennight to reach Silver Downs, or perhaps half that if he travelled by horse and was able to change them frequently. Another sevennights for a reply. It might be days yet before I could expect a response. I couldn't wait that long. Hearn's body would be burned tomorrow, and Brennus — and Ida — would be crowned within a day or two after that. Assuming they waited until after Hearn's funeral.

Derwa and Agata would be in immediate danger. If both women were to be kept safe, and Brennus and Ida stopped from ascending the throne, I had to act immediately. I had never had a head for strategy, but I needed a plan to stop a boy from becoming king, and to stop an imaginary woman brought to life, and to save both a queen and my sister.

My mind wandered through a few ideas, none of which were feasible. As long as Brennus lived, he would fight to be king. That was the one thing I was sure of. He had been raised with the expectation that the throne would be his eventually. The day might have come sooner than he expected, but that didn't mean he would relinquish the chance. Hearn was foolish and ignorant, but Brennus was cunning.

As the afternoon passed, I slowly figured out a plan. Maybe it would work. Maybe it wouldn't. If I failed, it would likely mean my own death. I didn't dare tell Derwa. She was in enough danger without being party to my treasonous plot.

As night fell, I fasted and meditated and when morning came my mind was clear. I knew what I had to do. As I walked to the audience hall, I tried not to think of all the ways my plan might go wrong. The doors to the hall were closed as usual. I hesitated, mindful of Derwa's words that I should have waited for Hearn to invite me in that first time. One of the guards finally looked at me.

"What do you want?" he asked, his voice uninterested.

"To speak with Brennus."

He opened the door and slipped inside. I could hear him even through the heavy doors.

"The druid wishes to see the king-in-waiting."

I couldn't hear Brennus's reply, but the doors opened to admit me. I had counted on Brennus being surrounded by advisors, and to my great relief he was. My plan wouldn't work without them.

Brennus wore an elaborately embroidered tunic that was far too big for him. He sat on a new throne positioned next to Hearn's. His head was held high and his face bore a barely concealed smirk. Ida wasn't in the room and I felt a rush of relief. She could obviously charm me to forget her, although that seemed to have faded since Hearn's death, but I was unsure whether she could also influence my thoughts or words. Without her here, I could be reasonably sure my thoughts were my own.

Four men stood in a group to one side of the dais. Lorne, a tall and skinny man with a face that looked far younger than his years. Cahan with his elaborate moustache. Teris, a short, stocky man who always looked as if his boots were uncomfortable. And Egan, who seemed more farmer than advisor. Iver, the fifth of the senior advisors, was absent. Had Brennus refused to have him or had he refused to support Brennus? He might be a potential ally.

I halted a suitable distance from the dais and bowed. It irked me to pay respect to this upstart of a boy.

"Druid." Brennus's voice echoed in the mostly empty hall. "Have you come to pledge your allegiance to me? I have use for a druid advisor."

"My lord." The words were bitter on my tongue. "I have come to tell you of a vision I Saw overnight."

Brennus forgot himself briefly and a smug smile crept across his face. He quickly wiped it away and nodded imperiously.

"You may speak," he said.

"My lord, I Saw our country. It had been ravaged by drought and fire and disease. People lay dead in the streets with nobody to prepare funeral pyres for them. The crops were stunted and wilted and there was not enough harvest to feed everyone. The livestock lay dead in their fields and crows feasted on their flesh. The rivers were dry and the land barren. The gods turned their faces from us."

I watched the advisors from the corner of my eye. They paid me little attention at first, but now they listened attentively. I noted the looks they gave each other, the little nods and whispered words.

"What nonsense is this?" Brennus's attempt to sound authoritative was ruined when his voice broke.

"I came to tell you as soon as I finished my meditations," I said. "There is more, if you will listen."

"I think I've heard enough," he said.

"My lord Brennus, we would hear the rest," Lorne said. "The druid may have information about how this disaster can be averted."

"I do," I said.

Brennus's face was conflicted, but at length he nodded.

"Very well," he said. "You may continue."

I bowed my thanks. "This vision I Saw was but one possible future. I Saw another future also. In this, our people were strong and healthy. The land was lush and well watered. Livestock grew fat and plentiful. The gods favoured us as they did many years ago. And our men were undefeated in battle."

The last was a gamble. Even if Brennus had no interest in what might befall his people, he would want his army to be victorious.

"And how do I make this second future come to pass?" Brennus asked.

My next words were intended for the advisors, not for Brennus, and I turned to face them.

"The difference is the king," I said. "In my first vision, Brennus holds the throne. He neglects the people and offends the gods and we all suffer the punishment intended for him. In my second vision, Girec is king. He is wise and patient and the land thrives under his guidance. He provides the gods with a sacrifice so great it ensures they look favourably on us for generations. It is in your hands to decide our future. We live or we die based on who you support as king."

"Blasphemy." Brennus stood and gestured towards his guards. "Guards, remove him from the room. Lock him in the cells. And don't let him speak to anyone."

They grabbed my arms and I offered no opposition. The advisors huddled together, whispering furiously. Brennus tried to get their attention, but his face turned red when they ignored him.

"Listen to me," Brennus roared. "The druid lies."

Lorne gave him a bow which was brief enough to be insulting.

"My lord, we have much to discuss," he said. "I beg our leave of you now."

"You will stay here," Brennus said. "All of you." He looked towards the guards. "Why are you still here? Take the druid away like I said."

As guards led me from the room, the four advisors left by another exit with Brennus screaming after them. They marched me along the hallways and down to the cells.

"One more for you," one said to the guard stationed at the door.

The guard gave me an inquiring look. It was Gwern, who had been on duty both times I came to visit Agata.

"So, druid, you've offended the kingling, have you?" he said, with something that might have been a grin. "Well, into the cells with you."

I answered his grin with one of my own and tried to look more confident than I felt. The advisors would be locked in private discussion until they decided how much weight to put on my "visions". If they decided to support Brennus, my execution was inevitable. But I had planted the seed of doubt and that was all I could do. The rest was up to them.

The other guards departed, leaving me alone with Gwern. I followed him to an empty cell, where he tossed me a blanket.

"Queen's order," he said. "Every prisoner receives a blanket now."

"Thank you," I said. "Would it be possible to send a message to the queen to tell her I am here?"

Gwern hesitated. "I could get into a lot of trouble for that."

"Don't worry about it then," I said. "I wouldn't want to cause trouble for you."

He considered me for another few moments, then nodded.

"If I have a chance to pass on your message quietly, I will," he said. "But I'm not promising anything. Brennus would have my head if he thought I was undermining him."

"Of course. I appreciate anything you can do."

Gwern closed the door and the bolt slid into place with a clunk. Only meagre lamplight made its way through the opening set high in the door, but I could smell well enough to know this wasn't one of the cells that were cleaned prior to the battle with Cullen. A mossy growth covered the floor and the air smelled of rot and mildew.

I wrapped the blanket around me and sat in the middle of the cell, where the stones seemed cleanest. The chill rose straight through the blanket. I pitied the prisoners who had been in here for days with no relief from the cold or the damp air. At least they had blankets now. I hoped Brennus's advisors would act quickly.

4 0

ARLEN

If Brennus was allowed to be king, he would undoubtedly have me executed. And he would claim Agata. I couldn't even imagine what he would do to her. Rape, certainly, but I was sure he would also have a special humiliation in mind. Something to punish me, even if I never knew about it. I would be dead by then and likely Derwa too.

All I could do was wait. I could do nothing else to influence the advisors. I focussed on my breath, on letting go of my thoughts, and sank into a meditative state. It allowed me to block out the cold and the damp and the occasional sobbing from other prisoners. Every now and then, the realisation that I would likely die within the next few hours sprang back up. I pushed the thought away and told myself I wasn't afraid.

Eventually the door to my cell opened. Lamplight blinded me and I could see only a dark shadow as I raised my arm to shield my eyes.

"I'm so sorry, Arlen," Derwa said. "I've only just been told you were here."

My feet tangled in the blanket in my haste to get up. I tried to bow, but my limbs were stiff and didn't seem to work properly. My heart pounded. Surely the advisors would not have allowed Derwa to fetch me if I was to be executed.

"Come," she said. "Your questions must wait until we can talk in private, though."

As I climbed the stairs, my legs wobbled but at least my eyes were adjusting to the light. Gwern was gone and another guard stood in his place. He nodded at Derwa as we passed. So, something had changed, for it seemed Derwa now had some authority within the keep.

Two guards waited at the top of the stairs. I recognised both their faces, but didn't know them by name. They fell in behind me as Derwa led us at a sedate pace to her sitting room. The guards took up positions in the hallway on either side of the door as she closed it behind us. Coals burned in the hearth sending off a wonderful wave of heat and I stood as close as I dared.

"Oh, Arlen," she said, looking me up and down. "I'm sorry."

"It was not as bad as it could have been." I finally noticed the blanket still wrapped around my shoulders and let it drop to the floor. "At least I had a blanket."

"I will be able to do more for the prisoners very soon." Derwa nodded to a table set with a platter of cold meat and cheese, a loaf of grainy bread, and a jug of ale. "Sit and eat. You've been down there for a day and a half as best I can tell. I'll tell you what has happened while you eat."

"Am I to be executed?"

She gave me a small smile. "No. Your plan, such as it was, seems to have worked."

The relief that rushed over me was immense and my hands shook as I reached for a plate. My mouth already watered at the aroma of roasted meat and fresh bread.

"Was no food offered to you in that time?" Derwa asked.

I shook my head, already filling my mouth with wild boar. It was succulent and juicy. I swallowed too big a mouthful and almost choked.

Derwa frowned. "I gave instructions for the prisoners to be fed twice a day."

I washed down the mouthful with ale and wiped my mouth, worried I had embarrassed myself in my haste.

"I apologise for my rudeness," I said. "I have become far too used to regular meals since I arrived here. It wasn't all that long ago that a day without food would have been a fast rather than torture."

"Eat," she said. "As soon as we are finished talking, I will ensure food is taken down to the cells. Much has happened since you went to the audience hall with your tale of two futures."

She gave me an appraising look, but if she doubted my visions, she didn't say it.

"The senior advisors spent a whole day in discussion before they came to me. I was distracted with Hearn's funeral and didn't note their absence. When they weren't present for his burning, I assumed it was their way of expressing disapproval of him."

I paused between mouthfuls. "Hearn has already been farewelled?"

"We burned him on a pyre and the remains were buried. I did wonder why you weren't there."

"I'm afraid I was otherwise engaged, my lady."

She didn't seem to find my comment amusing. I kept eating as she continued.

"I finally received a request from Lorne for an urgent audience. Truthfully, I nearly ignored his message. I assumed he wanted to discuss Brennus's coronation and I wanted no involvement. When I met with the advisors, they told me of your visions and that they were unsure whether they could support Brennus. They have taken to heart your words about Girec making a sacrifice. If Brennus doesn't become king, he will be the sacrifice. It has been many years since such a thing has been done here, but they consider this the strongest way to demonstrate their censure of Brennus."

I swallowed hard. I knew my plan would mean death for either Brennus or myself, but it was still difficult to hear.

"And Girec?" I asked.

"They are undecided. He is too young and has not been groomed for this as Brennus was. They may allow him to take the throne in a temporary capacity with myself as regent. An opportunity for him to learn and to show them he is suited to the role. If he has proven himself by the time he comes of age, they will support him."

"And if not?"

She shrugged. "He must succeed. There is no other option at the moment. If I had borne Hearn a child, the situation might be different."

"Does Brennus know?"

"He won't be told anything until they make a final decision. They want to speak with you again first. But there is another problem that needs to be dealt with before either boy can take the throne."

I waited. What had I missed?

"The woman who calls herself Ida."

For a moment, I had no idea who she meant, but then my mind cleared. Ida. I had forgotten again.

"I keep noticing her briefly, but then I forget," I confessed. "How is it that you remember her?"

"Everyone keeps forgetting her. I assume she has laid some sort of charm on the people here. As to why it doesn't affect me, I have no idea. Perhaps she didn't think me important enough to bother charming."

"You are the queen. She should have thought you important."

"You know how the people here view me."

"Perhaps that will be different now Hearn is dead. You said his advisors requested audience with you, that they want you as regent. That already indicates change."

"I hope it lasts. I don't know much about Girec as Hearn always kept both boys well away from me. But from what little I have observed, he is not like Brennus. I assume that is why your vision showed him to be the most suitable candidate."

The slight emphasis she placed on *vision* told me she believed I had fabricated it. Did the advisors suspect, too? I couldn't ask without admitting what I had done.

"So, we need to deal with Ida and I hoped you might be able to suggest how," she said. "Surely your training has given you some experience with creatures like her? Is she fey?"

I told her of Fiachra's letter explaining about Uncle Diarmuid's muse and how she escaped on his death.

"I don't know how to stop her," I said. "My uncles have already tried and failed. Uncle Fiachra has been a druid for some ninety summers as best I can figure. If he was not able to stop her, then I don't know what I can do."

"He must be very old."

"When I last saw him, he looked like a man in his sixties, but he must have been at least eighty summers even then."

"Would he come here, do you think? His advice and experience in this matter would be very valuable."

"I don't know where he is. He was leaving Silver Downs at the time of his letter. The message I left with you, would it have reached home by now?"

"I sent the messenger on horseback with instructions to deliver the message with all urgency. He was to change horses as often as needed."

"Maybe Uncle Fiachra is on his way here now."

"We can only hope he arrives in time to advise us. What do we do about Ida in the meantime? She will likely act against us when she finds out about your visions. You were fortunate she wasn't present when you went to see Brennus."

"He might have told her since then."

"He has been kept under guard in his bedchamber. For his own security, of course." Derwa stood and stretched. "I must go to the kitchens and arrange for food to be taken down to the cells. We can only wait, I suppose. Until the advisors make their decision, we can do nothing else."

As I left Derwa, I fixed the image of Ida firmly in my mind. I couldn't afford to forget her again. In my bedchamber, I looked longingly at my bed. I couldn't remember when I last slept. Two days? Three? It might be as long again before I could.

I sat on the floor and sought a meditative state, still clinging to the memory of Ida. It was harder than usual, perhaps because of my fatigue. But finally I reached the place where my mind could drift freely and I was no longer aware of the physical world. I held Ida's image in my mind and let my thoughts flow around her as if she was a rock in the middle of a stream.

I knew little of how she had been created, only that Uncle Diarmuid had somehow brought his tale to life. He had managed to confine her in his mind and keep her there for his last sixty summers. What could I do as a druid? Ida was a problem that needed a bard and a strong one at that.

I considered asking the Old Ones for help. I could go back to the fey realm and try to find the rock that called itself Orm or one of his fellows. But how would I recognise them when they looked so like their natural surroundings? And would they expect me to immediately help them take their land back from the fey? I still had no idea how, or when, I was supposed to do that and I couldn't afford to be delayed in the fey realm. There was also the risk that Titania would know I was there. But perhaps I could convince her to help me? Would she act if she thought Agata was in danger from Ida? But I couldn't be sure Titania cared anything for Agata, and it might do nothing other than bring me to her attention.

Could the elementals help? Fire or Earth or Water might restrain a living being. Air could transport one. But I didn't know how strong Ida was or how long I could persuade the elements to hold her.

When I opened my eyes, the room was dark. I hadn't found any feasible solutions and I was so tired I could barely think anymore. I eased open the shutters to steal a glance at the sky. Dawn was only a couple of hours away. There was nothing else I could do tonight. I crawled into bed and fell asleep.

41

ARLEN

When I woke, the sunlight shining through the gaps around the window shutters was pale, so I knew the morning was still young. I kept hold of the memory of Ida while I slept, but I still had no plan other than to hope Fiachra's reply to my letter arrived today.

It was only as I sat up that I noticed the figure sitting in the corner. Despite his age, his back was straight. Although his hair was now mostly grey, he still wore it in the many braids I remembered from my youth. His face might have held a few more wrinkles, but he didn't look anything near the hundred-odd summers I calculated he must be.

"Uncle Fiachra."

I straightened my tunic, wishing I had thought to change into clean clothes before falling into bed. He rose a little stiffly and I suppressed the urge to help him. Something told me he would not appreciate being treated like an old man.

"We came as soon as your letter arrived." His voice was deep and melodious. "How fare things here?"

I told him about Brennus and Ida claiming the throne. My "visions" that would mean death for either myself or Brennus, and how I had been locked away while the advisors debated. About Agata's situation and Brennus's interest in her. I kept my summary as brief and emotionless as if I reported to Oistin. Fiachra's face was thoughtful and he stopped me only twice to ask questions. When I finished, he nodded.

"I have Seen some of this. Frustratingly brief glimpses. I have always believed that the only one who can destroy Ida is a bard of Silver Downs. One who is the seventh son of a seventh son. But I begin to doubt myself."

"You mentioned an apprentice bard in your letter. Is that who you mean?"

"There is one who is a seventh son of a seventh son. Only one. His name is Tristan, and he is in the kitchen. He was hungry after our journey and I wanted a chance to speak with you privately."

"About what?"

"When I received your letter, I went straight to Silver Downs to get Tristan because I thought he would be the one who must stand against Ida. He believes it still, because I haven't told him what I Saw last night."

A growing feeling of unease squeezed my stomach.

"It's you, Arlen," he said. "You and Agata. You are the ones who must face Ida."

"I'm not a bard," I stammered. "Nor the seventh son of a seventh son."

"The two of you have both the blood of Silver Downs and also that of the fey running through your veins. We know nothing of the power such a combination might create."

"I have no power. I'm barely even a competent druid. My visions are few and brief, and I can't communicate with the air elementals."

Fiachra raised his eyebrows. "Interesting. Your mother has such a strong affinity with Air that I assumed you would too. But no matter. Those things are irrelevant. You must have some other ability you haven't realised yet. Something unique to you and Agata. Unlock that and I suspect the rest will come."

"Agata," I said. "What have you Seen about her?"

"Little more than that this requires the two of you. I assume you have reasons for not sending word to your mother about finding your sister."

Although his tone was mild, I heard the rebuke in his words.

"Agata found me," I said. "I didn't send a message because she wants nothing to do with the mortal world. She has been raised to believe she's fey and the daughter of Titania. I couldn't tell Eithne I had found Agata, but that she didn't want to know her family."

"And she is still in the cells?"

"The guards won't release her without authorisation from the king."

He shook his head and his tiny braids swung from side to side.

"We will go now and release her. I can compel the guards. But before we do, there's one more thing you need to know. You will need my strength to deal with Ida. She very nearly defeated Diarmuid all those years ago, and he was strong in his ability. Once we have Agata, I will explain more. I will give you everything I have in order to defeat her."

"Do you mean…"

His gaze was steady.

"I will die. I intended to give my strength to Tristan, although he doesn't know. He wouldn't take from me as much as he needed if he did. Ida will be far more powerful this time, but three is an auspicious number. With you, Agata and myself, I believe we have a chance of defeating her."

No words came to my tongue. I wanted to argue with him, to tell him Eithne would never forgive me if I let him do this, but he was calm and steadfast. This was a carefully considered decision and he had already made his choice.

"I'd like my body returned to Silver Downs," he said. "You remember the ancient oak just to the south of the lodge? My parents are buried there and I would like to be returned to the earth in the same place. Don't let them burn me."

How does one respond to a request like that? My throat closed and I could only nod.

"Is she here because of me?" I asked when I thought I could speak again. "You said she might be attracted to a son of Silver Downs."

"She has probably followed you here. But if not you, she would have found another of our blood."

"Are you sure about this? There might be another way."

"I'm the last of my brothers left living," he said. "I thought she might escape when Diarmuid died. I prepared him as best I could, but I always knew I would be part of her end, even if I don't have the ability to stop her myself. I regret we didn't try harder to prepare Diarmuid as a child. We wanted so badly to believe the curse had passed over him that we didn't see the warning signs. I share the blame for her creation and I'll share the burden of destroying her."

"Why didn't Diarmuid destroy her instead of returning her to his head?"

He sighed heavily. "He couldn't. She was as much a part of him as he was of her. It would have killed him, too. So instead he took her back into himself. He paid many times over for what he did in creating her. And now it's my turn. I don't regret this, Arlen. It is necessary. I only regret that I didn't act when I could have, before he ever created her."

"Is there anything you want to do first?"

"I've said my goodbyes. I'm ready. Let's retrieve Tristan from the kitchen and then we'll release Agata."

As I followed him along the hallways, Fiachra walked with his back straight and his head held high. His braids swung slightly, and to look at him, one would not think he was a man about to face his own death.

The kitchen smelled of hot porridge and fresh bread, and my stomach growled in response. A boy of about fourteen or fifteen summers sat on a bench. Like all of our family, he was dark-haired and dark-eyed. With his broad shoulders and strong arms, he looked more farmer than bard. But he nodded gravely at me and I could see he knew the importance of what we were about to do. His eyes were shadowed. Perhaps he suspected that the impact of this event would be greater than he understood. He swallowed the last of his bread and stood.

"You found him," he said.

"This is Arlen." Fiachra nodded in my direction. "Your cousin. There is another cousin we must find now, before we pursue our task."

The boy was clearly bursting to ask questions, but he was wise enough to restrain himself in front of the kitchen staff and the two guards who sat in the corner finishing their meals. I led the way down to the cells. The rank odour was familiar now, although no less unpleasant. We paused at the guard's station and I was a little regretful it was Gwern on duty today. I hoped he wouldn't be punished for Agata's disappearance.

"We have come to retrieve Agata," Fiachra said.

Gwern looked puzzled for a moment, but he nodded.

"Of course." He took the lamp off its hook and led us to Agata's cell. "Hey, fey princess. Come on, you're going out."

"Where to?" Agata's voice was sulky as she emerged into the lamp light. When she saw me, she glowered. "So you came back."

"We have to go," I said, praying she wouldn't argue for once. I didn't know how long Fiachra's compulsion would last.

"Am I being released? Can I go home now?" She moved too slowly.

I grabbed her by the arm and pulled her out through the cell door.

"Just walk," I hissed in her ear.

She finally stopped talking and walked a little faster. Fiachra passed me a cloak which I was sure he hadn't been carrying earlier. I draped it over her shoulders and pulled up the hood to cover her hair. We hurried out of the cells, leaving behind Gwern and his lamp.

"Will he realise what happened?" I asked quietly as we walked swiftly through the keep.

"He shouldn't," Fiachra said. "He'll remember that someone came to take her away and that they had the proper authorisation, but he won't remember who."

I led them out of the keep and across the courtyard. Fiachra was barefooted, despite the midwinter cold, and he walked gently, as if savouring the earth beneath him. The air was crisp and clean, and the sky was a brilliant blue with just a few scattered clouds. A raven cawed nearby. I wondered whether it was the one I encountered while seeking signs for Hearn's battle with Fingen. There would be significance in that.

We didn't stop until we were hidden behind the stunted birches. Agata threw off the hood, although she left the cloak around her shoulders.

"Is somebody going to tell me what's happening?" she demanded.

"This is our uncle, Fiachra," I said. "And our cousin, Tristan."

She dismissed Tristan immediately, but her gaze lingered a little longer on Fiachra.

"Thank you," she said, and her mouth twisted as if they were words she didn't like to say.

"We need your aid," he said.

"I need to go home," she replied.

"Help us and I'll ensure you get home safely."

Her gaze turned scornful. "I don't need help from a mortal."

"Agata, please," I said. "Will you just listen to Uncle Fiachra?"

She gave me a long look, but eventually sniffed and looked away. "Fine. I'll listen."

44 2

ARLEN

iachra explained to Agata about Uncle Diarmuid's death, Ida's escape and his plan to destroy her. As he spoke of his vision and his decision that Tristan would not be involved, the boy clenched his fists although he waited until Fiachra finished before he spoke.

"Uncle, this is not what we agreed."

"It is as it must be," Fiachra said.

"No, it should be me," Tristan said. "You said it yourself. It will take a bard who is a seventh son of a seventh son to do this."

"I don't understand it myself," Fiachra said. "But I Saw Arlen and Agata facing Ida. I fear..." His voice trailed away.

"You fear what?" Tristan asked. "I am strong enough. You know I am."

"Perhaps I didn't See you because you had already died trying to stop her."

"If it takes my death to stop her, it will be worth it," Tristan said.

"Eithne won't agree with that," Fiachra said. He shot me a glance I couldn't read. "You are like a son to her and I will not act against the vision. You will not be involved in this."

"The Sight can show possible futures," Tristan countered. "You've told me that yourself. How do you know this isn't just one possibility?"

"I have never been more certain of anything in my life," Fiachra said. "Trust me, Tristan. I know you came here expecting to do this yourself and I don't take this decision lightly. Now, I assume you have a tale prepared?"

Tristan nodded.

"Can you tell it to your cousins? Carefully. Don't draw on your ability and don't say her name. We don't want to attract her before we are ready. Arlen. Agata. You will tell the tale, so listen carefully to Tristan."

"And how do we access the bard magic?" Agata asked. For once her tone was interested rather than sulky.

"You won't," Fiachra said. "Or at least I don't think so. My guess is that your power is something to do with the two of you being together. Twin souls, or one soul divided between two bodies, depending on what you believe. There's something special about that. Something magic. It's different to the ability our bards have, but I think this duality of the Seen and the unSeen ones is what we need."

When I ventured into the fey realm to find Agata, something led me straight to her. Had she felt me, too, as I drew closer?

"Where should we do this?" I asked.

"Here will be suitable," Fiachra said. "My strength is greatest when I am connected with the natural world."

"Sadly there's little out here to connect to. As you can see, the trees are dying and everything else is already dead."

"It will be enough. I need only to have my feet in the earth and I can find the connections from there. Tristan, tell your cousins the tale while I prepare myself."

Fiachra took a stick from the ground and dug into the compacted earth, loosing it so he could dig in his toes. He placed his palms against a tree, seeking as I had to find the life within. There was much I could learn from my druid uncle and it would never happen now. My heart was heavy with regret for the knowledge that would be lost with his death. I listened carefully as Tristan told us his tale.

"Can you remember all of that?" Tristan asked when he finished. "The wording of the ending is particularly important."

I was well accustomed to memorising long passages, but Agata was flushed and looked unnerved.

"Can you say the last part again?" she asked.

What education had she received? I was taught lore and old tales and other arcane wisdoms. Oistin regularly tested our memory of such things. Agata had likely experienced none of that. While Tristan recited the end of his tale again, I went to stand next to Fiachra.

"What will happen if this works?" I asked.

"It should occur exactly as Tristan's tale says."

"And if it doesn't?"

He looked at me steadily. "She will be angry, we can be sure of that. She is strong. Probably far stronger than last time she was free. If we fail, she will likely kill us. From what you have said, she has already enticed Hearn into war twice over. Now that she has claimed the throne, who will she take her army against next?

"We thought the biggest danger to this country was at the battle front, where the southern armies still engage our forces. If they defeat us and sweep across the country, our whole world will change. They will force us to adopt their customs, their gods. Everything about our way of life will change.

"But I believe Diarmuid's muse is a bigger threat than the foreign armies. She sows discontent amongst folk in their own homes. For most folk the war against the invaders is happening a long way away. It has little effect on their lives except for the soldier sons who die in battle. But the muse sets neighbour against neighbour, brother against brother. The invaders might yet come and force us into submission. They want to rule us, but she would have us tear ourselves apart. There would be nothing left for anyone to rule over."

"That's why you are willing to die for this," I said.

His mouth twisted into a sad smile. "I've had a long life, Arlen. I'm the last of my brothers. My time is coming soon regardless of what happens today. If it takes my life to stop her, I'll be well satisfied with my choice."

Tristan and Agata were finally finished and came over to us. Fiachra pointed to a spot some distance away.

"Tristan, wait over there and don't do anything to draw her attention," he said.

"I can help," Tristan said.

Fiachra shook his head. "Stand back. I want to be sure you are returned safely home when this is over."

Tristan obeyed without further comment.

"Arlen. Agata," Fiachra said. "Come stand just in front of me."

We moved into position and he placed one hand on my shoulder and the other on Agata's.

"I'll send my strength into you as you tell your tale," he said. "You may or may not feel it, but trust it will be there. You must put everything you have into this tale. This is our one chance. She will take this as an attack and if we don't succeed, she will destroy us. With her on the throne, the entire country is in danger."

"Should we start now?" I asked.

He squeezed my shoulder gently.

"When you're ready, boy. When you're ready."

"There was once a bard," I said.

My voice didn't come out quite as strongly as I hoped and I wished I could start over. But Agata took my hand and the moment she touched me, I felt the connection between us renewed. Fiachra was right. There was power in the two of us being together. Strong power.

"He was not a very famous bard, nor a very good one," I continued. "But he was well loved by his family despite his flaws. In the pride of his youth he created a creature from nothing more than his words and the images in his mind. The creature came to life and when she left his mind, she committed terrible deeds. Eventually, and at great cost to himself, the bard secured her inside his mind again."

A tremble passed through the air. It was gone so fast I wasn't sure whether I imagined it. I hesitated and Agata took up the tale.

"Years passed and the bard kept the creature contained within his mind, right up to the moment he died." Her voice was clear and stronger than mine. "Then the creature broke free and emerged into the world again. Her name was Ida."

As if she had summoned the muse by speaking her name, Ida appeared in front of us. Her white dress whipped around her legs, although I myself felt no breeze.

"You fancy yourself as bards, do you, children?" she snarled.

I averted my gaze. Perhaps looking into her eyes would not affect me, but I wouldn't risk it.

"This time Ida was weaker than before, although she didn't know it at first," I said. "After the king to whom she had allied herself died, her power waned, for it was from him that she had drawn her strength."

"What is this?" Ida asked. "What are you doing?"

"Then came the arrival of a young man and woman," I said.

Tristan had obviously improvised here, changing the tale from what he had intended. Likely this section was originally about himself as a bard and the seventh son of a seventh son.

"Born of the same womb and in the same hour, they possessed but one soul between them," I continued. "And when the two halves of their soul were reunited, a mighty power was created. As they told the tale that would destroy Ida once and for all, they drew on the strength of a powerful druid, thus magnifying their ability many times over."

"Stop this at once," Ida shrieked.

She held out her hands towards us and I staggered as an invisible force hit me. It was only Fiachra's firm grip on my shoulder that kept me on my feet. Agata tightened her grasp of my hand as she took up the tale.

"Their words wrapped around Ida like chains." Her voice was still steady, although the hand that clutched mine trembled. "They contained her and confined her, and then they drained her power away, letting it siphon off into the earth, where it couldn't harm anyone."

Ida wailed, staring down at her own hands as if she had never seen them before.

"As her power drained, so too did her life force," I said. "Like her power, it drained into the earth, seeping slowly down into the dirt where it could never again come together to form a living creature."

As I finished, Ida's shape shifted. The edges of her form became undefined and instead of a woman, she was now a shining silvery blur. She sank down into the ground, screaming as the earth drank her up like a mug of spilled ale. In moments, she was gone. The three of us stood in silence.

"Is that it?" My voice was unsteady. "Is she gone?"

Fiachra swayed and collapsed. I wasn't fast enough to catch him. Tristan rushed over and stared down at him in horror.

"He knew this would happen," I said. "It was the price he was willing to pay for not preventing her creation."

"You took too much of his strength," Tristan said. Tears tracked down his cheeks. "He didn't tell me this might kill him."

"He did what he had to," I said and my voice was perhaps a little curter than he deserved. "And we should be grateful he was willing."

43

AGATA

My legs trembled as I stared down at the uncle I had never known. He lay with his limbs sprawled, his eyes unseeing. I had never seen death before. Was this how it would come for me, too, if I stayed in the mortal realm? Would I be alive one moment and fall down dead the next? My leg suddenly cramped and I fell. Arlen caught me before I could land on my dead uncle.

"You need a healer," he said.

"I'm just stiff from sitting in the cold for days on end," I said. "How long was I down there? Eight days? Nine?"

Arlen shook his head and didn't answer.

"Do you even know?" I asked. "I couldn't count the days in the dark, but you've been up here, free to come and go. Free to eat whenever you want and to bathe and to sleep in a bed. I'm sure you've been very busy while I was down there in the dark and cold, wondering if I would ever see the sun again."

"You have no idea what has been happening," Arlen said. "With the king dead and the succession in doubt, there were bigger issues that needed to be resolved."

I couldn't be bothered arguing with him any longer.

"Now that we've dealt with that creature, I'll be on my way," I said.

"You need a healer first and some decent food. You can sleep in my bedchamber tonight."

"I'd rather sleep in my own bed. I need nothing from you. I want to go home."

"I'm leaving for Silver Downs shortly. You could come with me. Meet our mother."

"No, thank you. I have no interest in meeting any other mortal relatives."

He gave me a dark look, then pointed.

"That path will lead you to the keep's gates," he said. "Keep following it to the town wall. I assume you know how to get back to the fey realm from there."

"I do."

"Agata, please, won't you at least stay long enough to eat?"

He gave me a look I couldn't interpret. It might have been sadness or maybe just weariness. I finally noticed the paleness of his face and the shadows under his eyes, and almost wanted to change my mind. This was my brother, after all. But he had left me in the dark for days.

"Farewell," I said. "Don't come looking for me again. I want nothing to do with the mortal realm. If our mother asks, I'm glad Titania took me."

The gate was open and nobody tried to stop me. Snow covered the road and masked the decrepit lodges as I ran through the town. Those folk who were out and about were bundled up in scarves and hats and patched cloaks. The breeze sent brisk fingers creeping in under my borrowed cloak.

My breath steamed in the cold air and as my muscles warmed, they loosened. Soon I ran smoothly. I didn't stop until I was back in the fey realm. I was badly winded, far more than I should have been. Perhaps the days spent in the damp cell damaged my lungs. Being back in the fey realm would cure that soon enough. I hoped it would also cure the horrible heavy feeling in my chest.

4 4

ARLEN

I left Tristan standing guard over Fiachra's body while I looked for Derwa. I found her in her sitting room, hunched over a table as she wrote on a piece of parchment. The room was warm and scented with a herbal concoction. Derwa was finally making this room her own.

I told her what happened and Derwa sent a pair of guards to retrieve Fiachra's body until we could take him home. They would look after Tristan also. I wanted him well away from me in case the next phase of my plan failed. Derwa promised to make sure he got home if I wasn't able to take him myself.

"Are you certain Ida won't return?" Derwa asked.

"Fiachra was confident she couldn't. We have killed her, in as much as a creature such as her can be."

"I'm sorry about your uncle. He sounds like a brave man."

"I doubt he would agree," I said. "But thank you."

A panting servant boy interrupted our conversation with a knock on the door. He sketched a quick bow to Derwa.

"My lady, the chief advisors request the druid attend them," he said, between puffs.

"Of course." Derwa stood and straightened her skirt. She looked unworried, although I knew her well enough to see through her facade. "Are they in the audience hall?"

The servant boy nodded and darted away.

"Are you ready, Arlen?" she asked.

I inhaled shakily. "I have to be."

She smiled and grasped my hand for just a moment.

"Good luck," she said.

My skin tingled where she touched me. When we reached the audience hall, the doors were already open, although guards stood on either side as usual. A brief *my lady* passed from the lips of one as we entered. Things were changing around Braen Keep.

I followed Derwa into the hall, walking a couple of steps behind her as was proper. Right now she was my queen, not my friend. And certainly not anything more. Brennus sat on his new throne. Beside him, Hearn's was empty. Was this where he expected Ida to sit?

Derwa stopped in front of the dais and looked coldly up at Brennus, then turned to the chief advisors, who were grouped to one side: Lorne, Cahan, Egan and Teris, along with Iver, who was absent the last time I spoke with them.

"Gentlemen." Derwa's voice was calm. "You wished to speak with the druid."

Her presence discomfited the advisors who shuffled a little closer together and hesitated before first one, then the others, bowed to her.

"My lady, we need to interrogate him about his visions," Lorne said.

"False visions," Brennus interrupted. His voice was overly loud and it echoed through the room.

"You will be silent," Lorne said to him. "If you wish to be present for this discussion."

"You can't talk to me like that," Brennus said. "I'm your king-in-waiting."

"That is yet to be confirmed," Lorne replied.

"Should this discussion not be held without Brennus?" Derwa asked.

"We have decided it would be appropriate for him to hear what the druid has to say," Iver said. "It is his future we discuss."

Derwa nodded and if she disagreed she held her tongue. I spotted Girec huddled against the wall behind the advisors looking as if he wanted to be anywhere but here. It was his future, too, being decided.

"Druid," Lorne said.

"My name is Arlen." I kept my voice pleasant. "And I much prefer to be addressed by name."

Lorne flushed faintly. "Well, then, Arlen, tell us again of your visions of the two futures."

I repeated what I told them previously, being careful not to embellish any details. I kept my words factual and unemotional so as not to seem as if I steered them in either direction.

"How certain is the future in which our country is laid to waste?" Iver asked.

"At this stage, I believe both futures are possible," I said. "We don't seem to have reached the incident that will force one or the other, although I feel we are close."

The men withdrew a little distance to talk amongst themselves. There seemed to be some disagreement amongst them, with the other four trying to persuade Egan. Heart pounding, I watched and tried not to look as if I strained to hear them. Girec was close enough to hear, but if anything they said gave him hope, he didn't show it.

Brennus sighed loudly and shifted on the throne.

"Will this take much longer?" he asked.

His voice held an unpleasant whine, and I stifled the urge to shake him by the shoulders. Maybe if that had happened to him from time to time, he wouldn't be quite as obnoxious. When the men ignored him, he repeated his question louder.

"Hush," Derwa said. "You are fortunate to be present, so try to act like a man instead of a boy."

Brennus glared at her.

"When I am king—" he started.

"Shut your mouth." Derwa held herself tall and glared back. "Right now you are a boy, and an insolent one at that. It is time I took some responsibility for your behaviour. Even *if*—" she put heavy emphasis on the word, "if you become king, there will be rules for you to obey and you will be required to respect your elders. Hearn allowed you to be ignorant, slovenly and rude, and that will change starting today."

Brennus opened and closed his mouth, but said nothing further. He continued to glower at her as the chief advisors finished their private discussion. Although I felt like cheering as she put Brennus in his place, now I wished she hadn't said anything. If he hadn't already been inclined to seek revenge on her, he certainly was now.

"Druid," Lorne said, then quickly corrected himself. "Arlen. Can you estimate how likely each of the two futures are?"

"They are equally likely," I said. "We are approaching the inciting incident from which the two futures will diverge."

"And do you know what that incident is?" he asked.

I hesitated as if choosing my words with caution, although this too was planned.

"It seems to me that the decision the chief advisors make regarding which boy will be king will determine all our futures."

"It's as simple as that?" Egan asked. His face was distinctly unhappy. It seemed he still disagreed with whatever decision the other four leaned towards.

I nodded. I was tempted to add more, but restrained myself. Too much now might push them in the wrong direction. The men retreated to speak quietly amongst themselves again. Brennus sighed, but wisely kept his mouth shut after Derwa fixed him with a glare. Eventually the advisors turned back to us.

"We will make our decision in the morning," Lorne said. "Both boys will be escorted to their bedchambers and kept under guard for their safety."

Brennus sat up straighter and opened his mouth to protest. At another look from Derwa, he changed his mind. Lorne nodded at me and I took that as my cue to leave.

I found Tristan in my bedchamber and a guard standing at the door. The boy lay on my bed and looked as if he had cried himself to sleep. I draped a blanket over him, then decided I should rest while I could. I lay on the floor and fell asleep almost instantly.

I woke to a soft knock on the door. My legs didn't seem to work properly as I stumbled the couple of steps to the door. I leaned against it to force it open and found Lorne waiting. The guard had retreated a few steps down the hallway to give us some privacy. Tristan was still sound asleep, so I stepped out into the hallway and eased the door shut.

"Have you made a decision?" I asked.

Lorne's face was grave.

"Girec will be king," he said.

My breath caught in my throat.

"And Brennus?" I asked.

"He is to be sacrificed. If your vision is true, then there is no other path open to us lest we destroy the country. We seek your guidance as to the most suitable method."

I swallowed hard. I was safe. So was Agata, and Derwa. And Girec.

"He should be drowned," I said. "Preferably in a body of water that is sacred to the gods."

"There is a pond a couple of hours' walk from here. Would that be suitable? Unfortunately there are no sacred sites in Braen Town. There were two some years ago, but Hearn had them destroyed."

"If there is nothing closer, that will have to do. Brennus should be given time to fast and meditate. Dawn is an auspicious time for a sacrifice. The chief advisors should come, and also Girec and the queen."

Lorne blanched.

"Is it really necessary for Girec to witness this?" he asked. "He is little more than a boy."

"And he's about to become your king. Let him see what his king-ship is forged from."

He nodded. "As you say."

I left Tristan sleeping with the guard at my door, and followed Lorne to the audience hall. Both boys stood in front of the dais. A distance of several paces between them indicated they had no desire to stand next to each other. They were both pale with dark circles under their eyes. Derwa stood a little way from them, her face composed, although she clasped her hands tightly. I suspected she already knew.

"We have made our decision," Lorne announced without preamble. "Girec will be king."

Girec seemed to grow even paler. He nodded and continued to look straight at Lorne. Beside him, Brennus started and clenched his fists.

"This is ridiculous," he said, loudly. "Hearn named me as his heir. You should obey his wishes. He was your king."

"And now he is dead," Lorne said. "The king may select an heir, but if the heir is underage his choice must be confirmed by the chief advisors. Surely you learned this in your lessons?"

"So what is to become of me?" Brennus's tone became belligerent. "Am I supposed to watch Girec stumble his way through a role he has not been prepared for? We will be a laughing stock. Is that what you want?"

"You will not need to watch," Lorne said gently. "To ensure the future we are trying to avert never comes to pass, it has been determined that you will be sacrificed to appease the gods."

"The gods don't care who is king," Brennus said, but his voice trembled a little. "Hearn never paid any respects to them and we have done fine."

Derwa interjected softly.

"Hearn was responsible for much damage and grief, Brennus, as I am sure you are well aware. Braen Town was respectful of the gods many years ago. We can be again, but we feel it necessary to propitiate them. I'm sorry, but the decision has been made."

"You will be permitted to fast and meditate for the rest of the day," Lorne said. "Arlen can assist if you need guidance."

Brennus shot me a venomous look and spat on the floor.

"Hearn thought you a fool and a spy," he said. "I wish he could have seen that you are also a traitor to the crown."

I didn't respond.

"We leave tonight at midnight," Lorne said. He turned to the guards. "Take Brennus to his room. Keep him in sight at all times."

To Brennus he said, "From your response I assume you don't want Arlen to accompany you. If you change your mind, you need only ask the guards to send for him."

Brennus's response was to spit on the floor again. Lorne nodded to the guards and four stepped forward. One took Brennus by the arm, but the boy shook him off.

"Don't touch me," he snarled.

"Let him walk if he will do so willingly," Lorne said. "If he won't, carry him."

Brennus glared, but didn't respond. He walked to the door with his head held high, surrounded by guards. The audience hall was silent for a few moments until Girec spoke.

"Is it really necessary to kill him?" he asked in a very small voice.

The chief advisors glanced at each other as if deciding who would respond.

"He will forever be a threat to your kingship if he is not dealt with now," I said. "This disappointment is not something he will ever forget. One day, you will turn around and discover he has led an uprising to take the throne from you. Or you will find yourself poisoned in your own dining hall or your throat cut as you sleep in your bed. The people are uneasy because of Hearn's lack of respect for the gods. They need to know we have done what we can to appease them."

"Will it work?" he asked. "Will the gods favour us if you kill Brennus?"

"I See possibilities, not certainties. I only know we can't afford to let him live."

Girec inhaled shakily and nodded.

"I would have you stay in my court if you would, Arlen." His voice was stronger now. "I know Hearn had little respect for druids, but I would like to have you at my side."

I bowed, oddly touched.

"Thank you, my lord but I am not suited to be a king's advisor," I said. "I believe my master sent me here for his own benefit, not for Hearn's. I beg your leave to depart as soon as possible. My uncle came yesterday to visit me and died. I need to take his body home."

One day, perhaps, I would tell him why Fiachra was here. But not today.

"You may leave if you want," Girec said. "But I'd rather you stayed."

A guard entered and spoke quietly to Lorne.

"The druid master has arrived," Lorne said.

45

ARLEN

"Oistin is here?" My heart lightened. He must have Seen what had happened. I didn't dare hope he would carry out Brennus's sacrifice himself, but I would value his advice. I badly needed to speak with someone who understood my terror at what I must do tonight.

"Arlen, you stand over there." Lorne pointed to a spot beside the dais, then turned to Girec. "My lord, you should sit on the throne. Hearn's throne, not the new one. My lady, would you stand over there beside Arlen? The chief advisors will stand in front of the dais."

"Is something wrong?" I was confused about why Lorne set such a careful tableau for Oistin's arrival. "He has surely come to advise me."

"I am not so certain of that," Lorne said. "I knew Oistin as a boy. He was ambitious and ruthless. It was many years ago now, but there are those of us who have not forgotten."

"You must be confusing him with someone else," I said. "Oistin would have begun his training in his tenth year. A boy of that age can't display much ambition."

"He went to the druids late," Teris said, surprising me as he had never spoken directly to me before. "I too remember. I was about fifteen or sixteen summers at the time and he was two summers older.

His father was involved in a plot to overthrow Hearn's father, Braen, and take the throne. Hearn happened to overhear a suspicious comment, relayed it to his father, and the plot was uncovered."

"Was there any evidence of Oistin's involvement?" I couldn't reconcile the druid master I knew with the ambitious boy they remembered.

"No evidence that he was, but also no evidence he wasn't," Lorne answered. "He left to train as a druid shortly after. I remember being surprised, for he had always been touted as his father's heir. If their plan had been successful, he would have been king after his father's death."

"We are not making any accusation against him," Teris said. "But the circumstances were strange and it is odd that he would come here now. As far as I know, he has never returned since he left to study with the druids."

A guard announced Oistin's arrival and we moved into our assigned positions. Oistin strolled in, taking in his surroundings as he did. He must have noted my presence, but gave no indication he saw me. He paused a few paces from the chief advisors, who were arrayed in front of the dais as planned. Oistin bowed and looked up to Girec on the throne.

"My lord Brennus," he began.

Girec looked down at him, but said nothing. Lorne stepped forward.

"Greetings, Oistin, it has been many years since we last met." His voice was courteous.

Oistin barely glanced at him, but continued to direct his words to Girec.

"My lord, I have Seen what has been occurring here and it is clear to me you need a more senior advisor than the one I sent previously," he said. "I have come to offer my own services to you."

Girec held his head high and looked to Lorne for a response. He managed to convey an impression of not deigning to speak to Oistin himself, rather than not knowing what to say.

"Perhaps you have not Seen as much as you think," Lorne said.

Oistin finally looked directly at him.

"You dare question my ability?" he asked with a sneer.

Never had I heard the druid master speak so coldly and arrogantly. I hardly believed Lorne and Teris's words, but it was clear there was a side of Oistin I never suspected.

"My lord Girec is the king-in-waiting," Lorne said.

"It hardly matters which boy it is," Oistin said, hurriedly. "The point is that we have a child about to take the throne and he needs a senior advisor."

"He already has senior advisors," Lorne said. "People who know him and know the court here. People who are accustomed to advising the king."

"He needs a druid, not mere men."

"He has a druid. You sent him yourself."

Oistin's gaze flicked up to meet mine briefly.

"He is little more than a boy himself, with no experience of the world outside the community," he said.

"It seems to me that you are the one with little experience of the outside world," Lorne said. "Arlen has been here for some weeks now and has proven himself a valuable ally. The king-in-waiting desires that he stay. You have no qualifications that would recommend you to such a post compared to the one who already holds this position."

"Arlen will be recalled to the community," Oistin said. "He is clearly unsuitable for the role here."

"As I said, the king-in-waiting has asked him to stay."

"Arlen belongs to the community. He returns if I recall him."

"I don't believe that was negotiated when you sent him here, which was, as you know, in direct defiance of Hearn's wishes. Nevertheless, you surely cannot think the druid master outranks the king. Do you?"

Oistin's face turned a deep red.

"Of course not," he spluttered. "But I am the more experienced druid and it should be me here, not him."

"The king-in-waiting has made his choice."

"The king-in-waiting was supposed to be Brennus," Oistin countered.

"It seems that what you have Seen may not be accurate," Lorne said.

Oistin started to reply, but Girec cut him off.

"Druid master, thank you for offering your services. However, I intend to keep the druid you already sent. With his agreement, of course."

"And who will be your regent?" Oistin asked, with a hastily added *my lord*. "You need a senior advisor who can fully assist you in such a capacity."

I suddenly understood Oistin's aim. He wanted to be regent. Was this his plan all along? Had he Seen Hearn's death and the succession of a boy king? If he became regent, would Girec soon have an unfortunate accident? Did he choose me for this role because he thought I would be easy to remove when the time came? It wasn't my place to ask questions, but I would dearly like to know.

"Queen Derwa will be my regent," Girec said, with a nod towards her. Derwa stood to the side of the dais, her hands folded in front of her. She looked serene as she returned his nod. "This has already been determined in consultation with the queen and my chief advisors."

"She is unsuitable," Oistin began.

"Do you think to criticise me in my own keep?" Girec voice turned cold. "You may leave, druid master."

I noted the subtle gesture from Lorne to the guards, who promptly stepped forward, making it seem as if they acted on Girec's words.

"But—" Oistin got no further before Lorne cut him off.

"The guards will escort you out," he said. "I regret that we are unable to offer you a bedchamber for the night, but the guards will take you to the kitchen so you can eat before you leave."

Oistin drew himself up tall and bowed to Girec.

"That won't be necessary," he snapped at Lorne before he turned on his heel and strode out. The guards followed behind him.

The door closed and we stared at each other.

"That was unpleasant," Lorne said.

"I have never seen him act like that," I said. Any respect I still had for Oistin was shattered.

"He is little changed from the boy I remember." Lorne's voice was sad. "I hoped I was wrong about him, but I fear I wasn't. He thought to take the throne for himself."

46

ARLEN

I sent Tristan to the kitchen, telling him to amuse himself for the rest of the day and to take my bed tonight. I would see both him and Fiachra home within the next couple of days.

Home. It had been so long since I had been to Silver Downs. Would Eithne even recognise me? A fierce homesickness swept through me as I remembered wide pastures and singing streams. A big flat rock near a stand of beech trees. Another rock beside a river where one could lie and listen to the water flowing over pebbles. The woods, which I had been forbidden to enter as a child. The big lodge filled with children, some cousins and others the sons and daughters of those who worked on the estate. The workers' children had never been treated any differently to the children of Silver Downs. We played together and were schooled together. I barely remembered any of them now. Did they remember the son who went off to be a druid?

I pushed away the memories to focus on what I must do tonight. A boy would die. Mine would be the hands that held him under the water until he stopped breathing. I pictured the scene, walked myself through every detail. Sacrifices who were willing were usually not restrained, but Brennus would likely fight his fate. So his hands would need to be bound. He would struggle. I might need help to hold him under the water. It was not ideal, but I would work with what I had.

Brennus had to die, I firmly believed that. Sacrificing him to the gods would be seen by the people as a sign that change was coming to Braen Town. That a new king would mean a return to the old ways. A renewed devotion to the gods. People feared what they had heard about the invaders from the south and their new religion which forsook the old gods in preference for one new god. A sacrifice would show them Braen Town had not forgotten its past. I spent the day in silent meditation and made my peace with what I must do tonight.

Girec and Derwa already waited in the audience hall when I arrived. Girec was pale and looked unsteady on his feet. He and Brennus were never friends, but they had grown up together.

"My lord, are you well?" I asked.

He nodded in my direction but didn't speak. I looked to Derwa and she came close to whisper into my ear.

"He is distraught. He understands this is necessary but wishes there were another way."

"As do I."

"I am at war with myself," she confessed. "Is it still murder when the death is a sacrifice for the gods? Brennus is a bully and unsuitable to be king, but he's still just a boy. I know this was our people's way many years ago, but I thought those days were passed."

"It must be done," I said. "He will forever be a threat if he lives. This will show that Girec truly intends to bring change. I know some think sacrifice cruel and unnecessary, but many folk believe we should never have left the old ways behind."

"This will be much harder for you than for me," she murmured. "All I have to do is watch."

"That alone will be difficult."

I let myself touch her arm gently. The fleeting contact filled me with longing — longing for a different world and a time and place where we could be together. That would never happen now. After tonight, when she looked at me, she would always remember watching me sacrifice a boy who would have been king. The chief advisors arrived before I could say anything else.

"The guards are bringing Brennus now," Lorne said. He held up a canvas sack. "I have the items you requested."

Brennus entered, flanked by six guards armed with swords. He wore a white linen tunic and trousers with a thick cloak draped over his shoulders. A guard on each side grasped his arms, but he walked docilely between them. His gaze was vague and wandering.

"Has he been drugged?" I asked quietly.

"We had to," Lorne said. "For his own safety. He was trying to tear out his throat, saying it was better that he died by his own hand."

Even a willing sacrifice was often dosed to keep them calm. I was ashamed at my relief that this would make my task a little easier.

Night fell as we left Braen Town. The snow was hard and icy, slick in patches, and I walked carefully. Brennus slipped several times and would have fallen if not for the guards holding his arms. Another guard walked close to Derwa, offering his arm when she needed steadying. The air was frigid and still, creeping under cloaks and beneath collars. I wrapped my cloak tighter around me and tried not to think about how much colder the water would be. We walked in silence and without torches, for the moonlight was strong enough to light our way.

We headed in the opposite direction to the standing stones and I had not gone this way before. Trees were sparse at first, but became more common the further we went from the town. Eventually we came to a small woods. The guards lit torches, for the canopy was thick enough to obscure the moonlight. The trees were a mix of oak and beech, ash and birch. Frost sparkled on the moss that grew up the trunks and spread over fallen branches.

We moved between the trees, following some path only Lorne saw. He probably explored every inch of the surrounding countryside in his childhood. If he was anything like my cousins, he would have gone as far as a boy could walk and still return in time for dinner. I watched carefully for any sign we might have inadvertently passed through a fey portal, but the woods around us never changed.

At length we reached a clearing, in the middle of which was a pond, its surface veiled with patches of ice. The edges were scummy and it was not as inviting as the one in the fey realm where I met Agata and Orm, but it would do. The lamplight reflected off the water's surface, obscuring its depths.

We rested on oil skins and passed water flasks around. There was little conversation as we waited for dawn. I huddled into my cloak and tried to calm my pounding heart. Despite the midwinter cold, sweat trickled down my back. Derwa reached for my hand. Her hand was warm, although her fingers trembled, and I wondered at the sensation of skin on skin. I eased the corner of my cloak over our hands.

Brennus sat between two guards, his eyes vacant and his jaw slack. Girec sat alone and stared off into the trees. He was pale, but I hardened my heart. One day it would be he who gave the order for men to die. Let him know now what it was to hold that sort of power over someone, while he was still young enough to learn to respect it.

When the small patches of sky I glimpsed through the canopy lightened and the birds began their morning calls, I rose. Lorne handed me the sack he had carried and I removed its contents, one by one. A small clay pot of dirt scraped from the packed earth in the keep's grounds. This I handed to Teris. A bronze bowl, which I passed to Derwa. The tiny oil lamp and tinder I handed to Lorne. The last item was a raven's feather and that I kept for myself.

"Bring Brennus forward," I said.

The guards pulled him to his feet. He looked at me briefly, but apparently found me uninteresting and turned his gaze to the pond.

"On your knees," I said.

The guards tugged Brennus's arms until he knelt. I glanced around at those who had accompanied us. Derwa's face was sympathetic but resolute. Girec held his head high and tried not to cry. The senior advisors were grave and distant. The guards' faces were carefully blank, although more than one swallowed hard. Brennus had given nobody reason to intercede for him, but it didn't mean that what we did this morning sat lightly with anyone.

"Brennus," I said.

He didn't respond. I repeated his name more sharply and he finally looked up from the pond.

"Do you understand what is happening?" I asked.

He nodded, but his eyes were dazed and I wasn't sure he really comprehended my words. I hesitated, wondering whether I should wait until the soporific wore off. A raven croaked loudly and I made up my mind. I raised my arms to the sky and took a deep breath.

"I request the presence of the elementals. I ask that you bear witness to what we must do. Our country has been led astray by a king who was wilful and selfish, conceited and blind to all but his own satisfaction. Tonight we make atonement for his failings, and for our failings in following him. Tonight we sacrifice the one who would follow his path. We pray that by our actions the gods forgive us."

I indicated that Derwa, Lorne and Teris should move forward. I had explained earlier what they needed to do and each now carefully performed their part. Lorne cleared an area of snow and leaves and placed the little oil lamp on the dirt. He struck a flame and lit the wick. Derwa filled the tiny bronze bowl from the pond, then placed it beside the lamp. Teris set the clay pot of soil down with them and I added the raven's feather. Our offerings stood in a row on the bare earth. The fire from the lamp played across the surface of the bowl and the water darkened and flickered. I didn't let myself look at what it showed.

"We offer these gifts to the elementals. Fire and Earth, Water and Air. Bear witness to the terrible task we do tonight."

I held my hand out to Lorne and he passed me two final items. A rope and a linen hood. I knelt in front of Brennus and took his hands. He offered no resistance but stared at me almost curiously, as if he was a child encountering someone he had never met before. I tied his hands together in front of him.

"If you have any final words, speak them now," I said.

He looked at me dumbly. With a heavy heart, I slipped the hood over his head. He tossed his head back, startled, and the guards tightened their grip on his arms. But he offered no further resistance as I tied the string that would hold the hood securely.

I rose and stepped into the pond. The water was near freezing and already my skin burned. I had feared we might need to cut the ice, but it was patchy and thin enough that I could easily break through it. The bottom of the pond was slippery and I kept my balance with difficulty. My progress wasn't terribly dignified, but all too soon I stood chest-deep in the water. My teeth chattered and I already couldn't feel my legs.

I nodded to the guards, who lifted Brennus by his arms and carried him into the pond. He kicked when he felt the frigid water, but they held him firmly. By the time they reached me, their shirts were soaked through and water dripped from their faces. Neither looked at me and I wondered whether they volunteered for this task or were chosen. Once again, I held my arms up to the sky.

"Bear witness to our sacrifice," I called to the elementals.

The guards lifted Brennus by his bound arms and his legs and tipped him forward. I placed my hands on Brennus's head and pushed him under the surface. He thrashed and struggled, but the guards grasped him securely as I held his head under the water. Time passed too slowly and he fought for longer than I expected. But at last his body stilled. I counted to one hundred, then released his head.

"Bear witness to our sacrifice," I said. My throat choked with tears I couldn't afford to shed.

47

ARLEN

We took Brennus's body back to Braen Keep, where a pyre had been built in our absence. I watched with dry eyes as the flames took him, and tried not to inhale the scent of his burning flesh. It was only later in the privacy of my bedchamber that I let myself cry for what I had done.

Lorne sent a carefully-worded message to Brennus's family, explaining only that he had died but not the circumstances. We assumed Brennus would have boasted of being named as heir, but his family were in no position to demand any explanation other than what Lorne offered. They gave up all rights to the boy when they sent him to be fostered as a show of allegiance towards Hearn.

Girec said little, but he listened carefully to everything Derwa and the chief advisors said. He would make a fine king, I thought, given enough time to learn all that Hearn hadn't bothered to teach him. Although I regretted the necessity of Brennus's sacrifice, I did not regret the deed. The country would fare far better with Girec on the throne. And those women who were important to me — Agata and Derwa — were safe.

Girec's first act was to order the prisoners from Cullen's and Fingen's estates be released. They were fed, given medical treatment, and offered work if they wanted to stay. Some would likely depart to live with families elsewhere, but most probably had nowhere to go. Here they would have a roof over their heads and the promise of a job.

It was almost dusk by the time I escaped the discussions with Girec and the advisors. I was fiercely hungry, having eaten nothing yet today, so I went straight to the kitchen. I took my bread and cheese and braved the cold outside to find a quiet place to eat. I wandered with no real direction until I ended up at the three birch trees. There was nowhere to sit as a fresh layer of snow covered the ground, so I ate leaning against a tree. It was a simple meal, but the bread was fresh and the cheese sharp. I rested my head against the trunk and closed my eyes. The tree's life force was weak, but even that small connection revived me a little.

Tomorrow Tristan and I would take Fiachra's body back to Silver Downs. I intended to stay there for a while, but I already knew I would return to Braen Keep. I would have dearly liked to ask Derwa to come with me so I could show her my boyhood home, but she had responsibilities here now and a king-in-waiting who needed her. So I would return and eventually there would be time and space for Derwa and I to find out what we meant to each other.

I dreaded telling Eithne about Agata. What would she think of me when she discovered I found my sister but failed to bring her home? In almost every letter I sent home during my training, I promised to search for Agata as soon as I could. Would Eithne think I gave up too easily? Or maybe she would think I hadn't even tried. I needed to make one last attempt to convince Agata to come home with me.

My feet already ached as I left the keep and the moon was high in the sky by the time I reached the portal. The night was bitterly cold and frost crunched under my boots. Icicles rimed the branches of beech and birch, sparkling in the moonlight. The air was fresh and clean, scented with woodsmoke and snow. Yet as I passed through the portal, the winter night disappeared, replaced with woods on a warm summery afternoon. The trees were lush with new leaves and blossoms. I heard the chirp of squirrel and the song of woodlark.

I wasn't sure I would remember the path to the pond, for it had been a long, winding route. But the woods seemed to lead me straight there this time. I didn't know how often Agata came here, but it was the only place in this realm that I knew she visited. I hadn't decided how long I would wait.

My feet were throbbing and blistered and I eagerly anticipated soaking them in the pond's warm waters. But when I arrived, Agata was already there. She sat in the moss in front of the pond. Her long dark hair cascaded over her back and I thought she might be crying. I cleared my throat to let her know I was there and Agata spun around, already scrubbing the tears from her face.

"You shouldn't be here," she said. "This is not a place for mortals."

"The portal let me through. Surely it would have stopped me if mortals weren't permitted."

"Fool," she hissed. "Titania will know. She Sees you now. She hasn't decided what to do about you yet, but if she knows you are here, she will come."

"Come home with me, Agata," I said. "Meet our mother. See the place where you should have grown up. There's a portal to the fey realm on the edge of our lands, so you can come straight back from there."

"I have no desire to spend any more time in the mortal realm," she said.

Before she could say anything else, a woman entered the clearing. She wore a blood-red gown and her dark hair flowed unrestrained around her shoulders. I recognised her instantly even without having seen her before.

"So, the mortal woman bore two children." Titania inspected me as if I was a squashed bug. "How fortunate for her, but why were you unSeen?"

I kept my face blank, not wanting her to know how much I feared her. The queen of the fey. The woman who tried to destroy both my mother and my sister. The one who featured in so many of my boyhood nightmares.

"The children of Silver Downs have always had special abilities," I said. "I thought you knew that."

Her eyes narrowed. "Impudent. Just like your mother."

"If I had half my mother's courage, I would be proud."

"Your mother was a sickly runt whose only achievement was bewitching a half-blood fey."

"My mother escaped a fey prison to bring home the man she loved," I said.

"Impertinent wretch. I should have squashed your entire line generations ago."

"I think you would have if you could."

She narrowed her eyes and put her hands on her hips.

"Do you dare suggest a handful of mere mortals are more powerful than I?" she asked, her tone scornful.

"I think you're scared of us," I said. "I know you watch us. What I've never figured out is why."

Titania's face registered surprise as she looked down at something on the ground. Orm had arrived. I reached down to touch the rock's smooth surface and Orm spoke in a slow ponderous tone.

"I'll tell you why, young druid," Orm said. "It's because she knows your line will be the end of the fey."

"What is that?" Titania hissed. "And where did it come from?"

"This?" I kept my voice casual. "You mean to tell me you don't recognise an Old One when you see one?"

"There are no Old Ones here," she said with a snarl. Her gaze didn't leave Orm for a moment. "They died out long before we ever arrived."

"No, actually, they didn't. They went into hiding because they didn't think you were worth fighting. But now they'd like their lands back."

Titania laughed. "You think we'll just walk away? We've held this land for thousands of years. It's ours now."

"I think you'll find you're outnumbered." I had no idea whether that was true, but I hoped it was.

"There are hundreds—"

Titania stopped as the clearing filled with a variety of rocks and logs and bushes and trees. They stood silent and patient. Agata let out a shriek as something climbed out of the pond and stood beside her. It was vaguely human-shaped, but its limbs were too long and its hands and feet too big. Water sluiced from its body and puddled on the moss.

"What is this?" Titania asked. "How are you doing this?"

"I'm not doing anything," I said. "They're the Old Ones."

"No point us trying to talk to her," Orm said. "She can't hear our kind. Only mortals can."

That's why they needed me.

"Well, if the fey need to leave, they have to go somewhere," I said. "Is there an unoccupied place they can go to?"

"An island a few hours off the coast. North and to the west. Occupied by wildlife but no mortals. None of our kind there."

"The Old Ones know an island," I relayed to Titania. "It is uninhabited. I can arrange transport if you will leave willingly."

Titania screwed up her mouth as if she tasted something bitter.

"We aren't going anywhere," she said. "And I have no patience for dealing with mortals right now. Come along, Agata."

She walked away. Agata didn't follow her, too occupied with staring at Orm. Could she hear the Old Ones? After all, she had as much mortal blood as me. As Titania reached the edge of the clearing, the weeping willows moved, interlocking their branches to stop her from passing between them. Titania gave a squeal of fury.

"Let me pass this minute or I'll burn you all to the ground."

"You can try," Orm said.

"I think you'll find they don't burn," I said. "And it seems there are more Old Ones than you realised."

"We are all around," Orm said. "The woods, your homes, your furniture. Did you really think the trees grew into shapes so convenient for you?"

"They're everywhere," I said. "They made themselves useful so they could watch you. They're your homes and your furniture. The woods. They're everywhere."

"That's nonsense," Titania said, but her voice shook. "The homes we use were left by the previous inhabitants of this land. We merely moved into them."

"I thought they were made by fey magic," Agata said.

"That's just what we tell the mortals." Titania's voice was distant and she missed the look of fury Agata directed at her.

"Will you accept the offer of transport?" I asked.

Fatigue washed over me in waves and I could barely follow the conversation anymore. If Titania resisted for much longer, I would simply lie down on the moss and sleep while I waited for her to come to her senses.

"Lies. It's all preposterous lies," Titania said. "I demand you let me pass. Whatever mortal magic this is, it's not amusing."

"I promise you this is no mortal magic," I said. "It's the Old Ones."

"I think he's telling the truth," Agata said. "They showed themselves to me, too, but I can't hear them like Arlen does."

"Yes, well, you're more mortal than anything else, so I'm not surprised you're siding with him," Titania said.

Agata gave her a wounded look and tears shone in her eyes.

"I've tried to be the best fey I could," she said. "Even once I found out I had hardly any fey blood. But you've never given me a chance. It was all about revenge, wasn't it? You never cared about me at all."

Before Titania could reply, a tree root burst out of the earth and wrapped around her foot.

"What is this?" she shrieked. "Get it off me."

"We are all around," Orm said in the usual slow way.

The root crept up Titania's leg, wrapping around her limb. She screamed and tried to tear it away. It climbed over her torso and encased her arms. It slid over her neck and head. Soon only her eyes were visible.

"This is what we'll do if they don't leave," Orm said. "To each of them."

"If you don't agree, they'll keep you like this," I told Titania. "And they can do this to all the fey. You'll be stuck forever, trapped inside the tree roots."

Agata stared at Titania in horror.

"We have to leave," she said. "Think of it. Everyone we know encased in those roots. We can't live like that."

Titania blinked furiously.

"I don't think she can talk," I said to Orm.

"Oh," Orm said.

The roots uncovered Titania's face.

"Do you agree?" I asked. "Because I've been up all night and I'm really tired. I don't feel like talking for much longer, so now's your chance."

"I agree," Titania said. She somehow managed to make the words sound imperious as if she did me a favour. "Get this off me and the fey will leave. But you will provide us with transport."

Even as the words left her mouth, wind swirled through the clearing. It was strong, almost knocking me over, and brought with it the scent of honeysuckle. Agata's hair whipped around her face and she had to hold her skirts down with both hands. Orm, steady as ever, seemed unperturbed, although I sensed a faint humming from him. Perhaps he communicated with others of his species.

"I think the air elementals are offering to transport you," I said.

The elementals responded by circling me, faster and faster, almost lifting me off the ground in their eagerness. Meanwhile, the root leisurely released Titania, easing down over her body and back into the earth until the only sign of its presence was some disturbed soil. Titania glared at me.

"I assume you need time to prepare," I said. "There is a ring of stones a couple of hours walk from the portal. Go there and call for Air when you are ready to leave."

"This is all your fault," she hissed. "I knew the children of Silver Downs were trouble. I'll see the end of your line yet."

"Protected," Orm said.

"I think you'll find we're under the protection of the Old Ones," I said.

Titania let out a squeal of rage, then marched out of the clearing. The trees let her pass.

"Come, Agata," she called over her shoulder.

"Stay," I said to her. "Come back to Silver Downs with me. If you go with the fey, you'll have to leave forever. The Old Ones won't let them come back again."

She chewed her lip, and for a moment I thought she actually considered it. But she shook her head.

"I belong with the fey," she said and ran after Titania.

Then it was just Orm and me left in the clearing. The rest of the Old Ones had disappeared without me even noticing.

"Well, that's that," I said sadly.

"The girl will be back," he said. "Maybe not in your lifetime, but one day."

4 8

ARLEN

y heart was heavy as I trekked back to Braen Keep. My relief at convincing Titania to leave was outweighed by dismay that Agata had chosen to leave with her. At least the Old Ones would have their home back shortly. I, however, would have to tell Eithne that she would probably never meet her daughter.

Tristan and I departed for Silver Downs later that day. The healers preserved Fiachra's body to give us time to get him home. Girec provided a cart and a pair of oxen and there was plenty of room for Tristan and me, even with Fiachra and our supplies. I didn't see Derwa before we left and I didn't know whether to be relieved or disappointed. Maybe there was no possible future that a queen and a druid could share, but there would be time enough to find out.

Tristan and I spoke only as necessary while we travelled. Midwinter passed and the days slowly became longer, although no warmer yet. We camped beside the road at night, wrapped well in blankets. Tristan turned out to be proficient with a bow and provided fresh meat to supplement our supplies. I often saw him staring at the wrapped bundle that was Fiachra's body, but didn't ask what he was thinking. He clearly knew Fiachra better than I did, so he likely grieved our uncle.

I recognised nothing of what we trundled past. It had been too many years and I was too young when I left. But after a full sevennight of travel, we finally approached the Silver Downs lodge. It stood proud above its surroundings, all grey stone walls with creeping mosses and vines. It was not as big as I remembered, or maybe Braen Keep had skewed my perspective. The gardens out the front were different from my memory. Shutters had been recently painted and the barn extended. But when I inhaled, the smell of home rushed through me. It might look different, but it still smelled exactly the same.

As we arrived, a pair of young girls were out the front, playing a fighting game with wooden practice swords. They waved and scampered into the lodge to announce our arrival. My hands trembled a little as I climbed down from the cart.

Eithne was the first to come out of the lodge. Her mouth trembled when she saw me. She moved as if to hold her arms out to me, but checked herself. I went to her and embraced her. She was far too thin and fragile, with bones that seemed almost to poke out of her skin. She returned my embrace and her shoulders shook as she sobbed once or twice. She released me and turned to Tristan.

"It's done," he said before she could ask. "She is destroyed forever. But Uncle Fiachra..."

She held out her arms to him.

"He knew even before he left," she said. "He told me this would be his final journey."

Tristan cried into her shoulder and Eithne allowed her own tears to run freely down her cheeks.

"He should have told me," Tristan said. "I could have helped them."

Eithne met my eyes with a questioning gaze.

"It was Agata and me," I said. "Fiachra Saw it would be the two of us who destroyed her."

"You found Agata?" She covered her trembling mouth with her hand. "Where is she?"

"She chose to stay with the fey."

Eithne smiled sadly and shook her head a little.

"I should have known," she said. "I should have expected Titania would make sure she never came back to us, even if she was found."

"It's all she knows. Titania raised her to believe she was fey."

"Do you think she will come home one day?"

I didn't want to lie to her, but it felt wrong to tell her the truth.

"Maybe," I said.

"At least I know she is alive and well," she said. "I had thought…"

I knew what she had feared, for I myself had often wondered how Agata lived. Whether she passed her years in the darkness and solitude of a fey prison.

"She has been treated as a princess, as far as I can tell," I said. "She hasn't been mistreated."

"Except in that she was stolen from her family." Eithne's voice was bitter. "But she is alive while we mourn my brother. Fiachra thought Ida would find you."

"Why me?" I asked. "I had little to do with her until Uncle Fiachra arrived. She charmed me and I kept forgetting she was there."

"It was one of our sons who created her. Fiachra believed her power would be strongest near those of our line. She needed to be near you."

"Hearn is dead. The news may not have reached this far yet. One of his foster sons is to be king." I couldn't tell her of my part in the death of his other foster son. Maybe that would be a tale for another day. Or maybe it would be a secret I would hold close for the rest of my life. "And Titania knows about me."

Eithne reached for me even as she clutched Tristan tighter with the other arm. Her fingers barely grazed my cheek.

"Oh," she said. "Will she come here?"

"No. She won't bother us anymore. The Old Ones have returned and the fey are leaving. They have been banished."

Her smile was hopeful, like the sun peeking out past a grey cloud.

"We don't have to fear her any longer," I said. "Mother."

4 9

ARLEN

spent the next sevennight at Silver Downs. Eithne and I didn't speak much for the first day or two. She would often walk past and hesitate, as if wanting to say something, then walk away. But gradually we both found our words and the years between us dissolved. She told me about what happened at Silver Downs in the years I was away. There were no other children for her and Kalen, out of fear that Titania would take them too.

I told her everything that happened with Agata and Titania. She understood why I hadn't brought Agata with me — perhaps better than I did — but it grieved her. I spoke sparingly of my studies, for there was much I wasn't permitted to tell, and of what happened at Braen Keep. If Eithne judged me harshly for the decisions I made, she didn't show it. The only detail I kept from her was my friendship with Derwa. It felt disrespectful to talk about her when things between us were still unspoken.

Once Eithne and I had said everything we needed to, my thoughts turned to Braen Keep and Derwa. Before I left, though, I wanted to explore the places I remembered from my boyhood. The hill where I could see out over the entire estate. The place where the twin rivers met. The woods on the edge of our land, not that I was ever permitted to enter them as a boy. I spent a morning walking across the estate, finding place after place that had some memory from my childhood attached to it.

I left the rock by the stand of beech trees for last. This place was special to Eithne, for it was here she fell in love with Kalen. I sat on the rock, listening to the wind whispering through the branches of the beeches, and imagining Eithne sitting in this very spot as a young woman. I could see why she liked this place. It was out of sight of the lodge and yet surrounded by Silver Downs land. The pastures were brown and mostly free of snow, for winter here had been mild this year. The rock was warm from the sun and weathered smooth. Woodlarks sang and somewhere nearby a raven cawed. Something rustled behind me. I ignored it, thinking it would be a vole or badger or squirrel.

"Arlen."

I jumped up when Agata spoke. She stood amongst the beeches, wearing a gown of forest green.

"Agata."

There were so many things I wanted to say and I had thought any chance of saying them was gone. But now she was here, my mind went blank.

"Just listen to me," she said. "I need to explain."

I nodded.

"I can't stay, so don't think that is why I am here," she said. "I need to remain with the fey. Titania has watched your family for a long time. Generations, I think. Your line — our line — has magic in its blood and she always feared we would become a threat to the fey. When Eithne was born, Titania thought she would be the one to rise up against them."

"Eithne would never harm anyone."

"She's strong and that makes Titania uneasy. She went into the fey realm and escaped with her mind intact. Very few mortals do that. And she was unSeen, which has always puzzled Titania."

"Eithne's birth was unSeen? Like mine?"

Agata's mouth twisted into a sad smile.

"Just like yours. She Saw me, but she only recently Saw you for the first time."

"That would have been after I finally accessed the Sight. I wondered whether it had broken something. Whether I would no longer be unSeen."

"I've never tried to See." Agata's voice was contemplative. "I wonder whether I have any ability."

"If you stay, I can help you find out."

"I can't. I've already told you."

"But this is where you belong." Having spent time with Eithne, I could see where Agata's stubbornness came from. "I've spent my whole life preparing to search for you. I promised Eithne I'd get you back. Everything I've ever done was about bringing you home."

Her eyes flashed and she scowled.

"It isn't your decision," she said. "It's mine."

"But you're mortal. I can understand you wanting to stay with the fey as long as you didn't know, but now that you do you should be here. With your family."

Agata put her hands on her hips.

"It's all about you, isn't it? It's about what *you* want for me, what *you* think I should do. What about what I want?"

"But how could you want anything else? You belong here."

"I belong with the fey."

I opened my mouth to argue, but she cut me off with a sharp swipe of her hand.

"Be quiet and listen. This is my life and it's my decision where I live. I know nothing about the mortal realm. Can't you understand that? The fey are all I know. They're all I understand. They're my family."

"Do they know you are mortal?"

"They do. It was difficult at first, but things are getting better since we went to the island. They're starting to accept me."

"Don't you want to meet our mother?"

"I don't want to give Titania any reason to go looking for her. Or for you. As long as I've chosen to stay, she's won. The fey might have lost their home, but she won against Eithne and I think that matters more to her than anything else."

I finally realised just how deep Titania's hatred of Eithne went.

"Will you come back one day?" I asked. "Spend some time with Eithne before it's too late. We will age much faster here than you will in the fey realm."

"I don't know. It's safer for all of you if I stay away."

Agata didn't stay long after that. She gave me a tentative hug before she left and I felt the connection between us renewed. As she melted away into the trees, I knew exactly which direction she went in. I would be able to find her again if I needed to.

It was only after she left that Sumerled revealed himself. We stared at each other and I supposed we each waited for the other to speak first.

"She hates me now," he said at last.

"Does she have reason to?"

Sumerled shrugged. "She thinks she does. That's all that matters."

"Were you following her?"

"I was looking for you."

I waited. He shifted his feet and looked out at the fields.

"So this is what he gave up the fey realm for."

"You mean Kalen? He gave it up for my mother."

"Can you give him a message for me?" His words came in a rush. "Tell him I'm watching over her for him. She's safe."

"Did you know she was his daughter?"

He finally looked me in the eyes.

"I suspected. She looks much like him."

"Why didn't you tell her sooner?"

"Because she would hate me. And I loved her."

"I'll tell him," I said.

He nodded and backed away into the trees. Just before he disappeared into the shadows, he spoke one last time.

"Tell him also that I understand. Tell them both."

"You understand what?" I asked.

But Sumerled was gone. His message might not mean much to me, but I suspected it would to Eithne and Kalen.

≈

The story continues in
Book 4: *Swan* (A mailing list exclusive)

Sign up at kyliequillinan.com/free-swan to claim your free copy.

ACKNOWLEDGEMENTS

There were times when I thought this book would never be finished. I had written a first draft some time ago but threw it out and started again just a few months before publication. There's not much left of the original story, except for Derwa, who was there all along. Although she's not a point of view character, she was always integral to the story that I wanted to tell.

I didn't set out to write three books about courage but somehow that's what happened. Muse was a story about a boy who didn't want to be a hero. Fey was about strong women who readily step up to be heroes. Druid is about a young man who is courageous in so many ways, even though he thinks he is failure.

Thank you again to Deranged Doctor Design for a lovely cover.

Thank you to Eliza Dee for fitting me into your schedule so urgently and for editing this beast.

Thank you to my uncle, Peter Abraham, who doesn't report me to the police when every now and then he receives a message that starts with something like, "I'm decapitating somebody and I need to know whether the blood will gush or ooze."

Thank you to Donald Maass for his comments on the story you're not telling that finally helped me to understand what Arlen's true problem was.

Thank you to Juliet Marillier for her comments on writer's block that finally loosened my words.

Thank you to Cathy Yardley for her help with tying things together at the end and brainstorming the final scene. There are so many elements that I finally managed to weave together thanks to those thirty minutes we spent talking.

And last, but not least, to Muffin, Lulu and Frehley: Thank you for being there waiting for me when I finished this book.

SWAN - PREVIEW

The sun sinks below distant mountains, sending a riot of colour through the sky. The lake in front of us reflects its hues: reds and oranges, purples and pinks. I inhale the crisp evening air and wish I could draw the sunset's beauty into me. Let its brilliant colours fill my emptiness and conceal the darkness that hides inside me. This is my prayer, although it is not one that would satisfy the priests. I exhale and let go of my bleak thoughts.

"Hilde." Drystan speaks barely loud enough to disturb my contemplation. He fears anyone else hearing. "They come soon. I feel it."

"I know, brother." My voice is just as soft, although it sounds harsher to my ear, not melodic like his. Drystan could have been a druid with that voice. When he speaks, the world around us quietens, as if the elements draw closer to hear him.

"You will protect them, won't you, Hilde?" He turns to me and his eyes reflect the red of the sunset, making it seem as if their depths burn with fire. "You must protect them. The priests will kill them if they find out."

"I will protect them with my life," I tell him. "Our brothers were wronged and it is our duty to provide them with safe harbour."

Drystan nods and resumes his vigil, scanning the sky for any sign the swans are returning.

"Soon, Hilde. Tonight perhaps."

I open my mouth to reply, but stop as I see something, far off in the distance, almost as far away as the setting sun.

"What is it?" In his eagerness, Drystan forgets to be quiet. He catches himself and lowers his voice. "Is it them?"

My eyes have always been keener than his, but still I squint, trying to make out shapes I'm not even certain I see.

"I can't be sure. Smudges against the sunset is all."

"They come."

His absolute faith in an old family tale shouldn't surprise me after all this time, and yet it does. Seven brothers. I recite their names silently, my lips swift to form each familiar name. Eremon. Yestin. Hael. Uistean. Inis. Eamon. And Fionn. Cursed Fionn. Their family had the three sons each man hoped for in those days. An heir, a soldier, and one for the druids, plus four sons to spare. It was the youngest who doomed his brothers: Fionn, the seventh son of a seven son. Fionn, the bard. He lived long enough to regret the deed and died of old age, weary and still heartsick at what he had done to his brothers.

There's magic in the blood of the children of Silver Downs. How many times had I heard that expression? It was usually said as a warning, sometimes with amusement, and occasionally as a curse. Fionn was the one who got all the magic in his generation. He was a bard with the power to bring his tales to life. They warned him, it was said. They told him what he could do. Whether or not he believed it, I've never known. But one day in a fit of rage, he told a tale of six brothers who turned into swans. Six brothers who took wing into the sky and flew off towards the setting son. Six brothers who in three hundred years would be restored to their human form.

The tale of the swan brothers has been passed down through the generations of Silver Downs, from heir to heir. Mayhap some didn't believe. It doesn't matter. The exact year of their changing has been forgotten, but we believe the time to be close. Drystan had thought it would be last summer. When they didn't come, he said it would be this summer. I am supposed to be at the battle front but was injured and sent home to recover. So as the sun sets each evening, we wait for them. Drystan and I stand beside the lake as the encroaching darkness slides its cloak over us, and we wait.

The smudge I couldn't quite see has grown closer and now it is not one, but six. I still can't make out their forms, but my heart pounds harder. I hadn't entirely believed Drystan when he said they would return during our days. I'm not sure I had even completely believed the tale of the six brothers turned into swans. Priest Pius would say it is a heresy. A test to trick us and turn our faces from Sulis Minerva, the One True God.

My heart hammers in my chest as I wait, my gaze fixed on those six tiny specks. They move so slowly. Beside me, Drystan is still and silent. I can't even hear him breathing. Perhaps he doesn't. This is the moment he has waited for all his life. As heir, the responsibility was passed from our father to him. It is Drystan's duty to wait and watch, to greet our brothers when they arrive.

"I see them," he murmurs. "Hilde, I see them. They come tonight."

My mind works furiously, planning for the moment of their arrival. The transformation. Will they be confused? Disorientated? We need to get them into the lodge quickly and quietly, before Priest Pius sees them. It may take some time for the brothers to fully return to their human minds, and if they say the wrong thing in front of him, it could mean their deaths. Better that they die, he would think, than that they live and challenge the truth of Sulis Minerva.

The specks come closer, closer, and finally I make out their forms. Six white swans, their wings moving almost lazily as they glide through the air. I can think of no more perfect backdrop than the brilliance of tonight's sunset.

"Magnificent," Drystan says, and I can only nod in agreement.

But then my sharp eyes spot something behind them, and the furious hammering in my chest slows. Disappointment seeps through me as I watch the seventh swan, its wings beating furiously as it tries to catch up to the flock.

"It's not them."

I am reluctant to say it, but he needs to know. The tale is very specific: seven brothers, but only six turned to swans.

"Of course it is, Hilde. You know the tale." His voice trails off as he, too, sees the seventh. "Oh."

His disappointment is palpable and I feel bad, even though it's not my fault. I was just the first to realise.

The swans come closer and closer. One turns its head, its profile sharp against the setting sun. It seems to look back at the swan fast catching up to them, and I'm sure I see its beak open and close. Encouraging or scolding, I can't tell.

I marvel at the sight of seven white swans in flight, even as I swallow my disappointment that this is not the day we have waited for. Drystan will be desolate. I reach out and clasp his hand briefly. His fingers are smooth, a contrast to my own hands which are chapped and roughened from weapons practice.

Now they are close enough to see their eyes, their beaks. I fancy I even see a feather that comes unattached from a wing and drifts lazily down to land on the water. Drystan and I stand tall as we watch their progress.

They are right in front of us now, and the seventh swan has almost caught up. One of the swans trumpets and I fancy it tells the trailing swan to go away, go back, don't follow. The seventh swan looks strained, breathless. I wonder how far it flew alone before it caught up to the rest of the flock.

The glint of sunlight on metal catches my eye a moment before the arrow pierces the side of the seventh swan. She screams — suddenly I am sure she is female — and crashes down into the shallow water.

The other swans are descending right beside us in a rustle of wings and a swirl of wind as it happens. Even as they land, they are already changing. The moment of transformation is too quick for me to make out the details, but suddenly six men stand in front of us.

Five of them step closer together, staring at us with wary eyes. One holds his arms out awkwardly, before remembering he no longer has wings. He lowers his arms to his sides. The sixth is already running.

ENJOYED THIS SAMPLE? *Swan* is a mailing list exclusive and is not available for sale on any retailer. Sign up at kyliequillinan.com/free-swan to claim your free copy.

ALSO BY KYLIE QUILLINAN

Tales of Silver Downs series

Prequel: *Bard*

Book One: *Muse*

Book Two: *Fey*

Book Three: *Druid*

Epilogue: *Swan* (A newsletter list exclusive)

The Amarna Age Series

Book One: *Queen of Egypt*

Book Two: *Son of the Hittites*

Book Three: *Eye of Horus*

Book Four: *Gates of Anubis*

Book Five: *Lady of the Two Lands*

Book Six: *Guardian of the Underworld*

Daughter of the Sun: An Amarna Age Novella

Standalone

Speak To Me

See kyliequillinan.com for more books, including exclusive collections, and newsletter sign up.

ABOUT THE AUTHOR

Kylie writes about women who defy society's expectations. Her novels are for readers who like fantasy with a basis in history or mythology. Her interests include Dr Who, jellyfish and cocktails. She needs to get fit before the zombies come.

Swan – the epilogue to the Tales of Silver Downs series – is available exclusively to her newsletter subscribers. Sign up at www.kyliequilli-nan.com.